Thomas Alexander Browne

The Miner's Right

A Tale of the Australian Goldfields

Thomas Alexander Browne

The Miner's Right
A Tale of the Australian Goldfields

ISBN/EAN: 9783743318090

Manufactured in Europe, USA, Canada, Australia, Japa

Cover: Foto ©Andreas Hilbeck / pixelio.de

Manufactured and distributed by brebook publishing software (www.brebook.com)

Thomas Alexander Browne

The Miner's Right

THE MINER'S RIGHT

A TALE OF
THE AUSTRALIAN GOLDFIELDS

BY

ROLF BOLDREWOOD

AUTHOR OF 'ROBBERY UNDER ARMS'
'THE SQUATTER'S DREAM,' ETC.

London
MACMILLAN AND CO.
AND NEW YORK
1893

First Edition (3 *Vols. Crown 8vo*), *April* 1890
New Edition (1 *Vol. Crown 8vo*) *October* 1890
Reprinted November 1890 ; *January* 1891 ; *June* 1891 ; *October* 1891, 1893

CHAPTER I

I AM in Australia at last—actually in Botany Bay, as we called the colony of New South Wales when Joe Bulder and I first thought of leaving that dear quiet old Dibblestowe Leys in Mid-Kent. More than that, I am a real gold digger—very real, indeed—and the holder of a Miner's Right, a wonderful document, printed and written on parchment, precisely as follows. I ought to know it by heart, good reason have I therefor, I and mine. Here it is, life size, in full. Shall I ever take it out and look at it by stealth in happy days to come, I wonder?

NEW SOUTH WALES.

No. 1163

MINING DISTRICT, AND DIVISION)
OR PLACE IN WHICH ISSUED.
Tambaroora and Turon

£0.10.0
Dad 6th April 1855

MINER'S RIGHT

Issued to Hereward Pole
of Yatala under the provisions of the "Mining Act 1854" to be in force until 31st December 1855

William D. Blake P.M.
Commissioner

Yes, I am here now, at Yatala, safe enough; as I said before, with my mates—Cyrus Yorke, Joe Bulder, and the Major. But I certainly thought I should never get away from England. One would have imagined that a younger son of a decayed family had never quitted Britain before to find fortune or be otherwise provided for. Also, that Australia was Central Africa, whence ingenuous youth had little more chance of returning than dear old Livingstone.

As for me, Hereward Pole, as I had but little occupation and less money, I was surely the precise kind of emigrant which the old land can so gracefully spare to the new. Gently nurtured, well intentioned, utterly useless, not but what I

B

was fitting myself according to my lights for a colonial career
—save the mark!—for I had been nearly a year on a farm in
Mid-Kent, for which high privilege I paid, or rather my uncle
did, £100 sterling.

So, I had learned to plough indifferently, and could be
trusted to harrow, a few side strokes not mattering in that
feat of agriculture. I could pronounce confidently on the
various samples of seed wheat submitted to me, and I had completely learned the art of colouring a meerschaum by smoking
daily and hourly what I then took to be the strongest tobacco
manufactured.

It wasn't bad fun. Jane Mangold, the old farmer's daughter,
who was coaching me, was a pretty girl, with rosy cheeks, a
saucy nose, and no end of soft, fluffy, fair hair. We were
capital friends, and she stood by me when I got into disgrace
by over-driving the steam-engine one day, and nearly blowing
up the flower of the village population of Dibblestowe Leys.
Now and then I had a little shooting, and a by-day with the
Tickham hounds. Life passed on so peacefully and pleasantly
that I was half inclined to think of taking a farm near the Leys
at the end of my term, and asking Jane to help with the dairy,
poultry, cider, and housekeeping department. Then a little
incident happened which changed the current of ideas generally,
and my life in particular.

It was one of the fixtures of the Tickham hounds, which
sometimes honoured our slowish neighbourhood. Old Mangold,
being grumpy, had told me that I might go to Bishop's Cote, or
indeed considerably further, for all the help I was to him. I
had cheerfully accepted his somewhat ungracious permission,
and mounted on a young horse I was schooling for Dick Cheriton,
a farmer's son of sporting tastes, I made my way over, pleased
with my mount, satisfied with my boots, and altogether of
opinion that I was better treated by fortune than usual.

I *could* ride, to do myself justice, and shoot. Second whip or
under keeper were the only posts for which I was really qualified.
I could make a fly and tie it : could somehow hit the piscatorial
need of most days and most waters. Mine was rarely an empty
basket. In fact, I was like a very large majority of the young
Englishmen of the day, in that I could do a number of useless
things, mostly relating to field sports and manual accomplishments. Tall and strong, with thickish dark-brown hair, I had
my mother's features and dark grey eyes, that didn't usually
look anywhere but in people's faces. For the rest I was wholly
ignorant of every conceivable form and method of money-
making, and could not have earned a crown to save my life.

Please to imagine me sitting sideways on my horse, thinking
whether there might be time to have a smoke before the hounds
threw off, then suddenly aroused by the rattle of carriage
wheels, which denoted a stronger pace than was generally
resorted to by county families assembling at a meet. Hastily

looking round I saw a pair of grand-looking brown horses, which had evidently bolted with a landau containing two ladies. The coachman was sitting still and doing his best, but he had only one rein; the other, broken short, was dangling from the near horse's head. I knew the horses, and, of course, the carriage. I had often remarked them at the village church; they belonged to the squire, who was my host's landlord. I knew, of course, the lady of the Manor by sight, having gazed at her afar off; but the girl, who was by her side in the carriage—pale and proud yet despairing, with a piteous look of appeal in her large, dark eyes—I had never seen before.

We were both early. The hounds had not yet come up. Save the village apothecary in antigropelos, and a stray horse-dealer or pad groom, there was hardly a soul near. My resolution was taken in an instant. I knew that the road they were speeding so fast along gradually commenced to descend. A longish hill, flint bestrewn, with a turn and bridge at the end of it, would soon account finally for all concerned.

I took my five-year-old by the head and raced for the hedge and ditch. He gave a highly theatrical jump into the road just by the side of the carriage. I saw both the ladies gaze with astonishment as I sent him up to the head of the reinless carriage horse. 'Help us, oh help us!' cried Mrs. Allerton, 'or we shall be dashed to pieces.' The younger lady did not speak, but looked at me with her pleading eyes in such a way that I felt I could have thrown myself under the wheels then and there to have been of the slightest service.

Nothing so sacrificial was required of me. Jamming my youngster, fortunately one of the bold temperate sort, against the near side carriage horse's shoulder, I got hold of the loose rein, and dragged at his mouth in a way that must have hurt his feelings, if he had any thereabouts. The coachman seconded me well and prudently. Between us we stopped the carriage within a quarter of a mile, and saved the impending smash. The rein was knotted, the bits altered to the lower bar, and peace was restored.

Both ladies were ridiculously grateful, though the younger, after impulsively placing her hand in mine, when her mother—as I found her to be—had shaken mine several times warmly, rather looked than spoke her thanks.

'Haven't I seen you somewhere?' at length asked the elder lady. 'I am sure I know your face and voice.'

I mentioned something about Dibblestowe Leys and Mr. Mangold.

'Ah, of course, I was stupid not to remember you before. You will tell us what name I shall mention to the Squire, as that of the gentleman who so gallantly saved the lives of his wife and daughter.'

'Hereward Pole,' said I, bowing and blushing—one blushed in those days; 'very much at your service.'

'One of the Poles of Shute, surely not? Why, I remember the old place when I was a girl. And your dear mother, is she still alive? I shall hope to see her again. What a wonderful coincidence. And, now I think of it, you are like her, especially about the brow and eyes.'

'Mamma, perhaps Mr. Pole would like to have his run with the hounds, now that we are all safe. We needn't stay in the road all day. I see they have put the hounds into Hollingbourne Wood. Papa says it was near Durnbank; so if Mr. Pole cuts across these two fields with that clever horse of his he will be just in time.'

'My dearest Ruth, you are a matter-of-fact darling; but I daresay Mr. Pole will enjoy the run after all. You young people are so strong. My poor nerves will be *agacé* for days, I know. May we hope to see you on Sunday to dinner, my dear Mr. Pole? I suppose Mr. Mangold can spare you on that day.'

'Or even on a week-day, perhaps,' said the young lady maliciously. 'You had better get away; I see something like business over yonder.'

I bowed low, and plunging in a dazed way at the hedge, was mortified to find that my steed adopted the tactics of *multum in parvo*, and got through rather by force of character than activity. However, I flew the next two fences in very creditable style, and reached the outer edge of the covert as Reynard had stolen forth, a few moments in advance of old Countess and Columbine, the detectives of the pack, and was well away with the leading hounds before the carriage was out of sight in the direction of Torry Hill.

The run was a cracker. How well I remember it still. I sailed along in the first flight all through. Indeed, so well was I carried, that I never had a chance of riding the young horse again, as he was promptly snapped up at a large advance upon his previous selling price. A single day with its occurrence brightens or shades a life. Fate takes the dial, and turns the hands with strong slow fingers, and we think we can carve out our own path in life, can choose the good or shun the evil that lieth around us. Now, like children, are we hurried forward or frightened back on the track of doom!

When I returned to the Leys late that evening Jane was most anxious to hear everything about the day. Had there been a good run? Was I well up? Did Dick Cheriton's horse carry me well? She didn't see why I should go riding other people's young horses. My neck was more valuable than Dick's —a gambling, drinking, good-for-nothing fellow. Was the Squire's lady there, and her daughter Miss Ruth? The undergardener had been down from the hall to see Deborah the dairymaid, and had told her that they were going to the meet because Lord Arthur Gordon was to be there. He was staying at the hall.

I must have been more curt than usual in my answers; perhaps I was tired or cross : men sometimes are, for no reason at all, like women. Anyhow, Jane was disappointed, and left off questioning me, saying that 'she supposed I would find my temper after a night's rest. Only she did think——' and here there must have been a few tears, as I found myself consoling her efficiently and protesting all kinds of palliatives, Mr. Mangold having as usual gone to smoke his pipe in the snug sanded kitchen, which he said was a hundred times more comfortable than Jane's smart parlour, which he never would call a drawing-room, much to her distress.

On the following Sunday I announced my intention of going to church, a practice to which I generally conformed on the ground of mixed motives, involving as it did a pleasant walk back through the lanes with Jane. To her wild astonishment and that of the parish generally, I was most cordially greeted by the lady of the Manor ; hardly less so by Miss Allerton, and finally carried off in the sacred hall-carriage before the eyes of the dismayed villagers, who looked upon it as something hardly less than a translation to realms Elysian.

On arriving at Allerton Court, a grand old Elizabethan pile, we were met on the steps by the Squire himself, who most warmly acknowledged his indebtedness to me for the signal service which I had rendered his family. Delighted to find that I was the son of his old friend Dunston Pole, while I was in the neighbourhood he hoped—indeed, he would take no denial—that I must look upon his house as my home. He was aware I was learning farming at the Leys with old Mangold. Very worthy old chap, and paid his rents with much more punctuality than many of the newer lights. Pretty daughter too, Miss Jane. Mind what you're about. Must not go about breaking hearts ; though girls look out for themselves nowadays pretty well, he must say that, however. I must come over and shoot. They always thought there was some of the best cock-shooting in England at Allerton Court, and as for hunting, he would mount me to the end of the season. I needn't ride five-year-olds after to-day ; though the one I steered to the Hollingbourne must have been a 'nailer,' if his informant spoke truly.

The Squire's address was fragmentary and conventional, but the tone of my whole reception was so truly sincere that I felt at once that my position as the friend of the family was assured. The lady of the Manor looked at me with a truly maternal warmth of affection, and from time to time recapitulated for the Squire's benefit every incident of our joint thrilling adventure.

'Never was so near being a widower, my dear,' he said. 'I wonder who there is in the county that would have suited me ? Never thought of it before ! One should always be prepared for those kind of things though ; couldn't have replaced my ladybird here though so easily, eh, Ruth!' and a tear gathered in the old man's glistening eye.

'You are a wicked old papa,' said she, holding up a finger reprovingly; 'you would have thought very little about successors and such rubbish, you know, if poor mamma and I had been dashed to pieces, which we should most certainly have been but for Mr. Pole's help and good riding.' And here I received a half-shy, half-grateful glance that made me consider myself a Paladin, and the lovely girl, the fairest of the fair, like her that was to reward *le brave et beau Dunois*, who of old returned from Palestine.

This was all very well, but one could not return from Palestine without having in the first instance gone there. It was no doubt mighty easy for such fellows as Dunois to go to foreign parts. Very little capital was required, and fighting, if a hazardous, is comparatively a cheap species of investment. Now, in these latter days, a man must either stay at home, leading an inglorious and unprofitable life, or be able to lay his hand upon a good round sum of money with which to be a backwoodsman in Canada, a squatter in Australia, a sugar grower in Natal, or an indigo planter in Nepaul. The days of cheap yet dignified adventure seemed, ah me, to be fled for ever.

Matters went on smoothly for me during the rest of my sojourn at the Leys. I learnt a decent amount of farming, and, indeed, gained a reasonable meed of praise from old Mangold. This advance in agricultural knowledge was due rather to increased attention on my part than to the time which I was enabled to devote to my duties; for, indeed, Miss Mangold told me with more acerbity than I had suspected her of possessing, I was always up at the Court, and, as she expressed it more familiarly than elegantly, in Miss Ruth's pocket.

I mildly repelled the accusation of living at the Court, excusing myself as to frequent visits by saying that one wanted a little change, and treating with silent scorn the unauthorised allusion to any part of Miss Allerton's sacred costume.

'You didn't want so much change once,' she said, tossing her head, which still looked pretty enough with her fresh colour and soft abundant hair; 'but times are changed I can see.'

'I shall have to go away next month,' said I, evading the latter part of her remark. 'You and I mustn't part bad friends, Jane.'

'I'm not bad friends,' she said, 'though some people are so fickle that they run after every new face they see just because people are high up in the world. I shall be sorry when you go, for it will be fearfully dull—worse than ever. But what will you do after you go away—take a farm about here? It will want money to do that, with the stock and rotation of crop you're bound to, and all the other fads for making farmers spend money instead of landlords nowadays.'

'I don't know what I shall do, Jane,' I answered somewhat reflectively. 'It appears to me that I have not much chance of doing anything in England.'

'But you wouldn't go out of England, Hereward—that is Mr. Pole,' said the girl hastily, while the colour left her cheek. 'You wouldn't go to America or India or any of those places, surely?'

'Why not?' said I bitterly. 'What earthly use is a fellow like me crawling about in England? I have no profession. I have no money. And the only thing I can try for is the post of a farm bailiff, a gamekeeper, or a second whip. Even these need recommendations. No; I'm a useless gentleman, and they might as well have drowned me like a blind puppy as bring me up to such a fate.'

'Oh, don't you talk like that!' cried the good-natured Jane, much moved by my unwonted bitterness and the tragic view of my position. 'Surely your friends will do something for you. Set you up in a farm, or get you a place under Government. You might be happy enough that way, if you would only be contented.' Here she sighed softly. Poor Jane!

'I could never be contented,' said I, 'with anything short of a decent position in the world. I hate the sameness of an everyday pokey life. I must travel, or get away from England and try my luck somehow.'

'Why don't you ask the Squire to make you gamekeeper at the Court?' she said mischievously; and then, marking my sudden change of countenance, said: 'Oh, don't be angry, Mr. Pole! But I hear father coming——'

Some days after this conversation I received a letter from my uncle, in which he drew my attention to the fact that the year during which he had consented to pay for my training at Dibblestowe Leys had well nigh expired. After that time he should be unable to do anything further for me, unless I chose to take a junior clerkship in the Treasury or a situation as farm bailiff; either appointment he doubted not that he could procure for me.

I was much minded to answer hastily, telling him that he need not trouble himself about such means of maintenance. Then I bethought myself that I ought seriously to think the matter over. Careless and reckless as I had been up to this time, a change had taken place in my position which swayed the whole current of my thoughts.

I had become sensible that my early admiration for Ruth Allerton had gradually ripened, from the opportunities which had been, perhaps unwisely, afforded us of knowing one another fully and unreservedly, into a deep, altogether uncontrollable passion. Gradually had our hearts become attracted, then inextricably intertwined in that mysterious bond of soul and sense—that complete instinctive union of every thought and feeling, which perhaps rarely occurs so indissolubly as in early youth.

We had spoken no word on the subject to each other. Yet had we discovered methods of divining each other's inmost thoughts. And as soon as I commenced to think about leaving the neighbourhood and ending the pleasant life of that most idyllic year, ah, me ! the whole truth flashed upon me with lightning-like revelation.

Curiously enough, I had scarcely realised it before. Utterly contented with the friendly liberty which I had enjoyed, I had, with the utter carelessness of youth, rested satisfied with the present. I was by no means so new to the world that I did not gauge the utter impossibility of my gaining the consent of Ruth's parents to an engagement—even were she favourable. County families don't usually arrange the marriages of their daughters on such terms as I had to offer. Granted that she was weak enough to assent to any mad proposition of mine, what possible hope could I entertain of carrying out an engagement ? I firmly believe, looking back to that time, that I had no other intention than loyally to abstain from compromising or entangling her. I would take my leave calmly of the old hall court and its loved inmates, and afterwards I would leave England. I was fixed in that opinion ; nothing would persuade me to remain pottering in this crowded old country, eating away my heart with a sense of poverty, inferiority, and misfortune. England was no place for a younger son. Without money, more than one of my ancestors had left it to seek his fortune. So would I.

I prepared then for quitting Dibblestowe Leys with something like method. I wrote to my uncle stating that I had no inclination to remain in England and commence a painful ascent to a competence by beginning at the bottom rung of the ladder. That my mind was made up to go to America, north or south, I hardly cared which. That possibly I should make for California, then in its second year as a gold-producing country. That he might help me to emigrate if he would. But that if he did not, I should go before the mast and work my passage in the first ship that would take me. His answer was that he thought I was mad, but that if I was determined to go, he would pay my passage, and find me a trifle by way of outfit.

I did not mention this notable determination to Ruth, reserving it to the last ; perhaps constitutionally unwilling to make a painful statement until it was absolutely necessary. Meanwhile, I commenced to use my practical opportunity effectively ; to that end I worked every day for a short time in the blacksmith's shop attached to the farm, for which fascinating work I had always had a boyish taste.

One bright morning I was relieving the striker for a short time, when he pulled a grimy newspaper from his pocket. He was a broad-shouldered, muscular young fellow of twenty, who had always been a kind of humble friend and ally of mine. Passionately fond of shooting and fishing, I had taken pains to get him a day's rabbiting occasionally, and had let him carry my basket now and then when we had an afternoon's holiday and set off for the trout stream. 'Would ye look at this, Mr. Pole?' said he. 'I ha' gotten it from a brother of mine in Australia, who went there in a big ship called the *Red Jacket* last year. Quartermaster, Jack was; and seems loike he's runned away, and gotten hissen up the country to a place they call Ballyrat, where they're a rootin' out the gold like spuds.'

'That must be all nonsense,' said I, unable to take in so much of the unusual at one gulp.

'Nay, but it is na,' he replied. 'He sent me the letter and two newspapers as I've got at the kitchen as ye'd like to see 'em. Here's the letter. Happen ye'd like to read it. It's Jack's fist sure enough. He wants me to go to him, and I'd go fast enou if I had any neighbour folk as 'ud go with me. But I can't think to face so far by mysen.'

'Ha! Joe,' said I, raising the heavy hammer and bringing down stroke after stroke with a strangely excited feeling, which made the heavy tool tremble in my grasp like a tack hammer. 'Wants you to go, does he? Well, maybe you might have a mate after all.'

I finished my hour's striking, shod a horse, and pointed some farm tools, thinking the while that I might find such skill valuable in rude lands. My task done, I ventured to the Grange, and, locking myself in my bedroom, opened the epistle of Mr. Jack Bulder. Thus it ran :—

'BALLARAT, October 10, 1851.

'DERE BROTHER—This comes from the land, and not from the good ship Redjacket, as I expected to write home from wen I left the Leys, in consekens of my having run away from the old ship, wich I never thout to have done, only every crew in Melbourne harbour has done the same, and your brother Jack isn't worse than other people. We all cut it, dere brother, because of the goold, which they told us was tremenjus, and too much to resist, and *so we found it.* Since I have cum here I have made three hundred pound besides two nuggets which i kep in a wosh lether bagg. There is plenty more ware that cum from. Dere brother, if I was you I would cum here at once, and don't let nothin' stop you, I send forty pound; it ain't much, but it will pay your passidge. Dere brother, let nothing kepe you from cummin' hear. This is a very nice country and we all xpeck to make our pile, that is fortun, in too yeares, at farthist. Dere brother, put yourself aboard a ship at once is the advice of yours truly, JOHN BULDER.

'*P.S.*—My mait has just found a lump of goold worth fourty pound. When you go to Melbourne, go to the Oriental Bank and ask for John Bulder; they will know my address. I send the *Star* and the *Herild*, as will let you know what is happening every day here, quite comman.'

I carefully read the newspapers after perusing this characteristic but conclusive epistle. They were well printed and respectably conducted. I marked the following paragraph with an instinctive feeling of relief and approbation, as follows :—

'We are glad to be enabled to chronicle the good fortune of our old friends Billy Watson and party. They struck good gold on the Monkey lead last month, and have washed up 200 loads to-day for 300 oz., worth at present price £1100, no bad result for six weeks' work for four men.

'The Blue Danube Reef has, we hear, come again on the lode at the 300 ft. level, and the specimens are excessively rich. Shares immediately went up, and it's reported that Mr. Smarter, by timely sales, cleared £2700 profit upon his original investment. We wish him every success.

'A bazaar was opened yesterday for the benefit of the local hospital, which we are glad to see was extensively patronised. Too much praise cannot be bestowed upon those ladies who have taken so much pains and bestowed such unremitting personal labour on this exceedingly attractive exhibition. More than £400, we hear, were collected and subscribed. When we think of the great uncertainty of life and limb existing in mining communities, it is obvious that such an institution, efficiently worked, is almost inestimable. We trust that the miners will rally round this unsectarian charity at another time. Meanwhile, may the Green Gully Hospital flourish and its founders meet with all manner of success.'

Here, in my circumstances, was a manifest revelation. It was plainly indicative of the country to which to go, and the reason for which to go. In other lands long toilsome years must be spent before there was even the chance of a fortune being made. In this wonderful country a single month might place one in that blessed condition of independence, that no amount of self-denial and labour in England could secure in half a lifetime.

I read and re-read the newspaper—the *Star*—from end to end. The more I read was I convinced of the *bona-fides* of the information, and the general advantages of the locality. I saw by the section of 'Police News' that offences were unsparingly punished in accordance with British law. Deeds of mercy and charity were by no means omitted from the daily life of the toilers for gold. It was not all *couleur de rose* as the record of casualties and accidents proved. Still the fact remained incontestable that fortunes *were being made* weekly, daily, in that favoured spot. The gold deposit was not likely to be worked out very soon. Other finds were referred to. It was the modern Eldorado. A two month's voyage would land one there. My mind was made up. I would try the gold region, and either win fortune, with whom fame is generally on speaking terms, or pay the usual penalty.

I informed Joe Bulder of my decision. Somewhat to my surprise he at once proposed to accompany me. 'I'm nowt but a plain lad, Mister Pole,' said he, 'but you might loike to see a Dibb'stowe face in foreign parts ; and I'll stand by thee hand

and foot, I reckon. I'm tired of working here for farmer Mangold. Doesn't thee see blacksmiths be a gettin' a pound a day oot there?—shoeing horses a pound a set. Why, thou'st' made a pound thysen this marnin', besides sharpening they picks at a shillin' each. Danged if I don't keep t' forge while thee goes a seekin' for gowd, and we can share and share loike.'

Joe little thought that he was advocating the great Australian mining custom of 'dividing mates,' by which most generously equitable portion of the unwritten law, fortunes have been made and shared on every goldfield in Australia. 'I shall be only too glad to have such a good fellow with me, Joe,' said I. 'It's a bargain. The next thing is to find a ship.'

My intercourse with Allerton Court and its inmates had continued as usual. A half-regretful tone had certainly characterised our latter interviews, since I had allowed it to be known that I should not remain at Dibblestowe Leys. May it have been that in each heart was still some unacknowledged feeling that I might not finally quit the neighbourhood, or, at any rate, go no farther away than the county in which my uncle resided. A few questions had been put by the Squire and Mrs. Allerton as to my future projects. To these I had answered without strictly defining my intentions. I had, in return, received good advice from the Squire, on the subject of making up my mind and taking a path in life. They little dreamed of the one I *had* chosen.

At length, however, the day before my departure arrived, and I rode over to the Court to pay my farewell visit. The Squire was away at a neighbouring farm, and Mrs. Allerton had accompanied him for a morning drive. I found Ruth in the old-fashioned garden, near the fish-pond, a place where a stone balustered terrace had been built, nigh which was a seat which commanded an unrivalled view in our eyes. There were Hollingbourne Woods and Torry Hill—the marshes by the sea, with the isle of Sheppy like a cloud in the hazy distance.

It was called the Lady's Seat, and was popularly supposed to have been placed there and much affected by an ancestress who had lost her lover in the battle of Long Marston Moor. It was the favourite resort of Ruth, who was of a contemplative and studious disposition. Here she was accustomed to take her sketch-book or a volume, and spend many a glad spring morning or still summer afternoon under the shade of the ancestral oaks. Half instinctively I wended my steps thither, when I heard that the Squire and Mrs. Allerton had driven over to Ollendean.

'You find me here all alone,' said she, 'and I am not sorry. I have been reading the *Bride of Lammermoor* over again, and making myself low-spirited over the woes of that most unlucky Lucy Ashton. Yet, I cannot but think, if she had acted with more firmness, and been true to her better nature, the tragedy need never have taken place. She was a victim of indecision.'

'What, in spite of her mother, that terribly despotic matron?' said I, 'and the prophecy?—

' " When the last Laird of Ravenswood to Ravenswood shall ride,
And woo a dead maiden to be his bride,
He shall stable his steed in the Kelpie's flow,
And his name shall be lost for evermoe ! "

What girl could stand against such a rhythmical doom, even leaving out the inexorable parent?'

'Some girls would—most of them, I hope,' she said, looking dreamily across the far wide landscape, over the greater part of which her ancestors had once held lordship. 'It might have rent her heart well nigh to resist her parents, but there was no other course to pursue.'

'Do you think *you* would have had strength of mind and constancy enough to have kept faith with the ruined, ill-fated Ravenswood?' asked I, with a sudden impulse ; 'think of the superior claims of a smooth, safe marriage with the prosperous Laird of Bucklaw.'

Her cheek flushed for a moment, but her eye met mine with an artless candour, which showed how little she realised the analogy.

'It's hard to go at once from romance to reality,' she said, 'and I can hardly imagine the situation occurring to any one in these modern days ; but, surely, if she had ever loved him, she must have clung to him *more* for his poverty and his banishment. As for agreeing to her mother's hateful project, she must have been mad, poor thing, as she afterwards proved to be, when she permitted them to speak of it to her. But suppose we leave Sir Walter here,' putting the book on the seat, 'and walk down the beech avenue this lovely morning. Have you had any sport lately? I don't think you have been over for a week.'

For a while, as we walked along the well-known avenue which followed the brow of the eminence, through the opening of which the hills, the valleys, with their woods of hazel and Spanish chestnut contrasted strangely with the dreary marshes, a momentary forgetfulness of my plans and purpose possessed me. We talked as usual upon the hundred and one subjects which were common ground between us. The state of the county politics, the new clergyman in a neighbouring parish credited with advanced views, the box of new books from Mudie's, the grand run from Staplehurst, in which the Squire had been well up with the hounds, a great dinner party which was to take place next week and to which I was to come and practise a part in a charade. A string of half-sisterly confidences which had always, since our first meeting, been open to me, and of which neither of us had ever thought, except as trifles, which might pass between ordinary friends or relatives of similar ages. My heart had only now undeceived itself. Hers was as yet strong and unfaltering, with the unspecting confidence of innocent girlhood.

I have often thought since that Ruth Allerton was a very uncommon type of womanhood, singularly unversed in the lore of the affections, in which knowledge girls of her age so often discover a premature shrewdness. Unlike most of her contemporaries, she was indisposed to the amusements befitting her age. The Squire abhorred London, and rarely went except when he could not avoid it. To Mrs. Allerton there was no happiness where her husband was not. And so it came to pass that Ruth had lived a life practically isolated from the gay world, fully absorbed in her own pursuits and resources.

When I recall the subjects upon which our long talks chiefly turned—such unusual ones, for instance, as what was the happiest state of life, whether to live for oneself or for others? This we decided very strongly in favour of the unselfish line, as who at our ages would not? A great and often resolved scheme for hers was, how to do the greatest good to the poor in this or any other neighbourhood, without destroying their independence and self-respect. How many plots against capitalists did we hatch in this behalf—as lawyers say.

What was the exact proportion of mental and bodily labour most fitted to produce true health of sense and spirit. Whether voluntary or involuntary labour was most beneficial.

Since then, how many different women of every creed and clime, rank and degree, have I known, only to confirm my fixed opinion, that she was a choice floweret of the rarest type of womanhood. For, old or young, rich or poor, wise or vain, homely or fair, I have never met with any woman like her.

Surely, there never was one more unconscious of her personal attractions. They were sufficiently visible to the ordinary gaze, yet she rarely troubled herself to heighten them in the slightest degree, never alluded to her form or face, hardly to those of others, and never but as illustrations of a fact. Plainness of apparel, except on occasions when she could not escape adornment, invariably characterised her, though she, perhaps, was a little *exigeante* as to material. I used laughingly to tell her that she would make an excellent Quakeress, but that her muslin would always be wonderfully fine, and cost more than any one else's.

Now, all this pleasant companionship must perforce come to an end. No more arguments when, with the pure light of truth shining from her earnest eyes, she would combat my utilitarian views, often adopted to arouse opposition, and to evoke the enthusiasm in which I delighted.

I did not, excited as I was with the idea, realise within myself the completeness of disruption which would be caused from all my old ties and life moorings.

'Ruth,' said I, 'do you know that a sense of mournful fore-boding is creeping over me, lovely as is the day and perfect the scene. I have bad news which I must tell you. I am about to leave Dibblestowe Leys, and, and, indeed, England, perhaps for some years.'

'Leave England,' she said, with such a sudden, sharp intona-tion, almost a cry of pain, that I looked up amazed. 'Oh, you are not speaking in earnest, Hereward ; tell me you are not.'

'I must go away from this place, happy as I have been here,' I said. 'And as I have no fortune, nor the slightest hope of making money here, I must go to some part of the world where I may, if I have luck, make it quickly.'

She had looked at me for one moment with a wild, piteous gaze of incredulity. Then she sank down on a rustic seat bench, and, turning away her head, sobbed unrestrainedly.

'Ruth,' said I, 'dearest, darling Ruth ! do not grieve so. I may, after all, only be a short time absent. Besides, most men have to leave their homes in youth. Why should I expect a better fate ? If I had dreamed that you would feel it thus, I might have——'

She interrupted me with a wave of her hand, as if forbidding me to continue my explanation. I sat down beside her and permitted her to give free course to her grief.

After awhile she turned her face towards me,—that sweet face I so often see in my dreams. It was calm and still, but with the strange unnatural look which comes when all hope has passed away.

'Why did you tell me so suddenly, Hereward ?' she said, softly. 'You see you have made me confess to caring so very much for your departure. If I had had more warning, I might have behaved like a young lady of the period, and hid my heart behind a cheerful farewell. Are you not sorry for your hasti-ness ?'

'I am more glad than I ever was at anything in the world since I was born,' I said, throwing myself on my knees before her, and kissing her cold hands, until they seemed to burn with the wild fever of my own blood. 'But I feel as if I had treated the Squire and your mother dishonourably, in winning their daughter's heart, under what they will consider false pretences.'

'We have both been to blame,' she said, sorrowfully, 'if people are to be blamed for loving each other fondly, without a thought of evil or deceit. But we could not help it, I suppose. And I can certainly declare, that I did not think I cared more for you than for a dear friend whose tastes and feelings seemed much to harmonise with and elevate my own. And now you are going away—for ever, perhaps ; *must* you go away ? Does love always begin by making people utterly wretched ?'

'I must go away,' I said, 'unless I am to ask the Squire to please to support me for the love of his child, or unless I am to content myself with a position of sordid penury, as hateful to myself as it would be dishonouring to you. No, dearest; there is but one path to me now—that of honour and adventure. The die is cast. But what are we to say for ourselves at the Court?'

'We must tell the truth, of course,' she said, proudly. 'There need be no concealment. I am not ashamed of my choice, my own Hereward—are you? Then let us go boldly to my dearest mother. I will tell her, as I have always told her, everything from a little girl. You are to dine here to-night, so you will have to tell my dear old father.'

'And what will he say, Ruth, do you think, when I mention my very handsome expectations?'

'He may be angry or grieved at first, but you must not mind that. The worst will soon be over. And he is so generous and just in all his thoughts—he will consider my happiness before everything. Tell him what you hope to do in—in—this far country; and that in a few years you will come to claim me. There is no more to be said. It is the truth, and the truth, he is fond of saying, always prevails.'

All this was very well, and as my darling looked into my face with her tender, honest eyes, I felt it to be in a way reassuring ; but the truth was, in the present case, that I was most horribly frightened, and having a clearer view than my unworldly love, of the extremely inadequate grounds upon which I had sought her affection, dreaded the dinner referred to, as if it had been a feast to precede dissolution.

Having made up our minds to dare the dreadful alternative of facing the Squire, Ruth and I, with the happy rashness of youth, commenced to look upon our joint future as a thing assured, in some form or other, and to make plans with the cheerful confidence of birds in a premature spring.

After dinner, during which Ruth had been very quiet, even *distraite*,—but as she was often so, less notice was taken of her mood than would have been the case with a girl whose spirits were ordinarily lighter,—I opened the trenches.

'I am afraid I shall have to say good-bye, soon, to this neighbourhood, and to all my pleasant visits to Allerton Court, Squire,' said I, gulping it out.

'How is that?' said the Squire, 'leave the country side! why, we couldn't do without you—who is to drive Mrs. Allerton, and get ferns for Ruth, and sketch ruins for Dame Ermentrude?'

This was an old aunt, a special patroness of mine, who lived in what was called the Old Dower House, and who petted me for want of much other kin to waste her loving heart upon.

'Why, we shall be altogether moped and desolated. I wanted you to ride that new horse for me this next season. Why not stay another year at the Leys? You won't know too much farming then, I'll be bound.'

'And what am I to do afterwards?' said I. 'No, Squire, the long and the short of it is, that I have made up my mind to

strike out a new path for myself, if not in this country, in some
other.'

Here Mrs. Allerton and Ruth left us, and I continued with a
boldness akin to recklessness.

'And I have something more to tell you, Squire,' said I, looking him full in the face, 'something, I am afraid, that you will
not approve of, but it cannot be helped.'

'What the deuce is the matter?' said the old man, 'you
haven't married Miss Mangold? I should consider that imprudent, I must say, but not my affair.'

'Never mind poor Jane Mangold, Squire,' said I. 'It is no
laughing matter. Your daughter and I have discovered that we
love one another, and have this day plighted our troth. You
will not suspect me of making dishonourable use of the confidence with which you have always treated me, but, the fact is, I
believe we neither of us suspected the state of our feelings, and
the avowal of them to-day was the purest accident.'

'What?' said the Squire, jumping off his chair with alarm
and astonishment, 'do you mean to tell me that you two young
fools have engaged yourselves to be married without asking
any one's leave in the matter? What in the name of everything
imprudent have you to marry upon, Master Hereward? What
geese — idiots — deaf - and - dumb blind incurables, have Mrs.
Allerton and I been, and, Ruth, too, the last girl I should
have ever thought would have dreamed of such folly. My
poor Ruth!'

'Squire,' said I, 'I will say good-bye, and get back to the
Leys. I see you are too excited to hear what I have to say to-
night.'

'No, no, boy,' he said, motioning me back to my chair.
'Mustn't turn you out like that. You've always been a good
lad, and one after my own heart. But the inconceivable folly
of two children like you wishing to be married. Why, it will be
time enough for you to be thinking of it this day ten years, and
not then, if you haven't a home to offer her. And to think of
my folly! I am the person most to blame in the matter.'

'But, Squire,' said I, 'suppose I make a fair thing, as fortunes
go, in five years, I shall then be six and twenty, and not so un-
pardonably young. Ruth is not eighteen, so she could afford to
wait till she was three or four and twenty, without wasting her
bloom.'

'Wait be hanged!' said the choleric old gentleman, 'she
would wait for twenty years. I know her nature; but do you
think I want to see my girl shrivelling up into an angular old
maid, with her temper and her health both soured together, her
good looks gone, and her life wasted for the sake of a fellow who
is, as like as not, racketing on the other side of the globe, and
taking the matter very coolly? And what is this wonderful
plan, may I ask, for making a fortune in five years?'

'I am going to Australia to try my luck at these goldfields

C

we hear so much about. There is no doubt they are wonderful places, and the yields are enormous.'

'All lies, I dare say,' said the distrustful senior. 'Anyhow, I have no great opinion of colonies; lots of people go there, who are no great good when they leave, and they come back a great deal worse.'

'Look at the paper,' I said, and I unfolded the Forest Creek *Herald*, which I had kept and read and re-read till I knew the names of all the people on the diggings as well as if I had lived there.

'People write queer things in newspapers, even in England,' he said, reaching out his hand for the journal in question. 'I hardly think they can be very trustworthy in a colony.'

'Read for yourself,' said I. 'I think the internal evidence shows intelligence and respectability. There are chapter and verse for the many wonderful things recorded.'

'Certainly, it is well printed and got up,' he said, relenting somewhat as he glanced over it; 'and really, it does seem all very wonderful and enticing. If I were a young man, I think I should take a run there myself. What does this mean? "We are gratified to learn that the shareholders in the Welcome Home Reef, who have been for more than a year hoping against hope, have struck good gold in their three hundred and fifty feet level. This at once sends up the shares to seventy-five and eighty. They were offered at seven ten last week. One gentleman whom we could name has realised twenty thousand pounds, in addition to his Sandy Creek profits, within the last fortnight."'

'It means,' said I, 'that a few energetic workers have been rewarded for their pluck and patience,—and after a fashion which would need half the years of a man's life to develop in England.'

'I must say,' he continued, looking over the alluring announcements, 'that such enterprises wear a very feasible appearance, as described here.'

And he began to quote afresh.

'"The Crinoline Claim washed up for four hundred loads on Saturday last; the dirt went well over two ounces to the load. Not so far off a thousand pounds a man for eight weeks' work. The shareholders are comparatively new arrivals." That sounds encouraging, I must say,' said the partly mollified elder. 'But there is no certainty, no certainty. Ah, here's another. "All previous finds on the field have been reduced to insignificance by the great find of the Welcome Nugget, at Whipstick, by Happy Jack and the Fiddler. Its net weight was 170 lb. 6 oz. Its value is estimated by the manager of the Bank of New Holland as not less than £8000 sterling." Ha! ha! we don't pull them up in old England like that, Hereward, lad! I suppose there'll be no keeping thee, I should go myself if I were young again.'

On the morning after the storm—the winds and waves having

somewhat abated—a calmer consideration of matters ensued.
Of course, Ruth had confessed all things to her mother, and
with feminine perseverance and entreaty had fully enlisted that
kindly matron on her side.

'When I married your father, my dear,' she said, 'he never
expected to succeed to this dear old place. Several lives lay
between us and its possession, all of which were inscrutably
removed. We had to undergo many things; but we never
repented of the tie which had joined us before we came to our
kingdom. Still, *some* provision is needed to be assured. I
must say, I think Hereward very brave for resolving to go to
such a horrid country, and not more adventurous than a young
man should be.'

It was finally settled that our engagement, which could not
be annulled without an amount of judicial cruelty which neither
parent had the heart to inflict, should be conditionally ratified.
I was to be permitted to seek my fortune in the far unknown
land, concerning which they had such very slender information.
Ruth would wait at home for five years, if that period should
be consumed in the not always speedy process of making a
fortune.

Have I before stated that the Squire and his wife were not
average specimens of the upper classes of the day? Strange to
say they elected to consult the feelings of their child. They did
not scoff, after the first natural outburst of the Squire, at youth
and strength, high hope and honest determination. Nor secretly
resolve to compel Ruth to accept the first middle-aged suitor of
indifferent morals and unexceptionable fortune that presented
himself. That such would have been the course pursued by a
very large majority of parents occupying the same or a higher
social position, my experience of life enables me to assert fearlessly. Thank Heaven, my darling had been blessed with a
father and mother of wholly different ideas; otherwise she
might not have been her sweet self, and the star which shone
so brightly amid the storm-clouds which enveloped my career
might have sunk for ever in darkness and despair.

We, happy and heedless children that we were, felt as trans-
ported with joy as if we had received permission to marry next
month. Ruth was one of those maidens to whom watching and
waiting have ever been nearly as suitable, indeed, quite as
secretly satisfactory as the immediate fulfilment of their hopes,
as affording scope for the self-sacrifice which constituted so
large a portion of their nature. And I, on the other hand, felt
moved with the natural passion of adventure, so strong in early
youth, to kill my dragons and slay my enchanters in decent
profusion, before I entered into the undisturbed possession of
the fairy princess and the enchanted castle.

Of course, Mrs. Grundy outdid herself in protestations against
the madness of the Squire for even sanctioning our engagement.
A young man without a penny in the world, who was going

to a rude wild country like Australia, from which he never would be heard of again. And really, it certainly was so difficult to believe—here they were permitting that nice, sweet girl—she had not much money to be sure, but she belonged to a county family—to engage herself to a penniless youngster, without money, profession, or expectation !

Fortunately for me, both the Squire and his wife treated such babble with supreme contempt. They were absurd enough to desire above all their daughter's happiness. They knew her steadfast disposition too well to doubt her constancy—to think of coercing her will. The affair was—even the marriage which it foreshadowed—a fixed and settled thing, not to be gossiped about but to be made the best of.

The Squire made an attempt to prevent my emigration which, like most English people of assured position, he looked upon as more bitter than death. He offered me one of his own farms at a low rent, with a promise of a loan of money sufficient to stock it. But my pride was fully aroused. My determination to do something worthy of the inestimable treasure they had confided to me was unalterable. So, in despite of all obstacles and hindrances, a month saw my passage taken, and all preparations made for my voyage to the other end of the world.

My uncle did not attempt to alter my heroic determination ; he acted sensibly, if not affectionately.

'I observe in the papers,' he said, 'that very astonishing finds have been made by the adventurers who have crowded from all lands to the Australian goldfields. You are young and strong, and totally without occupation. All the better for you that you have good blood in your veins. Your sisters will need every farthing of what was left by my brother. Still, I can make shift to pay your passage, and find you a decent outfit. You *may* make a fortune. Many as broken a ship has come to land. Write now and then and say how you get on. We have not, perhaps, been the most affectionate of relatives. When you reach my age you may, perhaps, understand some of the feelings of a disappointed man. Sincerely I bid God to bless and speed you.'

He shook my hand more warmly than I thought it was in his nature to do. My sisters hung weeping around me. In a few minutes the dog-cart came to take me to the station, and I left the home of my boyhood—for ever. Joe Bulder joined me at the station. That evening we slept on board the grand clipper ship *Marco Polo*, Captain Driver, bound for Melbourne, in company with four hundred and fifty other passengers, of every conceivable age, profession, and variety of mankind.

CHAPTER III

APPARENTLY we escaped all perils of the deep. To them I do not need specially to refer. For here we are at the Yatala diggings, I and my worthy mate and friend, Joe Bulder, both considerably altered in several ways. Two men are sitting by a large fire of logs, near the doorway of a small tent. They are old mates, and the other shareholders in the claim. Our party consists of four, which is much the most common number, particularly where the sinking is deepish as here at Yatala.

As to dress and general appearance, I don't think any one would have recognised the fresh-coloured, moderately well got-up youngster who used to sit in the Squire's pew at Bishop's Cote Church, or even the amateur farm-labourer holding the plough occasionally, or driving the engine at Dibblestowe Leys. The man who has just come out of the tent wears certainly a different appearance. He is arranging his raiment preparatory to commencing 'the night shift'—eight hours' uninterrupted work, nearly one hundred and fifty feet below the earth's surface. The which term commences at eight P.M., finishing at four o'clock in the morning. This man is taller and broader than the slight stripling who left England four years since in the *Marco Polo*. His arms are bare to the elbows, up to which is rolled a close-fitting flannel shirt. They are bronzed with exposure to a fiercer sun than that which ripens England's harvests, and the muscles stand out, cord-like, in relief. Round the waist, which is that of an athlete in high training, is a leathern strap tightly belted. He wears trousers of moleskin which, though clean and of fairly good cut, have, from constant washing with water holding a large proportion of clay in solution, become of a bright and cheerful yellow, altogether ineradicable. Yet, though the garb is plain and workmanlike, there is no trace of unnecessary coarseness of habit. The short hair and trimmed beard are those of the fashion-guided unit of humanity, while a studied air of cleanliness denoting regular baths and ablutions is plainly visible to the observant eye. This man is Harry Pole, the digger, myself, kind reader, after four years' steady, ill-rewarded toil at Aus·

tralian and, indeed, New Zealand goldfields—no nearer, as may be surmised, to the fortune which was to precede the priceless gift of the hand of Ruth Allerton.

Let us listen to the conversation of this man and his comrades.

'I don't see the use of going any furder with this confounded claim; here we've been bustin' ourselves for the last three months, night and day, and not a foot nearer to the gold than we was when the first shovelful was took out. We haven't a pound to bless ourselves with, and we're in debt to Mrs. Mangrove, at the Beehive store, that deep that I'm ashamed to go in for powder, or a bit of fuse. We're on the bottom safe enough, and there's not gold enough to put on the p'int of a needle. I say ding it this very night, and let's try for a show somewhere else.'

This encouraging speech, which most accurately described our financial position and prospects, capital and expectations, is made by Mr Cyrus Yorke, a young man of unusual physical power, but weak as to the reasoning faculties. He is of English descent, born in Australia, and though possessing many good qualities, is incorrigibly careless, besides being averse to sustained labour of body or mind. He is the only man of the party who is not a bachelor. His wife is a good-looking, good-tempered little woman, with twice as much sense as her spouse. She is the housewife for the party, and is treated on that account and for other reasons with great respect and consideration. Indeed, but for her conciliatory ways, it is most probable that some one of Yorke's many provoking sins of omission or commission would have led long ere this to his exclusion from the party.

'We're bound to see the end of this drive,' I say, in an argumentative tone. 'Everybody believes that the "lead" lies due west of us, and in thirty or forty feet we *must* strike it, if it's there at all. It would be foolish to throw away all our work and expense, perhaps, just a few yards from good gold.'

'We're bound to drive oot to the last inch,' said the square-set determined-looking man smoking a short black pipe. 'Harry here's marked and ciphered it all out, and we all agreed to it. What's the use of throwing up the sponge afore the fight's over? What dost thou say, Major?'

'I fully agree with Pole,' said the individual addressed, who, in monkey-jacket and generally rather roughish array, was lying on one of the stretchers reading an English newspaper. 'He has worked out the thing, as you say. I was too lazy to follow him. But he is generally right and Cyrus is always wrong; so, perhaps, he had better take his line and mind his immediate business, which is to tackle this night shift, and wire-in at the cross-cut without any more humbug.'

'Well, I'm blessed,' growled the unpopular candidate, 'if that ain't a nice way to talk to a mate and a shareholder, Major

One would think I was a wages-man, the way you three coves bosses it over me. You'll rouse the British lion one of these fine days, and so I tell you.'

Apparently Cyrus Yorke was minded to defer poking up that long-suffering royal beast, until a more convenient season—for he walked on to the 'brace' and commenced to peel off his heavier garments, preparatory to descending into the bowels of the earth, without more ado.

'You're all agin me,' he said, as he opened his vast chest and stretched his colossal arms above his head, as if trying whether his joints were about to act in their usual manner. 'But that's the way in this country, the majority always has the pull. It's time that kind o' thing was stopped, I think. Now, Mr. Joseph Bulder, you go and lead the old mare. I s'pose you don't want me to break my back, as bad as I am.'

'Thou'rt a rattlin' fine chap, if thou'd use thy four bones as is summot like, and drop botherin' thy old turnip of a head, as God Almighty never intended ye to do nowt wi' but tak' ither folks' orders. I'll back thee to put down a shaft agin any chap in Yatala. But don't thee go argufying, for it spoils thee. Ask thee wife else. Steady! Bess, old girl.'

Cyrus Yorke made no further reply, but clasping the rope with his hands above his head, placed one foot in the loop at the end and swung himself off the wooden stage, which is always built at the mouth of a mining shaft. A 'sprag,' being a stout piece of hard wood, was inserted between the rope and the iron roller on which the rope ran and thus the miner was slowly and steadily lowered down the deep, dark, apparently fathomless shaft.

In being lowered, dependent upon a single rope which, though apparently strong, has been known to break, the sensations are complicated if the depth be much over a hundred feet. The closeness of the sides of the shaft to the explorer gives a species of false security, by no means borne out by reason. An inexperienced cragsman would hardly consent to be lowered a hundred and fifty feet over the face of a Hebridean precipice, with the sea a thousand feet below, and nought but the sky and clamouring sea-fowl around—above.

Yet one adventure is fully as dangerous in reality as the other. Let but a sudden spasm, or syncope, attack the adventurer in the shaft, and if he loses hold of the rope, no power on earth can save him. The smooth hard sides of the shaft furnish no foot-hold, did the velocity acquired in falling not prevent him from making use of them. Down, down, he must fall until the end of the long cruel pit be reached—and then, let those say who have ever assisted to raise a man, who from carelessness, foul air, any one of the many accidents common to miners, has fallen down a deep shaft.

In this instance Cyrus was not fated to illustrate any of these dismal theories. Holding the rope easily with one hand,

and occasionally preventing by adroit touch of foot against the sides of the shaft the rope from swinging round, and so discomposing his equilibrium, he passed swiftly yet surely down to the bottom level, and having exhausted his small supply of ill-temper, crept along a gallery running at right angles to the shaft, where, seizing a pick, he commenced to knock down on to the floor of the gallery a stratum of mixed sand, pebbles, and small quartz fragments. Of these there was a layer about nine inches thick in the roof of the gallery, or 'drive,' as it is invariably called in Australian mining parlance. He had dragged after him a large raw-hide bucket which he found in the bottom of the shaft. This he set up on end, and quickly filling, drew to the shaft and attached to the iron hook at the end of the rope by which he had descended. He then pulled twice a small line which hung down, almost invisible, close by the wall of the shaft. This line moved a rude apparatus, in the nature of an indicator, at the mouth of the shaft. It was a hammer-like piece of hardwood above a plate of tin, on which, at each pull of the line, it smote smartly. The meaning of the percussion was, attention—all ready—or pull up, as the case might be. The old mare appeared to understand it, for she at once pricked up her ears, moved herself square to a singletree by which her trace-chains were fastened, holding herself in readiness to draw.

'Go on, old woman,' said Joe Bulder, 'haul away.'

The intelligent animal, long trained to this particular kind of work, needed no further urging. Setting herself staunchly to the collar, she drew steadily at the rope, now tightened by the weight of the leathern bag, with, perhaps, a hundred weight and a half of gravel therein. She walked along the track made by her own feet, called by miners the 'horse walk,' its position being formally indicated by two lines of very hastily constructed rail fence, and drew the auriferous burden yet nearer to the upper air. When she reached the limit of the horse walk, denoted merely by a sapling laid across two forked uprights, she stopped promptly, holding, however, the rope, and neither turning nor yet permitting it to slacken. At that moment the bucket appeared slightly above the brace at the shaft, and was taken by the topman, Joe Bulder, who, lifting it to one side, unhooked it and placed on the hook an empty bucket of the same construction, ready for the unpromising descent.

The lower portion of the rope is disconnected with the former one, and the mare being informed—one really does not see how —that her tenacity is no longer needed, complacently turns round and trots the whole way in, quite unaided, turning herself with great agility at the end, and disengaging the rope from her hind legs most cleverly. I then, in turn, take hold of the rope, place my foot in the leathern bucket, and go down slowly out of the sunshine in the humid darkness of the lower

earth, with the prospect of eight hours' continuous work before
me.

After all, it is not so hard to bear. We are, all four of us, in
magnificent health and condition, 'fit to go for a man's life,' as
Cyrus Yorke says, which means that we are hardened by toil,
trained down by exercise and regular diet, until very little improvement could have been made upon our condition, had we
to run a match against time, fight bushrangers, or accomplish
any of the feats of strength, speed, or endurance, which men
are foolish enough to attempt for cash or vain-glory in the pride
of early manhood.

We are gold miners, neither more nor less—diggers, as the
more general term is. Such we have been for the last three or
four years, during most of which time we have been together,
sharing the same toils or privations, transient successes or
protracted misfortunes. Joe Bulder and I have, of course,
been associated since we left England together. The Major
and Cyrus had by chance become mates in the colony of
Victoria, where we first met them, and by the merest hazard
joined forces with us. Since then we have journeyed together.
Quitted moderate goldfields where nothing more than an easy
liberal livelihood was to be had for the stern hazards of a new
rush, at a moment's notice. Here, 'dividing mates,' as the
mining phrase is, one half of the party, when times were bad,
working at bush or other labour, in order to provide food and
raiment, tools and lodging for the whole, while the other pair
tried the mining ventures of the locality, on the chance of
striking, at any moment, a fortune, small or great, to be loyally
and equally divided into four parts.

That the Major, as he was always called, had been an officer
in Her Majesty's army, and in the cavalry arm of the service,
no one doubted for a moment who had been in his company,
and who was capable of verifying the habitudes of an officer
and a gentleman. To what regiment he had been attached, he
did not think it apparently necessary to explain, nor did we at
any time ask him. Such examples of reticence were innumer-
able 'on diggings.' Silence was generally observed as to
people's antecedents. It being obvious that to go about questioning everybody as to what position he had originally occupied, and for what reasons he had concluded to adopt a miner's
life, would have been altogether futile, besides being patently
ridiculous and impertinent. And it will be conceded by all
who have gained their experience upon Australian goldfields,
that for whatever sins diggers may be responsible, bad manners,
and lack of genuine courtesy, cannot be reckoned among
them.

The Major, a man of four or five and thirty, was in the full
vigour of manhood. He had evidently seen a good deal of the
world, and in many phases of society, though he habitually
spoke little of himself and merely permitted such glimpses of

his European experience to escape him half unconsciously. He was extremely fond of reading, and though by no means zealous in the performance of manual labour for its own sake, performed his quota efficiently enough. He and I, with Joe Bulder, usually shared one of the smaller tents. We took our meals in common. This might have been distressing under the circumstances. But Joe's and Cyrus Yorke's original habitudes had become so altered by the influence of travel and cultured association, that few of their superiors would have objected to their companionship on the warpath.

Mrs. Yorke and the two children had the cart, with its tilt and other accommodations, to themselves, and, indeed, this nomadic dwelling was far from uncomfortable, with its divers and manifold contrivances for ease and comfort.

Does it occur to some, as yet unexpatriated, that the life I have roughly sketched was a dull, laborious, well nigh unendurable existence, to be led by men who had the hereditary title to move in good society, nay, who had at one time of their lives shared that lesser Elysium? Was such the case, when, added to the specific drawbacks, was that of hopelessness as to the future, quickly subsiding to dull indifference? Let us calmly consider.

As a matter of fact, we were far from miserable. Indeed, if I assert that we were in a condition bordering upon absolute contentment, even happiness, incredible as it may appear, I should be nearer the mark. For consider, in the first place, miners are absolutely their own masters, perfectly independent, *quamdiu se bene gesserint*, utterly free from fealty to all but the Queen and the commissioner. We were 'by many a league of ocean-foam' separated from Her Most Gracious Majesty, but the latter potentate was an abiding and highly vitalised fact.

I see him now. How many years have rolled by. Yet I stand up and feel inclined to lift my hat, as if it were yesterday. An erect, stalwart, middle-aged man, sitting his wiry thoroughbred with careless ease, bold-visaged, eagle-eyed, with the stamp 'of ours' writ large, like our mate, the Major, on every movement of his body, on every expression of his face, on every trick of speech, as he calls to the half-dozen greyhounds that follow him through the camp, as if his thoughts dwelt more with them than with the crowding miners who press and throng to get a word of audience, a passing nod, or even a look of recognition from the autocrat of the goldfields.

And, in good sooth, Captain Blake, formerly of Her Majesty's 11th Hussars, was an autocrat by instinct, habit, education, and circumstance, if ever there was one upon God's earth. He it was, certainly, who more inexorably than the Roman Centurion, was wont to say, 'Go here, or go there,' and to this man, 'Do this, and he doeth it.' For, from his decision, there was, at that time, no appeal. The Medes and Persians had

apparently drawn up the scanty Goldfields' Regulations of
that day. Crude and inapplicable to the multiform elaborate
complications of the mining industry, the largest discretionary
power was implied. And William Devereux Blake, well known
at many a mess-table in England and Ireland as the Devil's
Own Billy Blake, was precisely the man to accept all the
responsibility of the position. It would have crushed a weaker
man. But with a clear head, an utterly fearless, perhaps
aggressive, organisation, and a natural turn for acting as a
leader and ruler of men, he had hitherto avoided misadventure
in his consulship. Large were the issues with which he had to
deal, and puzzling were the mining laws which he had to administer. A bold, ready, decisive manner sufficed to carry him
through everything ; and though occasional dissentients might
object to his decisions as illogical, he was both highly popular
and legally successful.

To him were daily submitted the numberless questions of
mineral ownership which arose in such a community as ours ;
a gathering of men from every country under Heaven, where
each, by chance or choice, had come to occupy under certain
written and unwritten laws, so limited a portion of the earth's
surface that it was measured by feet. Under it might be the
hidden treasure, the reward of a lost youth—a ruined life—
the mere rumour of which had brought the greater number
of us so far over the main, across so many a weary mile of wood
and wold.

To decide equitably and rapidly, to maintain unswervingly,
and to enforce rigidly, the decisions arrived at after the hearing of such evidence as was forthcoming, required natural
gifts which few men possessed. But 'Billy' Blake had been
cast by Nature at his birth for the 'role' of a chieftain, and
most eminently qualified was he for the part which he was
called upon to play.

At one time his decisions were given in the modest
structure which served as the court-house, wherein were tried
daily such offences as opposed the statute law of the land. At
another they were delivered as he sat on horseback amid an
angry crowd of a thousand excited men. But in no instance
did the surroundings make the slightest difference in the
despotic tone of utter finality which clothed them. Men spoke
of his acts and words with bated breath. The commissioner
had 'decided' this or that point of mining law. He had turned
this man out of one of the richest claims on 'the field' and put
another into possession of it—and a fortune. He had sentenced
Towney Joe to six months' imprisonment with hard labour for
stealing five shillings' worth of wash-dirt. He had threatened
Red Dick that, if he heard of his beating his wife again he
should have twelve months within stone walls. He had told
Ned White, upon that worthy making sarcastic reference to the
commissioner's uniform coat as a fortunate protection to the

wearer, to put up his hands, and dismounting, had then and there so 'straightened' him 'inside of three rounds,' that Ned hadn't a word to say for himself, and was ashamed to show his face for a fortnight afterwards.

On the other hand, when Jim Black's wife had come crying to him, saying her husband hadn't the price of a miner's right, and it was very hard because he knew where there was some good ground, and he dursn't put a pick in it, because any one with a 'right' could take it away from him, he had sworn at Jim for a lazy blackguard, who was always trying to rob the Government, and declared, if he caught him digging without a miner's right he would send him to gaol straightway and then tossed a sovereign to the sobbing woman, telling her to take out a miner's right for her husband that very day, and to keep the balance for the children.

Every kind and variety of legend was current about the commissioner. He was the ogre of the fairy tale, the good knight of the romances, the wicked baron of the middle ages, the pitiless official—all by turns.

The great pro-consul had been away on leave of absence when I and my comrades first came to Yatala ; so we did not immediately meet. But daily, so much, and such extravagant reference was made to his acts and deeds, opinions and manners, that all unconsciously we looked forward, as did, apparently, the larger part of the population, to the momentous period when the Captain should come back.

In the meantime the interest of the dwellers and delvers of Yatala was divided by other social and official celebrities, some of whom were sufficiently characteristic.

Next to Zeus, the all-powerful, came the Inspector of Police, Mr. Merlin, an astute, fine-edged, courteously combative personage, who always reminded me of a Toledo blade, habited in the dress of the period. An animated rapier—if such a type of humanity be consistent with natural laws. Precisely that weapon and no other, being difficult to confront, to evade, to handle, or even to hold scabbardless. Only really innocuous when securely sheathed and placed on the shelf. There was little overt aggressiveness about him. He was the least egotistical of men, inasmuch as whatever ideas of superiority to his surroundings he might have cherished, he rarely expressed them. The exploits and adventures of which he may have been the hero he never narrated ; accomplishments he may have possessed, and did in several notably excel, but he never alluded to them. His reserve was impenetrable ; his caustic though courteous manner invariably the same. Yet few there were of the Yatala community who did not acknowledge pleasure in his society, coupled with a slight infusion of fear. There was an involuntary dread among the miners in his presence, lest he might rake up from the limbo of forgotten sins some deeply compromising charge. Men respected him, liked him, but, above everything, they feared him ; and, in consequence of this peculiar feeling he could walk through a crowd of five thousand men, and bear off a prisoner (if necessary) like a hawk appropriating a pigeon from a dovecot.

To him was chiefly owing what few British-born people could have realised without actual personal knowledge, the extraordinary state of order and good government which prevailed in our singular community. There was the utmost personal freedom and independence, as enjoyed in all Her Majesty's colonies, without lawlessness or licence. The reckless bullies of the Californian mining towns were as impossible here as Griffins and Enchanters. The great crowd of waifs and strays was sufficiently intelligent to know the laws, and apparently had reached a moral standard sufficiently high to obey them, and to yield uncomplainingly.

Our life, albeit so far unsuccessful, laborious, and monotonous, as some might have termed it, was not necessarily dull. Let it be remembered that we had the magician Youth on our side. Thus it rarely lacked interest, variety, even enjoyment.

For was not the population itself one ceaseless, never-ending mine of observation ? An unending wonder-book to him who had eyes to see and ears to hear, who, moreover, possessed the key to the cipher, and so read much that was sealed and closely locked to others.

Who were the men, the women, evidently gently born and nurtured, some of whom were daily encountered, performing the humblest tasks amid the rudest surroundings ? Was there not material for scores of romances in this privilege of companionship with them, which was our daily common lot ?

When some careless miner, or even a half-tamed bushman or ordinary labourer turned digger, suddenly unearthed gold which would have almost sufficed for a king's ransom, was there not novelty and romance in this ? in beholding the human grub swiftly metamorphosed into the butterfly—sometimes awkwardly fluttering amid his brilliant juniors, at other times soaring with adjustable wing, as if born to the inheritance of air and light ?

For the rest, albeit that our lot was that of daily labour, it was such a measure of exertion as came easily within the scope of the strong sinews and muscles of youth. There was in it nothing undignified, and the possible triumph at any given hour of any day glorified the drudgery which might, nay, daily did, for some comrade or other, end in splendour undreamed of and dazzling.

Our habitudes, maugre the daily labour, were distinctly those of gentlemen. The Major and I rose from our plain pallets to bathe in the neighbouring streamlet, or to 'tub' if such watercourse was not within reach, as regularly as when we lived in England. Our working clothes were of necessity plain and coarse, but the work over, or the holiday afternoon having arrived, on which all miners, however good their 'prospects,' make a rule of declining work, our dress was not widely different from what it would have been in a country town in England. Let all idea of long-haired unkempt ruggedness be rejected as the vogue of Australian miners. Even Joe and Cyrus wore their hair clipped to a most soldierly shortness of staple, as, indeed—barbers abounding, and doing a most lucrative business—do by far the greater majority of the miners everywhere.

I had, of course, arrived in Australia believing that I had only to establish myself upon any known and accredited gold-field to unearth a fortune without delay. Even in unknown and non-accredited regions I had visions of miraculous finds; visions of ledges of gold-bearing rock and nugget-strewed gravel floated before my eyes waking and sleeping. My limited knowledge of geology was pressed into the service of my imagination. I knew, of course, the leading formations in which gold chiefly occurred. Such knowledge would surely aid me in the discovery which was to mean home and friends and native land now rapturously regained, with the angel of my dreams, radiant at my return, as her celestial prototype.

Soon after I had fairly commenced my practical course of fortune-digging these flattering hopes vanished. I found gold-mining to be like any other profession, composed mainly of hard and unrelieved drudgery. A living was certainly to be made by it in a general way, barring accidents, sickness, or exceptional bad luck. The prizes were tangible and patent. But like those of all professions, or even lotteries, they were so few and far between, as merely to suffice to stimulate the crowd of unsuccessful toilers, who wore out their lives, their hopes, their strength, not unfrequently their morals and reputations, in the delusive quest.

Among the miners, though the community comprises and ever will comprise some of the best and noblest examples of manhood, were many who had suffered grievously from rude association and the corroding effects of disappointment. These men had accepted their destiny. They were life-long miners. The salvation of an exceptional find could alone restore them to the social surroundings they had once and for ever quitted. Working patiently while need was, they had lost the power to resist the temptation to spend in aimless dissipation the temporary gains which from time to time they secured. 'A good rise' was the signal for a week's revelry. Debts were paid; all necessary repairs to the mining requisites made. The remainder of the money received for their gold was wasted in excess.

In a few weeks the ex-foreign office clerk or university graduate was to be seen with a serge shirt and clay-stained clothes, patiently sinking, driving, sluicing, or reefing as the case might be—as fixed to his endless search as though he had been a gnome imprisoned in the depths of the treasure mountains of the Hartz.

We did not take Cyrus's advice. It would, financially, have been better for us if we had. But, of course, that could not be foreseen. If we knew for a certainty where the gold was not, we should probably be able to point unerringly to where it was, which would lead to the most astounding results, especially if the knowledge was disseminated simultaneously. The evil of this universal promulgation of knowledge was exemplified in the following digging episode.

Every one knows, that is, every one who has been a few years on a goldfield and carefully read up the regulations, omitting those which have been repealed, from time to time, that, when a 'frontage claim' is blocked off, that is, marked off as a permanent parallelogram, instead of being a 'chose in action,' or progressively developing mining tenement, any one can take up or seize upon the 'block off it,' or desirable section of land outside of the said frontage claim, by simply putting in four pegs before any one else.

Now the frontage claim or section upon the lead, or ancient river bed, was known to be rich because it had been worked, the gold extracted and turned into cash fortnightly, so that a very fair notion could be gathered of its richness. As, however, the shareholders were limited to an allotment of two hundred and forty feet in length, being at the rate of forty feet a man, along the course of the lead, it followed that the 'block,' or so much of the auriferous stratum as lay outside of this two hundred and forty feet by three hundred, would be tolerably rich also. The shareholders in the claim I allude to, No. 5 Sinbad's Valley, had made £8000 a man (there were six of them) in less than as many months. This I know of my own knowledge, and can prove if required. One of them was a Cornishman. Just before the claim was worked out he said to me—

'Harry, what do you think? I'm going home to Trevenna on Monday.'

'Are you, cousin Jack?' said I. 'I think you're a wise man. Have you written to tell them all?'

'Not a line,' said he. 'They think I'm dead or lost. How they'll stare. I don't think any of 'em ever saw a ten pound note in their lives. To-morrow's the last day's work as I shall do. Go by the coach Monday, and off by the overland mail steamer as sails from Sydney on Thursday next. Won't that be a holiday trip, eh mate?'

'It will, indeed,' said I, rather regretfully, and I am afraid, envying the poor fellow in my heart.

He was right. The next day *was the last day on which* he ever worked; but not in the sense in which he intended it. In lifting a heavy petrified fossil tree trunk which the waters of that long buried primeval stream had rolled down its golden sands, he overstrained himself. On Sunday night he was a corpse;

and on Monday, the very day he was to have taken the first stage of his trip home, we followed him to his long home, in the spacious newly-enclosed cemetery, already commencing to be thickly sprinkled with newly-dug graves. Later on I saw the cheque for seven thousand some hundreds of pounds (less expenses and the Curator of Intestate Estates' fees), which was remitted to the relatives in curious, old-fashioned, steep-streeted, pebble-paved Trevenna.

Well, the adjacent lot to the highly-satisfactory 'golden-hole claim,' as the miners phrased it, was to be had for the pegging-out first. The pegging-out, that is, the placing of four stout sticks, one at each corner, was easy enough. It was the 'first' business, the priority, which was difficult, if not impossible, of attainment.

The whole field was aware that at some time, not earlier than six o'clock A.M. on a certain morning, the shareholders of No. 5 Sinbad's Valley would mark out their claim for good and all. *One second* after which operation any alert persons might put in four pegs, one at each corner of the coveted adjoining block claim, and so hold the ground.

On the night before the battle, five hundred men, by curious coincidence, bivouacked on the ground, each man with a sharpened stick and gold-sharpened determination to secure a corner of the Aladdin-glorious treasure-chamber.

Precisely as the dawn's fresh pearly gray succeeded the misty cloud-wrack of the waning night, four shareholders of the frontage claim suddenly appeared with prepared stakes and marked out their carefully-measured earth-portion, none daring to interfere with them; but the instant that their task was completed there was a rush like the advanced guard of a charging regiment of grenadiers. The confusion which resulted defies description.

At each corner of the coveted block stood a couple of score of men, each wildly and frantically endeavouring to place his particular stake as near two of the frontage pegs as possible, and as accurately opposite and the regular distance. Men fought and struggled, cursed and struck and fell, as each raised high his stake or peg and strove to hammer it in securely. A few intimate friends or joint-operators with the frontage party were seen to appear on the scene suddenly, only a few minutes after the marking-off and essay to occupy. These were usually supposed to have 'the office,' or special information from the shareholders, and to 'stand in' with them; but these in their turn were swept forward and over in the mad rush of the eager crowd. For five minutes indescribably wild confusion prevailed. Then the crowd sullenly parted. Certain pegs and stakes were seen planted, sheaf-like, in each corner, and the 'blocking-off of No. 5 Sinbad' was over. The result of this attempt to symbolise priority of occupation, by means of pegs or stakes, possibly among the most ancient landmarks, has been accurately retained by the photographic art. 'The apparatus can't lie,' and a wandering artist, of that persuasion, attended the performance and faithfully reproduced both the pegs and their owners.

Mr. Commissioner Blake had no easy task, it will be seen. He was only required, in the exercise of his duty to take evidence and decide as to which four pegs had been placed in the corners of the block-claim off No. 5, first after the shareholders of No. 5, and, having decided, to place those persons to whom the pegs belonged in possession of the claim.

He did what he could. He rode down to the place attended by two troopers and a dozen dogs, and narrowly inspected the pegs. He even counted them, making one hundred and sixty-two in all.

'Who put in the first peg in the north-east corner?' he demanded.

'I did.'

'No, I did; 'twas me, Captain.'

'Me plenty plant 'm that one waddy,' said a civilised aboriginal.

'I put in first peg, Massa, sure as there's snakes in Virginny,' sung out old man Ned.

'No, no, my peg; I thrust it in with this meri,' yells Maori Jack, brandishing his war club, and showing his sharpened anthropophagic teeth.

'C'est le mien, c'est le mien, sacrés cochons que vous êtes, sortons,' grinds out a Frenchman.

'Das ist mein numero ein—ein—ein,' growls a German, 'haben sie der fader gesehn? er ist todten—spitzbuben—Donner un' blitzen.'

'Where are you shovin' to?' grumbles a —— but no, it is unnecessary to specify the nationality of the last speaker; 'd——n you all, you may take my share, if we ever reach within a hundred mile of Wingadee agin. I'm full up of these here blank diggings. Let me get out of this blank crowd. Call this digging? I say it's wild cattle meeting. I'll cut it while the play is good.'

'D——n the whole lot of you,' roars out the irascible Commissioner, charging right among the excited crowd. Why the blazes didn't you come and have it out earlier in the day. Get home, all of you, and mind that not a soul stirs the surface till I give leave. How the devil am I to tell who is the first man? I know no more than Adam. But, anyhow, I shall reserve judgment until to-morrow morning. Come up to the camp at ten o'clock and I will there and then deliver my decision. In the meantime, no one touches the ground with axe, shovel, or pick, or I shall know the reason why.'

On the following morning, as the Commissioner sat in his office, a small building, with a room for himself and one for his clerk, a back room and a passage, a large crowd gradually collected before the door. At ten o'clock precisely the office door was thrown open, and the Commissioner's clerk, standing therein, informed the crowd that the Captain was inside, and would receive the names of every man who had put in a peg in the block off No. 5 Sinbad's Valley.

His orders were these. Each applicant was to enter the passage by the back door. As he passed through his name would be taken down on a slip of paper by him, the clerk, and placed in a ballot-box, to be dealt with by the Commissioner afterwards according to his sovereign will and pleasure. A cheer was given as this announcement was made, and a string of men commenced to pass through the back door and out of the front, leaving their names in the course of transit. In half an hour all was completed. A hundred and sixty men, forty applicants for each peg, for *only four men could be shareholders*, awaited the fiat of the Commissioner. At a respectful distance a motley crowd of three or four times the number regarded them attentively.

This being completed, the Captain appeared at the doorway, and, amid loud cheering, commenced a brief oration. He said that he had given this particular case great consideration, that the confusion which had occurred was in consequence of the Government having framed some new regulations without submitting them to the commissioners. This one in particular —with regard to frontage-block claims—was a d——d stupid one, it seemed to him. He had no hesitation in saying so [loud cheering]; but however that might be, it was *the law!* And, of course, he would take care that it was rigidly obeyed.

He would now proceed to select the names of the four men to whom he should adjudge the ownership of the block off No. 5. He should do it by lot, as they would agree it was totally impossible to sift the evidence or arrive at any conclusion by ordinary methods, in the case of a hundred and sixty pegs, all put down about the same time. He was not going to try, at any rate.

' Mr. Watkins,' this to the clerk, ' would you please to bring forward the ballot-box. I turn away my head and select this ticket at random ; [reading] it contains the name of James Grant. The second, taken out similarly, is Patrick Mahony. The third is that of—a—Ewen Campbell. And the fourth is that of—a—John Smith. I hereby adjudge these four men to be the legal occupiers and shareholders of the block off No. 5 Sinbad's Valley. God save the Queen !'

The crowd cheered. The one hundred and fifty-six disappointed claimants said never a word, and the four men named received peaceable possession of the claim, which turned out a very rich one, and which they worked out to the last ounce. One man, whom I saw afterwards, bought a snug farm with his share of the gold ; and I visited him in a neat freestone cottage which he had erected.

CHAPTER IV·

WE worked hard, doggedly, persistently, and yet all was unavailing.

We 'hung on,' as the miners said, to our claim, driving and delving with pick and shovel, through the long hot days, or in the silent dark cold nights. No luck, no gold. Having no money was not the worst of it. Our balance on the wrong side had run up with the storekeeper, who trusted us to considerably over a hundred pounds. A large sum, when it is considered that our assets were almost nil, or such as, if sold, would have made a very slight impression on the account.

We became unhappy and despondent, more especially Cyrus Yorke, whose 'I told you so from the beginning,' was daily more aggressive and hard to bear. Our storekeeper friend, John Mangrove, did not seem to care so much. He had 'followed the diggings' for many a year. He and his smart, bustling, business-like wife were quite used to giving fabulous amounts of credit, to what they termed 'an honest crowd,' meaning a party of men who might be relied upon to pay when their luck turned. Mrs. Mangrove, indeed, laughed at our undiggerlike despondency when we came up one Saturday night and vowed we would not take some beef and flour for our married mate, having no money, and having that morning decided to 'jack up' or thoroughly abandon work at our present claim.

'We must go and fossick for a bit now,' I said, 'just for enough to make the pot boil; but we won't take any more of your "tucker," Mrs. Mangrove, without paying.'

'Bother the paying!' said the buxom, cheery woman, 'we shall get our money some time or other; but how are you and the Major to fossick, or anything else, without a scrap to eat. You must and shall take your rations till times mend. Luck always turns if you stick to your fight like men. Don't tell me you're down in the mouth. You've got to work till you make a 'rise,' for my sake, and how can you work without tucker?'

'All right, Mrs. Mangrove,' said the Major; 'you know what is good for us. We are your boys, you know. Can't you lay us on to anything?'

'Well, as you're good boys, I don't mind letting you hear of a little whisper I caught this morning of a rush out at the Eight Mile, that they say is going to be a regular fizzer. It is called "The Last Stake," and there are only half a dozen claims marked out. You'd be in time to-morrow morning early. I saw some awfully rich specimens that Tim Daly had.'

'Specimens are deceptive,' I say; 'but we will mark out four men's ground there to-morrow, only two need work till it's payable. Cyrus and Joe will go splitting or fencing until times improve a bit to pay the tucker-bill.'

'All right,' said Mrs. Mangrove, 'nothing like facing it. My old man and me was down to half-a-crown, and hardly a pair of boots between us once at Eaglehawk; but we dropped on to a shallow patch, and I puddled it in a washtub, didn't I, John? We made eighty pound out of that patch in two days.'

'You was allers a good 'un to work at a pinch, I will say that,' growled John, 'though you're tongue do run a bit fast sometimes.'

'If I didn't do a bit of blowing we might shut up shop,' she answered; 'you know that very well, Master John. Here, Harry, take this bottle of whisky with you; you and the Major want something besides tea just now. You're looking dreadful thin of late, and you'll be laid up with the fever if you don't mind. Give that Mrs. Yorke of yours a sip, it won't hurt her, a small drop. She's got a precious soft-headed husband, I can see.'

'You see a many things,' said John, 'can you see it's past twelve o'clock; the sergeant'll be turning everybody out directly. I shall shut up. Good-night, mates.'

After this interesting colloquy, by which we felt much cheered and invigorated, we went home and indulged in a glass of whisky punch each, which did not demoralise us much, not having touched anything for a month previously. We also insisted upon Mrs. Yorke joining us; she and Cyrus had not gone to bed. So we drank success to our next start, and slept very soundly afterwards.

The stars were in the sky when the Major and I quietly arose and wended our way out to the locale of The Last Stake Quartz Reef, alluded to by Mrs. Mangrove, and walking the four miles briskly reached it soon after daylight. Early as was the hour, others were there bound upon the same errand. We could see where the ledge of white silicate rock had been bared and workings commenced with a view of following it down. Carefully noticing the direction of the reef, we placed our two pegs, denoting two hundred feet in length along the line of the reef, and giving a title to the full width of one hundred yards on each side of the base line, whatever that might be. Once so placed, if only a minute before the next coming, this act constituted a perfect mining title to all gold within such defined boundaries. The law allowed three days' grace for occupation

and efficient work to take place. If such work were not commenced within three days, any other miners might summarily
take possession of or 'jump' the claim. Wending our way
back to breakfast, there being no necessity to take any other
measures at present, we explained the position of affairs to our
fellow shareholders. I took the initiative from habit, and laid
great stress on Mrs. Mangrove's kindness, which had enabled
us to begin again in a respectable and promising manner, instead of having to take to fossicking like so many 'hatters'—
solitary miners. Both the Major and I considered The Last
Stake Reef to look like 'a good show ;' but there were expenses
and of course food for the whole party. These we should not
get out of the reef for some time. And we were all averse to
sponging on kind Mr. Mangrove more than we could help. I,
therefore, proposed that Cyrus and Joe should take a job of
bush work, the wages of which—such labour being very well
paid just then—would suffice to placate the butcher and baker
for the whole party, until the reef turned payable, which it was
pretty sure to do. If not, we were only where we were before.

'That'll do,' said Joe; 'I was just a-longing like for a bit of
farm work this fine sharp weather. I ha' had such a spell of
driving that I'm regular cramped. It was pretty wet down
there, too, and I'm afeared of the rheumatiz. I saw Mr. Banks
this morning, and he offered Cyrus and me half a mile of fencing at good prices.'

'They just was good prices,' said Cyrus; 'I only wish I could
have tumbled across 'em down the country, I'd never have come
digging—would I, little woman ?'

'I'm sure I don't know, Cyrus,' she said, 'you were never
very contented, and if you had'nt come here, you'd have gone
somewheres else. But I do hope we'll make a rise on this
reef. We've been lower lately than ever I remember since the
party was a party.'

'We should have been lower down still, Mrs. Yorke,' said the
Major, 'if it had not been for these capital scones of yours, and
the way your good cookery saves the rations. I suppose it's
because Cyrus has such a tremendous appetite that you were
first driven to economise by method and high art.'

'If I've got a good twist, I can do a day's work,' said the
Hawkesbury giant, opening his chest and raising his great arms.
'But we'd better get away, Joe, and see Mr. Banks about this
fencing. I'd be sorry if he let it to any other chaps. The
Major and Harry can begin and rig their stage at the reef. I
don't think much of reefs. I believe in the alluvial myself.'

Then it was all settled. Next day we had cut our logs,
rigged our stage and windlass, and were soon 'sinking for the
reef,' which, whether volatilised from a lower chemical centre
or laterally secreted, was not visible on the surface where we
had put down our pegs.

In a few days we 'struck it,' followed it down, discovered

small specks of gold almost invisible to the naked eye, and at the first crushing were rewarded with a handsome dividend.

We thought our fortunes were made; we put on two wages men, and worked with renewed energy. The next, and the next, dividends were good; but one dreadful day it became apparent that the reef had 'pinched out,' become gradually smaller and more difficult to find. Finally, it disappeared altogether.

There was the alternative of sinking perhaps another hundred or two hundred feet, on the chance of its being struck at a greater depth, and 'carrying the gold better as it went deeper.' But this style of operation was only suited for men with capital. We resolved not to risk the little we had.

Altogether we got about a thousand pounds for our share of the gold in little more than two months. That, of course, was not so bad. Out of this the claim was in debt to Mr. Mangrove about two hundred and fifty pounds, which was religiously paid up at once, thus leaving nearly two hundred pounds per man. . Each, probably, had some few personal and private debts, which had to be liquidated. A certain refitting of wardrobes was imperative; other matters, too, had become attenuated during our longish term of ill-luck. A few presents to friends who had sympathised with us in our distress were also thought suitable. Eventually, the experienced goldfield's resident will have no difficulty in understanding that forty or fifty pounds each was about the outside amount which remained in our pockets, after a week's holiday and final settlement of affairs.

This statement but too often correctly describes the course of a miner's life even when there is no overt dissipation. His very virtues, his truthfulness, energy, and good faith aid him in extravagance, so to speak, for they enlarge his facilities for credit, which are so elastic while health and strength last that he can get as deeply into debt as he pleases.

When he *does* meet with a fair slice of luck, such as I have referred to, the greater part of his gains are swept away in repayment, while the balance remaining is so small that, to his easy mind, it seems hardly worth saving. 'Plenty more where that came from' is the most popular mining motto, which is true enough in a sense, but not always easy to reduce to practical application.

I had seen and encountered so much in my own person of this tantalising see-saw of apparent prosperity and real poverty that I had insensibly commenced to be drawn into the fatal vortex of indifferentism which is so apt to characterise the habitual miner, from whatever class originally drawn. I was beginning to be satisfied with the periodical intervals of ease and comparative luxury, to be more and more incapable of making any sustained effort to free myself from rude and unworthy surroundings. The fortune which I had hoped for, how much more accurately could I now gauge the slender probability of my winning it! The return to dear England, the union with my long-cherished darling, the transfigured angel of my dreams. How much more nearly this approached, with every flying minute, to the faint hopes of Heaven, and misty realisations of eternal bliss which visit the average believer.

In my despondent moods, when, after weeks of severe labour the end seemed no nearer, I allowed my spirits to droop to the lowest depths of despair. Why had I ever permitted my thoughts to range to such mad impossibilities? Had aught but the insane heedlessness of youth caused my fancy to soar so high, only to fall with more stunning shock? Was there the most distant hope of my ever realising ten or twenty thousand pounds by ordinary mining, with which to present myself in the course of the coming year to the Squire, and to claim the ecstatic reward? Midsummer, moonstruck madness the whole! No greater expectation, truly, as it *now* appeared to me, was there than if I were engaged in digging potatoes.

And yet such prizes *were* to be had, and did occasionally, at Yatala, fall to the grasp of the lucky—chiefly undeserving adventurers.

While I was in this undecided and, above all, agonising state of mind, I received a letter from Ruth. We had not been forbidden, in so many words, to correspond, but it had been explained to me by the Squire that while matters remained in such an extremely uncertain and precarious state, he thought I should agree with him that a regular correspondence would be inconsistent, etc., that, of course, he left it to me, and so on. The consequence of which was that, appreciating his consideration, I refrained from pouring out my heart as I otherwise should have done, and merely wrote, from time to time, certain matter-of-fact epistles. In them I stated my plans, described my place of residence, and gave my reasons for expecting good things in the way of gold discovery.

The hue of despair which had commenced to pervade my life of late had commenced to tinge my letters, doubtless, and so awakened a feeling of irrepressible tenderness and compassion in that dear heart that knew but one deep, still-flowing current of self-sacrificing love. Whatever the cause, I one day received from Mrs. Mangrove, who also officiated as postmistress, amid her other multifarious avocations, a letter; bearing the delicate characters so indelibly traced upon my heart.

'A letter from home, Harry, English postmark, come from your sister, your mammy, or your sweetheart. Don't be angry now; if you'll give me the address, I'll write and tell her what a good boy you are. Not like some of the swells here, who are the biggest rapscallions out, instead of setting a good example to us poor ignorant lower-class mullocks, eh, John?'

'What are you blowin' about now, old gal,' said the sententious John, removing the pipe from his mouth. 'I don't know about "mullock." God made all men free and equal, and though anybody can see as Harry and the Major are regular right-down swells, and so far and away ahead of us, what does Bobbie Burns say—" Who hangs his head for honest poverty "—and settera ?'

'Come, you're not so poor, nor over and above honest either, John,' retorted his better half—'that is, if you get a chance, and was dead sure of not being bowled out. It's I that knows you—still there's worse on the diggings. And now, here's your letter, Harry, and if you'd like to step into my back parlour and read it in comfort—there's no one in there, nor won't be till the Mildorah mail comes in. Take your beer with you.'

I accepted the offer of my worthy friend and banker ; so, sitting down upon the sofa and locking the door, I abandoned myself thoroughly to the half-painful thrill of memory ere I commenced to translate into half-whispered speech the loved and familiar characters.

Ere I opened the letter I gazed long upon the fateful scroll. How much of my former life came back to me ; how sharp the contrast appeared with my present existence ! I saw myself as I once was, how differently lodged and tended. The old Court, with its look of immemorial stateliness and reposeful comfort that now seemed luxury undreamed of, more than half forgotten in the rude surroundings to which I had insensibly adapted myself. And amid them my lot was fated to be cast, for how many years yet ? for my lifetime it might well be ! for how could I endure to return an unsuccessful, disappointed man—I that had so obstinately severed the links that bound me to the home of my youth—the position to which I had been born. I had seen men as gently nurtured, better educated, aye, with far higher attainments, after brave battling with hopeless odds, sink gradually year by year, yet more deeply into the slough of low companionship and sensual indulgence. They had despaired of returning ever to the dim, far-off world of their lost heritage ; had been contented thus to wear out the days of a despised, self-contemning existence. If such things happened to them, why not to me ? I was alone. My long pent-up dread of the worst for a moment overpowered me. I leaned my head upon my hands before the unread letter, and the hot tears, never before shed since childhood, rained down upon the tawdry table-cover.

The unwonted passion aroused me. I brushed the evidences of weakness from my eyes, and, rising to my sense of manhood, raised the precious evidence of woman's fidelity. I well knew what tender assurance I should find of fondly-cherished, brightly-burning love—unalterable faith, unswerving holy confidence. Yet, how many instances had I known where men, having trusted as deeply and loyally, had been heartlessly deceived. I had watched life-wrecks which had dated from the receipt of just such another letter in outward seeming. They, with deli-cate, deadly strokes, had yet rung the knell of hope—of faith

in woman's sacred truth. Such was not to be my doom, whatever else the Fates, which I had commenced to dread, might
have in store for Hereward Pole. How I drank in the sweet
sense of the precious, priceless symbols—thus dumbly that
spake—

'MY OWN DEAREST, EVER DEAREST HEREWARD—Your last letter,
written from Yatala, roused me from a fit of depression which had crept
over me, I hardly know why ; perhaps, from its being so long since I had
received one.   I re-read it before I could do more than gather that you
were well, and still bravely striving to discover that terrible, delusive
gold, which seems to be such a will-o'-the-wisp—in spite of the golden
tales which come by every mail from your far land.   I was unspeakably
cheered by this bare knowledge, and shall never fear gloomy presenti-
ments again.   But I had had so many.   I read—for I read all the papers
I can get hold of from Australia—about terrible mining accidents, till I
was half unconsciously in the habit of connecting my beloved with the
dangers and the deaths that seemed so common, and little regarded.   I
pictured you suddenly overwhelmed by a fall of earth in your subterranean abode, sometimes blown up by an explosion, like those awful ones
in coal mines.   What a dreadful one was that in Wales the other day.
We happened to be at Llanberis, for a change for poor mother, who has
been ailing lately.   I went down and saw the poor women, whose sons
and husbands, brothers and (alas !) lovers, had been reft from them in an
instant.   How many forms of grief were there.   Now, *I* could sympathise
with them, unlike many who merely viewed it as one of the far-away
calamities that we read or hear of, and turn from to the next excitement
or frivolous pleasure.   My aching heart found some relief in aiding and
comforting those whom I could reach.   I felt in a strange way cheered
and lightened when my task was done.   But oh ! how unspeakable was
the relief when I saw your dear hand-writing again, and knew that you
were safe and strong and hopeful as ever, though, so far, unsuccessful.

'Then, as I, for the sixth time, devoured your letter, I discovered a
desponding tone in your expressions, that I had never before noticed.
You did not speak with your old gallant disregard of present ill-luck, and
hope for future fortune, as you used to do.   My woman's quickness
divined a kind of dull resignation setting in ; a more than usual dwelling
upon your rashness in quitting England, joined to a deeper regret for
having, as you say, induced me "to link my life with that of a beggar
and an exile—to forfeit the paradise of my childhood's home for the
accursed outer-world of labour and privation, which would be my portion
if I followed you."

'All this, dearest, I look upon as sinful disbelief in God's goodness ;
besides which, to speak of an infinitely less worthy matter, it is very
wicked of you to doubt my love.   That you possess "once and for ever."
It may not be all that you fondly fancy, but such as it is, it is yours—all
yours—while life lasts, and beyond the grave, if there we retain the
feelings which animate our souls on earth.   Perhaps I am saying more
than I could ever express if we were nearer, but, separated by so vast a
distance, we may be doomed never again to hear each other's voices, I
feel as if I must give expression to every thought of my heart, lest you
might die and never know how its every pulse beats for you.

'After seeing the stony despair of some of these poor women's faces at
Pent-y-glas ; after hearing their dreadful agonising shrieks, as one after

another of the dead miners was carried up from the pit mouth and laid in his cottage; after witnessing the frantic delight with which the rescued were welcomed back to life, joy that sometimes threatened like to death, you must pardon me for believing mere want of success to be a small thing in true lovers' eyes, compared with those ghastly realities.

'Want of success, indeed! Why, what does it mean, that my high-hearted Hereward should not look it in the face, and frown it down, as of old. Have you not life, and love, and health, and strength! that stalwart form! that steady eye! When these fail it will be time enough to despond, to retract, to despair, to lose faith in God and man.

'But you will do none of these, my own darling. You will still work; you will still pray. Remember that there is another year, yet untried, before us, during which the reward of all your long labour and heroic self-denial may be found. My prayers may be answered, and your work, which according to the good old monkish legend, is also prayer, because done in a good spirit, will bring its reward. Keep up your heart for both our sakes—for the love's sake which is your Ruth's life. When that time is finished, come home to the old land, and be sure if you can quell that stubborn pride of yours—do I not love you the better for it—my dear old father will welcome you as a son. But if you will not or cannot come, I will never upbraid you, and more—so prepare yourself—no power on earth shall then keep me from coming to you, to follow your steps in weal or woe, so long as we both shall live.

'I have written you a woman's letter. It is the longest I ever sent. But I did feel so lonely and wretched. It has eased my heart. Would that it could lighten yours; perhaps it may. God keep and bless you, my own beloved.—Yours ever, in weal or woe, in the old world or the new,   'RUTH ALLERTON.'

I rose from the perusal of the heaven-sent letter an altered man. I pressed it to my lips, to my heart. Then I vowed silently, yet solemnly, to God, to work and deny myself from aught but needful rest and sustenance, until the time was expired, for her sweet sake—the best, the tenderest, the truest of mortal women, for her sweet sake—the angel that had stirred the dreary pool of doubt. I was healed; of that I had no doubt. Should I ever be suffered to thank her by my life?

'My word! I'll go bail there was a bank draft in that letter,' said Mrs. Mangrove, coming in suddenly; 'you look so cheered up by it. Must be good news, or something like it. I thought you were going to jack up at the claim when you came in, or had got the fever, or something. But now you look like a different chap altogether.'

'I am a different man,' I said. 'I believe my luck's going to change, Mrs. Mangrove; and if you and John will always back us right out, I believe we shall make our pile yet, and you will have a slice of it.'

'Never mind that,' said the good-natured dame. 'If you take all your stores from us, and pay your bill, that'll be enough for John and me. Our profits are pretty smart. We only want to get our goods off. But you and the Major and your other mates, you're a good crowd to work; I will say that for you;

stick to those new prospectors. There's something in that lead,
I'll go bail. There's no fear but what you'll drop on to it by
and by. John and I ain't afraid to speculate a hundred or two ;
we've not followed the diggings five years next Christmas to be
afraid of giving a bit of credit to rale out-and-out good working
men. No, nor five hundred at the back o' that ; you're right
for anything you want, tools, expenses, powder and fuse, as
long as we last out. Now, you'd better have a whisky, and get
home before the moon sets. Those holes is nasty things to be
walking through when it's dark.'

I declined the refreshment, but thanked the generous-hearted
creature with a warmth that made her and her husband exhibit
signs of distress. I then made off down the brightly-lighted
street, and following a narrow but well-worn track which
threaded the hundreds of shafts, wide, dark-mouthed in the
moonlight, like silent monsters watching for their prey, soon
reached the somewhat isolated spot, where our tiny camp was
situated.

My mates were all asleep. I was not sorry for that. I was
so filled with the deep pervading excitement which the reading
of my thrice-blessed letter had caused in me, that I should have
with difficulty compelled myself to interchange the ordinary
courtesies of conversation. I was as a man who had found a
huge and hidden treasure. I could no longer concern myself
with the poor coins and cares of daily life, until I had had time
to reflect upon my joy and good fortune.

'How good, how pure she is ; what more than mortal fidelity
has marked my Ruth's conduct,' I thought, as I lay down on my
humble couch. 'How many girls in her position would have
caught at the first excuse to free themselves from an engagement that must involve poverty and privation—that might even
end in exile ; and yet she had kept her faith, had been true to
the vow made on the well-remembered terrace, as we stood
looking over woodland vales. How had I deserved such fidelity.
Still, there was something in a man's strength, a man's hope
and struggle for success. She should have her reward, if a
single-handed swordsman could hew his way to success and
glory. There was a year of the precious granted time to spare
now. Perhaps the casuarina might not have changed her gloomy
filamental raiment once more before the tide would have turned
—the fulfilment would have been 'assured.'

The next day was Sunday. The Major and Joe had been on
the night-shift ; I had, therefore, all the day before me to
dream over my last found happiness, to permit my mind to
wander over the past, to hope and resolve for the future. No
mining, no work of any sort, was carried on on the Sabbath at
Yatala. An utterly unbroken stillness reigned over the whole
strangely assorted camp on the sacred day. In some countries
such would not have been the case ; men would have pleased
themselves as to the course they took. But here, the whole

sentiment of the place was as distinctly English as if the concourse of adventurers had been located in Surrey or Kent. The Australian colonies are not only in many ways contented to be English in act, manner, and thought. They *are* the English of a century back in many, in perhaps the highest embodiments of the national character. And there was no more thought in Yatala of Sunday work, or openly - avowed Sunday dissipation than of a carnival in Glasgow. Moreover, such labour was against the law of the land, which, as I before remarked, was by no means suffered to remain a dead letter at Yatala. Under 29 Carolus II. c. vii. sec. 7, an information would have been laid by the sergeant with exceeding promptitude; and the fine would have followed with mathematical precision of effect after cause.

CHAPTER V

NEXT day being Sunday, we breakfasted late, and by no means uncomfortably. When miners are provided with provisions at all, they are good of their kind. Fresh beefsteaks, grilled to perfection, and served up hot by our miraculous cook and good fairy Mrs. Yorke, baker's bread (there were five tradesmen of the craft in Yatala), fresh butter, and new laid eggs, with hot coffee, were all forthcoming. We had previously performed our ablutions and dressed ourselves with a trifling amount of extra care. The Major and I messed together in our weather-tight abode, wherein was a small extemporised table. Cyrus Yorke, his wife, and Joe Bulder had their meal at the family tent.

'Well, Pole,' said the Major, 'what was the result of your business interview with Mrs. Mangrove? Is she going to sell us up at the end of the month, or have you blarneyed her into another excursion towards the Insolvent Court?'

'She is a brick,' I returned, 'and John is not a bad fellow either. They have promised to back us until Christmas. After that we must take our chance.'

'By Jove!' said my friend, 'she is a tower of Shinar, in the brick line; a regular goldfield's guardian angel—a tutelar divinity! I don't know what all! We shall strike the gutter yet, depend upon it. And yet, consider my improper exultation! Depending for my daily steak (how famous and tender this one is; that little woman of ours has had it hanging up a week—bless her); depending, I say, for my daily bread and butter on a poor woman's bounty—what would the old 77th say to it. Conduct unbecoming an officer and a gentleman, eh?'

I had determined to spend the day in tranquil self-communion. To that end I sallied out, with some slight provision for a midday meal, for a long day's walk; the Major electing to pass the time on the broad of his back, working up his arrears of light literature, of which we always received from home a generous supply.

'Going for a regular all-day constitutional, Harry, are you?' he said. 'Well, every man to his taste: this is a free country. Seems to me we get a fair share of exercise without a twenty mile hump on Sundays. Keep your eyes open, for a likely gully for prospecting.'

He began to cut the leaves of his *Saturday Review*, and I departed. I was in no mood for the grim pleasantries, the instructive scientific articles, the scathing criticism of that magazine of pure English and merciless sarcasm. Welcome had been its arrival to us in many a dull unrelieved term of labour in the glaring dusty midsummer, or the dreary winter weather, when the rows of tents stood on a plateau of knee-deep mud. But now I longed to speed forth across the low green hills strewn with diorite, across the sharply outlined ridge, where the great white blocks of quartz gleamed in the morning sun, adown the long eastern slope, for miles through the park-like southern forest, where, over the thick greensward, the forester kangaroo and the wallaroo alone run, where eager green and gold parrots chattered and screamed—where the blue heron fished silently by the reed-fringed creek, where the eagle soared calm and peerless amid the loneliness of the firmament. And there I, too, could be alone and relieve my heart, that seemed almost bursting with unshared thought and thankfulness.

After hours of rambling and a gradual descent, I found myself in a defile which slowly widened, until it became a pleasant meadow-seeming flat, partly overgrown with high grass and patches of rushes. The hillsides had been precipitous, and an easier path having been found by the strayed horses and cattle of the miners, Nova Scotia Gully, as it had been called by a wandering Blue Nose, had been completely neglected.

A promising place for 'prospecting.' Yet nowhere did I see the shafts and heaps of rock or gravel which tell in a gold country of the hasty search for the precious metal. Instinctively reasoning on these passing thoughts, half looking out for a pleasant spot for my midday halt, I mechanically wandered to a depression where a lofty eucalyptus, fallen before a hurricane blast, lay with its bared roots sheer athwart a tiny watercourse. Below this natural embankment was a pool filled with pellucid water.

'Here,' I said, 'I will dream out the day, translating myself as nearly as may be in spirit to the pleasant land of my fathers, and linking my soul to hers, whose pure steadfast heart has so strengthened and lightened mine.'

Hour after hour, after my frugal midday meal, I lay on the grass under the vast trunk of the fallen forest-monarch, and dreamed of green England's meads and time-worn crumbling keeps, of the half-royal residences of the great nobles—the time-honoured halls of the squires and county gentlemen. I saw again the ancient gables of Allerton Court, the ivy-buttressed village church, the plodding unambitious farm-labourers, the old women in their caps, the clerk withstanding the ever troublesome boys, trying in vain to restrain from sounds and antics, secular if not profane, the calm voice of the clergyman reading the prayers, or preaching the sermon. How much out of keeping would any excited action or unfamiliar doctrine have been in that haven of repose and assured joys? And then, turning first to one side and then to the other, with a smile or a pleasant word, as either parent spoke, came my own, my beloved, my peerless Ruth Allerton.

Should I ever see her again, hear her voice, under the great lime trees I remembered so well, when we watched for the first shivering whisper as the evening breeze came sighing up over hill and dale? What a waste world was there between us! What a mournful, pale-gleaming, endless plain of ocean! Nor only such, but the great desert of Poverty, where the dwellers are for ever Bedouins, raiders, outcasts, desperate or despised dwellers on sufferance, by the border of the high-walled cities of wealth and respectability.

Thus did I think; thus muse during the little season of leisure which was allotted to me. The short day was fading fast ere I had completed my round of thought. Henceforth, action would obliterate contemplation. But I felt that in my life I had made a fresh departure. Kneeling on the turf by the gnarled tree-trunk, scarred and scattered as by the fire-storms of centuries, I swore solemnly that, until the year expired, I would neither pause nor slacken in my search for the magical metal. Magical—it would be the long lost Philosopher's stone. Would it not transmute the base dross of my present life into the minted treasure of honourable security—successful love?

The lengthening shadows, the more distinct woodland cries, warned me that I must tread the homeward path. At twelve o'clock that night I should have to go on to the 'night shift,' when eight hours of continuous labour were before me. But my heart was light, my purpose firm. Hope had never glowed so brightly in my breast since first I quitted England's shore, with all the sanguine strength of boyhood's expectation. As I stood up and faced the glowing west, where the rich hues of sunset poured a full glory upon the long green vistas of the waving woodland, a fragment of quartz attracted my attention. I picked it up and applied the usual miner's test. A few minute specks of the dull yellow, but unmistakable metal were visible. I hastily scooped out a handful or two of the surrounding earth, and improvising a dish from a circular bark covering of a hole in the nearest tree, washed it in the little rivulet. The result was a few grains of gold. This was fully satisfactory, as giving a few grains to so small a quantity of the gravel, the proportion to a cartload, the usual alluvial miner's measure, would be far beyond ordinary yields.

I decided to take possession at once of this lucky portion of the earth's surface, from which I anticipated the realisation of my fondest hopes, and commenced to cut four pegs, by placing which in the ground, one at each angle of the claim, I could, according to mining law, take perfect and inalienable possession. But all suddenly a feeling arose, vital and instinctive, which arrested all action—it was the Sabbath day. True, I had employed it most literally as a day of rest, of idle reverie, not availing myself of the regular preaching and prayers conducted by the minister of each denomination on the goldfield. Still, so strong was the reminiscent tradition of my childhood that I could not, for the life of me, commit so total a breach of all my early teaching and belief as to mark out a claim, thus doing actual work, and following my regular work-a-day avocation on Sunday. The old village chimes came back to my heart, to my ears, I could almost have sworn. My mother's voice, sweet, grave, low-toned—I seemed to hear the very words which inculcated self-denial, reading of the Word, heeding the commandments, 'Thou shalt not labour, thou and thy son, and thy daughter, and thy servant, and the stranger that is within thy gates.' I heard it all in memory's wondrous phonograph, as the full tide of life rolled backward, and I saw myself a schoolboy at the knee of a pale lady with wistful eyes and a radiance of holy love beaming around her worn features. All this I saw and heard. I could not sin against knowledge. I was not as one of the reckless gold-hunters with which the camp was thronged. I could not do the deed.

'It matters not,' thought I, 'the place is rarely visited. I will come to-morrow after my shift is over. That will surely be time enough ; and now I must stretch out if I wish to save the light.'

I cast down the stake, turned my back upon the temptation, and stepped out manfully towards the camp. As I left the spot the sun's level gleam seemed to light up the scattered quartz fragments with a glitter which transformed them into golden ingots. The strange laughing kingfisher of the south (*Dacelo giganteus*) perched upon a dead tree in my path, where his extravagant and ludicrous cachinnatory succession of notes, ending in a long-drawn ha-ha-ha, had a weird derisive chuckle to my ears. Was I turning my back upon a fortune, in obedience to the bidding of an outworn superstition? No, assuredly not! Yet my heart misgave me, and an evil presentiment commenced to depress my so lately exulted faculties.

The moon was up as I passed the track which for the last mile, running through an abandoned lead, was a narrow riband of safety amid a region of shafts of all depths and suddenness of approach. The lead with its hundreds of mounds, its black yawning pit mouths, had a ghostly appearance in the still clear, cold light as of a graveyard awaiting the unburied dead of a battlefield. The narrow path led onward, over, and around the lesser hillocks, passing the edge of sullen, narrow mine-mouths, where the displaced clod or pebble went rumbling and murmuring long—long—long—minutes it seemed, though but seconds in reality—ere the dull thud or splash at the bottom told of its completed errand. What would a man's fate be if belated or tarrying too long at the wine-cup he stumbled into one of those entrances to the nether world? I had known of such a fate happening to more than one stalwart miner, who had risen that day in rude health and well nigh giant strength. More than one skeleton had I known scooped out, months, nay years, after the disappearance of a comrade, only to be identified by the clothing that enwrapped the bones. But such would never be my fate. I knew every yard of the track. I rarely travelled the path but by daylight, and no living man could assert with truth that he had ever seen Hereward Pole under the influence of intoxicating liquor.

When I reached our camp fire, I found all preparation for our evening meal in such a state of perfect arrangement as induced me to suspect what indeed was the case, that the Major had been considerately awaiting my return.

'Thought you were never coming,' he growled, with affected sulkiness of tone. 'Mrs. Yorke, please to put the gridiron upon the fire at once, and the steak upon the gridiron one minute afterwards. I'm so delighted you've returned safe, Master Harry. I was just thinking how my supper was in a fair way to be ruined. Not that I was going to be fool enough to wait for you ten minutes longer; but how could a fellow—I put it to you as a gentleman and a man of the world—how could a fellow enjoy his steak knowing that he would have to go up to the camp and report his mate's probable death by flood and field—gunshot or suicide, or miscalculation of distance, in the morning.'

'A decidedly epicurean view to take of my probable decease,' rejoined I; 'but your friend the coroner will find no inquest necessary at present. It was very good of you to wait supper for me, dead or alive. How delightfully the steak hisses and simmers; wait till I have just time to dress the least bit, and it will be done to a turn. I have news, too.'

To change my outer coat for an old—very old—shooting jacket, but still distinguished as to cut, to replace the heavy walking boots by shoes, and to perform certain splashings, did not occupy many minutes. When I came forth from the recesses of the tent, refreshed and charitable of mood, the steak before referred to was in the act of being placed upon our humble board. Such it was, literally, being a section of a cedar plank about two feet wide, supported on trestles, which rendered transport and packing a very simple transaction. Covered with a clean cloth, it was sufficiently large for the present dinner party, the number of which never required to be increased. Potatoes baked in the ashes and served up hot, coffee, white bread in very excellent rolls, with honey and fresh butter, completed our meal. There was one rare and indispensable adjunct, that of appetite, which we rarely lacked, and which I may frankly confess to have provided in a very high state of perfection on this particular occasion.

E

We had eaten with satisfaction, we had washed down the solids with cups of coffee; we had lighted our pipes, and were miles beyond any of the lower unamiable forms of conversation, when I thus spoke—

'Major, I did not go out expressly with a view of prospecting to-day. I want to tell you that I came across something which I fancy will materially alter our worldly expectations.'

'Nobody said you were going prospecting,' observed the Major quietly. 'Nobody thought you had as much sense. *We* knew you would lie under a tree all day, and dream of the perfections of—what's her name—Miss Allerton. Besides, I know you have the narrow English notion of Sunday.'

'I didn't go out prospecting,' said I; 'as you kindly observe, I had not sense enough; but I made a discovery all the same. What do you think of that?' said I, suddenly producing one of my specimens.

The Major took it carelessly in his hand, looked narrowly at the sides and facets, moistened it with his tongue, squinted at it, and finally, with an air of high professional skill, said—

'To my mind it's awfully good, fine gold showing all through it—the best kind of stone, always. Rich enough for everybody . You took up a claim of course?'

'Well, no!' said I, 'Major, I did not. I have, as you say, some lingering traditions about my early days, and I could not disavow them. We can go and take it up early to-morrow after I come off the night shift. We must be all four there to put in the pegs, you know?'

'Yes, and an awful bother, too. Why can't one man, in the name of his partners, take up a claim—always supposing that they have the requisite number of miner's rights?'

'Well, of course; but there's something to be said on the other side. Occupation is the great fundamental principle of the miner. Otherwise the capitalist might, by proxy, delegate, and so on, monopolise half the good ground on a goldfield.'

'You be hanged,' growled the Major, 'you're talking now like an intelligent practical miner, a friend of the people, and so on. But we'd better all start at sunrise to-morrow morning, if it's a good show.'

On the next morning, accordingly, four men might have been observed wending their way eastward from Yatala, at an unusually early hour. They walked rapidly forward, silent, strong with steadfast resolve. It was the midwinter; the frost was white upon grass and shrub, the drooping points of which were bright and crystal-glittering.

'It occurs to me,' said the Major, after a long pause, in an ill-used tone, 'that we are most confoundedly cold, and most probably proceeding on a fool's errand as well. Ten to one there's nothing in this claim after we have pegged it out.'

'I allus reckoned this was a lucky gully out here,' said Cyrus

Yorke, 'and much about the lie of the place where Harry talks
of. I had a mind to peg out there myself once.'

'And why didn't you?' said I.

'Well, something put me off it,' said Cyrus, the most inconse-
quent of men. It was an excuse that we all eagerly accepted.

'This gully does shape like the real thing,' said Joe Bulder.
'I'll be bound when we get on a mile farther we'll all be of the
same mind. I wish we'd thought of it a week ago. All the gold
seems running this way. There's the Australian Maid, the Blue
Snake, and the Doubtful Card, all struck gold in the same line.
I believe we'll be on the gutter this time if we stick in to work
at once.'

'I can only say,' returned I, 'that in all my experience'—we
were beginning to talk, nay, to think, like men who had possessed
no interest but those allied with the search for gold since childhood—who dreamed of no other distraction for the years that
lay between them and the grave—'in all my experience I never
saw anything more promising.'

'Dare say not,' said the Major scornfully, 'all goldfield
ventures are promising. Devil mend them. They are *his* lures
specially and entirely. I should never be surprised at seeing
him come and carry away a miner, or elevate the editor of a
mining newspaper bodily. What lies—only inferior to those of
the Father of those inventions—must he have hatched, have
supported! What an atmosphere of dissimulation must he have
experienced, nay, have revelled in!'

'We have only to cross that ridge and we are in sight of the
spot. I am sure that you will be taken with it. Push on boys;
a fortune is waiting for you. I am as sure as that we stand
here that the Nova Scotia Prospecting Claim will run gold into
our pockets like a schoolboy making dumps.'

'Seeing's believing,' said the Major, quite inconsequentially.
'We have had not quite so much of that lately. Why, who is
this, and what is *he* doing so early? By Jove, it's Gus Maynard.
What's up, Gus?'

Gus Maynard, an American, ranked highly in our metallur-
gical phalanstery. Well-educated and well-mannered, he was
one of the enigmas which abound on goldfields, but which, after
the incurious mental habit which prevails in these societies,
doubtless for good and sufficient reason, no one attempts to
solve. Unobtrusive, yet manly and direct of demeanour, he
was equally *bon camarade* with the humblest miner and with
the educated, and what might be termed aristocratic section.
He was thoroughly practical, in spite of his rather advanced
geological theories, and had not wielded pick and shovel, from
Suttor's Mill to Hokitiki Beach-terraces, for nothing.

'I've been pegging out a fraud, I reckon, for the 999th time,'
he said, with the slow monotone which few northern Americans
contrive to evade. 'The early bird gets the worm, you benighted
Britishers are fond of saying. My notion is that he rushes out

before he completes his ciphering, and so gets "had" by a stock-broker, an insurance agent, or some other varmint.'

'Or by a betting man, eh Gus?' said I; 'but where have you been pegging out, and where are your mates?'

'Gone home; but I can show you their miners' rights, if you wish. Just marked out a prospecting claim, and if I hadn't sworn never to waste words on a hole till I saw the gold come out of it, I'd say it was a good one.'

'Show it to us, Gus,' said I faintly. As I spoke a sudden thrill of pain struck through me, while I saw in my mind's eye countless loads of ounce wash-dirt stacked around *my* spot.

'Know where there's a big fallen tree, a little well hole like, just in the dip of the flat? There you have it. I'd spotted this Nova Scotia Gulch for some time, and this morning I up and drove pegs, with the other three boys, because I had a dream four others were going to take it up.'

'Would you know any of them again?'

'One of 'em had a velvet coat on. I remembered that, for I never saw one here.'

'You're dream carried true as a pea-rifle, Gus,' said I. 'The fit took me to put on an old velveteen shooting jacket yesterday that I had in my kit. I wish it may bring you no ill luck, but it's *my claim* that you've just taken up. The Major and I and the other two mates are on our way to mark that very claim. I was there all day yesterday, but couldn't put in a peg because it was Sunday.'

'And a very good reason, too,' said Gus; 'suited us admirably. But hadn't you better come on and take up No. 1 South; it may be a good show. We've taken up five hundred feet square, and will set to work the day after to-morrow.'

The Major burst into a fit of immoderate laughter. 'Harry,' said he, 'we're not going to make our fortune this time. Fate and Gus Maynard have been too much for you. Let's have the melancholy satisfaction of seeing Gus's pegs, and noting whether they are all *en règle*. If not we'll "jump" him.'

I mechanically followed our transatlantic friend, though I felt more inclined to sit down and cast ashes on my head, in sincere imitation of the older races, who thus very naturally vented their emotions.

It was too true. The fallen tree—the pellucid basin, no longer stood unsoiled by the hand of man. They were in the centre of a square, at each corner of which was a substantial peg, with a trench cut to show the intersection of the angles. Every bit of ground which but yestereven I so fondly trusted to be the means of restoring my fallen fortunes, was now inalienably vested in others.

For, according to mining law, well known and carefully studied by us all, 'prior occupation,' if but of five minutes' standing, was sufficient to establish a right valid as that of an

immemorial freehold. I knew Gus Maynard too well to doubt
that he had neglected any of the necessary forms. My golden
estate was as completely forfeited as if I had remained in
England.

Not entirely to lose all our labour we marked out the first
claim, after the prospecting claim, in a southerly direction.
This, however, as by law established, would be but half the size
of the premier or prospecting claim, and to my jaundiced
vision did not appear to be half as likely to contain gold.

'What are you going to call it, Gus?' said I. 'It may as well
have a name.'

'We'll call it the Nova Scotia Lead,' said Gus. 'The man
this gully was named after was a friend of mine, and a real
smart chap, but so darned unlucky, that I believe if he bought
an axe the handle would split before he got home.'

'Perhaps his luck will turn some day,' said I, 'nothing like
perseverance.'

'Well, so it may,' said the mild-mannered, but somewhat
obstinate Gus; 'in about thirty or forty years, may be, he
might have a throw in. Then, most likely he'd pass in his
checks right away. I'm a great believer in luck. I never
had much myself, or I shouldn't be here, you bet. And an
old Indian woman told me once—but—let's talk of something
else.'

'What did she tell you, Gus?' said I, reckless in my despair,
and not disposed to acquiesce in any man's softly supersti-
tious moods.

'It's nonsense, no doubt, but all her tribe swore—I hunted
with them when I was a boy—that old Tacomah was never
known to be wrong, and more than a score of deaths had
occurred in the exact order she had predicted. It was this,'
continued he, while a shadow covered his face, like a dim
presage of coming ill—'She said I should go to a far land across
sea, to find gold; that I should have my desire, but that when
I had reached it to beware, for the end was nigh.'

'Every man's end must be nigh whose fate compels him to
live in this infernal place,' said the Major. 'We work like
niggers, and live like black fellows (this was rather unfair to
Mrs. Yorke); we never see any gold ourselves, and yet have the
privilege of looking at other fellows handling it and hugging it
as their own. Now, I *know* you'll be on it here, and as you're a
sporting man, let us have a wager.'

'All right,' said Gus, a born gambler, who, though prudent
and highly respectable, had a book always at the Metropolitan
Races, 'what shall it be?'

'I'll lay a hundred to two in fives,' said the Major, 'that you
get nothing payable out of this claim. If you win I sha'n't
miss the brace of fives. If it turns out a real golden hole, five
hundred pounds won't be worth considering—will it?'

'Done, and done again,' said he heartily.

The bets were written down carefully and methodically. After a while we returned to our old claim, crest-fallen it is true, but fully resolved to make a stand upon No. 1 South Nova Scotia Lead, and to free ourselves from debt, if possible, if we didn't make our 'pile' just yet.

We sold out our old claim for a ten-pound note; and in a couple of days, with our belongings at Nova Scotia Gully, had logged up and made a start with another shaft.

The sinking was good. No rock, no water. Gus and his party were soon down to the bottom. That is, the alluvial drift, the sand and water-worn pebbles, the gravel and debris of the long dead, deeply buried stream, which in past ages had rippled and murmured under the blue heavens, heard the birds call amid the trees, which lined its banks and reflected the still azure of a southern sky.

Now waterless, soundless—blind, dumb, and imprisoned it lay, with a hundred feet of the earth's crust upon its bosom— that bosom which was once more bared to the light of day, solely by reason of the gems and scattered treasure which lay amid the sands of shore and channel.

Man, the arch-disturber, burying himself deep below the soil, and groping, mole fashion, in his sunless galleries, was able to trace out all the meanderings of that sunless stream. Even the dark hard stone-like fragments of the perished forest did he exhume, scrutinising the grain of the timber which had fallen, the fruit which had ripened, the leaf which had withered in the long solitary æons of dimmest Eld.

When the first 'prospect,' the first pan of alluvial gold-drift, was sent up to be tested, we stopped work and joined the anxious crowd, who pressed around, deeply curious and, indeed, directly interested in its proved value.

The manner of separating the clay, sand, gravel, etc., from the precious metal, is much after this fashion: carrying his tin pan or dish to the nearest water, the miner—Gus himself in this present instance—dips the vessel beneath, and immediately commences a half-circular, half-vertical, rotatory movement, suffering the clay-stained water to pour off, to be replenished from time to time, and always leaving less and less debris behind it.

After successive washings and castings forth of the pebbles by hand, nothing is left but a narrow crescent of sand, on the edge of which a border of dull red grains, specks, small particles, and a few irregular yellowish fragments, are plainly visible. There is no mistaking the king of metals. As Gus holds up the dish first for mine, and then for the inspection of the eager crowd, each man takes a rapid, earnest glance, and draws back. Then a wild cry bursts forth, hats are thrown up in the excitement of the moment, and the more intelligible utterances can be translated into 'fine gold, mostly, some rather coarse and water-worn—half a pennyweight to dish.'

This was success, indeed, triumphant, intoxicating success. The rule of three sum under such circumstances, which every miner entrusts to his mental arithmetic, runs thus : two dishes to a bucket, sixty buckets to a load, which makes three ounces, or £11 odd to the load—the load meaning a reasonable quantity for one horse to draw in a box cart. The wash-dirt has in a general way to be subjected to a puddling machine, a shallow wooden cylinder, like a large circular trough, in which a species of harrow is drawn by an unlucky horse, which continues his unending round, like the traditionary mill horse, until he must be heartily sick of the whole concern.

Poignant regret and bitter disappointment were over, though so little a matter as the delay of a day's marking out had lost us what promised to be as good a claim as any on Yatala. In fact, 'a gentle fortune,' as Cyrus observed. We comforted ourselves with the belief that in No. 1 we had a claim which would almost necessarily be a good one—might, indeed, be as rich, or, indeed, richer than the prospecting claim.

Taking the general nature of 'leads' or dead rivers, it chiefly obtained, that if gold were found on one portion of them, it extended to all the claims within a considerable distance. Sometimes, of course, it was not so. All the gold in the locality appeared to have been shovelled by malignant gnomes into one crevice, in the familiar phrase of the miners, 'a pot hole,' leaving the rest of the lead non-auriferous and disappointing. This we knew to be possible, but did not think probable. We accordingly worked away, stimulated daily by the pile of wash-dirt rising high on the side of the prospecting claim's brace—a pile in which the gold could be seen with the naked eye. At length we bottomed. Our shaft was down amid huge gray boulders of limestone which formed the bed rock of the locale. The drift was reached. With what anxious eagerness did the Major and I carry out our first dish of wash-dirt to 'try a prospect.' Inch by inch the sand and gravel lowered in the dish, the clay-stained water flowed and flowed, till at length, in the full view of a hundred men, the last streak of sand and minute gravel was left. In vain we looked, with practised eye, for the faint red rim which had comforted us in the prospecting claim. I shook the dish, and with the action dispersed and reunited the remnant sand. It was of no avail. No trace—even the faintest—of 'the colour' could be descried. With a half angry, half humorous roar, the crowd parted right and left, while the verdict was proclaimed, expressively if not elegantly, by Cyrus Yorke himself, who cried aloud, plain for all men to hear.

'Bottomed a duffer, by gum, not the colour itself, no mor'n on the palm o' my hand.'

We tried a few more dishes, all with the same melancholy result. Not a scintilla of the magic metal. Our labour had gone for nothing. We felt humiliated in the opinion of the crowd, many of whom had a personal interest in our success, as their claims, following after ours, would have been enhanced in value. Others, in despite of the stern mining law, were evasive of regulations and were awaiting our success, in order to commence sinking on their own account. Others had speculated in shares for the rise, and now found themselves hung up in a falling market. All these persons regarded us, with more or less of justice, as having done them an injury.

About the same time or, indeed, within a few days afterwards, No. 1 North, with Nos. 2 and 3 on either side, bottomed with similar results. It was the more astonishing, as all the while the prospecting claim was raising any quantity of washdirt, and the market value of shares therein had risen to one thousand pounds per man. How I almost cursed my too rigidly puritanic education !

Cast adrift again, we struck out for pastures new in the mining-nomadic sense, and, disappointed — not despairing — commenced a fresh shaft some ten miles off—this time on a Saturday night, and in an extremely promising flat, in which, as usual, I sanguinely trusted to find my *schatz*, like the *drei reisende auf ihrem wege*. The *schatz*, however, was not, as yet, for any one—except Gus Maynard, it seemed. The Nova Scotia base line was changed by the commissioner, upon the impassioned application of scores of distressed miners, some with large families, others without any encumbrance, as they are politely termed in Australia. All kinds of efforts were made to trace the gold ; but no gold could by any means be traced, except in the unlucky-lucky prospecting claim—the shareholders in which were Gus Maynard and party, and not Harry Pole and Co., alas !

Then was the well-known frontage expedient tried of 'swinging the base line,' which the commissioner was empowered to do, when called upon by a majority of the registered claim-holders, on any given frontage lead. This somewhat remarkable operation, well-nigh impossible to explain to non-mining intelligence, and sufficiently confusing even to those who had the dear-bought privilege of mining experience, may be illustrated as follows.

CHAPTER VI

AFTER sinking in every claim to the bed rock, on the imaginary course of the lead, not only is no gold found, but, from the depth and character of the strata, it is evident that the lead or ancient river-bed *cannot* possibly run in that direction. Then, after due application to the Commissioner, the base line is altered or 'swung,' *i.e.* freshly marked on another imaginary course, and the registered claims only, of equal size and number of men—of precisely the same rotation—are marked out afresh on the new base line. All previous markings and occupations are thereby annulled. Only the new ones are valid.

This mode of procedure, originally framed by officers thoroughly versed in all mining law, had stood the test of experience. If not the fairest mode of distribution of risk, it was the best compromise that could be effected between opposing interests. Still curious contretemps were continually occurring. When No. 6, let us say, was measured off and allotted on the new line, it would be found, perhaps, that No. 5's shaft, seventy feet deep, the last twenty through basalt, and a highly expensive exploration, was *now* situated in No. 6 claim.

Thereupon the No. 5 men would come to the Commissioner and represent that they were all married men with large families, and that they had spent their last shilling in sinking the said shaft, and if No. 6 were allowed to have it what a hard case it would be; and wouldn't his honour allow them to work it still, and drive (or tunnel) into No. 5 their present claim?

A Commissioner who was soft-hearted or philanthropical would probably be disposed to assent to this very feasible suggestion. Thereby he would straightway complicate matters, and get the whole lead into confusion, inasmuch as if No. 5 got gold in No. 6's claim, there would be a very nice bit of work cut out as to the distribution of it.

Of course, Captain Blake, after years at the Meroo in the early days of Louisa and Lambing Flat, had seen far too much of that kind of thing to be taken in. He would simply tell them to 'go to the devil' and read the regulations. He and they alike were bound by what they saw there. They were

clever enough to read them, underline them, and worry the life
and soul out of him, William Devereux Blake, by taking
technical objections, God knows.   Then let them obey the law
whatever it was, and not come bothering him with ridiculous
applications.   It was as fair for one as another.   As to wives
and families, and such like rubbish (in the way of argument he
meant), it was waste of time to introduce such matter into the
question.   Lose their shaft?   Of course they must lose their
shaft.   And any block claim that the new base line, as newly
surveyed, took in, must stop work till the frontage line was
proved.   How were men to expend capital, and develop the deep
lead properly—answer him that—unless they were defended in
the possession of their duly registered frontage claim, he asked?
They must be protected in following the registered claims on
the lead wherever they were found to go.   Much grumbling was
occasionally heard, and threats were now and then used.   But a
commissioner of goldfields should know how to put down his
foot, and when once planted in accordance with his reading of
the law, should never raise it.   Firmness invariably, in the long
run, succeeds, with large bodies of men.

As I said before, we had the base line altered over and over
again at Nova Scotia Gully, until the south claim levels were
nearly turned into the north and *vice versa*.   The old shareholders in the prospecting claim were quite contented.   They,
of course, did not budge.   Their claim was central, measured
off by the mining surveyor.   It was daily turning out loads of
wash-dirt from half an ounce to an ounce to the ton.   It seemed
inexhaustible too.   The stratum of wash-dirt was the thickest
ever known in an Australian goldfield.   It was in some places
of the unparalleled—well-nigh incredible—depth of forty feet.
Think of that, said all the experienced miners; years and years
of work.   When would it come to an end?   But, jammed
between the fossiliferous gray limestone walls of a tremendous
'crevasse,' it seemed to be only what the diggers called a pot-
hole.   It apparently came from no other 'run of gold,' led to none,
certainly.   Hence was the disappointment deep and bitter in
proportion amid all the unsuccessful comrades of the hero of this
wonderful discovery, Gus Maynard.

Again we were disappointed.   Not for the first, not for the
tenth—the twentieth time!   We had simply, failing to find gold
in our claim, known as No. 7 North Nova Scotia, lost our time,
our labour, and every shilling which we had been compelled to
disburse for what are called in mining phrase 'expenses,' that is
rope, tools, iron work, wax candles (for working below), and
any other matters without which 'sinking' cannot be carried
on.   We had gone more deeply still into debt to our good friend
and backer, Mrs. Mangrove; and really, I felt quite ashamed
to face that truly generous and estimable woman.

'So you're "duffered out" again, Harry!' she said, in her usual
cheery accent; 'well, you *are* an unlucky beggar, I must say.   I

don't think that young lady of yours will have any great catch
of you. And the Major, he's just as bad. He generally buys a
few yellow books after he's had a regular march down like this,
and lies on his back and reads for a week. Your mate, Joe
Bulder, he always seems to me to take it to heart too much ; he
sits, and smokes, and grizzles about it, no end. And that
Hawkesbury chap, he never takes on at all ; he's too careless to
fret about anything : he leaves all that to the poor little wife—
just like you men, that is. But you are an unlucky crowd, and
there's no use saying you ain't.'

'I'm afraid we are, Mrs. Mangrove,' I said sadly, for my
heart was low enough, I confess. 'If I hadn't sworn an oath to
keep on till the end of the year, I'd throw the whole thing up.
As it is, I don't know what we shall do, for I can't think of asking
you for more credit.'

'You needn't ask for it, Harry, my boy; you shall have it
without asking, to the end of the year, as you've sworn such a
big oath about it. My word ! I haven't followed the diggings
all these years, me and John, without having to put the pot on
now and then. We'll chance it till your time's up, just for the
luck of the thing. Perhaps you'll make a rise, and pull us
through, and something over.'

'And suppose we don't ?'

'Then we can "blue the lot," and your tucker account can go
with many another good pound as we've seen the last of. But
mind you, it ain't all losings, not by a long way. Didn't Joe
Hall put us into that Mary Jane reef, as we're drawing good
divs. out of to this day. And German Harry gave us a half
share in the Fatherland. It was down a bit to be sure, but we
got eight hundred pound for that, and four good washings up,
too. So you go and fossick out another good show, and I'll
stand to you, whether the old man likes it or not. Take a nip,
won't you ; it'll keep your pecker up. No ? Then have a glass
of beer—it's only she-oak, but there's nothing wrong about it,
or we should have had a funeral or two by now, this hot
weather.'

I accepted the table-ale of the colony, said 'God bless you,
old woman,' to my kind and generous, if somewhat unrefined,
friend in need, and walked back to Nova Scotia Gully.

There I found the whole party so nearly posed in the different
conditions that Mrs. Mangrove had predicted of them, that I
burst out laughing in the Major's mildly-inquiring face. That
calm warrior was never truly and unaffectedly surprised—if
outward appearances were to be considered—at anything.

He looked up from a cheaply-published 'yellow-back' novel
of the period, which he had apparently borrowed since I left in
the morning, and which, lying flat upon his back, he had been
engaged in assimilating.

'Been drowning *atra cura* in the flowing B. and S., Harry ?'
he said. 'It's a terrible temptation when fellows have just

"duffered out," I admit. A debauch of light reading I find, however, has less reactionary vengeance about it. I don't seem to mind drinking so much, but I can't stand the repentance. That's what keeps me so virtuous.'

'I am not "on," most noble centurion,' I made answer; 'but I have just had a great yarn with Mrs. Mangrove—God bless the dear old woman—and she described so exactly the way you all took bad luck, that, when I found you with your yellow-back, whatever it is——'

'The *Count of Monte Christo*, my dear boy. Of course, I've read it before; but it's a fine, long, solid romance, and I thought this the most appropriate time for a big read, so I went and borrowed it from Burton—but go on.'

'Well, there's poor Joe, smoking and looking like a man who, having made up his mind to hang himself, is now devoting all his mental powers to fixing upon a suitable tree. She says, truly, that he feels it too much, and that Cyrus, who has gone fast asleep, leaving his wife at the water-tub, and all the plates and dishes to finish before she goes to bed, doesn't feel it half enough.

> ' "To each his sufferings: all are men
>   Condemned alike to groan,
>   The tender for another's woes (that's me),
>   The unfeeling for his own (that's you),'

quoted the Major with emphasis. 'I am at present so deeply penetrated with the scoundrelly ungrateful way in which his *monde* has treated the deserving Edmund Dante, that I have no tears to spare for our own apparently real misfortunes; but I do no mind quitting the "Château d'If" for a few minutes to inquire whether or no we are to starve, or whether we have eaten our last, or rather Mrs. Mangrove's last, beef and bread.'

'That admirable woman has pressed upon us a whole elysium of "tick," ' I say, 'that is until Christmas, when she will probably withdraw, leaving us to perish financially if we continue to be the prey of the gods.'

'But not until then?' the Major inquired, with a certain air of indifference, returning to his romance.

'No,' I said; 'our existence literally, and as a mining party, is secured until then. If we don't make a rise before that time, we shall have to become wages men, bush-rangers, or knock-about-men on a station—farm-labourers.'

'I was one once,' murmured the Major, with his eyes fixed on his book.

'What, a bush-ranger?' inquired I eagerly.

'No; not so good as that. But Mayne and I—remittances being disgracefully long in coming—contracted to dig a lot of potatoes for an old buffer near Tenterfield. We dug away with great industry; it seemed an easy sort of game, but I couldn't help cutting most of the potatoes in half. These I had to bury

to avoid detection, which led to old Baggs (that was our master's
name), referring blasphemously to the smallness of the crop. I
looked virtuously grieved.'

'Heroic virtue,' I said ; 'and how long did it last ?'

'More than a month, I assure you. One day our letters came
—Mayne's to the care of John Baggs, Esq., Bubbrah, and two
addressed Major Blank, you know, late 77th Regiment. How
old Baggs stared when I took mine from him. "These for you ?"
he said, gasping audibly. "Without a doubt they are, hand
them here, Baggs—there are not two ex-majors of the 77th
knocking about this beastly hot village of yours. Perhaps
you'll send for the spades, and let a boy bring our swags down
to the village. We're going there now. There's hardly time to
order dinner. Better drop in and join us ? one o'clock sharp."
"No, thank ye, er, er, Major. Well, I'm blowed," said he, and
walked off.'

Let me strive to produce, as we are out of employment, a
picture of that strange settlement, a mining community in its
first inception, while the colours are fresh upon memory's pallet.
What should I have thought of it, familiar as all things are now,
had I been suddenly deposited before the door of our tent, in
the old happy, sleepy days, at Dibblestowe Leys.

For as eye can see, the area of settlement—several miles
square—is denuded of timber, the felled or burned trees represented by unsightly stumps in all directions. Within this clearing every kind of building and tenement is carelessly strewed.
Tents, log-huts, with the walls built American fashion of hori-
zontal tree trunks ; slab-huts of split heavy boards, Australian
fashion, placed vertically, and for the most part not impervious
to heat or cold ; bark-huts, of which both sides, and sometimes
doors, are composed of sheets of the flattened eucalyptus bark—
this material composing the roof both of this and the previously
described architectural edifices. The more ambitious buildings
are of weather-board, sawn pine or hardwood boards, roofed
with large sheets of galvanised iron. These are chiefly confined
to the streets of the township proper. This is held to be the
maximum of architectural solidity, elegance, and durability,
from a digging point of view, beyond which no reasonable man
could frame an aspiration.

To the untravelled European mind such a picture of household habitudes would doubtless present the idea of ugliness,
squalor, and privation difficult to realise or exaggerate. As
with most superficial conclusions, the idea would be erroneous.
Among other factors of a beneficent nature the climate stands
prominently forward. The interior of Australia, for the most
part, enjoys seasons, mild, rainless, devoid of storms and
tempests, rendering unnecessary the durable abodes of more
northern regions. There is no want of space, land is cheap and
accessible. The Miner's Right—that talismanic document—in
addition to conferring the potentiality of untold gold, has other

powers and magic qualities. It provides the holder with a
perfect title to an allotment of the earth's surface, varying from
a quarter of an acre within town boundaries, to four times the
quantity in a suburban location, always supposing that 'payable gold' is not demonstrated to exist on or below the surface.
In such case any fellow-miner may claim to dig thereon, previously compensating the householder, as may be fixed by
arbitration, the Commissioner, as usual, being the final arbiter
for the affront to his Lares and Penates.

It follows hence that the thrifty miner who possesses the
treasure, not less common on Australian goldfields than in other
places, of a cleanly managing wife, is enabled to surround himself with ordinary rural privileges. A plot of garden ground,
well fenced, grows not only vegetables but flowers, which a
generation since were only to be found in conservatories. He
has a goodly array of laying hens, occasionally even a well-fed
pig. On a rainy day, when the claim is off work, the domestic
miner is often seen surrounded by his children, hoeing up his
potatoes or cauliflowers, or training the climbing rose which
beautifies his rude but by no means despicable dwelling.

Entering such a hut, as it is uniformly, but in no sense of
contempt, termed—a hut being simply lower in the scale than
a cottage—you will there find nothing to shock the eye or displease the taste. As in a midshipman's cabin, economy of space
may be the rule but untidiness is the exception. Not only is
the earthen floor scrupulously swept and perhaps damped with
sprinkled water every day, but the space to a considerable
distance in the rear of the premises. All scraps and refuse are
raked into heaps, and on Saturday, which is invariably a half-
holiday and cleaning-up day, carefully burned. The meal
to which the married miner sits down at mid-day is 'generally composed of excellent beef or mutton, roast or boiled,
bread of the best wheaten flour, vegetables and tea, à discrétion,
always supposing the claim to be 'in full work.' At less prosperous seasons, no doubt, there is occasional need for distinct
but seldom for distressing retrenchment. Before that stage
sets in the married miner generally betakes himself to hired
work of some sort, for the neighbouring squatters or farmers,
until he 'gets a show again' in a mineral point of view.

When the field becomes so worked out that there is no
longer hope of employment at his favourite occupation, the
domestic miner generally sells his improvements and the good-
will of his little holding to a more sanguine or more stationary
comrade, and packing wife and children, furniture, pots and
pans, shovels and picks, cocks and hens, upon his dray, catches
the old horse, and migrates to the next promising 'rush,'
whether fifty or five hundred miles distant. Arrived there, he
selects an unoccupied allotment, and proceeds to levy on the
adjacent forest for a fresh dwelling, which in a few days presents
in all essential respects a striking resemblance to the home he

had just quitted. This done, he attacks the green or gravelly garment which garbs the bosom of the Mighty Mother, with his old patient industry and a courage undaunted by a hundred defeats.

Among this class of miners, constituting a very large proportion of the mining population on every goldfield, it will be seen that the chance of lawless behaviour being supported is slight. Malcontents and criminals doubtless there were in due proportion to the exceptional circumstances which brought together the community, but the police being aided by the whole body of respectable miners, and still more strengthened by the propriety of public feeling, there was little probability of crime rioting and reigning unchecked, as (unless their own chroniclers are marvellously and unnecessarily mendacious) was the case on the American gold and silver fields.

Had such characters as Slade, and others, but presumed to have shown themselves in Yatala for a single day, they would have been hunted down and extirpated, I venture to say, with as little delay and compunction as the tiger which once escaped from a travelling showman in the neighbourhood of Dibblestowe Leys. Not a trace of sympathy would have been shown with their acts and braggart blood-deeds. I can fancy the speechless astonishment mingled with wrath unspeakable, with which Sergeant M'Mahon would have received the astounding statement that the portly host of the Freemason's Arms had been shot dead by Ned White or Bill Jinks, across his own bar. Hardly more surprise and incredibility would have been evoked had the news appeared in the Yatala *Watchman* that the Church of England clergyman, a Cambridge graduate, and a most highly respected personage, had been scalped by Bungarree, the black fellow, an aboriginal chieftain, who (when in liquor) was wont to assert his prior right to the whole goldfield, and his fixed determination to petition Queen Wikitoria for a share of the weekly gold escort.

The carrying of arms, that apparently natural and necessary habit in the United States of America, was here a monopoly enjoyed by the police. Even threatening to shoot was an offence punishable by law. A worthy Downeaster was, for that offence only, promptly apprehended and haled into 'The Logs,' as the strongly timbered lock-up was usually termed, for merely using the threat of shooting. He was called upon to find sureties to keep the peace in the sum of one hundred pounds, and, to his dismay and mortification, retained a night in duress for the first time in his life, he averred, such sureties not being forthcoming. The Commissioner, with his usual good-nature, sent word to one of his countrymen, who appeared and tendered bail to the amount, so that the free and enlightened citizen was liberated.

The town of Yatala, where the houses, huts, and cottages were so close to one another that every foot of frontage had its value, was composed of two principal and seven or eight cross streets and lesser thoroughfares. The larger shops, especially when lighted up at night, were gorgeous with plate glass, and brilliant in display of all the wares requisite for a mining community. There were haberdashers, grocers, fruiterers, tailors, shoemakers, butchers, bakers, booksellers, not noticeably different in the appearance of the warehouses and wares from their city prototypes. Paint and calico, varnish and gilding, with the glare of well-fed oil lamps, made the outer present-ment dazzling to behold. The tourist, walking down the main street at night, in the midst of a surging, stalwart, but most well-behaved crowd, must needs be struck with astonishment at the close resemblance of the mushroom town to the real, legitimate, accredited cities of an older world.

The back premises of these imposing structures would seldom bear close scrutiny, shading off as they did to bark and tin, and sometimes calico continuations. But commodious and weather-proof, they answered fairly well the purposes for which they were intended. The most prosperous establishments were naturally the licensed hotels and public houses. Of these there were a hundred and seventy in all. A very large number, doubtless, but any attempt to limit the licensing produced such a crop of 'shanties' or sly-grogshops, that the magistrates granted licenses to nearly every one who chose to apply The license fee, £30, was rather high. But, presumably, a demand for such entertainment existed, or persons would not be found willing to lay out their money on the speculation. Upon these establishments, which are generally suspected in rude com-munities of being seed-beds of disorder, a strong hand was kept. They were only permitted to have music with dancing at their saloons once a week. This permission was applied for in writing to the Bench, and liable to be promptly withdrawn at any time upon complaint by the police.

Gambling, in an open manner, was sternly repressed. Hotel keepers were fined severely if convicted, and every *particeps criminis* was similarly dealt with. Mr. Jack Hamlin, in spite of his engaging social qualities and latent nobility of nature, would have had a bad time of it at Yatala. Strictly under the surveillance of the police, Mr. Merlin's cold gray eye would have been invariably upon him; and it would have been un-safe to have offered long odds that the sergeant did not eventually run him in for contravening some of the statutes which he knew and loved so well.

Although many of the miners could not have been described as religious persons, yet was Yatala, on the whole, a very church-going community. The Protestant denominations were well represented. The Church of England, the Presbyterians, the Wesleyans, and the Congregationalists had all built, with-out a sixpence of Government aid, very neat and commodious edifices in which service was held, by ordained ministers, twice on each Sunday regularly. Sunday school, visiting societies, and other allied associations were as plentiful and well kept up as in any settled parish. The Roman Catholics had perhaps the most imposing building, except the Wesleyans; but then Cousin Jack Tressider, an opulent Cornish miner, had given eight hundred pounds to the latter, which had enabled them to have stained-glass windows with varnished seats, and divers other decorative distinctions.

I was never done wondering at what struck me first as the chief characteristic of this great army of adventurers suddenly gathered together from all lands and seas—viz. its outward propriety and submission to the law. Closely applicable was the description of the mixed host at the leaguer of Valencia—

> 'There were men from wilds where the death wind sweeps,
>   There were spears from hills where the lion sleeps,
>   There were bows from sands where the ostrich runs—
>   For the shrill horn of Afric had called her sons
>   To the battle of the West.'

And, indeed, swarthy, grizzled Californians, red sashed and high booted, with great felt sombreros that took all kinds of fantastic shapes—jostled stalwart 'Geordies' and Cousin Jacks, whose fresh faces told that they had never before left the shores of old England. Frenchmen and Spaniards, Germans and Italians, Hungarians and Poles, Greeks and—Trojans? Well, I may not swear that any unit of that richly variegated crowd had quitted the windy plains of Ilium, or the banks of Simois for Yatala Creek—but if that once famous nationality was unrepresented at the great Yatala rush, it stood alone in disfranchisement.

The compatriots of Achilles and Ajax, though not of Hector and Paris, were sufficiently numerous, proving, as one marked their stately forms, their flashing eyes and chiselled features, that the modern inhabitants of Hellas have not relinquished the birthright of godlike strength and beauty, which witched the world, when 'the fearless old fashion held sway.'

Yet, though the narrow streets actually trembled under the feet of the surging crowd of grand-looking athletes that thronged the well-lighted thoroughfares, and filled the shops and tavern bars after working hours, there was no lawless act, no wearing of deadly weapons, no foul language, no open drunkenness or offensive parade of immorality; far more decorous of demeanour and easy to thread than the ordinary crowd of a manufacturing town or a metropolis. What was the reason of this strange reserve, this almost unnatural decorum?

It was apparently a triumph of moral control! It was not wholly the spontaneous propriety of a highly intelligent, travelled, experienced community. Human nature, in the mass, though often unduly maligned, scarcely attains such results unaided or unrestrained.

F

A patent fact was, that the vast crowd was under the sway of a very smart officer of police, who, with two sergeants, a couple of detectives, and about a score of constables of the rank and file, about one man to each thousand, kept the whole of the great band of adventurers in perfect and admirable order.

Such, in other colonies, had not (*vide* Mick Hord, barkeeper, ex-miner, storekeeper, pugilist, etc.) always been the successful result under such circumstances. 'Perleece, Mr. Merlin,' he said one day to that officer, 'talk about perleece, and call this a "rush." I've known a rush of forty thousand men, and seen 'em kickin' the perleece from one end of the town to the other.'

'I was not at the Red Hills, my dear boy, nor Sergeant M'Mahon either,' said Mr. Merlin, smiling with that way of his that somehow did not tend to reassure people. 'I should not advise any one to commence that kind of thing here.'

Whatever the reason, no one did apparently care to take the initiative in any kind of disturbance, though such was often threatened.

The inspector, Mr. Merlin, was always extremely keen at knowing everybody and everything which it concerned him to know very thoroughly. Patient and calculating, too, always averse to use force when diplomacy would suffice. Yet utterly impartial and pitiless in the execution of his duty when need was. He was, therefore, respected by the miners generally, as a man of capacity, liked for his *bonhomie*, superficial as they knew it to be, and secretly feared by all those who recalled 'sins unwhipt of justice,' which were the precise traits of character needed by a man in his position.

Sergeant M'Mahon, the second in command of this somewhat minute battalion—have I described that good old warrior before?—was a man to whom not less than to Mr. Merlin the peace of the goldfield population was mainly owing. He was truly an astonishing combination of natural sagacity and acquired wisdom, as recognised in the force. Emigrating from county Mayo in his youth, he had passed his earlier manhood and middle age in the ranks of the New South Wales police. To say that he was shrewd, active, rarely at fault, was to give but little estimate of the unerring half-instinctive accuracy with which he pounced upon a criminal, if wanted, like a lurcher upon a leveret. An immensely powerful man, with a fair share of activity, he was invincible at close quarters, armed as he was with the terrors and majesty of the law, which he had, so to speak, incorporated with his own personal presence, until no man could separate them. His air of authority and grave official dignity soared far beyond all vain attempt at description. Kings might be regal of aspect and Emperors unapproachably grand, but the sergeant's majesty of demeanour was, perhaps, not exceeded by any crowned head in the universe.

A steady reader, he had mastered the intricacies and forms of ordinary police-court law to such an extent that few of the stipendiary magistrates, and none of the unpaid justices, could successfully contravene his legal dicta ; while, in the matter of foresight and discretion, he possessed a fund which would have set up an ordinary Lieutenant-Governor, or a couple of chairmen of Quarter Sessions.

The old Adam—not to mention the eager tameless spirit of the Western Celt—occasionally displayed itself, lighting up the dark gray eye, and changing the quiet, unimpassioned tones. But rarely was such a manifestation descried by the laity. Respectful to his superiors, firm yet reasonable with his subordinates, carefully civil or humorously polite to the general population, sudden and startling in any *coup d'état* the hour for which had arrived, the sergeant was a man whose successful aim in life was to prevent minor revolutions, and who only needed a national one to have become a General of Division.

Like many of the generals of the empire, a slight solecism here and there might be observable in his speech. But the courage, coolness, and organisation were there, and a natural consciousness of power about the man effectually prevented any appearance of incongruity, bordering on ridicule.

Mounted troopers and foot constables composed the contingent. Their duty was to arrest, or cause to be summoned to the police court, all such as betrayed themselves ignorant of the statute law of Great Britain, as adopted in the colonies, by committing breaches thereof.

It might seem futile to punish such offences as ordinary drunkenness or evil speech in the streets of a mining township by fine or imprisonment. Nevertheless the thing was done, and done effectually. Every offence against the law was taken cognisance of instantly, dealt with promptly, and punished sharply. All knew what they had to expect. The administration of justice was entirely impartial, and the law was backed up by the whole force of genuine diggers. They knew full well—being, perhaps, the most intelligent, experienced, and, so to speak, cultured class of *ouvriers* in the world—that the strong arm of the law would only be weakened to the detriment of the whole society.

As for petty mining thefts, the stealing of small articles of value, of wash-dirt or auriferous drift—these offences were so manifestly contemptible as well as immoral, that the whole field, as one man, worked for the detection and apprehension of the offender, who had no more chance than a lurcher among a pack of hounds. There was no lynching, however,—the invariable result of a weak executive. Once handed over to the 'secular arm,' all were assured that justice would be done. Six months' imprisonment, even in the case of the smallest value stolen, might be taken to be a sufficient deterrent penalty.

It was true enough that the whole population did not consist of industrious, straightforward miners. Every army has its fringe of camp followers, wretches who murder the dying and strip the dead. The great mining army of Yatala was not exempt from this ghoul-like accompaniment. Harpies of every length of beak and talon full surely congregate wherever gold is plentiful on this earth. There it was unearthed daily, to the value of thousands, of tens of thousands of pounds. Gamblers and thieves, men and women of the worst reputation, flock to a new rush. Among these there were men known to have committed one murder—suspected of more. But their persons were known, and their every act and word carefully watched. There was little chance of indiscriminate pillage or death-dealing at Yatala.

CHAPTER VII

SOME difficulty was encountered in quelling the gambling mania among the Chinese. Watchful and cunning, though they were in the habit of congregating to play 'fan-tan' for largish sums, the police never could catch them. One fortunate evening the sergeant surrounded the house of Mr. Lin Yun, and captured thirty-five Mongolians in all, bringing with him, in triumph, their strange instruments, their copper and brass counters, and all kinds of collateral evidences. A handy interpreter was found, and the upshot was that Lin Yun was fined ten pounds, and the rest five pounds each, with a threat of imprisonment for the next offence. This broke up the confederacy.

When the Chinese are in excess of, or nearly approach in number the white population, they are difficult to manage. It was not so as yet in Yatala, though a time came. As traders or labourers, house servants or gardeners, they were more industrious than and as trustworthy as the whites; while their breaches of the law were by no means numerous, considering their proportion to the population. After a quarrel in a gambling house, one Chinaman drew a knife and stabbed another, with whom he had an altercation. The others at once secured him, while a messenger ran to report to the sergeant, by whom the culprit was at once carried into captivity. He was subsequently committed for trial in due course, the court-house being crowded with his countrymen, and at the assizes found guilty and sentenced to death. His sentence was, however, commuted to imprisonment for life.

Looking back upon that exceptional, perhaps abnormal settlement, of which, however, I was for some years so completely a part that I doubted at times if my old life at Dibblestowe Leys, with my visits to Allerton Court, and my morning tramplings over the brown fallows, had not been a dream, and this my true and real existence, I see many things to be admired as well as some which were to be deplored and condemned.

Let me here testify of my own knowledge and experience to a much more than ordinary amount of Christianity. By this

I mean that adoption of the spirit of our religion, which finds vent in sympathy, charity, and abstinence from evil speaking and evil judging.

The main body of miners are, by circumstances, led to assume much of the demeanour and mode of thought which prevails in club life. They have graduated in the University of Travel, and are in a general way too experienced as gentlemen adventurers, and men of the world, to go blurting out their sentiments, like simple villagers, upon every tiny question of manners and morals that arises. Prompt and decided in action when need arises, they fully appreciate these qualities in their rulers. But they exercise a large measure of toleration, and have learned very thoroughly the high expediency of each man minding his own business. Only watch their bearing in the case of the family of a dead comrade, of hospital funds, of sudden misfortune or bereavement, of undeserved obloquy. I have never seen any body of men, in any land, so ready of hand in relief, so prompt and generous in aid, so delicate and effusive in sympathy.

A modern community is incomplete without its newspaper. At Yatala there were two, diametrically opposed, of course, in law, religion, and politics. One journal was strictly conservative, upholding the Government, with the administration of justice, and all things and persons pertaining thereto. The other, the *Watchman*, was democratic, not to say destructive, scoffing at the constituted authorities, sneering at the police, badgering the magistrates, impeaching the Commissioner himself, and continually calling on the great body of miners 'to assemble in the night and sweep away all tyrants and goldfields officials, together with the absurd contradictory regulations which hampered their honest efforts and trammelled their virtuous industry.' The editor of this exciting, not to say inflammatory journal, was named Fitzgerald Keene.

Clever, fairly educated, and morally unprejudiced, he, like another historical scribe, was quite capable of raising a wale upon that epidermis which it suited him to thong, whenever such to him seemed necessary for the purpose of the hour. Ingenious in discovering the weak point of an adversary, he would concentrate and exaggerate until the uninitiated were almost fain to believe that there *must* be some ground for this furious invective, this wholesale denunciation.

When once he had singled out an official for attack, no part of the whole moral surface seemed to escape him. Caution was cowardice and irresolution, pitiful indecision, conscious incompetence; firmness was obstinacy; decision was tyranny; coolness was contempt of the toiling masses; silence was dumb idiocy; speech in explanation was drivelling insanity or ludicrous display of ignorance. There was no pleasing him.

'The only cure (of course) for all this miserable official muddling and disgraceful apathy on the part of an effete and

corrupt government that stood tamely by while a great interest
was being plundered and blundered through daily, was that
the hardy and intelligent miners of Yatala should "roll up,"
and take the law, the government, the land, and the gold into
their own hands.'

After reading one of these anti-monarchical productions, Mr.
Merlin, with his customary coolness, intimated to the editor
that it was very well written—so much so that he himself would
not be surprised if some fine day it, or a similar proclamation,
did actually arouse the mining population to some mad revolutionary act ; in which case he would take upon himself to arrest
the author of the whole mischief—the writer himself—and that
he would so far honour him as to make the arrest with his,
Merlin's, own hands.

Mr. Keene turned rather pale at this piece of voluntary
information, which he did *not* work up into a 'paragraph.'
For some weeks afterwards there was decidedly less red pepper
in the leading articles of the *Watchman*.

It was not to be supposed that the rough and ready partition
of twenty or thirty tons of gold, to the value of something under
two millions of pounds sterling, was to be effected without a
little litigation. Law, of course, there was in abundance, and
a very good thing, too, though it bore hard upon our particular
party. The vulgar error arises that disputes are more easily
settled without law or lawyers. Such is by no means the case.
Unlearned people, when the *casus belli* is presumably important,
are tedious and difficult to deal with. Unaware of the nature
of evidence, they waste the time of the court far more than any
professional men, however prone to take objections.

In order to lay down the law there must of necessity be
lawyers. At Yatala there were four, who not infrequently had
their hands full between police cases, civil processes, and mining
suits. When it is borne in mind that the mining laws, as settled
by statute and the regulations founded thereon, were in some
instances intricate and, perhaps, ambiguous, that a large discretionary power was vested in the Commissioner, and that a
cheap and accessible court of appeal existed,—a rehearing before
two magistrates, who were empowered to reverse the most
elaborate decision of a Commissioner, if they saw fit,—it may
be calculated how many suits came on for hearing before our
administrators, and how crowded the court-house was on nearly
every day in the week.

The legal gentlemen consisted of duly qualified solicitors.
Such only were empowered to plead and conduct cases before
the court on behalf of clients. No miner was debarred from
pleading his own cause, but he was not permitted to cross-
examine witnesses, or to address the court on behalf of another.
It was held that such conduct would trench on the vested rights
and privileges of professional gentlemen. And as all matters
were settled at Yatala—notwithstanding it was a goldfield, and

a diggings in far-away Australia—principally and in accordance with 'the law of England, in that case made and provided,' and not as ardent reformers chose to suggest, so the status of the profession was upheld.

The chief personages among the band of advocates, who occasionally pocketed in a week fees that would have made a junior barrister's mouth water, were Mr. Markham and Mr. Cramp. They were nearly always employed on different sides, and either had or simulated a distinct personal antagonism—whether merely forensic or otherwise it was difficult to determine; but the fierceness of their tones, the bitterness of their sarcasms, the desperate tenacity with which they fought over the last shred of the probability of victory, with the power and elaboration of their addresses to the court, would have stamped them as advocates of a high order before any tribunal.

There was, perhaps, no great difference in their legal attainments. In mining experience they were level. Both had paid in hard cash, in common with all outside speculators, for whatever trustworthy knowledge of actual mining they had gained. No wonder that they threw sufficient energy into their advocacy of mining suits, when it was no uncommon thing in the flush times of a goldfield for the lawyer on either side to receive a half or quarter sleeping share in the mining property at stake. In one instance, a quarter share so given, or promised, realised within a short space of time no less a sum than two thousand three hundred pounds sterling.

Mr. Markham was a ruddy-faced, full-whiskered, middle-aged bachelor. He apparently kicked all care behind him, and thought of nothing but his business during the day, with a steady game of whist in the evening, and a few congenial friends with whom to share the flowing bowl, which regularly at 11 P.M. made its appearance in the shape of whisky and water. His friends said he was a man of regular habits, and knew exactly how much was good for him. His enemies said that he drank hard, if regularly, and was undermining his constitution. They called him careless, indolent, and fitful in the discharge of his duties. His friends (and they were many and less lukewarm than such easy-going well-wishers generally are) averred that no more watchful and *rusé* diplomatist ever veiled consummate art under a carefully careless manner. However that might be, Mr. Markham had a pretty high average of verdicts to score to his legal bat, and in all leading mining or criminal cases some curiosity was always displayed to know which side Markham was on.

A family man, of staid and austere morals, Mr. Cramp had his own good points, and was valued accordingly. He was closely and technically acquainted with mining and common law to an extent that made him a dangerous antagonist, when anything was to be gained by a fatal objection. When a point of law happened to be in his favour he would seize upon it and shake it, as a learned judge remarked, 'like a dog shaking a rat.' There was no fear of a Bench or a Commissioner forgetting his vantage ground, once he descried it. Painstaking and perspicuous, he was dangerous with a bad case, and irresistible with a good one. A tendency to irritability, of which his adversaries occasionally made use, was perhaps his weak point. But he was conscious of this defect, and under ordinary circumstances refused to 'rise' to any bait, however tempting.

Of the two other professional gentlemen, one was a Frenchman, who had successfully mastered the difficulties of our English tongue, as well as the intricacy of our laws. He was indeed a man of unusual talent—an orator, a logician, a tribune of the people, a republican of very advanced opinions. But for the genuine British distrust of a foreigner, Dr. Bellair would have taken a high rank as a political leader as well as a lawyer and a physician. But the invincible British prejudice against 'a Eyetalian, a Mossoo, or summat o' that there sort,' was sufficient to neutralise the fire of his oratory, the fervour of his philanthropy, and the ardour of his (adopted) patriotism. The Bench had occasionally great difficulty in controlling him ; his temper was utterly unmanageable, and occasionally landed him in disrespectful allusions to the quality of the law as at Yatala administered. The magistrates with much tact and kindness bore with him, trusting to his sense of propriety, which was delicate, to bring matters round. But the Commissioner, who was too awful a potentate to be bearded with impunity, had once sworn that he would incarcerate him in that provisional dungeon, 'the Logs,' if he did not then and there apologise and retract certain words, which he accordingly, with a bad grace, consented to do.

The fourth advocate was an elderly gentleman, who had formerly enjoyed a large metropolitan experience, and a well-deserved reputation for exactitude in the recollection of statutory enactments from Carolus I. upwards. He was scarcely so familiar with the subtleties of mining law and phraseology as his younger brethren, and though as good as ever in the labyrinth of common law, found a difficulty in adapting himself to these latter-day developments. However, so great was the general press of legal exercise that he had his hands full, and was rarely without more business than he could get through at his somewhat steady pace.

However, for some few weeks there came one of those lulls and seasons of depression which occasionally take place on goldfields. None of the claims, except the Nova Scotia, had been yielding richly for some time. We had cleared out from that unlucky neighbourhood, and were down fifty feet on the Liberator Lead, so called after the great Dan O'Connell, a party of whose countrymen had taken up a prospecting claim, of which strong hopes were entertained. So much confidence was felt that the value of shares all along the lead were steadily rising, and we, in No. 4, began to hope that we might be in for a good thing at last.

That man must be inconsiderable of mark, extremely cautious or unnaturally inoffensive, who does not possess enemies. Among these natural antagonists, who seem born for the chief purpose of working evil to foredoomed men and women, one individual always stands prominently forward. Whether fostered by chance, or developed by circumstances, the enmity is unmistakable. Deadly, unsleeping hate fills the whole nature of the creature. And they are exceptionally fortunate for whom the gods act as shield and buckler, so that the evil eye is dimmed, and the renegade from civilisation foiled.

The dangerous classes of Yatala, very fully represented at times, held among their evil celebrities a man named Algernon Malgrade. He had been known by name to me before I left England as a gambler and a low profligate. By birth one of an old county family, he was shunned by acquaintances and scouted by relatives. More than one shady transaction had left him not wholly unscathed. Toleration is long extended to the merely extravagant and selfish spendthrift, so long as certain society laws are not infringed. But at length a day came when a wholly unpardonable escapade caused Algy Mal, as his friends and humble imitators called him, to be 'cut' beyond all hope of rehabilitation. The fiat of expulsion from the inner circle is often delayed; but when it once goes forth the sentence is stern and irrevocable. Malgrade strove against it, with a sneer and a mocking laugh, for a while. But the odds were too great, and one fine day, like many another bad bargain, the goldfields of Australia were enriched by his presence and example.

We met at Yatala soon after his arrival. Flush of money, as not having wholly exhausted his outfit, he was looked up to by the, perhaps, not fastidious set with which he chose to ally himself. He was by way of greeting me as an old acquaintance. We had met more than once, but I repelled his overtures, and showed his companions plainly that I meant to keep clear of him. From that moment the whole evil nature of the man seemed to concentrate itself in a settled and passionate hatred, as violent as it was irrational.

In a score of different ways he soon announced himself as my sworn foe and antagonist. At all the meetings upon matters of local interest we invariably were ranged on opposite sides. He was not without talent; indeed, he possessed a superabundance of natural gifts, which he might have turned to material advantage had he listed. He had a persuasive manner of talking when he cared to hide the unclean spirit which dwelt ever within him. He was accomplished, graceful, and, as far as animal courage went, utterly fearless. Reckless and remorseless, he needed but mediæval power to have furnished a true type of the Visconti of old, sparing neither man in his anger nor woman in his lust. In these modern days, and under the democratic miner rule, such personages are only covertly dangerous.

At the amiable Algy, therefore, we could afford to laugh, and the Major, more than once, caused the evil sneer to deepen by carelessly inquiring whether he had heard from home lately, or whether a club to which they both formerly belonged was still as celebrated for its Madeira as ever. From this abode of bliss we knew that Malgrade had been driven forth by a well-nigh unanimous ballot of the members.

Though I had the worst possible opinion of his heart, and regarded the man's intellect as merely subservient to his appetites, I could not for the life of me return his detestation of me in kind, or cease to take a certain interest in his actions. For one thing, he was wonderfully good-looking. His recklessly indulged passions had, *as yet*, written no evil record upon face or form. The fair hair was still bright, the blue eyes still steadfast and clear. And a certain appearance of fallen-angel pride clung to him in the midst of his degradation. I could not help cherishing a dim hope that some day he might thrust from him the foul incrustation of vice and crime, and return to his natural position among men.

The Major never omitted to laugh at my credulous optimisms, and to sneer at my ignorance of the world, on these occasions.

'You ought to know a thing or two by this time, Harry, but I doubt if you ever will,' he would say. 'If a man doesn't pick up an accurate method of gauging the moral attributes of his fellow-men at a goldfield he will never analyse worth a cent. And here you are, just as much carried away by this infernal scoundrel's regular features and soft voice, as that handsome pantheress that he's stolen somewhere. She'll poison him some day or he'll knock *her* brains out, I feel certain. And what the loss to society would be in either case, I should fear to overestimate by the faintest expression of regret.'

'You are rather too hard on the other side,' I made answer. 'You have no sympathy for human weakness. I say it is a piteous thing to see the decadence of creatures originally noble and formed for higher things.'

'Bah!' retorted my unconvinced friend. 'Do you remember what Athos and Co. did with Miladi? That she-devil of a Dolores—she's no more Spanish than I am Greek—will give you a rough turn, as Cyrus would say, some day, if you let her so much as *look* at you—"I think I knows 'em!"'

All of a sudden, without any previous warning, a wonderful rumour arose that the prospectors in the Liberator Lead had struck incredible gold. Although they had not yet announced it, the excitement occasioned by this statement was astounding to those who had never known the tremendous force of the passions which, from time to time, stir the crowds which make up a goldfield's population. At one moment you would imagine them to be the most logical, law-abiding body of men in the world; at another time a brigade of red republicans would be liberal conservatives compared to them. In this instance no one but an eye-witness could have credited the turmoil which arose. As the report was soon passed around in every paper in the colony, strangers began to arrive within a month of the first announcement, whose worn draught animals and vehicles told of far and fast journeying. Every unoccupied person, male or female, young or old, from Yatala and within twenty miles of it, was apparently massed around the wings of the famed Liberator Lead. Daily the numbers swelled. The forest was felled. Huts were erected in all directions. Tents were like the sands of the sea for multitude, or the advance guard of an army. All was eager excitement and feverish expectation. The prospectors of the Liberator, as of every other lead or course of auriferous deposit, were bound by the regulations then in force to report 'payable gold' as soon as such had been struck, and to hoist a red flag as denoting the discovery. In default of such advertisement, for the general benefit, they were liable, according to custom and practice, to have their claim 'jumped' or taken forcible possession of by any party of miners who could prove that they were concealing the golden reality.

The prospectors made no sign. They refused to state precisely what the indications were. They simply declared that they had not as yet 'bottomed' or sunk down to the alluvial drift, immediately above the bed rock, and which alone is likely to be auriferous. Some of the impatient holders of claims on 'the line' frontage, and others, who were merely 'blockers' or the occupants of ordinary chance claims, anywhere in the vicinity, were more than impatient — they were threatening and abusive. They insisted that the shareholders were 'on gold,' for their own purposes hiding the nature of the deposit, cheating the public, disobeying the regulations, and injuring their fellow miners.

The chief man of the party, a grand-looking herculean Milesian, quietly rejoined that they had not bottomed yet, that they had nothing to show or report, though the indications were good, that when the time came they would at once report at the Commissioner's office. In the meantime they would answer no questions, nor let any one go down their shaft, except by order of the Commissioner.

That gentleman, who had condescended to appear on the occasion, and who began to realise that a crisis was approaching, asked Mr. Phelim O'Shaughnessy how long they expected to be, the sinking being easy, before they were on the drift?

'About a week.'

'Then, on this day week I will be here,' said Captain Blake, addressing himself both to the speaker and the mob, 'and on that day, whether gold be reported or otherwise, I will send down two men to examine the workings and to report to me.'

'All right, your honour,' replied Phelim. 'There's no two ways about us. Any one your honour likes to send down is welcome, but we're not going to let all the rapscallions in the country down our shaft just because they happen to think we're to slave and murther ourselves intirely for their convanience— to find gold for the likes o' them—coch 'em up, indeed ; the lazy naygurs.'

At ten o'clock in the morning of Monday, the 17th May, which was the day week following, the Commissioner sat on his horse beside the shaft, in much the same careless attitude as before. But the scene was changed in some important particulars. Gold had been duly reported. A red flag proudly flaunted from a lofty pole in front of the claim, while a crowd of five thousand souls, eager, earnest, dangerously roused at once by the strong passions of greed and anxiety, swayed and surged around the little group.

On a new and presumably rich lead it was no unusual matter to see a concourse of this kind. But rarely was there so much feeling shown as here. Rarely were there so many knitted brows and scowling faces ; rarely so much savage and insubordinate language. How had it all come about ? Mr. Merlin, with a couple of troopers, well armed and mounted, rode behind the Commissioner. Why was this semi-warlike accompaniment ?

The solution was this. A short time previous several fresh regulations had been drafted, and had become law, which to a certain extent altered the existing customs, more particularly as regarded frontage.

That which more particularly affected the present question was Regulation 22, reciting as follows :—

' When the sinking in new ground shall be found not to reach a depth of a hundred feet in dry ground, or sixty feet in wet or rocky ground, of which the bottoming of three or more shafts on the supposed line of lead shall be a sufficient test, unless the Commissioner shall specially sanction a further testing, all marking on the line of lead *shall be null and void, and the ground shall be open for taking up claims in the block form,* the frontage holders having a preference to select their claims in rotation, according to their priority of occupation on the supposed lead.'

This then was it which so agitated the seething human mass, which by this time included, as well as the true miner, men of every rank, trade, and occupation, lured to the banks of the Waraldah Creek by the wildly exaggerated reports which had gone forth.

So much depended upon the accident of the golden drift being struck at a foot or two *below* instead of above the magic number of a hundred feet.

Should this rich deposit be proved to lie at or beneath the specified depth, the rich claims, already numbered and registered as far as fifty, down the lead, would belong only and inalienably to those who had months before occupied and registered them according to law.

But should the golden seed of discord repose upon a drift shallower than the regulation number of feet, every man in the crowd might deem that he had a share in the golden subterraneous channel; possibly might delve within a fortnight into a recess as rich as that of Aladdin, or of the one to which Ali Baba procured the *entrée* at so great personal risk.

But would the Commissioner pronounce the 'open sesame'? For it lay with him—with him only rested the responsibility, graver than often befalls one man in a century, of dashing to the ground the hopes of a body of hardworking legitimate miners, or of unloosing the flood of half-infuriated physical force, which needed but one word from his lips to burst the bonds of restraint. The anxious chafing thousands were only too ready to scatter [themselves with pick and shovel, a swarm of human locusts, upon the golden ground which they seemed to devour with their eyes.

The word was 'Block.' But would Captain Blake utter it?

There was much to be done yet. Both sides were strongly represented—legally, officially, socially, as well as numerically.

> ' And many a banner will be torn,
> And many a knight to earth be borne,
> And many a sheaf of arrows spent,
> Ere Scotland's King shall cross the Trent.'

'In the first place, I shall send down two practical miners to examine the wash,' quoth he. 'I intend to satisfy myself as to the fact of payable gold to begin with.'

He looked around—scanning the faces of the miners nearest to him—on the crowd.

'Here, Tom Denman, and you, Geordie, my boy, get away down and send up a couple of dishes of wash-dirt. Then we shall all see if it's worth fighting about, and not have a row about nothing.'

Two stalwart miners stepped forward, and the man called Geordie, a middle-sized but tremendously muscular specimen from 'cannie Newcassel,' putting his foot in a loop of the rope, closed his hands upon it above his head, and was rapidly lowered down. In a few minutes the rope came up empty, and Tom Denman descended.

In less than a quarter of an hour the hammer indicator rose and fell upon its tin sheet, whereupon the rawhide bucket used for the purpose brought to light a collection of sand, quartz fragments, rounded pebbles, and gritty greenish clay-loam. This was unanimously pronounced a 'very nice wash,' and being

placed in a couple of tin dishes beneath the strict supervision of
the Commissioner, was taken to a neighbouring pool of water
and placed in readiness for the two miners who had excavated
it. These returned gnomes having been brought to light, at
once commenced to 'pan off,' according to the recognised rule
and practice.

Dipping the full dish into the pool, each man held the
vessel aslant while he washed among the gravel and small
stones, permitting the water to flow uninterruptedly over and
away from the wash-dirt. The clay-stained water assumed a
bright yellow hue. As the stones became cleared of the en-
crusting dirt, the miner carefully examined them for traces of
adhering gold and then threw them on one side. Gradually
the sand and clay disappeared over the rim, in the unvaried
steady flow of water, the dish being held slightly downwards
and off the level.

The sandy deposit at the bottom grew finer and finer, as
with a peculiar half circular motion the water and the outer
grains were ejected and the heavier particles retained. At
length there remained but a narrow segment of darkish sand at
the bottom of each dish, while plain for all to see was a streak
of deep though dull yellow particles, chiefly fine in grain, but
sprinkled with coarser grains, some of which were of the size
of wheat.

'Here you are, sir,' quoth Tom Denman, exhibiting the
residuum respectfully to the Commissioner. 'There's no mistake
about that. Geordie and I took these from different parts of
" the face." I haven't seen such a prospect for some time. A
good half ounce to the dish, and Geordie's, I can see from here,
is better.'

'I declare the Prospecting Claim of the Liberator Lead,' said
the Commissioner, passing the dish to the nearest of the eager
crowd, 'to be in possession of payable gold.'

The first man who looked at it shouted out, 'half an ounce
to the dish,' and threw up his hat. Hundreds, of course, were
not near enough to see, but the tone and the action were
sufficient. A cheer rose from the vast multitude that roused
the wallaroos in the sandstone spurs of the Dividing Range
miles away.

'The next thing to determine,' said the Commissioner, 'is the
depth of sinking. A good deal will depend upon that. One of
you men give my compliments to Mr. Underlay, the mining
surveyor, and ask him if he will come here. I wish him to
measure this shaft. I know he is not far off.'

'It's never a hundred feet sinking,' yelled an excited miner,
in a ragged red shirt. 'All the field knows it ain't much over
ninety. They may have bin and sunk through the bottom to
make it handy for their friends in No. 1 and 2, where they've
got half shares. But there's no hundred feet in it, and it ought
to be " block " out and out, this blessed minit.'

Here the multitude caught up the word, and sounded it over and over again in a vast reverberating chorus. For nearly a quarter of an hour nothing could be heard but 'block'—'block'—'block.'

'What the devil do you mean by making all that row, you fellows,' said the Commissioner irascibly. 'Do you think it will make any difference in *my* decision if you yelled yourselves hoarse and shouted till doomsday. Thank you, Mr. Underlay,' he continued, with a rapid change of manner. 'Will you have the goodness to go down this shaft and measure the exact depth from the surface to the top of the "wash." That I shall take leave to consider to be the real depth of sinking.'

Before he had well done speaking, Mr. Underlay, the mining surveyor, an active, resolute-looking youngster, had his hand upon the rope, and was on his way towards the lower regions. After a short sojourn he reappeared, holding a tape line, and after comparing and verifying his measurements, pronounced the words 'Ninety-eight feet eleven inches.'

Again a wild cheer rent the air, while the excited individuals of the outer crowd so pushed inwards under the impression that 'block' was to be declared, and claims given away there and then, that the Commissioner's horse began to get impatient, and Mr. Merlin and his troopers were under the necessity of turning round their chargers several times, which resulted in inconvenience to the toes and other portions of the frames of the vanguard.

'Understand once and for all,' said Captain Blake, 'that by Regulation No. 22 I am bound to allow three shafts to be bottomed on gold, on the course of the lead, before I finally decide upon the average depth of sinking, and before I declare the lead to be worked either under block or frontage. I shall, therefore, return this day week at the same hour. If the requisite number of shafts have been bottomed on the lead by that period, I will deliver my decision as to the question of block or frontage.'

Then a hoarse roar arose from the crowd, as of some hungry monster baulked of its prey. But further remonstrance or interference was not thought of. The Captain rode carelessly and peacefully homeward, lighting his cigar, and calling to his dogs, as if no such torments as gold and gold diggers, prospectors and claim-holders, frontage men and blockers, existed upon the hardly entreated earth.

CHAPTER VIII

IT is not to be supposed that our party added in any way to this state of incipient disorder, though we had taken up No. 4 North under the old frontage system and were sinking with might and main to get down and know our fate. We had every reason to think our claim would be unusually good. The indications in the prospecting shaft disclosed 'a show' of which the oldest miners spoke with bated breath.

But where the coming decision touched us, and the other frontage men, was in this wise : if we happened to drop right down on the 'gutter,' or main course of the lead, we were all right ; we should be allowed so many days to mark out our claim of a hundred and sixty feet, forty feet a man along the lead, and two hundred back, and it would be all right. That area of ground, *all on gold*, was a very fair allowance for four men.

But if we were *not* exactly on the course of the lead, but a little to the right or left of it, and if the block system was declared next week, matters would be very different. We should have to mark out our claim there and then. It could not afterwards be altered by a single inch. This would have to be done at haphazard, instead of by cautious 'proving' the ground, as under the frontage system. And if we missed the lead it might be taken possession of by any random blocker, just pitchforked here from another colony. We should lose the reward of months and years of work, the certainty we had a right to expect when we registered under the frontage system.

In the interim much agitation took place. Councils and caucuses were held. Letters and petitions despatched profusely to the Minister for Lands, who in those days held ultimate control over all mining affairs. The newspapers exhausted themselves in leading articles, each tending to exalt and glorify a different mining policy.

One gave a strictly conservative support to authority. 'The frontage system, framed as it was with the advice of experienced officials, was considered by intelligent miners to afford a highly needful guarantee for capital invested in mining enterprise.

Without capital there would be little mining worthy of the name, more particularly where, as in Yatala, the difficulties of piercing the basaltic strata, and of subduing the flow of subterranean streams, had to be surmounted. Still it was the opinion of many competent authorities that the frontage system had had its day. The field had been for some time in a languishing state. Many hard-working men were out of employment. There were specific regulations which had to be interpreted with a literal exactitude independently of personal feeling or private interest. And no one who knew Commissioner Blake doubted but that he would decide according to the letter of the law, and carry out that decision with unbending firmness.' Thus the *Beacon.*

This was the opportunity which the opposition journal had been waiting. And cheerfully did Mr. Fitzgerald Keene avail himself of the happy convention of circumstances.

'Many occasions had arisen during the last decade of shameless oppression and official incompetency, when the long suffering mining community, comprising a singularly large proportion of the intelligence, the energy, and the industrial enterprise of the land, might have spoken out with effect. True to their law-abiding instincts, they had hitherto remained loyal to the Crown, and obedient if not humble before constituted authority. But now the time had come, the hour had struck, when they must proclaim themselves to be freemen or for ever endure to be known and treated as slaves. Under the iniquitous mining statutes, and the still more contemptible mining regulations, their intelligence had been stultified, their freedom had been mocked, their opinions derided, and their industry fettered.

'Still there had been a pretence of fair play—there had been a tendency, erratic as had been the course pursued, in the right direction. Now, in this thrice accursed muddle which had taken place at The Liberator, would the herd of down-trampled miners, *numerically the strongest body* of labourers in the land, stand by and consent to their own ruin and spoliation? Was there not a man from old Ballarat to utter the magic words "roll up?"'

'And would a monster meeting separate without compelling present safety, and exacting material guarantees for the future?'

It was not altogether a sterile soil into which these seeds of revolution were so recklessly cast. It was a mob. Though vastly superior, as I have elsewhere stated, in its composition to most other mobs, it yet possessed their inherent characteristics. By the turn of a straw its action might have oscillated from good to evil, from patience and obedience to insubordination and wildest excess.

Among other expedients and demonstrations of the time, each party favoured large and imposing deputations. One day the frontage men and their adherents, backers, friends, acquaintances, etc., would march into town, several hundred strong, with banners flying and a band of music, to which a drum of sonorous, mysterious power lent effect. Forming in front of the Commissioner's office, they would request an audience.

When that gentleman sent word to say that he would consent to see them as soon as he had completed his immediate business, the crack speaker of the connection would be detailed for the occasion. When he appeared that gifted person would fire away at the unmoved Commissioner for twenty minutes or so without a check.

'He could inform him that the honest and legitimate miners whom he saw now assembled had come to lay their grievances respectfully before him, and to ask him if he was minded to have mercy upon them, upon their helpless wives and children, depending upon their rights as holders of frontage claims for bread? or, was he going to be carried away by the senseless clamour of a mob of strangers and adventurers, who had not a shred of title to the land they sought to plunder. Had not they, the frontage men, conformed to the laws laid down by the Government closely and obediently ; had they not duly registered their claims, incurred debts from their storekeepers and business men on the field on the strength of the security of tenure guaranteed by the frontage system? And now, after waiting for days, and weeks, and months, were they to be told that, because a new and unjust regulation had been made, because the first few shafts on the lead had not proved to be the full hundred feet in depth, were they to be turned out of their property—for it was as much theirs while they paid for their Miner's Right as the lands of Mr. Howard or Mr. Stanley, neighbouring country gentlemen? Were they to be turned out of their claims just when they were seen to be worth holding? No! They were honest men and loyal subjects, but there was a point beyond which men could not be urged. If justice were not given them in this matter bloodshed would be the end of it. They said it sorrowfully but firmly, and upon the heads of the Government the crime would rest.'

The speaker, who was a bachelor, and had last week had a quarter share in a frontage claim given to him as a retaining fee, almost wept at this point, and, with a look of sorrowful but manly appeal, closed his address amid cheers and applause.

The Commissioner always heard out such addresses, knowing from long experience that when a grievance has been rankling in the breasts of men, ordinarily silent about their dissatisfactions, nothing is more unsafe than to deny a hearing when they demand one.

'You may do as you please about granting their petitions,' he was wont to say. 'You may do what they don't like, or do nothing at all. But if you wish to rule large bodies of men peaceably, always hear what they have got to say. It is an inestimable safety valve.'

So Captain Blake listened to the eloquent miners' advocate, and gazed at him and the assembled crowd with an approving and benevolent expression. At the end of the oration he told them that 'he was sorry for them personally, if by any act of his, in carrying out the regulations, they should lose their claims on the Liberator Lead, some of which to his knowledge had been held in despite of difficulty and privation, for many months. But, above all, it would depend upon what proof was furnished to him of the depth of the sinking, and upon other particulars which would bring their claims under the provisions of the mining regulations. He would examine most carefully the evidence and those sections which bore upon the case in point. After that he would give his decision. He would frame that decision most elaborately, so that it should be in accordance with the law. And when it was given he should see that it was carried out. That was all he had to say to them.'

Whereupon they always thanked him for his courtesy and departed. The Commissioner went back into his office. The band struck up afresh, and the excited crowd dispersed, to walk six or seven miles back again.

A report would soon arise, that they had stated their case to the Commissioner with such power and pathos—the orator of the deputation would, perhaps, be responsible for this—that he had promised to decide in favour of the frontage men. The blockers being thereby infuriated would resolve to come in and state *their* wrongs. Being, as the proletariat, much more numerous than the frontage holders, who represented capital, they would 'roll up' so successfully that a crowd more than a thousand strong would, on the appointed day, be seen marching in a tremendous long line, four abreast, down the main street of the town, halting finally at the Commissioner's office. That much tried official would certainly begin a sentence with blank, and end it with the same, placing divers other blanks in the middle, all having reference to the eyes and future prospects of the majority of the members of the band and the personages of the deputation.

After thus blowing off the steam, he would meet them at the door, and listen tranquilly to what they had to say. Then the advanced democrat who was their philosopher and spokesman would thus open the trenches—

'As miners, and as men, they had come there to-day, not with any intention of threatening or intimidation,'—the Captain looked quietly at the speaker as he said this, who passed on to the next sentence—'but to protest mildly yet firmly, as became legitimate miners, against any monopoly of the field, whether it was by men claiming to be frontage-holders, or any others, he cared not who they might be, or what they were called.

'If they were not all experienced miners who were here

assembled this day, they all were the holders of Miners' Rights —many of them had families—many had helpless relatives depending upon them. Some had come from a distance it is true. But what of that? as long as they were at this moment dwellers in New South Wales, they had as much right to a fair share of any payable ground that turned up as the Governor himself. All they wanted was justice and impartiality. Let every man be allowed to mark out his claim, and get gold or not as his luck went. The law said, if the ground was under a hundred feet deep it was no frontage, and must be worked on the block. All they wanted was the law. The Commissioner was appointed to carry out the law, fair and equal, between man and man. They knew very well that the Liberator Lead was no frontage lead—but block, that is, ground to be worked in ordinary block claims. And block they hoped the Commissioner would declare it to be. It would be better for the whole field, and not leave the gold that was intended for the country at large in the hands of a few.'

' To this the Commissioner would reply that—'he would very closely examine the ground when three or more shafts had been bottomed on the lead, and would then give his decision in accordance with the strict law of the case. They might depend upon that being done when the time came, that is, when that number had been bottomed. Until that time came he could not, of course, tell them what his decision would be. He hoped it would be found to be according to law, and excepting by the Appeal Court there was not much chance of its being altered.'

The speaker then essayed to get another hearing, reminding the Commissioner that 'they represented four thousand men. They were not going to boast or make threats; but they were determined to have justice, peaceably, if possible, but if justice was denied them they would consider the advisability of using the power which their numbers gave them.'

At this point the Captain's patience—for the most part an algebraic or unknown quantity—abruptly gave out. He reminded the speaker that the miners had never gained anything by physical force in New South Wales, and as long as he had anything to do with mining, he trusted they never would. He had said all he had to say. They had fully explained their case, and could add nothing more, it appeared, but empty threats, which were utterly contemptible. He was busy now and begged to retire. Then he went in and closed the door.

In consequence of the reported 'bottoming' of certain shafts, punctually to the hour on the morning appointed, the Commissioner rode up to the Liberator Lead. There was hardly standing room for a mile around. The line of shafts could be traced by the flags which each exhibited. At the Prospectors', being 'on gold,' streamed a red flag, emblem of success. Also on three other shafts, Nos. 1, 2, and 3 North, which had bottomed on the supposed line of lead, thus forming a sufficient test of the depth of the ground according to the conditions of Regulation No. 22.

When the great man appeared, a deep hoarse sound rose indistinctly from the enormous crowd. Fully five thousand men had gathered hours since to await his approach. His fiat, to be given that day, was looked for with an intensity almost painful to a sympathetic bystander.

Upon Captain Blake alone, apparently, the immense concourse, the strained attention of the masses, the weight of responsibility, had no visible effect. He regarded the whole scene and its peculiar features with haughty immobility.

Riding to the first claim, he said to the men who were 'off work,' and standing at the mouth of their shaft, shareholders of No. 1—

'You are on gold?'

'Yes, sir, we've struck it all right.'

'At what depth?' is the next question.

'Well, about a hundred feet,' they answered.

'I shall send down two men first, and then measure your shaft.'

'All right, Captain.'

Two selected miners, as before, were lowered down the shaft, returning as hitherto, in the case of the Prospectors, with tangible proof of the highly auriferous nature of the deposit.

'So far, so good; now Mr. Richardson,' here advances the mining surveyor, 'have the goodness to measure this shaft.'

Mr. Richardson descends; then, after due delay, regains this upper earth, distinctly enunciating—'Ninety-seven feet five inches.'

At which statement a cheer from the blockers for the first time wakes the forest echoes, and a thousand caps or hats are thrown excitedly into the air.

The same formalities are carefully gone through with No. 2 and No. 3. Each is demonstrated to be 'a golden hole.' When measured, No. 2 is declared to be ninety-three feet and a half; No. 3 ninety-one only. Each declaration elicits a bursting cheer from the majority of the crowd.

Then the Commissioner braces himself, sitting squarely on his horse and confronting the assembled multitude. His address is brief. But rarely have words more power. This only does he say: 'I declare the Liberator Lead to be "on the block."'

This simple word would appear to have converted the whole assemblage into a crowd of raging lunatics. With one mighty cry rather than a shout the crowd broke up, apparently prepared to take immediate possession of the Tom Tidler's ground then and there handed over to them.

'Stop!' roared the Commissioner, in a voice of thunder which dominated the great mob, and almost immediately reduced those within hearing to a listening attitude. ' I give the holders of frontage claims twenty-four hours to mark out their claims in rotation, according to their priority of occupation — the ground will then be open for taking up claims in the block form.'

' I belong to No. 6,' said a tall miner ; ' we haven't proved it yet. We hardly know where to take our ground. Won't you give us a day or two more, Captain ? It's rather rough on us frontage holders.'

' Not an hour—not a minute,' replied the Commissioner. ' I have adhered strictly to the regulations. I didn't make them, and I can't help the ground not being deeper. That's your affair. I have given my decision, and by the Lord I mean to stick to it. Good-morning, all of you.'

A world of opposing forces and passionate feelings was seething in the hearts of the men to whom he thus bade adieu. That single word 'block' had sufficed to render possible hundreds of working parties, which to-day would be procuring timber, rope, tools, and provisions. At the same hour on the morrow they would be eagerly commencing a shaft, having previously put in the indispensable four pegs, which, with the more necessary Miner's Right, secured an unalienable title to the coveted landed estate.

On the next day, the spot so lately void and bare resembled a human rabbit warren. Everywhere trees were felled. Everywhere the miner was seen, mole like, burying himself in the orthodox narrow shaft, and throwing up the yellow clay which was the upper stratum. In a week the principal street of the village of O'Connell was a mass of gaudy-looking shops, filled with every kind of ware—every third house of course a public house. Vehicles of all kinds crowded the narrow way, and with difficulty threaded the crowd of wayfarers of every age, calling, and nationality. Within a month the four banks were all day long weighing, buying, sifting gold, while bundles of notes and handfuls of sovereigns were handed over the counter with apparently careless confidence.

As soon as the main body of block claims began to bottom, gold flowed in with almost fabulous profusion. And still the rumour grew and increased, until people from the uttermost ends of Australia commenced to leave their ordinary avocations and turn their heads towards the new Eldorado—the great, unprecedented, fabulously rich Liberator Lead near Yatala.

Our party had been exceptionally fortunate. We had No. 4 on the lead. There was neither rock nor water. We had the luck to bottom 'dead on the gutter,' that is, immediately over the defunct river, and to find the whole of its long buried bed, with the usual admixture of gravel, sand, and waterworn pebbles, richly studded with gold. Occasionally, indeed, we took several ounces of gold from a single dish of wash-dirt. When it is reckoned that two dishes, in miner's measurement, go to a bucket, and sixty buckets to a load—about a ton of earth—and that half an ounce *to the load* is thought a rich lead, it may be imagined what properties the Liberator claims were held to be.

Our fortunes were made, we all knew. We had about three years' work before us before we could bring 'to grass' our buried treasure—the sands of this long dead Pactolus of the South.

We were in the proud position of being able to 'put on wages men,' or hired miners, at three pounds each per week to assist us. We also bought a 'whip horse' for forty-five pounds, which staunch and well-trained animal drew up the precious gravel, and in many ways economised labour. We calculated that if the yield kept up at the present rate, we should clear from fifteen to twenty thousand pounds per man before No. 4 was 'worked out.' This was worth waiting and toiling for.

'Well, Joe,' said I, one day, 'this is better than striking in old Grimsby's forge at the Leys, isn't it? We've got our pile at last.'

'I doubt it is,' said he, as he leaned back for a moment, and then sending his pick into the face at which we were working, dislodged a quantity of the precious wash-dirt. 'We'd never ha' picked up a "slug" like this at yon old Dibblestowe—not but what I've wished myself back there many times.'

'Yes, Joe,' said I, taking from him the rough red heavy clay-stained lump, which looked like an ordinary bit of conglomerate, but which *we* knew to be a nugget of almost pure gold, weighing more than fifty ounces, and worth two hundred pounds. 'This didn't grow in Farmer Mangold's turnip fields, did it? I've wished myself at the old village, too, I can tell you. However, this is going to pay us for all.'

''Happen it is!' he said, 'and not before it's time, too. I was getting full about digging, and but for you I'd ha' ta'en my passage home again, worked it before the mast, long and long ago.'

'You'll go home and be a gentleman now, Joe,' said I. 'Anyhow, you can buy a big farm or two. You might settle down near the Leys and marry Miss Mangold yet, if she'd have you.'

'No fear,' said Joe, using one of the Australian idioms which he had grafted on to his homely Kentish speech. 'She'd a niver touched me with a pair of tongs, she was that proud and set up like then. But dost know what?' Here he made a pretence of whispering, though, being but the two of us in the 'drive,' a hundred feet from air, there was not much chance of being overheard. 'Jack Thursby told me he believed he seed her at Warraluen.'

'Jane Mangold at Warraluen? But how did he know anything about her?'

'Well, she got talking about Dibblestowe Leys, where she lived in England, as she should say. Then he up and told her he come from close about there, and as there was two chaps

Harry Pole and Joe Bulder, as was diggin' here,—he didn't know aught about you being a gentleman born,—and how as they come from the same place. Then she gave a sort of cry, and says, "Oh, surely it isn't Hereward Pole—don't you tell him I'm here in this hell, for it's nothing better." And then, he said, she cried badly, and went on terrible, till Black Ned, as she's married to, swore at her and threatened to knock her brains out if she didn't give over. I'd like to 'a bin there.'

'Good God,' said I, 'and is this the end of pretty, innocent Jane Mangold. How is it we never heard of it before?'

'Well, this chap, he kept it dark for a bit, but one day he and I was on a bit of a booze, and it all came out. It's a 'nation pity, ain't it now. Jack Thursby said he beats her awful, and some day he'll be the death of her—and it won't be the first he's made away with.'

'I wonder if we can do anything for her,' I said. 'Some day I must take a ride over to Warraluen and see her, though I hardly know how to help her. Still she shall have the offer of my assistance—poor—poor Jane.'

Then I fell to thinking how strangely intermingled our lives had been. More wonderful than any romance it seemed, if we two, who had wandered over the peaceful uplands and oakwoods of Dibblestowe Leys, hardly more than boy and girl, should now meet once more again in the far, strange, gold-town of Yatala.

CHAPTER IX

IT is generally taken for granted in Britain that every person in a colony must of necessity know, or be known by, everybody else. Mr. Smith, of Sydney, on furlough, is importuned to carry a letter to Mr. Jones's cousin in Queensland, while his disclaimer as to personal knowledge of Miss Thompson's brother in Victoria is evidently looked upon with suspicion. It seems hopeless to attempt to convey to old-world people correct ideas of the enormous distances which separate the settlements of a newly-peopled continent; impossible almost to explain the nature of those social divisions which still further tend to prevent the universal brotherhood which is held to characterise the Arcadian existence of colonists.

They cannot imagine the necessity for such lines of demarcation 'in a colony,' clearly as they are defined and rigidly enforced in every third-rate county town and old-fashioned village in Britain.

As a matter of fact, there are few places in the world, London excepted, where individuals may be more securely hidden from kith or kin, early friends, and later acquaintances than in Australia. And no place in Australia furnishes greater facilities for personal effacement than a large goldfield. A squarely built man in ordinary miner's garb, known as Jack Scott only by his associates, passes by carrying a tin dish and a shovel: how are you to divine that this particular Jack is the son of a clergyman, and the grandson of a general in the Indian army, who will presently die and leave him a fortune, when the whole thing comes out? You are summoned as a juror to attend the coroner's inquest held on a poor fellow found in an eighty-feet shaft, where he has fallen overnight, having missed his way in the dark. He was 'Bill Jones' to all men, and lo! his brother arrives from town to attend the funeral, and it seems poor, easy-going, unambitious Bill, contented with the society of 'equals'—the shareholders in the claim—and an occasional carouse, was the cadet of an ancient house, the members of which are broken-hearted at his early ignoble death. How many instances of this decadence had I noted? How often had

I dreaded in moments of despondency a like fate; shuddering to contemplate in myself a possible waif, hopelessly stranded on the shore of despair and evil hap!

It had easily occurred, then, that Jane Mangold and I, though we had been living considerably less than a hundred miles apart, had never met, had never heard of each other, until this recent chance. Now that I was assured of her near presence, an intensely eager desire, a thrill repeated from the ardent boyish period, when

'She was a part of those fresh days to me,'

urged me with resistless power to gaze upon that face once more of my old friend and playmate.

I had often analysed my feelings towards the girl who had so nearly been linked for ever with my destiny. I had never been absolutely 'in love' with her, as the phrase goes. But the vivid unreasoning admiration of early youth for the first fair form and face might easily have ripened into a passion. From this misfortune—the grave error of declining to a lower level of birth, breeding, intellect, and sentiment—I was saved by a loftier, a purer, a more absorbing devotion.

Yet he who has once been inspired by a woman, even with feelings short of the highest degree of admiring interest, rarely ceases to regard her with a peculiar tenderness. If there be generosity in his nature, he is ever ready to stand forth as her champion, ready with aid or counsel. And students of the human heart are wont to aver that the friendship which might have been love has ere now expressed itself in acts of sublime self-abnegation to which the world furnishes few parallels.

On the following Saturday, therefore, I borrowed a horse for the journey to Warraluen, 'putting a man on'—that is, hiring an experienced miner for the sum of ten shillings per diem, to perform my duty in the claim until my return.

Before the stars had left the sky, I rode quietly and steadily forth, thereby giving my horse, fresh from a run on grass but a few days since, a chance of settling to his work by degrees. As the sun rose higher I quickened my pace, and riding fast, but not unreasonably, the well-seasoned animal brought me within sight of the substantial little township of Warraluen before sundown.

As I rode up the narrow street, serpentine in construction, as in all gold-founded townships, I looked carefully for the hotel which I had been informed that Edward Morsley kept. The settlement differed in some respects from the one I had quitted. Its prosperity depended almost wholly upon quartz reefs. In their nature, the reefs or ledges of quartz rock are more permanent as to the gold crop than the alluvial deposits which can be rifled in a comparatively short time. Whereas the great depth of the matrix, as a rule, and consequently slow, steady extraction of the golden stone, necessitates a more protracted service, a more settled population. Hence the populations of 'reefing districts' are for the most part famed for comfortable cottages, well-grown orchards, and a general air of well-paid, contented labouring life.

The miners in this particular locality were chiefly Cornish-men, hereditarily accustomed to subterranean labour in their own land. Laborious, enduring, and efficient in their own occupation, to which many of them had served a life-long apprenticeship thousands of feet below old 'ocean's swells and falls,' in Wheal Maria or The Great Dungavel, they were said to be by no means so *suave* of manner or agreeable in associa-tion as their cosmopolitan brethren of the alluvial goldfields. The aggressive, sullen nature of the untravelled Briton was still uncorrected by association with the outer world. They formed a community within themselves, and, as such, shut up to the development of their own peculiar tendencies, some of which were less pleasing than remarkable.

At this particular time the reefs at one end of the line of shafts, upon a mountain crest far above the town, had been lately yielding enormously, and were renowned throughout Australia. The 'Cousin Jacks' were, therefore, in great force. Much given to brawling amongst themselves, they were more than likely to be uncivil to strangers. The small force of police, hitherto thought sufficient for their subjugation, was all inade-quate when a dozen reefs in line were sending up ten ounce stone—even better than that, it was whispered, and hundreds of wages men, employed by the great absentee companies, re-ceived their three pounds each as regularly as Saturday came.

In some respects, therefore, I had arrived at an inopportune season. Saturday night was pay night, and the vinous aspect of the groups I encountered — so different from the men at Yatala, except perhaps upon a high festival—convinced me that I had chosen a bad day for my entrance into Warraluen. However, I bestowed myself at the first available inn, and after needful refreshments and a couple of hours' rest, strolled out into the well-lighted streets.

'Well, lad,' said a short man, whose blue-black curly hair and deep-set eyes betrayed the 'Cousin Jack,' while his enor-mous spread of chest redeemed him from any imputation of insignificance, 'thou farest all as one as a stranger, loike? Where be'st bound?'

'To Morsley's Inn, if I can find it among these crooked streets of yours,' I said, slightly irritated at my want of success and inauspicious surroundings.

'Black Ned?' said the pocket Hercules, rolling himself around, and not resenting the imputation on his town, but steadying himself for a comprehensive look at me. 'Be'st a friend o' thatn? Not by the looks o' thee—danged sight more loike to be friends with yon pratty mawther as he's gotten boxed-up there wi' him—more's the pity.'

'Can you show me the house?' I asked, not much disposed for the sort of conversation that I foresaw could only be extracted from my acquaintance.

'Show thee t' house—why, I'm a gannin' theer, straight as I can go. There's a dance there t' night, man—a ball! and we'll fare there together, Billy Pentreath and a friend, an owd friend —eh, lad? I'll show thee the missis. Mayhap she'll dance with thee—thou'rt a tidyish soart o' chap.'

After a short walk, and a considerable amount of tacking indulged in by my guide before he could 'fetch,' as he expressed it, the 'main drive,' we fronted a large, imposing, two-storied brick building. Beyond doubt it was a gala night, as the profuse lighting up, the group of men and women round the doors, the sound of music which issued from the open windows, abundantly testified.

'Why, here's Billy Pen,' said a red-bearded giant, who looked like Odin or Thor about to enter a modern Valhalla. 'Here's Billy a coming to see the ball, and another chap. Who's yer friend; a Geordie, most like?'

'No fear, Red Gaffer—dunna thee moind about Geordies. Seems as he's a Yatala man, and a golden hole man, as I'm warned,' said Billy, improvising slightly for the benefit of his audience, and unaware that he was so far clinging to truth. 'Wants to buy a few shares in Frohmann's, and Barrell's, and Caird's. But let's in, boys, and don't obstrooct th' entrance.'

A shout of laughter greeted this imposing utterance of Mr Pentreath, performed with some difficulty. But seconding his expressed wish with an energetic shoulder movement, which even the giant did not care to withstand seriously, Mr. William Pentreath rolled through the open door into the hall of mirth, whither I followed with comparative ease.

'E. Morsley's Reefers' Arms,' as the large gilt letters on the front of the house proclaimed it to be, had always been celebrated as a 'dance-house,' where from time to time gatherings were permitted by the police for the avowed enjoyment of music and dancing. This privilege had always been fenced round with restrictions and sparingly conceded by the police authorities. It was found, in the early history of the goldfields, that these assemblages of men of all classes and characters, excited by liquor, flush of money, and urged on by the presence of women, more fair than honest, led to many undesirable results. It was then enacted that each hotel keeper who desired to have music and dancing in his licensed house, should apply in writing for the permission. This application was referred to the police officers, who recommended or otherwise. If broils had taken place, robberies been hatched, or bad characters been encouraged to frequent the house on former occasions, the police stated objections, when the application was sternly vetoed by the Bench of Magistrates. In no case was such permission granted oftener than once a week. It was, therefore, no scene of wild, unhallowed revelry upon which Mr. Billy Pentreath and I were about to intrude, no reckless orgy, but a fairly regulated entertainment, in which, if there was a certain license as to liquor and language, no great abuse of either would be possible. Still, I knew well that, had the woman I had come to seek retained her former feelings and principles, there would have been as much likelihood of her joining in a gipsy feast on the common near Dibblestowe as willingly lending the sanction of her presence to revelry like this.

The room was large and well lighted by lamps which hung from the ceiling. The floor good in a general way, although uneven towards one end, where the difference in the height of the wall showed that a smaller room had been annexed for greater public accommodation. A brass band of considerable power, and by no means inharmonious time, was at the moment performing a German waltz, to which about a hundred couples gyrated with orthodox slowness and precision. Of the women, some were handsome and showily dressed, others again were homely, middle-aged, and plain of attire, the wives of working miners who had a mind for once to enjoy themselves, and, at the same time, make sure that Sam or Joe would be back in time for his 'shift' at the claim. These were, in the main, reputable and hardworking women. It was easy to see many who deserved neither of these epithets. But whether fair or honest, there was one striking fact apparent, that women of *any* kind were at a considerable premium at Warraluen. More than half the couples were men dancing with *men*. The saltatory instinct must be, even when diluted by descent, of great original strength, if one may judge from the fact that men, long absent from the pleasures of ordinary civilisation, when met for purposes of amusement, will dance for hours contentedly with one another rather than not dance at all.

At the end of the room was a highly ornamental bar for the sale of liquors, behind which was displayed in tempting profusion every kind of alcoholic stimulant. Officiating here, in company with an assistant whose time was completely taken up in serving the drinks which were ceaselessly called for, was a tall dark man, showily dressed according to the taste of the locality, and affecting a kind of spurious gentility which I thought sat ill on a lowering, savage cast of countenance.

'Yon's Black Ned, blank him,' said my companion, 'as large as life, and twice as nasty if a' dared ; let's over and have a drink, and he'll tell us a' the lees as is agoin' about Frohmann's, Caird's, and Bolterman's, and the lot on 'em. You're a wantin' sheers for a Sydney company, eh lad ? That's your little game. I seed it soon as ye said fust word.' And here Billy winked at me with a portentous cunning, the effect of which was much enhanced by the difficulty with which he performed the feat.

Whether with characteristic shrewdness he had assumed that,

whatever my real errand, there was no need to advertise it, or
whether my appearance suggested an agency for the purchase
of reef shares, then popular with speculators and rising fast in
the market, I could not divine.   But I instantly saw the advantage of following the hint accidentally given, and being made
known to Mr. Ned Morsley under the style and title of a purchaser
of shares in the great reefs which were then sending all the
Australian world mad with hope, fear, and regret.

Such buyers were always, of necessity, provided with a
sufficiency of ready cash ; and the bearer of promptly available
moneys has always been a welcome guest at hostelries of every
grade since the days of the Tabard.

When, therefore, Mr. Pentreath lumbered up with diagonal
dexterity to the bar, narrowly avoiding the destruction of more
than one couple of performers, and further informed Morsley
that I was Mr. Poole, a friend of his, from Yatala, as was 'on
the gutter' in the best blank claim in the blank field, and was
bound to have the pick of all the sheers as was for sale in the
leading reefs on the blank Hill, the sullen face of the host
assumed an air of laboured welcome, and even an ominous,
half-gracious, half-sinister smile illumined his dark visage.

'You're only just in time.   I had some of Frohmann's this
morning, but they're gone.   There's a half-share in Caird's, and
two-quarters in Bolterman's, that I can put you on to.   The
men were here this morning ; one's off to Sydney, and the other's
just spliced—that's why they want to sell—d——d fools both.'

'Eh, thou'lt find him some, I warrant thee, as long as there's
a loomp o' quartz o' th' hill the soize o' a brickbat.   Whoy,
thou'st grinnin' aal over t' face loike a Cheshire cat.   But coom,
what'll thee tak', Mr. Poole ? let's booze up, summat near the
mark.   Ned, what's thine ? whoy, here's t' missis and Grizzly
Joe as is finished their dance aready.   Stir thee stumps, Ned.
It's Billy Pentreath's shout, all round.   Blanked if thee don't
own the handsomest wife from here to Los Angeles.'

Mr. Pentreath threw a five-pound note upon the bar and
looked defiantly around, as a tall American miner, with close
shaved face and heavy moustache, lounged up to the bar with
his partner, followed by the first detachment of the dancers,
whose waltz had suddenly come to a full stop.

I looked at Mr. Grizzly Joe's partner, guarding myself carefully from any appearance of unusual interest.   The first glance
showed me that it was Jane Mangold, the woman whom I had
last set eyes on as she bade me farewell at the Leys.   I could
recall her figure and dress even now, as I watched her run
hurriedly into the old-fashioned porch at the entrance to the
red-brown many-gabled farm house.

We had met again.   And here !

I was changed, as the boy changes to the man, when the days
of lightly carried duties and pleasures have passed away, and
those of the stern taskmasters of later years have worked their

will on mind and muscle. But I was still free—had I the
world's goods—to resume my former place in the land we had
both quitted, even, perhaps, with added fame and the prestige
of the roamer and adventurer. While she——?

Our eyes met, and for one moment the flush upon her face
faded so suddenly that I thought Mr. Pentreath's favourable
romance had failed in its effect, and that I should stand confessed before the jealous eyes of Ned Morsley, as a former friend
and admirer of his wife.

For the moment, however, he had been engaged professionally
—and hastily seizing the wine glass before her, she drank it
hurriedly, and, turning to her partner, with a forced laugh
made some commonplace remark about the heat of the room,
and her fatigue as mistress of the house and principal partner
at these troublesome balls.

The next minute Morsley returned from his spirituous search
and, with a peculiar look at his wife, introduced me as a friend
of Billy Pen's from Yatala, who had come over to buy a few
shares.

'Very glad to see him or anybody from Yatala in this rough
place,' she said, half looking down, but with assumed carelessness of manner. 'But I thought all the shares were sold that
were worth buying'

'Never you mind about that, Jenny,' Mr. Morsley said, with
a kind of jocular gruffness. 'Billy and I could find him some
shares if every claim on the hill had been sold twice over.'

'I've no doubt of *that*,' she returned, sarcastically. 'The
question is, whether Mr. Poole—I think you said—would care
to buy.'

Here the band struck up a popular war dance of the period,
and the room being immediately made noisily cheerful with
stamping and trampling to the somewhat exigent time, I
formally solicited the pleasure of Mrs. Morsley's hand for the
dance, thereby anticipating the intentions of half a dozen burly
aspirants, one of whom, evidently considering that a dance was
a dance, promptly thus addressed Mr. Pentreath—

''Ave a shottise, Bill?'

It was not for the first time that my arm had encircled my
partner's shapely waist. In old times there had been rustic
junketings, picnics, and other informal merrymakings, at which a
little dancing was allowable, if not ostensibly in the programme.
As soon as we swung clear of the encircling crowd at the further
end of the room, where there was an outlet to a small garden
with seats and other appliances for availing of the refreshments
ordered at the bar, we stopped by mutual consent and looked
in each other's eyes. For one brief moment they met, and then
hers, which wore a troubled and half-appealing wistful expression, sunk suddenly before mine, as she hurriedly broke the
silence.

'This is like—and yet how dreadfully unlike—old times, isn't it? Who would ever have thought that Jane Mangold and Hereward Pole would have met in Australia, in such a place as this, too. Oh, my God! who *would* have dreamed it? Don't say a kind word to me—don't—or I shall burst out crying—and then Ned will——'

'Are you afraid of him?' I said. 'Will he be angry if he finds you and I are old friends?'

'Of course he will. I am not afraid of him, or of any one else,' she said, turning on me with a sudden light in her eye and a defiant look which marked the change from the innocent country girl of old days. 'But I know he'll kill me one of these days. And now let us finish our dance, or these people will wonder. My miserable story will do some time when we can have a quiet talk together. I try to forget! Oh, if I only *could.*'

We whirled off to the familiar measure, to which with an odd, inexplicable impulse we addressed ourselves gaily. It afforded strange feelings of relief. We did not again stop till the dance was over.

So complete was the recognition of the once familiar face, that I had hardly asked myself whether or no the alteration in her appearance had been favourable or otherwise. Scanning her features more closely, I was astonished to confess that as far as outward seeming went, Jane was now incomparably more attractive than she had ever been. Her complexion still, as ever, wonderfully delicate, pure-tinted, and but faintly coloured with a warmer glow, was of the class so rarely seen save amid the green meads and sheltered vales of the British Isles. Her figure had but altered from that of girlhood to the more perfect symmetry of the more fully developed woman. The blue eyes, though their expression—ah me! had changed, were softly radiant, as of yore. Added to all, there was an air of self-possession—of higher resolution and quickened intelligence, that had been absent in the dear innocent old days of Dibblestowe Leys. She was then a bright-faced, merry, wayward country maiden—much resembling her whom Chaucer limned—

> 'Wincing she went as doth a wanton colt,
> Sweet as a flower, and upright as a bolt.'

Now, it may be that she had sinned and suffered, borne hard usage, and flung back bitter words; but the sorrow and the shame, the suffering and remorse, had been all powerless to deprive her of that gift, so fatal, alas! to many a possessor among Eve's daughters.

She was still graceful and striking-looking, nay more—a dangerously beautiful woman. I remained at Warraluen some days. I continued my for-tuitously-formed friendship with Mr. Billy Pentreath, who devoted himself to my service and entertainment, being, apparently, curiously anxious to justify his hastily-conceived description of my character and errand, by letting me into some of the confidential mining operations which had then financially so much interest for all classes of society in New South Wales.

I kept up the idea, which now thoroughly pervaded the larger portion of the community, by purchasing guardedly a few 'interests' from time to time out of the largish number submitted for my approval, and by assuming a gay and careless manner, much at variance with my habit and present inclination.

Thus Billy Pentreath, and his friend Harry Pole from Yatala, became fully accepted as the last novelty in speculative mineral society.

Even the suspicious Morsley relaxed his grim, menacing demeanour, regarding me, doubtless, as one of the harmless pigeons of the golden period, whose pecuniary pinions were fated to be even more completely and effectually plucked than usual.

Meanwhile opportunities were freely afforded me of hearing poor Jane's sad story. After my departure from the Leys she had become (she told me) restless and dissatisfied with her home and her ordinary duties. Her father was, as she thought then ('not now—not now,' she said, with how sad a look and sigh), hard and unkind. After several quarrels, resulting in settled home discomfort, she in a fit of pique and rebellion accepted Dick Cheriton's addresses. Marrying him without her father's consent, they emigrated to Australia, full of the golden expectations which, about that time, the great days of the Turon, of Ballarat, and Bendigo, lured so many hapless rustics from their homes, little dreaming of the ferocity of the dragons that guarded the Hesperides of the South. They arrived at Ballarat in the early days of that astonishing treasure-city, now with a population of many thousand souls, with banks and churches, railways and public schools, with parks on gala days crowded with school children, and regattas with fleets of boats upon Lake Wendouree; then a vast camp of cabins clustered beside the sodden banks of a muddy creek, or on the slopes of a gloomy forest, where in endless ranks stood charred iron-seeming stems of the great eucalypti. Some of the usual consequences followed.

Richard Cheriton, weak and dissipated, had, after a temporary run of luck, swiftly succumbed to the temptations of the scene and the period. Hard drinking and reckless gambling had made short work of him and his capital, and within three years of their landing, the ruddy-faced farmer, whose mild misdeeds in his native county would almost have counted as virtues amid the fierce whirlpool of vice in which he had lately revolved, was laid in the crowded cemetery, a shattered wreck, an imbecile, and a pauper.

Lonely and wretched, though flattered for her beauty and distracted amid the thousand excitements of the great goldfield, Jane had, half in despair, half in instinctive feeling of self-preservation, accepted the first apparently favourable offer of marriage made to her. Ned Morsley, apparently wealthy and successful, courted for his money, and veiling his villainy under a mask of careless dissipation, easily imposed himself upon her.

His wealth and his protection were alike shams. A wandering adventurer, he had dragged her from one goldfield to another, from colony to colony, or had deserted her, leaving her well-nigh to starve, unaided and unguarded. Used as a lure and a decoy, yet subject to paroxysms of causeless jealousy on the part of her husband, she had often experienced the vilest abuse, the grossest ill-treatment at his hands. Loathing herself and her surroundings, an inherent vigour of organisation, joined with the sustaining power of a false excitement, had hitherto served to keep her alive.

But how weary of her life she was, she again and again told me, with bitter tears. She would long since have ended it, but that her father was alive, and she clung to some half-instinctive hope that she might yet see him, and end her feverish wasted life near the cool brook and under the aged trees of the quiet village, where for generations her race had lived and died peacefully, innocently, happily.

'Oh! if I could only see the Leys again,' she sobbed, leaning her head against my shoulder in the abandonment of despairing and passionate grief, 'how happily I should die. I do not wish to live. I have long ago come to hate my life. Alas! false and wretched dream that it has been. But if I could only get away from these hateful heaps of earth, this miserable monotonous existence, this sickening endless turmoil about gold — the accursed gold—ruining alike in body and soul those who have it and those who have it not—I could sleep away my life peacefully and thankfully. Oh, Hereward, my friend, my brother, of the old glad, innocent days, you cannot think what a joy your coming has been to me. Do you think God will ever let me go back?'

I soothed the weeping woman, and offered such poor consolation as I could think suitable to her hopeless state. But that nothing could be done I was only too well aware. How can any woman of any degree be helped against her husband? She had chosen her fate and must abide by it, enduring torture only short of legally punishable violence, hardly restrained, indeed, within such bounds.

I was to leave Warraluen next day. I could not longer prolong my stay without causing inconvenience to my partners at Yatala, and probably exciting unfavourable remarks at Warraluen. I promised to aid and help my unhappy friend in all loyalty, and caused her to promise that if matters became dangerous or intolerable she would trust herself to my care at Yatala where I would do for her what a brother might.

In keeping up my character with Billy Pentreath, as an earnest mining speculator, I had purchased more shares in Frohmann's, Caird's, the Frenchman's, and Bolterman's than I had at first intended, but the money stood at my credit in the Bank of New Holland, at Yatala, and with the true mining disdain of the odds, I considered that a favourable rise was quite as likely to take place in their market value as the reverse.

When I returned to Yatala, after my week's unwonted recreation, I was accompanied as far as the first inn, about ten miles on my way, by Mr. Pentreath and a few friends, who were determined that I should not quit 'The Hill,' as Warraluen was familiarly called, without some sort of public recognition. We rode along, therefore, with a free rein as far as Spraggs's, as the hostelry of that gentleman was chiefly designated, irrespectively of a patently aggressive signboard, legended The Jolly Miner, and representing a suspiciously well-dressed individual in recent possesion of a fabulously large and brilliant nugget. Thither arrived, champagne was demanded, and my health was proposed by Mr. Pentreath as a legitimate miner and a true friend, as was a honour to his country and to Yatala, which tho' it was only alluvial—in a manner of speaking—had some tidy claims on it, and 'whoever met his friend Harry Pole from theer, would find him a man, whether the sinkin' was deep or shallow—and here was his jolly good health, with all the honours, three times three—hurrah.'

But for leaving poor Jane to bear unaided her miserable fate, I should have quitted Warraluen with a much lighter heart than I had entered it with. I made shift, however, to feign the requisite amount of hilarity, and parting cordially with my kind-hearted Cousin Jacks, I breasted the line of steep green hills around which the road wound, and 'they went on their way, and I saw them no more.'

.   .   .   .

Once more at Yatala, and again seated at our humble board, I had hardly completed my mutton chop, and commenced to extract the impartial local news from yesterday's *Beacon* when suddenly a low, rumbling sound attracted my attention. Something which I could not analyse, aroused a kind of sickening anxiety, and I looked out. God in heaven! what was that? I could see plainly the shaft and the staging of Gus Maynard's claim. As I looked I saw the woodwork on the top of the shaft driven up as by an unchained hell-blast, the bark roof of the sun-covering is burst upwards as by an explosion, and comes down in fragments all over the spot. Is it fancy, or do I see the heavy pile of crossed logs, ten or twelve feet from the surface of the earth, stagger—and fall ruinous to the earth? Does the adjacent ground disappear and finally remain stationary, as a hideous, dry, formless pond?

It is even so, and my senses have not deceived me.   There is a general rush from all sides to the place.   Men commence to work frantically for a time, and then stop, and say sadly that there can be *no help*.   Finally we discover the nature of the terrific accident which Providence has seen fit to suffer.

The Nova Scotia claim has fallen in.   All the present workings are for ever closed, and Gus Maynard and seven stalwart miners, who this morning were full of lusty life, are lying crushed lifeless clay in the sealed-up galleries, and a hundred feet from the day.   The heavy props which supported the drives had given way simultaneously, and an enormous mass of superincumbent earth fallen in upon the doomed miners. The suddenly expelled air, driven out through the shaft as by a tube, had produced the volcanic effect we had witnessed. There is no going down the shaft, no volunteering to risk life for the chance of saving dying or crippled men, as when the fatal fire-damp slays or only stupefies the miner in the ancient workings of British coalmines.   All such effort was useless.   All trace of shaft or drive was here completely lost.   Fresh shafts, of course, will be sunk, fresh galleries excavated, the old workings will be freshly scooped out of the jealous bosom of the dread mother—for the gold is still there, in fine dust and shot-like grains, and rugged, rough, red ingots.   Such prizes will always tempt the heedless heart of man.   Against these will he cheerfully barter afresh his life and limb, health and strength.

But Gus Maynard and his mates will never more be seen on earth, never more appear in the forms known and loved so well —for wives and orphans are weeping hopelessly now—till the sea gives up her dead, and the caves and dark places of the earth render up those that lie 'prisoned with them, awaiting the last dread trump.

When I dragged my feet back to our tent that night—for how unwillingly move the members when the heart is heavy— I felt as if a cloud of evil omen had gathered around our fortunes and prosperity.   All were silent, all desponding.   Gus was a universal favourite, and there were few at Yatala that night who did not sorrow as for a friend or a brother.

CHAPTER X

I HAD not, however, much leisure for the indulgence of grief in the matter of poor Gus Maynard, sudden and terrible as had been his fate. For we had no sooner quitted the sorrowful procession which had at length returned from the buried mine-works than Cyrus Yorke, who had been away all day, dashed in with the astounding intelligence, 'Our claim has been jumped.' The words were simple, but no addition could have exaggerated their significance.

From the first we had been almost instinctively aware of the framer of the plot which had done us so great an injury, which might even yet compass our ruin. Malgrade was the man whom each tongue amongst us simultaneously named and, with the sole exception of Mrs. Yorke, deeply and vengefully cursed. I am not sure now whether that prudent matron did not utter a wish connected with his prospective condition of existence which sounded less like a prayer than a prophecy. He had bided his time, and had dealt us a shrewd blow. In the long history of human strife, how unwise has it ever been to underrate a foe. Wiser than his fellows was he who said of old, 'Consider your enemies if you would be safe and strong—heed not your friends.' And, doubtless, what a coign of vantage has the stealthy, patient-watching brigand over the unsuspecting toilers—the heedless wayfarers of life. Daily, nightly, his thoughts are marshalled solely with a view to the season of opportunity, which sooner or later an ironic fate appears to grant. Thus had it been with us. The blow had found us unprepared. And though we had the ordinary means of defence, we were by no means sure that a joint in our armour would not be discovered, in which case no mercy need be hoped for.

But it was apparent Malgrade was not our sole antagonist. In all privateering on goldfields and other tempting vicinities, the initiated are aware that the alliance of capital with labour is indispensable. In the 'ebony' trade and other adventurous semi-mercantile enterprises, as well as Captain Kidd and his merry men, there must be the moneyed speculator, grave possibly, decorous of mien, but nevertheless not unwilling to furnish the outfit of the long low waterwitch of a schooner for a consideration. He 'planks down' the dollars requisite for the purchase of prints and necklaces, fetters and gunpowder, rum, small arms, and other necessaries. The crew must be paid and money found for the personal expenses of Captain Kidd as well, unprejudiced commander and thorough seaman that he is. In requital of which by no means paltry outlay a swingeing share of profits, when the middle passage is safely passed and the death-scared sable crowd 'sold and delivered,' is cheerfully yielded to the foreseeing man of money.

Such philanthropical individuals, loth to behold energetic men languishing for lack of means, have from the earliest records existed in every land. No more complete microcosm than a goldfield is to be found among human communities. It follows in natural sequence, therefore, that the sleek, remorseless trader in 'fellow-creatures' lives' was not far to seek at Yatala. Our ban-dog, Malgrade, had given him the office ; the calculation was simple and reassuring, and the matter being settled with the celerity characteristic of the locale, the funds were instantly forthcoming.

Mr. Isaac Poynter was a stout, florid, voluble personage, whose sleek black hair always shone in such oppressively lustrous fashion as to suggest that in his former trade as a butcher he had contracted the habit of anointing it with suet, and was unable to relinquish the practice now that less inexpensive pomade was accessible. He had followed many trades on various goldfields, including that of unlicensed liquor seller, and having accumulated a considerable capital by the consistent exercise of the strictest dishonesty, had settled down into the ostensible occupation of sharebroker and mining agent, with which elastic vocation he combined those of money-lender, gold-buyer, and receiver of property more or less disputed as to title.

This astute personage, as well as Mr. Algernon aforesaid, honoured our party by a grudge for several reasons hardly necessary to specify. The Major and I, he had been heard to say, were infernal stuck-up swells, who thought themselves too good for the society of parties in trade, while them fellers, Yorke and Bulder, had refused to stand in with him in a little safe speculation, and had had the cheek to offer to kick him off their claim. He'd had it in for 'em, and had settled in his own mind for to give 'em a rough turn some day, and now they'd see who they'd got to deal with.

Long practice of every conceivable evasion of the mining laws had made him familiar with modes by which, without infringing rules, the honest occupant of a claim could be harassed, ousted, besieged, and black-mailed. Any swindling device which Poynter was not acquainted with—and such an

acquirement was, in the opinion of the looser members of the
field, 'not worth knowing'—was promptly supplied by Malgrade.
It will be easily seen how difficult it was for our straight-going,
unsuspicious band to foil the machinations of foes so deliberate
and experienced.

The necessary arrangements having been made and the plan
of the campaign mapped out with Prussian completeness of
detail, nothing remained but to find the requisite number of
'honest hard-working miners' who were to be the ostensible
actors and moral scapegoats in the affair.

Such men, of course, were to be had. The price was
tempting, being no less than a half share each in the claim,
if the fortress fell and the condottieri were successful. This
was formally made over by legal transfer in the mining registrar's office, the rank and file being far too experienced to
trust their superior's promise in such an affair. Besides this,
it was agreed that they should receive wages at the rate
of half the ordinary tariff, amounting to thirty shillings per
week, during all the time occupied in professing to work
on the ground, attending court, or in any way furthering the
plot.

This was but the ordinary custom, and without such a payment the humblest miner on the goldfield would not have
given his services. The men, in addition to being average
practical workers, required also to be fully experienced in all
mining usages and regulations, lest they might be betrayed
into any illegal act which might jeopardise their title to the
property.

Each detail having been long thought out, was now executed
with a precision 'worthy of a better cause,' as the apologetic
formula runs, doubtless originated by some moralist, wondering
in his secret soul why the fiend's emissaries were always so
faultless in drill, so true to their colours, so zealous and so
sleepless.

And yet, the outcome of this recondite calculation was
the apparently simple and harmless proceeding of four men
putting in corner pegs, and going through the form of picking
a shovelful of earth from the sand surface of No. 4 Liberator
Lead.

Yes, long before that pawn had been advanced upon the chess-
board, whereon was to be played such an exceedingly stiff
game with live pieces, many a gambit, many a check and
counter-check had been conned over. Money had been lodged
in the bank, arrangements had been made for sub-dividing
shares, for forming a committee, for engaging professional aid,
for floating a company, if the need arose.

Mr. Cramp and Dr. Bellair had both received a retaining fee
in case of accidents, and with veiled but malignant expectation
the chief conspirators awaited the next move.

The requisite period, sacred to the law's delays, was fulfilled

All needful preliminaries were executed. The day of trial arrived. In all mining causes the method of procedure was this : every case must be tried before the Commissioner, who sat as primary judge. He heard the evidence in full and gave his decision ; but in view of the natural impatience of the mere *ipse dixit* of one man, even a man so widely respected and even feared as the Commissioner of all the southern goldfields, the Parliament of New South Wales in its wisdom had devised a mode of further trial. An appeal lay to a court composed of two or more magistrates of the territory, who were empowered to rehear the whole case, and afterwards to confirm or reverse the previous decision. If still further objection were taken to the verdict, and in any important mining case involving large amounts such proceedings were the rule rather than the exception, a last appeal would be heard before the Supreme Court, by whom the matter was adjudicated upon and finally settled.

Thus it came to pass that we looked despondingly along a vista of legal proceedings on protracted, if probably successful, action, but which was surely fraught with profuse expenditure along the whole line. However, there was nothing for it but to attack the beleaguering force and compel them to raise the siege, or for us to yield up the citadel. The last act we held to be impossible. We had, without an hour's delay, retained Mr. Markham, soon finding cause to congratulate ourselves upon our promptitude.

Punctual as usual on the appointed day, that gentleman arrived early, smiling and confident of mien. The streets appeared to us to carry an unwonted crowd. Many a miner left his work that day. Captain Blake rode up followed by his dogs, as was his wont, at ten o'clock sharp.

Throwing the rein to his orderly, he entered the court-house, and took his seat upon the bench with a stern and resolved air. He foresaw six hours of steady attention to a series of interminable technical details with which he was already painfully familiar, and all such methods of spending the bright summer days William Blake cordially hated, though, under compulsion, few men more successfully administered the apparently complicated but really equitable and comprehensive mining statutes.

Then, advancing with stately steps, the sergeant caused to be opened the principal door of the court-house. In a few moments it was crowded to the rails which protected the professional gentlemen, the parties to the suit, and the witnesses. Dr. Bellair and Mr. Cramp appeared for the other side. Both editors were in their places when the case—Pole and party versus Ingerstrom and party—was formally called on by the clerk of the Bench.

Mr. Markham stood up at once, and made the opening address.

'He was not there to defend illegal action; he trusted that he knew too well the principles of law, the requirements of justice, to attempt to pursue a short-sighted policy, whether on the part of his clients or any others. But he would say that a more scandalous outrage upon mining law, goldfields custom, and even the ordinary rules of equity which guided the transactions of society—as between man and man—had, hitherto, not been numbered among his experiences. However, knowing that there was a long day before the Court, he would not detain it further, but proceed to call his witnesses. Harry Pole, go into the box!'

I stepped upon the modern rack, where in this over-civilised age, heartstrings strain and quiver in agony, as that dread agent of the law, 'yclept the barrister, plies probe and scalpel. My operation was simple and painless.

'Your name is Hereward Pole. You produce your Miner's Right, of date January 185—, the present year.'

This was done. The important piece of parchment, about the size of a bank cheque, was handed first to the Court, and then to Messrs. Markham and Bellair, by whom it was as closely scrutinised as if, indeed, it had been an informal bank note.

Further judicious examination elicited from me the important facts that 'I had, on the 10th of August last, about a quarter past six in the morning, in company with Joseph Bulder, Cyrus Yorke, and Edgar Treseder Borlase, generally known as "The Major," put in a peg, not less than three feet long and three inches in diameter, and had affixed the same in an L trench not less than six feet long and six inches deep on the north-east boundary of the claim of four men's ground, known as No. 4 Liberator Lead. The three other shareholders mentioned put in similar pegs and cut similar trenches at the same time in my presence. The land was then vacant crown land, there being no one in possession or occupation thereof, or any pegs, shaft, or workings whatever visible. Furthermore, I had within three days thereafter, in company with the other shareholders, commenced to work the claim, now known as No. 4 Liberator, and had assisted to work it without intermission until the trespass by defendants. I had seen the defendant Ingerstrom break the surface of said claim with a pick. This was the trespass complained of.'

This cross-examined by Dr. Bellair: 'The measurement of the claim No. 4 was so many square feet. It was more than forty feet per man along the base line of the lead. It was not an exact parallelogram, but was of an irregular shape. There was not more than the number of superficial feet allowed by the regulations to a claim of four men's ground. The Commissioner had formally allotted us this claim soon after the Prospecting Claim struck gold. The quantity of ground so granted to us was not illegal by the regulations, so far as this deponent knew. Would not swear one way or another as to its being illegal to grant a claim in a form different from that laid down in the regulations.'

Here Mr. Markham objected. His learned friend was compelling the witness to answer a question which referred to a matter of law, not of fact. The witness's opinion as to a point of law was not relevant to the issue. The witness might hold an erroneous opinion as to mining law, or a correct one. In either case his opinion would, he submitted, be valueless as evidence. The Court was not concerned with what he *thought* with regard to mining law, or any other abstract subject, merely with what he *did*.

The Commissioner ruled that the question could not be put. As Mr. Markham had stated, 'the Court did not care a straw whether or not witness had the whole Act and Regulations at his fingers' ends, only what he did on that tenth day of August last.'

Dr. Bellair differed *in toto* from his friend Mr. Markham, and was not disposed to accept the dictum of the Court unconditionally. 'As a Doctor of Medicine, a Doctor of Laws, and a Barrister of the Supreme Court of New South Wales, he held himself entitled to contravene the ruling of any Chairman of a Quarter Sessions, much less a magistrate presiding over an inferior tribunal as was that of a Commissioner's Court. But he would proceed.'

The Commissioner was gratified to hear that. He was as little disposed to question Dr. Bellair's legal attainments as to make trial of his medical skill, but he wished him to understand most fully that he, William Devereux Blake, was judge in his own little court, and should demonstrate by prompt and decisive action (to which he trusted, however, that he should have no occasion to resort) that he would permit no disrespect or contempt of court as long as he sat there. He would remind gentlemen that much evidence remained to be taken.

Cross-examination proceeded with: 'Was certain that his party commenced work on the third day after pegging out No. 4. Had another claim on the Last Stake before that. Was working there till the 6th. Then abandoned it as they all considered the Liberator Lead the better show. Had more than one washing up at No. 4. Dividends were declared. Declined to state how much gold per man was divided. Were satisfied, at any rate, and did not want it stolen from them by defendants, or any other ruffians.'

Witness was here admonished by the Commissioner and told that he was only at liberty to answer questions, and not to refer to the morality of the defendants' presumed course of action.

Joseph Bulder is likewise sworn. He produces his Miner's

Right of date 1st January 185—, and gives corroborative testimony as to the occupation of No. 4 claim.

Edgar Treseder Borlase, sworn, states : 'Is a miner, residing at Yatala. Produces Miner's Right of date 1st January 185—. Assisted in the presence of the two previous witnesses and Cyrus Yorke in taking up the claim known as No. 4. Has worked regularly upon it ever since. Will swear that he has never been away more than a day at a time since they commenced work. If so has been employed in doing work for the benefit of the claim. Is a practical miner ; has worked at several other goldfields before coming here. Doesn't know exactly the number of superficial feet in the claim ; believes it to be about the right quantity for four men's ground. The right quantity would be so and so. If he had time could calculate it easily enough. Am not sure that he could do it accurately here. The Commissioner gave them their claim in that shape, partly because he chose to do so, and partly because in no other way, since the base line was swung, could they get their fair proportion of ground. Did not think that defendants acted otherwise than as——'

'Thanks, Major,' this from Mr. Markham. 'I will not trouble you any further.'

'Cross-examined by Dr. Bellair : 'Was formerly in the army, in the 77th Regiment. Have seen some service. Was not in any way compelled to quit the army. Would have knocked down any man who asked him this offensive question outside this Court, but was aware that it was his duty to treat all persons in that Court with becoming respect. Trusted that the learned counsel would assist him by his line of cross-examination in so doing. Did not wish to answer questions upon other than mining transactions. Was a miner here in every sense of the word, and expected miners' treatment—that of honourable consideration and manly fair play.'

(Slight signs of gallery approval promptly suppressed.)

Amos Burton called : 'Is the holder of a Miner's Right, but at present does wood carting. Was in the vicinity of No. 4, Liberator Lead, very early on 10th August, in the morning, and there saw the last witness and three other men marking out a claim. It might be No. 3, or No. 4. They took their time over it, and hammered in their pegs, and dug trenches all ship-shape and reg'lar. Saw no one there before they came. Believed the land to be vacant. Do not know the shape of the claim. Only, if any one took it up according to the regulations, these men did and no mistake.' (Is directed by the Court not to volunteer his opinion upon legal points.) 'Anyhow they were in occupation.'

Cross-examined by Dr Bellair : 'Is not a friend of the last witness, or the party, that is, not partic'lar. Knows Harry Pole, remember him at Cold Point. The Major was there, too. Always believed in 'em as legitimate diggers. Diggers

will take advantage sometimes if they can work it with
the regulations and the ground's good. Wouldn't do so
himself—that is, not unless it was a "clean jump," and the wash
was A 1.'

Ah Sing, storekeeper and general dealer, is next called, and
sworn by blowing out a match, repeating after the clerk of the
court a formula declaratory of the fact that, if he do not now
speak the truth his soul will perish as that match is blown out:
'Was on such a day on the line near Liberator Lead. Wantee
catchee that one piecee horsee dlive em cart Milliwa velly early
morning—sun come up allee samee wantee breakfast. See
Hally Pole, Joe, Major, and 'nother man—big man—peg out
claim, altogether. See um put in pegs, dig tlench, quite esure,
no foolee me, allee samee digger. Know digger way, catchee
claim once Myer Flat.'

Cross-examined: 'Digger buy things my shop, little boy, old
woman, young woman, allee samee Ah Sing. Suppose catchee
money, suppose swear lie, go to hellee quick, same as Doctor
and evlybody.' (Is requested by the Court not to include professional gentlemen in his theories of future punishment) to
which he replies, 'All lightee, Doctor stop at home, no tell lie.
Ah Sing no tell lie, Commish'ner. Commish'ner shutee up bad
Chinaman, logs, my word.' Being asked if he knows anything
about the present mining regulations, replies, 'Me plenty savee,
Hally Pole takee up No. 4, and that Dutchy man, plenty jumpee.
No more savee.'

Mr. Markham submitted that their heathen friend had shown
his ability to take a comprehensive grasp of the nature of the
suit. (Laughter.)

Dr. Bellair would not further examine this witness, whose
evidence he regarded as either venal or wholly untrustworthy
for want of intelligence and sense of moral responsibility.

Cyrus Yorke is called. He walks up through the closely-
packed crowd, who, partly knowing him as a shareholder in the
claim, and one of the parties to this *cause célèbre*, make way
for him as he slowly marches up, squaring his vast shoulders,
and taller by the head than the audience, composed though it
be of men of more than average stature. But Cyrus stands as
near seven feet as six in the Wellington boots which he always
adopts for great occasions; weighing besides over seventeen
stone, below which the hardest of regular work does not reduce
him. He is not a man to be jostled in any congregation, however dense. As he walks forward to-day, neatly dressed in suitable garments, he is the very pink of cleanliness, and does full
justice to Mrs. Yorke's talents as a laundress. His linen is spot-
less as that of a crack *espada* among the bull-fighters of Valencia.
A grand specimen of Anglo-Saxon manhood is Cyrus, as
developed by the kindly conditions of Australian life. I cannot
help contrasting him with the ordinary specimens of the English
farm labourers, from which he is sprung. Generations of un-

remitting toil, privation, and anxiety for the morrow, had in most of these instances stamped a look of almost painful endurance indelibly upon form and features, writing them down as hewers of wood and drawers of water, *adscripti glebæ* born thralls of a higher race and a more favoured class. But this man's external presentment bore the record of years spent in easily borne tasks and well-requited effort, of long intervals of repose and recreation, of seasons of pleasant social intercourse and free independent action.

CHAPTER XI

THE evidence, however, of Mr. Cyrus Yorke proved to be less striking than his appearance, save that portion of it of which the effect was on the wrong side.

He had pegged out on the 10th August with me, the Major, and Joe Bulder. He had assisted to commence work three days afterwards, and worked and occupied the claim without intermission until those four scoundrels, with other scoundrels backing them, whose names he did not know, but might find out some day, 'jumped' it.

Is told by the Commissioner that he must not refer to the moral tone of any of the parties to the suit. Replies that, as an honest man, he can't help it. Is assured by the Commissioner that his honesty will land him presently in the lock-up for twenty-four hours for disrespect of court, upon a repetition of the offence. Cyrus grumblingly subsides.

Is certain that there was no person in occupation when he and his mates took it up legally, and in proper digger fashion. If they have no right to it, no claim on this field is properly taken up.

Mr. Markham asks the well-meaning blundering giant no more questions.

The Doctor, with a look of evil triumph, rises quickly, looks at Cyrus with a vivisecting eye. In a voice of terrific acerbity, he thus began—

'Produce your Miner's Right, Mr. Cyrus Yorke, if you have such a document.'

There was a moment's ominous pause, during which the whole Court, to the smallest gamin, was pervaded by an intense, almost painful interest. The spectators stirred and leaned over towards the witness, silently gazing upon him as he was about to speak the words which, if in the negative, would seal the doom of the claim. Here was a man who, out of his own mouth, was perhaps about to convict himself of a breach of the law, which would have the tremendous consequences of depriving his party of the prize actually within their grasp—the well-earned reward of years of toil, hardship, suffering. Only

for the sake of ten shillings, too.   That was the price of a
Miner's Right for the first half of the year.   After June it was
reduced to a crown.   A claim worth fifty, sixty, perhaps a
hundred thousand pounds was going to be lost or held before
their eyes, for half a sovereign, and a shilling's worth of
trouble!   It was, indeed, as more than one bronzed, weather-
beaten spectator remarked under his breath, 'as good as a play.'

And was there no natural pity, no trace of sympathy among
the hearts of those who saw the blow, so crushing, so disastrous, about to fall upon comrades by whose side many had
worked, with whom they had interchanged the simple offices of
goldfields' friendship, who had tended one another sick and
wounded, who had knelt by the grave of each other's dead,
who knew that the man about to speak had a true wife and
prattling children to be helped or beggared by the upshot?
Truth to tell, the excitement of the spectacle much outweighed
the interest, and almost obliterated the sympathy.

For the rest—the miner belongs to a class with whom the
gambling element has ever been strong, even to apparent madness.   In his ordinary avocation he places upon the cast his
health, his fortune, his life, and, possibly, the food and shelter
of his wife and children, whom let no man say that he loves
less passionately and enduringly than his more stationary
fellow labourer.

But he is accustomed, from the commencement of his
perilous trade, to see fortunes approach with dazzling nearness,
then—

> 'like the Borealis race,
> Flit ere you can point their place.'

He has seen the treasure which was to crown and justify life's
toil, an existence of desperate adventure and untold hardship,
so often missed by a hair's-breadth, that he has lost the faculty
of wonder and pity at such mere daily occurrences.   He is not
hard-hearted, few men less so, only he is prone to regard all
human effort and temporal reward as the direct concomitants
of the world's grand demon 'Luck.'—All other explanation
seems to him futile.

So it might be our luck to lose this claim, the richest on the
lead, the best on the field, a fortune to each shareholder.   As
surely it might be another 'crowd's' luck to get it—they, and
their backers, the secret partners and abettors in this conspiracy, who 'stood in' with the actual operators, and found
the cash for these very expensive law proceedings, which, of
course, the actual jumpers, men of straw, could not furnish.

'Will you produce your Miner's Right, witness, I ask you
again?' thundered the irascible doctor.

There was not the slightest variation from his usual sleepy
monotone, not a change in his leonine countenance as Cyrus
placidly answered.

'I haven't got one—leastways, I haven't got it here.'

A suppressed sound, half sigh half groan, proceeded in a muffled involuntary way from the great assemblage at the fatal announcement.

'What do you mean then,' demanded the triumphant advocate, 'by occupying crown lands, and illegally mining for gold thereon with your companions, without a shadow of title? Answer me, do you hear?'

'I apprehend, Doctor Bellair,' said the Commissioner, 'that such a question is not relevant material to the issue. The Court is only concerned with facts. The witness's opinion as to the legality of his previous acts does not touch the point at issue.'

'I ask, Mr. Commissioner, do you disallow the question I have just asked?'

'Most certainly, for the reason I have just given,' said the Commissioner, with cheerful promptitude.

The Doctor gnashed his teeth, figuratively, and thus proceeded—

'Do you know, then, where your Miner's Right is?'

'I do not.'

'Will you swear, then, where you saw it last, or will you swear that you have one at all?'

The witness declared that 'he would do nothing either one way or the other. That he might, or he might not, have a Miner's Right. Anyhow, he had not got it then, in Court, that day—they must make the best of it.'

And here Cyrus looked defiantly round upon the crowd, with the air of the lion caught in the toils.

'I don't know that I need go any further with this case, your worship?' said the Doctor, with an air of the calmest assumption. 'The whole case is perfectly plain. The occupation is bad—has been illegal from the first, and ——'

'I must protest against my learned friend making his speech upon the merits of the case at this stage of the proceedings,' said Mr. Markham. 'He never was more mistaken in his life, if he thinks he is approaching a verdict for his clients.'

The real fact was, that Mr. Markham had, after hearing the damaging admission of Cyrus Yorke, given up all for lost, as far as it was in the indomitable nature of the man to do so. But he thought it due to himself and his clients to repudiate all likelihood of so dire a catastrophe, and to suspend his judgment till the evidence had been exhausted on both sides.

The Commissioner was of the same opinion. But years of experience, marking thousands of involved cases, had taught him the necessity of wearing the legend *audi alteram partem* close to his heart, metaphorically. He therefore said, 'If you have any witnesses, Doctor, I shall prefer to hear them.'

'VERY well, your worship,' said the Doctor, biting his lips. 'Call Carl Ingerstrom. Stop—I ask the last witness—Did you see this man on No. 4 claim on the morning of the 12th December, and if so, what did you say to him?'

'I did see him loafing about the claim on the 12th,' said Cyrus, 'and I told him if he didn't clear I'd kick him out of it that hard as he'd never find his way back.'

'Ha! that will do, Mr. Yorke. You give very good evidence indeed. Permit me to compliment you upon it.'

A large, respectable-looking Teuton steps into the witness-box. His name is Carl Ingerstrom. He produces his Miner's Right, completely *en règle*, and deposes as follows, with a clear, unhesitating air, though somewhat shifty as to the eyes—

'It vas de morgen of de dwelvth Tecemper I goes to numper vour of de Liperator Lead mit Mick Docheroty, Santy Mag Vails, and der Bommer. Ve dakes new begs and buds dem in de blases of dere begs. Ve vas occupy de ground — ve gommence do to vorks by beginnen to sinken anoder shaft. Dey rons and brevents us from vorken on our glaim—de last vitness, der breitmann, and anoder man. Ve has a sommons for de drespass. Ve knock off vorks dill de case is dried. Ve are here.'

Of course, this is a bare statement of the course of procedure necessary on the taking possession of a mining tenement, so as effectively to put the other occupants on their title. In the completeness of that title lies the gist of the whole action at law. And in that completeness very few of the more experienced spectators now believe.

Cross-examined by Mr. Markham. Is asked what induced him to peg out a claim in full work and occupation, and known to be on gold. Answer: 'Dat is de very reason—vould you hafe me beg out a glaim as is got nodings for do bay vages and du croob, and lawyer and alle teufels? I haf zeen Mr. Ikey Boynter, he adfice me not to shoomp noomber vour. I say I will do all as I d——n like, shoost like an honest miner. I belief as der didle of de glaim is bat. I know Mr. Malcrate; he is ein

herr hoch bes ahlter. I gif him one half share out of bure
freundlich. I haf zentimend—en sprach du deutsh. I lofe him.
I gif all my freunds half shares. Ve are all mades—hed and
fest, in dis glaim.'

Michael Docherty, Alexander M'Phail, and Thomas Bommer
(*alias* 'Tommy the Clock') are severally sworn and examined.
Their Miners' Rights are perfectly legal. Their evidence is, in
essentials, identical with that of Carl Ingerstrom. They have
legally taken up and occupied No. 4 Liberator Lead, always
supposing that the former occupation and tenancy were bad
in law.

Finally, the case for the defence is concluded, and Mr. Markham rises to commence his speech.

The Commissioner looks at his watch.

'I can sit until five,' he says, 'if that will enable you to con-
clude your remarks.'

'I think I shall be enabled, your worship, to bring my address to an end within that time,' says our counsel, 'though I
cannot promise, in view of the very important nature and
extent of the issue, to abate one iota of my privilege to address
the Court, in order to clearly lay before it any point of the case
that may seem material to the issue.'

'Certainly,' groans out the Commissioner resignedly. 'Of
course, this case will have to be adjourned, in order to permit
the counsel for the defence to be heard in reply. Now then,
Mr. Markham.'

Mr. Markham, availing himself of the permission, at once
commenced a lucid and masterly analysis of the whole mining
law and custom bearing upon the case, than which no advocate
was better fitted to display and unravel, no judge more qualified
by experience to deal with than the Commissioner.

Hasty and impatient by nature, William Blake was a man
whose clear intellect enabled him to comprehend with rapid
and comprehensive grasp the apparently involved cases that
were constantly brought before him. He could detect the
flaw in the most subtle of reasoning with unerring accuracy.
His attention never flagged, nor did his memory fail to retain
the most minute detail during the weary length of the protracted cases with which a crowded goldfield inundated his
Court.

Ours was one of the most important cases which had
occurred for a long time, and we had full assurance, as had
every miner in that great gold region, that every legal formality
would be scrupulously complied with. We knew that, if the
fortunes of himself, his family, and his whole kindred had depended upon the verdict, that our advocate could not have been
more tireless, more energetic, more watchful, more desperately
resolved to win, by the employment of his every gift and
faculty, than he was now.

He drew a picture of the long discouraging struggle with

fortune, which most miners had experienced. The travel and voyage from one colony to another. The terrible privations, by cold or heat, famine or poverty, silently borne or uncomplainingly defied! The weary waiting, the soul-sickness of hope deferred. The possible failure of health, the chances of accident, all the best gifts of mortality offered on the cast of the die. Life itself cast down recklessly as the last stake against gold.

Then the horizon brightens; a fortunate find is made. The last hope, when so many were vain, has proved successful. The old dream of home and native land and longing early friends is no longer a romance but a tangible reality. The richness of the claim is proved. The ceaseless labour is for once munificently rewarded. The toil of years is at length duly compensated.

But what then? Envy and greed, watchful and eager as harpies, swoop down. A sham title is set up to the property—so fairly, so truly, so honestly acquired.

'But not legally,' interjects the irrepressible Doctor.

'Am I to be interrupted in this way?' says Mr. Markham, appealing gravely to the Bench.

The Doctor is informed that it is hardly correct for him to interpose during Mr. Markham's address.

He apologises, and the speech proceeds.

'A sham title,' he repeats, 'is set up. These loafing scoundrels (he must apologise for the expression — but they are *not* legitimate miners, or self-respecting labourers of any kind) who had shammed occupation, shammed efficient labour, were set on by, if possible, greater scoundrels than themselves, only with a little more money, and who even now, in the background, were watching, spider-like, for the enmeshing of their prey. He trusted, however, that the web of deceit and chicanery would be rent on this occasion, would be swept into infamous oblivion by the besom of the law in the hands of Justice. (Applause.) Proceeding to quote a number of well-known decisions in mining cases he traced the gradual growth of the assumption—for it was no more—that all the partners in a mining enterprise should suffer in title, in property, in person, in their very mining existence, if but one had failed to provide himself with what, he admitted, was an indispensable preliminary to all searching for gold upon the public estate—on the lands of the crown—a Miner's Right. And he characterised as cruel, oppressive, and *ultra vires* of all the spirit and even letter of the common law of the realm, and, therefore, of the statute law under which the Commissioner was now adjudicating, this crushing and extreme penalty of forfeiture of the claim. If the work of men's hands, righteously won and manfully laboured at, was to be handed over to the first sneaking informer who discovered a paltry technical defect, then the goldfields would soon cease to be composed, as they were now, of the very flower of the working

classes. They would no longer have among them the more
stalwart and intelligent individuals of those above the grade of
labour, if such there were, but a concourse of thieves and
assassins, cut-throats and gamblers—the scum of the nations of
the earth.'

Not a single point which could by any means be brought to
bear upon the question at issue was omitted. Not a standard
authority or leading case was left unquoted. Not an appeal to
honest judgment, to good conscience and equity, as he maintained the Commissioner's Court as at present constituted to
be, not a single part of the evidence which was favourable was
left without reference; and when, candles having been procured and the hour of ordinary sitting long passed, the exhaustive oration was brought to a close by a solemn and
impassioned peroration, in which the high magistrate was
besought to right the oppressed and free the administration of
goldfields law from the reproach of constructive unfairness and
over-litigation which had so long clung to it, the Court adjourned with one universal feeling on the part of the crowd of
spectators, that justice was with the cause of the last speaker,
and that he had nobly cleared away all doubts from the minds
of his hearers.

On the morrow, punctually at the usual hour, the officials
of the Court were in attendance. Directly the doors were
thrown open by the police, an eager crowd of miners, business
people, and even strangers, attracted by the *cause célèbre*, poured
in, filling every seat and foot of standing room.

Dr. Bellair was to make his speech in reply, and all knew
that the Commissioner would then give his decision, that
important verdict, which though certain to be appealed against,
was rarely, in such cases as this, reversed.

But little time was lost. After a few moments the case was
again called on. The Doctor commenced his reply. His nervous,
eager countenance was toned down to a decorous appearance of
calmness and gravity much at variance with his volcanic tem-
perament, as he, with a great show of deference and respect,
addressed the Commissioner, 'whose experience and thorough
knowledge of mining law,' he said, 'had made his opinion
weighty, and his decisions all but immutable, wherever a goldfield gathered together its strangely constituted population.
He would implore him to dismiss from his mind all knowledge
of the different social footing of the parties to the suit; to
obliterate all fanciful ideas of presumed equity and false
generosity of sentiment, and to cling tenaciously and sternly,
as a British judge should do, to the only pure and unmixed
truth—the unquestioned and unquestionable law. This power,
this rock, this law of the land, his clients he should be able to
demonstrate, had most unmistakably on their side. Whoever
they were, whatever they were, he only claimed for them the
status of the ordinary legitimate gold digger, who, however,

with his Miner's Right, had the proud privilege of being able to occupy and search for gold every acre of the broad crown lands of this great colony of New South Wales. They had never forfeited their right to justice. He should not dwell on this portion of the facts, in opening his case, were it not that so much stress had been laid by his learned friend on the previous career of the complainants, on their long course of evil fortune, and their present prize, which it was asserted his clients had conspired to wrest from them.

'Whether it was so or not, he would submit, it did not touch the case in any shape. What was it to his worship, sitting here as judge both of law and of fact, how or with what success the complainants had laboured? If they had given their whole lives to an unsuccessful pursuit of gold, or fame, or happiness, had not others, all the world, indeed, with but few exceptions, done the same? The Commissioner did not sit here to redress the wrongs of society, and pose himself as a second-hand Providence, reading the hearts and rewarding the hidden motives of men, but to administer the law, not to make it—as the great Bacon, with almost divine wisdom defined it, not to consider probable compensations of fate, but to hear and determine within the limits of the statute, and only with regard to sworn evidence brought before him. He himself knew the Commissioner, and the whole tenor of his previous decisions—decisions which lent stability and assurance to the great interest he was called upon to control—too well to dream that he would otherwise think, otherwise act. But he ought, considering the quality of the *ad captandum* arguments used by his learned friend, due, no doubt, to the defects of his cause, not to pass over this aspect of the matter.'

The Doctor then, warming to his work, to our dismay briefly and trenchantly dealt with the evidence, bringing out the default of that unlucky Cyrus, as to his missing or wilfully evaded Miner's Right, into full and distressing prominence. He showed that, over and over again, claims which had turned out to be the richest and most valuable on their field had been ruthlessly forfeited in consequence of similar illegality. It was as firmly established as anything could be by a series of judgments, by the consensus of opinion, by the unwritten custom of mining law that in all such cases the default of one shareholder made *the whole occupation bad.* If the previous occupation was bad, the land was in the position of vacant, waste crown lands, which his clients had had a perfect right to enter upon. They had legally done so ; they had worked until prevented by force by the complainants. Their title was perfect. He defied any one to find a flaw in it. If a verdict was not given for them in this case, then the whole previous weight and authority of mining law fell to the ground, an unsubstantial and baseless fabric. All future decisions must rest on caprice and injustice, on personal feeling and improper partiality.

'But he had no fear of any such result, though, if it occurred, he would carry the case on behalf of his clients, poor and of small account as they were, through every court in the colony, including the highest, the Supreme Court, if it cost him every penny he had in the world. But,' he repeated, 'he had no fear of such a contingency, such a perversion of right, such a miscarriage of justice. The experienced magistrate, the pro-consul he might call him, before whose words of fate the fortunes, almost the lives of men, had before now trembled in the balance, could not, dared not (the Commissioner's eye glowed, and then rested fixedly on the impassioned advocate, who seemed transfigured into a tribune, shrieking forth the wrongs of oppressed humanity, and proclaiming gospel of the people's rights) *dared not*, in the clear light of his fame for strict justice and stern impartiality, record other than one verdict, one decree. He had no fear for the issue. He rested upon the firm basis of the evidence they had all that day heard. It was from first to last unassailed, unassailable ; the law was plain, the issue certain. He awaited but the formality of his worship the Commissioner's sanction to place his clients in possession of the ground of which they and the public at large had been illegally deprived.

Now came the exciting last act of the melodrama so likely to terminate in tragedy as far as we were concerned. The Commissioner calmly looked over his notes, and prepared to deliver his decision amid the ominous hush and suppressed excitement of the crowded Court. Not a sound was heard, though the spectators in the rear of the assemblage raised themselves on tiptoe, and strained every ear with deepest curiosity to hear the words of fate. The Commissioner, in whose hands lay life and death (so to speak), who had the power to take away from us all that made life worth living for, to doom us to the barren and hopeless existence of unrewarded toil and hope long deferred from which we had so lately emerged, commenced his address. It would not be long, we knew. It was not his wont to 'improve the occasion' in the hundreds of cases, more or less important, which he administered monthly. He was fully aware that his audience, whether as malefactors or parties to civil process, understood the consequences of legal wrong-doing on the facts of the case fully and accurately without explanation from him or any other magistrate. His duty was to administer the law, with which as a class they were singularly well acquainted, without favour or affection ; and this he always did shortly and decidedly. He was very careful in arriving at his decisions ; but once given they were as the laws of the Medes and Persians. If they could be shown to be *ultra vires* or informal, well and good ; let the higher courts see to that. But he, William Blake, had never been known to alter a decision, and as long as he was Commissioner of Goldfields never would be.

Thus he began—

'This was an information laid for trespass by Pole and party, complainants, who sought to cause Ingerstrom and others to abate trespass upon a certain mining tenement, known as No. 4 Liberator Lead.

'The gist of the matter clearly lay in the evidence given on the part of Pole and party, as to the legality of their prior occupation of No. 4 claim, before referred to. It had been proved before him this day in Court that they had taken up, that is, occupied and worked the claim, had sunk upon and traced the auriferous drift, had taken out wash-dirt, and received and shared dividends, long before the defendants had appeared upon the scene. If they had in all respects complied with the regulations, there was no doubt about the complainants possessing the prior right. Upon that proof being complete the whole title hinged. If it were not so proved, no natural feeling of sympathy on his part, no consideration of the crushing severity with which a breach of the goldfields' regulations would be visited on their heads, in the event of their forfeiture of so rich a claim as No. 4 had been proved to be, would prevent him from recording a verdict adverse to them. He, sitting there, had nothing whatever to do with the feelings, nay, the equitable right of individuals. He had always, he hoped, clearly interpreted and enforced the law, and the law only. Such he would continue to do, he trusted, to the end.

With regard to the occupation of Pole and party, it had been shown that three of the shareholders possessed Miners' Rights. But the fourth shareholder was unable to produce that indispensable permit. He must, therefore, be presumed to be without it, and, in such a case, he was an unauthorised occupant of crown lands, whether for residence or mining purposes. He had no *locus standi*. He could not legally apply for relief of any kind to that Court. Any share which he possessed must be forfeited. He was also liable to a fine, with imprisonment in default of payment.

'This, however, was not all. It had been long held by mining authorities that, unless all the shareholders taking up a claim were possessed of Miners' Rights at the time when they pegged out and commenced operations, their action was illegal as far as taking possession of crown lands for gold mining purposes, under the Act, was concerned. The occupation, he repeated, if but one even of the shareholders was not at that time the holder of a Miner's Right, would be bad in law.

'In this case, it had not been shown in evidence before him that Cyrus Yorke, one of the complainants in the trespass case now before him, was the holder of a Miner's Right when No. 4 claim was first by them taken up. That default, in his opinion, invalidated the whole title. Not the slightest doubt existed in his mind upon the subject. He would, therefore, give a verdict for——'

Here an uproar arose in the body of the Court towards the entrance door, of such a pronounced, ungoverned nature, that the sergeant, looking at first pained and then justly indignant, marched with long dignified strides and a sternly resolved air to the scene of disorder, as if to bring the offenders, there and then, before the Court for doom.

He reappeared, however, with an altered and relaxed visage, escorting gallantly our good friend Mrs. Cyrus Yorke, on the other side of whom was Mr. Markham, who ever and anon inclined his ear in confidential legal intercourse. The little woman held one hand triumphantly aloft, in which was something which stirred our hearts anew and caused the flickering light of hope to be freshly irradiated with a glow of celestial illumination.

'Your worship,' commenced the sergeant, 'I beg respectfully to state that the apparently disorderly conduct in Court was caused by the attempts of the friends of this witness to procure her admission to the vicinity of your worship.'

'Sergeant M'Mahon, the irregularity is fully explained. You desire to address the Court, Mr. Markham?'

'Yes, your worship. I tender this witness, the wife of one of the complainants, who has most important evidence, material to the issue, to give. I am aware that the proceedings on the side of the complainants have been closed, but, your worship's Court, as that of a Commissioner of Goldfields, is one of equity and good conscience, and I trust that such evidence as this witness may produce, will not be shut out.'

'I object to any such proceeding as monstrous, illegal, and perfectly unprecedented,' shouts Dr. Bellair, with a most excited air. 'The evidence has been closed. The whole proceedings finished, but the actual pronunciation of the verdict, in defendants' favour, of course; and now you ask to have the proceedings re-opened, for what possibly may be perfectly unnecessary evidence.'

'We shall see that,' said Mr. Markham, with a sanguine air. 'Will your worship admit the evidence?'

'The question with me, in such cases as I am called upon to try under the Mining Act and Regulations, is less whether the evidence be informally tendered, than whether the nature of it be material. In this case I will shut out *no evidence* that may possibly bear on the legality of my decision. Swear the witness.'

'Mrs. Yorke, go into the box,' said Mr. Markham. 'You are the wife of Cyrus Yorke, one of the complainants who has given evidence in this case to-day?'

'Yes.'

'Do you produce a Miner's Right, and, if so, in whose favour, and of what date?'

'I do. I took it out for my husband, one day in Louisa, knowing how careless he was in such things, and put it into a box for safety. It was hidden under the children's clothes, or I should have had it out in Court long before this. Goodness knows what——'

'Have the goodness to hand it to the Clerk of the Court,' interrupted the Commissioner.

The truly important document was inspected with eager eyes by that functionary, who respectfully handed it to the Commissioner. He read aloud the talismanic signs—

'Cyrus Yorke. 1st January 185—. Issued in the Registrar's office at Louisa. To remain in force till 31st December 185—,
       (Signed) 'William D. Blake, P. M., Commissioner.'

An utterly irrepressible sound of relief and amazement escaped the lips of the majority of the listeners. There was the missing link, the indispensable, vitally necessary legal act, in default of which this tremendously rich claim was about to be forfeited and transferred to the enemy, as sure as anything ever was in this world.

'Silence in the Court,' growls the sergeant, but with a sympathetic intonation noticeable through all his official severity.

'I demand to see this paper, this Miner's Right as it is called,' here breaks in Dr. Bellair, with a voice of mingled passion, regret, and disbelief. 'How do we know that it has not been manufactured for the occasion. I demand the fullest investigation as to how and when it was issued, and I protest against any notice being taken of it as evidence in this most improper manner.'

'You may protest, Doctor,' said Mr. Markham, good humouredly, 'but my client's case is complete. I am in a position to prove by the evidence of the Mining Registrar at Louisa, that the Right produced was taken out by witness during the week following Christmas of last year—she very properly determining to make sure that her husband should not be placed in a false position. I wish all wives were as careful on the goldfields. Now you can examine the witness, Doctor, and make what you can of her.'

'I shall do so, without your permission,' cried the fiery little advocate. 'Now then, Mary Ann Yorke. Is that your real name ; are you married to the complainant, Yorke ?'

'I'd soon show you, if I had you down on the Blue Lead,' said the little woman, trembling with passion, and suggestively raising her hand. 'What do you mean by——'

'Mrs. Yorke,' said the Commissioner, suavely but firmly, 'you must answer Dr. Bellair's questions, and I would remind you not to become excited in this Court. Answer the questions shortly, and to the best of your knowledge ; the examination will soon be over.'

'Yes, Commissioner, yes, your worship,' said poor Mrs. Yorke, already repenting her of her just indignation, in that it might imperil the cause ; 'but what does he mean by trying to make

out I'm not an honest woman, and don't have my right name?
I'll name him if he tries that on, as sure as my name's Mary
Ann Yorke.'

'I trust I shall be protected by the Court,' said the Doctor,
defiantly. 'It is necessary that I should test this woman's
credibility, which I have every reason to doubt.'

'Certainly, Dr. Bellair, but I must ask you not to put such
questions needlessly, as may be offensive to the witness's feelings of modesty and self-respect.'

'I claim the privileges of the Bar! and I defy your worship
to abate one jot or tittle of those privileges in my person. A
judge of the Supreme Court could not do so.'

'You will find, Dr. Bellair, that I am judge in my own court,
and that I will interfere very decidedly, if you pursue a line of
cross-examination which can only have the effect of distressing
the feelings, and outraging the moral sense of the witness—in
this case, a most exemplary and respectable woman.'

The Doctor snorted indignantly, and went on with his cross-
examination; but although he made himself sufficiently disagreeable to Mrs. Yorke, whose eyes became so round and fierce,
that we all felt alarmed, particularly Cyrus, at the probable
consequences, he did not choose to adopt the vivisecting process
permitted to counsel in the higher courts. He knew full well,
by experience, in spite of his bravado, that he would be peremptorily stopped by the Commissioner, one of whose fixed principles
it was, never to permit a woman, whatever might be her character and antecedents, to be needlessly harassed in the witness
box, or treated with unnecessary disrespect. So the day wore on.

'Why did her husband not take out his own Miner's Right;
wasn't he man enough to do it?' said the Doctor.

'He *was* man enough to work hard for his family, and had
never denied them anything—not like some folk, a spending
their money away from home, and isn't very particular what
company they went into on the sly; but he hadn't no head for
business like. And wasn't there many a good all-round man on
this field, as the same could be said of?'

All Mrs. Yorke's timidity gradually left her. Such is generally the case with female witnesses. And, being fully aroused
to a sense of the Doctor's antagonistic position to the party,
answered him with such vigour and unexpected epigram, that
the Court, more than once, felt compelled to interfere. However, nothing could be got out of her but that she had taken
out the Miner's Right for the use and benefit of her husband,
'as any wife as had any sense had good call to do.'

'Why, I might have one myself, Doctor,' she continued, 'for
all you know, or the baby in arms, bless him! The Act says,
"any person," don't it? It doesn't say man or woman, child or
sucking babe, does it? I shouldn't wonder if I knew as much
mining law as you do, Doctor, close up.'

'I opine that we do not come here to listen to this woman's

disrespectful maunderings about mining acts and regulations, your worship,' said the little man, loftily. 'I demand the protection of the Court.'

'Who do you call "this woman?"' Mrs. Yorke was just commencing to inquire, when she was told by the Commissioner that she might stand down after signing her name to her deposition.

'One moment, your worship. I wish to interpose one question, said Mr. Markham. 'What mining registrar did you get your Miner's Right from? who issued it?'

'Mr. Allen, of Louisa. I went over there about some quinces; and I saw him write it down in the but of his book. It'll be there, with the day and date, I know. There's no get away, you take my word, your worship.'

'That will do, Mrs. Yorke. We will not detain you.'

And the little woman retired to a seat, previously casting a look of withering indignation at her late opponent.

The Commissioner, apparently, did not see the necessity of making two speeches upon the same subject. Besides, it was getting late. He briefly gave the reasons for the decision he was about to pronounce.

'He had stated, he thought, in his first address that the missing link in the chain of evidence for the complainants was an important one—no less than the Miner's Right of Cyrus Yorke, one of the original and prior occupants. Had the defect in the evidence not been cured, a verdict must have been given by him virtually for the defendants—"No trespass committed."

'The last piece of evidence, although from circumstances tendered so late in the day, that some magistrates would have felt justified in shutting it out altogether, had clearly proved that the complainants were each and all legally authorised when they went on the ground. That they had prior occupation could not be doubted for an instant. They had worked their claim for gold, had washings out of it, and shared dividends. As to the size of the claim, and its irregular shape, that was partly caused by the course of the lead, and was a minor matter in his eyes. So long as they had no more than the number of superficial feet allowed in four men's ground, he saw no illegality in that circumstance. He, therefore, unhesitatingly pronounced a verdict for complainants, with one hundred and fifty pounds costs against defendants, who were hereby ordered forthwith to abate trespass.'

At this announcement a general impulse tempted the closely-packed crowd to cheer. The sergeant looked around with so horrified and severely surprised expression of countenance, that the audience relapsed into the dumbness of church-goers. Mrs. Yorke wept for joy, and infected with that strange contagious feminine luxury a young woman who sat next to her, and who, being a relation of one of the jumpers, might be said to belong to the enemy's camp.

'I give notice of appeal!' promptly said the fiery little advocate.

'Lodge your money within seven days, and a written notice in due form,' said the unmoved Commissioner.

'I desire to apply for an injunction also, to restrain Pole and party from washing up and getting gold from my clients' claim while this suit is pending.'

'And I oppose the granting of any such instrument,' said Mr. Markham. 'My clients have been placed in this position for no fault of their own. They have lost valuable time. They have been compelled to attend here without a shadow of reason, and debarred from their legal rights. And now your worship is asked, forsooth, to keep them idle for another three or six months.'

'Under the circumstances, I refuse to grant an injunction,' quoth the Commissioner.

'I shall only be compelled to apply to a judge of the Supreme Court,' replied Dr. Bellair.

'It is not for me to suggest to whom you may or may not apply,' answers the Commissioner. 'I shall grant no injunction, if every barrister in the colony made separate application. The Court stands adjourned to this day week.'

Whereupon there was a general stampede to the nearest hotels on the part of the witnesses, spectators, complainants, and defendants; while the Commissioner, evidently not in the humour for conversation, mounted his well-known hackney, which was brought to the office door by a trooper, and departed in the direction of the police camp, whistling, as he went, to his dogs, but evidently not 'for want of thought.'

The melodrama had been played. The *dénouement* was satisfactory as far as we were concerned. But more uncertainties and a further experience of litigation awaited us. The prize was too rich to be abandoned at the first check; Dr. Bellair, a man, when in the guise of an opponent, not to be lightly regarded. He had, it was reported, received a transfer of a 'sleeping quarter share,' that is, a proportion of the property of the claim, involving a sixteenth of the entire profit, without the necessity of representing or paying for the services of an able-bodied miner.

This might be worth a thousand—two—three thousand pounds. No doubt it was worth a considerable amount of trouble and legal research. We did not expect to be let alone for long. Of course notice of appeal had at once been given by the opposite side, and the sum of money, stated in the regulations, lodged with the registrar of the district court.

But we went to work again, and made haste to raise enough to complete a machineful of wash-dirt, which, when put through or puddled, produced a sufficiency of gold to pay all our late law expenses, and leave us a comforting surplus, thus demonstrating also the unabated richness of No. 4.

Hardly, however, had we completed this gratifying transaction than one of our late antagonists arrived in company with a police trooper, and called upon us to stop working on their claim.

' *Your* claim !' said Cyrus Yorke, striding up to him and lifting him off the ground, as if he had been a schoolboy, instead of a wiry, muscular labourer. 'You may serve out your injunction, or summons, or whatever it is that you've got the bobby to help you with ; but if you call No. 4 *your* claim again, I'll drop you down the shaft as sure as there's homminey on the Hawkesbury.'

We had seldom seen our easy-going, careless partner so excited before. Like most slow-moving intellects, his faculties were capable of great expansion when fully aroused. Once or twice we had marked him in the thick of an affray. Like Athelstane the Unready, when his blood was up, knight, and squire, and yeoman, and villain went down with wondrous suddenness before the South-Saxon giant of Wiseman's Ferry. On this occasion there was no need for deeds of valour. The miners of Yatala had long since discovered the futility of resorting to physical force.

'I say, Cornstalk, I shall have to put the bracelets on those mutton fists of yours,' said the trooper good humouredly. 'That chap's on the Queen's service, or all the same. Here's a Supreme Court injunction, which I hereby serve by giving to your mate, Harry Pole, here. D'ye hear ? Let go this honest old miner, or you'll drop in for it. I've seen as big a chap as you straightened afore now.'

Cyrus was too good a subject of Her Gracious Majesty to resist the law's representative. He relinquished Mr. Bommer with a gentle shake, growling to himself meanwhile like an interrupted grizzly. We capitulated. I called out 'below there.' The indicator rapped, and presently the Major and Joe Bulder emerged from the lower depths, clay-stained and disgusted.

'Blocked again !' quoth the Major, 'what an infernal shame. It's enough to demoralise a man altogether and irrevocably, this forced idleness. Enough to drive him to take to—well—Alison's *History of Europe*, or even Martin Farquhar Tupper. Do you ever reflect for one moment,' he said, facing the astonished jumper, 'what may be the consequence of your unprincipled litigation ? Heavy reading, incipient dementia, violent inanity, imbecility. And all because you won't respect the tenth commandment. Had you a mother ? Did you ever attend a Sunday school ? Had you so much as a maiden aunt ? Answer me.'

'You be hanged,' said the half-puzzled, half-irritated catspaw, who had evidently been drowning his sense of defeat in the flowing bowl, from his flushed and heavy-eyed look. 'You think because you and Harry Pole are swells that you can carry things all your own way on the field. But we'll learn ye different before we've done with yer.'

'And you think, because you're a pack of loafing blackguards,' retorted the Major, roused for the nonce, 'that you can interfere with fair working miners, and steal claims that you have no more right to than the bank in Main Street. We shall see you all in gaol for half a year for our costs, that's one comfort, and it's a great pity we can't put your underhand friends and backers there along with you.'

'You'll be pulled for using language calculated to cause a breach of the peace, Major,' said the trooper, 'if you don't stash it. Come along, my noble jumper, you've served your injunction, and that ought to satisfy you for one while.'

So the malignant departed, rather to my relief, for there was nothing to be gained by being summoned to Court, and fined under the 5th clause of the Vagrant Act. No. 4 was sufficiently near a public road, thoroughfare, or place, to tempt our adversary to swear that we were within the meaning of that very stringent clause.

Our wisest plan was to comply with the law, to hang up our buckets, put away the rope, and abide the issue. A deep claim is not a property that can be worked, or larcenously interfered with, without remark. The only way that our golden hoard could in any way be rifled was by the men in one of the adjacent claims driving or making a lateral gallery over our boundary below, when our washdirt might have gone up *their* shaft in the light of day, and no one been any wiser. This has been done before now.

In addition to this safeguard, the neighbours on either side were straightforward and honourable men. We also possessed another legal preventive. By application to the Commissioner we could at any time obtain an order to descend and survey either of the adjacent shafts, when, by means known to all miners, we could soon discover if any subterranean encroachment had been made.

We were stopped accordingly. It was a bore, but the other side could not work either; and being precluded from hard work, with plenty of money to spend, and no unpaid debts, or anxiety about the morrow, was a very different thing from our former experiences.

So we all preserved our souls in peace for the six weeks that elapsed before the appeal could be heard. The Major read every book in the library of the Mechanics' School of Arts, besides buying so many that they may seriously interfere with the comfort of our sleeping apartment. Joe Bulder smoked a good deal more than was good for him, and anathematised those scoundrels of jumpers with more fervency than propriety. While Cyrus ran his horse in several exciting sweepstakes, and won or lost as the case might be.

CHAPTER XIII

TIME, which brings all things to an end, and which had never passed so slowly for us before, even in our worst 'tucker' days, brought on the hearing of our appeal. It was heard before four magistrates in petty sessions assembled; and the whole weary evidence taken over again without the omission of a single detail. It certainly was a fact that Cyrus Yorke's being now the proud possessor of a Miner's Right led the opposite side to dwell with less persistent energy upon that point. But on the other hand they devoted the whole strength of their resources to bring out in strong relief their other allegation, viz. that the irregularity of the shape of our claim constituted a fatal objection.

An appeal lay to two or more magistrates under the Gold-fields Act of 30 Victoria, No. 8 (long since repealed), and was not so much an appeal upon certain clearly defined points of law as a total re-hearing of the whole case at issue. Hence the defeated party, generally being shrewd enough to discover the weak point of their evidence the first trial, not unfrequently took measures to strengthen that precise gabion or outwork when the appeal was heard. No doubt in some parts of the land the magistrates of the territory, not familiarly acquainted with mining law, constituted a wholly unsatisfactory tribunal before which to decide such delicate details and complicated issues. But the Justices at Yatala had been so thoroughly trained by a long series of mining cases and appeals during years past, involving vast sums and most important consequences, that the more important personages of the higher courts were hardly better up in the rule of evidence and the statutory necessities of their position.

So the whole lengthy evidence was fully and patiently heard; no detail was omitted; the irregular shape of the claim, and the number of superficial feet which it measured, must have been as well known to the habitues of the Court as a catch sum in arithmetic to the boys of a public school at examination time.

At nightfall the magistrates retired to confer among themselves. And after a quarter of an hour's council delivered their decision by the mouth of the chairman. The appeal was dismissed with seventy-five pounds costs against the appellants.

All recourse had now been exhausted but one. Of that one, however, our antagonists were determind to avail themselves.

Furious at defeat, and with a few sarcastic sentences reflecting upon the legal capacity of the magistrates, for which he was promptly called to order, the Doctor at once hurled his last challenge at our heads in the form of a notice of appeal to the Supreme Court.

He was informed that he could do so in the manner set forth in the regulations, by naming the points upon which he desired to appeal, and by lodging a sum of money as guarantee for the costs of the respondents in the event of the appeal being dismissed.

Money was still forthcoming, it appeared, as these expensive preliminaries were at once complied with.

Thus for the second time we were victorious. As we left the Court amid the congratulations of the crowd, Mr. Markham cheerfully asked the Doctor if he had made arrangements for sending the case home to the Privy Council after the Supreme Court had decided against him?

Frowning darkly, he replied that, 'It was not so very certain that he might *not* be compelled to take that step also. He had had reason to distrust the law of colonial judges before now.'

Here the crowd cheered him, evidently pleased with his indomitable courage. And we went straight to our claim, and put on a shift before midnight.

A week at least must elapse before the judge in chambers— in his metropolitan seclusion—could be moved to grant an injunction to further restrain us from working until the last appeal should be tried. We therefore concluded to make hay while the sun shone, or rather to dig gold while the coast was clear. To that end we put on a crowd of wages men, who extracted such a ceaseless output of washdirt that our foes used to come to the claim and declare that nothing would be left of their inheritance, so to speak, if we were not stopped.

The Doctor tried the Commissioner and the magistrates for a restraining order, offering to make affidavit that bloodshed would ensue. But the former said if a few rascally, loafing jumpers were knocked on the head it would matter little. And the other men in authority had doubts as to the legality of any but judicial interference at this stage of proceedings.

One fine day, though, an imposing document, with the judge's sign-manual appended thereto, did make its appearance, and was duly served upon us ; but before it arrived we had washed several machines of dirt, and extracted the best part of two thousand pounds in hard cash from the 'mining tenement' in dispute.

K

'Yon dirt goes better and better every load,' said Joe Bulder. 'Danged if I don't chuck that Doctor down a wet shaft if we're muddled about much langer a' this fashion.'

There was nothing for it, however, but to sling up the raw-hide buckets, and put No. 4 out of commission once more. It was hard, too, to see even other claims along the lead, with their red flags flaunting in the breeze, and the whip-horses hauling steadily at their ascending loads, or trolling back briskly and kicking playfully when the descending rope permitted such gambols.

We had, perforce, to endure more wearisome monotonous inaction and delay. Our appeal case in the Supreme Court was set down for hearing at the end of a crowded session, as luck would have it, and immediately before the long vacation. Australian judges are, as a rule, worked very hard, and have not the leisure of their European brethren. At this particular time the course of litigation, consequent upon an unprecedented period of inflowing wealth, had well-nigh exhausted the metropolitan bench, the bar, and even the sufficiently numerous solicitors. Two or three stupendous squatting actions, notably the great Terri-hi-hi Creek case, had swallowed up the last remnant of that admittable patience and attention to minutest details which so honourably distinguishes the British wearer of the ermine.

To the passionate grief and indignation of Dr. Bellair, who stopped but little short of a threat of impeachment before the British Houses of Parliament, the great appeal case in Pole and party v. Ingerstrom and party, which was beginning to be in all men's mouths, the value of the claim in dispute being variously stated from a hundred thousand pounds to a quarter of a million, was not brought on before the close of the session.

So it was left stranded with other forlorn argosies, and compelled to abide the humble position of remanet.

We were hardly less disgusted than our enthusiastic opponent that his frantic adjurations had beaten themselves vainly against the rock of judicial imperturbability. Whatever were we to do for the three or four, possibly six, months which would probably intervene before we could put a pick again into the tantalisingly rich washdirt of No. 4? How were we to spend our money or our lives in this confounded Yatala, thrice-read volume that it was to all of us?

Events follow quickly in those new lands upon which the Southern Cross looks down from the untroubled skies, fortunately for those sons of hazard and adventure, for whom the measured march of the old world has ever been too tame. I had wandered listlessly homeward one evening from a long day's walk, more than usually depressed with the thought that the waters of evil fortune were closing darkly over our heads in spite of our transient gold gleam, when I was struck by the unwonted appearance of activity displayed by the Major.

Our premises also had undergone a temporary alteration. The tent was down ; various articles of furniture were assuming their well-known travelling appearance. Joe Bulder was briskly busied in abetting the transformation of everything into light marching order. Suddenly I became conscious of an unwonted hum as of earnest voices amongst our circumjacent acquaintances. I began to recognise the symptoms of the complaint.

It was not for the first time that I had known a great goldfield infected by it. Forms were flitting about in the gathering twilight, lanterns were being lit in preparation for night work. Horses were driven up, the hobble chains and bells of which sounded their continuous characteristic chime. A word from time to time caught my ear, in which 'The Oxley,' 'Only a hundred and odd miles,' 'Five ounces to the dish,' 'Good sinking,' 'All block claims,' were increasingly distinct.

Before I stopped at the spot of earth which had been immediately before our own tent door, I was fully aware of the cause of the unwonted agitation which characterised the night.

A rush was on and a big one at that, as I heard an American digger inform his mate.

'You're a good fellow, Pole,' said the Major, 'in your way— a man of high principles and irreproachable morals ; but these infernally long walks amount to a defect in your character. Here have we been sounding boot and saddle all day, and couldn't get "tale or tidings of you," as Mrs. Yorke says. Lend a hand with this cord. Do you want to put anything else in this box of yours? I've packed it for you.'

'I'll see in the morning,' I said. 'Where's the rush?'

'*Where's* the rush?' echoed the Major, still tugging away at an obstinate cord with which he was securing a very bulging and battered portmanteau. 'Have you been in a cave all day? or where in heaven can you have deposited yourself not to have heard of the Great Rush to the Oxley—the biggest thing that's happened in Australia yet, and that's going to knock Ballarat and Bendigo into a cocked hat?'

'So good as that?' I queried languidly.

'Good!' shouted the Major. '*Nothing* ever heard like it, even in California or Eaglehawk. Three ounces, five ounces, ten ounces to the dish, regular chunks of gold, no rock, no water. All shallow sinking and block claims ; none of your confounded frontage, all law and humbug. I like the good old-fashioned blocks—when you get it, you get it and no mistake. There won't be a soul on the field in a week, except those who are on real good gold. And it *must* be good to keep fellows here after what we've heard.'

'How about No. 4; give it away?'

'No, most noble stoic, we are not exactly going to do that, badly as we have been treated by luck, law, and litigation. You and I and Joe are going "right away," as poor Gus would have said, and Cyrus will remain and be the dragon on guard.'

'I suppose we must start at daylight? It's a great nuisance,' I said, 'having this kind of thing to do over again.'

'You haven't gone mad by any chance,' said the Major, taking a light and peering into my face, 'as the defendant in Racker v. Smith did? A ten thousand pound claim *was* something to lose when all the world knew that he was in the right. No, we haven't quite lost No. 4 yet, in spite of the Doctor and all his works. But softening of the brain *must* be setting in, or you would never think of losing an hour, much less a whole night, when there's a rush like this on. No, we've hired a spring-cart and horse by the day, and the fellow will be here with it when the moon rises. You'll have to look slippy.'

'*You* seem in a wonderful state of sanguine anticipation, Major,' I made answer ; 'one would think you were totally unfamiliar with the chance of digging life. Doesn't it strike you that our ordinary luck will attend us—all the best claims will be taken up before we get there, or we shall most industriously bottom a duffer, or having by the strangest fluke dropped on to the gutter, it will be proved incontestably that some one has a better right to it. I am sick of the whole thing. I'll stay and shepherd No. 4, and you can take Cyrus and Joe.'

'You be hanged! you're malingering, and I want to shake the blues out of you. You'll be all right in a week. Besides, think of the glorious novelty of the whole affair. We're both ready to hang ourselves here. I don't believe there's a book I haven't read within fifty miles. And I ask you as a brother officer and a gentleman—I mean as a man and a digger, what *are* we to do till that blessed Supreme Court appeal is heard?'

'All right,' I murmured, 'I have no preference, as people in the provinces say about roast fowls at dinner. Who is the Commissioner?'

'Blake himself, no less—ordered off at a moment's notice. They think there's no other man in the service can handle such a crowd as is likely to be camped on the Oxley within three months. Nor is there, by what we hear. He'll have his work cut out for him, too, they say. There are vessels laid on from San Francisco already.'

'It will realise Mick Hord's mild exaggeration of a rush with forty thousand men. I say, are Merlin and the sergeant and all the rest coming too?'

'Everybody but the Clerk of the Bench they say. There's a new one appointed there, a fellow just out from England. Goring wrote me about him ; stammers a bit, but a great character they tell me. A deal of daring originality about him. I look forward to him as a kind of compensation in the circulating library line.'

'Going to keep Joe Bulder?'

'Not for long ; he must come back and help Cyrus do

nothing, more's the pity; but we can't trust the noble Persian's discretion; and Joe's head is a very good one, if he'd had any encouragement early in life to use it instead of his hands.'

The moon rose, the cart came, and we went. Nothing was placed in the vehicle but our indispensables in the way of clothes, bedding, our simple cooking utensils, and of course our tools. The road lay under our feet in the clear moonlight, white and dusty, between the withered grass and the tall tree-stems. The air was fresh. The heavens brightly azure. The horse was active and powerful, and his owner, well paid, drove briskly forward.

There was little trouble in finding the road, which led through the park-like forest which surrounded Yatala to the plains of the Oxley, on the head-waters of which this last-found Eldorado had arisen. Had we felt any uncertainty it would have been quickly removed, for in front, behind, on every side were wayfarers journeying to the same goal, of every kind, in every sort of conveyance, with every description of animal.

Bullock drays and horse drays, American express waggons, hand-carts drawn by men, and even wheelbarrows propelled by sturdy arms containing all the household goods of a family. Women laden with immense bundles were dragging young children by the hand, or as often carrying infants at their bosoms.

Sometimes a drove of cattle with wild riders behind them would come silently and all ghostly in the moonlight upon the strangely hurrying crowd. As silently, too, retreat, only to move parallel with, but far distant from, the disturbing concourse, whose physical needs they were destined to supply.

The whole movement had the appearance of something between a pilgrimage and a fair suddenly cut adrift from its moorings, and compelled to travel forward in grotesque procession to another land. So mixed and incongruous did the component parts appear. So unsuited and unusual to the rude travelling that was imminent, the yet ruder labour to come. I should have enjoyed the humorous contrasts of the scene, but hope deferred had indeed rendered the heart sick—sick unto death, with a despondency as new as oppressive, with a sombre presentiment I tried in vain to shake off.

We travelled day and night, only allowing ourselves needful rest and food, and bearing hard upon the good horse that carried our chattels. On the sixth day we reached the Oxley, and had a free and uninterrupted view of the Great Rush.

It was a strange sight. We, who had seen many goldfields, had never seen one exactly like this before.

The auriferous deposit had been so exceedingly rich in one particular point or cape of land which ran into the river that an unprecedented density of mining settlement had taken place there. This was the famous 'jeweller's shop,' where the very earth seemed composed of gold dust, with gold gravel for a variety. Thousands and tens of thousands of pounds' worth of the ore had been taken out of a few square feet here, and no blanks had been drawn for many yards immediately around.

We were fortunate in meeting a friend we had known in Ballarat, who immediately gave us the *carte du pays*.

He himself was such a man as one meets at goldfields, in the islands of the South Seas, in the desert, or in London, indifferently and apparently without any particular reason why he should be in one place more than another. But chiefly in the waste places of the earth, though he was as much at home in a West-End drawing-room as here where we found him, darkly handsome and cool as ever, leaning against a tall tree trunk, smoking a carefully coloured meerschaum, and gazing tranquilly upon the curious human mass below.

'Olivera, as I live! who in the world would have thought of seeing you here?' said the Major.

'My dear fellow,' said the stranger slowly and impressively, 'this is precisely the place where you *should* have been certain of finding me. Haven't I been at every great rush since California in '49?'

'Well, yes, I believe you have; you're a sort of auriferous wandering Jew. And what does your peripatetic wisdom think of this small assortment of the excellent of the earth. And hadn't we better join forces?'

'This will be one of the richest goldfields I have ever set eyes on. My geology and experience are both at fault, if it be not so. But I will not join you, for I have been so uniformly unlucky that I believe there is a fate involved in it.'

'Oh, that's all humbug, luck turns; try again.'

'Mine will turn, but not yet. I shall go on mining to my life's end, for my spirit has never yet yielded to evil fortune; but no party that I have ever joined has ever been successful, now these many long years, and I will never more share with others my disasters. I dig, as Harry of the Wynd fought, for my own hand. I have a claim, though, worked by wages men; and I will point out to you what I think a very favourable conjunction of strata.'

'All right, old man. We bow to your superior wisdom, and place ourselves in your hands—drive on the cart.'

We skirted the great throbbing hive of eager workers spurred up by greed and gain to such desperate efforts that an unnatural silence reigned over the scene. Even their looks were changed. Instead of the frank expression of the ordinary miner, always ready for a little cheerful conversation, these men looked like the worn and troubled artisans of a great factory, where an untimely lassitude or carelessness might lead to the rupture of machinery or the danger of dismissal.

We went down, however, with Olivera to the spot which he

pointed out, near which, indeed, his own claim was situated, and under his auspices pegged out four men's ground.

'You see,' he said, 'this is a place where the greenstone and the granite meet. In such a conjunction there is always gold, and heavy gold too.'

'But it was unoccupied before we came. Why did you not take possession of it yourself? You could not know that friends were coming either?'

'My dear boy, if I had taken it up, there would *not* have been gold in it. My luck would have prevented that highly desirable result.'

After pegging out our claim, we addressed ourselves to the task of putting up our tent and making ourselves comfortable for the time being.

We had forty-eight hours in which to arrange matters before we were required by law to go to work, so that there was time to spare. We had also to get hold of a fourth man as mate and shareholder, not so easy a matter in a community of strangers.

We wanted a man who could work, also one that would be reasonably easy to live with. A high moral standard we should not insist on; but neither did we care to be troubled with a dissolute rowdy or a drunkard.

The man with the spring cart had been paid off after depositing our baggage, and was taking a reconnoitring tour preparatory to returning to his family at Yatala.

We had put up our tent, and firmly secured it with pegs and ropes against wind or weather. We were standing aimlessly watching the unceasing crowd that passed to and fro, like ghosts in an Inferno, when Joe suddenly uttered a strongish ejaculation, and relapsed into the Kentish idiom.

'Danged if I didn'a think I should see 'un some day, and it's coomed at last.'

'See who, Joe?' I asked.

'Why *him*,' quoth my henchman, strongly excited. 'Dost see yon man a talking th' chap in th' red shirt and high boots. That un's brother Jack, sure enow.'

It had always seemed to us a curious thing that we should never have met with Mr. Jack Bulder in the flesh, though his memorable letter and remittance had been the proximate cause of our emigration. We had heard of him repeatedly, sometimes at one place, sometimes at another—in Queensland, Victoria, New Zealand by turns; but always something had interfered to prevent his looking up his brother during all the years that both had been in Australia.

I turned and saw a good-looking, well-dressed individual, who did not carry out my pre-conceived notion of a forecastle Jack. It was he, nevertheless. I watched Joe Bulder go up to him and say something which caused him to turn round sharply. I saw both men confront and look steadily at each other. Then followed a sturdy hand-clasp, which was all the greeting beyond

'Well, Jack, is't thou old man,' 'Why, Joe, I never thought you'ld turn out half as smart a fellow,'—which was considered necessary by the emigrant Britons after fifteen years' absence. They walked over towards me.

'This is my brother Jack, Mr. Pole, him as wrote the letter, as I show'd you at Dibblestowe forge,' said Joe, with some effort and shyness. 'You'll remember it.'

'I remember it well enough, Joe,' I said, 'but for it you and I would never have been here. I hope your brother has more to show for his time than some of us.'

'Glad to see you, sir,' said Mr. Jack Bulder, raising his hat, and discovering by his address that the university of travel had sufficed to impart a polish to which Joe had not attained. 'You're Mr. Pole that my brother came out with. It's a good sign, he's stuck by you so long.'

'It has spoken well for both of us,' said I, 'we have been firm friends and true mates all this time. And now, what do you think of this rush?'

'It's the best I've seen yet,' he said promptly. 'And I saw Ballarat at the start. I've been here since the prospector struck gold. I happened to be working in a gully nigh hand when the news came.'

'And how have you done?'

'Well, not so bad. Our party's just broke up, because we worked out the claim. We divided four hundred and fifty a man for three weeks' work.'

'That's good, isn't it,' said Joe; 'worth picking up, eh?'

'Pretty fair,' said the experienced miner, 'but nothing to what some of 'em's doing. I've banked my share, and I'm looking out to nip in again—while the market's up.'

'You can have a share in the claim which we've just pegged out,' said I. 'We want a fourth man, and were, indeed, looking out for one.'

'Whereabouts is it?'

'Close by here—near that greenstone dyke.'

'Oh, if it's there, I'm on. I had some notion of that spot myself; it's as likely a place as anywhere on the field. Now Joe, you and I can wire in and see which is the best man.'

'I'm on,' answered Joe, a ray of humour irradiating his honest countenance. 'I could'na work alongside o' thee when thou wast at Dibblestowe. But I reckon I can handle a pick with thee or any other man, now.'

This, of course, was a very fortunate concurrence of events. We had secured a really first-rate worker, and a man of experience on the field. Besides, I took much interest in him, as a brother of Joe's, one of the best and truest fellows that ever broke bread.

The Major, returning after a long talk with Olivera, was pleased to find that we had secured so good a mate. He went through the form of touching the pegs, to ensure strictly legal possession. (A burnt child, etc.) The brothers went away together, presumably to have a good talk, as Englishmen ever do, and unburden their minds.

Soon after daylight next morning they returned, bringing with them on a pack horse Jack's tent and worldly possessions, including various mining tools, and other articles more or less useful. This was a convenient arrangement for us, as the brothers agreeing to keep house together, the Major and I had the other tent to ourselves.

Little time was lost in preliminaries. The sun was not high before we had our stage and windlass up, and were delving away at mother earth as if we intended to solve the question of her central fires.

We were none of us new at the trade; there was a certain emulation between the patrician and plebeian element, for we worked in pairs. We were all young and in top condition. The consequence was, we got down at such a pace that more than one of the daily arriving parties stopped, all eager as they were, to wonder at the rapidity with which our beautifully straight and even shaft was boring, as if with a gigantic auger, towards the bed rock.

Olivera used to come and gaze at us, and then go back and inspirit his wages men with tales of our prowess, they naturally not being quite so anxious to strain every nerve in an enterprise in which they were less directly interested.

Though they had a week's start of us, we bottomed on the same day, and by nightfall the field was aware that Olivera's half-share men had bottomed another duffer, and that Pole and party, from Yatala, were so 'dead on the gutter' that every dish they took out was half gold.

CHAPTER XIV

IT was certainly one of the richest finds we had any of us encountered, and we had been where the gold lay as plentiful as shells by the sea shore. Directly we were down, we drove across to the outer edges of our boundary, lest some smart neighbour (for we were closely surrounded by this time) should subterraneously encroach and get into our treasure chamber, before we had full knowledge of its outer walls.

This sort of thing had happened before, within our own knowledge. More than once a too easy party of miners in rich ground had, when down upon the lowest stratum, suddenly found, as they said, 'the bottom drop out of their shaft,' all their hopes of wealth untold falling with it into an unknown abyss.

This abnormal proceeding had resulted from smarter neighbours having driven, or made lateral galleries all about their under world, taking the gold up their own shaft, and perhaps clearing out altogether to a distance before their iniquity became manifest.

There was certainly the method of legal recovery of damages and value of gold so abstracted, if wilful encroachment and felonious taking could be fully proved. But on a thronged and quickly-shifting alluvial goldfield, like the Oxley, the chances were against receiving satisfaction in full. Probably, too, the ill-gotten gold was sold or spent before the discovery was made, transferred almost as far beyond the bailiff's reach, if a judgment was obtained, as the quart of whisky which the Highlander defied the Customs officer to confiscate.

As I said before, our party was too *rusé* and experienced to lay itself open to such peculiar pillage. We drove and raised our washdirt without anxiety or molestation, and afterwards separated it from the attendant clay and gravel, by the old-fashioned expedient of a 'tom.' This abbreviation of 'long tom' is a sufficiently lengthy trough made of sawn boards with a plate of perforated iron at one end. The auriferous gravel, here placed, has a constant stream of water playing over it, the gold remaining in crevices specially prepared. Our wash-

dirt was so exceptionally rich that very little treatment sufficed
for it. At the end of the week's washing up, we discovered
that we were each making at the rate of a thousand pounds a
man, or fifty-two thousand a year. A most respectable income.
Even my friends of Mid - Kent would have allowed this;
though many of them maintained, to their dying day, that gold
digging was more or less an immoral occupation.

Well as we were doing, of course many others in our
vicinity and other places were as richly rewarded. Our claim
was soon well known as the Greenstone Dyke run of gold; one
consequence of which was, that every available yard of soil, for
more than a mile round, was taken up, thus preventing us from
extending our operations, or continuing further search in the
same direction.

We did not mind this, for, in addition to our present slice of
luck, we had, in deference to Jack Bulder's advice, bought up
all the 'interests,' that is, shares, half shares, and quarter shares
on or near the supposed run of gold that we had struck, which
were for sale. We had cash in hand, and so were able to speculate to advantage as many of our neighbours were poor men,
not long come on to the field. So that when the Greenstone
Dyke Lead became so notoriously lucrative, we had more strings
to our bow than one, and several sources of income.

Yet it seemed very hard that Olivera, who had shown us the
lead and demonstrated by geological facts that the gold *must*
be there, should get not an ounce of it; his claim being one of
the very few blanks that were recorded on the lead.

Besides, as all the claim holders had closed round as far as
could be seen in every direction, he was thereby shut out from
getting another claim, even within hail of his first favourite
spot. There was nothing for him but to go to a distant portion
of the field and try his fortune there. He did so, taking his
losses, as usual, very coolly, only saying ' Just my luck. There's
plenty more on this field, more than these blockheads dream of,
who have been crowding so eagerly here. But it is rather hard
to be almost the only man who has duffered out on *a lead of my
own discovering*. But you will do me the justice to say, that I
expected it from the commencement.'

So Mr. Dycecombe Olivera, whom we had got into the habit
of calling The Don, from his dark and somewhat foreign appearance, calmly departed with his vassals, and chose another
site for a probable gold-mine, about due west of the present
workings. This other was due east. Perhaps he thought that
a direct antithesis might break the spell.

While we were working together before the successful result
of our co-operative enterprise, I had instinctively occupied
myself with observing the characteristics of our new mate, Mr.
Jack Bulder.

His certainly was an organisation dear to the psychological
inquirer. He was much cleverer and more amusing than

poor Joe, whom he continually rallied about his simplicity
and the close - clinging rusticities he had been unable to
shake off.

'Hang it, Joe,' he used to say, 'why you're just the same
yokel as you were when I recollect you blubbering like a great
girl, when I went away to sea.'

'Happen I mightn't see so much to blubber about, if ye were
gannin' noo. When folks is young they're foolish like. I had
na been long from mother's apron-string then. I'm none as
forrard as thee, I'll allow, but I can do a many things as I
never thout to learn in foreign parts. And I can work and
haud a still tongue, lad.'

'I never could,' laughed the elder brother. 'I never could
in my life ; there you have the advantage of me, as you will
find some day. However, you *can* work, and no mistake, Joe.
I didn't think there was a man in Yatala, or here either, who
could work alongside of me, so easy and regular as you have done.'

Jack Bulder did himself no more than justice when he half
stated that no man on the field could work alongside of him
with pick and shovel in a shaft. He was one of the most
wonderful performers in the shaft-sinking line that we had
ever dropped across. Strong, quick - witted, and absolutely
tireless ; he had the ready-for-anything turn of mind of a
trained sailor. Full, also, of mechanical expedients in any
emergency, he displayed a fertility of resource which furnished
the most unaffected astonishment to his brother. Joe could
not sufficiently express his wonderment at such a genius having
appeared from out of the Bulder family, and their surroundings
in Mid-Kent.

'Danged if I know whether it be the sailoring or the digging as has made thee the man thou art,' said he, in one of his
vain attempts to explain the transformation which had taken
place in his elder. 'Seems to me as if they sent all the young
chaps frae Dibblestowe aboord ship for five year, and to the
diggin' for five year more, they'd never want no poor law nor
unions. Why, half-a-dozen chaps like Jack'd mak the fortune
o' a dozen towns like Dibblestowe ; they'd toorn all the ploughmen into farmers, and all the farmers into squires—danged if
they wouldn't.'

Without going quite so far as our worthy Joe in his theories
as to the best means of vitalising the latent forces of the
peasantry of Britain, the Major and I did full justice to the
merits of our new comrade. We had always regarded Joe as
the model Englishman of the labouring class ; but his senior
had all his unerring common sense, propriety of feeling, and
incalculable staying power, apparently, with far more initiative
faculty.

Whether it was the seafaring or the digging experience
which had made the man he was of him, we, of course, could
not determine. Anyhow, he was an interesting psychological

study, and as such, afforded endless matter for reflection and comparison to the Major and myself.

Not that we, after our dearly bought and curiously varied experience, were too prone to take the most attractive new acquaintance wholly upon trust. Hundreds of human disappointments, personal and vicarious, had served to cure us of the Arcadian trustfulness with which we might have entered Australia. Indeed, the half reproachful conclusion was strictly applicable to us, which passed sadly from the lips of a *détenu* in the cells of one of Her Majesty's metropolitan gaols.

Two prisoners in the exercise yard, serving their sentence, were heard one day conversing in earnest tones, such as aroused the attention of the warder, watchful lest plots for breaking gaol should be incubating. It proved merely to be the discussion of the probable success of an appeal to the Head of the Department—formerly a Commissioner of Goldfields—for some alleviation of duress.

'Do yer think we could gammon the chief bloke, Bill,' said the milder ruffian. 'He looked a good-'arted cove when we see him last?'

'I'm afeard it's no go,' croaked Bill, with despairing cadence, 'he's been too long at them bloomin' diggins.'

Such, alas! had been our too realistic destiny. Without losing our reverence for the higher qualities of our common nature, we had learned to distinguish between the true and the false ; and, for most purposes of deceit and imposture, such as are unblushingly practised upon the excellent of the earth—we had been 'too long at the diggings!'

'Confound the fellow,' said the Major one day, when we had had a lengthened discussion about him ; 'he's as good as a new novel, very nearly. But for him, and a torn copy of *Adam Bede*, I should have been out of all intellectual rations—perhaps, taken to beer and dominoes. Still (reflectively), he's got one fault, a very bad one, in my experience of character, real and fictitious. I can't call to mind a faultless hero, who hadn't a screw loose somewhere, connected with the leading machinery, too. Now, our friend's too d——d perfect altogether. I'm sorry for it. But mark my words, Pole, there's something *to find out* about him.

We, therefore, placed a percentage of our judgment, while basking in the sunshine, to the suspense account, so to speak, of Mr. Jack Bulder's energy and capacity ; for, did he not splice our rope, much worn and not to be replaced, improvise an anvil and point out picks after hours, manufacture a superior kind of windlass with a patent brake, and twice the ordinary power, besides fishing out a new auriferous gully, before Olivera, who, however, endorsed his judgment and took up a claim broadside on to us. This, of course, was after we had worked out our 'goldsmith's window' as the adjacent diggers christened it, and recommenced to dig out another fortune.

Our first claim possessed the very great advantage of being easy to work, besides being fabulously rich; that is, the wash-dirt could be got out and treated with almost a tithe of the terrible work and loss of time necessary at poor old Yatala. So Jack and his brother, working all the time like two bene-volent Trolls, with zealous emulation, it came to pass that we were clean worked out and had sold the good-will of our claim to some new arrivals for 'a cool hundred,' before many of our neighbours at Greenstone Gully were half done with their 'dirt.'

As may be easily imagined, this assimilation of the 'root of all evil' to the familiar tuber which merely needs in ordinary seasons to be dug up and put in bags (ours were chamois leather, to be sure), was not without its effect upon society at large, civilised and uncivilised.

Rumour had caught up, magnified, and sent fleeing on the wings of the wind to every quarter of the globe, sensational inflations, gold coloured and rose hued, until all Europe, Africa, America, and even Asia, to the bounds of 'far Cathay,' grew familiar with the gold farms on the banks of the Oxley, where the crops were gathered all the year round; where the streams trickled over treasure untold, and the very rocks were of virgin gold!

Our own astonishing successes, and, indeed, those of number-less fellow-workers, could not fail to produce a violent commo-tion among the floating populations of the earth. But Aladdin-chamber inventories must have been sown broadcast to account for the tidal-wave of stranger hosts which now came rolling in upon the river flats of the Oxley.

Not only did every colony of Australia, every province of New Zealand, send in, apparently, its able-bodied contingent, but Americans, Canadians, Germans, Frenchmen, Italians, Swiss, Cockneys and Highlanders, Scots and Irishmen, Spaniards and West-Indian Creoles, arrived, apparently in shiploads.

Moreover, and on this modern invasion our conscript fathers looked darkly and with sullen disapproval, long strings of Chinese, grotesquely attired, and heavily burdened, came thronging along the well worn trail which led from the arterial highways of the coast.

Simultaneously with the advance in force of the great army of miners, an official camp had been formed, where Captain Blake took up his headquarters, accompanied by Mr. Merlin, the sergeant, and a strong body of police, further reinforced a few days afterwards.

The Commissioner, with military prevision, selected as a site a high bluff or point surrounded on three sides by the deep and rapid waters of the Oxley. A stout palisaded fence was at once run across the neck (a narrow one) on the side facing the diggings, thus forming a convenient paddock for the troop horses, while, as a strategical position, it was capable of scientific defence, should the need ever arise.

The tents were pitched, pending the erection of the necessary buildings, the horses let loose, the Captain's dogs chained up, the Union Jack flaunted on a sapling appropriate for a flagstaff, and Her Majesty's Government was fully represented.

It was apparent to us that it would take the Commissioner and Mr. Merlin 'all their time,' as the diggers phrased it, to keep the field in the same state of order and subjection as had obtained at Yatala. A better *sous-officier* than Sergeant MacMahon they could not possibly have had. But, beside the enormously increased population which now gave every sign of being massed upon the ground, there were other elements likely to be infused which might lead to revolt and disorganisation.

On the first Saturday afternoon, after having heard that the new Clerk of the Bench had arrived, we went to call upon him. He was also Mining Registrar, Agent for the Curator of Intestate Estates, Registrar of the Small Debts Court, Coroner, Commissioner for Affidavits, and the holder of several other minor offices, which are generally appendages to the appointment.

We found him in the large tent which did duty as a courthouse, of one corner of which he had possessed himself. Evidently not a man of method, he was surrounded with books and papers relating to his office, all in such a state of inextricable confusion, that an average licensed surveyor (of all men, perhaps, most experienced in making a tent habitable and officially effective) would have swooned on the spot.

'Now then, w-w-what's your name,' he called out in a loud voice, without looking up, 'don't keep me w-w-waiting all d-d-day.'

The Major smiled. He looked up angrily. 'How d-d-dare you presume to l-l-laugh, sir, in Her M-m-m-ajesty's t-t-tent, sir, taking up the G-g-government time? D-d-don't you know every minute of my t-t-time's worth a g-g-guinea?'

The Major having by this time extracted his card, presented it, at the same time saying, 'Mr. Bagstock, I believe, permit me to introduce my friend Mr. Pole.'

Mr. Bagstock gave one hurried glance at the card, stared wildly at us, then with a rapid alteration of manner, got up and shook hands warmly with us.

'D-d-delighted to see you, I'm sure. Charlie Grant—b-b-best f-f-fellow in the world—s-s-said you were out here. W-w-wrote, I believe. Live near this p-p-pandemonium?'

'We live *in* it,' said the Major; 'we're familiar demons.'

'But wh-wh-what do you d-d-do, then?'

'Dig,' I said, 'and are not badly paid for it just at present.'

'Regular miners?' said our new acquaintance, still wonderingly. 'Good God! you don't say so. Got one of th-these and all?' Here he pointed to a book of Miners' Rights, upon which he had been scribbling names as fast as he could write before we came in which accounted for his unconventional reception.

This he explained as we talked afterwards, during which conversation he showed himself a most amusing man of the world. His habit of stammering was so repeatedly useful in giving point and accentuation to his witticisms, that we doubted seriously as to whether it was natural or assumed.

A vein of eccentricity, amounting to recklessness, pervaded his character, which I thought could either be accepted by the mining population as legitimate humour and pleasantry, or be seriously disapproved of, and so lead to the severance of official relations.

He freely confided to us his views as to the performance of his duties, as well as his general opinion as to the best mode of treating the heterogeneous population with which he was brought into contact.

'F-f-f-irmness, my dear fellow, and k-k-keeping them in their p-p-p-laces ; depend upon it that's the l-l-line to take, and cut s-s-short all their d——d t-t-technical details.'

'Hulloo! what is it ? Ex-c-c-cuse me M-m-major ?'

Here a burly digger advanced with a document carefully folded up in his hands.

'Are you the gen'lman as takes the hafferdavys ?'

'C-c-certainly; all I can g-g-get.'

'Well, Mr. Cramp said as I was to make my hafferdavy afore you, where you see my mark here, as I was the owner of these town allotments in Bathurst.'

'All r-r-right, s-s-swear away.'

Here he looked around for the official Bible, which ought to have been within reach, but which was probably buried under some of the piles of papers, books, forms of summons, warrants, informations, etc., which lay around as if in upheaval a corner of a stationer's shop had fallen in just then.

Not seeing it he continued : 'This is your signature, and the contents of this affidavit are t-t-true, so h-h-help you God. Half a guinea ! '

The man looked rather confused and uncertain, but produced the coin, and then said, 'I didn't see no Bible, sir ?'

'N-n-never mind. K-k-kiss the book when you g-g-get home !'

Overawed by the authority and impressiveness of Mr. Bagstock's manner, the miner, not one of the pestilent educated sort, departed, and we only awaited his safe clearing out to laugh heartily.

'Allow me to congratulate you upon your *savoir-faire*,' said the Major with much politeness ; for a newly-landed official, I don't recollect seeing your equal.'

Bagstock confronted us with a face of absolute gravity.

'Where do you s-s-suppose I should be if I d-d-didn't cut short these f-f-fellows' trifling objections. C-c-can't waste the G-g-government time, you know.'

There was a humorous twinkle in his eye as he said this, which nearly set us off again ; but his command of feature was perfect. So, arranging for him to dine with us and Olivera on the following day, and promising to send a guide to the camp before the appointed hour, we took our leave.

'By Jove,' said the Major, 'our friend will either be a distinguished ornament to the service, or he will be mentioned in such a way in Blake's despatches that the Government will require his services at Bourke or Wilcannia without delay.'

'I don't know about that,' I said. 'He has plenty of "pluck and assurance," as Deuchatel said the other day, and foreseeing rather wild times, I incline to the belief that he will develop into a celebrity.'

'Talking of distinguished people,' said my companion, 'I heard one of these Victorians, who are arriving in such hordes, address Jack Bulder familiarly by a different name. The man evidently knew him well. He acknowledged him, but little more, and went on with his work. He looked up afterwards and said something about "a purser's name being handy now and then in this country."'

'What did the fellow call him ?'

'Dawson, I think ; not his own name, at any rate.'

'It can't matter to us,' I said ; 'he may have married, and since he was on the diggings, as the men say, and have reasons not affecting his general character for not wishing to be brought back under a warrant, to answer a charge of maintenance. Such things happen now and then. Look at Westerman's case.'

'I am surprised to hear a man of your high moral tone talk in that way,' said the Major sarcastically. 'No, I don't think our accomplished friend, somehow, fears that the flowery fetters of matrimony may resolve themselves into prosaic handcuffs ; but I am convinced he has reason to dread some *éclaircissement* or other. In spite of his ceaseless work—and he is the devil, *bon diable* if you will, at that—he has a restless look. And I wouldn't give *very* heavy odds that he doesn't drink.'

'Why, he never touches anything,' said I greatly astonished.

'Bad sign,' replied the Major, 'very bad ; that is the reason why I think so.'

Our speculations, were, however, confined to our own breasts. In the daily increasing rout and turmoil of the greatest concourse of people ever gathered together upon (temporarily) the richest goldfield in Australia, it did not appear to matter much about private character, more than upon the moral standard reached by any given soldier in a decisive battle.

Our time was much taken up with our own highly exciting work, for which we were still rewarded beyond our most sanguine expectations. As all the early comers were similarly successful, and as it was from time to time requisite to defend one's ground against aggressive strangers, ignorant of mining or, apparently, any other laws, there was absolutely no leisure whatever. The Commissioner rode his horses almost to death, having to decide so many hundreds of cases on the ground daily; and though rapid and decisive as usual, the immense population of the field, with its daily multiplying gold areas, employed every moment of daylight, and still left a margin of small disputes undisposed of.

It was in one of these where our new mate distinguished himself by prompt action peculiar to himself. One afternoon we discovered that four unprepossessing-looking strangers had pegged out a corner of our claim, and were proceeding to sink thereon, under the pretext that we held more than our proper quantity, and that there was 'spare ground between us and the next claim.' It was merely a pretext, as we knew, but annoying, as it might be a week or two now before the Commissioner could come down and adjudicate. Before which time, as the ground was shallow, these fellows might have their shaft down and commence to rob us in daylight.

It must be explained that so rich was the yield of gold at this particular gully, every foot of ground represented no inconsiderable sum. A certain number of superficial feet only was allotted to each miner by the regulations. If he, working separately, or his party collectively, occupied more than the legal allowance, any other miner, making the discovery, might take possession of it, as ground held in excess, and if he proved his case it was allotted to him by the Commissioner.

Hence, in rich localities, it was customary for men to go round the claims with a tape line carefully measuring the areas. If they discovered a sufficient quantity of ground 'held in excess,' barely sufficient to sink a shaft upon, they made a practice of taking possession of it. In some cases they managed to work these fragments of claims, and secure a portion of the general treasure ; in others they effected a compromise, and sold out their titles to the original holders. This was not held to be a manly or reputable course of conduct by the miners generally, and, indeed, was chiefly adopted by the loafers and scamps of the goldfield. But, on the other hand, no miner had any right to take up more ground than he was legally entitled to, and if he was thereby damaged it was his own fault.

We however, and also Olivera, had always been scrupulously careful to measure accurately our due and lawful quantity, holding it for the reasons recited wrong and inexpedient to do otherwise. We were, therefore, convinced that the attempted occupation was only an impudent struggle for blackmail, by forcibly encroaching on our claim.

The Major and I had resisted by all means, short of personal violence, this invasion of our rights, and were engaged in a stormy altercation with the leading man of the party, a tall, fair-bearded, dissipated-looking personage. He affected an American accent, but was evidently one of those pernicious scoundrels, known as 'whitewashed Yankees,' who having been a few years in the States, make the fact an excuse for imitating the alleged license of the worst class of American rowdies.

'Now, look here, mister,' he was saying when the two brothers came up, 'ye don't allow, I guess, that we've come all the way from Bear Valley to let you Britishers freeze on to every likely gulch you con-clude to mark out on this all-fired rich placer. No, sirree. I reckon there's a smart chance of one handy now, and hyar goes my peg.'

Suiting the action to the word, he raised a stout pointed sapling end and prepared to drive it into the earth. At the same moment Jack Bulder with his brother Joe appeared on the scene, having both stripped to their working clothes for the shift.

Walking rapidly up, the elder brother appeared to have fully comprehended the situation, and backed up sturdily by Joe, was evidently ready to carry out mine or the Major's order. In the moment he cast eyes upon the tall man his manner changed suddenly and remarkably.

He rushed forward and, for a moment, his eyes glared at the stranger with an expression of hate, loathing, and wrath unspeakable, almost demoniac in intensity, which distorted his whole countenance. The direst earthly tragedy could furnish no fitter exposition.

His enemy—for such he was, doubtless, and the feud was not of yesterday—gazed at him with an air of deepest surprise, mingled with dismay.

'So it's you? blast you!' he hissed out, 'thief and betrayer that you are; hasn't the earth swallowed you up yet? Drop your peg and clear while you can. Why should I have your blood on my head? curse you! You won't?—then——'

Wholly dominated, as it seemed, by uncontrollable, furious passion, and, indeed, hardly giving his antagonist time to do anything, who stood speechless, still holding the peg, John Bulder dashed in upon him with the agility of a panther, and with scarcely less ferocity.

Pushing aside with his right hand the stake held cudgel-fashion as if it had been a walking-cane, he struck the stranger such a blow with his left as only an Englishman, early trained by the village *lanista*, can inflict. Down went the man prone, without sense or motion, and his antagonist stood beside him for one moment grinding his teeth and looking at the bleeding face, as one who hesitated whether he should follow up his natural instincts and stamp the life out of his foe as he lay beneath his feet.

At the same instant Joe Bulder walked forward and in a sort of mechanical manner knocked down the man nearest to him. All conflict being highly contagious, the Major and I advanced, upon which the others of the invading party threw up their hands with a gesture of disavowal, and declined the combat, temporarily.

'You seem rather hot property, mates,' said the more respect-able-looking one of the twain. 'I'm not agin a friendly round, when everything's agreeable; but it strikes me there's been enough rough and tumble for one morning. Yankee Jake brought us here; he said he knowed the ropes, and it was the regular thing to go in and jump a bit of ground or we'd never get none.'

'Well, now that you've discovered that it's a highly irregular thing,' said the Major, 'perhaps you'd oblige me by clearing out, and taking Mr. Yankee Jake with you, alive or dead. He looks like the last.'

That distinguished individual not being quite dead, slowly raised himself and looked around with an air of deadliest malice at his foe, who stood near him, as if with wrath unsated.

'Get up,' he said, 'you hound, and take your rotten carcass out of my sight. Why don't I drive my knife into you and make an end of it? It's almost worth while.'

Jack looked so tigerish, as he glanced at the bleeding wretch, laying his hand upon the sheath-knife which, sailor fashion, he always wore at his belt, that the man hastily, though with diffi-culty, arose, and, assisted by his mates, limped off the claim towards the place where their bundles lay. Before finally departing the tall man turned towards us, and with a face hardly human in its expression, bleeding and distorted as it was, groaned out,

'I owe you another for this, Ballarat Jack—d'ye hear? and I'll pay it yet, as sure as my name's Jake Challerson.'

The man whom he addressed made no answer, but with his hat over his eyes, and his breast still heaving with suppressed passion, passed into his tent. The only practical answer to the menace was that of Joe Bulder, who, tearing up their pegs, flung them after the retreating party.

There was no ulterior consequence to this rather serious affray, such as would on the morrow, as surely as it dawned, have taken place at Yatala. But the enemy, for reasons of their own probably, did not invoke the aid of the civil power. The police had their hands full of criminal cases and matters of more pressing import. And the Commissioner, when he heard of it, said he wished to heaven that other miners would take example by Pole and party, and not bother him about every trumpery jumping dispute.

We were not sorry to be done with our dispute on such easy terms, having had enough of law to last us our lives. Jack appeared to have done the right thing at the right time, as usual; still we could not help being impressed by the exagge-rated ferocity which he had exhibited in his encounter with the tall stranger.

'Those men were old miners, that was plain enough,' said the Major, 'and foes of no ordinary degree. I never saw mortal look more like a demon than Jack Bulder did after he had knocked the fellow down : and he did drop him, like a bullock. Never saw a straighter blow, fair in the mouth too. He won't eat or talk "worth a cent," as he would say himself, for some time to come.'

'And that ruffian hates him with no ordinary hatred either,' I said. 'I wonder what it is all about?'

'*Must* have been a woman mixed up with it,' mused the Major, with grim certainty ; 'no real hell-broth without *her* finger in it, trust me.'

'Pooh, pooh, Major, you're too hard upon the sex, altogether. Diggers quarrel about scores of things, apart from any question of that sort, as we know.'

'Quarrel, perhaps. But there is that kind of feud between those two men, if I mistake not, that only blood will quench, if opportunity serves. What did that scoundrel mean by calling him Ballarat Jack, too? Anything to do with the stockade affair?'

'Shouldn't wonder; but there were lots in it as well if he *was* there. He doesn't talk much about his Victorian experiences, I notice. By the way, how's Olivera?

'Well, I believe he's done rather better than usual for him. His party got £500 out of their last claim, which will about pay wages and something over. This is the fifth claim he has been in since he came here, and the first in which he has seen the colour. Isn't it wonderful? But I have known cases like it,' continued the Major, 'though rarely where the seeker was so persevering and scientific as our friend here. However, if the gold holds out, his luck *must* turn some day. No one ever knew the red to turn up for more than a certain number of times.'

'I suppose he'll be all right if the gold holds out, but a few years at this rate will see it out.'

'*He* says another generation won't, nor another after that,' replied the Major, 'that it's mathematically demonstrable.'

WHILE these minor events had been but ruffling the tide of time—ah me! what mere ripples upon the shoreless sea are all our lives, our deaths, all fateful agony between!—the great goldseeking multitude had swelled by constant influx to the population of a province.

There was no hill or dale within miles of the Commissioner's tents but was covered with tents and huts. The forest was crowded with grazing horses and working oxen. At night the vast illuminated area resembled an army encamped, an illusion to which the not infrequent rattle, as of musketry, as the miners discharged their firearms and loaded afresh, lent a reality.

When, in addition to the legitimate mining population, it was known that by far the greater number of the bad characters and escaped criminals from all the colonies had flocked hither in aid of whatever contingent might arrive from foreign sources, it may be guessed what a task lay before the officials in maintaining order and good government.

Certainly, trifling reinforcements had arrived, in the shape of more police, as also a couple of sub-commissioners, who, under Captain Blake's guidance, adjudicated in the less important cases which now arose in endless succession.

An escort, duly organised, left the camp weekly, with such an amount of gold stowed away in iron-bound boxes as would have gone far to induce the buccaneers in old Morgan's day to have landed at Sydney and marched across the continent for the express purpose of securing it. All things were apparently working fairly well in groove and gear, yet were there not wanting signs that awoke doubt in the minds of those who, like us, had for long years 'followed the diggings.'

'Strangers and pilgrims,' of all kinds and castes, were now so common that we should not have been a whit surprised to see the Cham of Tartary or the Sandjiack of Bosnia, each attended by a select body-guard in chain-mail, ride down Regent Street, as our main arterial thoroughfare, miles long, and crowded on every foot of frontage with shops and dwell-

ings, was designated. Nothing was more common than to see
tourists, whose every expression of speech and apparel showed
their total want of connection with the community, appear and
disappear after a short sojourn with magic suddenness.

One Sunday morning, resting from our labours, the Major
and I were at the camp, enjoying the rare luxury of a little
causerie with the Commissioner and his subalterns, when we
remarked four horsemen passing the outer edge of the palisades
towards a track which led adown and across a ford in the river.

Not ordinary bushmen, they were sufficiently near the type
to be recognised as Australians by people of our experience.
Their lounging seat upon their horses, yet with a certain air of
litheness and instinctive ease not so observable in riders of
European birth, settled the question in our minds. More than
one wore the loose cloak or wrap of stout woollen cloth, now
commencing to be in common use, borrowed from the wild
horsemen of the Pampas, and hence known as 'ponchos.'
Another peculiarity which did not escape our notice was, the
unusually high quality of the horses they rode.

'Come here, sergeant,' said the Captain, motioning to that
veteran, who at a short distance was intently observing the
cortége, 'did you ever see any of those fellows before ? I don't
like the look of them. Depend upon it, they are after no good.'

The sergeant saluted with due precision, and, standing very
erect, thus delivered himself—

'Well known to the police, Captain, every mother's son of
them ! The man on the black horse is Frank Lardner. The
big man next him is Ben Wall, one's a Victorian native, the
other hails not far from Yedden Mountain ; both have been up
for cattle and horse stealing, "done time," too. I don't see
O'Rourke. There's Gilbert Hawke and young Daly—dangerous
characters, the whole lot.'

'And can't you d-d-do anything t-t-to them ?' said Mr. Bagstock. 'L-l-lock 'em up or anything as a c-c-caution ; *pour
encourager l-l-l-les autres*, you know.'

'No charge against any of them at present, eh sergeant ?'
said the Commissioner. 'No warrant ?'

'Not so much as a summons, Captain, or sureties for the
peace—or it would be a grand chance entirely to take the lot.
I know where they're going to-night ; and I'm as sure as we
stand here that there's some villainy in the wind, if we could
only get to hear of it in time.'

'P-p-prevention's better than c-c-cure,' said Mr. Bagstock,
oracularly. 'I should l-l-lay them by the h-h-heels now, before
they've d-d-done anything.'

'Must act legally, my dear fellow,' said the Commissioner,
smiling ; 'we can't go beyond a reasonable amount of benevolent
despotism in a British colony. The law must be respected, and
the liberty of the subject.'

'What's the g-g-good of their being s-s-subjects, if you

c-c-can't take away their liberty ?' argued the advocate, somewhat before his age, of the yet undeveloped Jingoism. 'L-l-lock
'em up n-n-now, Commissioner, all for their g-g-good.'

As we thus discussed their characters and prospects, a turn
of the road brought the free companions in front of where we
were standing. One and all looked steadily at our group;
the leading horseman, indeed, touching his hat in a natural and
unstudied way as they rode by. I could not but admire, after
a fashion, the well-knit muscular figures, the keen, alert, hunter-
like appearance of these probable bandits. The careless abandon
of their horsemanship gave them a kind of picturesque air not
wholly devoid of romance, and I wished them from my heart a
better fate.

'*Morituri te salutant,* O Proconsul!' murmured the Major.
'I suppose all these fellows will be shot or hung within the next
year or two.'

'Very highly probable, indeed,' answered Blake. 'And before
that desirable event takes place, it will have cost the lives of
better men. It is a thousand pities I can't take Bagstock's
advice. In some countries that I have been in there would
have been a way of managing a *lettre de cachet* for such
known desperadoes.'

'I suppose trial by jury and all that kind of thing agrees
best with the British constitution in the long run,' said the
Major, 'but depend upon it there's nothing like martial law at
a pinch. The time may come when we shall be glad to resort
to it here.'

'Things are not so bad as all that,' said the Commissioner.
'Rather a serious row between the Donegals and the Cornish-
men on the South Lead last Sunday night. I hear two of them
and one of the Cousin Jacks were nearly killed outright. We
shouldn't have allowed that at Yatala. But here we have a
surplus population. Perhaps they'll reduce it in their own way.'

'Things are not going on as well as Blake thinks,' said the
Major, as we strolled homeward. 'He has had great luck in
holding down difficult populations, I grant. But his bridge
may break with him some day, and it is as likely to be here as
anywhere.'

'That other inspector of police that came over to stay a
week or so last month, said he believed all the "cross boys" of
all the colonies were congregated here; that there was bound
to be a row—by which he meant a revolt, I suppose—and that
nothing, in his opinion, could prevent it.'

'They can't hurt us if we're not slain outright, like Sir
Albany Fetherstonhaugh in the old border ballad by hard-
riding Dick Clym o' the Cleugh, and the rest. Our gold is pretty
regularly transmitted by escort. They won't rob that, I suppose.'

'Why not ?' I said. 'You don't suppose they have any
particular delicacy about stopping that or any other drag with
treasure aboard ! Fellows like those we saw to-day would be

an ugly lot to meet in one of those narrow rocky gaps, as they call them, over the line of ranges.'

'Not pluck enough,' said the Major. 'Horse-stealing and cattle-lifting are their favourite pastime, but standing before a police rifle, or a brace of revolvers held moderately straight, is not in the line of the native-born Australian brigand.'

'I hope you are a true prophet; but I hold a different opinion. These fellows, all unused to warfare as of course they are, are never averse to stand a shot or two for value received. But, like all Australians, when tempted to work or fight, they believe that the risk should not be disproportioned to the gain.'

'All the vices must be here by this time,' mused the Major. 'Even a modest assortment of the virtues is about to join us—from Warraluen, they say, even. The reefers, though on good gold there they say, are so worked on by the marvellous tales of the South Lead here, that they are nearly all leaving in a body, headed by your friend Black Ned. Have you seen Malgrade yet?'

'No, I heard of him though. He hasn't been here long. He camps down at that flat where those fellows we saw near the camp were making for. He and Poynter are working together, they say, and that big fellow with the whiskers, Harry Jefferson. He keeps the Pick and Pan public-house, and it's a rendezvous for all the horse thieves, homicides, and mixed ruffians on this side of the country. Blake told Merlin he ought to make a raid there some day; that it was a regular Alsatia.'

'There's something in the air I'm convinced. We shall hear news before long. There's a lot of these foreign fellows about that were at the Ballarat stockade. Joe Bulder says, too, there's a good deal of grumbling about the Chinamen.'

'It seems they have been mopping up some rich surfacing, and rather anticipated the European miners, who didn't like it.'

'Didn't they, indeed!' said the Major sardonically. 'Well I must say that for a nice, peaceful appointment, involving no special anxiety, or vexed questions of law or equity, commend me to the post of Commissioner on a large newly broken out goldfield.'

'I agree with you most thoroughly,' I replied. 'Taking the character of the population, the ceaseless complaints and disputes, the accidents and offences, the utter impossibility of foreseeing in what consequences the smallest ground of dissatisfaction if left unsettled may result, the complicated criminal and social ramifications underlying the whole fabric, on my honour, if I had a favourite enemy and could ensure his doing his work conscientiously, I would beseech

> 'The Fiend, to whom belongs
> The vengeance due to all our wrongs,'

to present him with the appointment.'

It seems unnecessary to state that nearly all our Yatala friends and acquaintances, as well as numberless strangers, were now located here.

Some of the streets were so full of well known names and faces that it appeared as if a portion of our old gold town had been lifted up bodily by a genie, as in the *Arabian Nights*, and dropped softly down upon the banks of the Oxley.

In all the earlier gold settlements, only those who had very good interests to represent stayed behind. As for Cyrus, he used to send disconsolate and wonderfully spelled letters, bewailing his lot at having to remain at a place where he could neither work nor play, where he had nothing to do but watch a shaft, and where there was now no more chance of a horse race than there was of a circus in a tea-tree scrub. He had a good mind, he said, to chuck up the whole thing and make tracks for the Oxley.

Not only friends but foes had naturally been borne in on the resistless wave of the exodus. Malgrade and Isaac Poynter, having joined unto them divers other evil spirits worse than themselves, were pursuing their old courses, from the circumstances of the place, with more unchecked license than of old. They had located themselves at a rich and strictly disorderly section of the goldfield, which had early gained an unenviable notoriety. More than one violent death had occurred there. Missing men, known to have left for town with gold, had never again been seen alive. A wild humorist had complimented it with the suggestive title of 'Murderers' Flat.' And, somehow, it had not lost the ominous name. Here were congregated, confessedly, the more lawless spirits of the place. Hither came outlaws from other colonies, over whose heads were warrants of apprehension certain to be executed if once their identity were established. This was the cover drawn by the police when any criminal of distinction was wanted; and on such occasions Mr. Merlin and his troopers invariably looked carefully to their arms, and neglected no precaution which might be necessary against surprise or resistance.

'From information received,' the sergeant was enabled to inform his superior officer that here the four mounted men who had passed the camp in the evening had remained during all the preceding day and night; that they had stabled their horses at the hostelry of Mr. Henry Jefferson, the Pick and Pan, where Malgrade had been seen in their company, besides other marked men; that in his, the informant's opinion, 'something good had been put up,' the nature of which benevolent enterprise he had not as yet been enabled to discover.

'So far, so bad,' Mr. Merlin condescended to remark. 'It would have been something to the purpose if you had got the least inkling of *what* they were going to have a shy at. I could have told *him* that Lardner, Wall, and Gilbert Hawke had something on hand. What it is we're all in the dark about.

What if we arrest the lot on suspicion of horse-stealing. I'll swear they never came honestly by their mounts.'

'Better wait,' counselled the sergeant. 'They're bound to be at some new game before long.'

'How do you know you'll have them then?' demanded Mr. Merlin fiercely. 'What with the confounded Donegal riots, and these infernal Chinamen, coming over here like locusts; and the cursed dance-houses; and just half the police here we ought to have—the superintendent keeps one so devilish short of men —the field is going to the devil; and I expect everything and everybody will come to grief.'

Really, there did seem to be some ground for Mr. Merlin's slightly bilious deliverance. His order-loving soul was daily vexed by reason of the irregularities which he was obliged to condone, knowing full well, too, that apparent trifles were prone to swell to dangerous dimensions.

Yet he relaxed not one jot or tittle of daily or nightly diligence; every one under his command was kept at the utmost tension of discipline possible to mortal man.

We, in a general way, thought that the greater concourse of adventurers massed together from so many different sources might, under unfavourable conditions, drift towards disaffection and revolt. But gold, the universal lubricator, was available in any quantity in those flush times, and to its efficacy we and all the moderates were fain to trust.

Truth to tell, we did not trouble ourselves deeply concerning the social life of the goldfields, or those difficulties which might beset a conscientious police officer in the discharge of his duties. We were sufficiently heedless of the morrow to disregard the future of the portion of Australia in which we found ourselves. We felt a benign trust in those who might come after. As long as we were not robbed or murdered—contingencies against which we felt tolerably certain of defence—we left all other considerations to fate and the lesser providences.

Then our daily labour was engrossing, its compensation profuse and exciting. If we could only manage to hold on, filling our pails at the golden spring which welled up so plentifully, all Australia might revert to a state of pliocene plasticity for anything we cared.

CHAPTER XVI

It is strange to note—stranger still to attempt to reason out the cause why, with such apparent unfairness, the gifts of fortune are in this world bestowed. Nowhere is the anomaly more glaring than on a goldfield. The widest divergence there apparently obtains between the abstractly just and the actual disposition of the prizes so long concealed by jealous Nature. The abstemious cultured toiler, careful for an absent wife and poorly-provided family, is steeped in endless ill-luck; while the bacchanal, the spendthrift, aye, the felon shedder of innocent blood, drives his pick into the golden heap at will. Who can reconcile these contradictions of circumstance with the eternal verities?

Thus, in despite of all moral obligations, and with but little apparent regard for the doctrine of compensation, the claims immediately around Murderers' Flat, unenviable locale as it might seem, yielded marvellously. Excepting the original 'Jewellers' Point,' there was no richer spot on the whole field. The prize-fighters and 'forcats,' burglars and bushrangers, who were said to be in a majority thereabouts, secured lawful gains of such value in a few weeks as should have converted them to virtuous ways their whole lives after.

So it might well have been. But the chief result of the wondrous gold spring, here so easily tapped, was a saturnalia comprehending a succession of terrible orgies, such as even in the darkest prison days the land had never known.

Here, fallen to the level of the dregs of humanity, could Algernon Malgrade reside, careless of all things but of the huge gains which he was apparently heaping up; while associating and carousing in his hours of abandonment with the vilest offscourings of society. Here was Dolores to be seen flaunting in extravagant silks and loaded with jewellery. And here, urged on by the same fatal thirst for gold, did Edward Morsley propose to settle afresh, bringing with him his wretched, despairing wife.

Of this fresh shuffling of the cards in the game of gold, amid the stakes of which my own life seemed so strangely commingled,

I was first informed by common rumour; more accurately soon after by a letter from poor Jane herself. The miserable, tear-stained missive ran—

'How can I find words to tell you that my husband has determined to leave here for the Oxley, and, worse than all a thousand times, to keep an inn at that horrible place, Murderers' Flat, of which I have heard such dreadful tales. He says we can make a fortune in a year. But I know the sort of life I shall lead there, the insults I shall be exposed to, the daily degradation in which I shall be compelled to share. I feel more than ever inclined to put an end to myself before this last horror comes upon me. I have borne enough, too much, and I solemnly swear that I will not consent to live there, whatever he may order me to do. If you wish me to keep this wretched life unended by my own hands, help me to get a passage home to England, dear, blessed old England—the very name makes me weep, how bitterly God only knows! You said you would do what you could for me—do this, the last and greatest kindness you can ever do for me, Hereward Pole, if you think the life worth saving of your most miserable, despairing friend, JANE.'

This was an appeal to which I could not remain deaf, unless I had had power to change my whole mental constitution. Whatever might be the consequences—and I foresaw some that were unpleasant, not to say dangerous and damaging, situated as I was—I was in honour bound to perform the service required of me. Had I not done so, I should have for ever regarded myself as basely selfish, cold-hearted, unworthy. Prudence strongly strove with me in my cooler moments. But had I listened to her dictates, I should ever have known inwardly that I had consulted my safety, so to speak, at the expense of every feeling of manhood, every thought of honour. I could not do it. I wrote at once to the forlorn creature to say that I would do what she wished: in the meanwhile I counselled prudence, and promised that I would at once take steps to carry out a plan for her escape, which I sketched out.

It involved, of course, no trifling sacrifice on my part, but I threw all such considerations to the winds. The die was cast. There was nothing more to be said. I immediately set about my preparations for going down to Sydney. Of course I explained matters to the Major, a preliminary stage which I rather dreaded. He heard me with an ominous silence. Then he thus delivered himself—

'I don't say you haven't acted generously, my dear fellow: it was very kind of you, and so on, but women are such confounded fools and so difficult to deal with, particularly when they belong to other people, that I shouldn't like to bet that you won't live to repent your good nature.'

'I shall never do *that*,' I said, 'whatever happens.'

The next thing necessary was to arrange for my journey by coach to Sydney, and, in this respect, fortune appeared to favour me. Mr. Bright, the Bank of New Holland manager, happened

to be going down at the same time. He had applied to the
Commissioner to go down with the escort, a privilege which
was on this occasion graciously extended to me.

'I know you're a good game shot, Pole,' he said. 'I saw you
shoot at Windaroo pigeon match when you beat Heathfield.
Bring that navy revolver with you, and we shall be a match for
all the bushrangers in the country. I always carry a brace of
"shooting sticks."'

'That's all very well, but they might take a sitting shot at
us, as O'Grady's father did at the sub-sheriff. I'm not so clear
that the escort's the best coach after all. There's a deuce of a
cargo this time, I hear, and we *might* drop in for "The Brigands
of the Black Forest" business.'

'All the better sport,' said the sporting financier. 'They
won't catch me napping, I'll be bound. And a bushranger's a
better mark than a blue rook, you must admit, Pole.'

'And a better shot, too, Captain,' said I. 'I wouldn't mind
a ruffle with some of your volunteers, but these fellows mean
business when they go on the war path. However, our passage
is taken.'

The first escort that left the Oxley after our claim had
washed up was an unusually rich one. Some of the others had
taken advantage of the late rains to do likewise. The result
was such an aggregation of the 'root of all evil' as sufficed to
set most of the unoccupied tongues on the ground wagging.
In any other country, perhaps, the transit of twenty-seven
thousand ounces of gold, worth more than a hundred thousand
pounds sterling, would have excited even more comment. But
we had been so much used to seeing bags and parcels, lumps
and handfuls of the precious metal handed about in dishes, tin
pannikins, and other homely utensils, that we scarcely thought
more of it as freight than of so much grain or potatoes.

In the hearts of others, however, there yet lingered, doubtless, covetous feelings and artful schemes more or less feasible
as to the illegal appropriation of what we held so lightly, one
parcel of which would in foreign lands yield perhaps a life-
long term of ease and self-indulgence.

Among the *enfans perdus* of the great mining army were
always a score or two of well-known men, always ready to
volunteer for a criminal forlorn hope, supposing the prize to be
sufficiently tempting.

The occasion of the escort leaving the police camp was one
which always involved critical observation and local excitement.
In every community there appears to be a distinct class, much
of whose time is devoted to the examination of contemporary
means of locomotion. They congregate to watch the steamer
arrive, the train depart, the coach come in, even the omnibus
roll heavily away with unfailing punctuality. At the Oxley,
the coach arriving bespattered or bedusted after the performance of a long fast journey over bad roads, was a daily miracle

at which, in despite of a sceptical age, the corps of observation never ceased to marvel. But the gold escort, combining as it did the prestige of a 'stage' with the mystery of a treasure-house, never failed to secure a yet larger and more representative body of spectators.

But that I had reasons of weight for visiting the metropolis at this particular juncture, I should not have quitted my post. I did not like leaving the barque before the anchor was down. I was wise enough to know that any break in a labourer's life makes return to steady work doubly difficult. But I was determined to arrange if possible for the passage to Europe of my old friend and playmate. I wished to save her from the dark fate, the final degradation, in which I had seen others as fair and erst innocent-seeming, engulfed before now. It appeared to me in the light of a sacred duty to my old home life, my old associates. And I was determined to carry it through at all hazards.

On this occasion Mr. Bright and I had from Captain Blake what was esteemed a rare and highly valued privilege on such occasions, namely, permission to 'travel by the escort,' as the phrase was, that is, upon the actual conveyance which carried the treasure boxes. Naturally such a permit was not granted indiscriminately; but from time to time a banker, a government official, or, as in my case, any resident of the place in whom the Executive had full confidence, was allowed to take his seat on the golden chariot. This equipage was represented by a strong, heavily-built American coaching waggon, which, with relays of four-horse teams, carried rapidly, and in general safely, the spoils of the alluvial drifts and quartz ledges.

'By Jove! you are a lucky fellow, Pole,' said the Commissioner, 'to be able to travel by Her Majesty's private conveyance with a thousand ounces of your own gold on board for pocket money when you get to town. I sometimes think I'll drop the service and take to digging in good earnest. What do you say? I'm afraid it's too late to buy into No. 4, or anything on the Sinbad Valley line. But just keep your eyes about you, Bright, when you are passing those confounded Eugowra Rocks. We've had a whisper that Lardner has been seen near Yedden Mountain, d——n him! You're armed, of course?'

I touched my left hip significantly.

'Of course. Too long in the country to travel unloaded. Bright has his battery, I know. Well, *bon voyage*. Remember me to the Chief if you see him. Tell him I'm worked to death.'

A stranger must have augured favourably of the early habits of the Oxley population who had witnessed the crowd assembled at five A.M. at the gate of the camp, at least half an hour before the departure of the escort. Certainly, the pure, fresh air of an Australian summer morn, dominating the stale and sickly odours of the tawdry bars and empty, dusty streets, might have seemed to some a sufficient reason. As the sun rose clear and ruby bright through the pale eastern pearl fringe, lighting up the sullen gorge of Eugowra, the frowning, sombre mountain range, my heart rose as if in unison with the gracious aspect of Nature, and each purer, more elevated feeling seemed strengthened and exalted. How mysteriously invisible is the form of coming evil at certain seasons ; how darkly soul-shrouding its very shadow at others.

On this day, however, success and hope encompassed me, bearing down all doubt and opposition. The Major and Joe came to see us off, and as I passed through the crowd I was sensible of respectful and admiring criticism.

'That's Harry Pole, of No. 4 Liberator, and the best claim on Greenstone atop of it,' said an old Yatala shepherd, charmed to have the opportunity of explanation. 'Richest claim on the lead, but disputed. Got £20,000 in the bank, and two thousand ounces in that bloomin' escort. Very awkward, ain't it ?'

'What's he want to go to town for ?' queried a cynical listener. 'What 'ud you or I, mate, want to go to town for, supposin' we washed up once a fortnight to that tune ? Wants to have his 'air cut Paris-fashion, or to see the theayter, or leave his card on the Governor-General, may be.'

'Don't they never rob the escort ?'

'Well, not much they don't, though I wouldn't say, mind ye, as it mightn't be done by men as 'ud stand a shot for a big touch. They'd have to work it to rights though. Here they come.'

At this moment the camp gates were opened, and the well-groomed, high conditioned team, fed with corn that cost a guinea a bushel, and with hay that was much dearer than loaf sugar (it was a dry year and the crops were bad and grass there was none), plunged at their collars, and the heavy but well-hung drag rolled out. The treasure boxes, to the number of half a hundred or more, were lifted out from Sergeant Mac-Mahon's room, and counted over carefully to the sergeant in charge of the escort. They were small, compact, and iron-bound, but judging by the way in which they were lifted, remarkably heavy for their size.

On the box sat a senior-sergeant of police, a tall, slight, soldierly-looking man, with a black beard which fell to his breast, and who handled the reins like one to whom such things were familiar. A trooper fully armed, with a Snider rifle between his knees in addition to the navy revolver at his belt, sat beside him. In the body of the drag, where I and Mr. Bright were accommodated with seats, were two more con-stables similarly armed. A couple of mounted men rode in advance, and as many a short distance behind. The distance was pretty accurately preserved, under all circumstances. These troopers carried short breech - loading carbines. Well mounted and admirably turned out, as to uniform and equipment—for Mr. Merlin's eye spared no slovenliness of dress on drill—they might have passed muster in any cavalry troop in Europe.

That distinguished official was there, of course, coldly observant, and with such an air of guarded approval as caused every person connected with the equipage and service, from the gold-receiver, Sergeant MacMahon, to the last pair of mounted troopers, to consider within themselves whether some detail of dress, duty, or deportment had not been left unperformed.

'*Bon voyage*, Bright ; good-bye, Pole ; good-bye, Harry,' were the last farewells that met my ear from the Major and the crowd. 'Good luck and a jolly trip to you !' And we were away.

The weather was superb, my companion cheerful and amusing ; the roads, though occasionally precipitous, by no means painfully uneven. The occasion was apparently fortunate. For a while I fully realised the pleasantness of change and leisure, the cessation of the daily revolution of the gold mill, a machine which becomes as wearisome in time as all other monotonously coercive occupations.

Unconsciously I commenced to dwell upon the still remaining obstacles to the homeward voyage, the contemplation of which, as too feverishly exciting, I always resisted. While at work, it had a tendency to unnerve and unfit for this dull unimaginative frame of dogged endurance which is labour's truest ally. Now I could for a short time revel in the roseate tints and golden haze wherewith the great scene-painter, Fancy, embellishes the dingy properties of life's dull stage.

A few more months' work, a few more washings up at the present most satisfactory rate of yield, No. 4 free from legal hindrances, fairly gone at, and, with the wages men we could afford to put on, worked out, the vein of auriferous drift would be quickly exhausted. Every square yard of it would be brought to the light of day, puddled, sifted, turned from gravel to minted gold by the rude skill of the miner—that latter-day alchemist.

Then, at last—would Fate permit such bliss ?—I should be in possession of a sum of at least fifty thousand pounds, perhaps even more. I should be firmly, indefensibly possessed of that title to respect, which every man holds who can point to a competence hewn by his own labour from the sterile, hard, at times adamantine quarry of labour. I should have done this almost literally. I should have disproved every word of disparagement that my enemies could have ever used against me ; have confirmed the faith of true friends ; have justified the sublime devotedness of my early love, my peerless Ruth ; have earned the right to a future of dignified ease, if not of unalloyed enjoyment.

In the sophisticated methods of approval which hold good, in this our day, it may well be questioned whether a man does not receive a larger meed of honour and respect who has been simply the recipient of an ancestral hoard. Such lands, such wealth, such rank, represent, rateably, the labour and the prudence, the valour and the wisdom, it may well be but the servility or the greed, of the dead men who have gone before. Their descendant, by no merit of his own, becomes the fortunate possessor not only of the lands and the money bags ; even by a curious fiction is credited with the possession of a large share of the valour and the intellect which he has but little chance of displaying, and of which it may be he is wholly devoid. He may never have done deed or uttered speech which the humblest labourer on his estate could not have matched. Yet, in this Pantheon of false gods and outworn idols, men and women make obeisance yet more lowly to the puppet of fortune than to the proved possessor of those qualities by which families are founded and races are ennobled.

Be this as it might I had become sufficiently democratic under my goldfields' training to believe that as Hereward Pole, the returned Australian miner, I should be able to hold up my head in my own country to some purpose with the proceeds of No. 4 and the Greenstone Dyke transmuted into a bank balance. Even as an unknown adventurer of fairly decent appearance and manners, with my trusty cheque-book by my side, that modern Excalibur, I could hew my way to the notice of the Queen of the Tournament. But though few knew, and fewer cared about such a matter of musty genealogy here, I was none the less Hereward Pole, a cadet of the ancient house of Shute, in honour and antiquity second to none of the companions of the Norman conqueror.

How the days would fly, after I had realised and gone to town on my final journey to take my passage by the first mail steamer ! What calm delight to rest from work, even from thought, long dreamy days, gliding on the breezeless, languorous Red Sea, or, in glowing sunset hours, to watch the unresting surge at play on the long mysterious coast-line of Africa, ancientest land of wonder and of dread. Past all mortal visions of happiness would be that day of days, *should it ever arrive*, ah me ! when the white cliffs, the emerald-green fields of long-lost, long-loved Albion would greet these desert-worn eyes !

Then would, indeed, heaven open for me—here below. Then would that whitest, purely radiant angel, gazing at me with the well-remembered, tender-glowing orbs of love——

'Curse that infernal tree—right across the narrowest bit of the gap ! Wonder whether it blew down, or whether those Yedden Mountain ruffians put it there on purpose ; blank, blank,' objurgated the sergeant. 'Jump out you two and take the axe ; we might shift it.'

Here was an interruption with a vengeance. Brought down from realms celestial to this saddest sordid sphere, where fierce or grovelling passions alternately debase hopeless humanity.

CHAPTER XVII

'THERE'S something like a gun-barrel behind that spotted gum-tree,' said Mr. Bright, who had dwelt in the bush in his youth, 'and I'll swear I heard a horse stamp. Save your powder and aim low all, of you, whatever you do.'

'Look sharp, men!' growled the sergeant. A cross-looking chap, on a black horse, was seen hereabouts yesterday, with another man answering Gilbert Hawke's description. If Darkie and his rider's anywhere handy now, it will be rough work in this beastly gap. Good God! here they are. Close up, men, and defend the escort—steady—fire!'

As the word of command left the sergeant's lips, a volley of firearms resounded, reverberating from each side of the rocky ravine, called The Gap, which we had a short time since entered. At the same time a body of nearly twenty men showed themselves from behind trees and rocks.

I awake—my dream, how rudely shattered—to a full sense of my immediate surroundings. We were attacked by bush-rangers. The far-famed pass known as Eugowra Rocks had been picked for the scene of conflict.

This now celebrated spot was on the saddle of a lofty granitic range of hills which intersected our road to the metropolis. A tedious ascent led to a spot where the escort coach had just space to wind between the huge monoliths that reared themselves frowningly in our path. The locality was densely wooded. No element was wanting for our discomfiture. A long stretch of gently descending ground led to the champaign below, where the road was easy and pleasant, without hill or wood to mar the path to the farthest horizon.

We had all been looking forward to this reward of previous anxiety, yet destined never to reach it. All the men were masked and otherwise fully disguised. They had apparently lain in wait in this narrow defile. Now we knew why our progress had been barred. The tree had been felled solely for that purpose.

Our return fire was quicker than they could have calculated upon. More than one shot told. It was not the first time I had burned powder in earnest. Mr. Bright fired as fast and steadily as if he had been engaged in his favourite sport of pigeon-shooting. There was little time for observation, but I thought I recognised a figure that stole from behind a huge rock to take up a nearer position to our ill-fated equipage.

For several minutes, long enough for hours they seemed to me, the fusillade was sharply kept up on either side. And more than one smothered cry or savage oath told that our ammunition was not all wasted.

The troopers who rode behind had closed up. Throwing themselves from their horses, and taking what cover they could from the wheels and body of the vehicle, they kept their Terry rifles busy. But we fought at a disadvantage in every way. The situation had been carefully calculated. The immense boulders on either side of the gorge furnished only too complete cover for the attacking party. Trapped and surprised, we had fallen into an ambuscade laid for us only too successfully.

Debarred from opening out into skirmishing order, we were exposed to a concentrated fire from hidden enemies. They were enabled to take sure and deadly aim at us from behind their more complete defences.

But no man flinched. The troopers—one of whom was a smooth-cheeked youngster, just newly landed in Australia, who had left the paternal rectory but lately for the force, *faute d'autre* —loaded and fired like veterans of the Old Guard.

'That's Malgrade, or the devil,' said I to Mr. Bright, 'he that just slipped behind the rock from the tree. I know his walk, d——n him : no mask can disguise him from *me*.'

'Just what I thought myself,' said Bright; 'let's give it him together, the next time he shows. We ought to nail him between us.'

At the first volley two of our men had dropped, if not mortally wounded, still decidedly *hors-de-combat*. We could not disguise from ourselves that our chance was bad of coming out unscathed or even of successfully defending our precious freight. With every fresh volley one or other was wounded, and every moment the impossibility of long sustaining the unequal fight was felt. Neither could we retreat and carry the gold with us.

Of the good team that had pranced so gaily out of the camp gates this morning one horse lay dead, and the other, badly hit, had broken traces and bolted through the forest. One of the wheelers was unharmed, but the other had two bullets through his body, and though still on his legs was evidently suffering internal agony, as ever and again he turned his eyes plaintively on us and backward to his bleeding flank, as if mutely asking why he should be mixed up in his master's combats.

The escort sergeant had been hit at the first discharge, as indeed had most of us, slightly or otherwise. He, however, held himself straight, and not only fired rapidly himself, but

kept the whole of his party well in hand, urging them not to
quit cover unnecessarily, but to aim steadily and surely whenever the bushrangers exposed themselves.

'They'll get tired of it if we can only keep them off for
another hour,' he said. 'I don't think they care about coming
to close quarters. We may get assistance before dark.'

It was not to be. Even as he spoke the brave fellow's face
was changing. I noticed the blood staining his blue uniform a
bright crimson, where it welled from his side in heavy, quick-
recurring drops.

They were the last words he ever spoke. The next moment
he swayed for a moment and fell heavily to the earth. A cry
of exultation at the fall of our leader rose mockingly amid the
crags, and a rush still nearer was made by the masked assail-
ants, who now exposed themselves more freely, as if sure of
victory.

The man whom I took to be Malgrade stepped cautiously
from behind his rock; at that moment Mr. Bright and I fired
without a second's loss of time at his left shoulder. He fell, but
was dragged behind the rock by some one, apparently also concealed there, and who was a taller and broader man than any
one we had as yet noticed. At the same time the whole fire of
the party poured down upon us, and both Bright and I felt
ourselves wounded again.

'Only winged, I think,' said Bright, raising his right arm.
'Might drop out of bounds, but I don't think they'll bag me this
time. How do you feel, Pole? where are you touched?'

'Under the rib, and I don't like the feel of it,' said I. 'I
wonder if we drilled that scoundrel Malgrade, if it *was* him.
By Jove, that young Rowan's done.'

Two troopers lifted up the poor youngster, shot through the
body and apparently dying.

'We can do nothing by stopping here, Mr. Bright,' said the
second in command, a grizzled sun-burned senior-constable,
who looked as if he had seen much service. 'We shall all get
potted and not save the gold, either; that's what I look at.
The best thing is to retreat across to that scrub alongside of
Stony Pinch. I know a track down it. I don't think they will
follow us there.'

'Leaving the ship while there's a plank to stand on is
devilishly mean work,' said Bright, blazing away in quick
succession as he spoke, 'but I suppose we can't do any good this
time. The Sergeant stone dead, poor fellow; that youngster's
little better, and Pole here doesn't look as if he'd hold out
long. I suppose we can take the horses and retreat in good
order?'

'We can manage that,' said the senior-constable. 'They
only want the gold, blast them; and the sooner we get the black
trackers on the trail, then the sooner we shall have a chance of
seeing some of it back.'

So, keeping our faces to the foe and maintaining a brisk fire, we commenced to retreat slowly, leading the unwounded horses and carrying the young trooper with us. As soon as it was seen that we had given up trying to defend the gold, no attempt was made to follow us up. Doubtless, it was thought that in our desperation we should not prove less formidable than at present.

One man only among the bushrangers had any personal animosity to gratify. This was Malgrade, if, indeed, it was as I supposed. And he had apparently received his quietus for a time. A few dropping shots followed us as we made our way slowly and with difficulty through the forest, which commenced to become more dense until it ended in a perfect thicket, or what to Australians is known as a scrub.

Here we struck after a while into a narrow, well-worn path, which led down a steep rocky defile, tortuously but distinctly. In less than a couple of miles we debouched upon a comparatively level and thickly-grassed meadow or creek flat. Here it was proposed that we should rest, while the senior-constable, who knew the country well, rode across to the nearest police station, whence the tidings could be at once sent to the Oxley, and half a hundred other headquarters. No time would be lost in setting a brace of black trackers on the trail of the robbers, who no doubt would have expended no unnecessary time in clearing out with the treasure. Assistance would, of course, be sent to us without a moment's delay.

The trooper dashed off on the best horse of the party, within three minutes of our halt, leaving us in the gathering twilight in no very enviable position. As fast falling shades of night commenced to gather around, the darksome trees which fringed the creek, the gliding waters which murmured along its channel, the heavy hanging cliffs of the dimly outlined mountain, gained a weird and melancholy tone. Our feelings were closely in unison with the solitary scene, the closing day. They could hardly be otherwise than mournful. We had started in the morning full, if not of high hope, of that cheerful confidence in the future, which is born of untried dangers, untempted perils. The gold which we bore with us was pleasantly connected with our tools and avocations. The day was bright, the journey little more than a pleasure excursion.

Now how darkly, how irrevocably all was changed! A dead man and dying horses lay beside the stranded carriage which had borne us forth so gaily in the morning. Stiff with our wounds, hungry, cold, and weary, our attitudes were gloomy and despairing. The pale countenance of the wounded man, streaked with blood, looked more ghastly in the flickering light of the fire which one of the others had at length lighted.

Is it a heated imagination, or are there other forms, strange shadows, gliding around the watch-fire and amid the dark-leaved water-oaks? They gather around upon the wounded man, whose

laboured breathing I seem to hear with ever increasing distinctness.

'Bright, I say, Bright! don't let those people crowd so closely
round Rowan, they will smother him. Good God! do you not
hear?'

'Your head must be going, Pole,' said the banker seriously,
who was sitting on a log smoking resignedly and watching the
wounded man. 'Come over and let me see where they touched
you. Take care——'

But I hear no more. I rise and stagger blindly forward, and
the blood pours from my side. I see a crowd of spectres hurrying towards me—my head swims, and my eyes are darkened as
in death.

When I recovered my senses I was lying under a tree in the
cool moonlight, with Bright bending anxiously over me. All
was over now, it seemed to me.

How joyously had I marked the sun rise over this very
mountain, as I rose from my humble couch at Yatala. And
now the same orb had but set, and with it the sun of Hereward
Pole's fortune. What a satiric comment on man's vain life and
vainer hopes. All was gone. Hope and fortune. Love, gold,
and life itself, and here I lay under this darksome forest tree
with the life-blood fast ebbing away, and scarce a trace would
be left of a wasted existence, blighted career.

Well, the news would soon reach Allerton Court; the country
busybodies would be enabled to verify their long cherished
foreboding that nothing would come of my gold-seeking
adventure, and that everything had turned out exactly as
they expected from the very first day of the Squire's sanction
to his daughter's ridiculous engagement.

Then I died! Can a man die more than once? Is it not a
real death when the flickering senses first dwindle down to the
lowest point of consciousness? Men arouse themselves as at a
faintly-heard summons once more to animate the sinking
frame, in pain and mutest agony, clinging with the might of
despair to every last buttress of the ruined citadel. Then an
appalling sense of general departure from this long accustomed
mortal tenement joined with a mysterious boding horror of
undefined doom. A time of coldness, numbness, deadly still-
creeping paralysis over the centre of sensation—then utter
darkness—extinction.

It would appear that I had not finally quitted this lower
earth; for I re-opened my eyes yet again. They rested not
upon satanic or celestial personages other than Mr. Inspector
Merlin, who was sitting by my bedside in an attitude of (for
him) great patience and amiability.

He rose quickly to his feet with a sigh of relief, remaining
silent for a short space so as apparently to enable me to realise
the fact that I was in a rude but neatly-furnished slab cottage,

accommodated with all the comforts which a small farmhouse could furnish. Then he spoke—

'Well, Pole, old man, you're worth a brace of dead men yet —a near thing, though. The doctor said that a shade closer to the main artery, and you would have been gathered to your strong-minded ancestor the Legate. Now you've got such a good-looking, neat-handed nurse to look after you, you're sure to come out right.'

'What has become of the other—fellows, and—the gold?' said I feebly. 'Who stuck us up?'

'Why, Frank Lardner, of course, b——t him!' said Mr. Merlin with perhaps allowable anger. 'We know that Wall, Gilbert Hawke, and Daly were with him, besides half a dozen other ruffians of less note. Sergeant Webber is dead and buried. Constable Rowan not expected to live. Watson has got a bullet in his hip, and will be lame for life. Bright was winged, and not much the worse for it. The gold was all taken of course, but the "wire" brought a cordon of police round them within twelve hours, and we know they can't have got clear off with it. We have great hope of recovering the lot within a month.'

'Thank God for that,' I said. 'I ought perhaps to think of my life first; but if all the gold was gone I shouldn't think the other very valuable. And so it was Master Frank, was it, with Wall, Gilbert Hawke, and the rest? What a pity such smart fellows should have taken to the bush and commenced with such a cold-blooded murderous outrage.'

'Pity,' said Merlin, drawing his lips slightly back, and showing his white teeth in a way which reminded me of the jaguar aroused. 'I'd find them pity if I saw them at the end of a half-inch line; and by —— you will see them there one day, as sure as my name's Mainwaring Merlin. Think of poor Webber, what a fine fellow he was! I shall never get such another accountant either,' he added reflectively. 'By God! I could hang them with my own hands. And now I must be off. Mrs. Morton, or whatever you call her, will be here directly. I quite envy you.'

Here Mr. Merlin took himself off, and went on the war-path, which indeed he had seldom quitted by night or by day since the terrible news of the Great Escort Robbery. Tireless, pitiless, even at the highest pitch of energy and alertness in mind and body, he was a dangerous enemy for the Yedden Mountain gang, as they were called, to arouse, and so indeed they found it before all was done. Had I been strong enough to smile, I must have done so at the *naïveté* of his regret for poor Sergeant Webber, whose clerkly qualities, plucky and clever officer as he was in other respects, mainly endeared him to Mr. Merlin's organising soul.

The sound of his footsteps had hardly died away when the rustle of a woman's dress told me that the nurse of whom he spoke was approaching. Strange was it that something.

even in that symbolical token of woman's presence brought
back to me a memory of the long vanished past. But I had
taxed my strength too much. Falling helplessly back upon the
pillow, I fainted. I had a dim, confused recollection of feeling
my forehead bathed, of the tender touch of a woman's hand
passing lightly over it, of a cordial held to my lips. With a
painful effort I raised my head and opened my eyes. I could
hardly trust the evidence of my senses. I thought I must be
wandering again, and that I fancied myself at Dibblestowe Leys;
for the face which was bending over me, full of womanly
tenderness, was the face of Jane Mangold.

I saw again the bright blue eyes, the soft fair hair, the delicate features of her who, before my knowledge of Ruth Allerton,
had been to me the embodiment of fairest womanhood. At the
first glance she seemed unchanged. Then I marked with pain
the deepened lines in her face, the saddened brow, the worn
anxious look, which had replaced the girlish defiant expression
which I had always associated with her laughing eyes and
saucy smile. The sad handwriting which the world and its
pitiless warfare inscribes upon its victims was there indelibly
imprinted.

'Jane,' I said, 'dear Jane, are we both at the Leys again; or
how do I see you here? Ah, why did you come to me?'

'How could I help coming to nurse you, when I heard you
were dying?' she said. 'Have you not been a friend—a brother
to me? Have you not saved me from what is worse than
death? And am I to do nothing for you to show my gratitude?
Mr. Merlin told me your life might depend upon careful
nursing.'

All this she uttered in her old quiet way of speaking when
anything moved her more than common. Once more vividly
real, under the shadow of death. How the old life career came
back to me.

'But, Jane,' I said, 'people will talk, and you know at
Yatala it does not take long——'

'If I am to be the cause of shame and disgrace to you, I will go
away and hide my wretched self the moment you have recovered
from your wound. It shall never be said that I helped to harm
you—you who have been better than a brother; but the doctor
says, even now, that you may not get over it. And I thought
that she, that Miss Allerton, might be glad to know that a
friendly hand, even if it was poor Jane Mangold's, helped to do
what only a woman can for man at the last.' Here she buried
her head in her hands and wept unrestrainedly.

'You are right, Jane,' I said, 'and I will answer for my dearest
Ruth, that she will be grateful to you, if I see her face no more,
for smoothing my pillow before the last sleep. We have always
been friends, why should we not be true to each other to the
last? Let us keep faith with ourselves and the absent, and the
world may say its say.'

She raised herself and looked wistfully at me.

'I only know that I should be glad if I were in her place,' said she, 'and would thank on my knees any one that did for my lover what I will do for you in your hour of need.'

Here I could no longer support the fatigue of conversation and, for a space, again 'effaced myself.'

THIS affair, of course, created an immense sensation, not only in the immediate neighbourhood of the Oxley rush, but throughout Australia. Certain lawless acts and deeds had been committed on all diggings. We were not, as communities, entirely free from crime, although, as I have attempted to describe, the average of serious offences against life and property was certainly lower than in many settlements of older date and higher pretensions to civilisation. But now any delusion as to the gradually improving tendency of the race was rudely dispelled.

A new, startling, and flagrant outrage had been committed. The affair had been arranged with laborious foresight. The details had been carried out with only too great elaboration. The result was complete and successful. Her Majesty's servants and lieges had been shot down in cold blood. The escort, always intimately associated with Government guarantee and protection, had been captured. Hard-working miners had been despoiled of their well-earned gold. And by whom had this been done? By whom planned, by whom carried out? Not by the fierce desperadoes of other climes, the probable outcome of piracies on the Spanish Main, of murders in Sonora, or gambling in the hells of San Francisco, but by 'sons of the soil,' as political patriotism forcibly expressed the fact, by men reared amid the forest-farms of the interior, who in their youth had been peaceful stockmen and station-labourers, who had followed the flocks or hunted the wild horse from boyhood, amid the streams and gullies of that very Yedden Mountain which rose dark and as if frowningly in the sight of the scene. It was to the philanthropist a grievous and discouraging fact. To the pessimist an unholy triumph. Well might the poet deprecate the *auri sacra fames*. Better hopes hitherto had been entertained. But now the country was obviously going to perdition; the men and women reared therein would be basely degenerate from a race whose flag the world had been forced to fear in war and respect in peace for a thousand years.

Such were the reflections of many honest Australian citizens, who deplored as deeply the nationality of the criminals as the criminality of the deed. In the meantime all imaginable steps were taken for the capture of the outlaws and the recovery of the treasure. With this latter attempt greater success was reached than with the former. So complete was the cordon with which the robber band was surrounded, so ceaseless the vigilance that left no hour of the day or night free from tireless tracking and close pursuit, that the heavily laden pack-horses with which they had commenced the transport of the gold boxes were abandoned, and the larger portion of the original gold recovered.

Among the treasure-trove lay, fortunately, sealed and accurately labelled, as were all the separate parcels, the leathern bag which contained the contribution of Greenstone Dyke, addressed to Mr. Hereward Pole, Bank of New Holland, Sydney. So that with the somewhat serious deduction of 'a vision of sudden death,' a gunshot wound hard by a vital spot, considerable loss of time, money, and peace of mind, matters in a few weeks would be much as they had been before my departure for Sydney.

But the capture of the band of outlaws was not so soon accomplished. Of all outlaws, the Australian bushranger has proved the most difficult to secure after a series of crimes has rendered him desperate.

'Native, and to the manner born,' he possesses natural advantages amid the wilds and fastnesses of the interior, with which the officials of the law find it difficult, in some cases impossible, to contend. A horseman of matchless skill and daring from childhood, with the best blood in England, aye even of the desert, often at his control, he is the equal of the Apache or the Comanchee in the saddle, their superior in strength and courage. In the broken and mountainous country near which he is generally concealed, he has the advantage of scouts of unrivalled activity and acuteness. These 'bush telegraphs,' as the modern robber slang has dubbed them, are of all avocations and both sexes.

The brown-faced urchin lounging after his father's cows on a three-legged screw, with a ragged saddle and green-hide girth, fixes his watchful half-savage eyes upon the troopers as they enter the forest and disappear up the winding slate-strewed ravine. They wear rough tweed suits, and old felt hats; they are riding on stockmen's saddles with rusty stirrup irons. But *he* knows them for all that, and marks them down unerringly. The bare-legged girl tending the small flock of sheep, or racing after the milker's calves, meets the strange horsemen then camped by a creek, and demurely answers their questions as to strayed bullocks. She knows 'the traps' by a dozen signs visible to the initiated. And at midnight or before dawn the robber in the traditional cave or the dismal deserted hut knows that the avengers of blood are on his trail, and flees noiselessly as the night-hawk to yet more secluded haunts.

How should they be run down, surrounded, or surprised? Well armed, well mounted, fearless horsemen, and for the most part quick-eyed and keen of hearing as the hunted deer before the questing hound; strong in desperate need, and brave with the demoniac feeling that liberty and life have been forfeited irrevocably, small wonder that the latter-day bushrangers of the Australian continent have, ere now, for months and even years defied the concentrated efforts of the respectable portion of the community to arrest or exterminate them. Such bands have for months, even longer periods, sufficed to keep a whole country-side in a constant state of peril and anxiety. Appearing here on a given day, robbing the mail, and parading every traveller on a certain line of road with almost ludicrous impartiality—within forty-eight hours besieging an isolated station, or robbing a bank two hundred miles away.

After more weary days Dr. Winthrop, who had ridden hundreds of miles in my case alone, at length thought I was well enough to be moved.

'By Jove! Harry, a narrow squeak,' he said; 'if the bullet had been from a navy revolver instead of one of those derringer toys, it would have made all the difference. Couldn't have gone a thread closer without rupturing the cœliac axis. Mrs. What's-her-name here has nursed you admirably. Old friend of yours, she says. Helped to save you as much as anything. Very pretty woman she is too. What's she going to do now she's left that brute her husband?'

'Going home to her friends in England, and so you can tell any one that takes an interest in my affairs,' I said, rather stiffly.

'Quite right, quite right, glad to hear it,' said the doctor. 'People *will* talk, you know, especially at the diggings. Glad to know there's no foundation, etc. Yarns get about. So the sooner you're back at you're own camp the better. I'll tell the Major or Bulder they can drive over for you any day. A mattress laid on one of those light American traps wouldn't shake you much. I suppose you heard about Merlin's men picking up the pack-horse, with ever so many gold-bags—Greenstone Dyke lot all right among them, and so on.'

'I did hear of it,' I said languidly. 'Caught any of the gang yet?'

'No, confound them, and not likely to. The police are worked off their legs. Though they've been very near them once or twice, they've always got off. Been sticking up people and places all over the country; might catch me as I go back—no knowing. They're never hard on the learned professions though. Sure to want them all some day. Good-bye, Harry.'

The day after this conversation Joe Bulder arrived with a quiet horse and a light tray buggy, the movable seat of which had been taken out. A mattress with all requirements in the shape of feather pillows, etc., contributed by a lady neighbour and Mrs. Yorke (for Cyrus had come over to work my share, and his wife refused to remain) was placed therein. With Joe's help and that of Jane I was able with great difficulty, pale, tottering, and death-like, feeble as I was, to stretch myself on my improvised ambulance. Jane sat by my side, while Joe walked by the horse's head, and patiently led the animal with a careful avoidance of all inequalities in the road.

'Yon's a queer start,' he said, after a long pause. 'If some of the folk at the Leys could see us three now, they'd think all the gold in Jewellers' Point wouldn't ha' tempted them to cross seas. When word coomed as you was killed along o' the sergeant and all the escort clean gutted, I felt loike as though I'd never stay another day in the land. I offered my share to Mr. Olivera for ten thousand down, and I'd ha' been off back next mail sure as there's hops in Kent. Dang the country and the people too. I'm nigh sick on it all. I could wish, loike some folk says, I'd never seen it.'

Jane gave a deep, half-unconscious sigh.

Joe had relapsed into his provincial dialect, as he generally did in moments of excitement, and doubtless failed for a short time to realise the very decided advance of his personal and pecuniary position, maugre even such adventures as gunshot wounds, escort robberies, and revolutions.

'Never mind Joe, the battle's not over yet,' I said. 'It's not like an Englishman to jack up and give these fellows best. We'll see some of these fellows hanged yet—those that are not shot, I mean. And talking of being hanged, was that fellow Malgrade at the township when the news came?'

'Nay, that he was na,' replied Joe, looking surprised, 'for a man I know told me as he should go to his camp to borrow a long-handled shovel early that morning. They was both away, he and his mate too; yon long chap, as he always called Harry, him with the big whiskers. This man tells me they didn't get back till nine o'clock; more than that, Harry's big bay horse was knocked up, and Malgrade's hadn't no more than a crawl in him. They'd come a goodish step by that'n, and no mistake.'

'How do you know, Joe?'

'Why, you see, Malgrade's horse is a bit of blood—only on the cross like himself; he's won a good many races on the sly like, droppin' in at country meetings on the quiet, and always in condition, and big Harry has been a cattle stealer every one says. He's a heavy weight, but yon bay horse of his can carry him like as he was a schoolboy. They'd ridden no twenty mile that night, nor fifty neither, it's my thinkin'.'

'Had they anything with them?'

'Not as he could see. Malgrade had a poncho on, and might have carried a bushel bag inside without any one being the wiser. But they didn't want to talk. Malgrade had a stiff arm —said his nag had fell with him and chucked him ont' the shovel, and he went off, as he was late for his work.'

'I'll lay my life both those fellows were in the robbery. I have a kind of recollection of a tall man on a big bay horse in the confusion, but of course they were all masked.'

'They'd both rob a church, it's my opinion of 'em,' said Joe, 'and Malgrade wouldn't stick at cutting the priest's throat after if there was aught to be made of it. As for big Harry, he's an old pal of all those Yedden Mountain boys, for I've heard him say as much.'

'If you talk any more you'll undo all my nursing,' said Jane with a wistful look, 'and you *do* want to see the Leys again, and —another place, Hereward, *don't* you ?'

When I found myself back at the tent at the Oxley things looked much as usual. Indeed the passing wave of excitement consequent on 'the unparalleled outrage,' as the *Beacon* for once truly characterised the late occurrence, had long subsided. Events of considerable magnitude are so quick and recurrent in large mining centres that, as human nature is constituted, the mental expense of prolonged interest is too great to be borne. So having well digested the facts, stupendous as they might have appeared in an old-world place like the Leys, that the escort had been robbed, policemen shot, the gold carried off and partly recovered, Harry Pole, of No. 4 Liberator, and Greenstone, badly hurt, and the bushrangers still at large, eating and drinking, work and play, digging and dicing, litigation and love-making, crushing and washing up, were all being eagerly transacted at the Oxley, much as though nothing had ever happened contrary to the ordinary course of life.

Jane was temporarily located with Mrs. Yorke, and Cyrus bidden by his wife to betake himself to the nearest hotel for the present.

'There'll have to be some one to nurse Harry for a good month to come,' said that matron, 'and I've not got the time to do it, though I'd be willing enough, as he knows ; but the cooking and the washing and the children's quite enough for one woman these short days. Jane had better keep with me till Harry's about again. She won't do me no harm, poor thing, and my belief is she'd have been straight enough only for that brute of a husband of hers. Of course us poor women are blamed for everything. But what's going to come of her when this hole through your poor side's mended, Harry ? She can't live here for ever. There'll be a lot of yarns about it as it is.'

'Of course, she will go home to her friends in England, Mrs. Yorke. I was going to see about a ship for her this time, if I hadn't been stopped. It's very kind of you to have her here, I know. You may take my word for it that everything will be done for her by me that a man could do for his sister. We're old friends, you know; and a man may have a true friendship for a countrywoman in her distress, I should hope.

'Oh yes, I suppose so,' said Mrs. Yorke, a little doubtfully, 'not that I hold with running it too fine ; when folks is young,

and one of 'em that pretty as people in the street turn round to
look at her, partic'lar on the diggings, where there's a lot of
curious women. Anyway, my character ain't to be shook that
easy, not if I was to take in worse than her for a spell. But I've
known you, Harry Pole, these years, so I'll take your word that
everything's on the square, and Cyrus says the same.'

'Thank you very much, Mrs. Yorke, you may trust me. I
hope I shall soon cease to be a bother to any one. And now
tell me some of the news. None of these scoundrels caught
yet?"

'Not a half a one. The p'leece is doing their best night and
day, nothing but telegrams and camping out and half killing
themselves and their horses. Merlin's lamed his old gray horse,
and got an awful cold, and is that savage no one durst speak
to him. Malgrade met him one day, though, in the street.'

'Ha! what did he say?"

'Oh, he stops as cool as you please, and says, "Good morning, Mr. Merlin, may I ask if you have any news of the escort
robbers?"   .

'"The ruffians are neither shot nor taken yet, Mr. Malgrade," and he looks as if his eyes was gimlets and would bore
two holes right through him in no time. "I believe they
receive intelligence from meaner villains than themselves who
probably shared the plunder without the danger. I have reason
to think there are men on this field even now that ought to be
arrested on suspicion."

'Malgrade looked just as straight at him, Cyrus says, you'd
have thought he was the honestest man in the world. Then he
smiles a bit and shows his white teeth.

'"Indeed," he says, "how very interesting. No doubt you
will get them all in time. Good morning."

'And he walks down the street as if the Banks belonged to
him.'

'Then Merlin suspects him?'

'Of course he does; he and big Harry was in it up to their
necks the diggers all say. But there's no evidence, and I
suppose law's law. Yankee Tom says if they'd been where he's
been they'd have been "lynched" afore now.'

'That's all very well,' I rejoin, 'when you're quite sure of the
right man. But it's awkward if mistakes are made. British law
is the best and fairest, and quite generally reaches far enough
in the long run.'

'Well, it ought to be sure, for it's awful slow at times; and if
we lose No. 4 I'll never believe in law nor justice again as long
as I live. However, this claim's shaping first-rate now. All
you've got to do is to get on your legs again, and we'll all have
enough to keep us without soiling our hands for the rest of our
lives, if every other man round Murderers' Flat was a bushranger, and I don't believe they're much better.'

'All's well that ends well, Mrs. Yorke—which means that a

good "washing-up" will fetch everything straight. We must trust in the Oxley "dirt" and a kind Providence.'

My wound, thanks to the tender tireless nursing of poor Jane, and the treatment of one of the cleverest surgeons in the southern hemisphere—a man well-nigh faultless, so that you could keep brandy from him and him from brandy—healed apace. Three months only had passed since the day when, with darkening eyes and flowing blood from a mortal-seeming wound, I was dimly conscious that our gold was in the hands of the spoiler.

Short seemed the interval, yet how had the great healer, Time, amended our lot. My hurt was as good as cured. I felt almost as well as ever. And the gold was all restored but a trifle of ten thousand ounces, hidden to this day. But Sergeant Webber lay quiet in his grave, and near him the young trooper, Rowan, poor, plucky, bright-eyed boy, not a year from England.

For a while now a season of unusual quietude seemed to have set in at the Oxley. There were no wars or rumours of wars as far as were known to us. The bushrangers certainly were not yet captured, but they did not again molest our district, and were beginning to wax faint as impressions on men's minds. My full strength returned and I found myself soon as well fitted as ever to do my work and enjoy 'God's glorious oxygen' again.

The washings-up were frequent and flourishing. Our credit balance mounted to a most respectable figure in the books of the Bank of New Holland. From time to time we saw Jane (who had resolutely refused to rejoin her husband) when she came out from her retirement to have a talk to Mrs. Yorke, by whose children she was held to be a beneficent fairy.

Having made so indifferent a start on this ever memorable occasion, it was only natural that I should postpone my next visit to the metropolis. The game was patently not worth the candle if one was liable to the trifling risk of losing one's gold and being shot through the body afterwards. So I decided to stay quietly at my work until Christmas-time at least, then five or six months distant, and go down by Cobb and Co.'s coach in regular orthodox fashion.

Then the question of Jane Mangold (I never could call her by any other name) was a difficult one to settle. She took a lodging in the town, at an inn kept by a very decent kindly widow, who allowed her the free use of her own private parlour, and in every way maternised her. But it was a dismal, unsatisfactory mode of life. She resolutely refused to make other acquaintances, male or female, secluding herself as much as possible, and only appearing on such occasions as were necessary for her health. A blameless sequestered life in every sense was hers. Still we thought it unnecessary that our friendly intercourse should be altogether broken off. I was her only friend, and from time to time we indulged ourselves in conversation and harmless friendly intercourse. I promised her also that she should follow me down to Sydney when I went at Christmas-time, when I would make all arrangements for her passage and see her on board ship myself.

'Oh, if you would!' she said. 'Sorry as I should be to see your face no more, still I should feel so utterly free from all care and anxiety—so uplifted to a region of bliss, if I were once fairly on board ship, homeward bound—that I could almost die for pure joy.'

'And that joy you shall have, Jane,' I said, 'as sure as Christmas comes and we both live. I will not leave till you are safe on board and the vessel sailing. So have no further care in the matter. It is only four months now.'

'But it is so much trouble,' she sobbed, 'and my passage money will be an expense to you. How shall I ever thank you, my only friend in this sore need?'

'Where should I have been if you had not looked after me at Eugowra?' I said jokingly. 'Why, the doctor told me that nothing but your good nursing pulled me through. You have saved my life, remember.'

'And you have given me mine in return,' she said passionately. 'A new life, a true and pure one henceforth, I swear to you, one that the angels will not blame when my hour comes. Always remember that, Hereward Pole; and may the good deed bring you the happiness you deserve, if ever man did, in the future.'

'But, Jane,' I said——

She lifted her hand with a rapid gesture of farewell—and was gone.

CHAPTER XIX

In the tiny forest-shaded pools, in lonely mountain tarns or stilly meres, amid placid restful surroundings, the influence of the fallen stone or branch agitates the surface for comparatively long protracted periods. The unwonted disturbance is succeeded by a series of ripples in ever-widening circles until the gazer marvels when the lakelet will subside into pristine unruffled calm. But in the roaring flood-tide of great rivers, or on the turbulent bosom of the mighty main, fleets with whole crews may disappear, or argosies laden with the treasures of Ind be whelmed with scarce a momentary displacement.

So in the wide and complicated goldfields society, had even my life fallen forfeit to the robber's aim, short would have been the moan made, and brief the requiem sung for me at the Oxley. The tribute of respect and regret would have been sincere if transitory. A day's cessation of labour would have been ordered at many a claim, doubtless. A long procession of vehicles in all grades, horsemen and foot, would have followed Hereward Pole, a brother miner deceased, to the often-visited cemetery under the pine-covered hill. But that duty well and truly performed, a few rough expressions of sorrow, a few extra glasses to the memory of a comrade 'gone where we all must go,' and the circumstance would be dismissed, myself almost as utterly forgotten as if I had never been.

What wonder then that even the still uncaptured band of bushrangers, *question ardente* as it was, commenced to lose novelty and interest.

The public were evidently beginning to think the piece had enjoyed too long a run, and that the management should bestir themselves to replace the tragedy with a genuine novelty.

That desired melodrama was already forward in rehearsal, if we had but known it, and the leading actors were becoming so perfect in their parts that the rise of the curtain bade fair to be demanded at no distant date.

In the early days of mining, when great yields of gold were freely won from the shallow alluvial deposits, a great influx of Chinese had taken place. These aliens, for the most part harmless and industrious, became stubborn and rebellious as their numbers made them formidable.

To the European miners, apart from their legitimate competition, they became especially distasteful. Their filthy habits when congregated in large camps prevented all ordinary residents from living in their vicinity. They swarmed over the alluvial diggings directly gold was found, monopolising the auriferous tracts. At the same time they rarely prospected for themselves.

For a year past the great body of miners had been sullenly enduring rather than acquiescing in this state of matters. The Commissioner had no love for the Mongolian or other dark-skinned aliens ; still they were all equal before the law, and as long as each man could produce his talisman, in the shape of a Miner's Right, he strictly enforced his privilege as against the most popular and influential miner on the field. He had, indeed, privately represented at headquarters that the rapid absorption of newly-discovered alluvial tracts by these swarming aliens would sooner or later lead to an *émeute*. He had gone so far as to suggest that they should only be permitted to work the abandoned portions of the gold areas, where their patient and frugal habits always secured them ample returns.

As before remarked, they were distasteful to the Commissioner, and one morning I had reason to note the Captain's autocratic acts and deeds. I had called early at the camp on some matter of mining business when the Commissioner, who was always afoot soon after daybreak, whatever had been the carousals of the previous night, espied me and insisted that I should breakfast with him. At that time the camp resembled a military mess, at which, besides the ordinary mining officials, there were sure to be a few strange guests, tourists, with perhaps a surveyor or other members of the Civil Service on leave. Blake's hospitality was unbounded, and a good cook was often available from among the crowd of wanderers who made their temporary home at the Great Rush.

So I cheerfully complied, and a very merry meal it was, save for one incident, which bordered on the tragic and might have been funereal. It would seem that his mightiness the Lord High Commissioner had been annoyed by the intrusion of certain irreverent miners upon the grounds immediately in front of the official residence. They had made a short cut to a dam on the creek, and the sight of all kinds of 'fossickers' and such small deer trampling across the sacred enclosure commenced to irritate our Czar. He immediately issued a ukase disallowing such trespass, and caused a notice to be affixed to the largest gum-tree at the entrance of the forbidden path.

Chatting carelessly, some one made an incautious remark reflecting upon the courage of his kangaroo dogs, a grand-looking, wiry-haired pair, which looked as though they might be 'black St. Hubert's breed.' This nettled our host, who was passionately attached to his dogs. He then and there swore that there was not only no old man kangaroo in the land that Ban and Buscar would not tackle, but they would go at any living thing that he (Blake) chose to set them on. A few moments after this slight *contretemps*, I saw his brow suddenly corrugate as he fixed his eyes upon the entrance to the path about which the late order had arisen.

We all looked, and waited the explosion. There, sure enough, were two Chinamen, heavily laden with pans, picks, and other mining implements, essaying to pass on. They looked for a moment with stolid faces at the warning placard, but, less enlightened than Mr. Jingles's historical pointer, dismissed the subject with customary 'no savey,' and clambered over the fence.

'Good God!' exclaimed Blake, with his brow as black as thunder. 'Am I never to be left in peace? Here, Wharton, Somers, Hayward, where are you all?' he roared out. 'See those infernal Chinamen—I'll teach them a lesson. Loose the dogs!'

The police troopers, who dwelt generally at the rear—his orderly and another or two—knowing from experience that when the Captain was in one of his moods he brooked no delay, ran at once to the kennel and opened the door, when not only Ban and Buscar aforesaid, but half a score of the other big greyhounds, came teeming out through the house like a canine avalanche on hearing their master's voice.

'Hold 'em, boys, hold 'em!' shouted Blake, and with one glance round the eager dogs dashed into speed, and sighting the luckless Celestials, by this time nearly through the enclosure, made for them as if they had been a brace of stray 'foresters' from the adjacent ranges.

The shouting had apparently only just reached the ears of the doomed ones, for they turned inquiringly, when, catching sight of the eager hounds stretching out, open mouthed, directly in their tracks, they dropped their loads, and with a yell of affright made for the high fence at the outlet.

Before they could reach it, the swifter savage brutes were upon them. Both men were down and apparently half worried before we could do more than start hurriedly to their rescue.

'By Jove,' said Blake, picking up his hunting crop, 'this looks serious. Run, boys, all of you, or that brute Buscar will have the throat out of his man.'

We did our best, I need not say; but just as we got up one man, rising to his feet, broke through the pack, climbed up to the top of the fence, with bleeding limbs and nearly every rag torn off him, and stood there yelling continuously in tones that might have been heard at Sailor's Gully, five miles off. As for the other poor fellow, old Smoker and Ban were dragging him along the ground by the arm, Ban with red jaws that showed he had found something other than cotton or silk to tear.

The troopers charged desperately with us in a body, and carried off both the men to the camp before the crowd of diggers which had begun to assemble could interfere.

'No harm done, "boys,"' said Blake, addressing them with his humorous audacity, which always stood him in good stead ; 'only a couple of Chinamen that couldn't read plain English, and I sent the dogs over to translate it to them. The big man was in luck that Smoker gripped his arm instead of his throat. His jacket was mighty well padded, for it tangled the poor fellow's teeth.'

The crowd laughed and dispersed ; and although the *Beacon* was loud on the 'man and a brother' question, nothing more came of it. Blake's sharp eye had discovered that the assaulted China-men, having lately arrived, were habited in garments thickly padded with cotton, which prevented the serious damage which might otherwise have taken place ; only an ugly laceration of the muscles of the arm showed where Smoker's sharp teeth had at length penetrated, but nothing more than the doctor speedily set right. And when Sing Foo and Chong Mow left the camp that evening with considerably more strong waters on board than they were in the habit of taking, each with a new suit of clothes and a couple of sovereigns of the Captain's money, the younger and less injured individual of the two was heard to express himself thus—

'Welly good man Captain Blake—welly bad dog. All litee.'

If the whole Chinese question could have been settled as promptly by the Commissioner and his dogs, much anxiety on the part of the Government, and, indeed, both blood and treasure might have been saved. *Dis aliter visum.*

Blake had in truth long foreseen the danger. He had drafted a series of regulations by the adoption of which all dissatis-faction might have been removed and subsequent evils pre-vented. Ever decisive and clear - headed, he would have cut the Gordian knot, as events proved, had a larger measure of discretionary power been allotted to him after his report went in.

It is in the nature of all great moral outbursts that minor matters should prepare the way previously. The fuel is laid, the combustive forces are gradually generated, the contact of metallic substance is alone wanting ; supplied through ap-parently fortuitous agency, the rending explosion follows, and the volcano bursts forth in Titanic might, whelming man and the labour of his hands with swiftest, resistless destruction.

At our eventful corner of the earth the proximate cause of the disturbance was the annexation by the Chinese of a newly-discovered and very rich patch of ground called the Green Valley. Distant some few miles from the actual township, it had been prospected by an old acquaintance of Gus Maynard, an ex-Californian of the wild old days—quite a different sort of person from the orderly and pacific Gus. Having fallen upon a remarkably rich patch at the head of what he called a 'gulch,' he had marked out his prospecting claim, had come in to report and register—as also to tell a few of his intimate friends—and to 'lay them on,' reserving a certain interest himself.

When he and his friends after a toilsome march returned, Sonora Joe hardly knew the lonely gully among the hills which he had left that morning. They could hear the hum of strange voices, too, long before they reached the place.

'It's them darned Chows,' said Joe wrathfully. 'If I was in hail of Suttor's Mill, and had a few of the old Forty-niners with me, I'd have the ragged bullet through some of their hides before morning. But there's no shooting worth a cent in this cussed country. These blawsted Britishers have no imaginations, darn 'em!'

The scene before him and his mates might have raised a better tempered man than the scared ex-trapper and Indian fighter. The broad gully was turned into a great Chinese encampment. Lanterns were flitting to and fro, giving a ghoul-like appearance to the strange-costumed, bare-legged figures that moved and chattered in the uncertain light. By the stakes and trenches which Joe's friends tumbled against they could see that hundreds of claims had been marked out, and every inch of the ground legally appropriated. Where did the foreigners all come from? There were not anything like the number at the Oxley, and what were there were chiefly employed at present on the River Sluicing Claims, about which there had been many quarrels and bitter disputes lately. One boss or headsman had indeed gone so far as to strike his pick into a dam in defiance of the Commissioner before his very face. But the Captain, snatching a revolver from a trooper, had put it to his ear, and dragging him out from among his astonished comrades, handed him over to the sergeant, by whom he was carefully locked up for the night. He was only released upon his payment of a fine of five pounds and a week's imprisonment for disobeying a Commissioner.

'Wal, I heard there was a big camp of these darned skunks, under two bosses, making their way across the mountains,' said Sonora Joe. 'They've had a fresh shipload or two for the Six Companies. But some of them, or this child, 'll have to go under before I lose my ground, if the whole British army was here, and the United States' regulars to help 'em.'

When they went up to the claim which he had left almost virgin in the morning, Sonora Joe cursed and swore with frightfully elaborate profanity. Beside his very pegs, which had been pulled up, sat a fat and stolid 'Heathen Chinee' whose gratified expression of countenance contrasted strangely with the deadly scowl which darkened the Caucasian features. The claim itself had evidently been rooted about in an unscientific and exasperating manner; while some of the wash-dirt, piled in a heap close by, showed that the Mongolian

instinct for gold had not been at fault. Sonora Joe rushed
forward and, seizing the astonished pagan by the pigtail,
dragged him to his feet, and then hurled him violently to the
ground.

'Clear out of this, you infernal yaller image!' roared the
infuriated miner, 'pig-rooting a man's very prospecting claim,
as if it was "old ground." Hav'n't ye eyes to see pegs and
trenches? By all the devils from here to Lone Mountain, I'll
have the next man's life that comes inside them pegs agin.'

But the men of a superior race were not likely to have things
all their own way on such an occasion. Numbers give boldness
even to the most timid animals. The man who had been thus
rudely ejected raised himself with difficulty and yelled out
several words in an unknown tongue. In an instant the
human hive was aroused—it was not long before it began to
demonstrate the possession of stings. Sonora Joe and his
mates were bold and hardy men, not unaccustomed to fight
against odds. They made for some time a desperate stand.
Fortunately they were not armed with revolvers, as would
have inevitably been the case in their own land. But with the
long-handled shovels and other mining tools which lay scattered
on the claim they made a desperate rally, and more than once
drove back the thronging foe.

Still they were powerless after a while against the forest of
sticks which appeared to surround them, with thickly-flying
stones, even more serious and disabling in their effects. After
a short but obstinate conflict they were compelled to beat a
retreat; and when they reached the Oxley about daylight,
sore and bruised, wounded and discomfited, to tell the tale that
the whole of the Green Gully, for which a large division of their
fellow-miners had been preparing to start that very day, was
monopolised by the invading foreigner, nothing was wanting
to supply the torch for the fires of insurrection which had been
smouldering so long.

The day which succeeded this occurrence was long re-
membed on the Oxley, at Yatala, and indeed throughout the
length and breadth of Australia.

Soon after sunrise, both the heralds of the community were
observed to patrol the streets with increased solemnity of mien
and preternatural importance of visage as they sounded forth
in the intervals of their tintinnabulary warnings, the customary
formula for convention of the goldfields *gemote*.

'Roll up, roll up. All true miners are requested to attend a
monster meeting at twelve o'clock sharp, opposite the Court-
house, to consider the injustice which has been done to the mining
community by the Chinese monopoly at Green Gully. Not a
yard of this rich alluvial find now available for Europeans
The prospectors ill-used and hunted. Roll up, roll up!'

CHAPTER XX

NUMBERLESS verbal invitations of this nature had been heard before at Yatala. At the Warraluen and other gold towns, time after time the ominous words 'roll up' had sounded forth, generally followed up by the gathering of a mighty crowd to listen eagerly to stormy, excited oratory. Then the throng would gradually disperse. A committee would be formed, with instructions to embody the wrongs of the mining community in a petition to the Minister for Lands, who at that period, before the inauguration of a special department with a Minister for Mines, swayed their destinies. Sometimes the wrongs complained of were imaginary, much fomented by demagogues and public-house politicians for their own ends. Sometimes they had real foundation in fact. In all cases they received recognition, oftentimes a measure of redress. This last was occasionally tardy.

The Commissioner and Mr. Merlin were wont to regard these mass meetings, with their fiery denunciations, as convenient safety valves. The sergeant, who knew more of the subterranean igneous agencies, assented in a general way to this doctrine, but thought 'the field' required ceaseless watch and ward in case of accidents. Wide as had been the experience of his superior officers, they had reached the stage of careless confidence, akin to that of the sea-captain who has weathered tempests and grazed a thousand shoals. High-handed and daring to apparent recklessness, how many a threatened goldfield's *émeute*, when battalions of stalwart, strong-willed men had blocked the narrow streets, making the very earth to shake with their tread, had they seen evaporate harmlessly? It would be so again.

On this morning, however, though all the officials appeared careless and unheeding as usual, they could not conceal from themselves that matters were different. There was something in the air that boded evil. All needful precautions were taken. The small force of police, mounted and on foot, were placed under arms and ready for immediate service. Even a detachment of troopers, passing through to another district, was impressed and added to the contingent; thus making up an effective army of about thirty men, to assail or defend themselves from thirty thousand! As rank after rank of miners gathered at the open space in the centre of the town near the camp, as every flat and gully within miles—for scouts had been sent forth from early dawn—furnished forth its quota of volunteers, the crowd became larger, denser, enormous. It was soon openly stated that every claim on the field was idle on that day. Yet there was hardly as much excitement as usual ; no loud talking, no eager gestures. A grave settled resolve— the most dangerous feature of a revolutionary crowd—appeared to have taken possession of the vast assemblage. The open space near the camp—the 'plaza' as the Spanish-American diggers called it—was one sea of human heads. The cross-streets were crowded far down on either side. A rude scaffolding had been erected some time since for the purpose of a hustings on the election of a member for the electorate. Upon this a man suddenly sprang and raised his hand, and as he did so a hoarse cry of greeting, a roar as of a herd of mammoths, rose from the vast far-spreading crowd. It was one of those sounds which, heard for the first time, instinctively thrill the heart and cause every nerve to vibrate. It tells of that vast unmanageable force, the physical power of the people, cast loose from all ancient moorings, and drifting into a sea of chaos. It tells of the unchained lions that are hungry for a prey. It pronounces, in trumpet-tones, the knell of legitimate authority. And it thunders the accusation against those whose task it is to guide mankind, that they have been slothful or incapable in the supreme hour of trial.

The man who was thus greeted was dressed in the ordinary garments of a working miner. His flannel shirt was open above his bare breast. His clay-stained boots and trousers showed that he had been summoned from daily labour. Yet one could see that he was a man of mark—one of those strange heralds of doom, arising suddenly, like storm-birds which sweep around the lowering horizon over the moaning sea when the tempest's hour is nigh.

As he raised his hand and stepped forward with a free unstudied gesture, and commenced in a resonant vibratory voice, that pierced even to the outer billows of the heaving human sea, Mr. Merlin observed to the Commissioner—

'It's that infernal scoundrel, Radetsky. I thought he was dead. Where has he been hiding all this time?'

'Faith, that's your business,' said the Captain. 'He's worth more than a thousand men where he is this day. After all, he's not a bad fellow that I know of—except that he's a rioter, a democrat *enragé*, and a Pole.'

'He's an infernal firebrand,' growled Merlin, 'and a deserter, I believe. I wish to heavens the Russians had shot him when they caught him, instead of letting him loose to plague us here. The sergeant knows him well.'

'It's me that does,' said that honest officer; 'didn't I know him at Turonia and Rocky Flat, and wasn't he nearly rising a ruction at both places, let alone Ballarat, where they say he was in the stockade. He's a dangerous man, none more so; but he never gave us a chance to run him in.'

'He has got his innings now,' said the Commissioner. 'And what he'll score before he's clean bowled no man can tell.'

The hour had come, and the man. So much was evident. As the burning words of the exile rolled forth in sonorous, telling periods, in spite of his foreign air and accent, the heart of every man in the vast congregation went out to him. He told them how their interests had been systematically sacrificed by those who should have conserved them. How they had been taxed directly and indirectly for the purpose of subsidising a costly system of management, which was as inefficient as expensive. How that their time and their industry had been swallowed up in litigation. How arbitrary rulers had coerced them, threatened them, degraded the very name of free miners, aye, of free manhood. How the whole system of tyranny and misgovernment had culminated in this one last intolerable grievance — this pandering to a monstrous wrong. This handing over the richest portions of the waste country they had civilised, the gold they had discovered, to a pagan horde, ignorant alike of the laws of God and man—human locusts sent hither by the Devil to eat up the reward of their skilled labour, of their arduous toil, of their weary exile. He spoke now to the hearts of men who, like himself, had left behind them for evermore, home and friends and Fatherland. (Here such a cheer rose from the foreigners and many of the British miners as seemed to rend the very air and echo among the forest glades for long moments afterwards.) They might suffer this if they pleased. They might humbly stand and look on while their comrades were plundered and their birthright given to dogs. For him, he was resolved. It was not the first time he had shed his blood for freedom. He might rot in gaol. He might die by the sword or the bullets of hirelings. But, if he tamely suffered these wrongs, he was no longer a son of slaughtered, betrayed, buried Poland, and no longer was his name Stanislas Radetsky.

He stood for one moment as he concluded his impassioned appeal, in which the words had poured forth in one unbroken torrent of sound, emphasised with action that seemed the very language of his physical being, an electrical co-ordinate of his nature. Then he waved his hand with a gesture of defiance as if to an unseen foe, and leaping lightly down from the rude rostrum was lost in the crowd.

Then arose, first a hoarse, deep murmur, as when the ocean slowly thunders against the rock-battlements ere the storm-wind arises in its might, bearing on its breath, in rudely rhythmical monotone, the doom of lonely barques, of strong- sailed navies and their crews. Then came a storm of cheers, commenced near the place where the speaker had subsided, and taken up from time to time till the furthermost edge of the vast concourse of people was reached. From time to time the menacing sound-waves ceased—only to be taken up and renewed at the slightest outburst.

'What do you think of that, Merlin ?' said the Commissioner.

'By ——! they mean mischief at last,' replied that official. 'I was always doubtful that those infernal Chinamen would lead to a row some day. I wish I'd telegraphed for a double supply of men.'

'Not the least use, my dear fellow,' said the Commissioner. 'If these fellows are as far gone as you say, a company of regulars would make no earthly difference.'

'That's impossible to say—and, surely, I need not explain to Captain Blake,' replied Merlin, with his most superfine bow, 'what a very small proportion of disciplined troops is sufficient to awe a crowd, however numerous.'

'There are crowds and crowds, my dear fellow,' answered the Commissioner, patting one of his greyhounds, who looked wistfully at the great array, divining with the instinct of his race that things were not as usual. 'Ban here knows that there's no kangarooing for him to-day, and he does not offer to run in any of the people as he generally does on Saturdays. Who is getting up now ? No foreigner this time, eh ?'

'It's Mark Thursby. I wonder at his making a fool of himself ; but they're all going mad together, it seems to me.'

'By Jove ! so it is. My favourite digger, if I have a preference for one of them. Serves me right ; but it looks bad when old Mark Thursby begins to "revolute."'

A very different figure from the eager, impassioned Pole now slowly arose and raised himself to his full height. A broad, vast-chested, long-armed figure, roughly clad, with heavy hob-nailed boots neatly laced up to the ankle. One of those children of labour whom the kindly soil and temperate clime of Britain have reared to till the fields, to work her thousand-fathom-deep mines, to build her endless iron roads, to be a marvel and a boast for strength and manliness the wide world through.

An Englishman he, and born north of the Humber ; so much was evident from his speech the moment he opened his mouth. That he was a representative man and popular with his fellows was also demonstrated by the cheers and favourable cries which greeted his appearance.

Standing erect and looking calmly at the vast surging mass, he spoke without a hint, gesture, or outward sign. His deep voice was but little raised, still it could be heard by those at a considerable distance away, so complete and wonderful was the hush. This was a proved doer, not a talker ; a man of immense personal weight and influence. And his every shred of utterance was valued according to its rarity. An untiring worker, yet a man of great organising power in mining undertakings. Utterly honest, fearless, true, and steadfast, there was not a boy on the whole of the Oxley diggings, out to the most distant unimportant gully, where a few ounces of gold were gathered weekly, who did not know, had not heard of Mark Thursby of Eaglehawk.

'I'm for the law mostly, you all know,' he said. 'Noan ivir seed me along o' the Coort, or in t' logs, and I've been diggin' since '49 at Suttor's Mill. But things has gotten too bad, though aw've nowt to say agin the Commissioner nor Mr. Merlin nor agin the sargint, as is a reet doon sensible chap as ever put the darbies on a Christian mon. But summat's gan clean wrong, and that bad as needs ravellin' oot, where yaller Chayneymen is gotten that bold as they'll tak t' brass and the land both, and drive out diggers as has paid for their Rights, and Englishmen as do'ant reckon to knock under to any folk on God's earth whatever colour or talk they've gotten. And if you're all good for gannin reet oot to Green Gully and takkin' it back from 'em, Mark Thursby's for makkin' one.'

The hoarse roar which greeted this proposition, unadorned as was the bare statement of fact with any flowers of rhetoric, was sufficient to denote that the deeper passions of the multitude were stirred. Those who listened were fully aware that something unusual was imminent. Of the nature and full extent they could hardly judge. Another and yet another speaker sprang forward and addressed the crowd, both representative miners, and men who had shared the experiences, the toils, and the burdens of those whom they addressed. Still no further manifestations of feeling took place. The great mass gradually became disintegrated, and the miners in small knots and companies departed. But it was known in the camp that the word had been passed round for a full muster at daybreak. What the result of that gathering might be all might surmise, but none could with certainty divine.

A sort of council of war was held, at which the sergeant, with Mr. Merlin and the Commissioner, assisted.

The sergeant looked so grave that the Commissioner, who had a strong dash of reckless hardihood about him, commenced to laugh.

'It's no laughing matter, Blake,' said Mr. Merlin. 'In my opinion the barricades are morally up, and to-morrow's sun will rise on the largest goldfield in Australia in revolt.'

'Against which we have a force?' queried the Commissioner.

'Of thirty strong, including all branches of the service,' said Merlin, with a mock solemnity; 'cavalry, infantry, with a reserve of two lock-up keepers.'

'Well, we must conquer or die, it seems,' said Captain Blake carelessly. 'I shan't retreat if there were forty thousand instead of thirty. I don't suppose they will thirst for our blood, however indignant they may be with regulations that don't exclude Chinamen. We must temporise as well as we can until the Government sends reinforcements, which they are quite certain to do within a week.'

While this movement was going on, it may be imagined that our party felt personally interested after no trifling fashion. We had everything to lose and nothing to gain by conflict with the civil power. Any overturning of the present state of society might be ruinous to us socially and financially. If we got mixed up with the rioters, we might be joined in their future defeat and punishment. If a general scramble took place, we might lose our claim. We had no fancy for being ruled over by the truculent scoundrels, of whom there were numbers among the mining body, only kept down by pressure of law and the orderly feeling of the masses. Our opinions were shared by large numbers of the better educated miners. Nevertheless, so strong was the *esprit de corps* which had grown up through years of mining comradeship, so fixed and clear was the conviction that in the matter of the Chinese our order had suffered wrong, that we felt bound in honour, and indeed irresistibly impelled to identify ourselves with the movement, disastrous though it might be to all our best interests. At the same time, we were not without hope that we might exercise a beneficial influence upon the crowd, thus possibly preventing bloodshed or overt acts of rebellion.

When, therefore, we were visited by the committee formed for the purpose of organising resistance to this present legalised Chinese occupation we gave in our adhesion, only expressing our hope that order would be maintained, and that nothing more would be done than was necessary to assert constitutional rights.

'You bet we're not going to let the rowdies have it their own way any more than the Chows,' said Sonora Joe, who was one of the selected chiefs of our auriferous republic. 'If any of them begin to show out and out ugly, we'll teach 'em what the Associated Miners' Executive Committee can do. There's some of 'em that remember San Francisco, and the old Vigilante days too well to make much of a muss. And, Major, I'm deputed to ask you, sir, in the name of the miners of the Oxley, now engaged in this little *pronunciamiento*, if you'll act as chief magistrate and commissioner in any cases that may be brought before you. We're bound to administer justice while we're working out the Magna Charta business; and I reckon Captain Blake won't feel free to act till things is fixed up square and monarchical again.'

'I don't expect he will,' said the Major, smiling rather grimly. 'And for two pins I wouldn't either. But just to keep things straight, I'll take office with you Roundheads temporarily.   But remember, if it comes to resisting the Queen's troops, I'm against you to the last drop of my blood.'

'We don't expect nothin' else, Major,' said the Republican. 'We don't expect any Queen's officer to desert his colours—we must all fend for ourselves then.   Mayhap it won't come to that.   But they must give us up the ground as we've toiled and moiled and wasted our lives for, or there'll be more than one as 'll stand a shot for it.   Daylight's the word and Green Gully.'

This important colloquy took place about midnight after the monster meeting in the town.   All the early part of the night preparations were made, sub-committees were formed, each having power to act in certain contingencies.   The miners have the faculty of organisation to a considerable extent, and for the necessity of self-government which has arisen under many circumstances of their migrating lives, are by no means so much at sea as large bodies of men suddenly cut loose from the social fabric would be apt to be.   Soon after midnight, therefore, all arrangements had been made, and the goldfield was in repose, which gave an utterly false impression of the state of tranquillity and the subsistence of lawless intent.

But long before the stars had left the sky the whole encampment was astir ; and as the sun rose the measured tread of ten thousand men marching towards the police camp commenced to shake the earth, and to warn the occupants with that strange indescribable hum which a large approaching force, however silently disposed, always produces, that the miners of the Oxley were at length under arms.

CHAPTER XXI

A STRICT watch had been kept at the camp the whole night through. In the ghostly dawn, gray creeping o'er darksome hill and hollow, the figures could be faintly discerned of armed men who, with their centurion, stood at their posts, as did the Roman sentinels in long-buried cities before the gloom and crash of the volcano. Yet, as the van of the great hosts of insurgents neared them, the wings of which stretched as far as could be seen, some natural anxiety must have arisen as to their intentions in approaching the tiny citadel. The police barracks and temporary gaol, popularly termed 'The Logs,' from the massive timber employed in all parts of their construction, were substantial if rude edifices, calculated to stand a siege against any reasonably superior attacking force. But the present league, if such it proved to be, would be as the tidal-wave of the ocean to the fisherman's boat-shed—the lake-flood to the beaver-dam. A few shots might be fired in desperation; a score or two of the rioters killed and wounded. And then every man in uniform would lose his life, had he a dozen to spare—might even be lynched or torn limb from limb by the infuriated rioters. Crowds, in their delirious hour, have been cruel ere now.

Still no sign of unsteadiness should be shown by the representatives of law. The officers were grave and resolved. The men firm, in their usual mechanical state of non-inquiring obedience.

'There are enough of them to eat us,' said Captain Blake. 'I wonder what the beggars are going to do? That's Radetsky in front carrying the flag. But they're not all such crack-brained enthusiasts as he is. Sonora Joe is near him, and our friends, the Major, Harry Pole, and that big Cornstalk. They will all be for moderation. I see some other fellows I don't like so well; but we must take our chance. Here they come.'

The leading body, having made a short wheel, now advanced to the edge of the open space in front of the police camp. I most unwillingly displayed myself in semi-martial array. All

who possessed them carried revolvers. Radetsky had girded on
an old cavalry sword.

'We must go out and meet them,' I heard Mr. Merlin say
distinctly. 'Hang it, we'll show them we're not afraid. Attention! left wheel! march!'

The police troopers and foot constables, who are always
instructed in infantry drill at an early stage of their career,
immediately stepped out after the immovable British fashion,
making as if they were about to advance in the very teeth of
the aroused multitude. Merlin himself, on his grey Arab, rode
on at their head as though he had the command of something
like an equal force. We could hear him say, 'Steady, men,
mark time!' as the little band executed their manœuvre with
most creditable precision.

The Commissioner, with his usual expression of half humorous gravity, loungingly sat on his well-known horse, close
to whose feet his greyhounds crowded, looking wistfully at the
multitude as if, with the fine instinct of their species, they had
divined that a storm was imminent.

So invariably accustomed were the greater portion of the
people to render implicit submission to the law as represented
by the personages now present, that even when their absurd
inadequacy as combatants was so sharply contrasted, a curious
feeling of schoolboy shamefacedness and moral inferiority was
uppermost for the moment. Then the reactionary element
prevailed, and with a mingled sentiment of admiration for the
dauntless front of the small army of regulars and a half painful
derision of their own instinctive deference, a storm of cheers
burst from the multitude, which was taken up again and again,
till the forest rang to its mountain buttresses.

The Commissioner promptly seized the opportunity, and in
a sonorous, resolute voice addressed them.

'Sorry to see you here, men, in open defiance of the law,
threatening the Queen's representatives. I do not deny your
grievances, but by constitutional means, and those only, they
would have been redressed. Now, at the bidding of bad
advisers, you have deliberately chosen to use physical force,
thereby placing yourselves in the false position of rebels and
outlaws against the Queen's Government.

(Here there was a hoarse ominous murmur, with cries of—
'We'll show the Sydney officials we're not to be trampled on.')

'You know I don't mince my words, and always speak my
mind to you. I shall do so now. Take my advice and go back to
your work. Represent your cause of complaint, which I will see
duly brought before the Government, and will back up with all
the means in my power, for in the Chinese question I am quite
of your way of thinking. (Cheers.) But, once commit yourselves to lawless acts and you'll all repent it. Mr. Merlin, here,
and myself, can do nothing with our handful of men, good as
they are. We cannot rout twenty thousand men or take them

prisoners. So we shall not try. But, mark my words—that you will have every man of the 70th Regiment, down to the drummer boys, up here within a month, the volunteers and all sailors and marines that may be on the station. Can't you see that you *must* be beaten if they bring artillery with them— perhaps some of you shot or hanged, who knows? You have not gone too far as yet, though your attitude is disorderly. Take my advice—don't be led away by foreigners, and trust to your own Government and your own officers. They have always dealt out justice, and will again.'

Here Mr. Bagstock, who had been an unwilling participator in the inconveniences of the bivouac, anticipating even yet more undesirable experiences, impatiently broke in, shouting to supplement practically and effectively his superior officer's speech.

'Look here, m-m-m-en,' he said ; 'w-w-w-hat's the use of all this m-m-mummery? it's b-b-beastly cold, this w-w-watching, I can t-t-tell you! Suppose you go and r-r-r-register block claims in G-g-g-reen Gully—most of those Ch-ch-chows haven't got Miners' Rights, you know—that's the easiest way to g-g-get possession, and quite l-l-legal too.'

A tremendous burst of laughter followed this proposition, made with the greatest coolness and apparent earnestness, joined with cries of—

'Well done you, Mr. Bagstock, you stay and stick to your papers. We won't touch a hair of your head,' etc.

The point of the joke, however, which was that Mr. Bagstock received a fee for each act of registration, and that in this hour of danger he had been sufficiently wide awake to his own interests to suggest the registration of a revolutionary mob at half a crown a head, so tickled the more humorous spirits that their infectious mirth went far to divert the rioters from their stern purposes. Even the iron-visaged police troopers could scarcely control their features, albeit under the terrible eye of Mr. Merlin.

The sergeant stared fiercely at an adjacent gum-tree, while the Commissioner slapped Mr. Bagstock jocularly on the back, and declared he would rise in the Civil Service, to which he was an honour and an ornament.

This ludicrous *contretemps*, joined with the sensible address of the Commissioner, whom all respected and believed, nearly had the effect of allaying irritation and sending most of the men back to their homes. But exorcists of all lands, since the world's dimmest eld, have ever found the fiend more easy to invoke than to lay. So it was in the present state of matters. All the worst characters in the various mining camps were now gathered together. Also, those mercurial spirits upon whom numbers and opportunity act as a spell for evil, found their fitting sphere and opportunity. The moderate men were over- powered by the subtle influence of an aroused multitude, while the wilder elements rejoiced recklessly in their hour of triumph. Scarcely had the legitimate miners raised their voices to cheer the Commissioner, and to suggest that after all they had better leave the matter in his hands, than a storm of cries, howls, and a surging rush towards the camp showed that the time of temporising measures was past.

'What!' shouted the fierce exile, maddened by the fear of losing his last chance of revolt against a settled government, and mingling in his excited brain a host of old-world wrongs with present grievances, 'are we to go back like beaten hounds at the beck of a tyrant, an oppressor of the people, who looks upon the toiling masses as dogs, the minion of a despotic government, based as are all governments upon the blood and labour of the foolish people, of us—of us! whom they chain and enslave and rob, and flog and slay—do I not, Stanislas Radetsky, bear the marks of their accursed rods? And are we to be lower than Chinese? But I will strike the first blow for liberty, let who will follow! Comrades, advance, we must have the camp!'

As he spoke he rushed towards the police, his eyes glaring with half-maniacal fury, and fired his pistol point-blank at Mr. Merlin, who sat unmoved upon his well-drilled horse, as one hardly believing that any actual overt act of warfare would follow. At the same time a few dropping shots were fired by men evidently acting in concert with Radetsky, who no doubt had been secretly working for a more compendious scheme of revolt.

The sudden report seemed to transform the impassive Merlin, who promptly gave the word—fire! and at the same time, raising his revolver without any appearance of haste, fired at the self-constituted leader, who staggered, but was immediately lifted up by those nearest to him and carried inward. At the same time an effective volley was fired by the whole body of police, who then retreated in good order towards their camp. I heard a bullet or two whiz unpleasantly near me. I saw the man on my left throw up his arms and drop in a ghastly heap by my side. And I was then hurried forward as by a resistless wave by the maddened crowd which passed onward with overwhelming force.

Then, indeed, ensued a tumult such as no man could imagine or describe, and such as in all my previous experience I had never dreamed of. Cries and curses, groans and shrieks, as an occasional bullet sped home, arose from all around. In vain did those in the van try to stem the mad rush onward, not willing to mix themselves up with the insane act of Radetsky, and unwilling to provoke a further firing from the police, who had only given a second volley, and stopped as soon as the fire from our side ceased. All order was lost. All feeling merged, apparently, in mad demoniac rage and thirst for blood and vengeance.

The police had retreated within their citadel, which was capable of being well and effectively defended, as long as their ammunition should hold out. Built with a view to resist a sudden onslaught, it was massively constructed of heavy hard-wood logs. The heavy doors were strong and clamped with iron. It was not particularly easy to set on fire, so that dead-liest of all resorts of the besieger was in abeyance. The iron-bark shingles defied hasty ignition, so that the besieged with their repeating rifles could have shot down any number of men engaged in carrying combustibles. Moreover, the timber cleared away by the reckless use of firewood by a large population left bare considerable space around the camp. Hence, even with the immensely superior attacking force, it was seen that they had a long and dangerous task before them in compelling the surrender of the little fortress. To storm it would have been a most useless expenditure of blood, and only justifiable in the case of the death of every single one of the garrison being resolved upon. Such few shots as had been fired by the police had been more deterrent than irrevocably disastrous fortunately. Radetsky was badly but apparently not mortally wounded. Others were more or less hurt, but no man had been slain outright. The rioters, much worked upon by all the moderate party, among whom Mark Thursby, the Major, the Bulders, and myself of course, canvassed unremittingly, began to consider whether it was worth while sitting down for a lengthened siege before the unpromising-looking camp, where the police could certainly hold out for several days, or whether they had better go on and drive out the Chinese, who after all were legitimate enemies, in possession of their gold and the cause of the whole disturbance.

Here Sonora Joe, who meant business rather than revolt, and who was extremely cute, like most of his countrymen, in the management of the sovereign people, saw his way to a diversion.

'I don't see,' he commenced, as soon as the turmoil had sufficiently subsided to secure him a hearing, 'what all this army work is going to do with getting back our shallow ground in Green Gully! Here's these cussed Chows working away and rootin' out the gold like spuds, while we're foolin' round these darned old logs and waitin' for the myrmidons of this all-fired, old Sydney one-horse Government to shoot some more of us. They can't well be off it—and when we've got all these boys' scalps in the block-house, I don't see how we can realise on 'em. They won't be half as good trade as those shallow claims, and we're losing them all the time. Guess we'd better make tracks ; put the prospectors back on to their claims ; wire in on the block, and send the hull darned lot o' those yaller niggers to h——l.'

This characteristic address, more particularly the concluding sentiment, seemed at this juncture to strike the fancy of the capricious crowd mightily. The artful allusion to rich gold in shallow workings, the miners' Eldorado, was difficult to resist. Nothing but hard knocks were to be got by staying where they were. Gold, adventure, revenge, were to be obtained by the onward march. Our party enthusiastically applauded and indeed took the lead for Green Gully, whither we had the satisfaction to find ourselves followed by the whole crowd, a comparatively small force being left to guard the guardians of the peace.

It may have been some seven or eight miles from the Oxley proper to the Green Gully. A concourse of individuals, whether brute or human, does not advance so quickly as a smaller number. Nevertheless, once started on the road every man apparently put his best leg forward, and very good time was made. Was it not a 'rush'? That magic word in mining parlance! How many times had we all seen people strip themselves of the last shilling, the last shred of property they had in the world, to improve their fortune by risking their lives to ensure their chances of being early at a rush which was perhaps utterly worthless and barren when they got there.

For the miner proper, splendid possibilities seem to be the resistless lure, and he is so constituted that the undefined mysterious future is quite sufficient to overbalance the prosaic present, however satisfactory and solvent soever.

In this case the majority had made up their minds that Green Gully combined the profits of a 'rush' with the excitement of a revolt, and their gamblers' nature was stirred accordingly to its lowest depths.

After little more than two hours' march, we came in sight of the far-famed Green Gully, the fame of which was soon to be so widely bruited abroad. There we 'saw a horde of yellow men, the Huns of this gold-empire of ours, spread over it apparently with the multiform ceaseless industry of an ant-hill.

A hoarse roar broke from the crowd as they marked the steady passage of lines of workers from the claim to the creek, bearing on their shoulders what they knew to be rich washdirt, —or why should they so sedulously keep up the laborious process of washing and 'cradling' the ore?

'There's my prospecting claim as thick as a bit of honeycomb with ants, blast 'em!' cried out Sonora Joe. 'Isn't that enough to make a white man own himself first cousin to a blind mule in a sugar-mill? Is this what we came across those infernal sage brush deserts to 'Frisco, and across sea hyar fur? Is the British Empire played out? and is this here Miner's Right a bit of waste paper?'

Then he drew out the parchment document so well known to his hearers, and flourished it on high, as though it had been the title deed of the whole Caucasian race.

The effect was electrical. By this time the main army of miners, with camp followers and concomitant personages of all kinds, had arrived, and were so to speak broadside on to the incurious automatons of Celestials, who went on without sign of doubt or trepidation, yarning up the yellow dross as though their privilege was to last to the day of doom. Such was it, in fact, to them.

With a hungry sudden rush as of one man, the vast crowd, like a tidal wave, rolled on and over the host of inferior race. It was an instant mean eclipse, followed by annihilation. The next moment, as it seemed, the whole superficial area of the Green Gully was occupied with European miners. In every direction were seen Chinese flying madly in panic, their pigtails floating behind them, their loose clothes fluttering in the breeze, their slippers discarded or only visible on one foot, their broad-brimmed hats flying in the breeze or lying prone and curiously suggestive on the earth. Picks and shovels were raised in the *mêlée*, not altogether in vain. The Chinese that remained were kicked, struck down, hustled, in every way maltreated until they joined, like the rest, the unreasoning panic of which they had been the victims. Sonora Joe, waving a brace of pigtails suspiciously resembling scalps at the thicker ends, bore down on the dignified and supercilious boss, who had so quietly sat down upon his prospecting claim. He was then running and yelling in the most ignominious manner. Joe could not avoid the triumph of sounding a war whoop over his departure, and intensifying by a simple stratagem his agony and despair at the onslaught of the white barbarians.

In half an hour all was apparently quiet. Sonora Joe was again in possession of his prospecting claim. Many of the others had apparently taken up claims with the greatest promptitude and despatch. There was not a bit of spare ground left in the whole Green Gully. A couple of thousand men were settled, apparently, upon as rich a bit of alluvial as had been seen or heard of since old Eaglehawk. The great thing was to keep it.

'Fancy a mob of Chinamen getting hold of a bit of ground like this,' said more than one steady-going old hand, delighted to quit the conflict for easy sinking. 'Let's see who'll turn us out again.'

As for the constables at the camp, they had nearly forgotten all about them. They could forgive them, and only trusted they wouldn't make fools of themselves and bring more bloodshed and danger on their heads.

In those days the area of the claims was small, so that, as the combatants carefully retained the legal measurement as between one another, the Green Gully, which was patently rich, absorbed a very large proportion of the leading miners, and also of the dangerous classes. In a comparatively short time the rapid transformation, therefore, had taken place from an invading army into a body of peaceful miners wielding pick and shovel, or marking out their claims with painstaking accuracy.   Of the routed Celestials, not a solitary individual remained.   After a hurried consultation they had formed themselves into some kind of marching order, and departed at a jog trot in the direction whence they had come.

CHAPTER XXII

For ourselves, we took no part in the attack and ill-treatment of the aliens. Of course we held such to be unlawful and indefensible, though from a miner's point of view we could easily understand an excited mob of mixed nationalities acting in that way. We had abstained from all complicity in the violence done, and took no share in the reward. We doubted not but that some kind of expiation was likely to be exacted for these high-handed proceedings, and were resolved to keep as clear of all blame as our comrades would permit us to do.

We, therefore, took the earliest opportunity of going back to the Oxley, though we had some difficulty in persuading Cyrus Yorke not to 'wire in,' as he expressed it, for 'a bit of shaller, with the gold sticking out a beggin', for half an hour, with a Chinaman's pick and shovel, cradle and everything complete.' We dwelt upon the anxiety such a proceeding would cause his wife, and finally carried him safely back with us.

On our arrival at the camp we discovered, to our great gratification, that the whole body of officials, with the police, had executed a flank movement and retired in good order, having evacuated their fortress and fallen back upon reinforcements. The force which had been left to keep them in check had found the task irksome, and gradually melted away. A scout had come in from Green Gully and given such glowing accounts of the extraordinary richness and shallowness of the ground, the best thing seen by living men since Eaglehawk in Victoria—that it was not in the nature of miners to stay away from such a rush. All the more energetic took their departure incontinently, leaving behind a gradually decreasing band of earnest political enthusiasts, with a sprinkling of loafers and camp-followers.

When these, towards nightfall, saw the Commissioner, followed by Mr. Merlin and his men, come forth in battle array, and take the road to Warraluen, they did not see their way clear to withstand them, and evidently thought, like that Provost of Edinburgh who considered the good town 'weel rid of that

de'il of Dundee,' that it was well to connive at the retreat of
such unpleasant, possibly dangerous adversaries.

On the following morning, therefore, when a contingent
from the main body of the rioters, having had leisure to
return temporarily from their claims and devote a little time
to public affairs, discovered that the camp was empty, they
took formal possession of the silent cells and echoing court-
house and offices in the name of the Committee of Public
Safety and the Associated Miners of Australia.

It is now certain that the bolder spirits among them entertained a hope that this revolt would spread through the whole
mining population of New South Wales, at that time numerically large and powerful, and that the working classes *en
masse* would next follow suit. To this end, and to fit themselves for future republican responsibilities, they commenced
to make laws for their own guidance, and to administer the
present code in a temper which showed that they would not
permit anarchy, violence, or petty crime among their own body.

Thus a few low-lived ruffians, who had presumed on the
social dislocation to pilfer and threaten outrage, were at once
arrested and lodged in the cells, being locked up with as much
promptitude as in the day of the sergeant's rule.

On the next morning they were tried before an elected
committee of miners and sentenced to a week's solitary con-
finement on bread and water, with a significant hint that on
the second offence the more severe Californian penalties would
be inflicted. This had the desired effect. An example was at
once shown and terror struck into those baser natures that
can be ruled in no other way. We and others who had valuable claims were not sorry to see that order would be enforced.
We, therefore, in every way assisted by personal influence and
otherwise to sustain so desirable a state of self-government.

That the bank officials did not by any means approve of
the present state of matters may be supposed. They saw themselves surrounded by a heterogeneous population from whom
the ordinary restraints had been suddenly withdrawn. At any
moment an organised band of desperadoes might arrange to
make a descent upon any given bank when it was well known
that thousands of pounds' worth of notes and sovereigns
besides large deposits of gold were in their safes. In a general
way these officials were highly popular ; such being the rule
among managers detailed for gold-fields work, and the ordinary
mode of life being favourable to a frank bearing joined with
business habitudes. But they had formerly had all the police
at their backs ; the strong arm of the law could always
be invoked for their protection. Now they were virtually
helpless, merely trusting to the good faith and honourable
feeling of a body of men who had openly defied the recognised
authorities. The position was not reassuring.

Superficial readers of the great book of human nature

might have deemed that it was a favourable time for the return of the bushrangers, who, since the police had been withdrawn, had no disciplined force to oppose. A fatal error! Had Frank Lardner's gang presumed upon any feeling of sympathy among the miners their career would have had a premature ending.

The mining community of the Oxley had revolted against their rulers and the Government of the day because they saw the hard won privileges of their order handed over to an in-ferior race, while their remonstrances were neglected or con-temned. They had openly stated their grievances and, failing adequate redress, had then taken arms against the authorities, in the light of day. But Lardner, Wall, and the rest of the gang had proved themselves assassins in the first instance, and robbers afterwards. They had stolen the gold which represented months of toil, often persevered in (for the diseases of camps claimed a daily toll) while the hand was heavy and the heart faint with sickness nigh unto death. And had they shown their faces on the Oxley at that critical period, Judge Lynch would have been assuredly presented with a commission, when a quick trial and a short shrift would very probably have stamped out robbery under arms, and saved the lives of scores of better men in the days that were to come.

No such sensational visitors, however, turned up. Even Malgrade, Big Harry, and a few others of the leading spirits of the Alsatia at Murderers' Flat, appeared somewhat subdued, having received warning, we afterwards heard, that a corps akin to the Californian Vigilantes was in process of formation.

The Committee plainly made it apparent that no irregularity would be tolerated by the mining commune so suddenly organ-ised, excepting that of disestablishing John Chinaman. Gold was plentiful in a general way. The Oxley was what is called 'a good poor man's diggings.' That is, most men—even those who were not lucky—were getting what they called 'wages and a trifle over'—meaning four or five pounds a week. A certain amount of ready money, arising from fairly remunerated labour, equally distributed among the populace, has always—and I speak from experience—an effect conducive to propriety and self-respect. Thus at the Oxley, though it came to my knowledge that a 'big thing' was planned and very nearly came off, no unlawful interference with the banking treasuries occurred in any one instance during the rule of the provisional government. Indeed, a kind of Utopian order and good guid-ance for a while prevailed—that kind of government 'of the people for the people by the people' for which so many ardent patriots have written and spoken, have fought and bled, died by sword and spear, axe and scaffold—from the dim darksome eld till now. How long this state of things might have lasted is another matter!

But it could not be denied by the worst enemies of democracy that, the *casus belli* effectually removed, nothing could have been more satisfactory to a philanthropist than the appearance and internal condition of the Oxley. In the streets of our strange city were seen none of the mournful degraded forms of poverty, no travesties of human nature, patiently carrying out a sentence of want, hunger, and degradation during their stay on earth. There were no poor in rags, no houseless women, no aged paupers, no gutter children, no street boys, no outcasts. All the viler types of humanity which deform great cities, and even the denser rural populations of the old world, were conspicuous by their absence. The schools were well and regularly attended. The churches of the various denominations, the pastors of which all remained at their posts, were crowded on the Sabbath. These good men had in truth never ceased to exhort to submission and to warn their congregations to keep from all riotous and violent proceedings. In a general way they possessed much influence. But this was one of the slow culminating crises — outbursts of human society—which kings, priests, or rulers are alike powerless to prevent.

I by no means wish to assert that our confederated community was free from the ordinary sins and breaches of the moral law under this provisional government. But there was, as under the old *régime*, a wondrously small amount of open or shameless evil. There was but little perceptible wrong-doing, nothing overt which would cause the lover of his kind to grieve and point to the bad influence of the *auri sacra fames*. Quite the contrary, in fact. Whether under our old-world despotism, or the newer lights of poor Radetsky, Mark Thursby, and the rest, a more serious, well-mannered, orderly-appearing settlement than that of the Oxley did not exist upon the earth. There were human beasts of prey among them, doubtless. They were but as the wolves and pumas which prowl around a herd of buffaloes. An isolated or heedless individual separated from its fellows might be occasionally beset; but on the least alarm there are a thousand trampling feet, a thousand glaring eyes and levelled horns, ready to crush to earth or toss lifeless in the air the base intruder, cowardly as savage.

Even those that were physically unable to endure the strain of manual labour found here rest and ease. A perennial side-stream of charity, flowing from the main channel of golden gain, enriched these weaklings and feeble brethren. Miners are always free-handed, so long as the tide of Pactolus runs not low, and in the patronage of the smaller industries, or in more direct alms-giving, the old, the worn-out, and the afflicted, found ready sympathy and ample aid.

One of those invaluable literary caterers for modern civilisation, ever ready to construct historiettes concerning lands which he has never seen and societies which he can never have entered, describes in one Australian novel (save the mark) a lovely and distressed damsel, reft from her friends, and chained to the pole of a tent by a ruffian band of diggers. In another improving tale the prepossessing, if not, perhaps, immaculate heroine, is publicly disposed of by lottery and carried off by the winner. How utterly, childishly impossible such occurrences could have been in the wildest days of mining adventure, let any digger say. Shades of the Sergeant! fancy his majestic indignation when, from information received, he started forth to arrest such flagrant and foolhardy criminals.

His strides would have lengthened to those which were conferred upon the wearer of the seven-leagued boots; his very gaze would have burned up the perpetrators of so unmanly, so unparalleled an outrage; and the shortest possible interval would have elapsed between the first whisper of the atrocities and the safe lodgment of all the parties to the disgrace in the historic logs, *en route* for the district gaol.

No! that strange scenes have been enacted in all mining communities I am not pledged to deny, but as far as my experiences of the Oxley and Yatala go, premier goldfields of Australia, on each of which twenty or thirty tons of gold had been unearthed within five years, where four millions sterling were divided among thirty or forty thousand men, such occurrences were not only never heard of, but were far more impossible of occurrence than in the very heart of London or Paris. Whatever the miners' shortcomings, the lack of a chivalric courtesy, of a deeply-rooted respect for womanhood is not among them.

Mr. Bright, the manager of the Bank of New Holland, was so far from being uneasy at the situation that he positively gloried in the warlike aspect and 'besieged resident' sort of business in which we existed. We all believed that he would have rather liked the bank to have been 'stuck up' with fair notice. A proverbially good shot and quick with his weapons, he carried a regular battery about with him for fear of being suddenly beset. We used to say that his customers were afraid to put their hands in their pockets to extricate a check for fear he might suspect them of feeling for a revolver and let fly at once. One day the Major and I, strolling down the street, heard a shot in the bank.

'Hallo! Bright has enticed in a band of robbers at last,' said the Major. 'It's a pity to spoil his pleasure, but we may as well look in for fear of accidents.'

When we got in it was another matter altogether. Our friend did not look so radiant and rubicund as usual. A fume of gunpowder and a hole in the floor suggested an accidental shot. It appeared that he sat down rather suddenly, and jarring one of the pistols which he wore round his waist, like the pirate captains of our youth, a six-shooter exploded, tearing through his coat-tail and burying a bullet in the floor unpleasantly near to his big toe.

Congratulations and libations having succeeded, he bewailed his lot in being cast in so fearful a region. Not even during a rebellion had any one the pluck to do anything out of the common. However, he had advices that military and even naval reinforcements were on the road. The rebels would be routed and discomfited in no time.

'How's Radetsky getting on? Poor devil! I shouldn't wonder, Major when the regulars come up if they hang all the leaders, yourself included, on that big tree in the camp reserve.'

'Radetsky will escape their clutches,' the Major said calmly. 'By Jove! I sometimes wish I was as near the end as he is.'

'Pooh, pooh!' said the banker good-humouredly, 'wait till that No. 4 of yours is in full work again, and even without that small property you can clear out for Europe and pick up your old form again. I wish I had the chance.'

'Something always seems to come in the way of our luck,' said the Major. 'First, those scoundrels of jumpers, and then this beastly *émeute* about Chinamen. I suppose we shall have a Russian invasion next, if the claim is proved good in law.'

On the following day it was announced that Radetsky was dying. The fiery enthusiast, the excited patriot, the descendant of an ancient line and representative of a gallant nation, was about to end his days in a rude hut in a mining settlement in a far, half-unknown land. He whose childhood had been passed among nobles and princes, petted by fond relatives, ministered to by devoted servants, was now dying alone and untended save by the charitable offices of his 'mate,' a peasant compatriot, and the neighbours, as even on a diggings the adjoining workers are called.

Not that much was wanting which could be of real benefit to the wounded man. The hut was small but scrupulously clean, and no care or watching was omitted that skill or kindness could devise. The principal medical man of the district, a duly qualified surgeon of high attainments and world-wide experience, had attended him from the day of his hurt. It was thought at first that he would recover, as the bullet had not touched any vital portion of his frame. But the man's tameless excitable nature was against him. He could not be induced to keep quiet during the first days of the campaign, and at length, when fever and delirium set in, and the sick man commenced to rave about the Austrian Cuirassiers and the charges against the Imperial troops he had led, to count up his wounds, and to name the name of Haynau with tireless execration, Dr. Burnside told his mate that his time was come.

'He will never make another speech, poor fellow,' said the kind-hearted medico; 'if he had been an Englishman or a

German I could have pulled him through, but these Sclaves are as bad as Celts, they *will* subordinate their reason to their emotions.   You might as well try to cure an untrained Norway falcon.'

So a few days before the important news of the arrival of the military put all other matters out of the miners' heads, the news of Radetsky's death, when announced, seemed to stir the heart of every creature on the goldfield. He had had a short lucid interval before his last agony, had lamented that he could not have died for Poland, but rejoiced that the blood of the last male of the ancient house of Radetsky had been shed for liberty. Every male of his line for three generations had perished by sword or bullet in the field in freedom's cause; and though he would leave his bones in this far land, the celestial spirit of freedom would hallow his grave. He thanked his comrades of every nation for their sympathy and noble kindness, and then died calmly and contentedly, believing that when the miners were again aroused to strike for liberty the occasion would always revive the name of Stanislas Radetsky.

That night it was announced in every form of public proclamation that all the honours of a military funeral had been decreed by the Executive of the United Miners to their leader and true comrade deceased, and that every miner was expected to attend, that the pall-bearers would leave the chapel at noon precisely, and that the procession would attend the corpse to the cemetery at Green Point Hill.

Never was such melancholy invitation more universally acceded to. It is a matter of fact and history that hardly a creature able to perform or provide locomotion, above the age of infancy, was absent from the gathering to do honour to the dead. Every shred and fragment of black cloth, crape, lace, or calico on the field was put into requisition that day. From early morning till midday the roads leading into the township were thronged with crowds so mixed and various that one would have fancied that an exodus was about to take place under pressure of national defeat or impending calamity. Men, women, and children, even to the toddling bairn and the babe that could not be left at home, were all there, all with one accord eager to pay the last poor tribute of respect to the gallant exile who had lived in peace and goodwill for long years unpretendingly and honourably with his humble comrades, and had now sealed with his blood his devotion to freedom and justice.

For long hours crowds pressed round his humble abode where this last descendant of the proud house of Radetsky had passed away, gazing with strong feeling and even with tears upon the calm face of the dead. The haughty regular features were still. There was a frown upon the tameless brow; they could hardly believe that the bright eagle eye had ceased to flash beneath the heavy lids which had been lovingly closed. It seemed hard to think that a form so highly vitalised, so infused through every nerve with eager force and restless energy, *could die*—could lie cold, motionless, unheeding of the hum and stir and beating hearts of the multitude around, whose pulses he knew so well how to stir with his wild, earnest, defiant words.

It was even so. The delicately moulded but sinewy hand was nerveless now, the hot pulse stilled, the tender, fearless heart cold in death. The tongue that could denounce or defy, persuade or command, was silent for evermore. The brave ally of the weak and the oppressed, the friend of the needy, the brother of the forlorn and deserted, had passed away to the land where truth is crowned and justice reigns eternal.

There was nothing left but to turn away and weep, and to tread with slow sad steps the familiar track to the grassy pine-shaded cemetery on the rocky hill. The dead man was carried to the chapel in his coffin by four compatriots—for the sons of betrayed Poland were numerous among the cosmopolitan roving gold-seekers, that great wave of humanity which first rolled from western and southern Europe to America in the days of the Californian wonder-treasures, thence to the half-fabulous land of the Antipodes.

There Father O'Rourke, an unobtrusively pious priest, who had never ceased to warn his flock against their illegal action and rash deeds, but had not quitted his post, read the prayers appointed over him. Again the coffin was raised on the shoulders of the pall-bearers, and slowly and mournfully the whole vast procession took their way to the pine-crested hill, where the Commissioner's fancy had decreed that the dead should lie. Behind the pall-bearers came a long array of vehicles—buggies, phaetons, dog-carts, express-waggons, every conceivable kind of carriage in use in the neighbourhood. Then, two and two, a thousand horsemen, winding in an immensely long undulating line. The guilds and brotherhoods and societies walked in array, all carrying the regalia of their orders, and rich with banners and plumes. Then an army of dark-clothed miners, followed by a confused multitude—men, women, and children.

Had any one visited the Oxley township that day, it must have looked like a fabled city of the dead, so thoroughly deserted was it. The day was cloudless and bright. The faint breeze caused the forest trees to quiver and rustle, the river murmured and rippled all unheeding. How strange a contrast with the day's bright tints, the sombre dark-hued crowd with their dread burden in the fore-front, and the Dead March in Saul pealing and reverberating through the hushed silence of the forest.

But a few weeks since, and he whom they mourned had been strong, eager, tameless by toil or ease, hunger or thirst, fear or favour. Temperate always, yet patient at his rude labour, there yet always seemed within the man a smouldering fire of hatred of injustice, of resistance to tyranny, of sympathy for the weak, defiance for the strong oppressor, which needed but a breath of sympathy or antagonism to fan into the red glowing blaze of revolt and resistance. His lot was latterly cast amid untoward surroundings, but of such material have the world's unforgotten brave, her patriots, heroes, and martyrs, been ever constructed.

Hours passed of the clear, bright winter day, and still the procession seemed winding along the road to the cemetery. When, however, the corpse with its attendant mourners, with the priest and the leaders of the procession, were seen to enter the cemetery, the line of march was broken up, and in open order those who were mounted rode at speed for the gates, while those on foot strove by short cuts and quickened pace to make up for other deficiencies.

When the grave was opened and the coffin lowered, the priest raised his voice and commenced the service for the dead. Every knee was bent, every voice was hushed, and the great crowd inside the enclosure and as far as the eye could reach knelt as one man, honouring in that hour him who, in their estimation, had fallen for the sacred cause of liberty and for his fellow-men.

More than half of those who thus bent the knee did not belong to the Romish faith. But this was an occasion when all men are equal in the sight of God, the Supreme Ruler of the Universe, before whom the wise and the unlearned are alike helpless, alike dumb. May none ever do anything more un-becoming to their own faith than to act as we did that day—falling on our knees by the grave of the man all had loved, and praying to God for his soul's rest.

In a few moments more the solemn and touching service was ended. The cemetery was speedily emptied, the crowd broke up, and each section of the assembly sought its home, those who were mounted returning at a pace very different from that of the morning.

CHAPTER XXIII

OF course the Government of the colony of New South Wales was not inclined to rest peaceably while its laws were being broken, its officers withstood, and inoffensive foreigners violently treated and driven out by force of arms. No one expected that for one moment. The British ensign, since it first floated to the breeze above the scarped sandstone natural fortresses of Sydney, has ever truly symbolised the good faith and firm rule of the parent land. The will of the people has never been pandered to by the ministries of the day, ever justly dreading that weakness of the Executive which has been the curse of all lands where its evil growth has been fostered.

No sooner had the official despatches reached Sydney than efforts were promptly made to march to the scene of revolt every available soldier, sailor, marine, and volunteer that could be impressed for the expedition.

By good luck, as some persons thought, a man-of-war was reposing peacefully in the harbour, and within twenty-four hours her gallant captain, his force of marines and bluejackets, with a couple of guns for siege purposes if necessary, had started with the regiment then in barracks and a strong body of volunteers, for a three-hundred-mile march across the Blue Mountains to the head-waters of the Oxley.

It was a toilsome and not over pleasant journey. There were no transmontane railways in those days, and many obstacles had to be encountered. The weather was cold, even frosty, as one of the sailors of the *Collingwood* discovered when, having committed an act of pillage, he was promptly court-martialled, tied up to a gun, and received three dozen at 6.30 A.M., to the surprise and consternation of the provincials.

However, though ranking beneath Sir Charles Napier's march through Scinde and other feats of endurance, the difficulties of the march were gallantly met and at length surmounted. The army, with guns in position, colours flying, and all the pomp and circumstance of glorious war, marched into the Oxley, and took up a position in the rear of the camp,

P

which had been promptly vacated at the rumour of their
approach. With them also returned the whole available police
force of the district, accompanied, of course, by Mr. Merlin,
Mr. Bagstock, and the sergeant. Captain Blake, who was an
old friend of the colonel of the 70th, accompanied that regiment,
and rejoiced in renewing his mess recollections and the routine
of military life.

As for our rebels, they were much disorganised, and as usual
intestine feuds had weakened their organisation. Now that
the Chinese had been driven forth and the coveted shallow
ground placed in the possession of the legitimate miner, the
revolutionary business became distinctly a bore. Much time
was wasted by the committee elected to administer justice in
the matter of mining disputes. It was wearisome enough to
listen to the interminable technical details which are indispensable in mining evidence, and apparently not more satisfaction was produced than of old. The suitors quarrelled
and wrangled and accused the mining assessors of being
partial, prejudiced, or indeed interested—charges which no
one ever thought of bringing against the Commissioner or the
magistrates.

Their total freedom from aristocratic and official guidance
was not such a grand thing after all. It was a white elephant,
costly, troublesome, and increasingly difficult to support.

The great body of the mining population was too intelligent,
well-intentioned, and respectable to succeed brilliantly in revolt.
They had no special aims of their own to serve, no restless
ambitions, no covetousness of wealth or power for their own
sakes. All that they wished was that they might be permitted
to enjoy their fascinating occupation in peace, and that no
hated aliens of inferior races should be suffered to swarm among
their camps, and spread themselves locust-fashion over their
beloved shallow ground—the prize and blue riband, as it were,
of the toilsome mining life.

And now the task was done, they did not longer care to play
out the farce of government and police administration. After
all it was better done by people trained to it and paid for it.
All this gratis magisterial work was a nuisance, and dreadfully
expensive in time to the few leading miners into whose hands
it fell. Such considerations as these were not suffered to sleep
for want of iteration and support by the Major and myself, as
well as by scores of men of the same calibre and higher logical
acumen, of whom the diggings are full.

Fortunately little blood had been spilled. Except Radetsky,
no man's life had been sacrificed. The Chinese, no doubt, had
been beaten and badly handled. Sonora Joe, and some of his
friends who had seen scalps taken, it is feared shore more than
closely in severing pigtails. They could bring actions for
damages.

Now that the soldiers had come, it became necessary either

to resolve to stand committed to an obstinate and bloody contest, sure to be a losing one in the end, or to lay down their arms.

For many reasons it was thought advisable to consider seriously of the latter course.

With the military and naval forces now near at hand, it was reported that the colonial secretary, Sir Charles Camden, a veteran politician, a native-born Australian, and a most able diplomatist, had accompanied them. This was considered by the moderate party to be a felicitous circumstance. Sir Charles was a man whom his enemies called the High Priest of the Expedient, and his friends knew to be uniformly successful when a dangerous difficulty needed the solvents of tact and timely concession. It is just possible to fancy that his occasional lack of uncompromising firmness led to political catastrophes. But once let the imbroglio be fairly developed and disaster imminent, there did not live in the southern hemisphere a man so effective in unravelling the tangled skein and reducing the chaotic elements to order and safety.

On a certain Monday morning, therefore, the advanced guard of the force, consisting of six companies of the 70th, marched with colours flying and bugles blowing into the camp reserve. Here they were presently joined by the volunteers, finally by the sailors and marines, the former dragging with them their two formidable pieces of ordnance.

To their astonishment they were loudly cheered on taking up position in front of the line, as they coolly unlimbered and got their artillery ready for action.

Before all this took place, however, Sir Charles had driven quietly into town in a dog-cart, with his servant behind him, while the plain, middle-sized, quietly-dressed man who sat behind and who slipped down and mingled easily with the crowd was a distinguished colonel of engineers, then in Sydney on leave, who had joined the expedition as a matter of interesting inquiry and novel experience.

When it was found that there was no disposition on the part of the miners to continue their independent government, but that the camp and other Imperial strongholds were delivered up in good order and condition, even with the addition of a couple of prisoners in one of the cells awaiting trial for petty larceny, negotiations were established between Sir Charles Camden and the leading representative miners. The upshot of this was that the Government revised the Goldfields Regulations, making, among other changes and alterations, by the Commissioner's advice, one which rendered illegal any occupation by Chinese for the purpose of gold mining upon auriferous ground which had not been worked and abandoned by Europeans for the full term of three years.

This satisfied the mining community, and healed the rankling sore which threatened such dangerous if not fatal results to the body politic. Shallow ground and new ground would henceforth be hermetically sealed to the Mongolian. The virtuous Caucasian proprietor and his followers of the true faith would be henceforth enabled to possess their souls in peace. I am not quite sure whether our ally, the Emperor of China, upon whom we forced our enterprising opium traders in and around certain jealously closed ports, would have considered it strictly in accordance with international justice. But it was a measure highly expedient, if not vitally necessary. For that reason, or because it was 'a far cry to Lochow,' or, in other words, a long way from the Oxley to Pekin, no protest on the part of his Celestial Highness reached us.

Sergeant MacMahon made a few arrests, including some of the leading rioters, against whom evidence of violence or special ill-treatment of Chinese was forthcoming, and they were duly committed for trial at the next ensuing Quarter Sessions. They were held to bail, and duly tried. But the juries refused to bring them in guilty, and with their discharge ended peacefully the great Oxley Flat *émeute*, now only of fading historical interest.

We, individually, were unaffectedly sorry when the troops left. There was an old comrade or two of the Major's among the officers, and though they chaffed him as having been found in arms against the Sovereign, and so on, we held high revelry, and had many pleasant excursions and rambles while the sailors and soldiers remained. Mr. Bright was also a favoured guest, and his warlike reminiscences gave the allied warriors much material for surprise and thought. He always averred that his counsels and influence with Sir Charles, to whom he was intimately known, contributed materially to the final and effective settlement of the question at issue. With the departing troops a gold escort service was improvised, which carried down all the gold which had accumulated, to the joint relief of bankers and depositors, among which last we were numbered.

The time had passed so quickly during all these abnormal and exciting proceedings, that we were quite surprised to find that our appeal case was on in the Supreme Court of New South Wales, held in Sydney.

Dr. Bellair went down in person to represent his friends and clients. But all his eloquence and fiery declamation availed him nothing with the modern Rhadamanthus and his peri-wigged compeers. The appeal was dismissed, with so swingeing an amount of costs as against the appellants that all thought of testing the merits of the case further was peremptorily abandoned. No higher court of judicature remained, except the Imperial Privy Council, with which ultimate legal resort, or indeed with the fraternity generally, the principal backers (on the Doctor's having tentatively defined its functions) refused, 'in Anglo-Saxon of the strongest kind that's made,' to have further truck or trouble.

Thus at length we found ourselves, after all our delays and anxieties, in indisputable possession of the celebrated and coveted No. 4. Our Oxley claim was doing so well that we felt a slight *embarras des richesses*, but after a solemn council we decided to send Cyrus and Joe back, with authority to put on men and place the claim once more in full working order. Mrs. Yorke at once commenced to pack up her effects; stating at the same time that she was 'full up of the Oxley, which was a rowdy, disagreeable gold-field as ever she was on, not a patch on old Yatala for comfort, which she had two minds never to have come away from, only Cyrus was a man that always wanted looking after, being that soft and good-natured as anybody might get round him, and run him to spend money on all sorts of foolishness, as well as taking shares in every duffer-lead on the field, as even his own children picked up from the shepherds was no good.'

While this full explanation of the defects of his character was proceeding, much to our amusement, though from our intimate knowledge of our mate's ways we had little to learn, Mrs. Yorke was working away most energetically and effectively, while Cyrus smoked his pipe with an air of philosophical calmness, as if his wife was opening up a subject of entirely new points of interest and abstract bearing.

As soon as we had finished the next wash-up, I was to go back to Yatala to supervise the management, audit the accounts, and so on, finally arranging for the carrying on of the two branches of our mining partnership, either of itself immensely lucrative, but none the less needing both energy and careful guidance to result in the splendid financial success we now so plainly saw before us.

In a couple of weeks, having had the satisfaction of seeing a goodly store of the unmistakable metal lying on the rude wooden receptacle of the machine, after all the clay and water-worn pebbles and extremely yellow water had been finally run off, thence transferred to a camp kettle and carefully banked, I returned to Yatala to look up Cyrus and No. 4.

The old town, though kept on its legs principally by the frontage claims of which ours was a sample, was comparatively deserted. Whole streets and suburbs appeared to have vanished, and the grass was growing on many a floor where we had been on good terms with the occupants, and occasionally spent festive hours.

Some of the old identities still survived, and among them were Mrs. Mangrove and old John who had so loyally backed us in our days of adversity. That speculative but forecasting matron was overjoyed at our return.

'I always stuck to it, Harry and his crowd would come out

all straight some day,' she said exultingly; 'didn't I, John, old
man? I always said the Major would drop in lucky, for all
those yaller books of his. Nothing like taking it cool and not
breaking out in the drink line when the party was down in the
mouth for a spell, as one might say. Some men would have
been on their backs for a week at a stretch with the hard times
you've gone through. But I always did like a party with a
smart clever woman like that little Mrs. Yorke of yours among
'em to do for 'em and keep 'em straight. And your sweetheart
at home, Harry, she brought you luck, you may swear. I
suppose you'll go back and marry her when the claim's worked
out and the Oxley regular done up, and forget all of us roughs
here.'

'I shall never forget you, old woman,' I said, 'you may depend
your life on that, nor John either; so make your mind easy.
See what a present I'll send you out from the old country.'

'I think John and me had better go home too,' said Mrs.
Mangrove. 'You might get another rough turn, and want
somebody as knew you to be your backer again, Harry my
boy.'

'No, no! none of that,' quoth John, laying his pipe pro-
visionally on his knee, a habit of his on the rare occasions when
he thought fit to confirm or contravene the course of the executive department. 'England's too far off to follow a rush, and
too dashed cold into the bargain. I couldn't stand it now.'

'What! worse than Hokitiki or Kiandra?' said his experienced helpmate. 'Don't you remember our getting snowed up
on the Long Plain, and having to feed the horses on the flour
they was a packin'?'

'Yes, that was rather a close thing,' assented John. 'We
was pretty near used up when they found us. I should ha'
been dead only for that spare flannel petticoat of yours; but
there's no get away in the old country, that's what I look at,
and no gold neither, except what you brings in your breeches
pocket. I reckon we'll stick to old New South Wales, for as bad
as it is, while our time lasts.'

'I reckon we may as well,' said his superior officer, 'unless
anything happen to you, and then up stick and clear out, John.
I never could fancy being shovelled in here; that graveyard
always puts me in mind of a shallow rush on purchased land,
where they make you fill in all the duffer shafts. We never did
no good on purchased land, did we, John?'

'Well, if that's all as troubles ye, old woman, you'd better
get the Commissioner to register you a fancy business allotment
there and you can make the improvements all ready for the
last decision, fancy marble crib, headstone and all complete.
Only some o' those fossickers would come rooting round with a
dish after a shower, prospecting, like, for any specimens ye might
have taken with ye.'

'Don't talk of such dreadful things,' said our usually unprejudiced *marchande*, shuddering superstitiously. 'As sure as your name's John Mangrove, some one will lose the number of their mess before the week's out. I've known it happen a score of times before now. You'd better be off to your bed afore you make any more pleasant remarks.'

This broke up the sitting, and we all departed; but strange and grotesque as were the ideas suggested, none of us treated the presentiment with such indifference as to jest upon it. Unlikely as were all the circumstances, and superior as was our position to what it had been of late years, I could not help confessing to an involuntary feeling of gloom and boding fear which I tried in vain to shake off.

On the morning after the conversation recorded we were hard at work arranging for future business. The claim was too good to be left alone for more than a day or two at a time, and the wages men, like all other day labourers, were none the worse for personal supervision. Cyrus Yorke and three miners were detailed for the day shift, and went on accordingly after breakfast, the others, with Joe Bulder, having their allotment of labour during the hours of darkness.

On our way to the claim, our large friend was in unusual spirits. He had made a match with his horse for the following Saturday afternoon holiday, and flattered himself that his antagonist had under-rated the pace and breeding of his nag. Like most Australians, and one Blount in the service of the late lamented Lord Marmion, Cyrus was a 'sworn horse-courser.' He was, indeed, a thoroughly good judge, and, heavy as he was, a first-class rider and whip. He had picked up a thorough-bred horse, which had found his way, more or less feloniously and unlawfully, into the Yatala pound, and had been sold out, poor, ragged, and studiously disfigured, for considerably under his value. By New South Wales law, and indeed by that of nearly all the other colonies, a pound sale gives a perfect and indefeasible title to any animal sold therefrom, no matter what equilarcenous acts may have led to his incarceration.

So Saracen, a great upstanding, weight-carrying bay, 'tower of strength, with a turn of speed,' a son of the well-known imported English blood sire Saladin, had at second-hand become his property for the sum of thirty pounds and a wash-dirt cart.

It was more than whispered that Larry Lurcher had stolen the animal, then in training, out of his stables on a great breeding station to the north, ridden him a hundred miles by day-dawn, and 'worked' him with the aid of, as it turned out, *untrustworthy* confederates into the Yatala pound. One of these said confederates was to buy him out of the pound and hand him over to 'the first robber' directly afterwards, thus to evade suspicion.

This worthy person *did* buy the horse, but utterly declined to convey him by legal receipt to his fellow thief. Larry of course could not explain the transaction sufficiently to regain his property by legal process. So the unjust one triumphed, and unblushingly resold Saracen (for his name had leaked out) for just double what he had given, and had the wash-dirt cart, with fifteen pounds more to the good—Mr. Merlin notwith-standing. This official was in possession of the facts of the case—the name of the former owner of the horse, the night upon which he had been stolen, the distance he had been ridden, and lastly the name of the thief. But he had *no evidence* to connect the adroit receiver with the stolen property. There was not material for 'a case.' So he had to acquiesce in hard fortune, and to smile upon the felon, mentally reserving him for a day of wrath.

Since Cyrus Yorke had become possessed of Saracen, he had improved immensely, and was now 'fit to go for a man's life,' as he said. I never saw Cyrus in better spirits, though to do him justice, hard fortune or good, he was always ready to enjoy himself, holding to such proverbs as 'care killed a cat,' 'a short life and a merry one,' 'it will be all one in a hundred years,' and other wise saws tending to decry undue forethought and anxiety for the morrow.

'My word,' he said, just before I put my leg into the bight of the rope and prepared to descend the one hundred feet of our shaft, 'we're getting rich now, and no mistake. I never ex-pected to see the cash rolling in, hand over hand, like this here. I feel as if I'd more than I know what to do with already. If it wasn't for the old woman and the kids I'd cut it, sell out, and buy a few farms on the Hawkesbury as would keep me the rest of my life. If I win this match with Saracen on Saturday, I don't know as I won't do it now.'

'Don't do anything rash, Cyrus,' I said ; 'better see the claim worked out, and then you can bank your money and live like a gentleman.'

'THAT's all very well, Cyrus,' I said, after a while, 'but you must either do one thing or another. This racing doesn't go well with digging. You'll have to be brought up before the Commissioner under the "efficient working" clause and fined, or else we'll put a man on and charge you a pound a day. We're all sticking to our fight and you're beginning to jack up.'

'All right, Harry,' he said good-humouredly, 'don't be afraid, old man, I'm good for a year's work yet, anyhow. Wait till I get down directly and I'll show you how a native can handle a pick. That Joe Bulder's a good man, but he can't do the day's work I can turn out, though he is a Britisher. Can he now ?'

'He certainly cannot,' I conceded, 'nor any other man in the claim ; only you're not quite so regular as he is.'

'You get out of my way, then, old Parson Harry. I'll be down directly after you send the rope up ; don't be long. Lower away.'

I slid softly down with my foot in the bight of the rope below the rim of mother-earth, and in the requisite number of seconds was safely on the shaft bottom, from which I retreated into a sideling gallery called 'a drive,' and was about to question a wages man as to how they were doing when I heard a sudden, rushing, unwonted sound, terminating in a horrible dull thud upon the hard earth at the bottom of the shaft. How my heart sickened ! How did my blood run cold as I *knew* it must be a *man !* I rushed to the shaft. Several men from the other interior workings met there. We raised the man, for it was one, and little but the outward presentment of what was once Cyrus •Yorke. He was not insensible, better had he been so. His first words were, 'Oh, my God ! my back, my back !'

When we raised him his whole frame was nerveless, dreadfully limp, and incapable of being supported in an upright position. Then we found, amid his groans and involuntary cries, that both legs were broken, an arm, with possibly internal injuries superadded.

He was fastened in an impromptu chair and drawn up with the aid of another miner, who went up with him, holding him as tenderly as a brother. It is in the time of real disaster, of mortal hurt, that one sees the true value of the manly heart. Little is said, there are no professions, but the proverbial feminine tenderness is often equalled by that of the chance comrades whose ordinary speech would lead a superficial observer to infer that not one grain of sentiment could abide with the rough exterior and ruder utterances.

Cyrus had full possession of his senses, and in answer to a question as to how he fell, groaned out, 'I forgot the sprag.' In the exuberance of his spirits he had jumped on to the rope and neglected to see that the wooden wedge, which when placed in the iron roller arrests and acts as a brake to the outrunning rope, was in its place. The unchecked rope ran through the roller with tremendous velocity, and poor Cyrus reached the bottom of the shaft almost as rapidly as though he had thrown himself down it.

There was no hope from the first. A messenger was sent to tell his wife that the earth had fallen in, and that her man was badly hurt. This is the most common phase of mining accident; for this every miner's wife is more or less prepared. In many instances they do not terminate fatally. There is generally some hope; but poor Mrs. Yorke fortunately dreaded the worst, and cried out when she saw the little procession—

'Oh, Cyrus! oh, my man! He'll never get off his bed. I dreamed of it the other night. If they've got to carry him, he's a dead man. I know before they tell me.'

However, she braced herself to the task, and with dry eyes was soon busied in making ready for him the bed, which, though in a poor tent, was neater and more scrupulously tended than in many a grander abode.

As the four men approached with the bark stretcher, upon which lay the huge frame of the magnificent athlete who had gone forth that morning in all the frolic spirits of youth rejoicing in his strength, there was already a small crowd collected near the tent door. His wife came forward, and giving one rapid despairing glance threw herself upon a low chair and covered her face with her hands. Then she walked forward, and bending down kissed the pale face of the death-stricken miner, already tortured by the spasms of mortal agony.

'Never mind, old woman,' he said, with an effort to make his big voice sound cheery and careless as of old, 'don't take on so. The doctor won't mend me, I'm thinking; but you'll have enough for your share of the claim to keep you and the kids for your lives.'

'Don't talk of the claim. I wish we'd never seen it. Oh, my God! have pity on me! Lay him down gently on the bed, please. Why can't I die too?'

There was no need to ask them to lay their ghastly burden down gently. A dozen willing hands were at once proffered, and as lightly as a babe by its mother was the injured man laid upon the bed he was never to quit alive.

Then almost mutely, but with looks and gestures full of heartfelt commiseration, such as could not have been surpassed in the most polished society of the old world, the crowd reverently and heedfully went on its way and left the mourners to their sorrowful duties.

The nearest doctor was at once sent for. He came with little delay; but beyond swathing up the wounded man, so that present pain was minimised, nothing could be done.

The wife looked long and searchingly at his impassive countenance, but found there no hope, alas!

'How long shall I have my senses, doctor?' said poor Cyrus.

'Forty-eight hours, perhaps,' said the man of sickness, wounds, and death. How many death-beds had he seen? 'You had better make any arrangements to-morrow, in case of accident. If you feel the pains coming on badly, take some of the draught I leave you, but not unless you can't do without it. Good-day!'

I walked out to the road with the doctor, and as far as the nearest hotel, no great distance.

'No chance of recovery, I suppose, doctor?' I said tentatively.

'My dear fellow, he has hurts enough to kill all four of you—severe internal injuries, fractured spine, broken thighs, arm, bah! he's a dead man now. Sensible woman, his wife—pity.'

'Poor Cyrus, it's a frightfully sudden end. What will you take, doctor?'

'Brandy, I think—three star.'

All the next day we watched over our poor comrade. Though the pain which he suffered was at times agonising to the limit of human endurance, he was perfectly conscious, and in full possession of his senses.

'That's what makes it so hard to bear,' he said, in one of the intervals when he lay calmed by the powerful narcotic draught, after a paroxysm of unusual fierceness. 'Here am I took, accidental like, all through a minute's cursed carelessness, and me as never had a day's illness, or knowed what it was to be sick or sorry, not once in my life afore. And just as I had my pile pretty well made, so as we'd no call to be grizzlin' and bustin' ourselves for money as long as we lived. Well,' he said reflectively, after a pause, 'I haven't been what folks call a religious cove, but I never wished anybody any harm, and I never done a mean act in my life. And I *do* feel it hard—precious hard—to be rubbed out like this, after followin' the diggings so long, just as I've made the first rise.'

Towards nightfall he felt easier, and as he lay with his wife's hand in his, one might have hoped, but for the cruel irreparable shattering of his whole frame, that a favourable change was at hand. He, however, mistrusted it himself.

'You've been a good wife to me, little woman,' he said to his wife, who now sat looking at him with a fixed gaze of grief, as if the fount of tears was dry, 'and I've not behaved bad to you, that is, as far as I knowed how. When I'm gone, you stick to your shares in the claims till they're clean worked out, and then you go and settle down on the Hawkesbury where we both was reared, and buy a good farm, and eddicate the poor kids well. And if you marry again, as women mostly does, and I don't see why you shouldn't, you pick a sensible, steady chap, as'll take care of you and them. I shan't have nothin' to say agin it. And now, kiss me, old woman, and bring in the poor young uns and the babby, bless his little round mug, for them pains is a comin' on agin, and they won't have their father much longer, I'm afeared.'

.   .   .   .

It was even so. An hour later a merciful delirium set in, and during the long night through Cyrus never recovered consciousness—talking mostly of his early days, among the maize fields of the old river, where so many of the early colonists were reared.

At dawn he passed away; and when the miners went forth to their daily work that morning, the giant frame of him whom all had known in robust health and spirits but two short days before lay cold and stiff for evermore.

We buried him near Radetsky, whom he had followed to the grave, little deeming that he himself was so soon to be laid beside him, and a crowd of mourners only inferior in number to those who formed the death march in honour of the patriot exile paid the last tribute of respect to the big, jolly, generous comrade whom they all knew so well.

As for Mrs. Yorke, she refused all comfort for a while, attending to her household tasks mechanically, but seeming as one whose mental faculties had received a numbing blow. By degrees, however, she rallied, and so far resumed her former nature as to resent a proposal made to her to go 'down the country,' as she expressed it, and settle in a quiet country town with her children.

' Poor Cyrus said I was to stop and see how the claims washed up till the very end,' she said, 'and so I shall as long as they're worth sticking to. I've followed the diggings so long as I should be lost at any other life; so I'll stop on and do for you boys, just as I've always done, till the party's broke up. There's plenty of good hard work, and that'll keep me from thinkin' too much and maybe losin' the little wits I have.'

So Mrs. Yorke abode with the party, knowing that she was among friends and brothers, and that her children were under the protection of the whole goldfield, every man in which would have gone far to aid them in any way. She gradually became her old cheery, sharp-spoken, energetic self again, and matters went on, as is the world's wont, with a gradually decreasing memory of the big, easy, good-humoured husband and father whom she used to order about with almost as little ceremony as the children.

As soon as I had reason to believe that No. 4 could be trusted to manage itself without my supervision, I placed Joe Bulder in charge, and returned to the Oxley. There was no very great difficulty in arranging poor Cyrus Yorke's affairs. He had, luckily for himself, taken a fancy to have his will made a couple of years before, being so much taken with the celerity with which Mr. Markham drew up that important document for a fellow miner *in extremis*, that he got that energetic gentleman to write out one exactly like it for him, leaving everything to his wife, as had his old friend, and actually signed it.

This was most fortunate, and saved all bother with the Curator of Intestate Estates and the necessity of commission to Mr. Bagstock—a result which that gentleman feelingly deplored. We had then only to place Mrs. Yorke's share of the dividends in the bank to her credit after each washing-up, and the poor thing knew to a fraction how much was added to her previous very respectable capital.

After I had returned to the Oxley, and these affairs, revolutionary and otherwise, were done and over, and we had time to think over matters in a calm and unexcited way, it occurred to the Major and myself one night as very strange that Jack Bulder should have taken such very particular care to keep himself out of the whole imbroglio.

'The very thing I should have expected him to have gone in tooth and nail for,' said the Major. 'He has often inveighed against the tyranny and harshness of the officials in the early days of mining, more particularly in Victoria, and occasionally shown an amount of ferocity that surprised me. Now, all through this row he has kept steadily to his work, avoided all meetings, almost ran the risk of being considered a traitor to a cause by some of the hot-headed rioters. Depend upon it he has a good reason for keeping so quiet.'

'He has shown his sense,' I said. 'There were many good reasons for keeping out of all this unfortunate affair. I wish others had thought the same.'

'Yes, but what I mean is, that he had some feeling beyond that of common prudence which would not have swayed such a savage beggar as he is when his blood is up. There is some mystery, I'll swear.'

'There is some mystery about every digger,' I replied. 'There is nothing wonderful about that. If one could only know the real history of nine-tenths of the people that we pass in the street or work alongside of for years, there would be the material for more startling romances than all the fiction-weavers in Europe could manufacture in a decade.'

'When one comes to think of it, perhaps if the Oxley Hotel

bars were turned into a veritable Palace of Truth instead of one occasionally witnessing the unveiling of a fragment of the statue, some novel effects and strong situations would result. But none the less do I firmly believe that our trusty acquaintance and mate carries about with him a secret as much more weighty and dangerous than the ordinary miner's possessions as a square foot of nitro-glycerine is to a canister of powder.'

'If your theory is right about his having a craving for drink, it will all come out the first time he has a "burst." I have noticed his being restless and excited lately. It may be that the enemy is crawling closer to him.'

'Poor devil! Perhaps it is so. I must say I pity those alcoholisers. It is so hopeless a case with them. And they are often such Bayards in their sane periods.'

'Poor human nature again!' said I; 'but isn't it bed-time?'

More important matters than John Bulder's strange mood had been passed over during the revolutionary and funereal period. So little had I dreamed of aught but war rumours and tragedies of late, that the absence of my accustomed letter from my darling Ruth did not unsettle and alarm me, as such an omission usually did.

When I began to reason on the subject I told myself that there was no fixed period for the sending of these priceless missives, and that they were occasionally delayed until the time of my eager expectation had passed.

I had certainly written very fully of late, and had dwelt with more than my usual guarded prudence upon the recent successes and wonderful expectations which had now fallen to our lot.

I had told of my wound, of the robbery of the escort, and of my slow and tedious recovery—all of which facts had elicited the most tender sympathy, the most fervent condolence. I had mentioned, perhaps in somewhat slight and formal manner, the good nursing I had received from Mrs. Morsley, which had so much tended to my recovery. But I had forborne to state that she was identical with the Jane Mangold whom Ruth so well recollected at Dibblestowe Leys.

My reason for this was merely an instinctive feeling that it was better not to go into the whole question of poor Jane's Australian career, and a doubt whether any one in England could completely understand and accurately gauge the nature of a goldfield's friendship, all innocent of wrong-doing as such friendships generally are.

Better for all and safer would it have been had I told the whole unvarnished truth, and trusted to Ruth's delicate sympathy and womanly sense of purity to have instinctively divined the real state of the case. As it was, my reticence gave point to the well-nigh fatal stab to my reputation, aided the deathblow to my happiness, which my mortal enemy had known so well how to deal.

I had tortured myself with the sickening foreboding of evil that sensitive spirits know so well for some weeks, when a letter came with the well-known beyond-sea postmark.

To my deep surprise it was in the squire's handwriting.

With mingled feelings I tore it open and read, with confused brain and mist-dimmed eyes, as follows—

CHAPTER XXV

'ALLERTON COURT.

'SIR—Circumstances have recently been brought to my knowledge connected with your present mode of life in Australia which have entirely changed my opinion of your character.

'Without further alluding to facts, with which I have been made acquainted through the correspondence of a resident at the Oxley diggings and former acquaintance (I enclose the communication), I may state here that I feel myself precluded from all future friendship or association with you.

'Deeply painful as it has been to me and others to decide thus irrevocably, you must be aware that your conduct leaves me no alternative as a father, as a gentleman. May God forgive you. I should be false to my heart's truest feelings if I could add that I did.—Yours obediently,

'GEOFFRY ALLERTON.

'Hereward Pole, Esq.,
  'The Oxley, N. S. Wales, Australia.'

More than once had I turned and re-turned this fatal scroll, like one who doubts and fears of doom irrevocable, spirit-crushing, eternal.

'What foulest slander, what devilish falsehood could have led to this astounding change in the warm-hearted old squire? And if he and his trusting charitable wife believed—as they must have done—the hateful lying slander, what would be the feelings of my pure, gentle, true-hearted Ruth?

And could she desert me at the first whisper of the breath of calumny, she whom I had known to be not less gentle than steadfast? Did I not remember with the vividness of yesterday our walk near the upland terrace along the beech avenue, our youthful sympathy with the Master of Ravenswood, and her scorn of the too easily-swayed Lucy Ashton?

As I sat staring at vacancy, rigid with despair and hate of my enemy—for who but Algernon Malgrade had, through some emissary near his old abode, worked all this misery and ruin— I could yet see Ruth's calm eye and severe features as she expressed her belief in the fond faith and clinging adherence to an absent lover, noblest, most exalted attributes of womanhood. Covering my face in an agony too deep for words, well-nigh too great for human endurance, I took comfort from the recollection.

Again and again I re-read the serpent-like scroll which had been cast into my Eden of love and faith, whence I was now, it would appear, for ever cast forth. It was addressed to an erstwhile companion and fellow-reprobate, sharer in Malgrade's darkest iniquities, but who, more astute or more fortunate than he, had never been actually convicted of dishonourable conduct, and was therefore still in the enjoyment of his social position. The poisonous extract ran thus—

'I daresay you remember something about that fellow Pole, who migrated to this strange quarter of the globe just before I did. I never liked the confounded prig, but did him the justice to think that he was hard-working and what the world calls respectable. Still I think poor old Allerton, who was ass enough to allow that nice daughter of his to become engaged to him, ought to know that he has been living in the most open manner with a woman named Morsley, who left her husband to nurse him when he received a wound in the escort robbery, and has remained with him ever since. She was said to have been a *tendresse* of his when he was playing at farming with her father, old Mangold, in Kent. People don't mind that sort of thing here, and *I* am not straitlaced, as you know, but I never was a sanctimonious hypocrite, and I can't stand fellows who sail under false colours.'

This artfully concocted missile had not failed of its effect. Like the frail dart, the keen point of which has been steeped in the festering relics of the charnel house, the merest scratch was sufficient to rankle and inflame into a mortal wound. 'The death of hope, love, friendship, all that is, except mere breath,' had followed. Should I ever be able to refute the calumny? Should I ever be afforded an opportunity to clear myself of this subtle, deadliest accusation? For the arch-assassin and conspirator in the matter was difficult to reach. We were already known to be sworn enemies. To charge him with the villainy, to assail him with reproaches, would serve no good end. He would probably reply with his polished, imperturbable sneer, well gratified to find that the barbed arrow had gone home. For an actual hand to hand conflict the time and place were not fitting. Men did not carry arms at our diggings, and though I felt as if I could have crushed every bone in his body, yet I knew that he was an adept at every kind of athletic exercise, and that an attack by me could only end in an unseemly scuffle and a separation by the adjoining bystanders, with an ultimate appeal to the police-office. Satisfaction was not to be obtained in that way. I must bide my time. He might yet be incriminated in the escort robbery. Merlin was following up the trail like a sleuth-hound. I should yet see him in the dock, thence to receive the full measure of his deserts.

A month passed. How I bore up under my burden I cannot tell. None can ever know. I was fortunate in having the inestimable distraction of full and exhausting bodily toil, which to the strong man, whose muscular power will bear the strain, supplies an anodyne to which none other is comparable. To the Major, who shared all my secrets, though I had not been put into full possession of his, I confided my griefs. He was less sardonic than I had ever known him.

'If I were weak enough to make an exception in favour of any daughter of Eve, which I don't say I do,' he answered musingly, 'I should do so in the case of Miss Allerton. She is, perhaps, one of the rare feminine flowerets which a certain consensus of persons of experience have decided to bloom once in a century. Were I in love, like you, which God forbid, I should hope against hope.'

Did the Major sigh? I could not tell. It would be too wonderful were it so. But after delivering himself of this most unusual sentiment, he departed abruptly.

I was approaching a phase of stony despair, which, apparently, no outward occurrences had power to change, when a letter was brought to me on which I instantly descried the long-loved, long-lamented characters of my love.

Had I been sick and like to die? Even in this hour of sanity and security, I fully believe so. That dull, darksome despair of life, the denial of all worth and value in existence, had set in, which kills in some races even as surely as the sword, though silently as the fatal cup. The Lascar casts himself down, saying I shall die, and by the simple exercise of will—hereditarily so directed—even thus *does* die. Why not the hopeless lover?

Never before had I opened one of her dear letters without being pervaded by a feeling of joy and serenity, which seemed as with some supernal influence to dispel the mists of doubt and danger by which my life was environed. Fearing, as I had good reason now to do, lest the *Argosy*, with all my freight of happiness, had hopelessly foundered, I yet had an instinctive reminiscent sensation of the well-remembered gracious influence. Nor was it illusory. Opening the letter with the obstinately-resolved feeling of one who knows that his charter of life or death, the release or the death warrant, lies between those delicate sheets, I read no farther than 'My darling Hereward,' when I threw myself on my knees and kissed the letter again and again in an agony of love and gratitude, as though it bore the pardon of a soul ransomed from the Inferno.

When my throbbing heart and whirling brain would permit me, I addressed myself more collectedly to the closely-written pages, which ran thus—

'I could not send you this before, though I grieved. They tell me all through the delirium of my illness that you would be left in doubt of your own Ruth, and of her love towards you, even after the wicked slander which has so injured you in papa's estimation. For I have been ill, very ill, my darling, and my poor brain is still weak and troubled with the dreadful imaginings which passed through it during the fever.

'But they tell me I am recovering now, and after the change of air which my dearest mother and I are about to take, I feel that I shall be quite well again and able to act with firmness. How much strength of purpose shall I need to cling to my love through good and evil report.

'Oh, what a dreadful thing it is that wicked people should be permitted to work such woe to those who have never injured them. I have barely heard of this Algernon Malgrade, whose fiendish letter has done all this evil to us. I was merely told that he was a man whom his friends had long cast off, and whose name was infamous in his own neighbourhood. That he could never have been a friend of yours, and is now a deadly enemy, I can well understand. And the deadliest foe he has proved himself to be.

'Before I go further I MUST tell you that, though I never believed the wicked invention, yet papa's anger, dear mother's sorrow, and my own vexation that any act of yours should have been capable of such a construction, combined to harass me with doubts and to produce the illness from which I have just arisen. It was also most unfortunate that you did not tell me in your letters after you were wounded that the nurse, to whom I felt so grateful, was Jane Mangold. Every one knew her here as a handsome flighty girl before she left England, and all were ready to believe the worst of her after the circumstantial falsehood which Mr. Malgrade's friend, whom I shall always consider as bad as himself, circulated.

'But oh, my own Hereward—long loved, only loved that you are, as from the first — I believed in your truth with all my heart and soul; so I do now. My father's bitter anger and disappointment at what he terms your ingratitude must yield to time and proof of your innocence. Dear mother is again on my side, and thinks he was over hasty in condemning you unheard. As for me, I am yours, in love and faith, as long as life lasts; and nothing that I can imagine would tear you from my heart, though I might die in the effort to sever myself from you.

'Write at once, calmly and prudently, to dear father and set yourself right, as you must be able to do, with as little delay as possible. When I think that but for this terrible escort robbery you might even now have been on your way home, I can hardly bear to think of the wretches who planned it, and are responsible for all the evils which have since flowed from the crime.

'Do not lose a moment in calming the fears about yourself which I constantly entertain, and in proclaiming your justification before my parents and all the world. But, whatever may be their opinion—and I pray that I may not be deemed wicked for opposing it,—I am and shall be always, your own   RUTH ALLERTON.'

I carefully folded up and put away among my hoarded treasures this the most rare and precious of them all—the assurance of a pure and loving woman's devotion. Encompassed as she was by apparently well-founded fears and anxieties, by the opposition of her parents and friends, and the opinion of the society in which she lived, what courage did she display! A difficult measure of antagonism for one so gentle and tender to withstand. Yet, for my sake, she repressed her natural desire to conform in all respects to the will of those tender parents with whom her life had been spent in willing obedience, choosing rather to trust in the fealty of one who, like me, was living in a strange land, the sport of wild adventure, of untoward fate, the undefended victim of calumny.

Whatever love mortal man could give, had ever given to woman, was her due; and if ever man had loved truly and with all the strength of his being, I, Hereward Pole, was that man. Why could I not at once take steps and in person defy my maligners and for ever put to flight all doubt of my good faith? I could *almost* do it. If I sold out now and quitted the goldfields I should leave with a fair fortune, a respectable competence sufficient to provide moderately for all my wants in days to come. But just now, at the crowning point of fortune, when *everything*, in a miner's point of view, was in our favour, it seemed too hard to quit the still running golden stream and leave to others the garnering of the wondrous treasures which were within our grasp. No! I had sworn to return to the land of my forefathers with such a portion of the golden store of this new world as should suffice to equip their descendant with something of the old splendour of the ancient house. I had wrested so much from the dragons which guarded the Hesperides of the south. I would reappear, laden with what would disarm the sneers and purchase for evermore the smiles of the fawning crowd we dignify as society.

Yes! in despite of the weary load of overworn patience, of the crushing sorrow, never more sharply mordant than now, the machination of fiends, falsely called men, I would adhere to my first resolution, never departed from, and fight out my life-battle to the close. The stubborn pride which compelled my expatriation forbade a premature return.

Meanwhile, all that I could do should be done. I would write both to the Squire and to my own unfaltering high-souled love, placing before them the fullest details, the most minute facts. My exculpation I would leave to a just and merciful God, to my Ruth's tender trust, to her father's honour and plighted word.

And yet, how was I to bear myself towards the ill-fated woman who was so closely, so ominously linked with my fortunes? Was I, with selfish dread of damage, to cast her off at the first storm summons of wave and gathering blast, as seamen, mad with fear or reckless in despair, cast forth the weaker comrade from an overladen skiff? Not for even her dear love's sake, not for the risk of withering up the life that remained to me, as a flame-scorched scroll, would I so far dishonour my manhood by the desertion of a trust.

This late-stricken victim, this forlorn creature, alone in a world which was thronged with foes and oppressors, had crept to my feet to die or to be succoured in sore need in the name of the old pure friendship of our joyous charmed youth, and was I to cast her off with calculating cowardice because her name had been used to forge a false indictment ?

No ! by heaven ! some men might do this thing, might hug themselves with the belief that the seeming cruelty of prudence was but the duty to themselves and their stainless reputation which all men owe. But might the Lord do so to me, and more, in the words of the ancient record of man's earliest tragedies, if I, Hereward Pole, stooped to so base a shelter from the storm of calumny which bade fair to whelm me.

So I betook me to the poor substitute for the spoken word, which those must ever employ who look to lighten the wrong which has been for ages the proverbial doom of the absent. I shut myself up, and devoted a long day to the careful compilation of a record of all that had occurred between us since I had first seen the unhappy Jane Mangold in Australia. I wrote humbly and patiently to the old Squire, solemnly pledging my faith as a man and a gentleman, that no tie existed between us save such as was almost a necessity of our positions, and which reflected honour upon our common nature.

I stated finally that she was about to sail for England shortly, that I had pledged myself to carry out arrangements to that effect, from which, of course, he would see that I could not now draw back, and that as she was returning to her father's home he might, if he pleased, and I earnestly besought him to do so, visit her at the Leys, and hear from her own mouth the true facts of the case. When face to face with her, I could trust to his clear head and knowledge of the world to unravel any apparent mystery.

My task over, my despatches sealed and posted, somewhat of my burning anxiety was allayed. Some portion of the load was lifted from my soul. I felt nerved to attempt the completion of my errand to this fair land, abstracted as it had been hitherto, as by all the evil genii of an eastern tale, and yet I had so lately yearned but to cease from penitent, aimless struggling against fate, to sleep the sleep of the tired wayfarer, to lie down and die !

Thus I sought out Jane ; told her—for I thought it well to do so—of the coward shaft that had been aimed against two lives. Her old fiery nature blazed fiercely out at Malgrade's treachery.

'Liar and coward that he is !' she cried. 'I could stab him with my own hand. *He* knew it was a lie—none better, but he hates me ' (here she blushed painfully) 'not less than he does you. He thought he would ruin us both with the same miserable slander. If I was a man I would tear his false heart out. And yet'—here the whole expression of her face softened and changed—'I only am to blame that my name could ever be used to injure yours, to cause you unhappiness and bring sorrow into your life and of those whom you love. I am indeed a most unhappy creature, born to do evil to my best friends, to those I love best; and I have at times a foreboding —oh! so dark and fearful, when I am long alone—that I shall yet work misery to you, Hereward Pole—my friend, my only friend! Why was I born? Why does God make such women as I have been—oh! why, why?'

Here her whole frame was shaken by a fit of passionate weeping which lasted for some time before I could interfere to comfort her and counsel a calm consideration of her future course. At length she controlled herself by a painful effort so piteously visible through every movement of her limbs and features that the hardest, coldest heart must then have permitted mercy to temper justice.

Raising her tear-stained face, and essaying at first vainly to speak, like a child who attempts to do so after abandonment to passionate grief, she again addressed me—

'I declare, as God hears me, that I would go away this moment where you would never hear of me more and no tongue could pierce this poor bleeding heart afresh, but for one reason, and one only.'

'Do not do anything so rash or foolish, my dear Jane. The worst has been said, no further harm can be done—that is one, if a small comfort. I will hasten my trip to Sydney. What I promised you nothing shall induce me to forego. Keep up your spirits, then. A few weeks will see you on your way to Dibblestowe Leys, bless the old place! Once there you can plead my cause, and clear yourself more effectively than all the letters in the world.'

'It is a glimpse of heaven,' she said, 'and do you not think I have been looking forward to it all these weary months as my only reason for living? But for that, as I said, I would start away for Victoria or New Zealand, change my name, and disappear from your life and all that ever heard the name of Jane Mangold. How I wish I had never borne another. But I shall stay, because—because—I am afraid.'

Here so strange and terrible an expression of fear, of mortal fear, passed over her countenance that a half thought her brain had given way under the strain of her sufferings crossed my mind.

'Jane, Jane,' I said almost harshly, 'what nonsense is this, what are you afraid of, or of whom?'

'I do not know of whom, she said in a strange low voice, with her eyes fixed on vacancy as one who peers into thick darkness; 'but I have a horrible dread, a kind of waking dream, of being *murdered*. And oh! how unspeakably awful, how fearful it must be to be killed in a second, in some cruel, painful way—sent to judgment with all one's sins upon one's head.'

'And who is there to kill you?' I said, trying but in vain to assume a cheerful tone. 'Of course—well——' here I hesitated; 'but why talk of impossibilities, these sort of things are never done.'

'They are done,' she said, still in the same low, murmuring, unnatural tone. 'Don't you remember that case of Clara Denver, poor thing? I saw her laughing carelessly the very day before. Still I don't think he would do it, though I used to think so once. Twice I dreamed of a man in a dark cloak, a sort of poncho. I could not see his face, but he had a knife, a horrid knife!' Here she shuddered and almost gasped for breath. 'I felt its sharp edge across my throat. Then I woke, screaming out. Twice I dreamed this. Do you think dreams are ever sent to warn people?'

'You have been terrifying yourself with fancies and imagining, my poor Jane,' I said, 'until you begin to see visions. Look at the clear sky and the bright sunshine. Where is the need for all this gloom and sadness? You and I are still alive and well in spite of the misery which others have caused us. Let us look facts in the face, do our duty, and trust in God. I must tell Mrs. Yorke to make you walk a little more—you shut yourself up too much.'

'You know I can't go walking about like other people,' she said; 'but you are always good and kind, and I feel better already. I will try and think of nothing—nothing—till you are ready to start for Sydney; and then God may pardon me and give me another chance for happiness in this life. Good-bye!'

She held out her hand instinctively, and then half shyly withdrew it, as if she recognised some additional reason why not even the minor greetings of life should be exchanged between us; then, as I grasped hers, said timidly, 'I suppose we may shake hands, mayn't we?'

I pressed her hand in mute disavowal of the tyranny of the idle or evil-speaking world to bind our every act and speech. As she turned and walked slowly, almost feebly away, I turned away my head, for I could not bear the sight of her altered mien and form, so changed from the bright womanly graces of old days.

It yet wanted some hours of sunset. There was no need for my returning to the claim. I had provided for my share of the work being efficiently performed in my absence. I shrunk from the idea of sitting or lying down aimlessly after the tumult of emotion which I had so recently experienced. I turned my steps towards the forest path which led outwards from the diggings, breasting the slope with rapid stride, and feeling the sunset breeze as it fanned my brow an indescribable relief to a fevered spirit.

I had crossed more than one crest of the slate-strewn ranges, and was threading the close shrubbery of a narrow grassy dell, when I saw the woman whom we knew as Dolores coming along the track. Bareheaded, with rapid pace and eager gesture, she turned at once towards me as her eyes lighted on my approaching figure.

Her head was thrown back ; her black hair, which was loose, fell in great masses down her back. Her eyes were flashing, and her white even teeth were set closely with a resolved, almost cruel expression.

I thought of passing her without appearing to take notice of her altered mein, but dismissed the idea as I marked her evident distress and agitation.

'Good evening, Mrs. Malgrade,' I said ; 'what's wrong with you? Has anything happened?'

'Happened!' she said, with fierce hate and scorn filling every line of her features, and blazing in her large dark eyes that seemed aglow with unearthly light. 'What should happen to a woman that's bound to Algernon Malgrade but wrong and ill-treatment. What have you to say of a man that strikes, that beats his wife. God help me! I am not THAT, but the miserable woman that bears his name ; and here I swear before God that I will never do so more, or break bread, or live under the same roof with him, if I starve or work my fingers to the bone for it.'

Here the excited woman fell upon her knees and raised her hands and face to heaven. 'I swear that I, Dolores Lusada, will never more live under the same roof with Algernon Malgrade, or take a morsel of meat or a piece of money from his hand, if I should starve ; and if I do not keep this oath may my brain wither and this hand rot to the shoulder. Look here, Harry,' said she, 'do you see the pretty mark?' here I saw that her face was bruised and cut as with a heavy blow. 'And see here,' she pulled up her sleeve, and on her white round arm was another livid mark that no light stroke ever made. 'And now you despise me. I know you do. Oh, Lord God! that ever I should have come to this!'

Then she threw herself upon the green turf, and covering her face with her hands wept and lamented with so dreadful an agony of tears, as if (in the phrase of childish days) 'her heart would break.'

It was not in my nature to abstain from offering such poor shreds of consolation as I had to bestow to any woman under such stress of circumstances. I certainly distrusted, and in a way disliked, Dolores as much as I could dislike a very beautiful woman, which was not, after all, a very active sentiment. I was fully aware that she might work me evil, and that to be seen with her would by no means conduce to my social reputation. For even on goldfields Mrs. Grundy is no obsolete puissance.

I calmed the frantic woman, and partly persuaded her to go to a respectable quiet lodging in Yatala, where she could remain until either she effected a reconciliation with Malgrade, which I knew was highly probable, constituted as women are, or made final arrangements for separation. Go back at present she would not, nor had I the heart to urge her.

I felt a grim half-bitter smile pass over my features as I said aloud—

'It is Kismet. Surely I am doomed to be the champion of every distressed dame and damsel on the goldfield. I am Amadis de Gaul or some other mediæval knight of romance, or perchance Don Quixote himself. If my heart is reflected in my face, there could scarce be a closer presentment of the knight of the sorrowful countenance. How the major will oppress me!'

I had brought matters to this more or less satisfactory stage, and was departing on my own track, leaving her to follow the path to the township which she knew very well, when a figure crossed the crest of the hill which caused both of us to start instinctively.

It was Algernon Malgrade. I noted the exact moment when he recognised our figures. He checked his pace for an instant, then advanced with a slow indifferent step and studied air of lounging carelessness.

He halted within a yard, and gazed steadfastly in both faces as if to read our very souls. Then he laughed. Devils laugh so. I felt certain of it, though I had, of course, no means of verifying the fact.

CHAPTER XXVI

'So you didn't drown yourself, *carissima !*' he said at length, in his soft vibrating voice, which he could render so melodious at will, 'but have concluded to console yourself and enlist the sympathy of Mr. Hereward Pole. *Je vous en fais mes compliments, monsieur,*' he added, taking off his hat and bowing with an assumption of respectful politeness ; then turning to Dolores, he added, 'I should have thought he had his hands full at present. If madame's temper, not to speak of other attributes, remains unimpaired he will have reason, like me, to bless the hour he first set eyes on you.'

Not prone to sudden outburst, rather of the older Gothic calibre, slow of incandescence, but capable under sufficient stimulus of being wrought up to a white heat, I had been inwardly raging since Malgrade first came within scope of my vision. I had refrained from violence, though at desperate cost of self-repression, not wishing to have it bruited abroad that Dolores was the *teterrima causa.*

But one swift thought of the ruin he had so nearly effected in my own case, joined to a sight at the same moment of the woman's bleeding face as it came between me and the westering sun, precipitated such a wave of wrath and desire for vengeance that I felt as if, like Ugolino, I could have passed an eternity in mangling the flesh of my foe.

Well was it said *Brevis insania furor est.* What is it but madness when the whole sensorium is merged in one reckless spasm of blood-lust, careless—if but the hate-hunger be appeased, the hate-thirst slaked—that fortune, fair fame, life itself be spent in the effort, lavishly as a child's toys of which he is awearied ?

Powerless then, too, the disciplined will, the instinctive inherited habit of prevision, to stand against the dire half-animal transport. The passion of Dolores, haughty and tameless as was her spirit, seemed to pale before the superior volume of mine, as with glaring eyes I confronted him, her enemy and mine.

"Base dog, and son of a dog !' I said. 'How dare you speak

to a man that you have wronged like me? You can beat a woman, you can lie behind backs. Look at that woman's bleeding face. Stand up to a *man*, you hound, and take the punishment you deserve, for, by ——, you shall have it now.'

A general misconception has gained credence that evil-intentioned people decline to look fixedly upon the countenances of the just or other sections of humanity. This may not infrequently occur; but the converse fact must have repeatedly impressed itself upon even the most superficial observer. Whatever his evil doings, and they were comprehensively numerous, man nor woman could ever say Algernon Malgrade's bright blue eyes and soft met them not fairly when he elected to deceive. Clear were they, and burning with the fires of hell when the demon within him was unchained; but always unwavering, lowered neither to friend nor foe.

As he stepped lightly forward with a mocking smile on his lip, I watched their cruel light deepen and glow, as might the gladiator's gaze in the old days of Rome, when the sword-play was before Cæsar, and the deadly inevitable stroke or thrust was impending.

In the matter of science as applied in the modern arena to boxing, no man on that great goldfield was his equal. But he had been lately leading an indolent dissipated life, while I had been taxing for the last few months, and therefore strengthening, every muscle and sinew in my whole frame.

Of these and other ideas I was dimly conscious as we went at each other with silent ferocity: on both sides the feeling of personal antagonism was too intense to suffer the intrusion of ordinary precaution.

From the first onset all notion of defence seemed to be abandoned, and the strange, curiously rare, sound made by the fall of heavy blows upon face and body, with our heaving breath, was the sole interruption for a space to the stillness of the sequestered spot.

I must have received a larger share of the first succession of blows that rained upon either form, but I felt or I heeded them not. I had iron muscles, a giant's strength in that hour, and, after fighting in to a 'half-arm rally,' which lasted for many seconds, I was less surprised than grimly triumphant when my adversary dropped senseless upon the turf, and lay without motion, prone and nerveless, as one dead.

Dolores had stood the while at a little distance watching the combat, her great dark eyes fixed upon us with an expression half fierce, half wondering, as though the contest, while ministering to her craving for revenge, was half painful from the mingled emotions which so inexplicably sway that most ancient and still unriddled sphinx of womanhood.

But when the man stirred not for a space, lying in an awkward position, as does a corpse, she slowly and unwillingly, yet as if drawn by a powerful influence, moved towards him, and then kneeling down by his side changed the position of his head, and loosened the kerchief carelessly knotted around his throat. As for me, I would not then have touched limb or feature to have saved his life, looking on him still with the loathing pitiless ire which the wounded serpent excites as we watch him writhing in the flames.

My evident feeling of abhorrence, ignorant as she was of the deeper reason I had for revenge, commenced to produce a counterpoise of sympathy on her part. Gradually he recovered consciousness, and, sitting up, gazed at me with a look of malice so intense, so devilish, that I could have deemed it in my excited state to have issued from a corpse re-animated by a fiend from hell.

Shaking his fist, he moved his mouth and essayed to speak. No words came, though a gibbering horrible sound was produced. I saw Dolores, with a softened expression akin to pity, place her hand upon his face; not till then did I observe with more curiosity than regret that the lower jaw was broken. My last left-handed blow, delivered with full force, had caught the lower face fair, at exactly the true distance, splintering the bone as if glass.

For the first time I felt partly avenged.

'You have shown yourself a man, Harry Pole,' said Dolores, as Malgrade fell over and apparently fainted, 'both in your pity and in your anger. I envy the woman who claims your love—the love of a good man. Once I had that treasure, but lured away by a villain, such a one as *he* (and she pointed to the prostrate man), I left home and happiness for ever—for ever. You had better return to your tent. I cannot abandon him in helplessness and pain, though in such a case he would not think of *me*. We part not this time, better for both if we did.'

Their cottage was at no great distance from the spot. When he recovered himself he would be able to walk there easily enough with her assistance. He was too well accustomed to feminine caprice to wonder at her change of humour. Doubtless they would effect a temporary reconciliation as they had done many a time and often before.

It was late when I reached our camp. I crept to my bed and slept as well as the pain of my sorely-bruised body would allow.

My appearance on the next morning naturally created great and general astonishment. But I kept my own counsel. Of course, it was shrewdly guessed that I did not so disfigure myself. And the multiform though not dangerous injuries I had evidently received were not to be accounted for on any 'ran against a post' theory.

But I have before stated that in no community in the world is the anciently wise precept of each man minding his own proper business more strictly adhered to than upon a goldfield.

If somebody had 'rolled into me' or *vice versâ*, it was doubtless
my own affair.   If I had reasons for not publishing the nature
of the combat, evidently a hardly contested one, why well and
good also.   It would come out in due time; and if it never did
so, what matter?   So my countenance was permitted gradually
to recover its normal contour and complexion without exciting
ill-bred remark or curiosity.

The great goldfield was still crowded and surging, as it had
been from its commencement, with human billows which foamed
ceaselessly around it—still ebbed and flowed the human tide
over its golden sands.   For the earth, pierced and torn and
riddled in every direction for miles upon miles, still gave to
the ceaseless toil of the excited and tireless crowd gold dust
and ingots in such profusion as might have excited the envy of
a gnome.

Some idea may be formed of the vast quantity actually produced by a glance at the official register of the period.   It is
there recorded by Commissioner Blake that within two years
not less than three hundred thousand ounces of gold were sent
to the metropolis by the Government escort alone.   Much was
also taken to Sydney or Melbourne by miners who preferred the
hazardous plan of carrying their own treasure.   Making all due
allowances, gold to the value of a million and a half sterling
must have been reft from the forgotten subterranean river beds
of the Oxley during the two years that we spent there.

And now the weather of the spring I refer to came in exceptionally wet and stormy.   For weeks heavy drenching rain
soaked the forests, the plains, the low-lying flats, making lakelets and pools of standing water where but lately the dust rose
in red or yellowish white clouds, and the tired eyes shrank from
the refracted glare of the glittering quartz-strewn streets and
the red massed mullock heaps.

The streams filled to overflowing ran foaming along their
channels, or raised above them by heavy rains amid the cloud-
capped mountains at their sources, ran riot in devastating flood,
sweeping away from the lower lands the cottage homes and
crops of farmers, the flocks and fences of the larger graziers, the
dams and water-races of the sluice-employing miner, while
every week brought news of deaths by drowning in the dangerous fords of the unbridged streams.   Coach passengers, or the
horsemen or ordinary post traveller, the peripatetic labourer of
the colonies, all shared and suffered alike.

What was curious was that the winter proper, which in Australia extends from June to August, had been exceptionally dry
and fine.   An occasional week of hard frost perhaps, with the
thermometer down to 25° Fahr., but on the whole glorious
weather—fresh, pure, invigorating, without tempest or inclement
weather of any kind.

But in September the weather changed with the rapid unheralded suddenness of the Australian seasons. Sleet-storms and heavy-driving gales of polar severity succeeded the bright noons and cloudless morns of the midwinter period.

Unprotected as our encampment was in the essentials of substantial buildings, the change of weather fell upon us like a Russian winter campaign.

A change came over the aspect of the whole settlement. The tents and bark-covered buildings, blown down or soaked through and through, looked bedraggled and forlorn. The women and children suffered much, doubtless ; for these last there was no play now outside of their homes, in which the narrow space precluded all but huddling and overcrowding for warmth and shelter.

The miners were now often hindered from their regular labour, and in the intervals, when the claims were ' off work,' might be seen grouped in or immediately around the bars of the hotels. These establishments did a roaring trade in hot grog, for the greater convenience of furnishing which, ingeniously contrived receptacles of boiling water were kept simmering all day and half the night on the counters.

I was sitting with Bagstock at the camp, at which palatial residence we were not disinclined occasionally to spend an evening, when a miner came to the door and requested to see the Clerk of the Court upon very urgent business.

This was no doubt informal, the 'government time' to which Bagstock was so fond of referring, only lasting from 10 o'clock to 4 p.m., as in more settled communities. But of course in real emergency no hard and fast line was drawn.

'What d'ye want, my m-m-m-an ?' said Bagstock, looking at the drenched figure and splashed garments of the messenger. 'Look sharp ! it's awfully c-c-cold.'

'I daresay it is,' said the man, looking down at his steaming horse, the heaving sides of which betokened the pace at which they had travelled. 'I hadn't time to think about it. I was sent to ask you to, if you'd come and marry a party to-night.'

'Marry a p-p-party ?' echoes the astonished functionary. 'Couldn't they c-c-c-come to me ? C-c-can't they w-w-wait till . m-m-morning ?'

'They can't come, and if they wait till morning it will be too late,' said the man solemnly, a tall gaunt Forty-Niner, as the Californian diggers were called who had been at the first discovery.

'Where is it, th-th-then ?' asked Bagstock.

'At the Gravel Pits,' said the messenger, naming a diggings more than ten miles off, on an exceptionally bad road, and with a dangerous creek to cross.

'The Gravel Pits ! said Bagstock. 'The G-g-g-gravel Pits, and on this sort of night !' Here the wind howled afresh and the rain poured down obliquely in swirls and eddies as if bent on finding its way into every cranny and corner by sideling intrusion. 'Why, I w-wouldn't go there to-night for f-f-fifty pounds!'

'I'll give you fifty pounds, half down,' said the unknown, feeling in his pocket, 'if you'll go at once ; there's life and death in the cards. What do you say ?'

'Well,' said Bagstock, 'that alters the c-c-case ; done with you ! I must muffle up, I s-s-suppose. I'll order my horse. Pole, you've got y-y-yours in the stable. C-c-come along for c-c-company.'

In five minutes we were mounted and all three riding as hard as we dared through the splashing sheets and streams of various depths that lay across our path in every way. Bagstock was not always painfully anxious about his work, but when actually compelled to his task there was no fault to be found with his energy and capacity. Our guide took the lead. I never rode in a wilder night, rarely along a rougher road. The ceaseless rain had filled all the minor water-courses, and every road-rut was running like a rivulet for hundreds of yards together. We waded through sheets of water or sand waist deep in unexpected pools. Best, our horses were tried and good. As for the message-miner, he rode ahead, keeping straight forward towards some unknown point, and his wiry middle sized mustang seemed to pass with instinctive cleverness the uneven blind tracks, dangerous to all horses not gifted with the marvellous surefootedness of the bush-bred Australian.

A two hours' ride landed us at the Gravel Pits, a section of the great stream of the 'deep leads' which formed the crowning glory of the goldfield. Wonderfully rich claims had been met with here, of which some, from the character and preponderance of the 'pay gravel,' as our Californian friends termed it, had gained their present name.

'Here's poor Jim's hut,' said our guide, pulling up at length with a jerk that brought us all almost on the haunches of his nag, 'and a better mate never handled a pick. But his time's up. The confounded low fever has about settled him. The doctor says he can't last another day anyhow.'

'But you told me some one w-w-wanted to be m-m-m-m-*married*,' said Mr. Bagstock, quite aghast. 'I'm not the undertaker. Who's the bridegroom ?'

'Why, poor old Jim is,' said the miner, taking the saddle off his smoking hackney, and letting her go with a pair of hobbles and a large bell which he affixed to her neck while he was talking. 'But you go inside, both of you, gentlemen, and you'll see all about it.'

He pulled open the door of the hut as he spoke, and held it open for us to enter.

The sight was a singular one. On a rude bedstead near the fireplace, scrupulously clean, and warm with all the usual coverings, lay the wasting figure of a man, the unearthly brilliancy of whose eyes and the waxen hue of his features showed that he was in the last stage of fever. Such a sight was by no means new to us. In crowded mining camps, as in all armies in tent or field, typhoid fever and its allied diseases claim their toll with fearful and awful regularity.

Day after day, when the weather was hot and humid in the late autumn, had we heard the 'Dead March in Saul' pealing and reverberating through the forest, and listened to the tramp of the long array of mourners.

But these terrible muster-rolls had long ceased, and save in exceptional cases like the present, when the Destroyer after being battled with through long months had finally triumphed, were beginning to be forgotten.

Another remarkable figure in the tableau was that of a handsome girl, whose whole form and face were plunged in deepest despairing grief — heartbroken, apparently, with the traces of undried tears on her cheeks. She was leaning over the bed, dressed in such finery, including a costly white silk dress, as would have excited the envy of most women on the field. She was dressed in bridal array evidently, a veil covering partly her long fair hair. She also wore heavy gold earrings, a broach of the same material, and a necklace of brilliants. A large bouquet of white roses and camellias, supplied by no provincial horticulturist, lay on the table near to her.

We at once took in the situation. Both of us knew the sick man by sight, as also by reputation. He had come here with his mate by way of California, where he had worked for some years, but had originally come from Australia, to which land he had at first emigrated from his native country.

He rose with the utmost difficulty, holding by a bar suspended above the bed, as we came in, and fixed his glassy eyes upon us.

'Glad to see you, gentlemen!' he said, in a thin reedy treble, which struck painfully on our ears when we recalled the strong man who now lay so feeble and childishly weak. 'I wasn't sure as Mr. Bagstock 'ud come, the weather bein' that bad. I was afeared I shouldn't be able to make an honest woman of poor Bessy there. I couldn't have rested in my grave if I hadn't done it — nohow I couldn't. Don't take on, girl. It wasn't altogether your fault or altogether mine either, as things arn't square.'

'Oh, Jim!' cried out the girl passionately, fastening her eyes upon him with the intense devouring gaze of love mingled with despair, 'don't talk in that way. I'm glad and proud enough to be made your wife; but I always knew that it would be so some time, and I trusted you, didn't I? Hadn't we better wait till you get well?'

'I'm not goin' to get well, Bess, and what ain't done this

night 'll never be done,' said the sick man grimly. 'So let's lose no more time. Bill's here, as 'll be best man ; and they can't say as you haven't a wedding dress and all complete, even to the bo-kay.'

Here the sick man tried to smile, but the extreme weakness of the facial muscles prevented the attempt from becoming anything but a ghastly contortion.

CHAPTER XXVII

It was but too evident that the strength of the principal performer in this strange travesty of the festal marriage rite would not last out much beyond the time necessary for the registration, so Bagstock took down the names, ages, nationality, and religion of the parties with methodical accuracy. The while the sick man watched and listened with painful eagerness lest anything should be omitted which might be material to the validity of the contract.

The girl made a flickering effort to appear calm and collected and then relapsed into her previous expression of deepest gloom ; while—how piteous to look upon—the sick man tried to rouse her, and actually forced her with tremulous fingers to take the bouquet into hers, clay-cold and unresisting as they were.

'What's the meaning of all this?' said I to our guide, who sat carelessly watching the proceedings with rather a satisfied expression.

'Well, you see, poor old Jim here, his wife—that's his first one—and he didn't hit it over and above well, and many a year ago in Victoria she made a bolt of it. All the boys tell me that it was her fault and not Jim's.'

'And so I suppose he takes up with this pretty young woman when he came on to the rush here, and they were not able to get married before.'

'That's about the size of it, Mr. Pole. This gal, she was the daughter of one of the selectors at Blue Gum Flats, and about two years ago she and Jim made it up to be man and wife, like. You remember what an upstanding good-looking chap he were.'

'Yes, indeed, he was. It's a sad change to see him like this.'

'Well, his time's up. A man must go when his time comes ; he ain't had a bad innings, but he used to fret awful at times when he thought as Bessy wasn't his wife. Now it's all right, and he'll die happy.'

'But how can he legally marry her if his wife——'

'Bless your heart, why he only got the news of his wife's death last week, and the moment he heard of it he orders the wedding dress, and the earrings, the brooch, and the bo-kay all regular, and sends me for the Registrator directly they come by "coach-parcel."'

The strangely environed marriage ceremony concluded, the new-made bride hid her face in her hands and retired into the inner room. The dying man lay back for a few moments, the strain upon his faculties having apparently utterly exhausted his failing strength. Bill lit his pipe, and seating himself by the fire seemed lost in meditation.

We prepared for our homeward ride, our horses being only hung up to the nearest fence, a practice to which they were well accustomed.

Suddenly the sick man raised himself.

'Bill,' he said, in a husky weak voice, 'come here.'

'All right, Jim, old man,' said the other, knocking the ashes out of his pipe, 'what is it?'

'You don't want another ride into camp to-morrow, do you?'

'Well, not particular. I'm on the day shift, too, and it's rather tidy work putting in them setts. The ground's none too good and won't bear playin' with.'

'Well, as Mr. Bagstock's here, and this job's over, he might as well do the other one, and finish this register business right away.'

'What other business, Jim?' said his mate in a low voice, while Bagstock looked from one to the other as if the mysteries of the night were never to cease.

'Why, you'll have to register my death, won't you?' pursued the sick man, fixing his unnaturally large fever-bright eyes upon us, 'and why not do it now? I shall be as dead a man by this time to-morrow as ever was stretched, and wot's the use of dragging poor Bill in and losing another shift in the claim? He told Lovett yesterday to have the coffin ready, so there's no call to waste a day over that.'

'Good God!' said Mr. Bagstock, 'who ever heard of s-s-such a thing, r-r-registering a man's d-d-eath when he's alive.'

'What's the odds?' queried the persistent moribund wearily. 'It's twenty mile there and back to the camp. As for dying, I've seen too many chaps go under with this blamed colonial fever or typho not to know the stages. When a man's like I've been all to-day he never sees another sunset. So just fix it up, Mr. Bagstock, and oblige all parties, will ye?'

Mr. Bagstock, during his short residence in the colonies, and moreover at the diggings, had rubbed off many of his British prejudices; but this request so transcended in its ghastly significance all his previous experiences, so contravened all his notions of the fitness of things, that he was on the point of flatly refusing when he caught the warning eye of the dying miner's mate. He whispered—

'Don't cross him, sir, he was allays the most obstinate cove out. It might do him a mischief to be disappointed, like.'

The sick man had again relapsed into a death-like stupor, but the strong calm spirit again rallied the fainting flesh—trembling as it seemed on the dread margin of eternity. He read in the official's eyes his request was granted, and then repeated for Bagstock's information, who took down the items in a large official-looking paper ruled and marked in spaces, the required details. It was soon over.

'It's the biggest day's work I've done this weeks,' said the sick man. 'I'm thankful to you, Mr. Bagstock, and to you, Harry Pole, for coming with him this perishin' night and keeping us company, like. Poor Bess is Mrs. James Bellinger now, and no man nor woman on the field can throw it up to her as she ain't. I shall die happy, though I never ciphered it out as I was to die on my weddin' day. Good-night and good-bye! for it's the long good-bye I'm thinking, and no get away this time.'

We shook the wasted hand of the doomed man, said a natural word of kindly farewell, departed for the world of light and life and strength and pleasure, where in a few hours all beneath the sun would still be strong and beauteous in heaped-up prodigality, and left the lonely bark to push off in the dread and awful hush of midnight on the dark waters of the shoreless ocean of eternity.

The moon had arisen, and by her silver light we rode slowly and silently forth along the lonely road that led from the little mining hamlet to the gold city. Our thoughts were full of the strong brave soul which was passing away fearless and un-shrinking from the dread summons that was even now rever-berating in his ears, careful in that supreme hour but for others, loyal in the very extremity of the weakness of the flesh to friendship and to love.

'I was t-t-told,' said Mr. Bagstock musingly, after a pro-tracted silence, 'that I should see some s-s-strange people on the d-d-diggings. There never w-w-was a truer word s-s-spoken.'

And he relapsed into a silence which lasted till we reached the camp. At that citadel all were still up, and unusual excite-ment prevailed. A telegram had come up to Mr. Merlin at a late hour which evidently was of importance; his manly brow was overclouded, and his utterances were more curt, not to say aggressive, than ever.

'What's the matter with you, Merlin?' said Bright. 'Bilious as usual, or is there any news about those confounded bush-rangers that seem to be always just out of reach, like crows when a fellow has a gun.'

'Read that!' said the inspector, throwing over the modern messenger of fate. 'Isn't it enough to make a man curse the day he was born? There, I've just sent away all my best men, besides Sir Watkyn, and now I haven't a tracker that could follow a working bullock over a ploughed field.'

Mr. Bright read out the telegram—

'Ben Wall, supposed to have stolen Grey Surrey out of Bowdler's stables last night, has been tracked through Forbes towards Jones's sheep station. Horse has a broken hind shoe.'

'The best chance I've had since they've turned out; and to think that it should be upset by such a casual accident. I was half a mind to keep the men yesterday. I knew it was a wild-goose chase. Well, sergeant, what is it?'

For that worthy officer, with cheerful visage, appeared in the doorway, and having duly saluted thus spoke—

'The men are back, sir, and Sir Watkyn the tracker with them.'

'Thank God for that!' said Merlin with unwonted piety. 'Is he sober?'

'Sober as a judge, sir.'

'How did they change route then without fresh orders?' said he sternly—for no deviation from the strictest discipline was suffered.

'They got a telegram from Sergeant Redmond about Ben Wall having been seen near Forbes. They afterwards met a man in a certain place, after which Senior-constable Evans acted on his own responsibility. Here's a letter, sir.'

'By Jove! we have him then,' cried out Merlin, 'unless the devil gives him better cards than usual. Have the horses fed. Lock up that fellow, Sir Watkyn, and have the men ready to start in an hour.'

The sergeant saluted and withdrew.

'The luck is changed, and the red hazard is coming up again,' pursued Merlin, with a gambler's joyous exultation. 'I see it all plainly. We shall have Mr. Ben as safe as a dingo in a dog-trap.'

'How's that?' I said; 'there have been so many false alarms.'

'It's all right this time,' said the inspector, opening his revolver case. 'The reward is a large one, and our friend has been "given away" at last by one of his precious pals. The worst of it is that we shall have to watch all the rest of this cursed cold night around a deserted hut in the ranges, and with the cold I've got I'm as likely to be a dead man as Ben is next morning. However, *vogue la galère*.'

While divers plans in the council of war were being discussed, Mr. Bright, after deep thought, contributed a suggestion.

'I can't go with you myself, Merlin, though I'd like to do it of all things, because it happens to be our quarterly balance day to-morrow, and though the General stands a good deal from me, I don't think he'd stand that. But I'll tell you what I'll do—I'll lend you my breechloader.'

'Sorry we're not to have the support of your presence, my dear fellow,' said Merlin with much politeness, 'but we're not going duck-shooting.'

'Nonsense. I tell you I'm serious. I wish to heaven I could have a steady pot at that fellow Ben Wall or Frank Lardner after the rascally way they took a sitting shot at us. But what I mean is this——' here his manner assumed an unwonted earnestness.

'Well, what is it? Unburden yourself of this dark and dreadful secret.'

'Now, you listen to me, Merlin.' Here Mr. Bright laid his hand upon the sub-inspector's arm, and in a deeply impressive voice spoke as follows: 'You take my advice—*use a smooth bore and green cartridge;* it's out and out the best business when you mean close shooting at anything under a hundred yards. Revolvers, I know by experience, are *most* uncertain, though, perhaps, as I should have been a dead man twice over if they had always been held straight, I oughtn't to complain.'

'Well, well, old fellow!' said Merlin, actually smiling and exhibiting a rare amiability, 'I don't know whether I won't take your advice for once. We've had such bad luck lately with this gang that I feel ready to do anything to change it.'

'I must say I can't congratulate you or your men on your success in stalking or shooting either,' said Blake; 'the civilians are having quite the best of it.'

'How's that?' demanded the inspector fiercely, looking up from his weapons.'

'Why, you know that Campbell of Goimbla shot Daly, and Keightly shot O'Rourke. Lardner's out of the colony apparently. Gilbert Hawke's flown away too, so if you want to make an imperishable name for yourself, you must come back with Ben Wall's scalp at your saddle-bow to-morrow.'

'D——n Ben Wall, and you too!' said Merlin, roused to unusual fervour by these taunts. 'Sergeant!' he roared, 'are the men never going to mount. By —— I'll break the senior-constable if my orders are not better carried out. There's no discipline, no decent punctuality of any kind on this infernal goldfield. I wish the devil had flown away with the first man that washed a dish of dirt on the Turon. Bright, where's that gun?'

'Here it is; and half a dozen cartridges.'

'Two will be enough,' growled Merlin, grinding his teeth; 'if I miss that infernal scoundrel after having to watch his damnable hiding-place in such weather as this, I wish my arm may rot to the shoulder blade. Good-night!'

'Take me with you,' said I, 'I owe Master Ben a turn, and this is as good a chance as I shall get. May I go?'

'You may go to the devil—that is, with pleasure, my dear boy,' with difficulty recovering his affability. 'Look alive and have your horse brought out. But you're half knocked up already.'

'I shall be all right when the shooting begins,' I said.

The night was now intensely dark—'the moonbeams broke and deepest night came down upon the heath'—bitterly cold, wet under foot, wet overhead, as we left the camp without beat of drum.

Well clothed and warmly wrapped up as we were, after the first mile the frost seemed to strike through all to the very marrow. No sound was heard but the occasional jingle of stirrup-iron or bridle bit, as the horses slipped and stumbled ; indeed, more than one fell in the perilous, rough cross-country tracks we were compelled to follow. More than one of the troopers was well acquainted with the locality, and could have ridden it like William of Deloraine—of whom the Last Minstrel's Lay avers —

> ' Alike to him was time or tide,
> December's snow, or July's pride ;
> Alike to him was tide or time,
> Moonless midnight, or matin prime.'

Still, between roaring torrents, abandoned shafts, black forest-arches where no ray of starlight penetrated, and dismal water-logged flats, where only the marsh-frogs made chorus, and the night-owl hooted, we should, it appeared to me, have made but indifferent progress but for the aid and leadership of the black tracker, Sir Watkyn, whose sobriety had been so anxiously inquired into.

This distinguished heathen was certainly on this occasion 'the right man in the right place.' Being commanded to take the lead at starting by Mr. Merlin, and to look alive and keep a straight track, as if it were the easiest thing in the world, Sir Watkyn rammed the spurs into his charger, and rode as straight 'o'er moor and fell, through wood and wold' as if he had a private understanding with the north star. Wonderful, indeed, is it that he and his kindred still possess this power, so often denied to the over-civilised individuals of the imperial race, of passing with unerring accuracy from point to point of the trackless wilderness, by night too even as by day.

Blindly and persistently we followed him, since better might not be. We rode in Indian file, the troopers and I in the rear, sleepy and over-fatigued, taking it for granted that we should reach some place or other eventually. It was, perhaps, hardest upon Merlin, whose cough, impossible of repression, sounded ever and anon in the most hollow churchyard-like manner as the icy dampness of the air irritated his bronchial passages. But no consideration could be extended to the personal circumstances of individuals, until the robber-gang was stamped out.

To their extermination the Government of New South Wales was pledged, and no detail or exertion was omitted which gave hope of successful capture. Many a trooper, and not a few of the subalterns of the force, dated the commencement of fatal chest ailments to the ceaseless watches and night marches rendered necessary by the prevalence of robbery under arms in the terrible winter of 186—.

It was long past midnight, and for all I knew to the contrary we might have been heading straight for Sydney, when our sable guide reined up short on the top of a flint-bestrewn range, where the corrugated stems of the great ironbark trees stood black and columnar against the ashen sky, sombrely regular, as though they had been fashioned from the metal itself.

Merlin and the senior-constable rode at once to his side. He pointed to a small open space below, dimly visible, as the heavens had cleared since midnight, and the stars commenced to make the contrasts of earth and sky faintly visible.

'You see um Sheep-station Flat,' he said, pointing downwards, while his teeth chattered like castanets with the cold.

'D——d if I do,' said Merlin, 'but what then?'

'Sam Towney's hut long o' that flat, that old lambing station. That fellow, Ben Wall, sit down long a that one hut, then Sam bring him tucker to-morrow morning.'

'We'll bring him something for breakfast too, eh?' replied Merlin with grim humour. 'But you're a sharp boy, Sir Watkyn, to bring us so straight; sober to a fault I see, too. Well, virtue must be rewarded. Give me that "tot" that I see tied to your saddle.'

Even in the dim light I could see the swarth face lighten up, with flash of eyes and teeth, as Mr. Merlin produced a capacious flask of spirits, from which he administered to the guide a carefully graduated dram, handing the flask also to the senior-constable and me, partaking moderately himself, and then sharing the remainder among the men.

'Now, our plan is, Pole, to lie quiet and surround the place till daylight. Master Ben's horse must be tied up or hobbled near the hut. He can't have him in the house with him. When he comes out we *must* drop him, unless the devil, who certainly has befriended him hitherto, comes to his assistance in person.'

The necessary orders were briefly given. Merlin, myself, Sir Watkyn, and one trooper were to spread around the front of the hut, taking such cover as the place afforded. The senior-constable and two other troopers were to take up their position at the rear. The horses were to be left where we stood, all tied up by their cavalry headstalls, with a couple of men who *sotto voce* cursed their luck to take charge of them.

Led onwards again by the swarth scout, who crept along sinuously adown the spur of the range, we silently and cautiously

took up our positions within about fifty yards of a dismal
deserted-looking slab hut with four sheets of bark off the roof
and a chimney which was all awry. Immediately at the rear
of the building was a thick scrub, one of those timber covers in
which a desperate active man on a good horse might foil
even a band of Comanche Indians let alone ordinary police
troopers.

'S——t,' sibilated our guide, 'me see um two horse, one fellow
gray horse, one fellow bay, like it short hobbles.'

'That'll do, very good boy, but hold your row and lie down,'
said Merlin. 'That's Mr. Bowdler's Surrey ; the game's netted.
All we have to do is to wait till he runs into the decoy.'

The black dropped on the earth, and straightway became
invisible after the manner of his kind, while we waited more or
less impatiently for the tardy dawn which was to rise for the
last time on the outlaw's career, or to add another to the list of
mortifying failures.

For myself, I had no great natural inclination to the trade of
robber-hunting. I could not help feeling some qualms of pity
for the human quarry, who in the prime of early manhood was
presently to be shot down like a beast of prey, or if captured
reserved only for an ignominious death. It needed all my recollection of the cold-blooded attempt upon the lives as well as on
the gold of others, in both of which departments I had suffered
loss and injury almost unto death, to harden my spirit to the
proper pitch of pitiless resolution.

Wearily the hours passed. Stiff and sore, cold and well-nigh
frozen was I, were we all. We could hear every faint sound of
the forest ; the cry of the night-bird, the rustle of the phalangers
and the smaller marsupials as they glided through the wiry
frozen grass or climbed the clear stems of the eucalypti.

We could hear the ripple of the tiny brooklet, its existence
mainly due to the late extraordinary rainfall. Gradually in
spite of my watchfulness a kind of drowsiness came stealing
over me, just as the first dim gray streaks of dawn were
visible in the east—the east that was so long of becoming
illumined with the day-god's fateful ray.

Near me, however, at that moment an opossum commenced to
make his curious half-chattering, half-mournful sound. This
unseasonable outcry became so persistent that both Merlin and
I, who were near each other in the night watch, were effectually
aroused. Indeed, the creature became so riotously and aggres-
sively noisy that I kept looking up first one and then another
of the white stemmed gums that were thinly scattered over the
flat, having completely banished the drowsy feeling which had
commenced to steal over me.

Merlin also was apparently disturbed, for he moved nearer
to me and peevishly devoted the obtrusive performer to the
infernal deities. As if the creature comprehended the uncom-
plimentary terms in which he had been referred to, the noise

suddenly ceased. And as the sound died away I saw by Merlin's sudden alteration of attitude that something had attracted his attention.

I looked towards the hut. Midway between it and the trees behind which we stood came a man walking slowly and heedfully, as if seeking for something near and well known which had not yet come within his sphere of vision. His dress, which was certainly of a dull grayish material, with a poncho over all, was so thoroughly in harmony with the neutral tints of the sky, herbage, and the struggling light, that he had actually quitted the hut and approached our position unnoticed.

But for our being accidentally aroused by the opossum, it is far from improbable that he would have passed our section of the cordon unchallenged.

CHAPTER XXVIII

HE was evidently searching for the gray horse which we had seen hobbled, and to secure which he carried a bridle in his left hand. He came unsuspiciously forward till within about thirty yards of our post. Then Merlin, stalking forward from behind his tree, cried 'Stand! in the Queen's name!' in a voice which sounded strangely loud and incongruous amid the hushed solitudes in the chill, gray, ghostly dawn. At the same instant, from beside the tree that had apparently sheltered the hilarious opossum, sprung the black tracker, uttering a yell which made the forest ring to its farthest extent.

Ben Wall, for it was he, showed no surprise ; he had carried his life in his hand too long, doubtless had foreseen precisely this description of *reveillée* far too often, to betray astonishment when the fated hour arrived.

Dropping the bridle, he faced round upon Merlin with wonderfully instinctive quickness, firing one barrel of his revolver with apparently the same movement of his arm, and giving Sir Watkyn the benefit of a second shot with the slightest change of aim. That agile son of the forest leaped high at the report, but whether from the result of the shot, or from natural elasticity of spirits, could not then be ascertained.

Mr. Merlin stood unmoved, but simultaneously with Wall's first shot he brought the breechloader to his shoulder and fired with deliberate aim. The robber threw up his arms with a convulsive motion, stood statue - like for an instant, during which every rifle and revolver in the party was emptied, and fell heavily upon his face—dead, and, but for convulsive graspings of the tufted grass and autumn leaves that strewed the soil, motionless.

We walked over to the body, headed by the tracker, who rubbed his fore-arm with a vengeful expression of countenance. It had been more than grazed by the second bullet, and the red drops fell fast across the sable skin.

'Turn him over,' said Mr. Merlin. 'I thought I should hold straight this time. There's the track of my green cartridge.

Bright was not far wrong. It's too cold for the pistol at this hour of the morning when there's no coffee to steady one's nerves.'

Merlin's aim had been true. The cartridge of heavy shot, hardly scattering at the short distance, had torn through the robber's breast like a grapeshot. Death must have been instantaneous. But every Snider and Colt in the party had left a mark. The corpse was riddled with bullet wounds.

'Ha!' soliloquised Merlin, 'there lies Ben, stark and stiff, and not the worst of the gang either. I know a man and so do you, Pole, that better deserves to be there. However, wishing won't hang people, more's the pity sometimes, so let us get back to our horses and return to the camp. I wish to heaven these fellows would choose decent weather to be shot in. I feel a precious sight more like a dead man myself than a live one.'

We betook ourselves to where the horses had been left, having previously had the corpse of the bushranger carried into the deserted hut whence he had issued, there to abide until a vehicle could be sent for it. We caught the noble gray horse with his companion, and led him back to camp with us whence he was restored to his owner, much to that gentleman's satisfaction. And ofttimes a merry girl, as in after days she felt his free elastic stride beneath her, as he stretched tireless over the forest turf, grew pale when told that this was the horse that carried the boldest bushranger of Lardner's gang on his death ride.

Of the final destiny of the gang mention may be made here. Nemesis, *pede claudo*, was in their case sufficiently effective in the long run.

Gilbert Hawke, like Ben Wall, was surrounded and shot dead. O'Rourke and Daly had perished before by the hands of gentlemen whose houses they had attacked. Gunn was captured and hanged ; while Frank Lardner, the Robin Hood of the Australian outlaws, the planner and contriver of an evil which far outran the original conception, escaped to a neighbouring colony, and there, as a storekeeper on a distant goldfield, lived unsuspected a life of quasi-respectability.

Discovered, however, at length, he was apprehended with singular dexterity and boldness by a member of the detective force, and safely lodged in the gaol in Sydney, there to abide his trial.

Strange as it may seem—and this is no fiction, but sober historic fact, which can be authenticated by official records— there were technical legal difficulties in the way of full proof of his identity and complicity in the wilful murders and attempts thereat which had been committed by his band.

So, in vindication of the unsullied ermine of a British court of justice, the highway robber and homicide was spared the last penalty and adjudged but to undergo a lengthened sentence of imprisonment. Even this, at the expiration of a term of years, during which he had earned a good gaol character for propriety and subordination, was commuted. And in answer to a mistakenly merciful popular request, he who had attempted deliberate murder, had compassed robbery under arms, and had indirectly been the cause of the loss of the lives of scores of better men, was permitted to go free. He now breathes the free air of heaven, and walks unchallenged in another land; while the victims of his lawless greed, his recklessness, and his evil example, lie rotting in premature or dishonoured graves.

The year 186— was evidently the commencement of a cycle of rainy seasons. It promised to be a year of flood and tempest. But the more widely the windows of heaven were opened, the weather keener, the blasts of the spring-time which, with storm and inundation, seemed never willing to ripen into summer, the more laden the alluvial levels of the Oxley appeared to be with gold.

The yield continued to be enormous. The escorts were fabulous; and save that the continuously severe weather necessitated heavier payments for carriage, and through this increased rates of prices for all things that the miner consumed, no other untoward result took place.

No one particularly cared. It was a land where all were rich; and men had lost the memory of the relative values of commodities dating from a period when money was scarce.

Olivera was perhaps the only man on the goldfield who had not at one time or another enjoyed his share of luck. He did, indeed, get sufficient of the root of all evil to live comfortably and pay all expenses. But he never seemed, somehow or other, to drop upon a 'golden hole,' though such might be above, below, even within a few inches of his claim, wherever he might chance to select it.

To him, however, a scholar, a traveller, above all a philosopher, this persistent run of ill luck made little or no apparent difference. He was always ready to explain the apparently inconsistent behaviour of Providence in his particular case.

'No doubt,' he would observe, 'this total absence of what ordinary people call success, would be dangerous to natures unaccustomed to take a widely comprehensive group of occurrences. For instance there's Ned Wright, ex-pugilist, rowdy, blackleg, what not; he is pursued by the police, and finally so much harassed that in despair he attacks honest work; he sinks with Tommy the Clock and two mates hardly better than himself No. 2 shaft on the Pink Lead; and what is the result? Why, that after getting down without rock or water, they bottom in the best claim on the whole lead, and make five thousand pounds a man in less than three months!'

'It's dreadfully aggravating,' says the Major. 'How you stand it, old fellow, I can't think.'

'Stand it!' said Olivera, carefully filling his pipe, 'what else is to be done? One can't bring an action against Providence. *My* idea is that I'm being reserved for something better than the Ned Wrights and Tommy the Clocks.'

'Harry Poles, Majors, Jack Bulders, and so on,' said I, laughing.

'Well, of course, there are several ways of looking at it. But after all (one's powers of mind and body remaining unimpaired of course) perhaps the longer the day of full fruition is deferred the better,' pursued Mr. Olivera musingly. 'Still I shall never give up mining until I die; and I'll take the long odds I land a big thing before I drop.'

Not so calmly philosophical by any means was our latest acquaintance and partner, Jack Bulder. Whether it was the wet weather and the unfriendly sky, or the absence of his brother, before whom he always preserved a comparatively dignified demeanour, or both these things, joined to the monotonous regularity of our washings-up and the swelling of our credit balance, which acted unfavourably upon his nerves, but so it fell out that John Bulder became careless and unpunctual in returning to the claim from the hotel where he had now permanently taken up his quarters.

It began to be whispered about that Bulder of Greenstone Dyke was going crooked, queer in his talk at times, not so steady as he had been when he first 'come on the rush.' Gradually—for gossip, so rife in older communities where events are rare and of modest magnitude, is singularly slow and accurate on goldfields—the rumour became confirmed that John Bulder 'drank.'

And one unlucky morning, after a lengthy absence of our defaulting mate, a messenger came up from the Ballarat Hotel with a note from the landlord—a very decent fellow who had known him in that gold city—that Mr. Bulder had been 'on the burst' for several days, and that some one from the claim, he thought, ought to come down and look after him.

This was not good news. But neither was it unexpected. The Major had prophesied as much. We did not moralise on it. We knew exactly how much it meant; how much and no more.

A certain percentage of men on every goldfield, on every large cattle or sheep station, in every country town in all the Australian colonies, is subject to this morbid phase of alcoholism. Not by any means the weakest or the worst members of society either.

The attitude of the public to the individual who may thus transgress is much like that of the gaoler in the *Old Curiosity Shop* on the occasion of Kit's incarceration. He did not reason much on the causes which led to parties being committed to his keeping. Crime, as he noticed it, was a variable and epidemic occurrence. Some had it, some hadn't, others mildly—much like measles, smallpox, or scarlet fever.

Many men in all the localities and societies referred to drink more than is good for them, perhaps become intoxicated frequently. But a man who has a regular burst, or 'goes on the spree' habitually and periodically, is classed in a different category. He is known both to friends and foes to be one who, while having the power to *refrain wholly* from intoxicating liquor for a given and definite, often a protracted period, must have his full swing, must yield in an uncontrolled state of utter abandonment to the craving for a debauch when the temptation suffices, or when his hour has come.

For weeks, for days, for months, years even it may be, the restraining power is known to last. Then chance or continuous pressure breaks the bond of self-denial, and over the broken embankment the pent-up passion seeks its lowest level, sweeping away tumultuously in its flow all good intent and manly resolution.

For a space, days and nights are recklessly devoted to the delirium of drunkenness. Then, wonderful to relate, the possessed one is suddenly discovered clothed and in his right mind, though grievously shaken by the 'unclean spirit which had come out of him.' A new era of perfect sobriety, energy, and propriety then sets in.

The Major and I, therefore, much as if we had heard that Jack Bulder had sustained severe accidental injury, or otherwise come to grief, concluded to set out and see about him.

'I'm sorry he's broken out,' said the Major, 'the fellow's such a strong nature, for good or evil, that there's no saying what he may not say or do.'

'It doesn't matter what he says, that I know of,' quoth I, 'and I don't see what he can do. However, we shall soon know all about it.'

When we arrived at the Ballarat Hotel, Mr. Hennessy the landlord met us with a very solemn face. He motioned us into the little room beside the bar which did duty as a snuggery and general office.

'Morning, Hennessy!' said the Major, 'what's up with Bulder; anything out of the common? All the same, Pole and I are obliged to you for sending us word.'

'Well, Major,' said our boniface, an extensively travelled man, who knew San Francisco, New York, and Panama better than the Australian capitals, 'I shouldn't have troubled about a little temp'ry kick-up, but I knew Jack at Ballarat, and it's worse than that.'

'How worse?' I inquired.

'In this way. He hasn't been sober for a fortnight, as one might say, till last Monday; since then he hasn't touched a drop but soft stuff and tea. The curus part of it is that he seems worse and worse. I'm afraid he's got the jumps coming on.'

'The jumps?' said I.

'Yes, the jim-jams, or whatever you make of 'em; the doctors call it D.T., or something of that kind.'

'Delirium tremens,' I returned, 'very likely, indeed. Is he noisy?'

'He 'asn't slep' for three nights, or stopped talking; keeps on gassin' about Ballarat, and the soldiers, that's why I sent for you. Some of the p'leece might tumble, you know.'

Here Mr. Hennessy looked extremely knowing.

'Well, suppose he does talk about Ballarat, who cares?' I said rather hotly, irritated with the show of concealment for which I saw no necessity. 'Suppose all the world knew he was there.'

'But not in Eureka stockade; not as Ballarat Jack, one of the principal leaders, for whom there is five hundred pounds reward offered, and who was strongly suspected of killing Captain Wayse.'

'Good God!' I said, 'you don't say so? I knew poor Wayse well, and used to dine at the mess with him in Melbourne. Do you think he was the man that stabbed him?'

'He's in there,' said the host in a low tone, pointing to a room upstairs. 'You can hear him talking and going on as soon as you get to the head of the stairs. Here's the key. I've locked the door at the other end of the passage; you take it with you and go up.'

We went quickly up the staircase, knowing that it led to a large room on the first story, which was used for masonic dinners, quadrille parties, political meetings, and other purpose for which more than ordinary accommodation is required. A dozen or more bedrooms were situated on the other side of the corridor. Of one of these Jack Bulder had permanently possessed himself. And the other occupants being absent on work or business, he had at this time the suite pretty much to himself.

We could hardly imagine that he was alone, for as we approached the door of the passage at the head of the stairs we could hear a voice denouncing, beseeching, defying, by turns, as if in earnest conversation with some one.

As we turned the lock in the door we heard him call out, 'Stand! not one foot farther! I'll shoot the first man that leaves the stockade.' We paused for one moment, doubtful whether he had arms, and then, smiling at our faint-heartedness, pushed open the door and entered the room.

It was a strange uncanny sight. Near the centre of the room, to which he had withdrawn himself, stood John Bulder, bare footed, in his shirt and trousers, much in the same state of apparel generally as he must have used when superintending the washing of his ship's decks in tropical seas.

His eyes, widely opened, were fixed with dreadful intensity upon a corner of the room. The expression of his face was utterly changed, so thoroughly that ordinary acquaintances might well have looked on him without recognition.

Then his eyes, dilated with horror, rested upon us. His head moved unwillingly and slowly away from the spot at which he had been gazing as he cried aloud, in tones of unutterable anguish—

'Good God! they are almost touching him, the blood from his breast drips over them! Will they carry his blood about to follow me through the world and torment me before my time?'

'What's the matter, old fellow?' said the Major. 'You're rather high-fed to-day. It doesn't do to play with D.T.'

'Who are you, and what authority have you to question me?' said the possessed, for such beyond doubt he seemed to be for the time, still turning back his head as if fascinated to the first point of his regard.

'Oh! you know us,' I said; 'it's only the Major and Harry Pole, your mates. You had better come home and have a good sleep.'

'How can I sleep?' he said in a quiet conversational tone, 'when *he* is there, night and day, by my bedside in the darkness, and here when I am awake and would leave him if I could.'

'Who is there?' I said, thinking to humour him, and knowing it to be an optical illusion, such as are common to those suffering from a disordered nervous system.

'*Who* is there?' he wailed forth, in tones that made me almost doubt his identity, so strangely awful were they with shuddering dread and despair. 'Who is there? who should it be but the man I killed at Ballarat stockade, while he was smiling in my face, Captain Wayse of the 80th. Don't you see the wound in his breast where my sword went through him, and the blood—the blood running still?'

Here the unhappy man threw himself down on his face as one who grovels in the dust, and drew his hands over his forehead as if to shut out the terrible sight.

'This looks serious,' said the Major. 'He may have been in the Ballarat riot, as a few men we both know here have been. But as to poor Wayse, who died of his wounds the next day, after pluckily leading his company when they stormed the stockade, he may have dreamt all about it.'

'I don't know that,' I said; 'it seems to have burned itself in on his brain in a way that another man's guilt could scarcely have reached. I met poor Wayse once. He knew the Leys well, and told me he had been shooting at a house close by the year before I went there.'

Here John Bulder raised himself on his knees cautiously, and then turning away his head, sat down.

'Who spoke about the Leys?' he said in a hoarse whisper. '*He* was there, too. I was a boy; he was little better—but a gentleman, just got his commission, and he seemed a little god to a country lout like me. How handsome he was, and jolly, kind to all and free with his money like a prince. Many a half-crown he gave me in the old days, for he used to take me out with him to carry the bag. Perhaps he'll forgive me yet before I die. Why can't I die? *I couldn't be worse in hell.*'

Here the wretched man sobbed and bewailed himself as if he had been the soft untravelled rustic his wanderings described.

After another interval he went on more collectedly, while we, seeing that unless he was placed in charge of the police for protection nothing could be done with him, and doubtful of how great a proportion of truth was mixed up with these revelations, listened without remark.

'One day I had snared a hare; I used to poach a little—most of us boys did, as much for the sport as anything, and I was just taking her out when the keeper collared me. I was being taken off to gaol—Lord, lord! how frightened I was—when *he* came by, and never stopped till he begged me off. I could have followed him over the world when he left the country. He gave me a sovereign, and told me either to 'list or go to sea, that I was too mettlesome a lad to make a ploughboy of. I went to sea, he went to his regiment, and now here am I, and he is—there. My God, my God!'

Here he leaped to his feet and commenced walking up and down the room like a sailor on a deck, always turning back at the same place and markedly avoiding the corner where, according to his delusion, the appearance still abode.

'Why did I join the rioters at Ballarat? why did heaps of good men? because the diggers were badly treated, hunted for their licenses, chained up like dogs, knocked down by bullies like Strongbow, and tyrannised over by raw lads fresh from England. I fought Strongbow fair once, and beat him too. He was as strong as a bullock, but I was too active. He was a man, too; he wouldn't let the troopers touch me. There was a lot of foreigners in it, too; some good, some bad, and Americans.'

'Wasn't Yankee Jake there, too?' said I, by way of a distraction.

'He! Curse him, wherever he is! He was not an American at all, only a white-washed one. He was an Englishman, of a good family, too, turned out for villainy of some kind. He was a traitor, too. He sold us at Ballarat or we should have had time to strengthen the stockade before the military came upon us. But that's not all he did.'

'Why, what else could he do?'

'What does a man like him do? work harm and misery all his days. I had a mate, a sailor-man, a real honest chap as ever pulled a rope or carried a tar bucket. He'd come over in a West Indian ship after one of his voyages, married a Spanish-American girl, the prettiest young thing you ever saw. Poor Dick used fairly to worship her, and she seemed that fond of him she was never happy out of his sight.   Dolores and he was like two children.'

'Dolores Lusada?' I said ; 'did you know her in those days?'

'Know her, yes, and respected her, too, and every man at the White Hills where we worked.   A neater, cheerier, better wife no man had, till this Jake, with his wheedling ways and lies and fine airs, flattered her out of her true and safe-sailing course, and persuaded her to dowse her flag and scud under bare poles before the wind with him.'

'And what did her husband do?'

'Followed them everywhere to kill him.   Then came back and drank—drank till he forgot all about his troubles.   But when he did, he was mad like me.'   Here he laughed in an unnatural ghastly manner.   'So they had to lock him up for a few months.   Then he came out quite quiet, poor Dick, and went away, and I never saw him again.   But why should he have gone mad ; he never killed any one.'

'Nor you, either,' said the Major.   'Somebody has told you all this.   You're only fancying these stories.   Come along home with us and tell Mrs. Yorke about it.   She'll make you some tea and you'll get a good sleep after it all, and that will set you right.'

'I would come, for I am sure you're kind,' he answered humbly, but as if he had never seen us before ; 'but he would come too, and in a small place it would be too dreadful.   His blood would run on the floor, too.   You could not help standing in it.   Ah-a——h !'

Here he again assumed an attitude and expression of fear and shuddering horror beyond all control.

CHAPTER XXIX

AFTER a while he commenced to pace restlessly up and down the room, studiously avoiding the corner where the awful spectre (as to his disordered mind it appeared) sat crouched with bleeding breast and sad reproachful visage.

'Why did I join with the rioters?' he recommenced. 'Well —some had good cause who had suffered cursed injustice—most of them, like myself, just followed on partly for the sport and partly because in a general way things wanted mending. I was young and foolish, proud of my strength and pluck, I suppose.'

'What sort of leaders had you?' said the Major, thinking it best to have his narrative concluded now so that relief might come to his overladen soul. 'Were they Americans or what?'

'Some of all sorts. There was Radetsky—a fine fellow too— they put a price on his head, though *he* fought for liberty. Then Peter Gawlor, the Irishman, who lost his arm in the fight, went in for devilment. A couple of Americans, backwoodsmen, and that scoundrel who calls himself Jake. He deserted the night before the attack ; they say he sold us, and brought on the military two hours before we were ready for them.'

'But what madmen you all were. How could you hope,' said I, 'to have any lasting success?

'Madmen then and now,' he groaned, 'but times were queer then. There was nearly a general rising. If we had beaten back the soldiers we should have been joined by the whole of the crowd, and then, if we had marched on Melbourne with an army swelling as it went, who was there then to oppose us?'

'Who indeed?' I said.

'A great Melbourne merchant told me,' said the Major, 'that they were prepared for the worst. Many of the young squatters and their friends armed themselves and formed the nucleus of an army corps at the Central Police Barracks at Jolimont.'

'The soldiers fought well,' said the dipsomaniac with his eyes fixed on vacancy. 'A messmate before a shipmate, a shipmate before a stranger, but a dog before a soldier, ha! I hate

them, all sailors do. But they fought like men. They came on
at the run, and many of them dropped as we fired, but they
charged with the bayonet in style, and our lot began to flinch.
I could see the captain at their head, an active, fair-haired,
young-looking man, his sword in his hand and a smile on his
face. I had a sort of feeling as if I had seen him before, but I
was too busy to look long. I saw the soldier that hit Gawlor,
and I took steady aim and dropped him. He fell on his face.'

'Well, that was all fair fighting,' said the Major, 'though you
were on the wrong side. Is that the worst of it? Your men
didn't keep steady, and the regulars marched over them. They
always do.'

'That was not all. God send it was, oh! how happy I should
be. A few of us made a stand, and the captain ran up close to
me waving his sword and cheering on his men. I felt a sharp
pain in my left arm as a bayonet went through it. At the same
time one of our men hit the captain a heavy blow with the butt
end of a gun. His sword dropped from his hand, and—God
forgive me—I snatched it up and ran him through with it. As
the handle jarred against his chest he looked me full in the face.
"Why, it's Keeper Jack" (that's what they used to call me about
the poaching) "all the way from Kent," he said half wonderingly,
"who'd have thought of meeting you here, old fellow. You've
hurt me, I'm afraid," and he fell backwards. I was the only man
who came alive out of the lot around him, his men saw to that.
I was wounded in seven places and laid up in hiding for three
months with £500 on my head. I don't know that it's off now.
But if he died why does he go with me everywhere—why is he
sitting there now?'

'It's a bad case and a thousand pities,' the Major said. 'Poor
Wayse, he was the eldest son, heir to a baronetcy and a good
estate. I knew him well, and never thought we should have for
a mate the man that killed him. But it's no use fretting; he
wouldn't have thought twice about cutting you down, Jack, I
can assure you.'

'But why should I have been picked out to kill him?' groaned
the homicide. 'He that was so kind—kind's no name for it. I
could have followed him round the world. He was never hard
to the rough country lad, as I was then, but as gentle as a
woman, though he was as brave as steel. It is no use. I shall
see him as he is there till I go to my own place. And then, then
he may forgive me. God have mercy upon us.'

There was now nothing more to be said or done. We descended, locking the door, and still could hear the unfortunate
victim of strong drink and remorse continuing his harrowing
entreaties to be pardoned and set free from torment.

We told Hennessy that we had tried all means in our power,
but that nothing save medical aid would be likely to benefit
him. So we wended our way homewards, and sent our doctor,
who had had considerable experience in cases of that nature.

That gentleman administered to him a very powerful sleeping draught to begin with, and followed it up with other remedies of such a nature that when, a week later, John Bulder presented himself at the claim he looked, though calm and composed, at least five years older, and moved as a man who is making a slow recovery after a fever.

'Had a heavy bout of it this time, mates,' was the only apology he thought it necessary to make. 'Gave a lot of trouble, and talked a lot of d——d nonsense most likely. You had a man on all the time, I suppose. Charge me with his wages in the next settlement, and any other expenses the claim's been put to through me.'

How marvellous is it that reason should so completely resume her sway after being so rudely deposed; that the reactionary feelings of energy and application are so powerfully experienced when the opposite tendencies have been so completely in the ascendant. But such is human nature, on the infinite variations of which mysterious creation 'twere vain to dilate in this brief chronicle.

When such a recovery takes place the mind and body after a while are so completely restored to their normal tone, that the sympathising observer might conclude not only that no criminal excess had been committed, but that such never could again intervene in the strong and well-regulated character.

'Until the next time,' quoth

> 'The Fiend to whom belongs
> The vengeance due to all our wrongs.'

This alarming outbreak did not, however, affect any one but the chief actor. Like my combat with Malgrade, it was no one's affair but his own. Other highly respectable people suffered periodically from the same kind of attacks. He had abundantly the means of delegating the work he used to perform personally; so that, if he had spent his whole time at Hennessy's, he was quite able to afford it. However, after a few days more he paid off his representative, and commenced to work his shift of eight hours with much the same patience and persevering energy which he had displayed on entering the claim. His spirits rose gradually, his appetite returned, and, as I said before, no one could have recognised in the cheery, hard-working miner the raving lunatic or the despairing hypochondriac we had so lately been compelled to succour.

His presence as a chief actor at the Eureka stockade, and his confession of having been the actual slayer of poor Captain Wayse, whom every one regretted, was much the more serious phase of the affair.

We knew, of course, that the Victorian juries had refused to convict the rioters when committed for trial for the same class of offence, and we doubted not but that they would pursue the same course in his case.

But actual homicide was different, and if arrested on suspicion of being one of the leading rioters at Ballarat, it would involve his being sent in irons to Victoria; for, of course, bail would not be taken in such a case, and that course we did not at all desire to see carried out.

Doubtless among the miners there were many who had recognised and could swear to him if they chose to give willing testimony; but the general feeling of the community was with the insurgents, and against the Government of the day in Victoria. And even if it were not so, no miner would voluntarily assume the hateful character of informer. The only fear was that the man known as Yankee Jake, who had reasons for personal enmity, might lay an information before a magistrate, and so compel the arrest of John Bulder on suspicion of having committed this high crime and misdemeanour.

However, at the present time, the said Jake, or 'The Count,' as he was indifferently called, had located himself in a quartz-reefing district, known as Mason's, about twenty miles distant, where he was understood to have made several lucky hits, to have been appointed a director in mining companies which had been successfully floated, and generally to be rising into a state of undeserved social splendour and distinction.

For the present, then, it was possible that this Cerberus had his jaws confined with a golden muzzle, on account of which his growling and tearing were temporarily suspended.

As for John Bulder himself, 'Damocles, his sword,' if thus above him suspended, did not produce apparent uneasiness. He worked and jested with the same careless ease as of old, and for a few short weeks care and strife seemed banished entirely from this our antipodean section of the universe.

. . . .

As suddenly as it had commenced, the wet, cold, inclement weather ceased. The sun shone daily with might and effulgence. The water-courses returned to their usual channels, the marshes commenced to dry up. The birds mated. The pasture grasses, hitherto hindered by the harsh winds and frosts of the late winter, made haste to shoot and burgeon with tropical rapidity of growth. All nature revelled in the rich bloom and wondrous luxuriance of the glorious Australian spring.

How different were the roads and tracks from those which we had lately plodded through and stumbled along. Every day added to the pleasure of living. Every change was in the direction of improvement and enjoyable existence. The days became insensibly warmer without being oppressively hot. The billowy prairies waved in the faint breeze which heralded the summer. The foliage of the slender-leaved eucalypti showed a tinge of softer green. And ever, in fine weather as in foul, the reputation of the Oxley goldfield, based upon the monthly unearthing of more than half a ton of gold, remained high and unwavering.

The weeks passed blithely along, and still so increasingly brilliant were our prospects, so satisfactory the dividends which we received at the Oxley, as well as those of which we had monthly advice from Yatala, that I at length fully made up my mind to settle my affairs temporarily the week before Christmas, and to take this long-looked-for holiday in Sydney, where I could arrange at the same time for poor Jane's voyage to her native land, whither, I doubted not, I should follow her before many months were past.

At our present rate our full shareholders would divide between forty and fifty thousand pounds a man—John Bulder's proportion being, of course, much less than this, as he had no original interest in No. 4 Liberator, of which we now held undisputed possession.

I was loath to leave off such engrossing exciting toil, but it came at last, the last week before Christmas, the second of the weary, hot, dry, dusty December, which had succeeded our matchless but too brief spring months.

I quitted my work that long-remembered day thoroughly exhausted, and, throwing off my working clothes with a deep sigh of relief, reflected that I should not need to don them again for a month. In the interim I should stand once more—oh, enchanting thought !—on the breeze-swept ocean beach, inhaling the briny odours of the half-forgotten main. At midnight, at sunrise, I should be free to watch the ebb, the flow of the mystic waters. In all my mining life I had not once happened to have revisited the coast since we returned from New Zealand. And now, excited by the near prospect of comparative rest and freedom, I exulted in the idea of exchanging the red-lined roads and yellow mullock heaps, the iron or wooden shanties, the sombre shadeless forest, amid which I had sojourned so long, for the cool streets, the lofty freestone walls, the massed flower thickets, and the unfamiliar luxuries of the City of the Sea.

Poor Jane, too, how innocently she would revel in the novelties and wonders of the Paris of the South, before commencing her voyage to the old land. I looked forward, like a boy, to the brief holiday-time we should have before we parted, perhaps for ever. My heart glowed at the thought that I had the means and opportunity of rescuing her from a hateful tyranny, from a life unspeakably wretched and degrading. The faded rose, once so fresh of petal, so delicate of hue, might, replanted in the ancestral soil, again bloom modestly, again put forth green leaflets, shrinking delicate flowerets.

In happy peaceful years to come we might yet see her, my bride and I, humbled and chastened of aspect, yet peaceful and respected in her village home, gathering with every added year a fuller measure of repose, of that divine peace that is promised to the heart's deep, sincerest repentance.

In all this sanguine, it may be in some respects imprudent

anticipation, I can swear it before the Lord of Heaven and Earth, my heart was towards her as that of a brother—of a brother only.

On the morrow early we were to start by the coach at day-light. When the sun set we should be a hundred miles on our way; ere the following midnight at our destination; once more in a land of civilisation, where art refines repose, and enjoyment rewards industry—fitting prelude to the life of unclouded happiness upon which I trusted to enter early in the coming year.

The sun had long since set. The night was sultry at the same time, but moonless, starless, rayless utterly. Some im-pending change in the elemental programme had covered the heavens with a robe of vapour so dense that when I rather im-patiently essayed to make my way from our tent to the town proper, I more than once got off the narrow track through the network of shafts, being compelled to grope back my way with extreme circumspection.

I attributed my restless and excited mood to the great change in my temporary surroundings. But I felt uneasy to an unusual degree. I had resolved to call at Jane's lodgings and warn her to have her luggage ready to the minute in the morning, as the coach-driver was of a ruthless and inexorable punctuality. And the disappointment of being left behind in my overwrought state of feeling would go nigh to break one's heart, I thoughtlessly said.

She appeared, poor girl, when I saw her, almost as childishly elated as myself at the prospect of the speedy deliverance from her prison house, and the translation to a higher sphere, a purer air.

We talked it over at greater length than was perhaps actually necessary, but our hearts were full, genuinely athirst for sympathy. As old friends, cognisant as were none others of a thousand circumstances of our bygone life that the loosened spring of a coming departure seemed to release from memory's coffer, we found a multiform and unexpected fund of mutual interest.

'I shall be a good woman to the end of my days, and, as far as my conscience will let me, a happy one,' she said, 'if I ever reach the Leys again and see the old man's face. And it will be to you, Hereward, and to you alone that I shall owe it—owe my salvation. God for ever bless you for it, and help you in your need as you have me.'

I had said farewell to her and had come out into the passage of the hotel, into which she followed me, being moved, as it seemed, to say these parting words. This thoroughfare—a kind of corridor between two sets of rooms—was unlighted. A gust from the rising wind suddenly blew to the door of the apart-ment we had just quitted. I had reached the outer door when some one brushed hurriedly past me. I thought it was one of the many inmates of the house, and walked on, when I heard a sudden sharp ejaculation, as in fear or anger, in Jane's voice, then a horrible, choking, gurgling, unnatural sound, which sent a thrill through every nerve of my body. I turned hastily to the doorway, and as I did so a man again rushed by me and was swallowed up in the pitchy darkness which now enveloped all things. Breathless with excitement I rushed to the spot near where I had left Jane. I felt along the wall and stopped, almost petrified, as something human clasped my feet, and again the hoarse unearthly sound struck upon my ear, though fainter than at first. Stooping, I raised Jane's fainting form, as I believed. Her face fell helpless forward against mine, and her arms clutched convulsively around my neck. At the same moment I felt something like liquid trickling down my breast and dripping with terrible distinctness on the floor. The hideous reality suddenly flashed across my mind, and I cried aloud for help.

Doors were quickly opened, lights appeared, trampling feet were heard. I was surrounded by the inmates and *habitués* of the house, a quickly increasing crowd. All gazed with widely opened eyes of surprise and horror. Full well might they gaze —for there stood I, Hereward Pole, in a pool of blood, with a dying woman in my arms, her throat cut with a dreadful gash which had nearly severed the head from the body.

For some seconds all stood silent. None seemed to have sufficient presence of mind to speak, much less to move for help, or in other act. Suddenly a voice from the outer edge of the crowd called out in husky strained accents,—

'Send for the police—let no one leave the place till they come. I accuse that man of the murder of my wife.'

I looked over the heads of the crowd. There was the grim form of Ned Morsley, while at his side, in ominous proximity, I marked the cold features and evil sneer of Algernon Malgrade.

At that moment the crowd parted, and the sergeant, accompanied by a trooper, strode up the passage.

'What is the meaning of all this? Ha!' he said promptly. 'some one call the women to take Mrs. Morsley and place her on a bed. Send for Dr. Bolton at once. Constable Grant, examine the spot closely, search the passage and room, try if you can find the weapon with which the wound was inflicted. Is the husband of the deceased here?

'Yes, I'm here. I wish to give this man Pole in charge for the murder of my wife.'

I stood as one bereft of reason when I had seen the dreadful, lifeless, unreal shape borne away by the women, all that was left of poor Jane, but a few moments since (or was it days, months, years since?) so happy and hopeful. And I with this miscreant's false charge ringing in my ears. I, Hereward Pole, her best friend on earth, accused of slaying her.

'Mr. Pole,' said the Sergeant, without betraying one atom of surprise, 'disagreeable duty, painful of course, only a matter of form, but I must trouble you to come along with me. Constable Grant, Mr. Pole won't think of escaping I know, but for fear of accidents, dark night, and so on, allow me, sir—thanks,' and I felt cold iron, for the first time, grate upon my wrists, and was on my way to the cells where all *détenus* of whatever kind or caste were primarily incarcerated. The clock struck ten. So early in the night too, to strike the knell of hope, life, liberty, good fame. Alas! poor human creature, thou that callest thyself man, made in thy Maker's image, and boastest thyself of will and energy, and election of the better path, how darkly ironic is Fate in its dealings with thee.

One moment happy, healthful, bright with the light of love and life, hope and joy in days to come. In the next, all thy vision red, gloomy with the savour of blood, thy liberty exchanged for the felon's cell, thy fame the sport of falsehood and evil hap, thy life blotted and future marred. Wherefore dost thou not follow the counsel of the patriarch's wife—curse God, and die.

CHAPTER XXX

THROUGH the long hours of that hateful night, which made a true inferno of the close-walled, low-roofed cell, I paced its narrow limits. My brain lay quiescent in dull stupor, or with feverish rapidity ceaselessly revolved the scenery and action of the terrible tragedy, in which I could scarcely realise my part as leading actor, accused criminal. Heaven, surely, without abrogating all functions of justice and mercy, could not suffer my conviction upon so false, so hellish an accusation! Could it be believed for one moment that I, with no conceivable reason for anger, had hurt one hair of her poor head?

No. But it might be proved.

I sprang upwards, as the fiendish suggestion passed through my brain and passed into the darkness as if to look for some subtle imp that had personally whispered the damning thought. The links of circumstantial evidence were not so far apart, but that malice and persistent ingenuity might forge the fatal chain. Men as innocent had ere now ascended the scaffold proclaiming their innocence.

What are the facts?

I am discovered in darkness, in solitude, with the dying woman in my arms. I am naturally covered with blood. Angry voices, one of them a man's, had been heard sounding exactly where she was last seen alive. Then the passionate refusal to 'go home'—a phrase of double meaning. Then cessation of speech and the awful unhuman death tones which so strangely thrilled me.

I sickened with fear. I thought how such evidence would have tended in the case of another so arraigned before me.

At an early hour of the day, now dawning, I knew that I should necessarily be brought before the bench of magistrates, charged in due form 'that I did on such a day unlawfully kill and murder one Jane Morsley, etc.' There was no escape from that. I saw myself standing in the dock, compulsorily exhibited for the pleasure of the curious and idle crowd, a spectacle of guilt or shame, as opinion might incline. What had I done in my short life that such misery, such undeserved torments should be heaped upon me?

Worn out at length by racking alternating paroxysms, my aching eyelids are sealed by kindly nature; a blessed sleep enfolds me mother-like, strikes dumb and motionless the crowd of evil shapes that flit through the unguarded portals of the brain.

But anon the busy, babbling, and remorseless day is not to be cheated. The sun, that sun which I fondly hoped to have watched arise as Jane and I were borne swiftly towards the sea, towards hope and happiness, and renewed life for both of us, soon streamed through the apertures of my cell upon me, half a felon, half a maniac, as in my excited imagination I then deemed myself. His beams illumined the silent chamber where she lay a corpse. What a mockery was it that there should be aught but clouds and tempests in this melancholy star, misnamed a world? Was it not rather a hateful prison-house, where souls ruined and doomed in a former state of existence roamed endlessly, cheating themselves with the hope of happiness, amused by the malice of friends, with dreams of impossible bliss?

One of the constables fully aroused me by bringing in the wherewithal for a rude lavation. He respectfully advised me to dress and have a cup of tea, which would help, as he said, to straighten me a bit before court time.

He meant well and kindly, as did all the men of the police force stationed there, knowing me well by sight and reputation. Whether guilty or innocent in this matter he possibly did not consider himself bound even approximately to decide. It was not his 'case.' The sergeant would have the getting up of the evidence, and so on. But it was hard, he thought, to see a man like me, who had seen better days, as the common phrase runs, locked up on such a charge. Was I guilty? Who could say? Wonderful things in the history of crime had happened, even in his experience on goldfields, and he was a young man; and where there was a woman in the case, who was to say with certainty what might or might not take place?

So Police-constable Grant calmly arranged my basin and towel, with a small looking-glass and comb, placed a tin measure of tea with a plate of the same material, containing bread and meat, at the farther end of the cell, mentioned that court would be open at ten o'clock sharp, and departed.

It was later than I thought. I had scarcely more than time to lave my burning brow and breast plentifully with the ice-cold water, which indeed wonderfully refreshed and relieved me, drink freely, and partake of the smallest morsel of bread, when the iron-bound door again clanged and Sergeant MacMahon entered with another trooper to escort me to the court-house.

'Brushed yourself up a bit, Mr. Pole?' he said, with a kindly gravity. 'It's a dreadful business, but there's no use taking things too much to heart before the real time comes on. Have you any legal gentleman engaged to defend you?'

'Defend me!' I said, 'what necessity is there for that? who could think for one moment that I was guilty of such a crime?'

'Never mind the crime, Mr. Pole,' said the sergeant, his keen gray eye resting upon me meanwhile, as if there was a printed page on my heart which he was deciphering slowly but accurately; 'take my advice and have Mr. Markham. You're not fit to conduct your own case. But I daresay your mates have sent for him long before this. Please to follow me into court.'

I walked out of the cell dreamily and did as I was told, constable Grant following within arm's length, as was *de rigueur* in case of attempts at escape. I was then taken through the crowd which filled the court, and permitted to sit down in the vicinity of the table usually devoted to professional gentlemen, strangers of degree, and parties to civil suits. I saw the sergeant look over at Blake, who nodded his head affirmatively.

The court is crammed. Even the approaches are so thronged that those afar off desist from endeavouring to gain nearer 'coigns of vantage,' and content themselves with sitting on the fence of the camp reserve. There is a sickening feeling at my heart, which still keeps throbbing with the thought that Jane lies dead, foully murdered, and that I stand here this day in the sight of all men charged with being her slayer. Truly my enemies had triumphed—so far I was beneath their heels.

Of course, my friends muster strong on the occasion. I see the Major, Olivera, and Jack Bulder, also Mrs. Yorke, the latter weeping profusely, with a large solemn baby in her arms, Mrs. Mangrove and other female sympathisers, all with their best bonnets on as if they were going to church. The Commissioner is seated on the bench with two other magistrates. They look at me with an air of not seeing me, which long practice has enabled them to assume. It is not for them to take for granted guilt or innocence on the part of the accused until the evidence be concluded. There is a man charged with being drunk in a public street. He having been locked up all night, and not being an habitual offender, is discharged with a caution. I watched him passing into the body of the court, and metamorphosing himself into a spectator, with features quite relaxed and free of care. Another indiscreet has been drunk and disorderly. He is adjudged to pay a pound or to undergo seven days' gaol. He pays, and lightly changes front.

'Hereward Pole, stand up! You stand charged with wilful murder; how do you plead?'

I start as though I had been struck.

'Not guilty,' of course I exclaim.

'Swear Sergeant MacMahon,' says the Commissioner. And

the sergeant enters the witness box. On his oath he thus deposes—

'I am a senior-sergeant of police stationed at the Oxley goldfield. About half-past ten or a quarter to eleven o'clock, P.M., yesterday, while on duty, I was attracted by seeing a crowd at the licensed house of Mrs. Simpson. I immediately proceeded thither, and on entering the house perceived the prisoner standing at the top of the passage with a woman in his arms. She was apparently in a helpless or dying state when I approached. There was a pool of blood at the feet of prisoner. Examined the appearance of the woman, whom I recognised to be Mrs. Morsley, whom I had known at Grenville and Warraluen diggings as the wife of a man named Edward Morsley. Her throat was cut almost from ear to ear. (Sensation. The women cry piteously.) She could not speak. I heard one sound, a kind of unintelligible moan. I caused her to be placed upon a bed and sent for Dr. Bolton. When I saw her she appeared to be quite dead. Edward Morsley called out from the crowd and said, "I charge this man with the murder of my wife." I said "Very well." I arrested the prisoner and confined him in the lock-up. I then charged him with the wilful murder of Jane Morsley. He said, in answer to the charge, "I could not have hurt her for all the gold in Australia."'

Cross-examined by Dr. Bellair, retained for the prosecution : 'Prisoner looked pale and horror-struck, as any one would have looked under the circumstances.'

Dr. Bellair : 'What, even a policeman ?'

The sergeant, with dignity : 'Yes, anybody but a doctor.'

Dr. Bellair : 'I appeal to the Court for protection. It is most improper of the witness to address the counsel for the Crown in this way.'

The Bench is of opinion that no disrespect was intended. The witness is merely desirous of eulogising the professional nerve of surgeons.

Sarah Simpson, sworn, states : 'I am the landlady of the hotel where deceased lodged. She had been with me several months, and was most quiet and well-behaved in every way. Understood she was going home to England. Mr. Pole, whom she told witness knew her in England, used to come and see her now and then, but not often. Remembered his coming last night. He said to me, "Mrs. Simpson, please tell Mrs. Morsley I want to see her about being ready in time for the coach to-morrow. If she's gone to bed it doesn't matter. Be sure and have her called early." I told her and she went into the front parlour where Harry Pole was. When Mr. Pole was gone, or say a couple of minutes afterwards, I heard the parlour door slam. I heard her say, "I won't go home, I'll die first." Ran out with others directly after when Mr. Pole cried "Help." Saw him holding her all bleeding in his arms. Oh, my God !'

(Here the witness fainted, and the proceedings had to be stayed till her recovery.)

By Dr. Bellair : 'Can't think who did it. Will never think it was Mr. Pole ; he always acted the gentleman, and was a good friend to her.'

'Too good a friend, perhaps ?'

'No, sir, he were not—not as I ever see or thought on, and won't believe till my dying day.'

'Perhaps I ran in and killed her, then ?'

'Perhaps you did, sir ; little men is that vicious when they takes the turn, as they might do hanything. But some one come from somewheres and did it, and not Harry Pole, and that I'll live and die on, poor dear !'

John Henderson sworn : 'Is a commercial traveller, and had been several days in the house. Was just going to bed when he heard some one cry out for help. Ran out into the passage, other people having come with lights. He saw prisoner standing near the end of the passage supporting Mrs. Morsley in his arms. Had seen her in the hotel several times. There was blood on the floor, on his clothing, everywhere. Deceased was bleeding from a large wound in the throat, which had been cut, as the phrase is, from ear to ear.'

Cross-examined : 'Did not hear any one speak before the cry for help. Might have been some talking without his hearing. Had been going over his accounts before going to bed.'

'Was that his way of saying his prayers ?'

'Not exactly—it was minding his business, however, and he would recommend other people to mind theirs.'

'Was the prisoner very pale and unnerved ?'

'Not more so than any gentleman—himself for certain would have been—on suddenly encountering such a dreadful task. Could not form any opinion as to who had committed the crime ; would as soon accuse his Worship on the Bench as prisoner of having done it.'

At this stage of the proceedings a note was placed in the hands of the Commissioner who, after reading it, gave it to his brother magistrates for inspection. After a short consultation, he spoke as follows—

'A letter addressed to the Bench has just been placed in my hands. In it Mr. Markham, who is employed on behalf of the prisoner, states that he has been prevented attending to-day on account of other professional engagements, and requests that the Bench will remand the prisoner until Monday next in order that he may have the opportunity of securing professional aid. Have you any objection, Dr. Bellair, to the course indicated ?'

'Under the circumstances of the case, none whatever, your worship,' said the little man, with stupendous dignity.

'Call up the witnesses, Sergeant MacMahon, and let them be bound over to appear on the day named—Edward Morsley. Algernon Malgrade, Sarah Simpson, John Henderson, are you content to be bound in the sum of forty pounds each to appear on Monday next at the court-house on the Oxley at ten o'clock, there to give evidence in the case of Hereward Pole charged with wilful murder? are you content to be bound?'

'Yes, your worship.'

'This Court stands adjourned till to-morrow morning at ten o'clock.'

The crowd passed out and separated into groups to talk over the all-absorbing topic, with the interesting uncertainty, doubtless, of my innocence or otherwise in the affair.

In a few minutes the whole enclosure was cleared, the court-house locked up. I was again sitting on my bed in the cell upon which I had thrown myself in dull despair as I re-entered.

Was this, indeed, *my* life? or had I changed souls and destinies as old writers dreamed?

It seems the first thing the Major did after quitting me at the lock-up when I first entered it, was to send off a messenger post-haste to Mr. Markham, with a note briefly detailing the circumstances, and enclosing a substantial check as retaining fee on my behalf in the preliminary inquiry which was imminent.

On the Sunday afternoon, therefore, that gentleman was ushered into my cell, and, shaking me by the hand with his accustomed warmth and heartiness, appeared only to perceive, like a skilful and courtly physician, a slight social indisposition which regular treatment would be sure to remove.

'Unpleasant affair, Harry, my boy,' he said; 'dreadfully unpleasant; temporary inconvenience, eh? and all the rest of it. No bail allowed either, or of course you needn't have been ten minutes in the logs. Not but what there are worse places— delightfully cool this broiling weather. Got a crib all to yourself, eh? I say, sergeant.'

'Well, Mr. Markham,' said my chief custodian, 'what can I do for you?'

'Why, send me a chair, of course. You don't expect me to stand for a couple of hours while I am having a good confidential yarn about this business with my friend, Harry, here. When it comes you can lock us in; only don't forget to let me out about tea-time.'

'All right, Mr. Markham,' said the sergeant. 'Is there anything else I can do for you?'

'Nothing, except you were to let me have some brandy and soda. But as that's against the regulations, we must wait for happier times, I suppose. Thanks, that is a good substantial chair—good afternoon for the present.'

And he sat himself down with the greatest ease and deliberation, while the bolt was shot to, the door clanged, and we were alone in the cell.

Mr. Markham's face underwent a sudden and complete change. The expression of rollicking good humour faded away as the door swung on its hinges. When the key had turned and

T

the bolt shot to, nothing was to be seen but a keen concentrated gaze, whence all levity had fled for ever.

I returned his gaze with eyes as unfaltering as his own.

'You never did it, I can see that,' he said, as if in answer to an unspoken question. 'I had my doubts before I saw you. Don't speak now; if you knew as much of human nature as I do, you'd believe anything or nothing in any case where a woman was concerned. You didn't do it, as I said before. Now, the question is, who did, and how is he to be fixed ?'

'I can't tell,' I answered wearily. 'I did not, as you truly say and believe. Why should I have harmed a hair of her head ? Poor Jane. I would have done anything in the world for her that a man might do.'

'So I have heard,' he said drily. 'It's a pity that this brother-and-sister business should so often be misconstrued. I don't blame you, my dear boy; young men will be imprudent. But it would have been better for both of you if you had let her go her own way, and you had stuck to your work.'

'It may be so,' I said. 'It is too late to talk of that now.'

'Well, yes; and I didn't come here to moralise. The point is, who do you think killed her, and why ?'

'The man who brushed past me in the entry was the only person who had time or opportunity. It was too dark to recognise him.'

'And you have no idea who or what he was like ?'

'Something, for a moment, put me in mind of Ned Morsley. I can hardly say why. But it could not have been him.'

'Why not ?'

'Because he was among the crowd with Malgrade hardly two minutes afterwards, when I had poor Jane's body in my arms. He could never have stopped and joined the crowd after such a deed.'

'Humph !' said my adviser, 'the night was dark, you said ?'

'The very darkest that I have seen for years. There was a thunderstorm at midnight. I heard it coming as I paced up and down this doghole for an hour before.'

'Poor Harry !' he said compassionately. 'You expected to be in Sydney, somewhere about Batty's hotel, by this time. Life's another word for disappointment, isn't it ? You have a sheath knife, I see.'

I knew what he meant. I handed it to him. I had picked up the habit of carrying such a knife attached to my belt from the sailors on the outward bound voyage, and had found it come in too handily in a rude wandering life to relinquish it.

'Humph ! point ground down, edge like an old meat axe, very fine knife to cut butter. What have you been doing with it lately ?'

'The fact was that we came to a quartz vein at 120 foot level, and I picked out some very good coarse gold with the point till I broke it off, and had to grind it round. The edge was gapped by young Dawson the other day. I lent it to him to go kangarooing. I didn't think it worth while sharpening it, and indeed was going to give it to Mrs. Yorke for a kitchen knife to-morrow.'

'Humph!' said Mr. Markham again. After this he sat in silence for a few minutes. Then he aroused himself and changed the conversation, encouraging me to talk of old English days, of my life at the Leys, of Jack and Joe Bulder, of my fixed determination to have cleared out in six months, whatever may have been the ebb or flow of the treasure-tide. Lastly he commenced to ask in a general way whom I had seen that day, with whom conversed, what well-known miners, loafers, or quasi-criminals I had seen about the town. Finally, he exhorted me to keep up my spirits, and to go over and over the few minutes before and immediately after the tragedy, lest haply some important fact may have escaped my observation.

Then he took leave of me, and knocked at the door, first moderately, then impatiently. There was no answer. The sergeant had been called away, and there was no one to release the captive until he returned. Mr. Markham lit a cigar and appeared to take the forced incarceration easily enough.

While accepting the profuse apologies of the sergeant, when he arrived in high glee, having captured a horse-stealer—the show criminal of the division—Mr. Markham seemed by no means fully satiated with prison experience for the time. He lingered in the vicinity, putting careless half-questions that were half-assertions to the sergeant and Grant. Finally, he thanked that official most warmly for the pleasure of his visit and the confidence with which he had honoured him, and strolled off with a last injunction to me to keep up my spirits and try to 'remember up' any facts and details even up to the most minute shred of speech or action during the few minutes preceding and following the tragedy, or otherwise I should do him no credit as a client, and the enemy—even Dr. Bellair, who was retained for the Crown—would have cause to triumph.

CHAPTER XXXI

THE door was shut behind my kindly, good-humoured advocate. He had succeeded in raising my spirits, albeit imperceptibly. A vision of future safety and peace rose, faintly tremulous, amid the dread shadow-land of the dim horizon. Of happiness I did not dream ; it could never more be mine. The insatiable Fate, which had so mercilessly dogged my footsteps in this southland, was still relentless. My reputation stood shamefully linked with the ill-starred dead. Her very name was all - powerful still to injure me with those whose good opinion I valued most in the world. Strangely impalpable Slander ! How subtle, how dire a poison art thou ! Conveyed in the touch of a hand, in the whispered breath, in the motion of the body, the glance of the eye. As by those wondrous, deadly mediæval agencies, the life, nay more, the memory, the soul's weal is blasted, shrivelled, stricken dead, and dishonoured before the magical missile, viewless as the wind, secret as the sea, cruel as the grave. Brinvilliers and the Borgias have gone to their appointed place ; but modern society still holds those who smile and betray to doom, who stab with words and slay with medicated tongue. Dead or alive, poor Jane had worked me woe. Was I now to be overwhelmed, crushed, obliterated ; and was there no hope of succour ?

As these and kindred thoughts passed through my mind, already crowded with morbid and gloomy images, my dull ear became increasingly sensible of a deep yet distant murmur, which gradually swelled in volume and nearness to my cell. Half instinctively, as I listened, the sound waves resolved themselves into a familiar rhythmical noise. It was the tread of a large body of men marching in rank.

What was the occasion ? Scarcely another *emeute ?* What then could it be ? In another moment the band of one of the great associated guilds struck the first notes of that grand composition long associated with the dead, with the last pageant in which they hold formal association with the living. With stupefied unawakened intelligence, as to an overture, I listened indifferently. The solemn awe-inspiring movement was familiar

to the ear, yet bearing no message to the heart. Then flashed
with electrical suddenness across me the terrible truth—it is
Jane's funeral. How had I not earlier realised the possibility
of such a ceremony, natural and inevitable as it was?

How inexplicable are the movements of the mind. But a
moment since I had schooled myself to a stoical mood of endurance of the ills that might henceforth come upon me. I
felt even a feeble kind of reactionary resentment against the
course of events which had stricken me down so suddenly, had
laid me so low. Mr. Markham's condolences had not been without their effect. After all I was not wholly to blame. I had
done everything for Jane's best interests that a man could have
done for his own sister. I had been actuated by the best and
purest motives if such there be within this strangely concocted
entity, this jumble of 'made ground' (to use the miner's phrase),
that we call humanity. And what had been the result?

She lay dead, a disfigured corpse, denied even a seemly
appearance in death, she that was so fair. I was in a felon's
cell, justly so prisoned in the opinion of a section of the society
in which I lived, irrevocably humbled and injured in my own
eyes, and in those of my fellow-men. One thought of the sea-
washed pier we had both so longed to tread again came through
my brain at the same instant.

One breath of the ocean breeze fanned my face in visionary
freshness. The contrast, even in glamour and delusion, un-
manned me. I cast myself down on my pallet and wept like a
child. Long and passionately I wept as I lay there, while the
sunshine streamed through in golden flakes telling of the bright
blue cloudless skies without, and of the dry dusty street which
our feet had so often paced. Adown this she was now passing
for the last time—the last time, ah me! to the pine-crested
cemetery. There dwelt many guests that had never dreamed
of being bidden so early to take their part in life's last promenade, to taste 'Death's coal-black wine.'

Radetsky had gone there. How strange and unnatural that
his restless heart was stilled. Cyrus, of the mighty arm, was
never more to raise so much as the weight of the dry grass
stems that fluttered in the summer whirlwinds. And now,
Jane Mangold, fresh-tinted, bright-hued, innocent wild rose, as
I first remembered her in her country home; the sad-eyed,
haggard woman of these last sorrowful months, *she* was gone to
be alone with Death—when the train of kindly mourners should
return, who paid the last token of respect to a foully murdered
sister, a repentant fellow-sinner.

Should I be the next?

In my weakened and excited state the idea assumed a
horrible distinctness; it gradually increased to the dimensions
of a fear, almost of a form, until, with throbbing burning
temples, like to burst with pain, with beating overcharged
heart, of which the pulsations seemed to clang intolerably and

loudly, I pictured myself carried past my prison, along the self-same well-known road, and saw the familiar faces of friends and acquaintances, decorously downcast, at the same distance from the bier at which I had a score of times walked myself.

It seemed to be a fitting end for this accursed, feverish, treasure-seeking life, in which the gold was so rapidly turning to ashes and bitterness, to dead leaves, as in the folk-lore of childhood's days.

'Why,' I once more moaned out, 'did I not die by the robber's bullet? A quick shrift, a clean death, worthy of a man, if premature and sudden? Then I should have left behind but fond regrets, but passionate loving tears and manly sorrow for a lost comrade——'

While now——

.   .   .   .   .   .

I must have been weakened as by a wound, become morbidly nervous and sensitive, for this womanly passion and hysterical weakness to have come over me. But I had hardly tasted food since first the prison bolts closed behind me. Sleep had been either entirely absent or broken and disturbed with frightful images. I had heard of men going mad under such circumstances, and I at times probed and tested my mental powers as if to discover whether or not reason was shaken.

The tramp of feet passed and ceased; the deep tones of the funeral march died away in the distance; the shadows darkened, and finally the cell, which in hot summer evenings felt intolerably stifling, became filled with darkness. I slept or lay in unconscious stupor. I hardly knew which. But I started up from time to time. In my ear sounded the awful words, 'dust to dust, ashes to ashes,' as if spoken within my cell, and still, ever and anon upon the night breeze came the dirge-like echoes of the Dead March in Saul, still the wailing wind voices of the night cried aloud of death and of doom.

.   .   .   .   .   .

Pale, unstrung, tremulous should I have found myself before the crowded court on the appointed morning, but Mr. Markham, who has called in before breakfast, will not have it so. His cheering voice breaks the spell.

'I say, Harry my boy, this sort of thing won't do at all. I can't have you grizzling and doing the handkerchief business like a peculiar Christian or some of those repentant sinner-parties that intend to sin again when they get another chance. You must pull yourself together a bit or you'll do me no credit, and any goldfield's jury will bring you in guilty for not having pluck enough to bluff it off like a man.'

'I say, governor,' this to the sergeant, 'I'll send him in a cup of coffee from Jones's of my own particular brewing, and you'll see that he takes it, won't you?'

'All right, Mr. Markham, you may depend on me,' said the sergeant good-naturedly, 'and it's what I'd advise him myself,

to hold up his head a trifle higher in the court. There's no
saying what evidence may be brought forward.'

'Perfectly correct, sergeant, as usual,' said my professional
adviser, with a meaning look.

'Now, I wonder what that old fox has got in his head,' said
he to me, as the worthy official departed. 'He's the closest old
file I ever met, and I know the police have been hunting up
every scrap of evidence they can lay their hands on. I shouldn't
wonder that Bellair gets a slight surprise himself to-day. But
don't expect too much, Harry, old fellow. You never can tell
till the numbers are up.'

Mr. Markham's coffee was, probably, flavoured with something more potent than milk and sugar, or I should hardly
have felt so much relieved in mind as I did when my cell door
opened, and I saw the Major, Jack Bulder, Olivera, and Mrs.
Yorke, all waiting to give me a reassuring word and smile as I
came out.

Their strong undoubting faith acted as a cordial to my
worn senses. Here, at any rate, were kindly, honest, and
withal shrewd people, who believed undoubtedly and uncom-
promisingly in my absolute innocence.

'*He* kill her,' said Mrs. Yorke to a large female with a dull
distrustful countenance, showing a *soupçon* of the asperity
which had occasionally flavoured her discussions with Cyrus.
'I wonder if there's people alive with so little sense as to think
of such a piece of rot. Not but what there's plenty of women
on the field as wants killing, Mrs. Muggins. I don't say there
ain't, but every one knows as he was that softhearted about
females, young or old, good-looking or homely, it was all one to
poor Harry—he had a pleasant word and a smile for all of 'em.
More than that, there was nothing he wouldn't do for the
humblest of 'em in the way of kindness and rale downright
politeness, as I call it. Didn't I see him pick up a big bag of
chaff as old mother Shea, the milkwoman, was a-carrying to the
cows one dry time, and hump it the best part of a mile for her
through the town, too. He kill anybody with a petticoat on,
not he! Only he was too dashed soft, and so was run into
things as artfuller cards kep' out of, that's what he was, and I'd
like to have stuck Merlin and the old sergeant into the logs
themselves for potting the wrong man, and see how they'd
like it.'

Here Mrs. Yorke's frightfully revolutionary sentiments were
brought forcibly to an end by the onward movement of the
crowd, which separated the disputants and surged into the
building directly the large door of the court was opened by the
sergeant. By the favour of Mr. Merlin, to whom she had
alluded so disrespectfully, she was, however, accommodated with
a seat on the form set apart for witnesses, and otherwise treated
with distinction. The known fact of her being 'a golden hole
woman,' as the miners called her, doubtless operated to her

advantage. Wealth has its privileges all over the world, even at the headquarters of the chief of metals.

The court was now formally opened. Mr. Markham, cool and confident, advanced with a cheerful mien. The Commissioner and his brother magistrates sat with unmoved countenances, like Rhadamanthus and his peers. Dr. Bellair rose with tragic brow and a mien of awful dignity.

'Your worships, I demand that all witnesses leave the court.'

The Commissioner nodded to the sergeant, who, in stentorian tones, repeats the formula—

'All witnesses are ordered to leave this court, until called on to give evidence.'

With this several persons, some not previously known to me, or indeed apparently to one another, prepare to leave the court, with some difficulty, indeed, on account of the crush and crowding.

'Call Algernon Malgrade,' says the Doctor, with additional majesty, and that gentleman lounges forward and goes into the witness-box, with an air of calm indifference to the hundreds of eyes that are at once directed upon him.

Mr. Markham looks him all over in a keen, yet leisurely, manner, with the air of a surgeon regarding a subject upon whom he proposes to undertake a serious and critical operation. Malgrade places one hand on the witness-box and stares back in return with his habitual insolence of manner. Mr. Markham softly rubs his hands and smiles severely, with an air of peculiar benevolence.

Being sworn, the witness thus deposes : 'My name is Algernon Malgrade, formerly in the army. Am at present a miner, residing at the Oxley, where I hold interests in mining properties. Have known the prisoner for many years. Knew him slightly in England before either had sailed for Australia. Have also known deceased and Morsley for several years since they were married, when they lived in Ballarat ; knew them well as acquaintances ; always thought they lived on the usual matrimonial terms. They quarrelled, as a matter of course, occasionally. Deceased was a high-spirited woman. Like all handsome women, and some plain ones, she had a violent temper ; would not swear to that physiological fact, but such had been his experience. Had heard, cursorily, that Morsley was jealous of prisoner. Thought it likely enough, prisoner's conduct had been most imprudent. Saw Morsley when he came to the Oxley a few days since. He did say he should prevent his wife going to Sydney with prisoner. Thought he intended to let matters slide—that is the course he himself should have taken under the circumstances. Recollected the night of the murder?—Y-e-es ! He was walking up Mayne Street, and came up while smoking to the door of Simpson's hotel. Was leaning against the outer door, when Morsley came up. They heard voices inside the passage; deceased, as he thought, called out, "I will not go home, I will die first." Morsley said, "That's my wife's voice," and rushed in. In a moment or two he came out gasping for breath and greatly excited. I asked him what was the matter? Just then we heard prisoner call for help, and we all went in. I saw prisoner standing supporting deceased, who was bleeding from a wound in the neck and apparently dying. The police came soon after, and Morsley charged prisoner with the murder of his wife.'

'Call Edward Hill Morsley,' continues Dr. Bellair, with solemnity unspeakable.

The spectators drew back. There was an audible murmur as the husband whose wife had been foully murdered answered to his name, and walked slowly and firmly towards the witness-box. I gazed at his face. Save one, he was the man I hated and despised most on the earth. His dark face had a stern, almost savage, expression, which gained intensity as his deeply-set black eyes met mine; aflame with the lurid light of all the baser passions, they seemed to glow with demoniac lustre. If there was any tremor of body or quailing of the spirit as he lifted the sacred book and bound himself, as God should help him, to 'speak the truth, the whole truth, and nothing but the truth,' he did not show it by quiver of muscle or outward sign.

Dr. Bellair commences the examination, and extracts with practised ease his sworn statement, the more readily, perhaps, that every word of it is prejudicial to me, and accords with the most favourable hypothesis of the witness's own conduct.

'My name is Edward Hill Morsley. I am a hotel-keeper, and reside at the Miners' Home, Warraluen. I was the husband of the deceased Jane Morsley. We were married at Wendouree Street, Ballarat, and have followed the diggings since then, about four years. We have had quarrels now and then. Last year prisoner came to Warraluen. He formed some acquaintance with me and deceased, whom I afterwards found he had known in England. Deceased did not tell me so at the time, nor did prisoner. I assisted him in the purchase of shares in the Holman Company, and others, and was very friendly towards him. After he left, deceased kept up a correspondence with him, and seemed restless and dissatisfied—talking of going back to England. I gave her no cause of complaint. At the time of the escort robbery, when prisoner was wounded, deceased insisted on going over to Eugowra to nurse him, and did so against my will. She refused subsequently to come back; she stayed at the Oxley where prisoner lived, and said she would go to England. I came over to the Oxley to see her, and if possible to prevail on her to return to me. I went to Simpson's Hotel where I heard she was staying. As I came up to the door about twelve o'clock, or perhaps nearer half-past eleven o'clock, I heard deceased and some one talking in the passage of the hotel. Deceased said in an excited tone of voice, "I will never go home with you, I will die first." I ran into the passage and found prisoner holding deceased in his arms; she appeared to have been wounded. I ran out to give the alarm, but was so taken by surprise that I could not speak. In the meantime prisoner called out, and other people came in. I followed them into the passage, and when the police came gave prisoner in charge for murder. Have had quarrels with deceased like other married people, I suppose, but had no ill feeling towards her. She was very fond of admiration, and had a violent temper when roused. This led to altercation of course. She was much worse after prisoner came to Warraluen. Saw Algernon Malgrade at the hotel on the night of the murder. Did not remark him before until the crowd came up. May have spoken to him in the forenoon of that day. Did not have a long conversation with him on that day—to the best of my knowledge, that is; if so have forgotten it. Is not a particular friend of mine, not more than a diggings acquaintance. May have seen him the day after the escort robbery. Did not see Wall or Gilbert Hawke the day after the robbery; saw plenty of other persons that day. Do not carry a knife on ordinary occasions; have not got one now. May have borrowed a knife since I came to the Oxley to do some trifling act. If so, do not remember. Do not know a man named Luke Weston. Did not borrow his knife the day before the murder; may have borrowed one from some one. May have said that deceased should not go to Sydney with prisoner, but never to my knowledge that I would cut her throat first. Have said such things in the heat of passion—people often do; never intended her any harm.'

CHAPTER XXXII

THUS far the examination-in-chief. It was now Mr. Markham's privilege to cross-examine. Rising quickly and facing the witness one moment, his features changed visibly as he gazed at him until they wore an expression of rigid determination well-nigh akin in sternness to those of his opponent. Morsley, on his part, took an attitude, half of weary expectation, half of dogged defiance, like a swordsman who watches his antagonist's eye and hand.

'You have stated to the Bench that you were married in Ballarat about the year 185—. Is that so?'

'Yes.'

'Within a month of that time were you bound over to keep the peace towards your wife under heavy penalties, having committed a brutal assault upon her?'

'I was bound over; we had a quarrel, but I did not assault her as she stated.'

'Oh, you had not assaulted her; she imagined it?—imagined that her face was cut and bruised also?'

'She fell down and bruised her face.'

'How did she fall down? was she running in fear of you?'

'She was leaving the room hastily when she fell.'

'No doubt she was—very hastily. She was probably afraid of her life, as she had good reason to be. Did you then leave Ballarat and proceed to Granville Rush?'

'Yes.'

'Did the last witness, Algernon Malgrade, accompany you, and was he a partner with you in the Granville Arms Hotel?'

'He came with us, and had an interest in the hotel.'

'Did he suddenly leave the hotel a few weeks afterwards in consequence of a disagreement with deceased?'

'They had some words, and he left.'

'Did not the deceased say that she would not live in the same house with him; that he was a villain and a traitor?'

'She did abuse him, if I remember—but she was in the habit of using strong language. Her temper was always violent.'

'Just so; and yours was particularly lamb-like. You wish the Bench to believe that. This made no difference in your friendship with Malgrade?'

'None at all. I bought his share of the house, and he went to Yatala diggings when it broke out.'

'Did you say in your examination-in-chief that Malgrade was no particular friend of yours?'

'I may have said so.'

'May have said so? You did say so, sir, most distinctly. How do you reconcile that with the fact of your having been a partner with him, and having taken his side in a dispute with your wife? Answer my question.'

'A man may have business transactions with another man without being his intimate friend.'

'Of course, of course; may purchase a property together, after having come away from another diggings together, live in the same house, and be so bound up together that you take his part against your own wife. You don't call that friendship?'

'Not particularly. I'm not bound to take up all a woman's quarrels. A man on a goldfield would have nothing else to do.'

'Certainly. I see your point, Mr. Morsley—you have proved yourself to be a very prudent, self-controlled, amiable person. But how did you come, at Granville, to have knocked down a man named Albert Hoffmeyer, and broken three of his ribs, in a quarrel arising out of jealousy?'

'That is another affair. I had good reason for what I gave him.'

'Was your wife treated in the hospital immediately afterwards for a broken arm, of the cause of which she could give no account?'

'Yes, I believe so.'

'Another accident, I suppose: fell down, probably.'

'I submit your worships,' here broke in Dr. Bellair, who had been restraining himself with frightful exertion of self-command all the time, 'that this line of cross-examination cannot by any possibility bear on the case. The witness may or may not have been a model husband, that peculiarly British institution, but I assert that his patience or amiability is not here called in question. Your worships have only to deal with the point as to whether there is a *prima facie* case against the prisoner upon the charge for which he stands in custody, when it will be the plain unavoidable duty of the Bench to commit him to the next Assize Court.'

'Your worships are doubtless aware,' quoth Mr. Markham, with studied impressiveness, 'of the great and peculiar importance that this witness should be subjected to a searching cross-examination. The issues of life and death are involved, and though this can be but a preliminary examination, it is indispensable, if I am to do full justice to my unfortunate, and I fearlessly assert, innocent client, that no limit be set to my privileges as an advocate.'

'Innocent!' shrieked the inflammable doctor. 'Innocent! when the very stones in the street cry out for vengeance for the blood of a murdered woman.'

'Murdered, ay—but by whom?' said Mr. Markham in a low deep voice of concentrated feeling, bending forward and fixing his eyes with mesmeric force and earnestness upon the witness.

It may have been fancy, but I thought I saw the cruel eyes quail before the sudden challenge; the form lose something of its rugged boldness of defiance.

A vivid motion of surprise then possessed me. Could *Morsley himself* have been the murderer? I had hitherto dismissed the idea from my mind. It seemed utterly impossible, in the short space that elapsed between the time in which the dark figure in the poncho brushed past me in the passage, and Morsley standing on the outskirts of the crowd demanding my apprehension as his wife's murderer—dressed also in a lightish gray tweed suit of clothes, that he should have presented so entirely different an appearance to that of the unknown in the poncho.

Mr. Markham evidently was following up some clue. I held my breath and controlled the beating of my heart.

'The Bench is of opinion,' here interjected the Commissioner, 'that Mr. Markham is justified, in cross-examination, in testing the credibility of the witness in any manner which he may consider suitable.'

'I shan't trouble you any further as to your domestic habits, Mr. Morsley,' said my advocate. 'Will you please to answer me a question of quite a different sort? You remember the escort robbery?'

The witness nodded.

'It was on Friday, the 14th April 186—, was it not?'

'I think so.'

'You think so; don't you know it was, sir?' thundered the terrible interlocutor. 'And very good reason you had for knowing it. Now, did you or did you not meet the last witness at a place called the Rocky Springs, in company with two other men, whose names I needn't mention, when you and he received a parcel from those men?'

'I did not.'

'You did not? now be careful, you are on your oath. Was one of the men Harry Jenkinson — commonly known as Big Harry?'

'No. I never saw the last witness or him either.'

'You swear that? You did not meet either of them on the day mentioned?'

'I may have met them in the course of a week or two.'

'But not on that day—the day after the escort robbery?'

'No, certainly not.'

'Do you know a man named George Roper?'

'Not that I know of. I can't swear.'

'Call George Roper, sergeant.'

The name is called outside of the court, and a quiet, sleepy-looking agriculturist appears.

'Do you see that man; do you know him?' The man grinned sheepishly.

'I think I have seen him. He sold me some corn once. I see so many people that I can't be expected to recollect everybody.'

'Of course not, of course not, Mr. Morsley; we must try and refresh your memory. That will do, Roper. You can leave the court. And you didn't see that man the day after the robbery at Rocky Springs?'

'I can't swear one way or the other. I may have done so.'

'At Rocky Springs?'

'No, not that I remember. At another place.'

'Very good. Now, Morsley, attend to me; be very careful in your answer as the question is important. How were you dressed on the night when deceased came by her death?'

Here more than one spectator leaned forward, as if anxiously awaiting the result of his question.

'In the same dress I wear now,' he answered with perfect composure.

'Just so, a gray tweed suit. I think coat and waistcoat of the same colour, trousers slightly darker; allow me to look at them —a very serviceable suit, quiet, and so on. The second button seems different in colour from the others, and—just permit me for one moment—rather clumsily sewed on: no woman's hand did that, Morsley; comes of quarrelling with your wife, eh? You don't recollect how it came off, I suppose?'

'My barkeeper noticed that it had come off before I left Warraluen,' said the witness, scowling darkly at his questioner. 'He offered to sew it on for me. Would you like to have the tailor's address that made the clothes?'

'Why, yes,' said Markham, as if he had expected the question, 'he might be able to tell me *if this button* (here he took one from his pocket) *exactly matches the others in colour*, shape, size —and also in the shade of silk twist with which the others are sewed on. He might be able to swear to that Morsley, or the reverse, but perhaps you can do so.'

'How can I swear? how do I know where it comes from?'

'*It was found clenched in the dead hand of your murdered wife*, as I shall be enabled to prove,' said Mr. Markham with slow pitiless severity of tone, 'does that help you to recollect how you lost it?'

The swarthy hue of the man's face, which had gained him

the sobriquet of Black Ned, visibly paled, and his strong frame shook before he answered sullenly—

'If you wish to accuse me of killing her, you had better say it out at once, but I thought I was a witness and that man in the dock the prisoner.'

'You will be quite clear about your respective positions in a short time, I daresay,' said Mr. Markham, with cheerful confidence.

'I must again protest,' broke in Dr. Bellair fiercely, 'against the extraordinary latitude taken by the counsel for the defence in this case.   Are the feelings of the witness to be lacerated by references to the unfortunate deceased at every turn.   Surely your worships will not tolerate this sensational style of examination.'

'My learned friend's client will have to submit to more sensational treatment before he leaves the court, I feel confident,' said Mr. Markham; 'in the meantime I must request that no restriction be placed upon my undoubted legal right to the severest cross-examination.'

The Commissioner nodded affirmatively, and the intensely interested audience gave a kind of half-murmur, as of strained anxiety, as Mr. Markham proceeded.

'You had on no other coat but the one you now wear, on the night referred to?'

'No; it was a warm night.'

'You did not wear a poncho, for instance?'

'No.'

'Have you got such an article of dress?'

'Yes.'

'Where is it?'

'I left it behind at Warraluen.'

'Oh! you left it behind.'

'Yes.   The weather was dry and hot.'

'And you have not worn one here?'

'No, certainly not.'

'You are in the habit of wearing a sheath knife, I believe?'

'No, I am not.   I have a pocket knife.'

'Please to show it to the court.'

The knife is produced.   An ordinary knife, with two blades, one much blunted cutting tobacco.   It is handed up to the Bench.

'That is the knife you had in your pocket on the night of the murder?'

'Yes.'

'And you had no other knife in your possession?'

'No.'

'Not at any time during the week?'

'No.'

'Of that you are certain; you didn't borrow a knife from any one?'

'Not that I remember. It is possible that I may have done
so during the week, but I have no recollection of it accurately.'

'Quite right, Mr. Morsley, to be careful—*you can't be too careful* in your present position, I assure you. You can go now;
sign your depositions first, though.'

Morsley had turned as if to leave the box, glaring at his per-
secutor with ill-concealed hatred and malice. An evil look of
triumph half gleamed in his eyes, as he took the pen in his hand
to write his name with studied coolness. Yet his hand shook in
spite of all his efforts. Others, doubtless, noticed this. But many
a strong man in that court had been similarly affected, concerning
whom there was no question of guilt or innocence. The symptom
was but too common. And the only effect on the bystanders was
to confirm the notion that Black Ned had been 'on the drink'
lately, perhaps on account of his trouble. And that was quite
sufficient in their eyes to account for tremulous penmanship.

He raised his head menacingly as he stepped from the
witness-box, and swaggered down the body of the court with
his usual insolence of demeanour palpably exaggerated, probably
for the benefit of myself and Mr. Markham. Dr. Bellair cleared
his throat and prepared to address the court with a highly
confident air when the sergeant strode forward with one of his
characteristic seven-leagued movements, and laid his heavy hand
upon the shoulder of the retiring witness.

Morsley turned hastily with a face of surprise, almost of fear,
which he vainly tried to control, while the sergeant thus spoke
in tones which filled the court—

'I arrest you, Edward Morsley, in the Queen's name; and I
now charge you with the wilful murder of your wife, Jane
Morsley, on the night of the 16th instant.'

The astonishment of every living soul in the court, Mr.
Markham alone excepted, was extreme and patent. The crowd
positively gasped in amazement, as the sergeant, exerting his
great strength, pushed the prisoner into the dock, the door of
which was opened by one of the constables and closed upon him,
he appearing like a man in a dream, dazed and incapable of
offering resistance.

As for me, I sat staring before me, almost incapable of collect-
ing my ideas upon the subject. All that I could gather from
the action of Sergeant MacMahon was that he, for some reason,
believed Morsley to be the murderer of poor Jane. Mr. Markham,
from his questioning as to the poncho, evidently leaned towards
the hypothesis that he and the man in the poncho were one.
But where was the proof? where the connection with any act
of his, and the blood so pitilessly, so cruelly shed?

Dr. Bellair was the first to awake to the need for action.

'Your worships, I beg, I demand redress against this proceeding, this most unprecedented, most unparalleled outrage
upon the person of a witness, this insult to your authority by
this autocratic policeman, after all a subordinate officer of the

force. He seems to think that he can arrest any one he pleases.
I suppose' (here the little man stood up to his fullest height,
and puffed out his chest heroically) 'I suppose he will arrest
me next!'

'Dr. Bellair,' said Blake, 'Senior-sergeant MacMahon is fully
empowered to act in this matter at his discretion. He is
responsible to the head of his department. He, no doubt, has
his own reasons for the action he has taken. It is not within
the province of the Bench to direct any alteration of the mode
in which he has chosen to effect this arrest.'

'Of course,' returned the doctor, foaming with rage, 'if the
police are permitted to arrest witnesses in court during a trial,
and indecently to interrupt the course of law in any way they
please in order to trump up a case, I have nothing more to say,
further than that I shall lay a special complaint before the
Minister for Justice, the head of the Crown Law Department.'

'Take what steps you think fit, Dr. Bellair,' said the Commissioner, 'but I must ask you, however, to refrain from entering into a detailed description of your probable action. You
wish to make an application to the Bench, sergeant?'

'I pray for a remand of the prisoner, Edward Hill Morsley,
for eight days, your worships, at the end of which time I shall
be in a position to bring most material evidence against him.
In the meantime, I desire to apply to your worships to discharge
Mr. Hereward Pole from custody, as I have decided not to proceed further with the charge against him.'

A murmur of approbation filled the court, which fell on my
ears like the sound of a far-off torrent, so confused was my
brain, and dulled my every sense, at this unexpected course of
events.

There was a pause of perfect silence while the Bench de-
liberated. Then Blake looked boldly and cheerily across the
crowd.

'The accused, Mr. Hereward Pole, was discharged,' he said.
'The Bench was unanimous in their opinion as to the extreme
hardship of his having been placed in his present painful position at all. Unhappily circumstances appeared to be against
him at the time of the death of the unfortunate deceased.
Sergeant MacMahon, whatever might have been that officer's
private suspicions as to the real criminal, was therefore justified
in arresting Mr. Pole. But he, the Police Magistrate, had now
much pleasure in stating, on the part of the Bench, that after
hearing the evidence brought forward that day before the Court
not the slightest suspicion attached to Mr. Pole, and he left the
court, most emphatically, without a stain on his character.'

This announcement was received with a general burst of
cheering, promptly suppressed by the sergeant.

CHAPTER XXXIII

THE Court was immediately adjourned.

Surrounded by my friends, I was marched off in triumph, escorted by a great crowd that insisted upon following us down the principal street in triumphal procession. A small band of musicians even, on the watch for opportunities of profitable patronage, seized the occasion, and headed the cortege, playing ' See the conquering hero comes,' ' When Johnny comes marching home,' with other airs appropriate, in their opinion, to my circumstances.

For me, like the victims of those death ceremonies of the olden Asiatic communities when stupefied by narcotics, I felt confused with a blare of trumpets and beating of gongs and cymbals. One glance as I left the court had shown me my enemy being conveyed to the cell I had just quitted. His face was a study for all evil passions, baffled malice, blind rage, and hate unspeakable. As Malgrade departed he was hustled and hooted by the crowd. The women had come to gradually but distinctly connect him with the tragedy in some shape, and he had become scarcely less unpopular than the principal criminal.

The crowd left us at the cross street which led down to our dwelling, previously calling for three cheers for Harry Pole, which were given with great heartiness and enthusiasm before they separated.

I walked listlessly into our humble dwelling. It looked like a palace after the hateful bare walls of the cell. Throwing myself down on my bed I felt inclined to sleep for evermore. And, indeed, so utterly wearied was I, so worn out with stress of mind and body, with sleeplessness, anxiety, and pain, that I fell at once into a deep slumber which lasted unbrokenly until sunrise on the following day.

.   .   .   .

How wondrously complicated, how tremulously, delicately fine are the first mental movements as our being, truly unwillingly, extricates consciousness from the trance which so strangely simulates death ! How clear yet impalpably minute is the semitone of thought which indicates misfortune already realised, or looming dim and powerless in the future. Magically sudden also is the thrill of relief when the soul, signalling the dread incubus with electrical flash, simultaneously registers the facts of safety and freedom.

So wakes the pensioned soldier, with the well-remembered sounds of parade and drill in his ears, to contrast only more effectively with the blessed independence of rural life in his long-lost village-home. So wakes the newly-enriched heir, half encompassed by the shifts and straitened ways of his ungilded manhood, to rejoice even more vividly in his lofty halls and the tokens of unfettered expenditure. So comes the blissful morn to the freed captive, whose first movements seem guarded by his prison walls, upon whom the quick joy of realised freedom instantly breaks with the beam of heaven's light.

As the sun streamed unimpeded through the window of our cabin, my soul seemed to be irradiated, my whole being pervaded with a gratitude so deep that for a moment I shrunk from it as disloyalty to her who lay so cold and still in a blood-stained grave.

'Well, Harry!' said the crisp, unsentimental voice of Mrs. Yorke, 'you'd better come and have your breakfast if you're ever going to get up again. You've had enough sleep by this time. Don't take on overmuch—it's no use doing that. Poor Jane's gone, and there's an end of her. We're all sorry enough for it, but fretting won't bring her to life, and there's no use your grizzling all the health and strength out of yourself if she is dead. I'd clear, if I was you, and cut digging for a spell. The claims 'll go on all the same as long as they're worth sticking to.'

'I am going away, Mrs. Yorke,' I said wearily. 'I shall leave my interests in the Major's hands. I know I can trust all the mates. My loathing of this place, and all things connected with it, I can't describe. I hope I shall never see a diggings again.'

'I feel pretty full up about the field myself at times,' she answered, 'and good reason I had.' Here her face softened, and the tears streamed down her cheeks, suddenly as an April shower. 'But I don't know as I could better myself living in a strange town among a lot of people as couldn't tell washdirt from mullock, and never saw a tin dish used except to set milk in. I was quite a girl when Cyrus and I came on the diggings first, and I've followed them so long that I can hardly content myself anywhere else. But it's different with a man; and I should up stick and be off to England by the first mail steamer if I was you.'

'I daresay I shall do something of the sort directly, but just now I feel as if I were some one else. The change that has come over me has taken all my old feelings away. I can hardly describe it.'

'There's one thing would keep me for a bit if I was you,' she said in a lower tone, 'and I'd wait a year to see it if I was dying to get away.' A hard bitter look came over her face as she spoke.

'Why, what could that be?'

'To see that villain, Ned Morsley, hanged,' she said below her breath.

'Ha!' I returned, 'I had forgotten the brute. Still I don't see how the guilt is to be brought home to him, though I have a conviction now that his hand alone could have struck the blow.'

'Of course he did,' she said, 'every child on the diggings knows that, and me blackguarding the poor old sergeant and Merlin for running you in when they only did it to throw that wretch off his guard while they hunted up the evidence.'

'Is that the reason why they did it?' I stammered out. 'How little my feelings seem to have counted in the matter.'

'Well, you see,' said Mrs. Yorke sagely, 'the police can't afford to consider people's feelings, it's the "case" they have to give their minds to, as Mr. Merlin told me. He's away at the Fish River on the track of Gilbert Hawke; but I'll go bail the sergeant's got a few bits of evidence that Mr. Black Ned don't reckon upon. They've got Mr. Markham for the Crown now, and Morsley's got the little doctor to defend him. The case will be on next Monday, and I'll be there if I'm spared.'

'I suppose I shall not be away either,' I said. 'I may as well see the thing out. It is only the next shifting of the scene in my life's drama.'

There were yet several days which must elapse before Morsley could be put upon the preliminary examination, the prelude to a final trial before judge and jury.

This interval was more difficult to dispose of than any period which I could recall since my arrival in Australia. I had entirely lost the spring of action which had formerly incited me to labour. The hope of success then lured me on. Now that success had come, the bitter blight of sorrow, the settled night of adversity had destroyed all hope. The future was filled with impenetrable gloom. I had had no letter from home either since the last one from my darling Ruth, in which she had avowed her unfaltering belief in my innocence, and her resolution to abide by me at all hazards.

What might have happened in the interval? I trembled to think. Had she been induced by her parents, justly, as they would argue from their point of view, incensed against me, to marry one among the well-born, perfectly unexceptionable suitors, who doubtless were but too eager to offer themselves to the heiress of Allerton Court.

The hours, the days, the long bright days of an Australian midsummer, seemed as if they would never come to an end. Yet the weariest work was over. My prison doors were opened. My trial, in the face of the curious crowd, with all its racking torment and corroding anxiety, had been concluded. I was triumphantly cleared in the face of the society in which I lived of the frightful accusation under which I had lain prostrate.

Once more I stood a free man under the broad blue sky of heaven, without trammel or fetter. How strange it was to feel thankful for such a boon. I that had hitherto been as free as the bird that cleaves the sky, without thought of cage or knowledge of captivity!

For the first day or two levees of sympathising friends and acquaintances gave me no time wherein to think over plans for future action. People to whom I had never spoken came from comparatively distant diggings to shake me by the hand, and congratulate me on my acquittal. I found that a widespread belief had existed throughout the goldfield, that my being arrested at all was an outrage and an injustice. They had not dreamed of interfering with the administration of the law (there being no 'shallow ground' in the case), but were not the less united on the score of my having suffered wrong and injustice.

I had not, indeed, slept the second night in our joint abode when an influential deputation, consisting of some of the leading miners and business people of the goldfield, waited upon me for the purpose of ascertaining if a certain day would be convenient for me to be entertained at a public dinner specially arranged in my honour, and designed therein to exhibit the unanimous public sentiment in my behalf.

I was not, as may be believed, in the humour for festal assemblages of any sort or kind. My first impulse was of unqualified denial. But the feelings which prompted the invitation were generous and manly. I knew that my refusal would be construed by many as, if not an insult, at any rate as implied personal superiority to my entertainers. I had decided at no distant period to leave the locality, and to let drift my miner's life behind me for ever. And I could not deny but that this would be a fitting opportunity to say farewell to those with whom I had so long worked and dwelt on terms of perfect social equality.

How utter was the change, the revulsion of my feelings. The goldfield, with its surroundings and associations, had all become hateful to me. I could not walk down the street, or take part in ordinary duty or pleasure without being reminded of the dear dead Jane, and of the pleasant aftertime we had dreamed of when she should be restored through my instrumentality to her old quiet home and a life of peace, in which, shielded from every evil, she might devote her days to good deeds and repentance. Ah me! All such pleasant pure imaginings had been blasted, shattered into more than oblivion—into a bitter and bloodstained memory; into a horror and a crime which must suffice to render barren of joy years of my future life.

I had announced my intention without delay to the Major

and my other mates in the claim. I should take away the cash which stood to my credit in the bank, and leaving the Major as my authorised agent, by power of attorney, trust to him to guard my interest and remit whatever further monies might accrue to me up to the time when Greenstone Dyke and No. 4 were worked out, and either abandoned, or made a present of to the wages men, as the case might be.

I should have more than sufficient for all my needs, and for whatever life I should elect to lead in England or on the Continent. I could travel. I could lead a society life, if it so pleased me, among the *haute volée* of the great cities of the world, to which a man of good family, if duly gilded and not disqualified by manners or morals to which exception can be taken, can always procure the *entrée*. I could live quietly and luxuriously in the land of my birth, in town or country, which ever might best suit my humour. In a word, I was free to choose the perfectly untrammelled heartless life which so many people consider to be the most precious result of realised wealth.

Such had not been the goal to which my thoughts had turned when I placed the warm quick pulses of youth, the settled purpose of manhood, in the scale — trusting to the hazard of brave adventure, and the goodness of a merciful Providence for success, after a few years more or less of honourable toil, of manly endeavour.

No! far otherwise was the pinnacle to which I had essayed to climb. A height which should be irradiated by love and honour, as well as by personal happiness, by the gratitude of the poor, the respect of the rich, the encircling belief which alone finds life worthy and leaves it ennobled.

And to what kind of stagnant existence was I now doomed ? To the selfish withdrawal from all of the honourable cares of humanity, to the well-clothed, well-fed, well-amused passage through barren hours, which, as by the subtle action of a mineral fountain, turns the heart and every moral tissue to stone.

.   .   .   .   .   .

During the period which elapsed between my liberation and the examination of Morsley by the bench, the probability or otherwise of his being the murderer of his wife was the chief centre of thought, the leading topic of conversation among all classes at the Oxley. Curious half-forgotten scandals were exhumed, giving colour to the most extravagantly improbable theories as to the actual slayer and his presumed motives.

'It was a former admirer, driven to madness by her coquetries, who had offered to elope with her by the next American mail steamer, and to settle ten thousand pounds upon her.'

'It was no man at all but a jealous woman-rival, who had sworn years since to be avenged on her, and included in that evil prayer the promise that she never should quit the goldfield alive !'

'It was a mistake from beginning to end. Fitzpatrick, just returned from Granville Bar, had heard that his wife was stay-ing at Simpson's and carrying on "top ropes," as the phrase for "light life and conversation" then obtained, had rushed over maniacally and seeing the unfortunate deceased parting with a stranger on terms of friendship never stopped to reason, but, the likeness being curiously close as to figure and height, rushed in and committed the fatal deed. He and his wife were off to California within forty-eight hours.'

These and other mournful or ludicrous versions were (as I heard afterwards) freely bandied about and accepted as true or probable statements.

A strong general feeling of belief in the guilt or complicity of Morsley pervaded the minds of the more closely-reasoning portion of the population, from the man's known savage and pitiless nature—from the bad terms on which he and poor Jane had notoriously lived—most of all from a general instinctive habit to think ill of him and Malgrade, which showed the deep unpopularity which now encompassed him.

But if in reality guilty how had he so suddenly appeared among the crowd, ready and willing to charge me with the crime? Was it in the nature of things, was it credible that any man should commit so diabolical a deed, and appear within five minutes apparently on a level with other spectators, and suffi-ciently free from all trace of crime to fear the searching scrutiny of the police?

Thus reasoned by far the greater number of the miners and residents on the goldfield, and thus in good sooth did I myself incline, strong as was my distrust of every word and deed of the ruffian to whom poor Jane had been so fatally bound.

Could there be any other human creature so strongly in-terested in the death of the unhappy woman? It could not be so.

Morsley, and he alone, must have filled up the measure of his iniquities by dyeing his hands in the blood of the helpless creature whose life he had ruined, sending her into the presence of her Maker, as she had foreboded, poor soul! without one moment's preparation for the dread ordeal.

The frank vengeance of the middle ages, when rulers had the power to enforce personal expiation of unusual crime, would have torn to pieces such a man by wild horses ; the populace, greedily curious and critical, would have gloated over the ghastly spectacle, watched the rending of the living muscle, the dislocation of the tortured limbs. And could not I, too, have shared the fierce pleasure with calmness if not with exultation? And there was wild justice in the custom. Why should the arch-criminal, the cool contriver, the remorseless agent in a plot of devilish bloody deed, bear but the same penalty as the frenzied foolish rustic, the half-besotted maniac, who slays in fury and weeps over the deed he has committed?

However I might suffer personally, I determined not to quit the Oxley until I had witnessed the trial of my enemy, and heard the nature of the evidence to be brought against him.

I knew that the sergeant would not have taken the decisive step of arresting Morsley in court and applying for a remand, unless he had something more than ordinary circumstantial evidence *in petto*. Whatever it was, the outside public, myself included, were left in total ignorance of the nature of it. Mr. Markham was now retained on the part of the Crown, a recognised practice which obtains in important police cases. Dr. Bellair was special private counsel for the accused, and I knew could comport himself with his usual intensity and aggressiveness.

As regarded my partners, nothing could have been more considerate, more delicate than their every word and act. The same might have been said of every chance acquaintance of the goldfield generally. The miners, better than most men in more conventionally apportioned communities, understood the difficult position in which I had been placed—appreciated the loyalty in which I had striven to carry out my trust.

'Why didn't the darned skunk put a head on his devilry while the *pronunciamiento* was out?' queried Sonora Joe wrathfully, 'then we could have lynched him quite high-toned and respectable like. Now, I bet the nigger will be indulged with a judge and jury foolin' round. Couldn't do no more if he'd been a full-sized Chow destroyer in the Flat troubles.'

'We're not quite so quick as you are, Joe, and we like to hang the right man, you see. But I'll back British institutions against Yankee ones any day in the long run. You'll see an infernal scoundrel get his deserts, or I'm much mistaken, and everything done ship-shape and Bristol fashion.' So spoke Captain Blogg, late of the *Maid of Avon*, merchantman, which, having been deserted by her crew, from the boatswain to the cook's mate, was long a sheer hulk in Hobson's Bay. Finally, the captain and mates had to go, unless they elected to become a band of Flying Dutchmen without the ability to fly out of the great land-locked Bay of Hobson, where the navies of the world might ride.

'Wal—I don't reckon to dispute John Bull's ways, not so much as I did when first I came on these diggings. I surmise that he's a critter as knows what he wants and mostly hez it. But you mind me, Joseph L. Jefferson, that if there's no rope twisted for that woman-murdering hound, there's a rifle or two will crack, as mostly carries true when the bead's drawn on a man.'

The Major, to do him justice, never recalled any of our

conversations in which he had warned me against imprudent
entanglement, and the dangerous companionship of any one of
Eve's daughters, young or old, married or single—they were all
alike to be avoided and distrusted by the wise man.

'You're weak and low now, Pole, old fellow,' he said;
'nothing but change — change from this confounded New
World, which has become old to us—will set you up. You've
had the fever, so have I, so have most men, the wise and the
unwise—Edgar Borlase among the number, who was left among
the dead on one of life's battlefields many a year ago. But he
arose and staggered off, finally was cured and became strong,
outwardly at least. So will you. But you must change the
landscape, from these endless forests, these monotoned mullock
heaps, to green England's glades and meadows. Ha! the
thought is entrancing. What do you say, Olivera?'

'I quite agree with you,' said that calm enthusiast, who now
strolled up, meerschaum in mouth. 'We should be justified in
getting the Commissioner to send Pole down in charge of the
police, only to be released on shipboard. He has so unhinged
his nervous system that nothing but sea air and his boyhood's
home will have power to cure.'

'Why don't you come back to Europe too?' I said rather
thoughtlessly. 'You might as well come, for all the good you
are doing here?'

Olivera's eyes flashed, and he stood for a space without
speaking. I thought I saw a slight flush pass over his dark-
hued countenance.

'You are right, perhaps,' he said, 'though you cannot know
the reasons which I have for longing once more to set foot on
English soil; but it is my destiny to remain here till the hour
of success and triumph arrive. It may be that a generation
shall pass before that result. Till then I shall continue to
be a miner wherever on this broad continent the gold lure
beckons.'

'You are not to be discouraged, then,' I said, 'no matter how
unfortunate you may continue to be,' charmed momentarily out
of my own sorrows by this man's imperturbable fatalism.

'Fortunate and unfortunate are relative terms,' he replied
calmly. 'I believe firmly that before my destiny is accomplished in this land I shall amass wealth by means of mineral
discoveries, whether by means of gold, silver, copper, or tin, I
cannot say. But that my fate is connected with one of these
metals I am as certain as that we stand here. Good-night.'

'I shall leave directly after this trial, Major,' said I, as we
prepared for rest. 'You need have no fear further of indecision
on my part. But I cannot go away till I have heard the fresh
evidence which has evidently been procured by the police. I
feel as if it was a sacred duty which I owe, not only to myself,
but to *her*.'

On the day to which Morsley stood remanded, I once more entered the court-house, under very different auspices from those of my last appearance there.

Accompanied by the Major and Olivera, I was warmly received by Captain Blake, and we were accommodated with seats by special permission of the Bench, whence we could observe the proceedings at our leisure.

The time of opening the Court had been purposely anticipated by us, as we wished to be freed from the inconvenience to which the inevitable crush of the crowded building would have given rise.

The hour, however, arrived, and the man.

Had I been of a persistently revengeful nature, every feeling of that kind must have been gratified when I saw my enemy brought in, carefully guarded by the police, and placed in the dock. The sergeant's expression, it is true, betrayed no other feeling but that which might have actuated a zealous naturalist in possession of a very rare living specimen liable to take flight at any moment. On his calm brow, in his watchful gray eyes, was no faintest sign of moral reprobation or even partial disapproval. Nothing but unsleeping vigilance, nothing but inflexible determination, nothing but the most careful reminiscent accuracy, as of a dux in a mental arithmetic class continually examining himself lest he might have forgotten his calculation.

As for Edward Morsley, his fierce features were clouded, as of old, with the look of sullen defiance which was natural to them. I looked at him from time to time, wondering in my own mind whether prejudice caused me to see guilt in every line of his face, or whether I did him wrong and translated the shadow of past crime into a reflection of the deed still untracked and unavenged. Who could say? Was it real, true, actual fact, that Jane had been foully done to death, was buried, lost to all things beneath the sun for evermore? Why could not the dead for one short space return and avouch the truth, confound the guilty, and absolve the innocent? Mystery of mysteries!

Portals inscrutable of the silent eternities! what secrets do they not enfold?

Again the court is filled. The Bench is seated. The witnesses are in attendance. Mr. Markham and Dr. Bellair, like heralds in the mediæval tournaments, are busy with preliminary arrangements, on which hang the issues of life and death.

Before progress can be made with the new trial, all proceedings are read through which have been initiated on the former occasion.

Then the Bench inquired of Sergeant MacMahon if he had procured additional material evidence in the case on account of which the prisoner had been remanded.

'On most insufficient grounds, your worships,' said Dr. Bellair.

Mr. Markham smiled in a gratified manner. The sergeant stroked his immense beard, which concealed the third button of his uniform coat, and merely remarking—

'The Bench may be of a different opinion shortly, Doctor,' said, 'Call George Corbett.'

A respectably-dressed, open-countenanced miner stepped forward and went into the witness-box. When sworn, this was his statement—

'I am a miner, and reside at the Oxley, where I am a shareholder in the Crinoline claim, Red Hill. On the 20th instant, on the night of the murder, I was coming up the town, when I saw a man covered up with a poncho come out of Simpson's Hotel and run down Mayne Street. He stopped just opposite to me and turned into a side alley near a butcher's shop. There is a deep shaft close to the edge of the lane. He stopped for a second or two and walked quickly up to the hotel again. His clothes then looked of a lightish colour, and he had no poncho on. To the best of my belief the prisoner now before the Court is the man. I did not speak to him, but followed him to the hotel. There was a crowd collected there, and I heard the man in the light clothes say, "I give that man (meaning Harry Pole) in charge for murdering my wife." Then I heard that Mrs. Morsley was killed, and I saw the police take away Harry Pole. Showed Sergeant MacMahon the shaft afterwards, which I spoke of, near the butcher's; it was an old shicer and pretty deep. It could hardly have been two minutes between the time the man in the poncho came down the street and returned.'

Cross-examined by Dr. Bellair: 'Have no acquaintance with prisoner. Have seen the deceased, Mrs. Morsley, several times; did not know her to speak to. Know Harry Pole, as a digger merely; am not a friend of his. May have passed him the time of day. Told the sergeant that I saw a man run down the street at the time of the murder. Showed him the shaft afterwards. It was one of the old block claims before the main lead was struck. Must be about sixty feet deep. Have no interest in the case one way or the other, but would do anything in my power to bring a murderer to justice. Any man worth calling a man would do the same.'

'That will do; you can go down,' said the doctor. 'Your moral ideas are not called in question, and your evidence is not important one way or the other.'

'You will see more about that, Doctor,' said the sergeant with marked respect. 'Your worships, I desire to tender evidence personally in the case, and request to be sworn.'

'I also desire to know whether the police are to be Crown prosecutors, advocates, gaolers, and witnesses all in one, and acting in the same case whenever they may see fit to try and procure a conviction,' cried out Dr. Bellair. 'I submit, your worships, that the fact of a police officer usurping all these powers is monstrous; in every way most improper and unauthorised. In the name of my client I demand the protection of the Court.'

'The Court is of opinion, Dr. Bellair, that Sergeant Macmahon has a perfect right to tender evidence in this or any other case which, from circumstances, may be most material. Swear the witness.'

The sergeant is accordingly sworn with due solemnity. He deposes as follows—

'My name is John Fitzgerald MacMahon. I am a senior-sergeant of police stationed at the Oxley. On the 20th instant I was on duty at the lower end of Mayne Street, when I observed a crowd forming in the vicinity of Simpson's Hotel. I proceeded there as quickly as possible, thinking it might be a fight or a fire, and passing through the crowd I saw Mr. Hereward Pole supporting in his arms the deceased Mrs. Morsley. She appeared to be in a fainting or dying condition. Blood was flowing from her throat freely, and Mr. Pole's hands and clothes were covered with her blood. I had her placed upon a bed. About a minute afterwards the prisoner called out to me from among the crowd to take Mr. Pole into custody, whom he charged with the murder of his wife. I did so. I noticed at the time that prisoner was dressed in a gray tweed suit, as at present. I saw that one button was missing between the upper or throat button and the third. I looked at his hands; they were free from stain. I left Constable Grant in the house with instructions to him to search closely around the spot where the deed had been done. After locking up Mr. Pole (which I did to throw the guilty party or parties off their guard)——'

'Mr. Pole is very much obliged to you, sergeant,' said Mr. Markham, 'I feel certain. No doubt he will recognise the compliment when he has a little leisure for consideration.'

'We have to manage these things in our own way, Mr Markham. It was a little hard on him. I beg to resume my evidence.—I returned to the house, and very closely and carefully examined the corpse of deceased. In the right hand, which was clenched, I found this button (already produced by Mr. Markham); it corresponds with the buttons upon the coat at present worn by the prisoner, from which a button similar in size and shape has been lately torn and replaced. I caused this button to be compared with those upon prisoner's coat when he was asleep, and can produce the witness who so compared them. There was a small piece of silk thread, known by tailors as "twist," in the button. It is the same as that used in the sewing of the other buttons of prisoner's coat. A few hairs, as from a beard, were tangled in the clenched fingers of the left hand of deceased. I produce them wrapped in paper. They are black, curling, and slightly tinged with gray. They correspond with the beard of the prisoner. The hair of deceased was light brown, almost flaxen.'

The sergeant stooped down and placed before him on the ledge of the witness-box a formidable parcel, which he commenced to open carefully.

'From information received, I went on the following day to a shaft in a narrow lane close to Simpson's Hotel. I caused myself to be lowered down it, taking a candle, and examined the bottom. I there found a pair of loose dogskin gloves; they were on the poncho produced (sensation); it is of dark cloth, and of a size suitable to prisoner. There are fresh stains upon the gloves, chiefly on the right hand one. There is a dark reddish stain upon the outside of the poncho on the front, as if a sudden gush of liquid had produced it. I also found a knife, which I now produce. It is a sheath knife, ground very sharp, and slightly curved inwards. The blade and handle are stained with blood—recently stained and hardly dry. In the pocket of the poncho was a handkerchief (which I produce); it is marked in a woman's handwriting E. H. M. There were also a newspaper unopened, and two letters unopened, addressed to Mr. Edward Morsley, Warraluen.'

Cross-examined by Dr. Bellair: 'Have known prisoner for several years, ever since he came to Granville Rush. Am not prepared to say that he has committed offences against the law, but he has always been an associate of bad characters. Have had him watched since the night of the murder; do not consider that kind of espionage improper when men are suspected of crimes such as prisoner is now charged with. Cannot swear that prisoner is the man whom the witness Corbett saw running towards the shaft, but consider that the evidence produced tends strongly in that direction. Prisoner in his evidence in Pole's case distinctly swore that he did not own a poncho. Have more evidence to bring forward.'

'Call Luke Weston.'

A short, broad-shouldered, swarthy man with earrings now steps forward, whose rolling gate betrays acquaintance with the high seas, and leads to the suspicion that he left his last ship without applying formally for leave.

He is sworn, and, hitching up his trousers, makes the following answers to Mr. Markham—

'My name is Luke Weston. Am a miner. Came out in the *Cambysus*. Have been here about three months digging. Know the chap in the dock ; saw him at Pegleg Gully last week. He was chucking his money about, but seemed down on his luck, like. We were talking about knives, and I threw my knife and made it stick in a board. It's a trick I learnt of the Spaniards when I was hide-droghing in South America. He looked at it and said the edge was sharp, too. I said it was, and no mistake. I wanted a job, and he said he'd give me a line to a friend to put me on as wages man at a reef at Warraluen. I took it very kind of him. He advanced me a pound to pay my coach fare. We had a couple of drinks before we went to bed. Just as he was going away he looked at my knife, and I said I'd give it to him if he fancied it. I took off the belt and sheath and all. He laughed and walked away with it. I went to Warraluen early next morning. I look at the knife produced ; it is my knife. I will swear to it by the wood of the handle, which is a Brazil wood. I also look at the belt and sheath produced. They were my belt and sheath. The sheath is not leather—it is raw horse-hide dressed in Spanish fashion. I swear prisoner is the man I gave my knife to.'

By Dr. Bellair : 'How did I leave my ship ? Well, ran away, if you want to know particulars. Lots of other sailor men did the same. Had been drinking a little during the evening with prisoner. Was not drunk, nor even half seas over. Got work at Warraluen on prisoner's recommendation. Do not think it mean to give evidence against him. Believe him to be a bloody murdering land-pirate that ought to be hung at the yard-arm.'

'Call Constable Grant.'

He is sworn, and thus gives evidence—

'My name is Donald Glencairn Grant. I am a police constable stationed at the Oxley. I remember the night when Mrs. Morsley was murdered. I saw her conveyed to bed. I remained when Sergeant MacMahon arrested Mr. Pole and conveyed him to the lock-up. I remained behind, and, in accordance with instructions, examined carefully the room where the murder took place. I found a gold sleeve button or sleeve link, such as shirts are fastened with, which I produce ; it was down on the floor and was stained with blood. It has the letters "E. H. M. Ballarat" engraved on the inside. It is rather a large stud, and is of Australian gold, I should say. I was present when Sergeant MacMahon found the button and the hair produced in the hands of the deceased. He sent me to call Mrs. Simpson before we touched them. We had great difficulty in getting them, as the hands were so tightly closed. Immediately upon prisoner being arrested last week, I went in accordance with previous instructions to the room which he had occupied at the New Zealand Hotel. I found Mr. Malgrade, who has given evidence, about to enter, but I prevented him from doing so, saying I was about to seal up the door. I searched the room and found at the bottom of a trunk the belt and sheath which have been produced during the examination of the last witness. The trunk had " E. H. Morsley " painted on the outside. It was a leathern travelling trunk or portmanteau. I also discovered the fellow to the sleeve link produced, which I found on the floor at Simpson's Hotel, stained with deceased's blood. The sleeve link which I now produce was not stained ; it is exactly like the other, and has the same letters engraved, also Ballarat. I then sealed up the door and came away.'

By Dr. Bellair : 'I was told to watch prisoner in a general way after the murder, as evidence might be forthcoming against him. Do not know why Senior-sergeant MacMahon did not arrest him on suspicion if he suspected him. It was his case ; I suppose he had reasons for what he did. Do not know anything about prisoner or his wife. Have only recently arrived on this field. Was formerly stationed at New England. Have heard in a general way that prisoner was jealous of his wife. Did not trouble my head about that part of the affair, it was no business of mine. Believe it to be my duty, as a police constable, to prevent crime if legally possible, or to aid in apprehending criminals.'

Mr. Markham suggested that if the doctor wished to examine the witness as to the 'whole duty of man' as applicable to the police force, he could not do better than consult that admirable manual of regulations lately issued by the Inspector-General, and save the time of the Court.

Dr. Bellair submitted that he had a perfect right to test the credibility of any witness, and was not inclined to take for granted the good faith of the whole police force, believing that they were too fond of getting up sensational cases and manufacturing evidence which rested upon the most fragile foundation.

As the details, which had been so carefully collected by the sergeant, wrought themselves one by one into their appointed places, links in the chain of circumstantial evidence which gradually environed the prisoner, every eye in the Court was fixed upon him with horror and reprobation. For him, he seemed wholly absorbed in his own reflections, and apparently failed to perceive that he was the centre of a thousand unwavering, unfriendly regards.

It was only towards the end of the protracted proceedings, as he leaned heavily upon the front of the dock, that I marked a gradual sinking of his muscular frame—a pallor approaching ghastliness overspreading his features. Once only did his eye meet mine, when arousing himself he stared me fully in the face, leaning on his arms. If a look could have killed, my life would have ended there. Rarely do mortal men encounter so dreadful a gaze. Such eyes may glare hopelessly from forms tormented, accursed, in the Inferno devoted to arch-criminals. Wretched and degraded as are the dwellers in the dark places of the earth, even among them such demoniac malice is rarely exhibited. I shuddered instinctively, and felt relieved to think that this was in all human probability our last meeting.

Mr. Markham made a short telling speech, carefully confining himself to those parts of the evidence which in his mind most conclusively connected the prisoner with the crime. Whatever doubt their worships might have in their own minds, it was not for them to usurp the functions of a jury, to whom would be left the duty and responsibility of deciding whether or no the evidence established the prisoner's guilt. The plain duty of the Bench was to commit the prisoner for trial at the next ensuing Court of Assize.

And this view of the case the Bench unanimously took in spite of a tremendous *ad captandum* speech from Dr. Bellair, who inveighed passionately against the insecurity and danger of circumstantial evidence, and defied the magistrates to connect his client personally with the deed which had been committed.

'The Bench desire to remind you, Dr. Bellair,' at length said the Commissioner, 'that we are only acting ministerially. This is but a preliminary proceeding. Many of your arguments, the Bench think, would have great weight with a jury, but we have made up our minds to commit. I would suggest that you are only wasting your own valuable time, and perhaps that of the Court.'

'If the Bench have made up their minds, if they are resolved, no matter what arguments may be brought forward, to take a particular, a prejudged course, I of course cannot prevent it,' said the doctor, at a white heat. 'With regard to the closing observation of Mr. Commissioner Blake, I will observe that I bow to the decision of the Bench as to questions of law ; but the assertion that I am wasting the time of the Court deals with a question of fact, concerning which I am as competent to form an opinion as any man living, be he who he may.'

Here the little man folded his arms and frowned ferociously at the Bench, presenting a not inapt likeness to a frantic terrier confronting a kennel of staghounds.

'Edward Hill Morsley,' said the Commissioner, deigning no further notice of the irate advocate, and as he spoke the slightest sound was audible throughout the Court, 'you are not obliged to say anything, and what you say will be taken down in writing, and may be used against you at your trial. Do you desire to say anything ?'

'Nothing whatever,' answered Morsley, with the most perfect *sang froid.*

'My client reserves his defence,' said the doctor defiantly.

'Edward Hill Morsley,' again said the Commissioner, in

measured and grave accents, 'you stand committed to take your trial for wilful murder at the next ensuing Assize Court, to be holden at Russell on the 20th January next.'

'Call up the witnesses, Sergeant MacMahon, and let them be duly bound over to appear.'

This was done.

The prisoner was removed, amid the muttered execrations of the crowd, who pressed to gaze at him as he was hurried away.

The Court was adjourned, and as I and my comrades walked silently away, a load seemed lifted from my mind, in that the innocent blood that had been shed would be avenged, and no mourning ghost, as sings the rude folk-lore of her own land, would flit over the hearthstone of poor Jane's birthplace, waiting in the midnight hour for justice denied both of God and man.

CHAPTER XXXV

WITH no longer any reasons for lingering at the Oxley, I accordingly made preparations for my departure at an early date. Before that event could take place, however, the farewell demonstration in my honour, which I had pledged myself to attend, was to come off. A few days still elapsed before the preparations would be finally completed. Then I should take my farewell of goldfield life; quit for ever the avocation so familiar to me, the associates among whom I had dwelt for long years, to embark afresh upon a path in life, if not new, so long untrodden that it would be virtually strange.

My heart should have bounded with delight at the idea of once more treading the soil of my native land, of mixing with my equals, beholding my kindred, enjoying the thousand and one luxuries of which the faint echo only reached us occasionally through books and newspapers, or a stray denizen of those unknown far lands who appeared without notice and departed as suddenly as he came.

But though I could not give a logical denial to this chain of reasoning, the spring of my nature had been overstrained by my late misfortunes, so that no prospective pleasure of any kind seemed to me possible. What might happen when I had fairly cut adrift from my present surroundings I could only dimly conjecture. I was willing, nay, languidly eager to change the scene, but entirely reckless as to the consequences.

To all my other griefs were added the crowning misery that I had not heard one single word from Ruth since the last letter upon which I had founded so large a superstructure of hope and gladness. What was I to think of this continued silence? I could not believe that the whole family had cast me off without another word. The Squire, choleric as he occasionally showed himself, was far too high-bred to have omitted to acknowledge the circumstantial narrative which I had so patiently compiled in my defence.

But if not so, how was this persistent protracted silence to be accounted for; what could have happened? I knew, or thought I knew, the unwavering loyalty of my darling's nature, not less firm than gentle, though loyal to parental sway. Had long-borne anguish of mind proved too harsh a trial for that delicate frame, fit casket for the ethereal spirit which it clothed? Had she passed from earth? And had her parents, agonised with hopeless grief, been too careless of forms and ceremonies to put upon record the unutterable sorrow to which they dwelt ever a prey and a sacrifice?

Or had absence and doubt, with parental pressure added, sufficed, as in hundreds of cases which I had known or heard of, to sway the girlish determination; to invest a newly accredited suitor with the charm and glamour which once were the privilege of one alone; who could say? All things were possible during absence and misconstruction. I deemed that I had good cause to be aweary of my life—to loathe the sight of the sun.

Sadly resigned to the approaching fete in my honour, I took but little heed of the great preparations, which were proceeding at a rate which interested Mrs. Yorke deeply and caused quite a sensation in the immediate neighbourhood of our claim. That worthy matron had just been up to town to make some purchases at Mrs. Mangrove's store, and had brought back the most astounding rumour. The Commissioner was to take the chair at the dinner; all the magistrates were to be there; all the legal gentlemen, among whom Dr. Bellair and Mr. Markham would allegorically couch together, even as the lion and the lamb. Nearly all the business men and every miner of mark on the field had taken tickets. There had been nothing like it since the great Sunday-school gathering in Verjill's paddock last Michaelmas day. Everybody was talking about it, and Mrs. Mangrove said she was going to listen to the speeches, and she, Mrs. Yorke, would do so too.

Kind-hearted Mrs. Yorke's prattlings did not particularly raise my spirits, and I shrank from a festive gathering and the after-dinner florid eloquence, which I did not doubt would take place. Nevertheless, I would go through with it. And, after all, was it not as well to have a permanent record of the universal good-will and confidence of the most respectable inhabitants of the district, showing their entire belief in my innocence of the charge laid at my door?

I had strolled down a mile or two towards the lower end of the 'lead,' on the upper part of which we were working, and was calming my mind with the contemplation of the far-off pearly sky-line with its crimson shafts and quivering lances of tremulous flame, when, as I passed along a narrow street, my attention was aroused by a small crowd. Angry voices, one a woman's, rose in tones of altercation.

I felt more than half inclined to retreat, but the old feeling which always impelled me forward in such cases was still strong within me, and I obeyed it.

To my very great surprise I saw that the disputants were Algernon Malgrade and Dolores. Both were excited beyond all bounds of restraint which ordinarily could have controlled such temperaments. Her nature was, I know, passionate and tempestuous, uncontrollable as that of the roused tigress. He, to do him justice, would not have committed himself to an unseemly brawl in the open streets, but he had been drinking— his face was darkly flushed, and his utterance thick. There was no want of steadiness in his movements, but I knew that he must indeed have been drinking hard, and not for one day only, to have brought himself to this condition. He was savage and reckless in consequence, and having had, as he thought, some occasion of complaint against Dolores, had given rein to his brutal nature and beaten her.

She, as before, was most wildly excited, shrieking aloud, calling down the vengeance of heaven upon him for his cruelty and injustice, and upon herself for her weakness in ever attach- ing herself to so detestable a villain, cursing with dreadful intensity the hour she was born and that in which she had first set eyes upon him.

All this was uttered rapidly and emphatically in a loud voice, with the excited gestures and vehement action which belonged of right to her hot southern blood. A crowd had gathered, evidently sympathising with her wrongs. Anything more dis- tasteful to all the instincts of a man like Malgrade, low as he had fallen, dulled and deteriorated as was even now his every moral sense, could not have been imagined.

'Stand out of the way, you fools,' he said, in a voice trembling with rage, and with a look which caused those nearest to him to draw back rapidly without further warning; 'and you, you jade, come home if you don't wish me to knock your brains out where you stand. Can't we have a few words without your calling all the field to share it, and making as much noise as if you'd hired the bellman for a roll-up? Come home, I say.'

His words were more or less jocular as he advanced towards her; but whether the miserable woman distrusted him, or feared a repetition of his unmanly violence, or whether, thoroughly exasperated, she had become utterly reckless, no one can tell.

'Don't come near me,' she said, in a strange and lowered tone. 'I made a vow before, but this one I'll keep. If you lay a hand on me, you never were in such peril of your life since— since—you——'

Seemingly anxious to stop her mouth, fearful that she might repeat something dangerously near the truth, Malgrade was apparently incapable of further restraining himself. He muttered something and rushed towards her as if with some violent intention. As he approached she drew backward, still facing him, until she reached the open door of the shop—that of a butcher—opposite to which, in the long street which traversed that suburb, the altercation had commenced. In retreating she was arrested by the large butcher's block which stood just in- side the doorway. She glanced at it with lightning-like rapidity.

On it lay several knives. She snatched up the largest, sharply pointed and keen edged, and, making one desperate lunge at her pursuer, buried it to the hilt in his body. He threw up his arms ; one spasm contorted his features ; his eyes stared, widely opened but unconscious. Then he fell forward, prone and motionless, at the very feet of the angry woman. The jaw dropped. Algernon Malgrade was a dead man.

Casting off my lethargy, I bounded to the spot. The features had resumed their habitual calm. Blood was flowing from a deep small wound immediately under the right ribs. He who but a minute before was my enemy, her oppressor, was now a lump of lifeless clay.

With all the inconsistency of her sex, Dolores—the moment the deed was done, and he whom with all his faults she, ay, so many women, had loved, lay dead before her eyes, slain by her own hand—threw down the blood-stained weapon and, with a curdling shriek, cast herself on her knees by his side, imploring him to speak but one word, and calling him by every fond and endearing name.

The crowd which had closed around the corpse here opened to make a passage for Dr. Bolton, who being in the neighbourhood had been skilfully captured by an active young constable on duty and brought to the spot.

He looked calmly and all unmoved upon the frantic woman, the curious crowd, and the calm face of the dead man.

'Why, Pole,' he said, 'you and I appear to come in for more than our fair share of tragedies. Deep incised wound, ex-act-ly above the region of the liver ; couldn't have been more accurate in her anatomy if she had tried. Subject dead ; not the least use in remaining. Death must have been instantaneous. Constable Dickson, have the goodness to inform the coroner that I shall be at his service at three o'clock P.M. Better lock up that poor Dolores, or she'll do herself an injury. Nervous twitching of the muscles of the face, incipient dementia. Good-morning.'

This terribly tragic occurrence almost again unhinged my nervous system, although at the proceedings which necessarily followed I was fortunately spared personal reference. There was a cloud of witnesses beside me ; so that at the coroner's inquest, which terminated in a verdict of manslaughter as against the miserable woman whom Malgrade had driven by his ill-treatment to the rash deed, I was not called. She was of course committed to take her trial at the next assizes, her fate being in some inscrutable way destined to be again mixed up with my name. For she had unwittingly been the instrument of vengeance against the man who of all others had set himself most deliberately to work me evil. He had succeeded in part, as one's enemies often do in this world. But his punishment— was it the lottery of fortune or retribution?—had come upon him swiftly and irrevocably. How strangely ordered apparently that Morsley should be lying in gaol charged with the murder

of his wife, while his principal ally, coadjutor in many an evil
deed, lay dead by the hand of a wronged and insulted woman.
I believe *now* that Malgrade was in some form or other connected with the murder of poor Jane.   Either that he had
supplied the information as to the exact time of her starting in
the coach to Sydney, or that he had known that Morsley came
up to the hotel that night with murder in his heart.   Cautious
as Malgrade was ordinarily, I believe that he would have dis-
suaded his more savage companion from open outrage, but his
intensely malignant feeling towards me, deepened since our
conflict, held him back from interfering.

Yes, I had been avenged on mine enemies.   Swiftly, too, had
the wheel of destiny turned, far more so than is often given to
wondering man to witness with awe-stricken submission.   One
lay within prison walls, whence the chance was slight that he
should ever again see the blue vault of heaven, save on the day
when he was brought forth to die.   And Algernon Malgrade,
whom but a few short hours since I had seen serene, smiling,
scornful as of old, apparently defiant of all men as of the Lord
on high, lay dead by a woman's hand in a street brawl.

And this was the end of the handsome, well-born, cultured
aristocrat, whom I well remembered meeting for the first time
at Woolwich, when, as a military cadet, he was the pride of his
family, the idol of doting relatives.   Clever, brave, accomplished,
popular, there lacked nothing apparently which goes to make
one of the most successful men of the age.

Lacked there nothing ?   Yes, one thing might have been
wanting.   The key-stone of the arch, supporting the fair edifice
which now lay prone and ruined.   Algernon Malgrade had
never possessed a *heart*.   Callous to the claims of others, and
habitually self-indulgent from boyhood, the moral sense, originally feeble, had been by degrees totally obliterated.   He had
lived for long years a life utterly devoted to sensual gratifica-
tions, stoically indifferent to the feelings, the interests, the lives
even, of all who might cross his path.

And now, the victim of his own base passions had perished
by the hand of a companion in evil, whose soul he had dragged
down into even deeper degradation than her own reckless
courses might have sought out.

Dolores had spoken truly at the time of our encounter when
she said it would be better for both of them if they never again
met.   She was his fate, though then he knew it not.   And his
death was virtually hers.   For upon the trial her manner so
obviously told of a mind diseased that by direction of the jury
she was sent to a lunatic asylum, where the sad remnants of
humanity, once known in their perfection as the beautiful
Dolores Lusada, passed from mortal ken.

The dinner given in my honour was indeed a very grand
celebration in its way, perhaps excepting the Sunday-school

picnic alluded to, and the Chinese riot, the very largest and most popular demonstration known since the opening of the gold-field.

In conjunction with a natural regret at the departure of a comrade, there was no doubt a widely-felt desire to convince me that the popular sympathy was wholly with me in the matter of my trial and unjust incarceration. And in this sentiment all classes, all orders and conditions of men, appeared to share, from the Commissioner to the bellman.

At a certain hour, late in the afternoon, I walked up to the long room at Hennessy's, the very apartment indeed in which Jack Bulder had transacted his delirium. That worthy and energetic personage now accompanied me, as also the Major, Olivera, and my true follower and henchman Joe. They formed a sort of bodyguard on the present occasion, as did the sons of Torquil of the Oak to the youthful and lucklessly irresolute chieftain of the Clan Quhele.

In the room above referred to were about a hundred and fifty persons assembled, while the gallery was filled with the feminine contingent, who had mustered in great force, in order to witness the ceremonial and hear the speeches.

It would be easy and apparently natural to say that all this kind of thing is a bore and an infliction that people would decline thankfully were the opportunity afforded. But few men are so constituted as to be totally indifferent to the nature of the feeling with which they are regarded by any community in which they have long resided. And when, in spontaneous unbought goodwill, an attempt is made to formulate the silent opinion of character and conduct which has grown up in the course of years, cold must be the heart, and strangely impervious to the strongest natural impulses of humanity, that is not stirred to sympathetic appreciation and manly grate-fulness.

Calmly, well nigh indifferently, as I had schooled myself to regard this demonstration from a distance, when I looked around the room and saw the stalwart forms of the representa-tive miners from many a well-known locality, men of worth among their fellows and of trans-Australian celebrity—I saw the officials, the lawyers, the magistrates, the tradespeople, even some of the lowest members of the community, brought there by approval and pure good-will alone—my heart swelled and seemed for a moment nigh bursting when I thought I should see their faces no more.

The Commissioner stepped forward on my entrance with his usual prompt initiative, and thus spoke—

'Mr. Hereward Pole, I have been deputed by the gentlemen here assembled, representing, I am pleased to see, all classes of residents upon the goldfield and its vicinity, to present you with an address, in which sincere regret is expressed for your approaching departure, approbation of your conduct as a miner, a man, and a citizen, during the years of your residence among us, coupled with the fullest sympathy in the matter of the late unhappy occurrences to which I will not further allude. This address concludes with an earnest hope that your visit to Europe may be productive of lasting happiness, and that all good fortune may be in store for you which your sincere friends on this goldfield can desire.'

Then the address, handsomely engrossed and illuminated upon vellum, and containing more than a thousand signatures, was handed to me by Captain Blake.

I read my reply, in which I thanked all my very good and true friends of the Oxley for the warm-hearted and encouraging manner in which they had supported me in the days of my adversity. I could hardly express my sense of the delicacy which they had shown in arranging that I should leave the Oxley fresh from receiving evidence of their kindness and goodwill. This token and expression of their faith in me, I should treasure and value to my life's end. On the goldfields, working among them, I had always, despite of adverse circumstances, been happy and contented, and I assuredly should recall with pleasure all the days of my life the manly character of the miners of the Oxley and Yatala. I again thanked them for thus ending my sojourn among them in a manner so honourable and satisfactory.

I really had great difficulty in reading my humble composition. In spite of all attempts at steady self-control, my voice would falter as I thought how I had been forgotten by my friends and kindred, renounced by my plighted love, and cast off by her parents; how I had been apparently abandoned by God and man—left to the tender mercies of my enemies. Yet the men around me, merely comrades in toil and privation, many of them rude of speech, and such as at one time I should have thought shame to have associated with, had stood by me staunchly, and had nobly, delicately, considerately thus assured me of their firm faith in manhood and in my innocence. Such are truly periods in men's lives far beyond the reach of ordinary words, ordinary emotion. One of these supreme moments I felt this to be, and my heart welled over with genuine gratitude as it tremulously responded to the appeal.

Host Hennessy, according to the *Beacon*, displayed his well-known administrative powers which, combined with an exceptionally *recherché cuisine*, had raised his establishment to its well-deserved intercolonial pre-eminence. However that may have been, there was a very creditable display of matters edible and potable, particularly the latter. Wild and tame turkeys were plentiful at the Oxley, and the highly respectable wild fowl known as the wild duck—the 'canvas-back' of Australia —were as the sands of the sea-shore. Barons of beef and saddles of mutton preserved the British flavour of the entertainment. Kangaroo-tail and ox-tail soup disputed pre-eminence;

but according to Merlin and the Major, who were both authorities, the dinner was extremely well cooked and well served.
The claret and hock, sauterne and champagne, with the other
wines in ordinary use, had been specially selected by the
committee, and were such as no reasonable gourmet, especially
in such hot weather, could find a word to say against. After a
fair amount of law had been granted for the exercise of the
knife and fork, the chairman, Commissioner Blake, arose and
requested attention to the usual loyal and formal toasts to
which are granted precedence in all gatherings of Britons. In
due time he requested all glasses to be filled, as he was about to
propose the health of the guest of the evening.

'When I mention the name of Hereward Pole,' he said, 'you
will agree with me, gentlemen, that we are met to-night to do
honour to no unknown man. He has dwelt among us for years,
and as a man, a miner, a citizen, and a gentleman, he has fully
entitled himself to our genuine respect and cordial liking. He
has shown by his consistent behaviour on this goldfield that it
is possible, while working like a man, to live like a gentleman.
(Loud cheers.) He has, as you know, staunchly performed his
daily labour in the mine. He has never in any way declined
association with the respectable and intelligent miners of the
goldfield. Yet he has lived in all essentials as truly the life of
a gentleman as if he had occupied chambers in the Albany
and had taken his daily promenade in the parks of Rotten Row
—ay, more so, far more so, if honourable labour be placed before
indolent self-indulgence, the soldier in the camp before the
courtier in the palace. That there are others I am aware, many
others, equally well born, well educated, well conducted,
among the great army of industry, which I am proud after a
fashion to rule over. Such men, as long as they are true to
themselves, will always be treated with all proper respect by
their fellow-miners who have not had the same early advantages.
They were indeed more popular for being gentlemen by birth
than otherwise. A manly workman, no matter what his occupation might be, was always proud and pleased to associate with
a comrade better instructed than himself. The benefit was
mutual and mutually recognised. Turning from these considerations, which, however, had impressed themselves upon his
mind during a lengthened experience, he would call upon the
gentlemen assembled, residents of all classes upon the goldfield,
to confirm his statement, that no miner more respected and
generally popular than their guest had ever bade them farewell.
He remembered him when he and his friends, Major Treseder
and Mr. Joseph Bulder, and the late Mr. Cyrus Yorke, commenced mining at Yatala. Their conduct had always been
honourable, straightforward, and manly. One and all in the
claim had made good their title to be so esteemed. And no one
grudged them the remarkable, the well-deserved success they
had attained. (Loud cheers.) He would allude, and but lightly,

to a subject which would always have a thrilling interest for their guest. It would be painful, but he had a reason for speaking. A grave criminal charge had been brought against Mr. Pole. Circumstances had led to his being arrested and tried on that charge. He had been discharged, having been thoroughly cleared from all suspicion, even the slightest. They were here to-night representing every class in the community—official, commercial, and industrial—and as one man it would now go forth that they affirmed the perfect blamelessness of Mr. Pole throughout the whole affair. He had acted with an unselfish generosity and pure friendliness which was not often paralleled, and they—men of the world as most of them were—were proud, for the honour of human nature, to testify to their admiration of Mr. Pole's manly conduct throughout the whole affair.'

Long and enthusiastic cheering resounded after Blake concluded his peroration, wherein he wished me all the gratification the Old World could furnish to the fresh powers of enjoyment which I should bear from the regions of the New. In which pleasure pursuit he heartily wished that he could accompany me.

If the amount of good feeling then and there existent in my case was to be measured by the heartiness of the applause which greeted the conclusion of the Captain's speech, and the sincerity of the contempt with which heeltaps were avoided. I was that night one of the most popular and well-beloved individuals south of the line. It was some considerable time before it all came to an end—a large number of my quondam pick-and-shovel acquaintances being specially anxious to catch my eye before draining their glasses to my health and long life.

When matters had settled themselves somewhat I returned thanks as follows—

'Friends and fellow-miners, I stand up with the feeling that it is most likely the last time that we shall look upon each other's faces. Thus I feel impelled to speak out with perfect unreserve the feelings of my heart. Those among you who are miners—and it is as a miner only that I wish you to look upon me now—have had that opportunity of knowing me which years of association of similar labour done within each other's sight can give, and alone can give. In such a life no man can hide his nature, his character, from his fellows. They know his manner of speech, his acts, almost his thoughts. His life is as a scroll spread out for their inspection. If they believe the record to be true, honest, manly—always making due allowance for the weaknesses of human nature—they will be good comrades to him. They will be friendly and courteous in prosperity, in adversity they will stand by him like brothers —ay, as a man's own kindred often do not stand by him. It matters not whether his rearing or theirs may have been different, his former surroundings, his social position ; if he has come up to their standard of manliness and honourable dealing during his career on a goldfield, the miners of Australia will yield him that respect, that cordial good-will, and that help in his sore need which is unknown, I believe, among any other body of men. I have lived to experience the truth of what I am saying in my own person and in my own circumstances, some of which have been, as you all know, painful and unfortunate to the last degree. But I wish you all now to believe, if it is any satisfaction to you, that I have been supported and encouraged more than I should have thought possible by the kindness and manly sympathy of the miners of the Oxley goldfield. When I leave, as I intend to do on the morrow, never to return, I shall carry away in my heart the undying remembrance of kindness received from all classes of the people among whom I have lived and toiled, on the whole happily. I thank my friend, and your friend, the Commissioner for the generous way in which he has been pleased to allude to my mining career and character ; and I beg of you all to look upon Hereward Pole, wherever he may be, as a comrade and a friend.'

When I concluded it seemed as if everybody was more or less affected with the sadness of farewell sentiments. Mrs. Mangrove and Mrs. Yorke, with some of their acquaintances in the gallery, were all sobbing audibly, while even the guests, hardened as they might have been supposed to be against the softer influences, looked rather lugubrious. This was brought to a close by Mr. Bagstock who, perceiving a change of programme to be necessary, took occasion to rise and propose the health of 'the unsuccessful miners'—an idea which took immensely, and speedily restored hilarity. It was responded to by Olivera, who declared his belief in the ultimate good fortune of the class—say in twenty or thirty years—with such gravity that it produced fresh bursts of laughter.

CHAPTER XXXVI

EARLY next morning I quitted the Oxley for ever, perhaps, and turned my face southwards. The journey was this time truly uneventful, and I found myself on the third morning once more in that picturesque city which the sea-roving Anglo-Saxon has reared on the strand of the peerless Haven of the South.

How divine a sensation, how blessed a relief was it to my worn spirit to lounge aimlessly adown the crowded streets, and permit the novel units of the surging crowd to imprint themselves half mechanically upon my brain. Of all rests and solaces, surely none is greater, more efficacious, than the abiding for a season in a city of strangers, where no man bids you greeting, where none disturb the mystic peopled solitude in which the spirit bathes and revels.

The ordinary adjuncts of civilisation were to me an aspect fresh and fascinating beyond description.

The season was that of midsummer, often arid and desert-bare in Australia, but the showers which the sun distils from the clouds which flit across the broad bosom of the Pacific had refreshed the groves and gardens which line the shores and heights. The verdurous glades were emerald green between the flower thickets ; the air was heavy with the perfumes of a thousand gardens and orange groves ; and the nights, jewelled and bedecked with the lustrous stars that shine wide-glittering around the Southern Cross, were to me almost magically full of restful harmony from the measured rhythm of the surges which rolled their soft murmurous monotones beside my couch.

As a matter of strict business I transferred my funds to the head office of the Bank of New Holland, which amounted to fifty-three thousand some odd hundreds of pounds sterling. I also made arrangements for the periodical payments to the credit of my bank account of such moneys as might result from the periodical 'washings-up' of No. 4 and Greenstone Dyke. These were to be my last mining ventures. I was too loyal to the sentiment of my order to relinquish my interest in the good claims that had done so much for my partners and myself. But I did not intend to tempt fortune again, or, as far as I could control my destiny, have another hour's work or anxiety about money as long as my life lasted.

Whatever might be my future course on the ocean of fate on which, after this pleasant island sojourn to refit, my barque was likely to drift so aimlessly, I intended to preserve myself from the sordid cares which eat up the heart of man—'the rust and moth which corrupt' but too often the best treasures of existence.

After a short but satisfactory interview with my banker, who, studiously affable and courteous, assured me that the whole civilised world of finance was deeply interested in the progress and prospects of the Oxley, I proceeded to attire myself once more in accordance with the family tradition of my order, and to that end placed myself unreservedly in the hands of Mr. Knolley, the Poole of Sydney.

He must have justified my confidence; for a week afterwards, as I took my afternoon stroll down George Street after a morning spent in some more pronounced exercise, I could hardly resist the conclusion that the well-dressed, hatted, booted, gloved individual whom I encountered suddenly in a gigantic mirror of Palmer's palace of silken sheen, and drew back respectfully from, must be somebody else, certainly not Hereward Pole, late of No. 4.

By degrees I became accustomed to my long disused second self, the Hereward Pole who was wont to bow to and *causer* with ladies, to dine *à la carte* at good hotels or fashionable cafés, to mingle as of right only with persons of a certain rank and position, to be posted up in all the *petite histoire* and esoteric gossip of society, and to bear myself—so soon do use and wont effect a change—as if I had never known any other habitudes.

It is true that my face and neck were bronzed and tanned, burned deeply dark where exposed to the merciless sun of the interior wastes. And my hands were hardened and roughened out of all similarity to the delicate feminine extremities which ornament the non-manual toilers of the world. Still, I had always tended them after a fashion. Brown and muscular they might be, yet still I flattered myself that in shape and otherwise they still indicated gentle blood. I adopted gloves with much trouble and weariness of the flesh at first, but adhered to them religiously after I found they were working wonders in the complexion of my unconventional digits.

And the sea—oh! the sea—glorious, unbounded, freshly beautiful as each sun arose, lighting up the great sandstone battlements, the scarped bastions upon which ages of storm and the unresting surge had beaten vainly. How did I draw daily fresh health and inspiration of tangible joyousness from the ocean breath, from the ever-changing various wave beauty —'from calm or storm, from rock or bay,' all savoured of the airs of Paradise, to me so long *habitans in sicco*, sojourner in the monotoned wastes of the great Gold Desert. Ah! if but she, my ill-fated friend and companion, had been permitted by a tender Providence to have made this the first stage on her home-ward-bound path of love and duty. But it had been ordered otherwise. And though at times the terrible scene in which I had borne a part came as freshly back to my mind as if the whole occurrence was stereotyped amid the nerve tracks of my brain, yet the impression waxed feeble with each repetition—thanks to that very feebleness of our nature which so often acts as a safeguard from the persistent arrows of remorse, the undying bitterness of a haunting memory.

I had selected for my residence a well-known principal hotel, situated in what was once a fashionable portion of the city proper, but long since abandoned to wharves, warehouses, and strictly mercantile purposes. In the good old days when Sydney was a green-swarded town, with a growing coast and island trade, and about thirty thousand inhabitants, here dwelt some of the leading colonists and merchants. Here they built themselves handsome freestone houses, with noble verandahs and balconies and Moorish-looking high-walled gardens, within which grew the banana and the orange, the loquat and the guava, in tropical luxuriance and profusion. These pleasantly-secluded retreats were towered over by the great fronds of the *Araucaria excelsa*, and often in the clear summer nights, lights and music, graceful flitting shapes and rippling laughter mingled effects with the gleaming waters of the bay and the murmuring wave.

But all these things had passed away with the *bon vieux temps* that is bewailed everywhere and which returns no more. The merchants had become too rich to live among the haunts of commerce; they had migrated to more newly fashionable suburbs, or sailed away across the sea to lose themselves in older agglomerations of realised wealth and restless hyper-civilisation. The gardens had become too valuable as town allotments to be devoted longer to bananas and araucarias. So the walls —old, true, massive walls, such as we see in Italian and Spanish cities, behind which dark-eyed damsels wait languorous and expectant for the soft-hued eve—were pulled down. The glorious spreading trees were ruthlessly felled or rooted up — the Southern Dryads notwithstanding—and the sacred soil auctioned at per foot to make way for a mushroom eruption of stucco terraces and panel-gilt villas.

One of these fine old lofty, many-roomed, double-veran-dahed mansions, carefully constructed of great freestone blocks, when labour was cheap and leisure abundant, had been utilised for the use of strangers and pilgrims, and was known as Batty's Hotel. It enjoyed a wide free view over the bay and islets of Sydney Harbour, while from the upper balconies were visible the grand and towering masses of the North and South Heads—frowning lofty sandstone capes, through which, by an entrance comparatively narrow and apparently more so than in reality, the great liners, the huge ocean steamers, the white-sailed fleet of coasters and seagull-fashioned yachts, could be seen threading their way into the noblest, safest, most picturesque harbour in the southern hemisphere, in the British possessions, in the known world.

This was one of my favourite bits of amusement and occupation when I was not sitting or lying on the short thick doub grass turf which lined the paved but disused streets which led down to the old wharf and to the water's edge generally. Here I would lie by the hour gazing at the moss-grown steps, with heavy iron rings rusting and unused, wherever the light pleasure boats, the gondolas of the South, were wont to be moored. In this new land, the necessary scarcity of ruins makes all edifices that savour of decay or vanished greatness inexpressibly touching to the contemplative wayfarer. In imagination I wove romances which fitted the circumstance of their crumbling porticoes and trade-encumbered apartments, far otherwise occupied in the past. I felt myself cast for the part henceforth of a dreamer, a spectator only in the theatre of life. My career as an actor, as a probable *jeune premier*, was past—irrecoverably past. Henceforth I should sit mute, anonymous, in an unnoticed back seat, listening all unamused to dialogue, the music, the oft-repeated *dénouement*, until eyes grew dim and hearing dulled with age.

It was a dreary prospect, but what other could I hope to realise? Mine was not the spirit of tireless philanthropy, which could go on toiling for the benefit of the race without enthusiasm yet without cessation — *ohne Haste, ohne Raste* — till the worn frame and wearied mind lapsed simultaneously.

No! I had not so learned the gospel of life, neither had I practically come to believe that human beings were in a general way much the better for being helped. The world was full of shams and impostors as it was. A large indiscriminating charity only created its own environment of beggars and almsrecipients, as in old times the abbey produced its crop of sturdy beggars, as the mushroom springs up from the suddenly enriched and newly watered soil. When I felt aweary of the purely sensuous, harmless, convalescent existence that I was at present leading, I could put myself on board a mail steamer, and perhaps brace myself to active virtue in the sterner clime of the historic North.

There was one of these anachronistic mansions which I particularly affected, appealing as it did in the character and beauty of its architecture and surroundings at once to my surviving æsthetic tastes and to the loneliness of my present circumstances; built upon the natural terrace which sloped upward from a lovely and secluded bay, and girt by a larger area of grounds, in which a small portion of the primeval wilderness, left wholly undisturbed, had been most artistically blended with every horticultural device which could heighten the beauties of nature.

Much attached to the sight from early association and other reasons, the proprietors, colonists of high consideration and great wealth, had long resisted the encroaching tide of mere commercial enhancement of values which had threatened to swallow up their cherished heritage.

At length, however, the golden flood could be dammed back no longer, an enormous price had been accepted for the property. The mansion had been cleared of furniture and now lay untenanted. The grounds were no longer 'kept up,' and though no actual outrage upon the long sacred privacy of the demesne had taken place, the sentence had gone forth and Charlotte Bay was doomed.

There was something in the façade of the house—a noble mansion in the Elizabethan style, built of pale, pink-veined, creamy freestone — that strangely reminded me of Allerton Court. Otherwise there were no characteristic features in common. But memory has a thousand strange ever-recurring links and tentacles which cause the heart to stir and tremble at the merest chance symbols, to others meaningless as the mid-day sun, the evening breeze.

In this particular instance, I had no sooner set eyes upon the imposing, almost feudal-seeming pile, standing in lonely grandeur amid the strange semi-tropical woodlands, than the memories of Allerton Court flashed before me with such suddenness and strength that I could scarce control the impulse that urged me to passionate exclamation. So vividly before me

> 'The old mansion and the accustomed hall,
> And the remembered chambers and the place,
> The day, the hour, the sunshine, and the shade,
> And she, who was his destiny, came back,'

that I sank down upon one of the carved stone benches beneath the gloom-greenery of a vast wild fig-tree, which had power to eclipse the bright noonday sun ; sat down and groaned aloud in freshly-summoned agony of spirit.

Long did I sit there, half reclining in the deep shade and solitude well nigh as perfect as when, in the previous century, the pre-Adamite savage crept through the interlaced boughs in pursuit of the wild-wood game. Long hours passed ere my throbbing heart commenced to be at rest, and the paroxysms of my keen-edged regretful memories to be lulled. When I arose the sun was sinking, the westward flame-pageants visible in dimly burning gold behind the waving spires of the tall feathery-stemmed Indian bamboo. Birds were calling to each other from haunts deep in these rarely disturbed solitudes, curiously near as they were to the hum and bustle of a large city. Slowly I moved homewards. The waters of the bay, seen over the parapet of a low stone wall, without intervening break of fence or building, seemed magically mirrored into silver, gem flashing with the sunset cloud pageant. Sullenly frowning down upon the placid glories of sea and sky, reared itself Titan-like the great North Head. I paced along a winding avenue leading to the outer gate. It was a garden of Armida. Above, below, around were masses of brightly-flowering tropical shrubs. Palm trees were mingled with the strange pale-foliaged trees, the eucalyptus, casuarina, and banksia. The earliest discoverers had found and named the very spot. A stone bridge, itself almost venerable with age, and clasped with close lianas, spanned a narrow creek which ran under great fern fronds and evergreen moss-velvet bars plashingly to the sea. Insensibly the beauty of the hour, the fairy-like strangeness and charm of the surroundings, acted as an anodyne to my tortured spirit, and when I debouched from these sacred groves, as they seemed to me, on to the red gravelled undulating highway, I felt like one who had been redeemed from his appointed sojourn in Elfland, and from whose eyes the glamour had fled for aye.

So strong, however, was the impression left upon me that on the morrow and each succeeding day I sought the same enchanted spot, and spent amid its shadowy lawns and sunless retreats the long bright hours of the summer day. The sultry eve which in that southern clime lengthens far into the silent, clear-hued, starry night often found me still unwilling to change the realm of fancy for the abode of men.

I had made myself known to the under gardener, who alone lived on the premises, chiefly as a watch against thieves and tramps. By a liberal douceur, I had fixed myself among his mental machinery as primarily a species of harmless lunatic prone to insensate wanderings, but secondarily as the possessor of good clothes and current coin, therefore well-intentioned and worthy of toleration.

Thus, though we seldom interchanged a word, an armistice, even an acquaintance, was arranged and ratified between us. I was suffered to roam unheeded through every secluded nook, every natural fastness, every artificial addendum and improvement to the grounds. I came to know at length every feature of the ample-seeming demesne, from the cave in the natural sandstone rock, the fishpond, and the fernery, the bath grotto, and the sea wall, to the lawns, where strange flowering bulbs grew among the close-shorn grass, appearing annually as regularly as the season, and yet with no record of their original introduction. I knew every banana tree, the broad, delicate, pale green fronds of which were alone to be seen unbroken and of perfect shape in that sheltered segment of Paradise. I knew the birds which dwelt amid the leafy thickets and darkly-shaded recesses; they built tame and unharmed as if on an uninhabited island in the South Seas. As I lay luxuriously

day-dreaming in the mimic wilderness to which I had become
so strangely attracted, deeper and yet more deep became the
feeling daily that in some mysterious way this lonely romantic
mansion, these picturesque fragments of a world foreign to all
the prosaic realities of a sordid modern life, were connected
with my destiny and that of her who had been during all these
weary years a loadstone and a beaconlight to my heart—to my
innermost soul.

Yes, Ruth, love and worship had alike centred in thee.
Stormclouds might have obscured thy divinely clear effulgence,
gross earthly vapours might have mingled with the ethereal
essence of my spirit homage, but thine image and thine only
has ever been shrined in this heart.

As the summer days drew on and the shadows lengthened, I
made my way for the most part to the boat wharf or jetty,
which, constructed of huge blocks of rough sandstone, had been
run out into deep water over the shelving sands. This piece of
simple engineering interested me greatly. I loved to lie at
length upon the cool flags or sit upon the steps at the end and
think of how long since the trim delicately-fashioned yachts
lay at anchor close to it, while adown these very steps, now all
unused and moss-grown, had light feet tripped, while musical
voices and the gay converse of youth sounded where now alone
the wavelets of the rising tide plashed mournfully, or the
wheeling sea-bird shrilly screamed.

Hour after hour would I lie at length watching the sunset
hues as they gradually paled, and the bright tints died out of
the sky, as from a human face the warm tints when pain or
grief has sapped the sources of the blood ; the evening breeze
as it stole whisperingly through the darkening shades, stirring
the leaves which fell not the winter through, and fretting the
silver surface of the great water-plain which lay so still and
solemn under the star lamps as they gradually grew into golden
fire from the pale shimmering lights which faintly trembled
into being amid the azure depths.

Calmness, repose—soothing, consoling to a degree unutterable,
—did I find there in the long vigils which I ever and anon kept,
rousing myself with difficulty at midnight and pacing dreamily
back to my hotel. As the days wore on and the year had
entered upon its second month, that one which is esteemed of
the highest in temperature, the most scorchingly severe even
in the fierce summer of the South, I felt that my spirit had
entered upon a fresh stage of existence, that I had acquired
anew the strength and endurance of ill which would enable me
to recreate the fragments of my long past trust in a beneficent
Providence.

Gradually, in these day-dreams and midnight musings, there
came to me an immeasurably deep and solemn conviction of the
folly of resisting the immutable decrees of Fate. What was I—
what was a nation of such atoms in the sight of the Omnipotent—

that one should dare to complain of the preordained, eternally immutable course of events? Were the colossal forces of Nature, the dread laws of existence which governed the immensities and eternities, to be set aside that such an ephemeris as I should sport its hour in the sun? What were all the ills of life compared to the furies which were evolved from a man's own conscience? These I could confront with clearest countenance. For the rest, let worse or better come, I was prepared for all.

CHAPTER XXXVII

ONE sultry morn, according to my custom, I sought my favourite haunt, to which I now considered myself to hold a kind of title, and lay dreamily upon the shaded greensward in true southern abandon. During the earlier part of the day the heat had been intense ; and as I thought of the parched uplands of the Oxley, at that season so burning and breezeless, I wondered how I could have endured so long the Sahara-like summers which there prevailed. Here, in this wondrous Eden shade, all sun-glare was banished ; the sun rays seemed only to penetrate the leafy screen to be transmuted into the languorous summer warmth that was free from all tinge of earthly discomfort—a lotus-eating, luxurious sensation, nothing more.

Noon had long passed. The ocean breeze came sighing over the burnished wavelets, the yellow shore, the silent groves. All nature hasted to revive and revel in the approach of eve. I had strolled out to my station on the end of the stone pier, and mechanically gazed at one of the ocean liners which had arrived that day from Europe, and was anchored at no great distance.

I fell to speculating idly upon the intentions and probable projects of the passengers, who were even now commencing the long, and perchance wearisome, sojourn of colonisation. Were they doubting and fearing, or hoping all things, even as I had done in the same long past period which I could so distinctly remember. Then I saw a boat put off from the ship and row towards the shore.

It was an eve superb in tropical beauty—such a one surely that, if placed with absolute correctness upon canvas, would provoke the taunts of those critics who condemn all apparent richness of colouring as unnaturally heightened, and thus false to nature. The numberless tiny headlands, wooded or greenswarded, with shining waveless bays nestled between, harbours for fairy fleets, the long incline of groves and gardens, the lawns and terraces of which in so many instances seemed crowded, as in old Italian pictures, to the sea rim, presenting in their half-wild, half-cultured condition the effective contrasts of a new land. The tall araucarias stood columnar on every height, giving dignity and ordered beauty to the landscape. The white walls of stately mansions and trim villas gleamed freshly bright among the dim woods, shining like Grecian temples in the olden days of earth's glory ; while, as the western sky became gradually empurpled and aflame with the gorgeous pageantry of the dying sun, an unearthly brilliancy appeared to illumine the scene, more akin to theatrical effects of light and colour than the mere summer splendour of the hour.

As the boat was rowed, a fairy bark through a gold-empurpled sea, to the shore, being steered, as it seemed to me, on a course that would bring her nearer than I at first thought to the solitary disused pier, I arose and prepared to retire, a growing dislike to strangers having become with me intensified of late.

An inexplicable feeling restrained me. I remained. I looked earnestly, fixedly, at the occupants of the boat. Besides the crew and an officer of the ship, who steered, there were two ladies and a gentleman, an elderly man I conjectured from his way of sitting.

Whether it were fancy or not I could not tell, but they appeared to be likely to land upon the pier, *my* pier. After spending some time, with stationary boat, in looking long and with interest at Charlotte Bay House, the boat moved swiftly up to the stone steps, and the man whom I had correctly taken to be an officer of the newly-arrived vessel leaped ashore and fastened the rope in the boat's stem to an iron ring affixed to the largest block.

'This is the place,' he said. 'This is Charlotte Bay, I think the most beautiful spot in all our beautiful harbour. The pilot said it was for sale ; but if it has not been sold, we shall be able to look over it. We have just time to see the house and garden, Miss Allerton, before it gets dark. Perhaps this gentleman can tell us if we are trespassing ?'

At the sound of that name, of *her* name, I drew myself up with a sudden impulse, and gazed eagerly at the individuals composing the little party. An old lady, a gray-haired elderly man of distinguished air, and a young lady walking feebly and closely veiled. Gracious Lord ! Could it be ? Had the God of infinite mercy and wisdom heard my prayers, and did I again behold my lost love in this half-enchanted wild, on the strange far land on which I never dreamed that her foot should press ?

'No one will prevent you,' said I, quietly, to the sailor, a bright-eyed, stalwart youngster, one of those gallant offshoots of the old Norse brood, whom the Motherland sends out yearly on the decks of her still increasing fleet to plant her standard and win new empires on the furthest bounds of the round world.

'The young lady wishes to see the house—a fancy of hers puts her in mind of home,' he said in explanation to me, as of a matter in which he scarcely, but for courtesy's sake, sympathised. 'Perhaps you know the paths hereabouts—they are not quite plain sailing?'

I bowed and walked ahead, closely followed by the whole party. I had felt too deeply agitated to think of making myself known as yet. I could not see her face, but I fastened my eyes on the form, the outlines of which I so well knew.

'What a beautiful house!' said the young lady, for the first time drawing up her veil. 'What a delicately-coloured stone; and oh, what a fairy land of a garden. How glad I am that we came to this country, darling mother, though I am afraid you and my father do not share all my rapture. I feel as if I must soon get well now. I am ever so much better already.'

'My darling,' said dear old Mrs. Allerton, 'your father and I live only for you. You do not need to be told that. And this certainly is a most beautiful place, and the climate deliciously mild when it is not too hot. But what made you take such a fancy to come and see this particular house? There seem to be many beautiful ones on the shores of the harbour.'

'Don't you know, mother dearest; surely you *must* see,' she said. 'Why, that part of the southern wing is just like the one at Allerton Court. It has a tiny rose garden and lawn just like the one the new gardener made for me the year *he* left England. Oh, I cannot tell why, but the feeling came over me at once as I saw it from the ship that in some sort of way connected Hereward with this house—the one I saw in my dream the week before we left England.'

'But, Ruth dearest, you said just now that this house put you in mind of the old Court,' said the Squire.

I thought the frank face changed, the form aged, the bold, undoubting, fearless regard altered, and my heart sank as an inward monitor suggested that I was not wholly without responsibility for the decadence.

'Oh, but I told you at the time, my own good daddy, that the house I saw in my dream, where we should hear of or meet with Hereward, was like Allerton Court. Indeed, I never expected to see any house half so beautiful as this at the other side of the world. I feel convinced that this is the very place. My hope is renewed now that we may see him shortly; then all doubt will be explained and disappear.'

'God grant it,' said the Squire fervently. 'But for your health's sake, my darling, we should never have taken this long voyage, which now seems to me the wisest thing we could have done. But the stars are coming out. How large and bright they are. We must get back to our good ship. We shall be all sorry to leave her to-morrow.'

During this conversation I stood like a being of another planet. I felt as might the fabled possessor of the ring of Gyges, as though, myself invisible, I was privileged to see the acts and hear the speech of those who were to me at present the most important personages on the earth's surface.

They knew me not. How should they in that dim half-shadowy atmosphere connect the tall bronzed muscular man with the fair-faced English stripling who had quitted England nearly seven years since.

And now my prayers had been granted, though in a way that in my blindness I had never for one moment thought of, deeming it a thing impossible that the Squire and Mrs. Allerton, representatives of those English families which seem firmly rooted as their ancestral oaks, should ever set foot upon Australian soil. Yet, though I felt a well-nigh irresistible impulse to declare myself at the first moment when the well-known voice fell like long-remembered music upon my ears—the face which to me was as that of a seraph's was again presented to my astonished gaze—yet another feeling equally strong caused me, inexplicable as it may seem, to hesitate and finally to refrain.

When Ruth's veil was lifted it was at once apparent to me that the almost transparently delicate features, the pathetic expression of the bright wistful eyes, the too slender though still graceful form, betokened but too surely the recent inroad of disease. Without doubt a happier period of change and improvement had set in, most probably with the voyage. Still I read but too plainly in the undisguised anxiety with which both the Squire and his wife regarded their charge and her every movement that but a short period must have elapsed since the most torturing phase of fear and doubt had existed for them with regard to her very life. And dared I now hazard, in whatever slight degree, that precious, that inestimable gift of heaven, the health of this fragile maiden? Had I said impulsively, 'I am Hereward Pole,' what nervous injury to an already weakened frame might not the sudden shock have produced?

No—patience and self-command must still be mine. They were to leave the vessel to-morrow, and I should have no difficulty in discovering their hotel, if indeed they did not come to Batty's and locate themselves beneath the same roof as myself.

In a few moments the plash of oars told me that they had sought the protection of the noble ship which had brought them across the ocean in safety. As favoured passengers they had been made welcome to stay during their convenience after their arrival in port. To-morrow I gathered that they had decided to establish themselves for a season in Sydney.

They had departed. I was left alone to determine upon my course. Wonderful and astonishing as were the events which had now manifested themselves, they had not confused my brain; rather I had felt more cool and composed than at any time since the commencement of my misfortunes.

I could see it all now. Part of the history I read aright in

the face of my own beloved Ruth when I had the first brief
glance of her countenance at Charlotte Bay.   There was graved
the whole tale of my unanswered letter, of the silence and uncertainty under which I had languished so long.

This was the key to the mystery.   Strong in her immortal
love she had borne all too patiently, and with mute inward
struggling against the gnawing worm of grief, the pangs of
doubt and fear, her brave pure spirit had been loath to suc-
cumb.   Then her health had suffered, nearer and nearer still to
the dark bourne had her fragile frame, the tremulous casket of
the love-lamp, drifted.

The Squire had suddenly decided as the most direct and
satisfactory method by which the mystery could be solved to
set sail for Australia.   Once there it would be comparatively
easy to find out the rights of the matter.   My character, my
acts would be then manifested clearly.   If my career had been
stainless, then my name and fame would for ever be established.
If not, for her sake, for all our sakes, it were better that no
further doubt or hope should exist.

Their necessary preparations, though serious, were not com-
plex or numerous.   The family was small.   Be sure that the
Squire had the right kind of man as bailiff by whom the property could be managed, and rents handed over to his agent.
The voyage of course was long, possibly tedious.   But what
were wind and wave or unaccustomed travel to the fact that
health and happiness might again be the portion of their beloved
daughter.

It should be well understood before we take these imprudent unconventional people to task for their incredulity and
indulgent weakness that they had no other aim or project in
life but to see the happiness of this child of their heart's best
love fully assured ere they themselves passed away.   Strange as
it may appear, and eccentric to the verge of lunacy, they did
actually believe that mutual love, based upon simple natural
predilection would, if circumstances permitted its fruition,
result in perfect happiness, or as near to that ideal condition
as mortals here below ever aspire to.   Money, position, fashionable brevet, rank and consideration, they had the clearness of
vision to regard as the trifles in the great tragedy of human
destiny.   They were prepared, even if they found in Hereward
Pole a toiling unsuccessful man, discouraged by ill fortune, and
despairing of the long-desired goal, yet straining onward as
through the dashing wave and gathering storm the seaman
gazes at the swaying symbol, to stand by the promise made to
him.   If they had found me thus toiling honourably, poor, yet
loyal to the vow in making which I left England, they would
have said—

'Come back with us and be as a son in our old age; there is
the love of your youth, in her eyes truth in absence is still
shining.   Come with us across the wandering sea.   Let us see

our children happy in this short life of ours, in the old home
where your place is still vacant.'

So much of the end had now come. My eyes had seen the
sight I had never imagined in wildest fantasy, the denizens of
Allerton Court actually domiciled in the South. All was well.
All was tending in the direction of my dearest hopes. On the
morrow I should seek out their residence, and presenting myself
before the Squire, invite him to search into the records of my
goldfield life, and form his own conclusions as to the allegations
made against me. I at least should not shrink from the closest
scrutiny—my conscience was unclouded.

But apart from any doubt which might arise with reference
to these considerations, a terrible and paralysing fear arose in
my mind lest, after all, all plans and projects might come too
late. What if the insidious wasting disease, the unseen foe
that mocks the hues, the aspirations, the sanguine confidences
of health, should prove inexorable—if death should claim his
victim even in the arms of love !

I had seen the pallor of Ruth's beloved face even in the few
moments at Charlotte Bay ; had noticed the slow weariness of
her step — that step that was wont to be so light, so fairy-
tripping adown the woodland paths of her home.

Was I doomed after all, when my earthly treasure had been
borne to me across the waste of ocean, to stand sadly by and
watch the gradual fading of this floweret of Paradise ? What
would be my agony were her pure spirit to exhale now, pre-
maturely wafted to the realms of bliss ! And what a pilgrimage
would be ours were the sorrowing parents, with myself, to cross
the ocean homeward-bound, with every mile of wave and foam
increasing the distance between us and the grave which held
all we loved or could ever again love on earth !

Then I reviewed my own prospects. Would my altered form
and face have power to rekindle the torch of love, or would I
find a foe in the ideal of my own personality which had so long
been cherished in Ruth's gentle breast ? Had the sterner traits
of manhood, the traces of toil, hard fortune, and anxiety worn
away all the bright hues of youth, all the fabled graces of the
halcyon time that memory unwillingly recalled ? I knew not.
But the very doubt caused me fresh pain.

I passed a sleepless night, and as the east slowly, almost
imperceptibly, raised a bank of pearls amid the gray dim cloud
wrack, I was pacing feverishly adown the balcony watching the
gray plain of ocean gradually beam into life. As the long
tremulous gold line gleamed in shimmering ripples across the
pale wavelets of the slumbering main, no sign of that daily
miracle, the marvellous birth of dawn from night and chaos,
escaped me. The life of the great city, as if painfully, awoke
and stirred and laboured. Seabirds, and light graceful boats
with sails as white and speed as free, swept over the enfran-
chised sea-plain. A huge steamer came through the harbour

portals breasting the churning waves, and throbbing as if with pride throughout her mighty frame. Power, freedom, and volition seemed granted to all but me, as if by some magic spell, upon the folding of the trailing garments of the night. I alone felt aweary of the sun, sadly distrusting what the day had in store for me. I strolled down to one of the hermitages which once were piers and bath-houses, and casting myself recklessly into the briny water swam far out into the bay, only returning when forced to own to myself that the long swim had taxed even my practised muscles. But the tone of my nervous system was braced and renovated by the exercise, and I felt strengthened for the endurance of the day's ordeal.

CHAPTER XXXVIII

I CONSUMED the first hours of the morning in a quest among the large hotels, those modern caravanserais where the solvent stranger in a new land chiefly finds a home. To my great surprise I found no trace of the Allerton family. I sought with gradually increasing anxiety. In vain I hurried round the city at the utmost speed that my hansom cabman, stimulated by wild offers of increased payment, could sustain. Apparently no such persons existed among the travelling public, easy to trace as European passengers of distinction generally are in Sydney.

I cursed my negligence in not procuring their address from the officers of the *Somersetshire*, who no doubt had heard of the Squire's destination, and were certain to be entertained by him after landing.

As a last resource I thought of the Clubs. Of course—how dull I was not to have known that the Squire must have introductions, which would secure his being at once made an honorary member of the Australian or the Junction.

Driving up to the senior establishment I dashed into the hall, and with an air of anxiety which evidently puzzled the waiter inquired if Mr. Allerton was a member, and, if so, at present in the house?

That seraph in livery replied deliberately, but in accents to me resembling the music of the spheres.

'Hon'rary member, sir. Mr. Allerton have just gone into the billiard-room, sir. What name shall I say? Please to walk into the strangers' room, sir.'

I almost tottered as I entered an apartment which conveyed no idea of the proverbial luxuriousness of club upholstery. Seizing a pen, I scribbled 'Hereward Pole' upon a sheet of note paper and handed it to the angelic messenger.

I stood before the fireplace bracing my nerves, like one who awaits the dread summons of fate, striving in vain to appear cool and collected. I roused myself after a few seconds with the consciousness that I had done no wrong; nay, had indeed achieved the task which in the pride of my youth I had so lightly set myself to accomplish.

In another moment the quick active step sounded in my ears, which I remembered so well in the corridors of Allerton Court. The door opened, and the Squire stood before me.

He gazed for one moment at me with strange, unrecognising air; then his frank features lighting up with their old kindly expression, he exclaimed—

'Good God! Hereward, my boy, is it you at last? And to think that I should not have known you. By Jove! though, what a man you have grown.'

He was holding out his hand, which I shook warmly. What memories did that touch evoke. I tried to speak, but no word would come. The tears rolled down my cheeks as if indeed I had been the sensitive boy he remembered at the old Kentish village, against whom he never dreamed of guarding as a suitor for his daughter's love.

Mr. Allerton looked steadfastly at me with an eye still bright and piercing in its regard. Then his face softened still more, and he turned away his head visibly affected.

'My dear boy,' he said at length, 'there need be but few words between us. That I have doubted, I frankly confess. Appearances were against you. I see before me, in spite of all that has come and gone, the same true-hearted fellow that left old England, and that I was proud to call my son. But come along outside. My heart is too full for talk in a house. Let us have a stroll in this lovely sea-park of yours.'

In a few moments we were passing along the avenue which leads towards the Bay, bordered on the hither side by shining tropical-foliaged trees, comparatively old, through the stately pleasaunce which a former governor reserved for the citizens of the nation yet unborn. Safe from interruption, and shut out from all sounds but the low whispering of the great fern fronds and thick-massed foliage, stirred by the faint ocean breeze, I poured out my heart as to a father, soon convincing the placable and trusting Squire of the falsehood of all aspersions upon my loyalty and truth.

I roughly sketched the circumstances of my mining career, describing my companions and detailing the history from first to last of my friendship with Jane Mangold, fated to so tragic an ending.

'Poor girl, and poor boy, too,' said the kind-hearted Squire, 'you have had a hard time of it; your gold has not been cheaply purchased. I am glad that scoundrel will be hanged at any rate. I am not sure but that you would have done as well to have stuck by old England in the long run. And we, that is poor Ruth and ourselves, should have been spared more misery than I can tell.'

'Many a time and oft I have repented, Squire, that I ever left the Leys; but youth is rash. The hazards that lead to fortune will never lack volunteers from Britain.'

'Well, I suppose we mustn't grumble. It has made a man of

you,' he said, looking admiringly at my broad shoulders and stalwart frame. 'I hardly thought you would spread out into such a heavy-weight champion. It must be a fine climate. Hard work seems to have agreed with you at all events. I wonder if Ruth will know you?'

'She did not recognise me at Charlotte Bay yesterday,' I said, 'but it was late.'

'Yesterday—was that you? Good heavens!' cried out the Squire, deeply moved, 'what an astonishing, almost incredible, coincidence. I shall believe in dreams all my life after. Did you hear what she said about the house she saw in her dream before she left England?'

'I did catch something of the sort,' I answered, 'but her dear face so enthralled me when she raised her veil that the full sense of her speech was lost upon me.'

'Most strange—passing strange,' mused the Squire. 'There is nothing wonderful in her not knowing you yesterday. I had not the remotest idea of you other than as a perfect stranger, though courteous and considerate as we all agreed.'

I smiled.

'When did the dream occur?'

'Before we quitted England. We were debating the question of leaving for Australia, a most unlikely thing to have happened, you must confess, when our poor girl, then hardly recovered from a terrible attack of brain fever, informed her mother and myself that she had had a dream of astonishingly clear and circumstantial nature. That she had seen a stately stone mansion, unique and remarkable of appearance, standing on the shore of a southern harbour, embosomed in a strangely beautiful garden; *that she had seen you lying on a stone bench under a vast wide-growing shady tree with tropical foliage.*'

'That has been literally true, during every day of the last month,' I answered. 'But how almost incredibly strange that the vision should have been so presented to her.'

'Once I should have classed such a matter,' said the Squire solemnly, 'with frivolous fanciful imaginings and harmless delusions; but of late I have learned that there are more things 'twixt heaven and earth than were dreamt of in my philosophy. I am in that respect, perhaps in others also, a changed man.'

'And what fixed your determination to cross the sea?' I said. 'I should never have believed it if I had not seen you all in the flesh. The Dryads at Allerton Court must have wailed audibly.'

'It was a wrench, God knows,' said the Squire, 'but one will do much for life—and our life is bound up in the welfare of our beloved child. She, poor dear, clung to her dream-revelation as though it had been gospel. And as the idea had given her fresh hope, and the doctor counselled change of scene, we made the plunge. And,' continued the Squire, looking kindly in my face and then at the blue waters of the bay, over which the white-sailed boats were darting before the western breeze, 'I shall never regret the step. Now I declare I have talked till I am hungry and thirsty both. Come home with me and plead your own cause with Ruth. We are in lodgings.'

'That accounts for my not finding you. I made so sure you would be at one of the hotels, and was half inclined to go back to the *Somersetshire* to find out if I had not been dreaming in my turn that I met you at Charlotte Bay.'

'Why did you not make yourself known then?' commenced the Squire; but looking at my face he read the answer, and went on. 'A natural feeling on your part, my boy, quite of a piece with your old self. I see the digging and all that has not changed Hereward Pole much. In poor Ruth's delicate state—for though she is quite a new creature now, she had to be carried on board ship—the shock might have had ill effects. Still I think you will find her more or less prepared—thanks to this wonderful dream.'

'And what was your fancy for lodgings? I almost thought you would go to Batty's where I am staying. Nothing could be more delightful or more luxuriously commodious.'

'Well, the fact was that one of our fellow-passengers, who hailed from Sydney, recommended our present abode so strongly, the lady being the retired widow of a military officer he knew, and a most estimable person, that we took his advice. So our address is 580 Macquarie Street, where my wife is spoiled and Ruth petted as if Mrs. Pemberton was her great aunt.'

'I have heard of Mrs. Pemberton,' I said. 'You could not be in better quarters, and as dearest Ruth's health I could see had grievously suffered——'

'You say truly, my dear boy; nay more, she has been raised up almost from the grave, but by God's great mercy she has improved in health and strength almost from the very hour we began the voyage; so perhaps from this lovely land, where all things are new and interesting to her, she will return fully renovated. It only needed in my opinion that she should have her faith in you justified. Come and tell her so.'

It was not deemed advisable even now to risk a sudden interview. The Squire confided the important news of my arrival and rehabilitation to his wife, who with prudent limitations imparted it to her daughter. Finally my long-lost, long-loved faithful one was told that I was come, was actually in the house —that I awaited her in the next room.

The door opened, she came forward. One glance was sufficient. No need of careful searching inquiry of feature for love's swift vision.

'Oh, Hereward! oh, my love! and do we then meet again? God is indeed merciful,' were her faltering yet eager words as she sank fainting in my arms. I supported her to a couch, and there, with her head leaning on my shoulder, we sat steeped in bliss so rarely granted to lovers in this changeful world. Sorrow and trial had disappeared ; our passion, which had been tried and tested as by fire, was still fervent as ever after the lapse of years. I had wrested from fortune her favours and smiles. Our hopes were about to be crowned with triumphant, if long delayed, fruition.

The happy moments lengthened to hours, which fled unheeded, and still we sat hand clasped in hand as she listened with deepest interest to the tale of chequered existence, until, fearful of her failing strength, I commenced to use my newborn authority by vowing that the Dinarzade business must be over for that day.

'I could listen for ever, love,' she said. 'What romance could be half so interesting as Hereward's real adventures to his poor Ruth. Poor Ruth ! Poor Lucy Ashton ! How often have I thought of you as my absent Edgar Ravenswood. Never has *my* heart wavered ; but, unlike her, I had the best, the most tender of parents ; but for them I should have died. I am not strong now ; but oh, if you had seen the shadow I was a year since.'

'But you will be strong again, my darling,' I said. 'In this fair new land the soft airs and bright hues will work a magic charm, which my love will deepen,' I whispered.

'Darling,' she said, clasping my bronzed face with both her delicate lily hands. 'I know that I shall be restored to my old self. I feel assured of it by some inward feeling. The cloud is for ever lifted from my life. From the morning after I dreamed about that house—it will ever be The House Beautiful to me, I shall love it till I die—I have felt myself a new creature. And now it has come true. My love was there, even while I gazed upon it, and now we are here together—the love of long ago is illumined. I am too happy to die. Death has no power over those whom joy transforms.'

We were aroused at length by Mrs. Allerton, who came to suggest that dinner could not be more than ten minutes distant ; that the Squire, on learning the hour at which we returned from the domain, had refused on principle to partake of lunch ; that, as he was walking up and down on the balcony, frequently consulting his watch, punctuality on this occasion might be judicious.

'Poor, dear old Pappy !' said Ruth. 'It is a long time since he gave me a lecture on punctuality at meals, as he occasionally did at home, for reading up to the last minute, and coming down after the guests had assembled.'

'It is a good sign,' said the kind old lady, with a sigh and a tender look at her daughter. 'I hope you will follow papa's example at dinner, though I must say you have been a very good girl of late. Your country, Hereward, will have the credit of curing her. I had no idea that you were so civilised, I must say.'

' Many English people, my dear Mrs. Allerton, think that we Australians are just emerging from barbarism. I hope to show you some things and places which will bear describing when you return.'

'Oh, I promise you we are not going back till we have seen all that is to be seen,' said Ruth. 'I find that I am passionately fond of travelling now that I have fairly commenced ; and I love this country for your sake and all the people in it, except the bushrangers, and they might have been worse when one comes to think, poor fellows. I intend to go to the mines to begin with.'

'You may go anywhere you like, my darling,' said the Squire, who now entered the room, 'as long as you eat your three meals a day with a becoming appetite. There goes the dinner bell at last. How any one can be as hungry as I am this moment, with the thermometer at 85° in the shade, is more than I can make out. I should never have believed it in England. I wonder if they have got any of those delicious garfish for us which we had at breakfast ?'

I had realised the ancestral paradise. A child of Adam, vicariously driven forth from those wondrous shades, those emerald lawns wet with heaven's first dews, the woods and waters of a world fresh from its Maker's hand. I had been suffered to re-enter. The angel-guarded portals, rendered invisible to mortals since that day of expulsion, as goes the mediæval legend, swung wide for me. To me, alone blest among mortals, was it vouchsafed that I should wander amid groves hallowed by the presence of a pure and perfect love, gazing in the eyes of an Eve pure from every stain of mortal sin, as her guileless untempted prototype.

Day after day Ruth and I strolled together adown the endlessly varied woodland paths with but the whispering surge-voices for all friendly auditory. We watched the moon rise over the silver lakelets of the harbour, or threaded the mazes of the great garden-park, as the sun drooped low amid the empurpled splendour of the wave. At such moments life seemed distilled into a draught of supernal happiness at which we trembled.

The days, while we gazed, glided. The summer waned, and the long-drawn lingering light insensibly yielded a longer interval to the soft appeals of night. My darling's strength returned apace, her step regained its elasticity, her voice the fuller rounded tone which, though subdued in ordinary moods, I remembered so well.

Meanwhile the Squire and Mrs. Allerton were not wholly unamused. The former made numerous acquaintances at the Australian Club, and even took short excursions into the country, where he looked with deepest interest upon the high-bred herds and flocks and studs of noble horses which had flourished under scientific culture so far, strange to say, from old England.

'Most astonishing, truly wonderful country, this Australia of yours, my boy,' he would say to me on his return from these excursions. 'Never could have believed that such stock could have been produced out of England—and on grass, nothing but grass, too, that's what beats me; no roots, no hay, no cake! How they do it I can't tell. It's the climate, I suppose, and their being able to run out all the year round. If we had such soil and climate in England our farmers would get too rich.'

'But the labour, you forget that, Squire,' said I mischievously. 'You don't pay your ploughmen and hinds a pound a week, with board and lodging, and fuel thrown in.'

'Ah,' said the Squire meditatively, 'there's something in that. The weekly wages bill at Allerton Court would mount up if we paid at such rates. But it's a splendid country, a magnificent country. If I was a young man and hadn't my bread and butter ready cut and spread for me, like some folks, I'd emigrate. It's the only career for a youngster of spirit, I can see that now.'

'So poor Hereward did the right thing after all, daddy?' said Ruth, putting her hand into the Squire's, and nestling her head against his shoulder. 'And yet I know some people who said he was so foolish to leave England.'

'Of course he did, pussy, and so did we do right in coming here to hunt him up. There's no knowing what might have happened else. And I know one obstinate young lady whose cheeks are beginning to look very much rounder than they did. It must be the fish or the fresh bread and butter, or ——'

'Happiness, my dear old father, pure happiness,' said Ruth, blushing and throwing her arms around that most indulgent of men. 'The doctor in England, you know, said if my mind could be at rest, that health would certainly follow. And here,' she continued, taking my hands with both of hers, 'I have found peace and happiness, if such are permitted on earth.'

'To that God, who in His infinite mercy has brought this to pass, and to whom our prayers have ever been raised, even in our deepest anguish, be all the praise,' said the soft loving voice of Mrs. Allerton, who had joined us noiselessly.

And from every heart, as from every voice, in tones of deepest gratitude and sincerity, rose to heaven the prayer of thanksgiving.

It was arranged that the whole party should remain in Sydney until the approach of the mild Australian winter, when by quitting these southern shores for England, we should reach home either in the merry month of May, or when leafy June had summoned the full glory of a northern summer.

To employ a portion of that interval, and at the ardent entreaty of Ruth, I finally consented to guide the whole party

to the Oxley diggings, where their full comprehension of one
section of Australian enterprise would certainly be effected.

For several reasons, it may well be imagined, I had no great
liking for the arrangement. I had quitted the scene of my
labours ostensibly for ever. Customary, even exceptionally
farewell rites had been performed. There would be a species
of awkwardness in re-appearing upon the scene after my social
demise.

I was to play also the new character of a gentleman at large
in the company of distinguished visitors from Europe, one of
whom would be speedily known to be my affianced bride.

Such difficulties and awkwardnesses as there were in the
way, I had full confidence that I should surmount. But there
were difficulties, even probable embarrassments, which the unrelieved *dolce far niente* of my recent life disinclined me to
encounter.

I made more than one attempt to dissuade my wilful princess
from the enterprise. I exaggerated the discomforts. I used
the customary English arguments: 'it was a rough place,
and not, perhaps, exactly fitted for people of her delicate
nature,' etc.

But she turned the tables upon me by saying—

'Oh, now you are untrue to your good comrades and friends.
I am ashamed of you. Besides, you told me that there were
quantities of such *very* nice people there. I want to see the
Commissioner, and Mr. Merlin, and Mr. Bright, besides that
delightful Major, and my old acquaintances Jack and Joe
Bulder. I remember Joe quite well, frightening the rooks at
sixpence a week for farmer Giles. In a word, I want to see the
romance of the goldfields before I leave Australia, and see it
I will.'

Here my future proprietress stamped her foot, and looked so
deliciously incongruously fierce that we all laughed.

'Who would have thought that this was the little pale girl
that was carried on board ship?' said the Squire, patting her
cheek with intense pride and satisfaction. 'My darling, you
must not take us to the South Pole, because it is as cold as the
North one, though you might not think so ; but we will go with
you to the end of the world if you will only keep strong enough
to order us about. Hereward, my boy, you'll have to take out
three more Miners' Rights, I see.'

This joke, in which the Squire with pardonable exultation
displayed his knowledge of Australian institutions, brought
down the house, so to speak, and for the first time, half-seriously,
realising the fact that feminine steadfastness of character may
demonstrate itself in more directions than one, I surrendered
unconditionally, and prepared mentally for a newly-flavoured
experience of goldfields life.

CHAPTER XXXIX

MRS. ALLERTON, like most elderly ladies who have led carefully-regulated existences in the ancestral mansions of an English county, was not blessed with much curiosity. She held that the inconveniences of travel more than counterbalanced its advantages, and, somewhat to our joint relief, made up her mind to stay where she was. In the lady of the house she found a most pleasant well-informed companion, ready to afford her every kind of information about Australia without going off the balcony. She feared naturally the altogether untried hazards of a coach journey, and distrusted a goldfield as something between a mining camp and a barricade. Thus she pleased herself and contented every one by giving us three full permission to conduct the journey on our own responsibility, and remaining in Macquarie Street till our return.

'Now that dearest Ruth is so strong,' she said to me, 'and her father and you are in charge, I think every change must benefit her. As for me, I feel quite at home with Mrs. Pemberton. I never thought hot weather would agree with me so.'

So, partly by rail, partly by coach, we made the eventful journey, and much to my relief the latter part of the adventure was free from any of the *contretemps* which occasionally happen to the best regulated stage companies. The coaches were not unpleasantly crowded, nor were there any inebriated personages involuntarily obnoxious and impossible to quell except by the strong measure of leaving them behind.

We had scarcely reached the grand Alpine chain of mountains which divides the coast lands from the interior plateaux, ere the greater freshness and dryness of the atmosphere was sensibly felt by my companions. Ruth's spirits seemed to rise with every change of scene, and the appearance of the country, the open park-like forest, the flocks which fed by the roadside, with such strange Arcadians in charge, the occasional droves of cattle with their attendant stock-riders, the packhorses, the swagman, pipe in mouth, stepping cheerily along the highway, all these characteristic scenes and sounds of a far land, were to her and to the Squire sources of unfailing surprise and interest.

'How different all these people look from our labouring hinds and villagers generally,' said Ruth. 'Nobody looks poor, nobody looks depressed or dependent. You have no poor in Australia, have you, Hereward?'

'We have plenty of people who haven't any money,' I say, 'but one could hardly speak of them correctly as "the poor" in the collectively contemptuous way we used to do in England.'

'That's because it's always warm here.' ('Is it though?' interjected I.) 'People can't be really poor unless they have no fuel and very few clothes as well as hardly any food. Now look at that man making such a nice fire with dry wood in abundance. What is he doing that for? he can't want to warm himself.'

'He is going to boil a quart potful of water to make himself some tea. He has probably some bread and meat in his pouch. Off these, with the tea, he will make a sufficient meal, after which he will walk ten, twelve, or fifteen miles as the case may be.'

'Why don't they drink beer?' said the Squire. 'Our washerwomen and ladies' maids are the only people who drink tea in that way in England.'

'Beer is neither so cheap, so portable, nor so wholesome a drink in all weathers and seasons. Bread, meat, and tea carry the Australian labourer from one side of the continent to the other, not but what they drink beer and strong liquors, generally, with all too little unreserve when they can get them.'

'And suppose our friend's store runs out, and his money, what does he do then?' asked the Squire.

'Present himself at the first sheep or cattle station at the time of sunset, where he receives the dole of food and lodging for one night, almost as a matter of right.'

'And can he do this for any length of time?'

'Virtually, the time is unlimited—until he obtains work to his taste. If the employment or wages do not suit him he will walk hundreds of miles before taking service.'

'So that, practically, the proprietors support a strike against themselves, by giving sustenance to labourers who perhaps have decided not to accept their rate of wages.'

'It amounts to something of the sort. But, at the same time, it brings the labour to their doors, even at the outskirts of civilisation. In the main, any differences of opinion on these points between pastoral proprietors and their employees arrange themselves easily.'

'And have you ever travelled in that way, Hereward?' said my fair questioner, looking with the deepest interest, as the driver was walking his horses up a hill, at the wayfarer sitting down on a log and commencing his repast.

'Dozens of times, between one diggings and another, when we

were hard up—there was nothing else for it. You should hear
some of the Major's stories.'

'Poor Hereward!' said the girl, looking into my face with the
deepest tenderness and commiseration. 'How much you have
undergone, and for my sake! We must try and make it up to
him, shall we not, papa?'

'You mustn't think that sort of thing the worst part of our
life,' I said, 'any man with moderate health and constitution
may laugh at such hardships under a sky as blue as this.
Anxiety, settled bad luck, sickness, debt, doubt of your ability
to pay just demands, other misfortunes, these are the true evils
of a miner's life. And from these,' I said, taking her delicate
hand in mine, 'we may now, without boasting, say that Hereward Pole is freed for ever.'

'Quite so,' said the Squire. 'A young fellow just about to
be married to a young woman, who has been waiting for him
for half a dozen years, who has made a fair fortune by his own
exertions, and has an old father-in-law who believes in him, has
a very fair prospect before him, as things go in this world ; so
don't let us have any more melancholy talk—do you hear, Ruth,
darling. I feel like a schoolboy out for a holiday. I'm going
to enjoy myself in every way, and talk all sorts of nonsense till
we get back to Sydney. So don't oppress me with moralising.
Your mother and I will have time to do all that on the voyage
home.'

I had written to the Major, and apprised him of my intended
reappearance on the field thus accompanied, and asked him to
arrange at the leading hotel for suitable rooms and accommodation. He was also to inform the Commissioner and Mr. Merlin,
as well as Mrs. Mangrove, with other tried and trustworthy
friends.

I did not wish to arrive at the Oxley entirely without notice.
At the same time I knew that I could trust to the consideration
of the mining population generally, as well as to that of former
associates and acquaintances, that nothing that could wound
the most fastidious delicacy would meet the eyes or ears of my
companions.

In due time the Oxley, scene of so many toils and troubles,
failures and life-wrecks, triumphs and successes, was reached in
safety.

Strange, and yet curiously familiar, looked the characteristic
features of a great goldfield. The winding streets, the net-work
of shafts, the parti-coloured mullock heaps, the thronging
miners, the toilers and camp-followers, earnestly energetic and
yet so unlike any other class of labourers, the throbbing
clanking engines which worked in such near proximity to many
of the houses, the dull reverberating clash of the quartz-
crushing batteries—all things long familiar, even to irksomeness
in my own case, were viewed with the deepest astonishment by
the Squire and his daughter.

'What a wonderland! what a new world!' said Ruth, 'and what a perfect treasure-house of tone and colour. I quite envy you, the picturesque life you must have led here. My sketches will set me up for life when I get home. There never were such opportunities for "genre painting."'

'H—m!' said I. 'The vivid interest you display fades away in time, I can assure you. All the same, there are worse places than a goldfield.'

Old Hennessy, issuing from his well-ordered hostelry, received us with respectful attention, and promptly provided the most comfortable rooms. All traces of the journey effaced, the appearance of an appetising breakfast interested the Squire and myself temporarily more than the unwonted surroundings. He was specially complimentary as to the cutlets and broiled chicken, and beheld with unaffected surprise a magnificent cold round of beef, which occupied a secondary and strategical position.

'You don't live on pork and molasses, eh, Hereward, my boy, in these, ahem—diggings? I shall get quite Australian by and by. That corned round would be hard to beat in old England. Beautifully marbled, and just the right colour too, properly pink and not too much saltpetre. How that piece of beef would astonish an old butcher at the Leys. He never would believe that there was anything but kangaroo to eat in Australia.'

After breakfast appeared the Major, 'showing great form,' as he would have said himself, scrupulously turned out, and looking in every detail of appearance and manner the high-bred personage he undoubtedly was. With him, after a while, we sallied forth for a walk through this golden land, where fresh signs and wonders met Ruth's eager gaze at every step. Everything excited her observant faculty. The thronging miners, the shops, the women and children—these last so sturdy and self-reliant—the great heaps of red and yellow earth, which she made no doubt were largely mingled with gold.

'This is like a town in Hans Andersen's Tales,' she said. 'How I should like to set him down in Main Street—isn't that the name?—and make him describe it in his charming simple fashion. All would be gold-coloured, the bread, the butter, the beef and mutton, the picks and shovels, the hair of the women and the beards of the men. I do observe the lower garments of your fellow-diggers, Hereward, are decidedly auriferous looking. Talking of that, sir, why don't they come up and greet you; they haven't forgotten your expressive countenance, have they?'

'It is a proof of the courtesy which characterises a mining population, as I have often told you. They know me well enough, but do not consider this to be an appropriate time for renewing acquaintance. They are chiefly in their working clothes for one thing, and acknowledging you and the Squire as distinguished visitors, they have the sense to defer their recognition of a comrade.'

'Very remarkable set of people I must say,' said the Squire. 'I never saw so many grand-looking well-set-up fellows together out of a regiment of Horse Guards in my life. They don't look much like our home mining or manufacturing population, I must say.'

'No finer fellows does the world hold,' I reply. 'Moreover, the effect of travel has stamped itself plainly upon face and form. They have most of them enjoyed a liberal education in that sense.'

'I thought there was something distinctive about them,' said Ruth ; 'but now I demand to be taken to our claim, Greenstone or Bluestone, which is it ? As I shall be a shareholder I ought to go and inspect the mine. Don't you think so, Major Borlase ?'

'Most certainly, Miss Allerton. I know they are not prepared, but you will be able to see how gold is actually brought from the depths of the earth.'

'I quite long, I assure you, to see Mrs. Yorke and the Bulder brothers, Jack and Joe,' she continued. 'How different they would have been if they had remained at the Leys. I saw one of their old comrades just before we left England, and he said— "Be you and Squire aiming to fare to Horsetrailier all the way, Miss Ruth ?" I said, "Yes, William." "Only for to think now ; moind ye bain't took by them kangaroos, Miss. They do tell I as they be main fierce in some parts." Just fancy the different degrees of development between such a man as William Wicker and his travelled comrades.'

'I have an idea, Ruth,' said the Squire ; 'you must get up an entertainment, give a lecture on Australian goldfields, and so on, when we all get back. Talk of development, it must be in the air, my darling. Some folks are becoming positively alarming. Are your Australian young ladies so full of speculative theory, Major Borlase ?'

'We have them of all kinds,' said the Major, 'I believe, just as in England. But I'm hardly an authority. Hereward will tell you.'

'He affects to decry your sex,' I said mischievously. 'You should consider yourself highly honoured, Ruth, by the Major's attentions.'

Ruth glanced quickly at our comrade. The expression of his face was, as usual, utterly impenetrable. But her quick womanly intuition apparently read something in the melancholy eyes and haughty brow which did not lead her to prolong the badinage.

'A man to love once and always,' she said to herself. 'He has been a victim to some cruel woman, and has distrusted us evermore. Poor fellow—why are the best men so often singled out for ruin ?'

Then the Major's deep tones were heard.

'I used to think I had reasons to urge for my scepticism. But Miss Allerton bids fair to shake my most cherished unbeliefs. Be content with your own happiness, Pole, and don't add point to the misfortunes of your less enviable fellow-creatures.'

The shaft of Greenstone Dyke and all its surroundings were much as I had left them. The claim, though fallen off from its original splendour, and no longer sending up dirt to the tune of eight and ten ounces to the load, was still sufficiently rich to be regularly worked. The Major himself had not felt called upon to continue his manual labour. He supervised the management only. Jack and Joe Bulder still preferred to work their shift as usual—the latter for want of knowing what else to do with himself if he were suddenly to discontinue the occupation of years, and the former justly apprehensive that evil might result to him, in case he gave that opportunity to the Adversary which idle hands are popularly held to furnish. Wherefore, Ruth enjoyed the opportunity she had so much wished for, of seeing her old acquaintances of the Leys.

John Bulder had finished his shift and arrayed himself in a quiet, rather well-cut tweed suit and round hat, much like that worn by the Major and myself before our arrival.

When he therefore took off his hat, and bowed with a certain ease and quiet air of politeness to Ruth and the Squire, they looked wonderingly, as if they had never seen him before. Then Ruth walked forward, followed by the Squire ; both shook him warmly by the hand.

'I never should have known you, Jack,' said she. 'Why, whatever have you done to yourself ? Now I can recognise your face again. Do you remember picking me up once when I fell off my pony and the nurse was so frightened ? Oh, how curious it is to see our old friends so changed and, if I may say it, improved.'

'Thank you very much, Miss Allerton,' said Jack, with much composure, but, at the same time, with great respect. 'I've led a roving—rather a wild life since I left the Leys, and I daresay I am a good deal changed. It's a miracle, though, to see you and the Squire here, looking so well, too.'

Joe was even then coming up the shaft, and so arrested the colloquy.

This proceeding Ruth watched with the greatest interest, being much astonished to see how steadily and cleverly our famed whip-horse, Roan Bessie, effected the process. Joe, too suddenly shooting into upper air and seeing Miss Ruth and 't'owd Squire,' as he would formerly have called them, standing near the mouth of the shaft, was much more astonished, and gasped for breath, looking from one to another, as they both warmly greeted him, as if they had been denizens of another world.

'You see, Joe, I have come all the way from the Leys to look at the claim and the party,' said Ruth. 'You and Jack have been good friends and true mates to Mr. Pole all through. He and I will always be grateful to you for it—depend upon that, Joe.'

Joe was altogether too much overcome to say much. He stammered out something about Mr. Hereward having brought him across the sea, and that he'd promised to stand by him like an Englishman, and that he had done so, he hoped. His service to Miss Ruth and the Squire, and he was glad to see them looking so well.

'You look very well, too, Joe,' said the Squire, putting his hand kindly on the broad Saxon shoulders, 'a good deal browner and not quite so full of flesh as you used to be at the Leys, but in first-rate condition and as hard as nails, I'll be bound. Well, you've worked to some purpose I'm told, that's a comfort. I suppose we shall see you back again some day?'

'May be,' said Joe, rather doubtfully, 'when the claim's worked out. But that won't be this year, Squire. There's no use in leaving good gold behind us, and Mr. Hereward here'll want all we can send him in the old country, I reckon.'

'I suppose that's what you call being "dividing mates," Joe,' said Ruth with a smile which completely overpowered the honest fellow, who gazed at her as if she had been the tutelary divinity of all miners and such as dive into the bowels of the earth for a living.

As for Mrs. Yorke, she completely won that matron's heart by walking down to her cottage after lunch and spending a couple of hours quietly with her, during which time Mrs. Yorke related to her most of the events which had occurred at the Oxley and Yatala for the last five years, with annotations of her own, winding up with the accident to poor Cyrus which had made her a widow, and tearfully drawing attention to the infant Cyrus, whose plump features wore much the same grave uncompromising expression which had characterised his late father.

Apparently Ruth found special favour in Mrs. Yorke's sight, for she subsequently informed me that nothing but actual eyesight could have made her believe that such a young lady existed in the whole world, let alone in England, 'which the people as comes from there is mostly stuck-up till they get their experience,' and that if I had waited for her till I was gray it would have been nothing but reasonable.

Mrs. Mangrove also fell a victim at the first assault. We went there together, and John was brought in to see the young lady from England that he had often heard his wife rally me about. That worthy second lieutenant found his custom of leaving all the talking to his superior officer very convenient on this occasion, only he mechanically began to fill his pipe, and being warned by a portentous frown put it back into his pouch and stared helplessly around.

His wife received Ruth's thanks for the help which she had extended to me in time of need with much good feeling mingled with dignity, and would have it that she had done nothing out of the way, only in the way of business, and such as any other storekeeper would have readily furnished.

'The fact was, Miss,' said she, bending her keen gray eyes upon the soft countenance of her visitor, 'that Harry here (Mr. Pole, I mean) and the Major, and Joe, and Cyrus, they was such a straight-goin' honest crowd, as no one could help backin' them. Storekeepers you know, Miss, has to keep their eyes open. They know a man when they see him, bless your heart, and can tell a good sort from a loafer or a rowdy, you believe me. Many a time I've seen Harry here come in for his letters, when they were getting nothing, looking as if he hadn't had a good meal for a week. I never could help getting ready something for him. And if he got a letter of yours, Miss (for of course I always knew the home postmark), he'd look as if it was meat, and drink, and gold, and everything to him for a month afterwards.'

Here the tears came into Ruth's eyes, the harrowing picture of my probably emaciated condition proving too much for her.

'Come, Mrs. Mangrove,' I said, 'things were never quite so bad. I must appeal to the Major. You took care that we didn't get so low, I'm sure, and Mrs. Yorke, too. Don't you remember those beef-steaks and the bottle of grog?'

'Well, what of that? You were both fools enough to have laid down and died rather than run up a bill, and nothing coming in and no show going. Bless your heart, Miss, we had to force it on 'em, hadn't we, John? *We* knew their luck would turn, didn't we, John?'

'Truest word you ever spoke,' said John, surreptitiously filling his pipe, and keeping a match in readiness for Ruth's departure.

'And now we've all seen you, Miss,' said Mrs. Mangrove, falling back on a sense of power derived from a long course of important and complicated business transactions, 'I can tell you this, that when you go away there'll be only one opinion on the whole field—that Harry has dropped upon a bit of luck that's worth No. 4 and Greenstone Dyke twice over.'

'Couldn't ha' laid it out neater, not from the Bench,' affirmed John, striking a lucifer match in the enthusiasm of the moment and blowing it out again.

'Do you know I shall be quite spoiled if I stay here much longer,' said Ruth, laughing, and shaking hands warmly with the worthy pair; 'but I shall know how to think of Hereward's good true friends when we are far away. That's the reason I was so anxious to come to the goldfields.'

'They'll all remember you, no fear,' said Mrs. Mangrove; 'won't they, John?'

John all but dislocated my wrist in token of full approval and private personal leave-taking, merely committing himself to a guttural sound which might have been an echo of his helpmate's concluding words.

He winked at me solemnly as the door closed, and an expression of ineffable satisfaction overspread his features, while the subtle aroma which simultaneously pervaded the atmosphere announced that the unnatural separation between man and pipe had terminated.

CHAPTER XL

ALL the 'county people,' who are just as much a caste sacredly set apart in Australia as in any other place, called upon Mr. and Miss Allerton with prompt cordiality. After a few days invitations to dinner and to visit them at their pleasant homes, for periods more or less extended, poured in upon us. With some of these magnates the Major and I, Olivera and others, whose social status was acknowledged, had always been on intimate terms. And now, the tinge of romance which clung round the fact of my long engagement being known, seemed to intensify the proverbial hospitality of the district.

I managed by the daily use of Hennessy's well-known trotters and double buggy to return the calls; to show Ruth and the Squire by degrees pleasant homesteads and the great estates which lay outside of the auriferous region. Nothing could exceed the admiration and interest which each fresh experience evoked from both the emigrants. Ruth's quiet high‑bred manner, joined to the innocently joyous air which had of late become habitual to her, gained favour with all her Australian friends, while her genuine interest in the marvels of Nature which everywhere surrounded us in this new world, gratified her entertainers as a flattering tribute to the attractions of Australia.

Very much to my satisfaction, her tact—perhaps still more her unselfish kindness of disposition—enabled her to strike the fortunate medium between the indiscriminate heedless praise which colonists distrust and the supercilious disapproval which they disdain. She examined and compared everything of which she had former experience in Britain; in the great majority of instances giving warm unqualified praise to the product or custom of the new land.

Most of all, perhaps, did she please by her praise of the climate.

'I have good cause to do so,' she would say, 'for it gave me new life. From the first moment that I breathed the faint odorous breezes on the Australian coast till now, when I am revelling in this beautiful, dry, pure atmosphere, an indescribable lightness of heart has possessed me. No! Hereward, it was not altogether the sight of you, miraculous as that appeared, it was the balmy nature of the atmosphere. At any rate I shall live and die in that conviction.'

The Squire on this point was hardly less optimistic.

'How much we lose,' he said, 'by not travelling, by not being acquainted with our own empire! Here I see England over again, only under more hopeful conditions. Never saw finer meadow land in my life, finer grain, finer cattle and sheep, while as for the horses, our friend's four-in-hand, beautifully matched, turned out and driven, would take high rank in the Four-in-hand or the Coaching Clubs. Wonderful country, most wonderful! And to think that it used to abide in my mind as a sandy waste, very hot and bare—a kind of second-hand Sahara.'

The days wore on, and as we rode or drove through the great estates, some inherited through more than one generation from the original founders, more thoroughly gratified was the Squire with his experiences, more deep in his denunciations of people who lived at home at ease, and talked ignorantly of the labours and successes of colonists.

'How little we know at home,' he was wont to say at the day's close, when we were chatting over our claret in some of the well-appointed mansions of the district; 'how little we dream of the empire which is being built up here at the other end of the world, upon the true old English foundations. And the people, too, regular Englishmen to the backbone; that's what delights me; couldn't tell 'em from Kent or Devonshire men, except that they're bigger, better fed, better taught, and consequently more alive to their own interests and what's going on in the world. Look at those teamsters we saw to-day, all native-born Australians, I'm informed, not a man of them under six feet high, broad shouldered, light flanked, as poor old Maxwell used to say, and as upright and well set up as if they'd lodged with a drill sergeant. We have plenty of good fellows among our farming men, and the breed's not to be beat, but these are finer men, sir, finer men, though I never thought I should live to say so.'

No wonder the Squire became so popular with all the gentry of the neighbourhood. He was enabled abundantly to gratify his desire to become practically acquainted with all the ins and outs of the semi-pastoral, semi-agricultural life which surrounded him. He was taken over and through great farm-steadings, where were hundreds of acres of grain and hay crops, single fields as large as an English farm, where droves of high-bred Shorthorns, Herefords, or Devons dotted the meadows. He saw the woolsheds where fifty thousand high-caste merinoes come annually to be shorn, and grieved much that he could not witness the operation. There were mills and forges, race-horse and training stables, shops and stores, butchers and bakers, all necessary for the needs of the large population of workers, which sometimes a single estate maintained. And in some of these large and complicated establishments there was not a nail wanting, a rail out of place, the smallest evidence of a day's delay or neglect.

'Another old-world delusion knocked on the head, Hereward, my boy,' he would say. 'Always understood that you colonists, particularly the Australian-born part of them, took life uncommonly easy, naturally disposed to be indolent and so on. What do I find to be the case? that for energy—not blind unreasoning force, but intelligent scientific persistence—they exceed us, if indeed they do not beat us hollow. The old country will last my time, Hereward, and there may be something for your children, please God; but old England's going down, my boy, and these new Englands across the Atlantic and Pacific are going up.'

The Squire might not have been so patient and persevering in his research into the very roots of Australian institutions had it not been that the climate so entirely suited Ruth's constitution, that her rapid restoration to perfect health was almost daily visible to both of us. The drier air of the interior, perhaps the most pure, light, and invigorating in the known world, joined to the subtle penetrating aroma of the vast forests of eucalyptus, completed the cure which the voyage had commenced. Her light form regained its exquisite proportions, her eyes the rare brilliancy which a pathetic incident, or a touch of true humour in the old days ever evoked. Even at times a *riante* and sportive tendency, which I had never before noticed, told truly of the marvellous change wrought by the soft airs and bright skies of the charmed south.

'We must get back to Sydney, young people,' said the Squire, with a half sigh one morning as we sat in the breakfast-room of one of our kindest hosts, looking adown the course of the winding river, the red bluffs of which marked its course in contrast with the great meadows which, dotted with sheep and cattle in their various enclosures, stretched away to the spur of a volcanic range of hills. 'If we had that land in Kent what hops we could turn out—eh, Ruth?'

'It is wicked to covet, Pappy. I am afraid you are growing avaricious.'

'Perhaps so, but *apropos* to our return I really have noticed a shade of mild inquiry in your dear mother's letters of late. I have been obliged to put it all on the score of your surprising improvement in health. And truly, darling, the bush air or the hospitality of our kind friends, or the gum leaves, or the diggings, have made a new girl of you. They won't know you when we get back to Allerton Court, positively they won't.'

'And I feel quite grieved to go away,' said Ruth. 'Indeed, if Hereward here had not disappointed me by getting so alarmingly rich, just as I came out, I should have enjoyed keeping

house for him at Greenstone Dyke, I should indeed. Mrs.
Yorke would have taught me how to bake bread in a camp oven,
and I should have been perfectly happy.'

'H—m!' say I. 'It's very good of you, my dear Ruth, but
things are just as well as they are.'

'Very much better,' said our hostess smiling—a wise approving smile. 'Miss Allerton is a true woman, and we all pine for
self-sacrifice secretly now and then, but *les agréments* are not to
be despised in the long run.'

When we returned to the Oxley, where we proposed to stay
only two or three days, *en route* for Sydney, we found all our
friends ready to receive us. To them was added Mr. Bright,
who had been absent on leave. This gentleman had long been
an object of deep interest to Ruth on account of his association
with me in the terrible affair of the escort robbery—a fellow
combatant as well as a fellow sufferer.

The gallant banker was not at all averse to the *rôle* of first
soldier, and presently gave Ruth, at her request, all the details
of that memorable engagement, describing circumstantially the
death of the sergeant in command, and the almost fatal nature
of my wound, with attendant incidents.

Ruth's newly acquired roses paled during the recital, to
which she listened with subdued earnestness, arising with the
conviction that Mr. Bright was a modern Bayard, and that my
life was mainly due to his valour and promptitude.

'What has become of Bagstock?' I said. 'The Squire promised to take home some curios for his friends.'

'He has gone out to Back Creek on official business, I believe,'
said the Commissioner. 'Started before daylight.'

'Energetic young man,' said the Squire, 'nothing like attention to business—most praiseworthy.'

Here the members of the assembled group exchanged
smiles.

'It's something about a coroner's inquest, or an intestate,'
said Blake gravely. 'You were sleeping in the next room at
the camp, Olivera, what did you hear?'

'I was awakened,' said that gentleman, with his usual grave
deliberation, 'by Bagstock's clerk, who came to the window
about three o'clock. I just caught the words, "Glorious news,
Mr. Bagstock, butcher at Back Creek got drowned going
home drunk last night. No will they say—lots of money in
the bank," but probably there was no connection between the
expressions.'

'Probably not,' said Blake, observing that Ruth looked
deeply pained. 'Careless young fellow that clerk. What did
Bagstock do?'

'He said, "Shocking occurrence, you mean, Bunce; order
my horse to be saddled, and ask the sergeant to send a trooper
to take charge of the effects." I presume he started soon afterwards. I went to sleep.'

'The butcher has three or four thousand pounds to his credit in our bank,' said Bright. 'Bagstock will get ten per cent as Curator of Intestate Estates.'

'You don't say so?' said Olivera languidly. 'As good as three or four hundred pounds legacy to our friend then. That accounts for, but does not excuse, Bunce's reprehensible levity.'

'The butcher was bound to go soon anyhow,' said the Major. 'It is rather a windfall for Bagstock. If two or three more of the same sort occur, Mr. Allerton, he will be able to visit his friends in England soon.'

In despite of our pleasant round of country-house visits, when we returned to the Oxley, Ruth averred that she felt as if she were coming back to the society of old friends.

'I must have an undeveloped tinge of Bohemianism in my nature, Hereward,' she said, 'or I never could feel such an interest in a community like this; perhaps it is a natural feeling of gratitude because of their staunch kindness to you. There seems to me such endless variety of character to classify, that if I lived in this neighbourhood I should never become *ennuyée*. Our dear old home is sacred and delightful, but I must own that there is a dead level in manners, customs, and conduct in an English village which rarely rises above the monotonous.'

'You would make the same complaint here after a protracted experience of the life.'

'Impossible,' she answered. 'Now look at that man walking towards us. A most picturesque figure, is he not? you would not meet any one like him at the Leys in a century.'

'He is an old acquaintance of mine,' I said. 'How goes it, Marco?'

The miner, a stalwart Genoese, with a grand black beard and a tranquil pleasant countenance, carefully put down his pick and shovel, and lifted his hat, bowing low with the courtesy which seems natural to all foreigners. He then shook hands with me.

'On the whole, well; but our last shaft has just proved a failure. We are now going to sink on a new level.'

'How long were you at it?' queried I.

'Nearly four months, six in the party.'

'And got nothing?'

'Not so much as would pay the blacksmith.'

'Oh, what a pity,' said Ruth sympathetically, probably picturing Marco with a wife and family dependent upon him for support. 'It grieves me that such things can happen in a rich place like this.'

'It is the fortune of war, madame,' said the miner, with an air of philosophical resignation. 'We must hope the luck will change. Meanwhile, permit me to say adieu, and thank you for your kindness.'

He bowed again to Ruth, shook hands with me, took up his tools, and strode onward.

'Now, there is a tragedy in real life,' she said, as he passed out of hearing. 'I suppose such things daily occur here. What a grand-looking man, so clean and neatly dressed, too. How nobly he bears his misfortune. Could we help him in any way, Hereward? Perhaps he has children and a wife in distress.'

'Marco Dorazzi is a bachelor, and is known to have several thousand pounds in the bank,' I answered, smiling at Ruth's impulsive charity. 'A lost shaft, more or less, will not be the ruin of him.'

Bent upon making the best use of the short time now left to us, Ruth persuaded me to accompany her to the homes of many of the married miners, being most anxious to find out for herself, she said, how the domestic business was managed. She so completely avoided all appearance of condescension—sitting down and presently making herself at home with the children where there were any—that the hard-working matrons felt impelled to open their hearts to her on the spot. For the most part, cleanly well-dressed children met her view, the elder ones, perhaps, just returning from school, the younger ones, in all respects, well provided for. Often a neat vegetable garden with a few flowers and rose-bushes gave an air of comfort and slight embellishment to their humble abodes.

'After all,' Ruth would say to me, as we strolled homeward, not seldom meeting the man of the house returning from his 'shift' with the evidences of toil plainly visible, 'these people live a much more enjoyable and natural life than our English peasantry. Their cottages, if not very substantial, are clean and suited to the country, such a summer land as it is. You don't see those curiously-patched garments so common in England. The terrible grinding poverty, with the workhouse in the distance, that overshadows our poor is absent here. I could have been very happy here myself living in a hut just like that woman we just quitted. I am sure her rose-bushes were beautiful, and nothing will make me think otherwise.'

'But the comforts of a home,' I remonstrated.

'What are the comforts of a home,' she replied, almost impatiently for her, 'to a woman whose heart is eaten away daily and hourly with torturing doubts or bitter griefs? She has a soft bed on which she cannot rest, delicate food which no longer nourishes her, the external shell of a life which is slowly perishing.'

'But you could not have lived here,' I persist. 'How could I have asked or permitted you to come?'

'Why not?' she again asked, with the same earnestness of tone, 'because all the true woman is pared away, do you suppose, by the refining process of high civilisation till no longer faith, nor steadfast endeavour, nor patient endurance are possible to her for true love's sake, unless under a lofty roof and amid crowds of servants? That would be to make a puppet and a butterfly of her who has the misfortune to be born among the

2 A

higher ranks—not a loving woman,' she added with ineffable tenderness. 'No, Hereward,' she continued, 'it is all well ended I humbly trust. A merciful God be thanked for my present happiness; but I vow to you that I would a hundred times rather have lived in one of these huts and cooked and washed for you as that humble woman there does for the man we just saw returning, than have waited the weary solitary years which have passed.'

'Why didn't you take somebody else?' I said. 'A man's heart more or less does not matter much in modern society. I have thought a thousand times that I had no right to keep you in pining uncertainty about my fate.'

'That is possible to some people,' she said softly, 'and I do not think I should altogether blame a girl who did so. But not possible to me—not to me, darling. I feel now as I have never felt since the first year you went away. I suppose you cannot well be poor any more; but whatever happens we must never, *never* be separated again in this world. You will have to make the best of it.'

Probably the best man living is wholly unable to gauge the depth and tenderness, the ethereal pervading essence of her very nature which expresses itself in woman's devotion. As I heard the soft chords of that beloved voice vibrating with unshed tears, eloquent with half-uttered tones, I was fully conscious that, deeply as I appreciated her love and truth, I had but too often resigned myself to an apathetic despair, while she, the solitary watcher in her far-off home, was hourly a prey to corroding fears, palpitating on the rack of mute unutterable woe.

How unworthy was I of her heart's best blood, of her purest affections, offered up on the altar of virgin love, for my sake, for my sake only!

I could only tremble and wonder at the priceless sacrifice— could only vow inwardly with a fervour which the uttered promise often lacks, to partly repay by the lavish dedication of my future life the soul's treasure which was to be entrusted to my guardianship.

.   .   .   .   .   .

On our return Mr. Bright and Mr. Bagstock greeted us with much cordiality, the latter apologising for his unavoidable absence, but laying all the blame upon the inconsiderate action of the butcher, who might (he alleged) just as well have waited another week.

Ruth looked grave at this, and apparently to turn the conversation walked forward to an aboriginal woman, who with a small bright-eyed picaninny at her back and another by her side, was soliciting 'tick pence' in a dolorous whine.

'What a thin dress, poor thing,' said her compassionate sister on the side of Eve, 'and a torn blanket, too.'

'That's all Bagstock's fault,' said Mr. Bright jocosely. 'He has a bale of them at the police-office, sent up by the Government to be given to these dark predecessors of ours. You ask him, Maria.'

'You gibbet blanket old Maria, Massa Bagtock?' whined the gin, 'all about blanket I believe you got long a Guv'ment.'

'That one stealem blackfellow blanket, I believe, Maria,' chuckled Mr. Bright mischievously, 'big one sell 'em along a storekeeper, mine thinkit.'

To Maria, under the influence of more than one glass of grog, unfortunately, this appeared a very feasible suggestion. On the strength of it she immediately raised her voice and began to threaten Mr. Bagstock with condign punishment.

'Me yabba Massa Commishner,' she said, 'put you long a logs, I b'leeve taken from blackfeller—me know, now, me tellum sargint—me tellum. Me seeum blankit along a courthouse.'

We all exploded with laughter. Bagstock looked annoyed, and Ruth rather terrified, as Maria began to perform a kind of war dance round the badgered C.P.S.

'Hold y-y-y-your tongue, you s-s-sable storyteller. Bright, you ought to b-b-b-be ashamed of yourself. Of course I have the blankets. They are to be given out to the whole tribe on the Q-Q-Queen's b-b-birthday.'

'What a thoughtful act,' said Ruth, 'do they give all the poor creatures blankets once a year; and how many are in the tribe?'

'Once a y-y-y-ear,' said Bagstock, 'and about a h-h-h-hundred in this tribe.'

'How I should like to see them gathering,' said Ruth. 'I have hardly ever seen any of the Indians of the land. I think all savages most interesting.'

'Then we'll m-m-make it the Queen's b-b-birthday, the day after to-morrow, Miss Allerton,' said Bagstock, with decisive gallantry. 'Tell 'em it's because the winter's s-s-setting in early.'

'Oh, Mr. Bagstock, thank you,' said Ruth, 'how kind of you; but can you do it?'

'Not the slightest d-d-difficulty,' said he, 'almanacs scarce on the g-g-goldfields.'

'Bravo, Bagstock,' said Mr. Bright, 'and I'll tell you what I'll do, I'll give a picnic to the school children and let Miss Allerton see what Australian youngsters are like.'

CHAPTER XLI

IT did not matter much, presumably, at the antipodes about the ante-dating of Her Gracious Majesty's birthday by a month or two. So Bagstock sent round a herald announcing that in consequence of a cold winter being expected, the Queen's birthday would take place on the following Thursday, when blankets would be distributed punctually at ten o'clock A.M.

It was wonderful how fast this piece of intelligence circulated among the scattered aboriginals of the district. Whether the fiery cross was borne around in the shape of a rum bottle, or the picture - writing of the Aztecs resorted to, cannot be known. It was curious to observe, however, on the day preceding the supposed royal birthday, how many of Her Majesty's sable subjects were seen making, by the shortest routes known, by hill and dale, by wood and wold, towards the Oxley township.

Not that the Australian *indigène*, dark of hue and strongly suspected in these free-thinking evolutionary days of pre-Adamite proclivities, has been found invariably incapable of the humanities. More than one philanthropist has tested the question of pan-genesis, so ordering that the swart son of the waste should receive his due allowance of Eton, Latin grammar, and Euclid, in company with the children of the White Conquest.

Indeed, the tale is told of a newly-arrived European wayfarer, sore troubled about a variety of tracks where 'you can't miss the road,' coming unexpectedly upon a black fellow lying under a shady tree, wrapped in a blanket, and engaged in the perusal of one of Sir Walter Scott's novels.

The white man stared, then said—

'I say, which of these three is the proper road to Mildool station?'

The 'savage' rose, bowed courteously, and thus delivered himself—*Medio tutissimus ibis.*

'What?' shouted the Englishman.

'Don't you understand?' said the congener of the Scholar Gipsy, pointing to the middle path—

> 'The middle is the safest way,
> Take it, and rest ere close of day.'

The amazed Anglo-Saxon put spurs to his horse, and, arriving at the station barely with the light, gasped out that he had met the Devil under a tree in the forest, who had quoted Latin and talked poetry to him.

'To be sure,' quoted the Scottish host, as he sent the stranger's hack to the stable.

> 'The De'il or else an outler quey
> Gat up and gae a croon.'

'It was either Old Nick or Bungaree—I did not know he was back.'

'And who the deuce is Bungaree?'

'He was a smart little black boy enough twenty years ago, when the idea occurred to old Moxon to send him with his own sons to the Normal Institution in Sydney, Dr. Lang's pet school. There Bungaree learned to read and write—moreover, Latin and Greek, with all other sophistications of the human animal, bringing home (for he was highly intelligent) more than his share of prizes. His success gratified all the good people mightily until he approached manhood.'

'And then?'

'Why, then, the wolf cub growled and broke his chain, took to the bush, blankets, and a wild life among his peers, learned to love the fire-water and to hate work and settled abiding places. It was he whom you saw to-day.'

During each forenoon Ruth was uncommonly busy, and visited so many shops that I inquired whether she was going to load a vessel with soft goods souvenirs of the Oxley; but I could not extract any satisfactory explanation, and was therefore fain to leave things to find their own level. I also discovered her deep in colloquy with Mr. Bright and Mr. Bagstock, and made no doubt but that with the assistance of these worthy gentlemen she was concocting some scheme by which the guests at the approaching school feast, or members of the aboriginal tribe, would profit.

Mr. Bright, with his usual munificence, had invited all the school children within a radius of ten miles to partake of his bounty, and had arranged that, in addition to a substantial lunch, with cakes and oranges and ginger-beer at discretion, suitable presents should be allotted to all the girls over ten years old. This was the department Ruth wished to supplement.

When the fateful day arrived, Ruth could hardly eat her breakfast for excitement, and immediately after that important meal I was dragged into the Police Camp Reserve, where the remnant of the once powerful and numerous tribe of the Oxley (long feared of the pioneer settler) had bestowed themselves.

It was a strange and perhaps a piteous sight. War and

disease, the fire-water of the white man, and the curses which ever accompany civilisation, had pretty well cleared out the 'braves' of the tribe. The men who had slain stockriders and speared cattle, killed shepherds, and caused stations to be abandoned a score of years agone, were chiefly absent. They lay on lonely sandhills or beside marshy lagoons, whither they had fled in vain hope of escaping the vengeance of the white man. A few stalwart survivors, sullen of aspect, showed in their bloodshot eyes and sodden countenances that they had found a panacea for all evils in the debasing habits which they had copied from the whites. Only the gray-beards of the tribe exhibited dignity and the true stately savage unconsciousness.

Each sat on the earth awaiting his turn of distribution ; and yet betrayed no eagerness to receive the gift to which they attributed so much value. They understood but little English and disdained all the arts by which a largess is stimulated.

The women and children predominated as to numbers, and these were the objects of Ruth's deepest interest and sympathy. Some of the half-caste children were exceedingly good-looking, and it was all I could do to prevent Ruth burdening herself with a pretty saucy five-year-old, whose mother offered to sell her in so many words for twenty shillings sterling. Though the woes of civilisation had worked much evil upon most of the women of the tribe, some of the younger gins, especially those whose complexions were 'dishonestly fair,' were lithe of form and pleasant to look upon. On these Ruth gazed with the deepest sympathy and unfeigned tenderness of pity.

'Poor things,' she said, 'what a lot theirs must be ! How I wish I could help them, could shape their lives into what charity and thoughtfulness might make of them. I feel quite sad that I shall go away and never see these strange, half-childish, fawn-like faces again. In their natural wistful expression I can fancy I see the half-formed forest creature we read of, not wholly human, yet all graceful and redolent of the old classical myths.

'My dear Ruth,' I remonstrate, 'you really seem to discover so many wonder-treasures in my country that you will never consent to return to your own. You ought to have married Bishop Selwyn, or some other evangeliser of the heathen instead of plain Hereward Pole.'

'I cannot imagine a more grand and ennobling manner of wearing out one's life,' she said, 'and you are not to laugh at me on such subjects, sir, or I shall think that the fire of trial has left some dross behind. Ask Mr. Bagstock when he is going to begin.'

That worthy and decisive official here advanced and saluted Ruth with flowing courtesy. With him were the Commissioner and Mr. Merlin. These gentlemen had been most assiduous in their attention to Ruth and the Squire since their arrival at the Oxley.

Considerably less than twenty-four hours, indeed, had been suffered to elapse before the higher officials from the camp presented themselves and duly left their cards upon the new arrivals, taking the opportunity of congratulating me cordially upon my return under such favourable auspices. The pleasure derived from the introduction appeared to be mutual. Ruth professed herself perfectly charmed with the Commissioner, whose air and bearing, she alleged, possessed a distinct flavour of chivalry hardly ever seen in these degenerate days. Mr. Merlin's flawless courtesy and carefully veiled satire created a natural astonishment in the Squire's mind that such a perfect and entire chrysolite, socially speaking, could be found in the wilds of Australia, while Mr. Bagstock's truly English appearance prepossessed him at once in favour of that gentleman, more especially when he discovered that his family lived in an adjoining county to Allerton Court.

Ruth had, very properly, though partly at my instigation, not attired herself in what some people consider to be suitable travelling raiment, which means their oldest and plainest garments. She had not set out with the notion that she was never to meet with any more ladies and gentlemen, or that, such being the case, it did not matter how unbecomingly she was dressed. On the contrary, she wore her last consignment of costumes, not very long from Paris, the freshness and fashion of which caused her to be regarded with a much deeper interest than would otherwise have been the case. Her manner being gracious, and her conversation original and piquant, she fulfilled thus all the conditions of pópularity.

The sergeant and a brace of picked troopers attended in charge of the coveted blankets, as well to dispense one by one those useful articles as to moderate any excessive eagerness which might be displayed by the wilder denizens of the forest.

As they approached—the old men coming first in order—each was asked his name, which was formally entered in a book by the clerk, when his woollen donation was delivered and duly debited to him. After the graybeards came the weird and awful beldames of the race. Savage women, after youth and middle age have passed by, are certainly the most unpleasing, not to say revolting specimens of humanity the traveller is called upon to view. Ruth shuddered as the chattering scolding crones came up, whining and entreating for a double allowance of blanket, always trying to smuggle an additional one for some fabulous grandchild, whose existence they were utterly unable to prove.

Gradually the ranks thinned. The fortunate recipients envelóped themselves in their prizes, or, folding them, sat down in majestic serenity upon them. Then came the boys —shy or bold, shamefaced or impudent—with roving hawk-like glances, rivalling those of the forest dwellers in piercing acuteness and wandering restlessness of vision. Lastly, the shy timidly-stepping girl children, with great gleaming dark eyes and dazzling white teeth, half-unclosed in wonder and half in terror.

When all, even to the tiniest elf, were supplied, Mr. Bright called one of the troopers to roll over another great package, and, opening it, commanded all the women to stand in a row. Then Ruth took my arm and walked over to it, producing a bright, coloured print dress and a warm garment fitted for winter wear. This she delivered to the oldest 'gin' with her own fair hands and in most genuine expression of goodwill. The poor old thing looked with perfect amazement at the fair and gentle benefactress for an instant, and then, realising the astounding fact, threw herself on her knees before her and kissed the delicate hand of the giver.

Then were handed out to the delighted foresters similar presents all down the line, until each one of the women and girls was made proud and happy by the same thoughtful gift. The men, indeed, looked jealous and awkward as not deemed worthy to partake of the bounty of this celestial visitant, as they appeared to deem her, but upon Mr. Bright saying a few mysterious words in their own tongue all discontent vanished and a pleasant anticipatory expression pervaded the party.

Finally, Mr. Bagstock called for three cheers for Her Majesty Queen Victoria, upon which a tremendous long-drawn cry, swelling and increasing in volume rose to the heavens, all eyes being turned to Ruth, as if with a conviction that Her Majesty had personally deigned to honour them with her presence ; but upon Mr. Bright making another short speech in the aboriginal tongue, which he had learned in his early outpost days, a deeper gratitude expressed itself in a gathering round of the whole tribe as if disposed to kiss Ruth's shoe latchet in reverent worship. Tears of joy and gratitude rolling down the faces of the younger women and girls showed that the darker complexion of these children of nature denoted no essential difference in the emotional qualities of the sex.

A portion of the tribe subsequently adjourned to the ground wherein the sports of the children's picnic were to be arranged, and gazed on the relaxation of the white man with edifying gravity. But, in the interests of truth, it must be related that the greater number of the adults betook themselves later on to the lower sort of public-houses, where they in too many cases sold the Queen's bounty for grog. Mr. Bagstock narrowly escaped holding a coroner's inquest upon one of the younger 'gins,' who had excited the wrath of her sable spouse, and was supposed to be lying at the bottom of a deep pool in the Oxley. Indeed that gentleman, at the first bruit of the affair, picked up a worn copy of Shakespeare in his hurry upon which to swear the jury, and was only prevented from completing his preparations by the return of the supposed corpse, but little the worse for blows and immersion.

There was ample time, owing to the early hour at which the ceremony had been initiated, for the completion of this preliminary performance before Mr. Bright's *clientèle* arrived.

This they presently commenced to do in great force, the rendezvous being the paddock of a friendly farmer, who granted the privilege of strewing his grounds with countless fragments of paper parcels and other debris of lunch to all such companies and associates as desired to make merry in the vicinity of the Oxley.

The spot selected was within a mile of the township. One of those natural forest parks peculiar to Australia, where green turf under the century-old trees and a moderately level surface permitted foot races, dancing on the green, kiss-in-the-ring, and other time-honoured rustic pastimes.

Mr. Bright, whose hospitable tendencies were unlimited, had made it understood that though the children were specially invited their relatives and friends were also expected, and would be equally welcome.

The day was of course fine. It was also moderately cool and breezy, so nothing could be more appropriate. Buggies and carriages were in attendance—a general holiday had been proclaimed by the Commissioner, by whom alone miners could be allowed to be legally absent from their claims. We all drove to the spot.

There stupendous preparations had been made and were still being made under the orders of Mr. Bright, who had preceded us and stood in the midst like a General of Division, ordering autocratically and issuing commands for fresh supplies, as if he was going to banquet the southern district *en masse*.

'I like to see things well done when one is about it,' said the Squire, as band after band of happy school children marched in, carrying banners and insignia, perfectly wild with happiness and youth—synonymous mostly. 'But, what a spread it will have to be; there must be a thousand children at least.'

'What a beautiful sight,' said Ruth in a tone of the deepest sincerity. 'I certainly never saw so fine an array of nice looking intelligent children before. So well dressed and well cared for, as they all look. Such bright intelligent faces, too. There is also a distinct refinement and high mental development which I don't think I ever observed among village children before.'

'I'll back the youngsters of this district, Miss Allerton,' said Bright effusively, 'against those of any part of Australia. I've been all over it, and I never saw anything to compare with them, I assure you.'

'It's a theory of mine,' said Olivera, who had joined our party, looking as if he had just quitted a London club, 'that the fusion of the different branches of the Aryan family, more than usually feasible in the concourse of a goldfield's population, is favourable to a high standard of mental and bodily excellence.'

'I don't doubt but you're right,' said the Squire. 'A border population is always a vigorous one, chiefly superior to the races of which it is compounded. It is to be hoped that you colonists will educate these youngsters thoroughly. There will be nothing commonplace about them, for good or for evil.'

'Miss Allerton shall examine them by and by,' said Bright. 'You should hear them sing, too. Most Australian children are musical, and all our schools attend to their chorus singing.'

'I am so pleased we were able to wait for this delightful spectacle,' said Ruth. 'I suspect you did it partly to please me, Mr. Bright. It was very kind of you, I could not have enjoyed anything more.'

'I don't suspect it at all,' I said. 'Bright's quite unable to resist any new lady visitor. It's a good thing you're going back to Sydney, there's no end to the extravagances he is capable of committing.'

'I hope he will never do anything that he will regret more. When we get back I must take this for a pattern for my school feasts at the Leys. But oh! if we could only be sure of such lovely weather.'

'There's where they have the advantage of us,' said the Squire. 'But I hope to see Mr. Bright and our other good friends there some day. Old England has its good points, and we must try if we can't show them something in return for all their kindness. When do you expect to see England again, Captain Blake?'

'Some of these fine days,' said the Commissioner, 'if my old uncle does the right thing by my brother Jack and myself, I hope to be able to keep a dog and enjoy a little hunting before I get too old, if I ever do. You can't get it good out of England.'

'Have to fall back upon coursing Chinamen, eh, Blake?' said Mr. Merlin, who had now joined us, looking refreshingly cool and as innocent as if there was not a criminal within a hundred miles. 'I am certain Miss Allerton would not have countenanced a chase we witnessed one morning, eh Pole?'

'Purely accidental, I assure you,' said Blake, turning graciously to Ruth, whose face became shaded over at this untoward allusion. 'Fact is, my poor dogs got demoralised by living in the camp with police and other man-hunters. Had to send them into the country, I assure you, to rub off the effects. But here's a movement along the whole line of infantry.'

The luncheon hour being imminent, a decided convergence had taken place towards the tents, of which every available one had been secured by Mr. Bright and his emissaries that the neighbourhood afforded. Besides this, large booths, walled and roofed with boughs and decorated with great fern fronds and tapering slender pine trees, had been erected.

Within these a generous supply of eatables and cautiously

composed concoctions for assuaging thirst had been provided.
The simple needs of childhood were amply gratified, while their
proud happy parents and friends did justice to the good cheer,
and inwardly chaunted the praises of their generous enter-
tainer.

'I think the last spread we had was a dejeuner at Hennessy's
to that distinguished novelist, Anthony Towers, wasn't it, Pole ?'
said Bright; 'only it was attended by children of a larger
growth.'

'Yes, I remember,' said the Major. 'Cuisine very fair and
Heidsieck's dry monopole to wash it down. The old Turk grate-
fully acknowledged it in his book on Australia by a faint
allusion and a statement that the cookery was better than the
speeches.'

'Comes of trying to give honour where honour is due,' said
Bright, 'but he did mention the oysters we had that night.'

'Yes, confound him ! You will go down to posterity with
the Bishop and Mrs. Proudie, and all that lot, as the munificent
banker who provided them.'

'What was it he said to you, Jack ?' inquired Mr. Merlin,
with suspicious softness of manner, 'when you asked him confidentially if he would have taken you for a native ?'

Bright hesitated for an instant, and then answered—

'"Not for an aboriginal certainly." What the deuce did he
mean by that ?'

We all shouted again. And Ruth 'came nearer,' as an
American friend would say, to a hearty laugh than I had seen
her for many a day.

The day wore on. Though warm, the atmosphere was so
tempered by the sighing breeze, which ever and anon came
whispering through the forest trees and over the sun-glinted
hill tops, that the most delicately constituted organisation could
not have felt oppressed.

The sports were nearing their close ; the little ones had eaten
and quaffed and romped and played and raced to their hearts'
content. Mr. Bright had made them a speech, praising their
proficiency at the various schools, on the Board of Management
of which he was a sort of perpetual chairman, complimenting
their parents and guardians upon their robust appearance and
polite manners, and winding up by formally inviting them all
to a similar picnic to take place, if he were well and at the
Oxley, on that day twelve months. If he was prevented from
attending, he was sure his friend Mr. Merlin would be happy
to take his place, knowing his warm interest in the education
question, and his proverbial liking for children.

This address, whatever might have been its rhetorical merit,
was sufficiently telling to 'bring down the house,' being
specially adapted to the audience, and boasting a peroration
more attractive than are many more ambitious efforts.

After this was over, one of the head teachers made a short

reply thanking their friend Mr. Bright, whose goodwill and kindness were proverbial from one end of Australia to the other, and calling for cheers for the lady from England whom they were all so glad to see among them and for Mr. Allerton.

Then a little voice which I fancied I knew called for three cheers for Harry Pole, a suggestion which apparently met with general approbation, and with a terrific storm of cheers for Mr. Bright the great array of happy children formed into their original ranks and companies and moved away to their respective homes.

Just then a trooper came galloping up, and saluted his officer.

'Mr. Merlin, a gentleman wishes to see you.'

'Indeed,' replied Mr. Merlin, in somewhat acidulated tones. 'Lead on at once. *I very seldom see one.*'

With this Parthian shaft, and his lowest, most courteous bow, Mr. Merlin departed, leaving us with a sensation of *sic transit gloria mundi*, and a disposition to move slowly homeward.

For my part, I thought that Ruth had undergone rather much fatigue and excitement for one day, and I was not sorry when our comfortable rooms at Hennessy's received us, and all further exertion was relegated to the indulgent future.

CHAPTER XLII

THE next morning's issue of the *Beacon* was filled up in great measure by the reports in detail of the blanket ceremony and of Mr. Bright's picnic, dwelling much upon the munificence therein displayed, and holding up for imitation the generosity of spirit which had always characterised that gentleman. 'We were pleased to observe among the spectators,' the editorial went on to say, 'the distinguished visitors from England who have lately honoured our goldfield with their presence. Miss Allerton and her father—the Squire of Allerton Court, in the county of Kent—accompanied by Mr. Pole, attended on the ground during the whole day, and took the most lively interest in the proceedings. The lady before mentioned, indeed, showed by her generosity on both occasions that her sympathy was truly genuine; and in the name of the residents of this goldfield generally we beg to thank her most cordially and respectfully for the intelligent interest in social and mining matters she has exhibited during her stay. Such visitors from the old country, even when, as in the present instance, of high social rank, do themselves honour as well as the mining population by temporarily relinquishing the privileges of their order, by mingling and conversing on equal terms with those around them. Such truly aristocratic conduct meets with genuine appreciation on a goldfield, and in no community is it more accurately gauged.

'Turning from such agreeable reflections, we regret deeply to have to allude to a presentment of the darker side of goldfield life, to verify the rumours of a tragedy enacted in our midst on the very day when far different scenes were witnessed at the Oxley.

'Our readers have been made aware from a perusal of our exhaustive mining reports of the daily improving character of the reefing industry at Mason's, and of the unprecedented rates to which certain scrip has lately reached.'

Such was then the nature of the summons by which Mr. Merlin had been reft so suddenly from the festal scene, and from the prospect of a *soigné* last dinner at Hennessy's, to which we had invited him, in company with the Major, Mr. Bagstock, Blake, and Olivera.

I was just in time to secure the copy in the breakfast-room, and to give Hennessy a hint to suppress that and any following issue, as far as our apartments were concerned.

What had happened was only hinted at, no further particulars being then obtainable, but on Merlin's return late at night (he had been officially present at the coroner's inquest) the ghastly details were brought out in the smoking room.

It would appear that the Great Columbia and Undaunted Quartz Reefing and Pyrites Reduction Company (Limited) had been paying so surprisingly well of late that the management, among whom Mr. Jake Challerson was a leading director, owning, indeed, one-eighth of the whole immensely rich claim, determined to give a lunch in entertainment of the metropolitan shareholders. Special coaches had been put on and the supposititious birthday of the Sovereign had been a gala day in every sense at Mason's.

Strangers, much wondering, clad in unwonted raiment, escorting prepossessing personages of the gentler sex, thronged the chief and only street of Mason's. Simple questions were asked as to familiar goldfields sights, and pretty expressions of wonder and delight issued from cherry lips. *Facile princeps* among the perhaps unconventional magnates of the directory, the illustrious Jake Challerson, unapproachably apparelled, redolent of fabulous wealth, was regarded with fluttering interest by the ladies, with ill-concealed awe by the younger members of the party.

Flags were flying along the narrow thoroughfare which, macadamised with glittering white quartz, and bordered by acres of plate-glass windows, looked like a street scene in an opera. Those miners whose labour was not actually necessary in the working had leave given, or had given themselves leave, as the case might be, to make holiday. The guests were hilarious and jubilant when not awe-stricken at the statistics blandly poured forth from the well-practised lips of their hosts. The entertainers were flowingly gracious and generous, as only gatherers of gold *au naturel* ever are. Many a quaint fragment, or matrix-encircled nugget, the weight of which astonished the fair recipient, was transferred 'without registra:ion' during a visit to the strong-room on that auspicious day.

Mr. Challerson, tall, languid, romantic-looking, posed as the Comte de Monte Christo, and gave on all sides with the thoughtful yet unqualified profusion of that illustrious *revenant*.

The guests enjoyed a full survey and fuller explanation of the great steam-driven quartz-crushing machine, with its celebrated battery, where scores of steel-shod stampers fell ceaselessly with regular irregularity upon heaps of pale stone throughout the long long summer day, the star-stream silent night. They shuddered as the ground, the whole strong edifice, seemed to quiver with earthquake tremor beneath the tremendous thuds of the tireless Briareus. They saw, when the streaming water carried off in solution the sand to which the matrix had been reduced, the thin lines of gold which the water was powerless to move, awaiting the hour of cleaning-up. They saw the very spot where the Chinaman fell last year, shot in the act of robbing the sluice boxes by night. Having undergone as much wonder, excitement, instruction, and intimidation as could be borne without refreshment, it was no wonder that the summons to lunch was hailed with deepest approval.

Lunch was served in one of the engine-sheds, which was brilliantly draped for the occasion, and ornamented out of its work-a-day appearance. Champagne flowed; the service was costly; the rarest fruits and flowers, specially forwarded by express, graced the board, which groaned under dainties and delicacies uncatalogued.

Mr. Jake Challerson was the life and soul of the whole party. After the refection was over, the 'cage' was brought into requisition and the whole party, prepared for fresh adventures, arrived safely at the lower level, and walked along the great main drive which, lighted up with coloured lamps for the occasion, presented somewhat the appearance of Aladdin's Cave.

The miners stood respectfully at the angles of the cross-cut drives, and listened with pleased astonishment to the soft voices and rippling laughter which aroused the unaccustomed echoes.

At length the cage began to make periodical upward ascent. By degrees the whole joyous party, assisted in safely bestowing themselves by Mr. Challerson, who chivalrously remained below till the last moment, regained the upper air.

Here Mr. Merlin, from whom the above sketch of proceedings had been elicited by incessant questioning, declined further interrogation. Handing in the depositions which he had brought back with him, he desired us to read for ourselves. I was chosen lector, and amid a silence which showed how deep was the interest, read as follows—

'This deponent, Hans Bunsen, on his oath states: "I am one of the wages men in the Columbia and Undaunted Company's workings. I remember the day of the picnic and lunch. A large party came to see the workings; they were lowered down the shaft in the cage, both ladies and gentlemen. I saw the deceased, Mr. Jake Challerson, there. I knew him as one of the principal shareholders in the Company. He was at Ballarat when I was there in 1851. He used to be called Yankee Jake. I do not know if he was an American. He had been in America I believe. He talked like one. I also knew deceased, Old Man Dick, as we called him; he had been working for the last two

years for the Company; he was a very silent man. We used
to think him a little touched—not quite right in his head. He
was a good man to work. I have heard that he was married,
and that his wife had run away from him; did not know of my
own knowledge or care, certainly not — what was it to me?
Every man's business is his own affair. There was a shot going
to be put in just at the bottom of the shaft; we wanted to take
down a bench there. The drill had been put in, and Old Man
Dick was waiting with the fuse until the party should go up.
Jack Martin and I, with two more men, were waiting in the
second cross-cut till the blast went off. Old Man Dick was in
the bottom of the shaft, and helped to send up the ladies and
gentlemen. Mr. Challerson was the last. He said, 'It's my
turn now.' He was just putting his foot into the cage when
Old Man Dick pulled him down. I heard him say 'No, you
don't. We'll go together directly. Yankee Jake, your hour
has come.' 'Who are you?' says Mr. Challerson. 'You old
madman, how dare you? let me go this instant. Help, murder!'
'Blast you,' says Dick, not loud, but very deadly like, 'don't
you know Richard Dunstan, whose wife you stole? Where is
she now. Chained up and whipped, may be, in a madhouse!
I'm a miserable half-mad wretch, and you're a fine gentleman,
Jake Challerson; oh yes, with money and white shirts and
diamond rings and a gold watch and friends, ha! ha! You
left me in hell—when you stole Dolores; now I'm going there
for good — and *so are you.* Then we saw them struggle—
very hard Mr. Challerson fought, till Dick picked up a drill and
struck him over the head with it. He fell upon his knees;
then Dick gave the signal and the cage was drawn up empty."
      'By the Coroner: "Why did not you and the other men rush
in and interfere?"
      '"We were going to do so, of course, but at the first start we
saw Dick had a lighted candle always close by him, and the
keg of powder open with which he had been filling the drill hole."
      'The Coroner: "What happened then?"
      '"We saw him drag Mr. Challerson close up to the keg; he
then took the candle in his hand. We ran for our lives along
the drive, and the next minute there was an explosion like a
thunderbolt, and we knew what had happened. The whole
place was filled with smoke, and stones and gravel sent along
the drive like shot. After a bit we went to the bottom of the
shaft. There we found two bodies. The roof of Mr. Challerson's head was gone, one of his arms was blown right off. Dick
was lying on his face stone dead but not torn about. He looked
as if he had been smothered. We signalled for the cage, and
with assistance sent both the bodies up."
      'John Martin, also sworn, corroborated the evidence of the last
witness. "Had been only a short time on the claim. Knew
Old Man Dick as a mate. Appeared to him to have something
on his mind. Could not be a better working man. Told him

(witness) one day that his wife had left him years ago, and that
he had never done any good since.   Believed, from what he had
heard, that the woman known as Dolores Lusada was the wife
of the deceased, Richard Dunstan."

'Egerton Wilson, being sworn, states : "I am the teacher of
the school established at Mason's, and have been resident there
since the reefs opened.   I knew the deceased director at Ballarat,
New Zealand, and in England.   His name was not Challerson,
nor was he an American, though he had lived in several
States and been in California.   For reasons of his own, he
assumed the American accent and professed to be a native of
that country. ; He was the youngest son of the Earl of Venhamsley.   I knew him as a boy, later on, when he was in the army.
He was compelled to sell out on account of a dispute at cards.
He left England immediately afterwards, and was some years
in America.   He came over from California to the Turon, where
I first met him.   He left afterwards for Ballarat.   When I met
him in New Zealand, a woman named Dolores was living with
him as his wife.   She went by the name of Mrs. Challerson.
Have since heard that she left him, and is now in a lunatic
asylum.   Decline to state whether deceased was connected with
the Ballarat riots, or whether I was implicated in the affair
myself.   We were both residents in Ballarat at the time.'"

John Bulder, it seems, had also to be called upon to give
evidence, his name having been mentioned by the miner known
as Old Man Dick to his comrades in the claim as an old friend
and acquaintance.   He went to Mason's without mentioning
his errand; we were only aware of the fact upon reading his
sworn testimony.   It was as follows : 'I recognise both the
deceased men before this inquest.   I knew the deceased, Richard
Dunstan, many years since, though I have not seen him since
he left Victoria.   He, I, and the other deceased, known as Jake
Challerson, but whose real name and title was the Honourable
Charles Dormer, he being a younger son of Lord Venhamsley,
worked together as mates at Ballarat in the year 1852.   The
fourth man was a Swede, named Dirk Olafsen.   Richard
Dunstan's wife, to whom he had lately been married, cooked
for the party.   Some months afterwards, when the Forest Creek
Rush was at its height, deceased Challerson and Dunstan's wife
eloped, and it was said lived there together.   Dunstan's reason
became unsettled through grief.   He was placed in the lunatic
asylum at Yarra Bend, where he remained for several years.   I
have seen Dunstan's wife at the Oxley since I have been on the
field.   She was then known as Dolores Lusada, which was her
name before she was married.'

By the Coroner—"Richard Dunstan was an honest hardworking man, whom every one respected.   He was always most kind
in his behaviour to his wife.   As to my opinion of the character
of Challerson or Dormer, I knew him to be one of the most
infernal scoundrels that ever walked the earth.   Am aware that

I am speaking of the dead. He ought to have been dead long ago. Decline to say whether Challerson was connected with the Eureka Stockade revolt; if so, it is a pity he was not shot when better men met their fate. Decline to state whether I took part in the rising myself. Am not aware that it concerns the facts of this inquest. Have no intention of being dis-respectful."'

John Bulder's was the last testimony, and, with Bunsen's, placed the motive of the deed in a light so clear and distinct that no further elucidation was needed.

It was a sad termination to the gay party, which, full of pleasant anticipation and ephemeral joyousness, had touched the glaring streets of Mason's with such unwonted brightness of colouring. The glamour of wealth, the false splendour shed by prosperity, however acquired, had dismally disappeared. The guests had fled in panic-stricken rush. The miners, save those needed as jurymen and witnesses at the inquest, had returned doggedly to their work. Two shattered corpses lay in the great engine shed, still incongruously gay with gaudy flags, which flapped all forgotten and unheeded. And still the quartz-crushing machine, with its ruthless ceaseless stampers, went thundering on from mid-day to midnight, unchecked, unslackened, still keeping up the same hungry sullen roar, as of a troop of lions.

The verdict of the jury, when divested of the legal phrase-ology with which it is considered still necessary to clothe such decisions, was to the effect—'That the deceased Jake Challer-son, otherwise Charles Dormer, and the deceased Richard Dunstan, had come to their deaths from injuries received con-sequent on the explosion of a cask of gunpowder, ignited by the said Richard Dunstan while in a state of temporary insanity.'

Such was the verdict of the jury, which no after legal action disturbed, but the stern sure verdict of the public at large, many of whom had known the slayer and the slain in years gone by, was that the prosperous criminal, the traitor, the betrayer, the false witness, and the shedder of innocent blood, had deservedly perished in the hour of his triumph by the hand of the most deeply wronged of his many victims.

'It is rarely,' commented the *Beacon*, 'that the painful duty is cast upon us of recording such awe-striking occurrences. The affair has naturally created a widely-spread sensation throughout the district, both the actors in the tragedy being well known among the mining community, although the more prosperous performer, he who had been so suddenly called upon to meet his fate, was of late more prominently before the public. As for the slayer, who assumed the terrible responsi-bility of compelling his own and his enemy's appearance before the bar of Heaven, let us assume that long brooding over his wrongs had deranged his mental powers, and that for the deed which hurried two unwarned human beings, with all their imperfections on their heads, into eternity, he was but indirectly responsible.'

These reflections and allusions only appeared on the day of our departure from the Oxley, and I had in the confusion of leaving no great difficulty in keeping them from Ruth's knowledge, not wishing to shock her unnecessarily, or to mingle her pleasant experiences of the goldfield with such darksome shadows. The locality being a few miles distant from our town favoured my efforts at concealment; nor was it until some months afterwards that Ruth learned why Mr. Merlin, John Bulder, and other acquaintances had been compelled to visit Mason's on the day after Mr. Bright's *festa*.

I arranged, on this occasion, with the obliging and ubiquitous firm of Cobb and Co. to have a special coach put on for our party, of course for a consideration, but one which I cheerfully paid for the very great additional comfort. Our party was to be augmented by the Major, who had at my solicitation consented to take a short holiday in the metropolis and leave the care of the claim temporarily to our trusty partners.

CHAPTER XLIII

IN view of our approaching departure, Ruth most conscientiously performed all valedictory duties and ceremonies, as to which she recognised a binding obligation. Little was left undone which might in after years afford cause of regret.

She had revisited the bank and refreshed her memory anew with the sight of the heavy masses of gold dust which lay darkly red in the metal shovels which were used to weigh and apportion them. She tried to lift again, with wondering exclamations, the mass of retorted gold which had come in from the quartz reef—one, indeed, the heaviest of all, from the last crushing of the Columbia and Undaunted Company Amalgamated. She smiled afresh at the old goldfields joke, wherein the courteous manager made a present to her of a bag containing a hundredweight and a half of the root of all evil if she could carry it away. She had paid special and exhaustive visits to Mrs. Yorke and Mrs. Mangrove, leaving with each of these representative matrons delicately-devised tokens of her goodwill or souvenirs in the time to come. Mrs. Yorke, indeed, parted from her with tears in her eyes, and averred that she never had taken to any one in her life so much since a certain lady who lived in the vicinity of her old home at Campbelltown used to have her in and teach her on Sundays and hear her read the Bible when she was a little girl, 'and a deal of good it did me, if you'll believe me, Miss Allerton,' she said. 'I've seen some rough people and rough doings since I've followed the diggings, but many a time when I've been tempted to turn on poor Cyrus that's gone, or do something foolish, the thought of Mrs. Blundell's kind, gentle, beautiful face would come before me just like the face of an angel, and I'd hear her sweet voice reasoning with me for my good, just as plain as I did in the happy old days. I never could do anything to displease her, and though it is twenty years ago, and she in her grave, the very thought of her makes me feel like a little child again. Yes, you're like her, Miss Allerton. You have the same voice, and you're the only living soul that ever reminded me of her.'

The term of our pilgrimage was completed. It had passed

over even more satisfactorily than I had anticipated. Nothing save the last harsh flapping of the wing of fate had occurred in the least degree to mar Ruth's enjoyment, to subtract aught from the kindly interest which she had from the first taken in the gold hive and its working bees.

No social duty, no farewell ceremony had been left unperformed by us. Everything had been scrupulously carried out, as with a tender fidelity, towards a spot we should neither of us revisit on earth.

Together had we stood again beside the grave of poor Jane Mangold, on which now the roses were blooming and the turf was green with the first autumn showers. Ruth's tears fell fast as she recalled how she had nursed me with unfaltering care and vigilance during the long weary days and nights when I was delirious after my wound, when (as she afterwards told me) I used to make the room echo with the name of Ruth, believing her to have forsaken and renounced me.

'But for her you might never have been spared to meet my eye again, Hereward, and I might have died, doubting, or at least not fully convinced of your love and truth, and to think that she, to whom we owe this, lies here beneath our feet, under this turf, dumb, voiceless, darkly blind to all beneath the sun. Ah me! what a tremulous, fearful joy is this life of ours. May God give us grace to live aright, and so order our lives that we may not fear the death summons that seems so perilously near at hand. Oh Hereward, "the pity of it!" if she could but have returned to the Leys, as you hoped and intended for her, what a joy it would have been to me to help to make the rest of her life happy. Poor, dear, ill-fated Jane! we must bid thee farewell on this earth for evermore, but you will not be forgotten or unmourned.' Here she stooped, and plucked one of the pale roses from the well-cared-for grave, and sighing, placed it in her bosom as we slowly left the spot.

It had somehow leaked out that we were to leave the Oxley 'for good and all' on the morning after. Long before our breakfast was concluded the Squire noticed that the streets seemed unusually crowded in the vicinity of Hennessy's corner. He inquired if there was a public holiday, or if any ukase of the Commissioner had gone forth proclaiming such to be lawful and of due force and weight.

'Not that I know of,' replied the Major, who was our companion at the morning meal, being indeed necessitated to bear us company even to the metropolis.

'Surely they can't be intending to say good-bye publicly and officially to us all?' asked the Squire. 'Who is it that is so popular? They can't have formed a profound admiration for an elderly country gentleman whom capricious fate has whisked away from his paternal acres. Hereward they know of old. It must be you, Ruth! What is your "charm," as a Frenchman would say?'

'A case of mutual admiration, love at first sight of the most pronounced type,' said Ruth, her whole face lighting up with enthusiasm. 'I really have taken an extraordinary fancy to Hereward's fellow-miners; I suppose they are gallant enough to return the compliment. I really believe they are gathering to see us off.'

This appeared to be the correct reading of the demonstration. As soon as the light American coach with its four well-matched well-conditioned greys drew up to the hotel door with our baggage carefully packed in the rack—a precautionary task I had supervised at an early hour—the street was seen to be crowded on both sides down to the farther angles. As I led Ruth towards the vehicle, a man stepped out of the densely-packed array, and raising his hat with a gesture of greeting essayed to speak. We arrested our steps. It was Mark Thursby.

'Happen ye'll stop, Miss,' he said, swaying his stalwart frame slightly, as though to accentuate the words, which with some difficulty he appropriated for the occasion, 'while I mak shift to givè ye my respects, and the o-pinion o' the miners on this field, as they've bidden me to do. They reckon as Harry Pole was allers a right-down, plucky, good-hearted chap, as worked like a man, and allers went straight, come fair weather or foul—a man as the miners was proud of, and a credit to the field. They wish him luck, and you too, Miss, and the Squire, wherever you go. They've made bold to ask you to accept of this here bit of a wedding present, a trifle of gold that'll make up into ornaments like, to remember the miners of the Oxley by when you're far away i' th' old country.'

Here the strong man bent his head in token of obeisance, and almost timidly presented Ruth with an assortment of metallic fragments, enclosed in a wash-leather bag. As she took them in her hand she knew by their weight the value of the offering, and also by the touch that one was a nugget of somewhat uncommon size.

She looked for one moment at the grand simple face of the miner, showing a power and dignity of its own, born of the consciousness of vast strength, calm courage, and unswerving honesty—the cardinal virtues of manhood. The light came to her eyes and a flush to her cheek—less rare in these days of returning health. Then the colour faded and her eyes filled as she said with a child's sweet unconscious pathos, tremulously resolved, as she tried to keep her voice steady: 'I thank you sincerely, Mark Thursby, and my future husband's comrades, for your rich and rare gift, which I shall wear on my wedding day. I am even more deeply grateful for the message of good-will to me and mine. I came here for the purpose of seeing the place and the people among whom Hereward had worked so long, and who had been so true to him in good and evil fortune. I shall be glad all my life that I have done so, and I now say farewell, and pray from my innermost heart that God may bless you all.'

I lifted her into the carriage. The Squire and the Major were already on the box seat. The high-conditioned leaders reared as the driver not unwillingly let them have their heads, when such a storm of cheers rent the air as caused the team to take the southern road, fortunately level, open, and well gravelled, at such a pace as freed the driver from any anxiety about being 'on time' for the mid-day stage. As we passed the camp we saw the whole force turned out in full uniform. Ruth raised her tear-dimmed eyes in time to view the majestic figure of the sergeant, whose ample beard seemed even more voluminous and imposing than usual; to mark Mr. Merlin on his gray charger; to recognise and return the military salute of the whole troop; and thus we bade adieu to the Oxley for ever. Hill and dale succeeded each other as quickly as the shifting scene of a panorama; plain and woodland came into view and receded beneath the tireless rattling hoofs of the game impatient team, which now rushed excitedly at their collars, and taxed the muscle of the driver's arm, even, with occasional aid from the brake. The Squire was the first to break silence.

'A twenty-mile stage to be run out from end to end at this pace, and no gruel thought of! What would they say in England, Major? We shall have to send here yet for our carriage horses, I foresee.'

Sydney once more. Again the blue wavelets of the peerless haven, the Italian sky, the white gleaming Grecian villas, the tropical foliage, the breath of the ocean, the murmur of the surges throughout the silent night. How these unwonted sights and sounds acted upon our sense and intensified the beautiful effect of change—mightiest agent, rarest of the luxuries purchased by wealth.

'Is this Sydney, or, by any pardonable mistake, Paradise?' murmured the Major, as we disembarked from our hansom at Batty's, Ruth and the Squire having preceded per four-wheeler from the Redfern terminus to Mrs. Pemberton's. 'It was very rash of me to come down before I was in a position to cut the whole thing, eh, Pole? Do you know I feel inclined now to toss up whether I shall go back at all. Write a line to the Bulders, telling them to take the claim themselves and send my share after me.'

'Why not? you and I have enough. What's the use of making oneself miserable for more? A few thousands more or less are "neither here nor there," as Cyrus used to say.'

'H—m!' meditatively replied the Major. 'I must consider that part of the case during the next fortnight. Try how the half-pay business works; haven't had any previous experience. This is almost too awfully jolly, I must say. Wonderful thing the sea, when you come to think of it, isn't it? as that brown-bearded stock-rider said, do you remember, who confessed that he saw it for the first time. Ha! ha! a breakfast under these circumstances isn't a breakfast, is it? No; always assuming that garfish are in season, it is a feast for the gods!'

Mrs. Allerton duly expressed and reiterated her extreme and unaffected surprise at the appearance of her daughter, whom she and Mrs. Pemberton asserted to have returned from her sojourn in the wilds of the interior in positively rude health.

Sydney appeared to have agreed passably well with Mrs. Allerton, *maugre* the heat and mosquitoes, these latter beasts of prey being kept at bay by the integrity of Mrs. Pemberton's curtains, while a daily walk in the Domain and the *entrée* to the Botanical Gardens had quite compensated for the minor inconveniences.

Matters being in such a highly satisfactory state, no valid reason could be adduced for deferring the ceremony which was to seal my long-deferred, now ofttimes despaired-of, happiness. The day was actually fixed, incredible as it may seem, and such perspective arrangements made as included the appointment of the Major as groomsman and such other necessary selections as befitted a very quiet wedding, where few but the actual personages and Ruth's parents were likely to attend.

So the great, the glorious day being decided on, after such interval as was required absolutely by the not altogether un-chronicled *modistes* of Sydney, the wedding raiment put in hands, *nous autres* had nothing to do but to wander about and enjoy ourselves, if possible, until my happiness could be transacted.

Somewhat to our surprise, the Squire joined us in all our excursions, and, like Dr. Johnson with Bennet Langton and Topham Beauclerk, professed himself keenly eager for the diversion of a 'frisk' in our company.

'I shall regret Sydney and these pleasant rambles I know when I return,' he would say. 'I wish the South Head lay within hail of us elderly country fogies!'

'Surely,' pleaded the Major, 'when you can run over to Paris in half-a-day, and have the capitals of Italy, Germany, Russia—what not—all within a week or so when you want a little change, and can pay for it, is there not enough to satisfy a reasonable Briton!'

'You didn't quite see my point, my dear Major. What is the advantage of Paris, Rome, Venice, half-a-score of capitals, with all the grandeur and glory of the world packed up among them, to me, Geoffrey Allerton, *ætat.* sixty? I'm too old to take pleasure in merely watching the parti-coloured stream of life flow by. "The brave days when we were twenty-one" have passed away with all that gave them joy and savour. I can't stare at picture-galleries all day long or listen to music by the hour either.'

'Then what do you want?' quoth the Major, 'for I can't for the life of me divine.'

'Does it not occur to you,' queried the Squire, looking at him with the kind, wise smile I remembered so well, 'that a man of my age and country tastes would much rather run across to a younger, a greater, and a newer England if he could do it by a week's travel, than to any of the places you have named? There he would see the agricultural problems that he had studied all his life worked out—by his own countrymen too—under other and more favourable conditions.'

'Now I begin to perceive,' said the Major. 'A light breaks in upon me. Hereward, the governor is a bigoted agriculturist; he has contracted the cockatoo complaint, I'm afraid; on the part of the "legitimate miner" I protest against him!'

'Not at all,' I say, coming to the rescue. 'It's the big grazing areas that have fetched him—hearing of Jimbour with a couple of hundred thousand sheep, and Boorooman with forty thousand head of cattle. Besides, we did see a hundred and fifty mares and foals in one paddock at Wendalong.'

'And not a bad one among them,' broke in the Squire. 'Well, I confess I could spend the winter here with the greatest possible enjoyment. These are the things which would interest me, and I own it. Besides, all the great properties are in the hands of Englishmen, managed more or less in English fashion. I don't take the same interest, I admit, in the operations of foreigners.'

'I can sympathise with you, Squire,' I said. 'For many a day I used to watch the farmers at their ploughing near Buninyong on a fine spring morning and long to have the stilts in my hand again. It always put me in mind of the Leys.'

'Australia has only to bide her time,' continued the Squire, who had become serious; 'but the march of events does not lag in these days of steam and telegraph. As the races swarmed westward in the old-world days when corn land and grass land became scarce, as the Norsemen later on took to their war galleys in search of free forage and brought home gold and captives, so now the surplus strength of Europe is passing over both oceans. Columbia will absorb one wing; but Australia, rich in minerals, soil, and sunshine, will bid high for the other. We are standing here in one of the great capitals of the world that is to be.'

'How you will surprise your old neighbours at Allerton Court when you return, Squire,' said I.

'I have gained food for thought, my boy, which will last me for the remainder of my days,' he answered earnestly, 'besides some comprehension of the prospects of my fellow Britons in the south, and that is more than most country gentlemen can say. Besides, mark my words, both of you—we have nothing to do but talk for a day or two, you know—a great change is coming over the British farmer, and, through him, over the landlord. With cheap corn from America, live stock and meat from this country, an enormous trade, hardly yet thought of, but, it strikes me, feasible enough, how can farmer Giles pay the rent he does now? Answer me that. He and his son must emigrate, I say; and where can they come to with half the chance of doing well as to a country with kingdoms of cheap land like this? And they will come—they must come; I feel assured of it.'

'It is a thousand pities, as you say, Squire, that Botany Heads are not within a week or ten days' trip, like America. They get the pick of our English immigrants; the voyage is so short that they are safely landed in less time than would have served to make up their mind about starting for Australia.'

THE day of days arrived at length, lingering as had been the diurnal periods—or rather ages, æons, eternities—which preceded it. But for the punctual appearance of the sun, that unfailing wonder-sign in southern lands, I might have imagined that some especial disarrangement of the solar system had taken place for my express discomfiture. Good kind Mrs. Allerton, in spite of my entreaties, would not abate an hour of the stipulated time which had been agreed upon as necessary for the awful preliminaries so incomprehensible to men. Ruth, too, was unkind enough to smile, and remark that as we had waited years an additional month could not matter so much. In vain I brought forward arguments as to the frightful uncertainty of human life, the prevalence of epidemics, the recklessness of cabmen, the tempests of the equinox, probable earthquakes, all things, and each which might occur to frustrate our new-found happiness if longer delayed. Nothing availed me. I was compelled to solace myself, as had other impatient lovers, with reflections on the curious obstinacy of a sex which poets and romancers have, for some inscrutable reason, conspired to depict as soft and yielding.

But the winds and the waves, the stars in their courses, the forces of nature, with the lesser powers of human life and society, combined to favour the votive and supreme ceremony of our love.

The sun-god of the south, celestial, effulgent, rose on the most entrancing day that had dawned since first the summer breeze whispered to the ocean 'neath the lone headlands or by the silver sands of Rose Bay; surely on that charmed strand the fays of the southern main first danced to the mystic moon. Clear and bright as the 'gold bar of heaven' I watched God's glorious messenger of light and warmth majestically uprise through an azure cloudless sky. It was the pale dawn flushed and glowed. It was the city of the Apocalypse—amber and pearl, rose, amethyst, and jacinth. All things were transfigured. It was from a fresh creation I seemed to issue forth, redeemed from a world of strife and labour, henceforth to inhabit a sphere of peace, of radiant happiness, which was to know no time or limit. We were but a small party as we met at the massive, old-fashioned, but still favourite and venerable church, with its alleys of araucaria and Moreton Bay fig-trees. Hard by was Mrs. Pemberton's house and the glorious sea-terraced garden pleasaunce wherein we had wandered so many happy hours. With the Major, whose faultless attire defied the most fastidious club critic, came Mr. Bright, whose leave of absence appeared perennial. The Commissioner, with Mr. Merlin and Olivera, had managed to sever themselves temporarily from their onerous duties, and to stand by me on that day. Certain delicate-featured willowy - figured Sydney demoiselles, friends of Mrs. Pemberton's, who had professed themselves quite too awfully charmed to assist at such a touching ceremonial, officiated as bridesmaids, and these were the only stranger guests in all the company. Ah, how different would it have been at Allerton Court !—a remark which Mrs. Allerton could not help making in the maternal fulness of her heart. But she saw the bright hues of health again mantling on Ruth's cheek. so long a stranger to the warmer tints, and marked the love-light which glowed and sparkled in her soft bright eye. The flower-laden ocean breeze stole through the open windows of the old church, and during the hush and stillness, with the solemn tones of the aged clergyman, mingled ever and anon melodious surge-voices, chaunting their deep rhythmical anti-strophe. The beauty and strangeness of the surroundings, where we now indissolubly sealed our union, overcame her motherly o'ercharged heart, and the tears of joy and thankfulness filled her eye and rolled unheeded adown her cheek.

Our wedding dejeuner, though a tiny festival, was complete ; and, thanks to Mrs. Pemberton's taste and sympathy, utterly perfect in detail.

Merlin confessed that he had never tasted such champagne since his last dinner at Very's. Mr. Bright proposed the health of the leading performers with effect and feeling. The Major was compelled to undertake the toast 'The bridesmaids,' which doubtless he did under a mental reservation equivalent to 'without prejudice.'

The Commissioner and the Squire arranged to meet in North-amptonshire, not far from the historic Kirby Gate, in two years' time, which appointment, strange to say, did come off, by reason of the uncle of him (Blake) dying in the meantime and making testamentary dispositions of astounding liberality.

We had planned to pass our earlier wedded days amid the fern-fringed glades and weird primeval forests of New Zealand. The month had not ended when we were steaming south over the restless sea which heaves and moans evermore before the still fathomless fiords of the West coast and the snow peaks of Treble Mount. We explored the hot blue springs of Waiwera, and luxuriated by starlight in the alabaster shell baths of Rotomahana.

We saw the magic lake that divides the pink and the white terraces ; more marvels of the land of the Maori ; the yellow and green mosaics ; the silver-fretted fairy rock-work, so beauteous seeming to the eye, so wondrous soft to the touch. Ruth's state of mind almost approached intoxication ; her admiration was boundless.

'I can imagine all about those people who came here and never returned to civilisation. The lotus-eaters were no myths after all. This is the land of enchantment.'

Ruth now congratulated herself that she had, early in her *suzeraineté*, signified her intention of thoroughly acquainting herself with this new world before she returned to the old for the remainder of our days.

'We are young and adventurous now,' she said, 'or at least I am. Before we settle down to the dear unchanging English country life, why should not we see as much of this wonderful land of yours—the land which has done so much for both of us—as we can ? In the long dark winters and not too sunshiny summers of our northern home will it not be pleasant to recall this free untrammelled life — this wandering hand - in - hand through the Eden that now lies around us ?'

'I never heard of a female Vanderdecken,' I say musingly. 'Can it be our fate to travel everlastingly, "prospecting" for hidden treasures of knowledge till we are too worn and gray to utilise them ?'

'You are the laziest creature,' she says, pretending to frown. 'I believe you never would have made anything more than tucker—isn't that the expression ?—if it hadn't been for your mates and your backers, male and female, eh, sir ?'

'May I be permitted to express a hope that Mrs. Hereward Pole will not come out with expressive colonialisms when—I mean if—we return to England.'

'Mrs. Hereward Pole—how very grand a title—is generally *en accord* with her surroundings, social or otherwise. But seriously, Harry dearest, you are not in a hurry to find yourself *planté là* in the dear old kingdom of Kent ? Can we be happier than we are now, without a thought of the morrow, without cares or engagements, and with "a new heaven and a new earth" uprising before our gaze with every morn. In the after time, if we are like other people, we shall have sufficient same-ness and settled life to content the most *exigeante* of British matrons.'

'I will go with you to the end of the world,' I mur-mured ; 'we will sail on thus "till the sun grows cold and the stars are old," only let me lie at your feet and gaze into your eyes, love-illumined and tender-bright, for ever, as I do now !'

The Squire and Mrs. Allerton did not desire to explore

further the earth's surface, and having, as they thought,
sufficiently improved their understanding with travel and
adventure, they placed themselves on board the Peninsular
and Oriental Company's majestic steamer *Hindostan* without
unnecessary waste of time. Mr. Allerton much congratulated
himself that they had evaded the rigours of an English winter,
and would arrive just in time to welcome the budding leaves of
spring.

For ourselves, we carried out Ruth's programme, to which I
secretly inclined all the more for having observed that the
free unmonotoned life of 'riding o'er land, sailing o'er sea,' was
building up her constitution to a point of vigour and endurance
which I could scarcely have hoped for in her early Australian
days.

So beneath the Southern Cross we roamed far and wide
and saw many things, and ere the winter winds commenced to
howl, like wolves baying around the ice-peak of the Pole, we
fled away towards the summer isles of the purple sea, and there
possessed our souls in halcyon enjoyment.

Hand in hand we watched the graceful flower - wreathed
maidens of Hawaii dance, as the earth's first-born daughters
danced beneath the broad moon's silver ray ; saw the Kanaka
dive through the transparent water of coral-fringed bays, and
watched the cocoanut palm wave welcome to the fleets of swift-
darting canoes with their joyous oarsmen. We brushed with
careful foot the smouldering lava of Kilauea, through the
crevices of which Ruth, shuddering, marked the red glowing
eternal fires of a nether visible and palpable hades. We gazed
on the vast blocks and silent halls of the great temple of Iono—
built by the hands of the spectral dead. At midnight we were
lighted on our homeward path by a heaving sea of molten fire,
through which the red domes of lava arose to heave and fall—
in hissing fragments, amid pale green films of vapour, and a
faint lace-tracery of mist.

Still another moon and we are on board the *New York City*,
among the passengers, who were regaled with ice still pure as
when first from the caves of Lake Wenham, and salmon fresh
as when congealed the first day of its capture. Entering by
the Golden Gate we saw the other great gold city of the earth
—San Francisco, and were entertained by a cousin of poor Gus
Maynard with the royal hospitality in which Americans excel
all the nations of the earth. Under his guidance, or rather in
his train, we 'did' the Yosemite, Los Angelos, the Mammoth
Tree, and even, what interested Ruth most, the wall of the old
mission St. Pedro, whereon were traced legends not unconnected
with 'the old, old song,' old when these old walls were young,
'Manuela of La Torre.' Onward again by trains which threaded
the awful snow solitude and lone peaks of the Rocky Mountains,
through great cities which had been waving forest solitudes
but yesterday, over prairie-oceans where the far horizon showed

nor hill nor tree—naught but endless flower-strewn plains, as league after league stretched beneath the tireless swift-speeding iron steed, over billowy waving seas of giant grasses and lavish herbage products of the boundless generosity of nature in the far west, over tressel bridges which trembled and vibrated as the long train wound its oscillating way across shuddering abysses. We reach the ocean of the north, again the wondrous Atlantic shore ; we dwell in great cities, wondering and awe-stricken at the labour results of the Briton left free to develop his many-sided nature and boundless energy in a new land of limitless resources. We commence to feel restless — only a week and then home, home!—ah, me! The wanderers have reached home—England, the dear old chalk cliffs of Albion—at last.

From my old friends and true comrades can I now part for evermore without further mention? Can I leave the generous sympathetic reader of these rambling pages to pine in uncertainty, rendering herself uneasy as to what became of Mrs. Yorke and Mrs. Mangrove, whether Mr. Merlin married, if the Commissioner returned to England, or Mr. Bright became chief inspector of banking institutions, with *carte blanche* for champagne and oysters, and unlimited leave of absence? He who indites even so humble a chronicle of men and manners as this, which now draws to a close—and time, too, perhaps grumble impatient youth, when the heroine is married—cannot complete the task without a tender feeling of regret. Have we said farewell, and for ever, to all the personages, fair and friendly, loyal or false, gentle and simple, which have moved, have spoken, have strutted their hour upon our tiny stage? Shall we never meet again in this world? Alas! some are dead and gone ; even in the world of fiction there is a savour of reality ; and we could mourn—if we might—for the bright eyes that have 'forgotten to shine,' for the brave hearts whose pulses are for ever stilled. When the golden holes known to this day as Greenstone Dyke and No. 4 claims were exhausted and utterly worked out, the party was broken up for good and all. The whole plant, the whim, the tools, the huts, the Major's cottage —every mortal thing down to a worn-out hide bucket—was sold by auction and the proceeds divided among the shareholders. Roan Bessie, the whip-horse that had drawn up so many thousand buckets of washdirt, was bought in by Joe Bulder, who had made up his mind to purchase an estate on the Hawkesbury and settle down to his old occupation of farming. In this resolution he was supported by Mrs. Yorke, who had definitely consented to become his wife, and to entrust her 'pile,' as she phrased it, and the welfare of her children to her late husband's comrade.

'Now the ground's worked out and the party broke up,' she said in explaining the matter to Mrs. Mangrove confidentially, 'I feel that unsettled that if there was a new rush broke out in

the middle of Californy I'd be bound to follow it, which must
be foolishness with all the money I've got in the bank. So jest
as I was thinkin' how awkward it 'ld be not to have a soul to
cook for or to chaff a bit when they come in from work, and
grizzlin' over poor Cyrus as is dead and gone, this old Joe must
come and ketch hold of my hand and offer to take a half share
in all future interests. Well, I agreed to transfer, with the
parson for registrar, and I don't know as I could better it much.
Marryin's a long lease not easy cancelled if the labour conditions ain't carried out as we've all seen on this field. But Joe
and poor Cyrus was always good mates. He's as sober and
steady as Roan Bessie, very nigh ; never was off his shift, hot or
cold, wet or dry. He'll be a good dad to the young 'uns, and
he's that used to doin' what I tell him that it won't come
strange to him by and by, as it might to some chaps as never
worked in the party.'

So Mrs. Yorke, holding that it would simplify matters, was
married first, and travelled down country afterwards with Roan
Bessie and another horse in a cart with the children and other
portables much in the same fashion as they had come to the
rush. They could begin to be top sawyers, she said, when they
got to Sydney, and then they could make a fair start and launch
out at their leisure.

I am bound to say that their wedding, as reported in the
Beacon, was an imposing affair, and in a manner far more
splendid than ours. The Oxley Church of England building
was so full that seats were not procurable, and numbers of the
friends of the bride and the bridegroom, who had rolled up in
force, were constrained to stand outside.

A stupendous breakfast at Hennessy's is yet quoted in mining
circles, at which the health of the happy pair was drunk in
every conceivable liquor, from lager beer to maraschino, while
the benediction was pronounced in more tongues than had been
set going at once since the Tower of Babel. And the ball at
night, at which the happy pair led off the first dance, was such
an entertainment as recalled the 'brave days of old' to all old
prospectors and 'forty-niners.'

Next day, before the sun was well up the camp was deserted
and Joe and his wife on their way to Sydney.

Jack Bulder had, fortunately for himself, joined the ranks of
the Good Templars some months since. He, therefore, was
enabled to appear at the marriage and subsequent festivities
without risk, and on those somewhat dangerous occasions—
teetotally speaking — he conducted himself with a perfect,
though somewhat pensive propriety. He consistently declined
matrimony on his own account for the time to come, residing
at intervals with his brother, to whose children he willed his
fortune in anticipation of the sudden death which he always
prophesied would be his fate. Some years afterwards he was
drowned by the foundering of his yacht, the *Favourite,* in a

gale, between Melbourne and Sydney, when his bank shares
served to consolidate the increasing prosperity of the Yorkes
and Bulders, the second generation of which, well educated
and well endowed, may yet take rank among Australian
notables.

Some weeks after we had left the Oxley, Edward Morsley
was put upon his trial at the Assize Court held at Russell, and
after a careful and protracted examination of the evidence
found guilty of wilful murder and sentenced to death. Beyond
reiterating a statement that poor Jane had taken her own life
in despair at being at the last moment prevented from sailing
for England, he made no attempt to exculpate himself or evade
his doom.

Remorseless ruffian though he might be, he was 'brave with
the she-wolf's courage grim, dying hard and dumb, torn limb
from limb.' When the drop was finally arranged, and after he
had been pinioned, he motioned to the hangman's assistant as
if wishing to speak. The clergyman came over—he had in vain
urged him to confess—and listened intently. These were the
criminal's last words : 'Now look here, what I want to know is
this : am I standing perfectly square and straight?' The good
man sighed and commenced the prayer for the dying. The
drop fell, and the innocent blood was avenged as far as human
justice could compass such expiation.

It was a fact—let us say a coincidence—that within a year
of our departure by easy stages for Europe, unlooked-for good
fortune commenced to shower its benefits upon nearly all the
members of our *camaraderie*. The Commissioner's uncle died,
leaving him and that brother with whose name and fame we
were tolerably familiar, a considerable fortune. Mr. Jack
Blake acted up to his Christian name and family traits (was
there ever a Jack of sordid soul?) He divided the inheritance
with the Commissioner, whereupon that high official swiftly
departed for England, taking two couple of his kangaroo dogs
with him. Smoker and Spring he could not leave behind,
while Forester would show some of the home coursing men that
in roughish country a 'dawg' reared in Australia could make it
very hot for the hares of the period.

The last sensational legend that will ever be told by Australian camp fires about 'The Captain,' arose out of the grand
farewell dinner in his honour the evening before he started for
Sydney *en route* for Europe. The officials of the goldfield, the
gentry of the district and the neighbouring towns, mustered
strong. The wines were undeniable. The honour of the Civil
Service stood involved ; there was but little flinching. Towards
the end of the evening a slight difference of opinion arose between Blake and an argumentative surgeon formerly in the
army ; moreover born north of the Tweed. It referred to a
question of genealogy, leading to that of the county rank and
precedence of his family, anent which sacred subject Blake was

wont to be unusually stiff and dignified towards the small hours.

As ill-luck would have it, the contumacious doctor accompanied him and Bagstock towards the camp after all was over, when he was ill-advised enough to recommence the argument.

'It's a vara odd thing, noo I come to think o't,' he said musingly. 'I was quartered in Galway, close to Tuam and Dunmore, for three years. I can recollect fine the Dillons and Brownes, the Frenches and O'Malleys, by the score, but the de'il a Blake I can ca' to mind for the life o' me.'

'By —— !' growled the Commissioner, and as he spoke he seized him with both hands, and exerting his enormous strength, lifted him high in the air as if he had been a child. 'You'll remember one of the Blakes after this night, I'll go bail.'

A deep-water race just then crossed their path in which the ice-cold waters led from a mountain stream hurried, gleaming in the dim light. Into this Blake dashed the unlucky Doctor, and striding forward, left him to struggle out the best way he could with Bagstock's aid, whose only consoling remark, as he dragged out the dripping and sputtering victim, was 'I should have thought you had more s-s-sense, Doctor, than to argue with the Commissioner at t-t-two o'clock in the m-m-morning.'

A bronzed soldierly-looking man, whose straight going and utter indifference to obstacles are somewhat at variance with his snow-white hair and beard, has for some seasons been well known with the Pychley—a dead shot, an authority on greyhounds which brings him nearly on a level with Stonehenge as a referee and authority, the latter days of the erstwhile 'Billy' Blake of the 11th Hussars—whose name was the synonym for feats of daring, beside which foolhardiness was cautious prudence—pass peacefully and happily. But still in all parts of Australia, when miners gather round a camp fire, or the tongues grow lissom under the influence of good fellowship and potent liquor, some racy saying or autocratic act of Commissioner Blake's is quoted, and for long years yet the name of 'The Captain' will be a spell to conjure with on the banks of the Oxley.

Mrs. Mangrove and John, true to their principles, were among the earliest arrivals at the great Matamora rush, which occurred years after the Oxley. There they erected the first hotel and sold it at a large profit. They built another, specially retaining the name, and stocked a large store before the second detachment of new arrivals flocked in. As the first American coach arrived, carrying about fifty odd passengers, and the reins of the seven horses handled by a gigantic Canadian were thrown to the helpers, there was such a rush to Mangrove's Hotel that the inexperienced felt sure that a fight or a bushrangers' raid was on (so the *Matamora Herald* pleasantly put it).

'It's only "the boys," John,' said the long - experienced hostess, as the bronzed and bearded faces, fresh from Queensland, New Zealand, Victoria, and Kiandra, welcome breathing, thronged the hotel, hustling one another like school boys, and casting their swags recklessly on the verandah.

Mrs. Mangrove expressed herself to the effect that it was quite like old times. John, who had been smiling silently throughout the whole performance, merely replying as he gave expressive nods to the hearty greetings of old acquaintances, 'regular stunning good rush, boys ; 120 oz. nugget got by one man simply.'

Mr. Bright, like the Commissioner, was indebted to a considerate relation for a bequest which, somewhat to his regret, absolved him from the necessity of forming branches at new goldfields and defending the property of the Bank of New Holland like a mediæval champion against all comers. He and Mr. Merlin met in Paris the following year, when the latter gentleman was enabled to display his proverbial knowledge of gastronomy under the most favourable conditions, and together they experienced such dinners as can only be realised in dreams south of the line. We had the pleasure of talking over old times with them during the shooting season at Allerton Court, where Australian stories were reproduced for the benefit of some of the magnates of the county—tales of wonder to which Mr. Bright's exceptional shooting, when we got to the preserves, lent ample corroboration.

Surely it is decreed and fore-ordained that the lives of some men should be divided into periods of war and peace. The youth of those who, like myself,

> 'Have striven and toiled and fought it out,
>   Under the hard blue sky'

of a far land is filled full of the hazard and the glory, the grim perils and the stormy joys of war, of dreary watching in trenches, dogged endurance of defeat, intoxicating triumph of victory.

To some men-at-arms it is given to march proudly in through the gate of the beleagured city of Fortune, with drum and trumpet and banners flying, while comrades lie dead in the breach or disabled on the plain.

Let him who emerges from the battle of life safe, enriched, and honoured by all men, be more than content, be humbly thankful to the great Being by whose mercy he, all unworthy, was spared while so many perished on the march or the stricken field.

For me, Hereward Pole, the reign of peace has distinctly set in, now and for ever. Henceforth, save when the shadow of the wing of Azrael the Death Angel, from whom no household rich or poor may claim immunity, darkens my threshold, no faintest fear of fate or trace of care or grief was mingled with my life.

I was fortunate in being able to purchase an estate which marched with Allerton Court, and which the Squire, in a mild and Christian-like way, had always coveted. The house was delightful—perhaps too large and complete for the land which surrounded it. But for that we did not particularly care. My son would be the heir of Allerton Court, and in the fulness of time, upon the death of the Squire, which apparently will not take place for long years to come—would that he may become a centenarian—we shall occupy that time-honoured pile.

And do I manage to fill up satisfactorily the great intervals of absolute leisure in this wholly new and untried life, free from all necessity to work with head or hand—a pensioned idler and non-combatant, guaranteed against all the ills of mortality except *ennui* ?

Well, yes, I get along, and find unalloyed happiness a fairly payable claim. Ruth and I are nearly as much at Allerton Court as at Combe Hall, our own, our very own place, which is almost too comfortable, not to say luxurious. The Major has pretty well taken up his abode with us, and the Major's room is one of the recognised apartments of the house. He is a confirmed bachelor; our friendship is, therefore, unlikely to alter in degree. When country life palls upon us, we are graciously permitted by Ruth to fish in Norway, to hunt in the shires, to run down to Scotland in the grouse season, and even, one particularly cold winter, to try a little lion-stalking in Algeria.

I am a magistrate, and thus moderately interested in county business. Besides, London is not such a very bad place for a few days now and then. Rome and Venice we think we know something about; but we are forbidden to go to Russia, or to stay more than a fortnight in Paris at a time. With a few of these distractions, always accessible within forty-eight hours or a trifle over, it is surprising how the year gets disposed of. Every now and then a fresh Australian turns up that I hear of at the Reform Club, the Travellers, or the Athenæum, and I bring him out to Ruth's great interest and satisfaction. Olivera himself appeared one day, having 'at long last,' as his Irish mate said, made a fortune suddenly in tin, and become one of the leading capitalists of Stanthorpe. He had played a waiting race, and won fortune's sweepstake on the post in the last heat.

In my study, as the modest apartment is called which contains my private and personal effects, hang many prints, pictures, and other delineations, more or less *en souvenir* of far lands and strange adventures. But the one which I occasionally find Ruth and the children gazing steadfastly at — our nursery is pretty full and Hereward the second, commonly called Harry, is growing a big boy and clamorous for a Shetland—is a small much-crumpled piece of parchment, framed in wonderful dead gold Venetian, and which, after detailing for the hundredth time some spirit-stirring goldfields adventure of which papa was the hero, she proudly describes, for the benefit of any youthful visitors, as a talismanic document without which no one can dig gold in Australia—none other, in fact, than a real, true, authentic 'Miner's Right.'

THE END

Printed by R. & R. CLARK, *Edinburgh.*

MESSRS. MACMILLAN AND CO.'S PUBLICATIONS.

MACMILLAN AND CO.'S POPULAR NOVELS.

Crown 8vo, Cloth extra, 3s. 6d. each.

BY F. MARION CRAWFORD.

MR. ISAACS : A Tale of Modern India.
DR. CLAUDIUS.
A ROMAN SINGER. | ZOROASTER.
MARZIO'S CRUCIFIX.
A TALE OF A LONELY PARISH. | PAUL PATOFF.
WITH THE IMMORTALS.
GREIFENSTEIN. | SANT' ILARIO.
A CIGARETTE-MAKER'S ROMANCE.
KHALED : A Tale of Arabia.
THE WITCH OF PRAGUE. | THE THREE FATES.

BY CHARLOTTE M. YONGE.

1. THE HEIR OF REDCLYFFE.
2. HEARTSEASE. | 3. HOPES AND FEARS.
4. DYNEVOR TERRACE. | 5. THE DAISY CHAIN.
6. THE TRIAL : More Links of the Daisy Chain.
7. PILLARS OF THE HOUSE. Vol. I.
8. PILLARS OF THE HOUSE. Vol. II.
9. THE YOUNG STEPMOTHER.
10. THE CLEVER WOMAN OF THE FAMILY.
11. THE THREE BRIDES.
12. MY YOUNG ALCIDES. | 13. THE CAGED LION.
14. THE DOVE IN THE EAGLE'S NEST.
15. THE CHAPLET OF PEARLS.
16. LADY HESTER AND THE DANVERS PAPERS.
17. MAGNUM BONUM. | 18. LOVE AND LIFE.
19. UNKNOWN TO HISTORY. | 20. STRAY PEARLS.
21. THE ARMOURER'S 'PRENTICES.
22. THE TWO SIDES OF THE SHIELD.
23. NUTTIE'S FATHER.
24. SCENES AND CHARACTERS.
25. CHANTREY HOUSE.
26. A MODERN TELEMACHUS. | 27. BYE WORDS.
28. BEECHCROFT AT ROCKSTONE.
29. MORE BYWORDS.
30. A REPUTED CHANGELING.
31. THE LITTLE DUKE.
32. THE LANCES OF LYNWOOD.
33. P's AND Q's, AND LITTLE LUCY'S WONDERFUL GLOBE.
34. THE PRINCE AND THE PAGE.
35. TWO PENNILESS PRINCESSES. | 36. THAT STICK.
37. AN OLD WOMAN'S OUTLOOK.

MACMILLAN AND CO., LONDON.

MACMILLAN AND CO.'S POPULAR NOVELS.

Crown 8vo, Cloth, 3s. 6d. each.

BY J. H. SHORTHOUSE.

JOHN INGLESANT.
SIR PERCIVAL.
THE LITTLE SCHOOLMASTER MARK.
A TEACHER OF THE VIOLIN.
THE COUNTESS EVE.

BY MRS. CRAIK.

(The Author of "John Halifax, Gentleman.")

OLIVE. With Illustrations by G. BOWERS.
THE OGILVIES. With Illustrations by J. McL. RALSTON.
AGATHA'S HUSBAND. With Illustrations by WALTER CRANE.
HEAD OF THE FAMILY. With Illustrations by WALTER CRANE.
TWO MARRIAGES.
THE LAUREL BUSH.
MY MOTHER AND I. With Illustrations by J. McL. RALSTON.
MISS TOMMY: A Mediæval Romance. With Illustrations by FREDERICK NOEL PATON.
KING ARTHUR: Not a Love Story.

BY MRS. OLIPHANT.

A BELEAGUERED CITY.
JOYCE.
NEIGHBOURS ON THE GREEN.
KIRSTEEN.
HESTER.
HE THAT WILL NOT WHEN HE MAY.
THE RAILWAYMAN AND HIS CHILDREN.
THE MARRIAGE OF ELINOR.
SIR TOM.
THE HEIR PRESUMPTIVE AND THE HEIR APPARENT.

MACMILLAN AND CO., LONDON.

MESSRS. MACMILLAN & CO.'S PUBLICATIONS.

THE CRANFORD SERIES.

THE VICAR OF WAKEFIELD.

By OLIVER GOLDSMITH. A new Edition, with 182 Illustrations by HUGH THOMSON, and a Preface by AUSTIN DOBSON. Second Edition. Crown 8vo. 6s. Also with uncut edges, paper label. 6s.

TIMES.—"We cannot conclude without mentioning an attractive reprint of an old favourite, *The Vicar of Wakefield*, with a preface by Austin Dobson, and illustrations by Hugh Thomson, sufficiently recommended by the congenial pencil of the artist and the congenial pen of the author of the preface."

PALL MALL GAZETTE.—"Mr. Thomson shows infinite invention and variety in the two hundred drawings—some of them decorative head and tail pieces, but most of them illustrations to the text—scattered through the volume."

SATURDAY REVIEW.—"One of the best illustrated *Vicars* we know."

QUEEN.—"The edition is most profusely and most graphically illustrated by Mr. Hugh Thomson, who has most truthfully retained the costumes and represented the customs of the period, without in any sense losing the individualism of the characters represented."

SPEAKER.—"The delightful story has never been illustrated in a more pleasing fashion than in this charming little volume—for this is an edition of the *Vicar* to be read, and lovingly cherished on the book-shelf in the chimney corner where one's favourite companions stand side by side, instead of being relegated to the formal pomp of the glazed and wired bookcase, or left to lie upon the drawing-room table. It is delightful alike to hold, to read, and to scan with an eye to the illustrations. . . . Such an edition as this of Goldsmith's prose idyll will be welcome everywhere as an old friend in the daintiest of new attires."

CRANFORD.

By Mrs. GASKELL. With Preface by ANNE THACKERAY RITCHIE, and 100 Illustrations by HUGH THOMSON. Crown 8vo. 6s. Also with uncut edges, paper label. 6s.

PALL MALL GAZETTE.—"One is almost tempted to think, as one turns over the pages of this delightful edition, that Mrs. Gaskell must have written *Cranford* with a prophetic eye for Mr. Hugh Thomson as an illustrator. All the characters in the little village society gain by Mr. Thomson's sympathetic delineation."

DAILY NEWS.—"It is no small feat to have added a chapter to *Cranford* which will enhance the pleasure of the reader of that delightful sketch."

DAILY TELEGRAPH.—"Never have Mrs. Gaskell's charming sketches of *Cranford* appeared in daintier guise. . . . *Cranford* can now boast of a preface that is as near perfection as possible."

DAYS WITH SIR ROGER DE COVERLEY.

Reprinted from *The Spectator*. With Illustrations by HUGH THOMSON. Crown 8vo, elegant. 6s. (Uniform with "Cranford" and "The Vicar of Wakefield.") Also with uncut edges, paper label. 6s.

MORNING POST.—"It is not the first time by many that the worthy knight has afforded subject for the artist's pencil, but he has never received happier treatment. Mr. Thomson's *Cranford* was excellent indeed, but his *Sir Roger de Coverley* is even better. Among the many drawings it is hard to find those that are especially admirable, for the general level of merit is so high."

QUEEN.—"I count it quite one of the most charming gift-books of the season. Sir Roger, the pretty widow, Will Wimble—they come back to us from Addison's wellnigh-forgotten pages with irresistible charm."

DAILY TELEGRAPH.—"Both in paper and type the reprint leaves nothing to be desired, and Mr. Thomson has evidently found the task of illustrating the diversions of the famous old squire extremely congenial to his tastes."

ST. JAMES'S GAZETTE.—"If ever a charming book deserved to get into a third edition it is the *Days with Sir Roger de Coverley*, the *raison d'être* for which was Mr. Thomson's beautiful and humorous little illustrations. The artist has thoroughly entered into the spirit, the delicate style and humour of Addison's essays. It is from both points of view an admirable little gift-book."

MACMILLAN AND CO., LONDON.

A CLASSIFIED
CATALOGUE OF BOOKS
IN GENERAL LITERATURE
PUBLISHED BY
MACMILLAN AND CO.
BEDFORD STREET, STRAND, LONDON, W.C.

For purely Educational Works see MACMILLAN AND CO.'s *Educational Catalogue.*

AGRICULTURE.

(*See also* BOTANY; GARDENING.)

FRANKLAND (Prof. P. F.).—A HANDBOOK OF AGRICULTURAL CHEMICAL ANALYSIS. Cr. 8vo. 7s. 6d.

LAURIE (A. P.).—THE FOOD OF PLANTS. 18mo. 1s.

NICHOLLS (H. A. A.).—TEXT BOOK OF TROPICAL AGRICULTURE. Cr. 8vo. 6s.

TANNER (Henry).—ELEMENTARY LESSONS IN THE SCIENCE OF AGRICULTURAL PRACTICE. Fcp. 8vo. 3s. 6d.
—— FIRST PRINCIPLES OF AGRICULTURE. 18mo. 1s.
—— THE PRINCIPLES OF AGRICULTURE. For Use in Elementary Schools. Ext. fcp. 8vo.—THE ALPHABET OF THE PRINCIPLES OF AGRICULTURE. 6d.—FURTHER STEPS IN THE PRINCIPLES OF AGRICULTURE. 1s.—ELEMENTARY SCHOOL READINGS ON THE PRINCIPLES OF AGRICULTURE FOR THE THIRD STAGE. 1s.
—— THE ABBOT'S FARM; or, Practice with Science. Cr. 8vo. 3s. 6d.

ANATOMY, Human. (*See* PHYSIOLOGY.)

ANTHROPOLOGY.

BROWN (J. Allen).—PALÆOLITHIC MAN IN NORTH-WEST MIDDLESEX. 8vo. 7s. 6d.

DAWKINS (Prof. W. Boyd).—EARLY MAN IN BRITAIN AND HIS PLACE IN THE TERTIARY PERIOD. Med. 8vo. 25s.

FINCK (Henry T.).—ROMANTIC LOVE AND PERSONAL BEAUTY. 2 vols. Cr. 8vo. 18s.

FISON (L.) and HOWITT (A. W.).—KAMILAROI AND KURNAI GROUP. Group-Marriage and Relationship, and Marriage by Elopement. 8vo. 15s.

FRAZER (J. G.).—THE GOLDEN BOUGH: A Study in Comparative Religion. 2 vols. 8vo. 28s.

GALTON (Francis).—ENGLISH MEN OF SCIENCE: THEIR NATURE AND NURTURE. 8vo. 8s. 6d.
—— INQUIRIES INTO HUMAN FACULTY AND ITS DEVELOPMENT. 8vo. 16s.
—— LIFE-HISTORY ALBUM: Being a Personal Note-book, combining Diary, Photograph Album, a Register of Height, Weight, and other Anthropometrical Observations, and a Record of Illnesses. 4to. 3s. 6d.—Or with Cards of Wool for Testing Colour Vision. 4s. 6d.

GALTON (Francis).—NATURAL INHERITANCE. 8vo. 9s.
—— RECORD OF FAMILY FACULTIES. Consisting of Tabular Forms and Directions for Entering Data. 4to. 2s. 6d.
—— HEREDITARY GENIUS: An Enquiry into its Laws and Consequences. Ext. cr. 8vo. 7s. net.
—— FINGER PRINTS. 8vo. 6s. net.
—— BLURRED FINGER PRINTS. 8vo. 2s. 6d. net.

M'LENNAN (J. F.).—THE PATRIARCHAL THEORY. Edited and completed by DONALD M'LENNAN, M.A. 8vo. 14s.
—— STUDIES IN ANCIENT HISTORY. Comprising "Primitive Marriage." 8vo. 16s.

MONTELIUS—WOODS. — THE CIVILISATION OF SWEDEN IN HEATHEN TIMES. By Prof. OSCAR MONTELIUS. Translated by Rev. F. H. WOODS. Illustr. 8vo. 14s.

TURNER (Rev. Geo.).—SAMOA, A HUNDRED YEARS AGO AND LONG BEFORE. Cr. 8vo. 9s.

TYLOR (E. B.).—ANTHROPOLOGY. With Illustrations. Cr. 8vo. 7s. 6d.

WESTERMARCK (Dr. Edward).—THE HISTORY OF HUMAN MARRIAGE. With Preface by Dr. A. R. WALLACE. 8vo. 14s. net.

WILSON (Sir Daniel).—PREHISTORIC ANNALS OF SCOTLAND. Illustrated. 2 vols. 8vo. 36s.
—— PREHISTORIC MAN: Researches into the Origin of Civilisation in the Old and New World. Illustrated. 2 vols. 8vo. 36s.
—— THE RIGHT HAND: LEFT-HANDEDNESS. Cr. 8vo. 4s. 6d.

ANTIQUITIES.

(*See also* ANTHROPOLOGY.)

ATKINSON (Rev. J. C.).—FORTY YEARS IN A MOORLAND PARISH. Ext. cr. 8vo. 8s. 6d. net.—*Illustrated Edition.* 12s. net.

BURN (Robert).—ROMAN LITERATURE IN RELATION TO ROMAN ART. With Illustrations. Ext. cr. 8vo. 14s.

DILETTANTI SOCIETY'S PUBLICATIONS.
ANTIQUITIES OF IONIA. Vols. I.—III. 2l. 2s. each, or 5l. 5s. the set, net.—Vol. IV. Folio half morocco, 3l. 13s. 6d. net.
AN INVESTIGATION OF THE PRINCIPLES OF ATHENIAN ARCHITECTURE. By F. C. PENROSE. Illustrated. Folio. 7l. 7s. net.
SPECIMENS OF ANCIENT SCULPTURE: EGYPTIAN, ETRUSCAN, GREEK, AND ROMAN. Vol. II. Folio. 5l. 5s. net.

1

ANTIQUITIES—continued.

DYER (Louis).—STUDIES OF THE GODS IN GREECE AT CERTAIN SANCTUARIES RE·CENTLY EXCAVATED. Ext. cr. 8vo. 8s. 6d. net.

FOWLER (W. W.).—THE CITY-STATE OF THE GREEKS AND ROMANS. Cr. 8vo. 5s.

GARDNER (Percy).—SAMOS AND SAMIAN COINS: An Essay. 8vo. 7s. 6d.

GOW (J., Litt.D.).—A COMPANION TO SCHOOL CLASSICS. Illustrated. 3rd Ed. Cr. 8vo. 6s.

HARRISON (Miss Jane) and VERRALL (Mrs.).—MYTHOLOGY AND MONUMENTS OF ANCIENT ATHENS. Illustrated. Cr. 8vo. 16s.

HELLENIC SOCIETY'S PUBLICATIONS —EXCAVATIONS AT MEGALOPOLIS, 1890— 1891. By Messrs. E. A. GARDNER, W. LORING, G. C. RICHARDS, and W. J. WOOD-HOUSE. With an Architectural Description by R. W. SCHULTZ. 4to. 25s.

—— ECCLESIASTICAL SITES IN ISAURIA (CILICIA TRACHEA). By the Rev. A. C. HEAD-LAM. Imp. 4to. 5s.

LANCIANI (Prof. R.).—ANCIENT ROME IN THE LIGHT OF RECENT DISCOVERIES. 4to. 24s.

—— PAGAN AND CHRISTIAN ROME. 4to. 24s.

MAHAFFY (Prof. J. P.).—A PRIMER OF GREEK ANTIQUITIES. 18mo. 1s.

—— SOCIAL LIFE IN GREECE FROM HOMER TO MENANDER. 6th Edit. Cr. 8vo. 9s.

—— RAMBLES AND STUDIES IN GREECE. Illustrated. 3rd Edit. Cr. 8vo. 10s. 6d.
(See also HISTORY, p. 11.)

NEWTON (Sir C. T.).—ESSAYS ON ART AND ARCHÆOLOGY. 8vo. 12s. 6d.

SCHUCHHARDT (C.).—DR. SCHLIEMANN'S EXCAVATIONS AT TROY, TIRYNS, MYCENAE, ORCHOMENOS, ITHACA, IN THE LIGHT OF RECENT KNOWLEDGE. Trans. by EUGENIE SELLERS. Preface by WALTER LEAF, Litt.D. Illustrated. 8vo. 18s. net.

STRANGFORD. (See VOYAGES & TRAVELS.)

WALDSTEIN (C.).—CATALOGUE OF CASTS IN THE MUSEUM OF CLASSICAL ARCHÆOLOGY, CAMBRIDGE. Crown 8vo. 1s. 6d.— Large Paper Edition. Small 4to. 5s.

WHITE (Gilbert). (See NATURAL HISTORY.)

WILKINS (Prof. A. S.).—A PRIMER OF ROMAN ANTIQUITIES. 18mo. 1s.

ARCHÆOLOGY. (See ANTIQUITIES.)

ARCHITECTURE.

FREEMAN (Prof. E. A.).—HISTORY OF THE CATHEDRAL CHURCH OF WELLS. Cr. 8vo. 3s. 6d.

HULL (E.).—A TREATISE ON ORNAMENTAL AND BUILDING STONES OF GREAT BRITAIN AND FOREIGN COUNTRIES. 8vo. 12s.

MOORE (Prof. C. H.).—THE DEVELOPMENT AND CHARACTER OF GOTHIC ARCHITECTURE. Illustrated. Med. 8vo. 18s.

PENROSE (F. C.). (See ANTIQUITIES.)

STEVENSON (J. J.).—HOUSE ARCHITECTURE. With Illustrations. 2 vols. Roy. 8vo. 18s. each.—Vol. I. ARCHITECTURE; Vol. II. HOUSE PLANNING.

(See al

ART AT HOME W. J. LOFTIE, B.A THE BEDROOM A BARKER. 2s. 6d. NEEDLEWORK. B Illustrated. 2s. MUSIC IN THE HO 4th edit. 2s. 6d. THE DINING-ROO With Illustration AMATEUR THEATE POLLOCK and LA by KATE GREEN.

ATKINSON (J. B NORTHERN CAPIT

BURN (Robert). (S

CARR (J. Comyns). 8vo. 8s. 6d.

COLLIER (Hon. Jo 18mo. 1s.

COOK (E. T.).—A THE NATIONAL GA collected from the 3rd Edit. Cr. 8vo Large paper Edition

DELAMOTTE (Pro DRAWING-BOOK.

ELLIS (Tristram).— TURE. Illustr. by and the Author. 2

HAMERTON (P. ART. New Edit.

HOOPER (W. H.) ar A MANUAL OF M PORCELAIN. 16mo

HUNT (W.).—TAL Letter from Sir J. Cr. 8vo. 3s. 6d.

HUTCHINSON (G ON LEARNING TO I

LECTURES ON A POOLE, Professor POYNTER, R.A., and WILLIAM MOR

NEWTON (Sir C. T

PALGRAVE (Prof. Ext. fcp. 8vo. 6s.

PATER (W.).—THE In Art and Poetry.

PROPERT (J. Lun MINIATURE ART. 4to. 3l. 13s. 6d.—Bo

TURNER'S LIBE DESCRIPTION AND Rawlinson. Med

TYRWHITT (Rev. SKETCHING CLUB.

WYATT (Sir M. Sketch of its Histo Application to Indu

ASTR

AIRY (Sir G. B.).- Illustrated. 7th E —— GRAVITATION. tion of the Princi Solar System. 2nd

LAKE (J. F.).—Astronomical Myths. With Illustrations. Cr. 8vo. 9s.

HEYNE (C. H. H.).—An Elementary Treatise on the Planetary Theory. Cr. 8vo. 7s. 6d.

CLARK (L.) and SADLER (H.).—The Star Guide. Roy. 8vo. 5s.

CROSSLEY (E.), GLEDHILL (J.), and WILSON (J. M.).—A Handbook of Double Stars. 8vo. 21s.

— Corrections to the Handbook of Double Stars. 8vo. 1s.

FORBES (Prof. George).—The Transit of Venus. Illustrated. Cr. 8vo. 3s. 6d.

GODFRAY (Hugh).—An Elementary Treatise on the Lunar Theory. 2nd Edit. Cr. 8vo. 5s. 6d.

— A Treatise on Astronomy, for the use of Colleges and Schools. 8vo. 12s. 6d.

LOCKYER (J. Norman, F.R.S.).—A Primer of Astronomy. Illustrated. 18mo. 1s.

— Elementary Lessons in Astronomy. Illustr. New Edition. Fcp. 8vo. 5s. 6d.

— Questions on the same. By J. Forbes Robertson. Fcp. 8vo. 1s. 6d.

— The Chemistry of the Sun. Illustrated. 8vo. 14s.

— The Meteoritic Hypothesis of the Origin of Cosmical Systems. Illustrated. 8vo. 17s. net.

— The Evolution of the Heavens and the Earth. Illustrated. Cr. 8vo.

— Star-Gazing Past and Present. Expanded from Notes with the assistance of G. M. Seabroke. Roy. 8vo. 21s.

LODGE (O. J.).—Pioneers of Science. Ex. cr. 8vo. 7s. 6d.

MILLER (R. Kalley).—The Romance of Astronomy. 2nd Edit. Cr. 8vo. 4s. 6d.

NEWCOMB (Prof. Simon).—Popular Astronomy. Engravings and Maps. 8vo. 18s.

RADCLIFFE (Charles B.).—Behind the Tides. 8vo. 4s. 6d.

ROSCOE—SCHUSTER. (See Chemistry.)

ATLASES.

(See also Geography).

BARTHOLOMEW (J. G.).—Elementary School Atlas. 4to. 1s.

— Physical and Political School Atlas. 80 maps. 4to. 8s. 6d. ; half mor. 10s. 6d.

— Library Reference Atlas of the World. With Index to 100,000 places. Folio. 52s. 6d. net.—Also in 7 parts. 5s. net ; Geographical Index. 7s. 6d. net.

LABBERTON (R. H.).—New Historical Atlas and General History. 4to. 15s.

BIBLE. (See under Theology, p. 32.)

BIBLIOGRAPHY.

A BIBLIOGRAPHICAL CATALOGUE OF MACMILLAN AND CO.'S PUBLICATIONS, 1843—89. Med. 8vo. 10s. net.

BIBLIOGRAPHY—continued.

MAYOR (Prof. John E. B.).—A Bibliographical Clue to Latin Literature. Cr. 8vo. 10s. 6d.

RYLAND (F.).—Chronological Outlines of English Literature. Cr. 8vo. 6s.

BIOGRAPHY.

(See also History.)

For other subjects of Biography, see English Men of Letters, English Men of Action, Twelve English Statesmen.

ABBOTT (E. A.).—The Anglican Career of Cardinal Newman. 2 vols. 8vo. 25s. net.

AGASSIZ (Louis): His Life and Correspondence. Edited by Elizabeth Cary Agassiz 2 vols. Cr. 8vo. 18s.

ALBEMARLE (Earl of).—Fifty Years of My Life. 3rd Edit., revised. Cr. 8vo. 7s. 6d.

ALFRED THE GREAT. By Thomas Hughes. Cr. 8vo. 6s.

AMIEL (H. F.).—The Journal Intime. Trans. Mrs. Humphry Ward. 2nd Ed. Cr. 8vo. 6s.

ANDREWS (Dr. Thomas). (See Physics.)

ARNAULD, ANGELIQUE. By Frances Martin. Cr. 8vo. 4s. 6d.

ARTEVELDE. James and Philip van Artevelde. By W. J. Ashley. Cr. 8vo. 6s.

BACON (Francis): An Account of his Life and Works. By E. A. Abbott. 8vo. 14s.

BARNES. Life of William Barnes, Poet and Philologist. By his Daughter, Lucy Baxter ("Leader Scott"). Cr. 8vo. 7s. 6d.

BERLIOZ (Hector): Autobiography of. Trns. by R. & E. Holmes. 2 vols. Cr. 8vo. 21s.

BERNARD (St.). The Life and Times of St. Bernard, Abbot of Clairvaux. By J. C. Morison, M.A. Cr. 8vo. 6s.

BLACKBURNE. Life of the Right Hon. Francis Blackburne, late Lord Chancellor of Ireland, by his Son, Edward Blackburne. With Portrait. 8vo. 12s.

BLAKE. Life of William Blake. With Selections from his Poems, etc. Illustr. from Blake's own Works. By Alexander Gilchrist. 2 vols. Med. 8vo. 42s.

BOLEYN (Anne): A Chapter of English History, 1527—36. By Paul Friedmann. 2 vols. 8vo. 28s.

BROOKE (Sir Jas.), The Raja of Sarawak (Life of). By Gertrude L. Jacob. 2 vols. 8vo. 25s.

BURKE. By John Morley. Globe 8vo. 5s.

CALVIN. (See Select Biography, p. 6.)

CAMPBELL (Sir G.).—Memoirs of my Indian Career. Edited by Sir C. E. Bernard. 2 vols. 8vo. 21s. net.

CARLYLE (Thomas). Edited by Charles E. Norton. Cr. 8vo.

— Reminiscences. 2 vols. 12s.

— Early Letters, 1814—26. 2 vols. 18s.

— Letters, 1826—36. 2 vols. 18s.

— Correspondence between Goethe and Carlyle. 9s.

BIOGRAPHY—*continued.*

CARSTARES (Wm.): A CHARACTER AND
CAREER OF THE REVOLUTIONARY EPOCH
(1649—1715). By R. H. STORY. 8vo. 12s.

CAVOUR. (*See* SELECT BIOGRAPHY, p. 6.)

CHATTERTON: A STORY OF THE YEAR
1770. By Prof. DAVID MASSON. Cr. 8vo. 5s.
—— A BIOGRAPHICAL STUDY. By Sir DANIEL
WILSON. Cr. 8vo. 6s. 6d.

CLARK. MEMORIALS FROM JOURNALS AND
LETTERS OF SAMUEL CLARK, M.A. Edited
by HIS WIFE. Cr. 8vo. 7s. 6d.

CLOUGH (A. H.). (*See* LITERATURE, p. 20.)

COMBE. LIFE OF GEORGE COMBE. By
CHARLES GIBBON. 2 vols. 8vo. 32s.

CROMWELL. (*See* SELECT BIOGRAPHY, p. 6.)

DAMIEN (Father): A JOURNEY FROM CASH-
MERE TO HIS HOME IN HAWAII. By EDWARD
CLIFFORD. Portrait. Cr. 8vo. 2s. 6d.

DANTE: AND OTHER ESSAYS. By Dean
CHURCH. Globe 8vo. 5s.

DARWIN (Charles): MEMORIAL NOTICES,
By T. H. HUXLEY, G. J. ROMANES, Sir
ARCH. GEIKIE, and W. THISELTON DYER.
With Portrait. Cr. 8vo. 2s. 6d.

DEÁK (Francis): HUNGARIAN STATESMAN.
A Memoir. 8vo. 12s. 6d.

DRUMMOND OF HAWTHORNDEN. By
Prof. D. MASSON. Cr. 8vo. 10s. 6d.

EADIE. LIFE OF JOHN EADIE, D.D. By
JAMES BROWN, D.D. Cr. 8vo. 7s. 6d.

ELLIOTT. LIFE OF H. V. ELLIOTT, OF
BRIGHTON. By J. BATEMAN. Cr. 8vo. 6s.

EMERSON. LIFE OF RALPH WALDO EMER-
SON. By J. L. CABOT. 2 vols. Cr. 8vo. 18s.

ENGLISH MEN OF ACTION. Cr. 8vo.
With Portraits. 2s. 6d. each.

CLIVE. By Colonel Sir CHARLES WILSON.
COOK (CAPTAIN). By WALTER BESANT.
DAMPIER. By W. CLARK RUSSELL.
DRAKE. By JULIAN CORBETT.
GORDON (GENERAL). By Col. Sir W. BUTLER.
HASTINGS (WARREN). By Sir A. LYALL.
HAVELOCK (SIR HENRY). By A. FORBES.
HENRY V. By the Rev. A. J. CHURCH.
LAWRENCE (LORD). By Sir RICH. TEMPLE.
LIVINGSTONE. By THOMAS HUGHES.
MONK. By JULIAN CORBETT.
MONTROSE. By MOWBRAY MORRIS.
MOORE (SIR JOHN). By Col. MAURICE. [*In prep.*
NAPIER (SIR CHARLES). By Colonel Sir
WM. BUTLER.
PETERBOROUGH. By W. STEBBING.
RODNEY. By DAVID HANNAY.
SIMON DE MONTFORT. By G. W. PRO-
THERO.　　　　　　　　　[*In prep.*
STRAFFORD. By H. D. TRAILL.
WARWICK, THE KING-MAKER. By C. W.
OMAN.
WELLINGTON. By GEORGE HOOPER.

ENGLISH MEN OF LETTERS. Edited
by JOHN MORLEY. Cr. 8vo. 2s. 6d. each.
Cheap Edition, 1s. 6d.; sewed, 1s.
ADDISON. By W. J. COURTHOPE.
BACON. By Dean CHURCH.
BENTLEY. By Prof. JEBB.

ENGLISH MEN OF LETTERS—*contd.*
BUNYAN. By J. A. FROUDE.
BURKE. By JOHN MORLEY.
BURNS. By Principal SHAIRP.
BYRON. By JOHN NICHOL.
CARLYLE. By JOHN NICHOL.
CHAUCER. By Prof. A. W. WARD.
COLERIDGE. By H. D. TRAILL.
COWPER. By GOLDWIN SMITH.
DEFOE. By W. MINTO.
DE QUINCEY. By Prof. MASSON.
DICKENS. By A. W. WARD.
DRYDEN. By G. SAINTSBURY.
FIELDING. By AUSTIN DOBSON.
GIBBON. By J. COTTER MORISON.
GOLDSMITH. By WILLIAM BLACK.
GRAY. By EDMUND GOSSE.
HAWTHORNE. By HENRY JAMES.
HUME. By T. H. HUXLEY.
JOHNSON. By LESLIE STEPHEN.
KEATS. By SIDNEY COLVIN.
LAMB. By Rev. ALFRED AINGER.
LANDOR. By SIDNEY COLVIN.
LOCKE. By Prof. FOWLER.
MACAULAY. By J. COTTER MORISON.
MILTON. By MARK PATTISON.
POPE. By LESLIE STEPHEN.
SCOTT. By R. H. HUTTON.
SHELLEY. By J. A. SYMONDS.
SHERIDAN. By Mrs. OLIPHANT.
SIDNEY. By J. A. SYMONDS.
SOUTHEY. By Prof. DOWDEN.
SPENSER. By Dean CHURCH.
STERNE. By H. D. TRAILL.
SWIFT. By LESLIE STEPHEN.
THACKERAY. By ANTHONY TROLLOPE.
WORDSWORTH. By F. W. H. MYERS.

ENGLISH STATESMEN, TWELVE
Cr. 8vo. 2s. 6d. each.

WILLIAM THE CONQUEROR. By EDWARD
A. FREEMAN, D.C.L., LL.D.
HENRY II. By Mrs. J. R. GREEN.
EDWARD I. By T. F. TOUT, M.A.
HENRY VII. By JAMES GAIRDNER.
CARDINAL WOLSEY. By Bp. CREIGHTON.
ELIZABETH. By E. S. BEESLY.
OLIVER CROMWELL. By F. HARRISON.
WILLIAM III. By H. D. TRAILL.
WALPOLE. By JOHN MORLEY.
CHATHAM. By JOHN MORLEY. [*In the Press*
PITT. By LORD ROSEBERY.
PEEL. By J. R. THURSFIELD.

EPICTETUS. (*See* SELECT BIOGRAPHY, p. 6

FAIRFAX. LIFE OF ROBERT FAIRFAX OF
STEETON, Vice-Admiral, Alderman, and
Member for York, A.D. 1666—1725. By CLE-
MENTS R. MARKHAM, C.B. 8vo. 12s. 6d.

FITZGERALD (Edward). (*See* LITERATURE
p. 21.)

FORBES (Edward): MEMOIR OF. By GEORGE
WILSON, M.P., and Sir ARCHIBALD GEIKIE,
F.R.S., etc. Demy 8vo. 14s.

FRANCIS OF ASSISI. By Mrs. OLIPHANT
Cr. 8vo. 6s.

FRASER. JAMES FRASER, SECOND BISHOP
OF MANCHESTER: A Memoir. By T.
HUGHES. Cr. 8vo. 6s.

GARIBALDI. (*See* SELECT BIOGRAPHY, p. 6

GOETHE: LIFE OF. By Prof. HEINRICH
DÜNTZER. Translated by T. W. LYSTER
2 vols. Cr. 8vo. 21s.

'LE. (*See* CARLYLE.)
SKETCH. By REGI-
8vo. 1s.
RAL C. G. GORDON
GORDON. 4th Edit.

y W. S. ROCKSTRO.

STORY OF. By the
D. Cr. 8vo. 4s. 6d.
TED WORKS, p. 22.)
OF REV. FRANCIS
Son, Rev. JAMES T.
s. Cr. 8vo. 18s.
LETTERS AND JOUR-
WIFE. 8vo. 14s.
A. McMurrough): A
pers chiefly unpub-
Cousin, SARAH L.
t. 8vo. 14s. net.
ERS, AND MEMORIES
y HIS WIFE. 2 vols.
Edition. 1 vol. 6s.
CHARLES LAMB. By
M.A. Globe 8vo. 5s.
—GOLDEN BOOK OF
s.
CT BIOGRAPHY, p. 6.)
MEMOIR OF DANIEL
MAS HUGHES, Q.C.
8vo. 4s. 6d.—Cheap
d. 1s.

WORK. By JAMES

(*See* SELECT BIO-

E OF CHARLES J.
CHARLES DICKENS.
8vo. 25s.
FREDERICK DENISON
REDERICK MAURICE,
8vo. 36s.—Popular
2 vols. Cr. 8vo. 16s.
R CLERK MAXWELL,
L. CAMPBELL, M.A.,
Cr. 8vo. 7s. 6d.
BIOGRAPHY, p. 6.)
OIRS OF VISCOUNT
M. TORRENS. With
vols. 8vo. 32s.
OF JOHN MILTON.
SON. Vol. I., 21s.;
V. and V., 32s.; Vol.
(*See also* p. 16.)
S LIFE OF. With
s by K. DEIGHTON.

TORY OF. By P.
8vo. 30s.
LIFE OF NELSON.
Notes by MICHAEL
obe 8vo. 3s. 6d.
ECTIONS OF A HAPPY
graphy of MARIANNE
J. A. SYMONDS. 2nd
8vo. 17s. net.
ECOLLECTIONS OF A
8s. 6d. net.

OXFORD MOVEMENT, THE, 1833—45.
By Dean CHURCH. Gl. 8vo. 5s.
PARKER (W. K.)—A BIOGRAPHICAL SKETCH.
By His Son. Cr. 8vo. 4s. net.
PATTESON. LIFE AND LETTERS OF JOHN
COLERIDGE PATTESON, D.D., MISSIONARY
BISHOP. By C. M. YONGE. 2 vols. Cr. 8vo.
12s. (*See also* BOOKS FOR THE YOUNG, p. 41.)
PATTISON (M.).—MEMOIRS. Cr. 8vo. 8s. 6d.
PITT. (*See* SELECT BIOGRAPHY, p. 6.)
POLLOCK (Sir Frdk., 2nd Bart.).—PERSONAL
REMEMBRANCES. 2 vols. Cr. 8vo. 16s.
POOLE, THOS., AND HIS FRIENDS.
By Mrs. SANDFORD. 2nd edit. Cr. 8vo. 6s.
RENAN (Ernest).—IN MEMORIAM. By Sir
M. E. GRANT DUFF. Cr. 8vo. 6s.
RITCHIE (Mrs.).—RECORDS OF TENNYSON,
RUSKIN, AND BROWNING. Globe 8vo. 5s.
ROBINSON (Matthew): AUTOBIOGRAPHY OF.
Edited by J. E. B. MAYOR. Fcp. 8vo. 5s.
ROSSETTI (Dante Gabriel): A RECORD AND
A STUDY. By W. SHARP. Cr. 8vo. 10s. 6d.
RUMFORD. (*See* COLLECTED WORKS, p. 23.)
SCHILLER, LIFE OF. By Prof. H. DÜNTZER.
Trans. by P. E. PINKERTON. Cr. 8vo. 10s. 6d.
SHELBURNE. LIFE OF WILLIAM, EARL
OF SHELBURNE. By Lord EDMOND FITZ-
MAURICE. In 3 vols. 8vo.—Vol. I. 8vo. 12s.—
Vol. II. 8vo. 12s.—Vol. III. 8vo. 16s.
SIBSON. (*See* MEDICINE.)
SMETHAM (Jas.).: LETTERS OF. Ed. by
SARAH SMETHAM and W. DAVIES. Portrait.
Globe 8vo. 5s.
—— THE LITERARY WORKS. Gl. 8vo. 5s.
TAIT. THE LIFE OF ARCHIBALD CAMPBELL
TAIT, ARCHBISHOP OF CANTERBURY. By
the BISHOP OF ROCHESTER and Rev. W.
BENHAM, B.D. 2 vols. Cr. 8vo. 10s. net.
—— CATHARINE AND CRAWFURD TAIT,
WIFE AND SON OF ARCHIBALD CAMPBELL,
ARCHBISHOP OF CANTERBURY: A Memoir.
Ed. by Rev. W. BENHAM, B.D. Cr. 8vo. 6s.
—Popular Edit., abridged. Cr. 8vo. 2s. 6d.
THRING (Edward): A MEMORY OF. By
J. H. SKRINE. Cr. 8vo. 6s.
TUCKWELL (W.).—THE ANCIENT WAYS:
WINCHESTER FIFTY YEARS AGO. Globe
8vo. 4s. 6d.
VICTOR EMMANUEL II., FIRST KING
OF ITALY. By G. S. GODKIN. Cr. 8vo. 6s.
WARD. WILLIAM GEORGE WARD AND THE
OXFORD MOVEMENT. By his Son, WILFRID
WARD. With Portrait. 8vo. 14s.
—— WILLIAM GEORGE WARD AND THE CATHO-
LIC REVIVAL. 8vo. 14s.
WATSON. A RECORD OF ELLEN WATSON.
By ANNA BUCKLAND. Cr. 8vo. 6s.
WHEWELL. DR. WILLIAM WHEWELL, late
Master of Trinity College, Cambridge. An
Account of his Writings, with Selections from
his Literary and Scientific Correspondence.
By I. TODHUNTER, M.A. 2 vols. 8vo. 25s.
WILLIAMS (Montagu).—LEAVES OF A LIFE.
Cr. 8vo. 3s. 6d.
—— LATER LEAVES. Being further Reminis-
cences. With Portrait. Cr. 8vo. 3s. 6d.
—— ROUND LONDON, DOWN EAST AND UP
WEST. 8vo. 15s.

WILSON. MEMOIR OF PROF. GEORGE WILSON, M.D. By HIS SISTER. With Portrait. 2nd Edit. Cr. 8vo. 6s.

WORDSWORTH. DOVE COTTAGE, WORDSWORTH'S HOME 1800—8. Gl. 8vo, swd. 1s.

Select Biography.

BIOGRAPHIES OF EMINENT PERSONS. Reprinted from the *Times*. 4 vols. Cr. 8vo 3s. 6d. each.

FARRAR (Archdeacon). — SEEKERS AFTER GOD. Cr. 8vo. 3s. 6d.

FAWCETT (Mrs. H.). — SOME EMINENT WOMEN OF OUR TIMES. Cr. 8vo 2s. 6d.

GUIZOT. — GREAT CHRISTIANS OF FRANCE: ST. LOUIS AND CALVIN. Cr. 8vo. 6s.

HARRISON (Frederic). — THE NEW CALENDAR OF GREAT MEN. Ex. cr. 8vo. 7s. 6d. net.

MARRIOTT (J. A. R.). — THE MAKERS OF MODERN ITALY: MAZZINI, CAVOUR, GARIBALDI. Cr. 8vo. 1s. 6d.

MARTINEAU (Harriet). — BIOGRAPHICAL SKETCHES, 1852—75. Cr. 8vo. 6s.

NEW HOUSE OF COMMONS, JULY, 1892. Reprinted from the *Times*. 16mo. 1s.

SMITH (Goldwin). — THREE ENGLISH STATESMEN: CROMWELL, PYM, PITT. Cr. 8vo. 5s.

STEVENSON (F. S.). — HISTORIC PERSONALITY. Cr. 8vo. 4s. 6d.

WINKWORTH (Catharine). — CHRISTIAN SINGERS OF GERMANY. Cr. 8vo. 4s. 6d.

YONGE (Charlotte M.). — THE PUPILS OF ST. JOHN. Illustrated. Cr. 8vo. 6s.

—— PIONEERS AND FOUNDERS; or, Recent Workers in the Mission Field. Cr. 8vo. 6s.

—— A BOOK OF WORTHIES. 18mo. 2s. 6d. net.

—— A BOOK OF GOLDEN DEEDS. 18mo. 2s. 6d. net. --*Globe Readings Edition*. Gl. 8vo. 2s. *Abridged Edition*. Pott 8vo. 1s.

BIOLOGY.

(*See also* BOTANY; NATURAL HISTORY; PHYSIOLOGY; ZOOLOGY.)

BALFOUR (F. M.). — COMPARATIVE EMBRYOLOGY. Illustrated. 2 vols. 8vo. Vol. I. 18s. Vol. II. 21s.

BALL (W. P.). — ARE THE EFFECTS OF USE AND DISUSE INHERITED? Cr. 8vo. 3s. 6d.

BASTIAN (H. Charlton). — THE BEGINNINGS OF LIFE. 2 vols. Crown 8vo. 28s.

—— EVOLUTION AND THE ORIGIN OF LIFE. Cr. 8vo. 6s. 6d.

BATESON (W.). — MATERIALS FOR THE STUDY OF VARIATION IN ANIMALS. Part I. DISCONTINUOUS VARIATION. Illustr. 8vo.

BERNARD (H. M.). — THE APODIDAE. Cr. 8vo. 7s. 6d.

BIRKS (T. R.). — MODERN PHYSICAL FATALISM, AND THE DOCTRINE OF EVOLUTION. Including an Examination of Mr. Herbert Spencer's "First Principles." Cr. 8vo. 6s.

CALDERWOOD (H.). — EVOLUTION AND MAN'S PLACE IN NATURE. Cr. 8vo. 7s. 6d.

DE VARIGNY (H.). — EXPERIMENTAL EVOLUTION. Cr. 8vo. 5s.

EIMER (G. H. T.). — ORGANIC EVOLUTION AS THE RESULT OF THE INHERITANCE OF ACQUIRED CHARACTERS ACCORDING TO THE LAWS OF ORGANIC GROWTH. Translated by J. T. CUNNINGHAM, M.A. 8vo. 12s. 6d.

FISKE (John). — OUTLINES OF COSMIC PHILOSOPHY, BASED ON THE DOCTRINE OF EVOLUTION. 2 vols. 8vo. 25s.

—— MAN'S DESTINY VIEWED IN THE LIGHT OF HIS ORIGIN. Cr. 8vo. 3s. 6d.

FOSTER (Prof. M.) and BALFOUR (F. M.). — THE ELEMENTS OF EMBRYOLOGY. Ed. SEDGWICK, and WALTER HEAPE. Illus. 3rd Edit., revised and enlarged. Cr. 8vo. 10s. 6d.

HUXLEY (T. H.) and MARTIN (H. N.). — (*See under* ZOOLOGY, p. 43.)

KLEIN (Dr. E.). — MICRO-ORGANISMS AND DISEASE. With 121 Engravings. 3rd Edit. Cr. 8vo. 6s.

LANKESTER (Prof. E. Ray). — COMPARATIVE LONGEVITY IN MAN AND THE LOWER ANIMALS. Cr. 8vo. 4s. 6d.

LUBBOCK (Sir John, Bart.). — SCIENTIFIC LECTURES. Illustrated. 2nd Edit. 8vo. 8s. 6d.

MURPHY (J. J.). — NATURAL SELECTION. Gl. 8vo. 5s.

PARKER (T. Jeffery). — LESSONS IN ELEMENTARY BIOLOGY. Illustr. Cr. 8vo. 10s. 6d.

ROMANES (G. J.). — SCIENTIFIC EVIDENCE OF ORGANIC EVOLUTION. Cr. 8vo. 2s. 6d.

WALLACE (Alfred R.). — DARWINISM: A Exposition of the Theory of Natural Selection. Illustrated. 3rd Edit. Cr. 8vo. 9s.

—— CONTRIBUTIONS TO THE THEORY OF NATURAL SELECTION, AND TROPICAL NATURE: and other Essays. New Ed. Cr. 8vo. 6s.

—— THE GEOGRAPHICAL DISTRIBUTION OF ANIMALS. Illustrated. 2 vols. 8vo. 42s.

—— ISLAND LIFE. Illustr. Ext. Cr. 8vo. 6s.

BIRDS. (*See* ZOOLOGY; ORNITHOLOGY.)

BOOK-KEEPING.

THORNTON (J.). — FIRST LESSONS IN BOOK-KEEPING. New Edition. Cr. 8vo. 2s. 6d.

—— KEY. Oblong 4to. 10s. 6d.

—— PRIMER OF BOOK-KEEPING. 18mo. 1s.

—— KEY. Demy 8vo. 2s. 6d.

—— EXERCISES IN BOOK-KEEPING. 18mo. 1s.

BOTANY.

(*See also* AGRICULTURE; GARDENING.)

ALLEN (Grant). — ON THE COLOURS OF FLOWERS. Illustrated. Cr. 8vo. 3s. 6d.

BALFOUR (Prof. J. B.) and WARD (Prof. H. M.). — A GENERAL TEXT-BOOK OF BOTANY. 8vo. [*In preparation.*

BETTANY (G. T.). — FIRST LESSONS IN PRACTICAL BOTANY. 18mo. 1s.

BOWER (Prof. F. O.). — A COURSE OF PRACTICAL INSTRUCTION IN BOTANY. Cr. 8vo. 10s. 6d. — Abridged Edition. [*In preparation.*

CHURCH (Prof. A. H.) and VINES (S. H.). — MANUAL OF VEGETABLE PHYSIOLOGY. Illustrated. Crown 8vo. [*In preparation.*

GOODALE (Prof. G. L.). — PHYSIOLOGICAL BOTANY. — 1. OUTLINES OF THE HISTOLOGY OF PHÆNOGAMOUS PLANTS; 2. VEGETABLE PHYSIOLOGY. 8vo. 10s. 6d.

GRAY (Prof. Asa). — STRUCTURAL BOTANY; or, Organography on the Basis of Morphology. 8vo. 10s. 6d.

—— THE SCIENTIFIC PAPERS OF ASA GRAY. Selected by C. S. SARGENT. 2 vols. 8vo. 21s.

HANBURY (Daniel). — SCIENCE PAPERS, CHIEFLY PHARMACOLOGICAL AND BOTANICAL. Med. 8vo. 14s.

HARTIG (Dr. Robert).—TEXT-BOOK OF THE DISEASES OF TREES. Transl. by Prof. WM. SOMERVILLE, B.Sc. With Introduction by Prof. H. MARSHALL WARD. 8vo.

HOOKER (Sir Joseph D.).—THE STUDENT'S FLORA OF THE BRITISH ISLANDS. 3rd Edit. Globe 8vo. 10s. 6d.
—— A PRIMER OF BOTANY. 18mo. 1s.

LASLETT (Thomas).—TIMBER AND TIMBER TREES, NATIVE AND FOREIGN. Cr. 8vo. 8s. 6d.

LUBBOCK (Sir John, Bart.).—ON BRITISH WILD FLOWERS CONSIDERED IN RELATION TO INSECTS. Illustrated. Cr. 8vo. 4s. 6d.
—— FLOWERS, FRUITS, AND LEAVES. With Illustrations. Cr. 8vo. 4s. 6d.

MÜLLER—THOMPSON. — THE FERTILISATION OF FLOWERS. By Prof. H. MÜLLER. Transl. by D'ARCY W. THOMPSON. Preface by CHARLES DARWIN, F.R.S. 8vo. 21s.

NISBET (J.).—BRITISH FOREST TREES AND THEIR SYLVICULTURAL CHARACTERISTICS AND TREATMENT. Cr. 8vo. 6s. net.

OLIVER (Prof. Daniel).—LESSONS IN ELEMENTARY BOTANY. Illustr. Fcp. 8vo. 4s.6d.
—— FIRST BOOK OF INDIAN BOTANY. Illustrated. Ext. fcp. 8vo. 6s. 6d.

PETTIGREW (J. Bell).—THE PHYSIOLOGY OF THE CIRCULATION IN PLANTS, IN THE LOWER ANIMALS, AND IN MAN. 8vo. 12s.

SMITH (J.).—ECONOMIC PLANTS, DICTIONARY OF POPULAR NAMES OF; THEIR HISTORY, PRODUCTS, AND USES. 8vo. 14s.

SMITH (W. G.).—DISEASES OF FIELD AND GARDEN CROPS, CHIEFLY SUCH AS ARE CAUSED BY FUNGI. Illust. Fcp.8vo. 4s.6d.

STEWART (S. A.) and CORRY (T. H.).— A FLORA OF THE NORTH-EAST OF IRELAND. Cr. 8vo. 5s. 6d.

WARD (Prof. H. M.).—TIMBER AND SOME OF ITS DISEASES. Illustrated. Cr. 8vo. 6s.

YONGE (C. M.).—THE HERB OF THE FIELD New Edition, revised. Cr. 8vo. 5s.

BREWING AND WINE.
PASTEUR — FAULKNER. — STUDIES ON FERMENTATION: THE DISEASES OF BEER, THEIR CAUSES, AND THE MEANS OF PREVENTING THEM. By L. PASTEUR. Translated by FRANK FAULKNER. 8vo. 21s.

CHEMISTRY.
(See also METALLURGY.)
BRODIE (Sir Benjamin).—IDEAL CHEMISTRY. Cr. 8vo. 2s.

COHEN (J. B.).— THE OWENS COLLEGE COURSE OF PRACTICAL ORGANIC CHEMISTRY. Fcp. 8vo. 2s. 6d.

COOKE (Prof. J. P., jun.).—PRINCIPLES OF CHEMICAL PHILOSOPHY. New Ed. 8vo. 19s.

DOBBIN (L.) and WALKER (Jas.).—CHEMICAL THEORY FOR BEGINNERS. 18mo. 2s.6d.

FLEISCHER (Emil).—A SYSTEM OF VOLUMETRIC ANALYSIS. Transl. with Additions, by M. M. P. MUIR, F.R.S.E. Cr.8vo. 7s.6d.

FRANKLAND (Prof. P. F.). (See AGRICULTURE.)

GLADSTONE (J. H.) and TRIBE (A.).— THE CHEMISTRY OF THE SECONDARY BATTERIES OF PLANTÉ AND FAURE. Cr. 8vo. 2s.6d.

HARTLEY (Prof. W. N.).—A COURSE OF QUANTITATIVE ANALYSIS FOR STUDENTS. Globe 8vo. 5s.

HEMPEL (Dr. W.). — METHODS OF GAS ANALYSIS. Translated by L. M. DENNIS. Cr. 8vo. 7s. 6d.

HOFMANN (Prof. A. W.).—THE LIFE WORK OF LIEBIG IN EXPERIMENTAL AND PHILOSOPHIC CHEMISTRY. 8vo. 5s.

JONES (Francis).—THE OWENS COLLEGE JUNIOR COURSE OF PRACTICAL CHEMISTRY. Illustrated. Fcp. 8vo. 2s. 6d.
—— QUESTIONS ON CHEMISTRY. Fcp.8vo. 3s.

LANDAUER (J.). — BLOWPIPE ANALYSIS. Translated by J. TAYLOR. Gl. 8vo. 4s. 6d.

LOCKYER (J. Norman, F.R.S.). — THE CHEMISTRY OF THE SUN. Illustr. 8vo. 14s.

LUPTON (S.). — CHEMICAL ARITHMETIC. With 1200 Problems. Fcp. 8vo. 4s. 6d.

MANSFIELD (C. B.).—A THEORY OF SALTS. Cr. 8vo. 14s.

MELDOLA (Prof. R.).—THE CHEMISTRY OF PHOTOGRAPHY. Illustrated. Cr. 8vo. 6s.

MEYER (E. von).—HISTORY OF CHEMISTRY FROM EARLIEST TIMES TO THE PRESENT DAY. Trans. G. McGOWAN. 8vo. 14s. net.

MIXTER (Prof. W. G.).—AN ELEMENTARY TEXT-BOOK OF CHEMISTRY. Cr. 8vo. 7s. 6d.

MUIR (M. M. P.).—PRACTICAL CHEMISTRY FOR MEDICAL STUDENTS (First M. B. Course). Fcp. 8vo. 1s. 6d.

MUIR (M. M. P.) and WILSON (D. M.).— ELEMENTS OF THERMAL CHEMISTRY. 12s.6d.

OSTWALD (Prof.).—OUTLINES OF GENERAL CHEMISTRY. Trans. Dr. J. WALKER. 10s. net.

RAMSAY (Prof. William).—EXPERIMENTAL PROOFS OF CHEMICAL THEORY FOR BEGINNERS. 18mo. 2s. 6d.

REMSEN (Prof. Ira).—THE ELEMENTS OF CHEMISTRY. Fcp. 8vo. 2s. 6d.
—— AN INTRODUCTION TO THE STUDY OF CHEMISTRY (INORGANIC CHEMISTRY). Cr. 8vo. 6s. 6d.
—— A TEXT-BOOK OF INORGANIC CHEMISTRY. 8vo. 16s.
—— COMPOUNDS OF CARBON; or, An Introduction to the Study of Organic Chemistry. Cr. 8vo. 6s. 6d.

ROSCOE (Sir Henry E., F.R.S.).—A PRIMER OF CHEMISTRY. Illustrated. 18mo. 1s.
—— LESSONS IN ELEMENTARY CHEMISTRY, INORGANIC AND ORGANIC. Fcp. 8vo. 4s.6d.

ROSCOE (Sir H. E.) and SCHORLEMMER (Prof. C.).—A COMPLETE TREATISE ON INORGANIC AND ORGANIC CHEMISTRY. Illustr. 8vo.—Vols. I. and II. INORGANIC CHEMISTRY; Vol. I. THE NON-METALLIC ELEMENTS, 2nd Edit., 21s. Vol. II. Parts I. and II. METALS, 18s. each.—Vol. III. ORGANIC CHEMISTRY: THE CHEMISTRY OF THE HYDRO-CARBONS AND THEIR DERIVATIVES. Parts I. II. IV. and VI. 21s.; Parts III. and V. 18s. each.

ROSCOE (Sir H. E.) and SCHUSTER (A.).
—SPECTRUM ANALYSIS. By Sir HENRY E.
ROSCOE. 4th Edit., revised by the Author
and A. SCHUSTER, F.R.S. With Coloured
Plates. 8vo. 21s.

THORPE (Prof. T. E.) and TATE (W.).—
A SERIES OF CHEMICAL PROBLEMS. With
KEY. Fcp. 8vo. 2s.

THORPE (Prof. T. E.) and RÜCKER (Prof.
A. W.).—A TREATISE ON CHEMICAL PHY-
SICS. Illustrated. 8vo. [In preparation.

WURTZ (Ad.).—A HISTORY OF CHEMICAL
THEORY. Transl. by H. WATTS. Cr. 8vo. 6s.

CHRISTIAN CHURCH, History of the.
(See under THEOLOGY, p. 34.)

CHURCH OF ENGLAND, The.
(See under THEOLOGY, p. 34.)

COLLECTED WORKS.
(See under LITERATURE, p. 20.)

COMPARATIVE ANATOMY.
(See under ZOOLOGY, p. 42.)

COOKERY.
(See under DOMESTIC ECONOMY, below.)

DEVOTIONAL BOOKS.
(See under THEOLOGY, p. 35.)

DICTIONARIES AND GLOSSARIES.

AUTENRIETH (Dr. G.).—AN HOMERIC
DICTIONARY. Translated from the German,
by R. P. KEEP, Ph.D. Cr. 8vo. 6s.

BARTLETT (J.).—FAMILIAR QUOTATIONS.
Cr. 8vo. 12s. 6d.

GROVE (Sir George).—A DICTIONARY OF
MUSIC AND MUSICIANS. (See MUSIC.)

HOLE (Rev. C.).—A BRIEF BIOGRAPHICAL
DICTIONARY. 2nd Edit. 18mo. 4s. 6d.

MASSON (Gustave).—A COMPENDIOUS DIC-
TIONARY OF THE FRENCH LANGUAGE.
Cr. 8vo. 3s. 6d.

PALGRAVE (R. H. I.).—A DICTIONARY OF
POLITICAL ECONOMY. (See POLITICAL
ECONOMY.)

WHITNEY (Prof. W. D.).—A COMPENDIOUS
GERMAN AND ENGLISH DICTIONARY. Cr.
8vo. 5s.—German-English Part separately.
3s. 6d.

WRIGHT (W. Aldis).—THE BIBLE WORD-
BOOK. 2nd Edit. Cr. 8vo. 7s. 6d.

YONGE (Charlotte M.).—HISTORY OF CHRIS-
TIAN NAMES. Cr. 8vo. 7s. 6d.

DOMESTIC ECONOMY.
Cookery—Nursing—Needlework.

Cookery.　-

BARKER (Lady).—FIRST LESSONS IN THE
PRINCIPLES OF COOKING. 3rd Ed. 18mo. 1s.

BARNETT (E. A.) and O'NEILL (H. C.).—
PRIMER OF DOMESTIC ECONOMY. 18mo. 1s.

MIDDLE-CLASS
Compiled for th
Cookery. Fcp. 8

TEGETMEIER (W
AGEMENT AND CO

WRIGHT (Miss
COOKERY-BOOK.

N

CRAVEN (Mrs. D
TRICT NURSES.

FOTHERGILL (D
INVALID, THE CO
TIC, AND THE GO

JEX-BLAKE (Dr.
INFANTS. 18mo.

RATHBONE (Wr
PROGRESS OF DIS
TO THE PRESENT

RECOLLECTION
E. D. Cr. 8vo.

STEPHEN (Caroli
THE POOR. Cr. 8

Nee

GLAISTER (Elizal
8vo. 2s. 6d.

GRAND'HOMME
DRESSMAKING.
E. GRAND'HOMME

GRENFELL (Mrs.

ROSEVEAR (E.).
ING, AND CUTTIN

DRA
(See under L

ELE(
(See under

EDU

ARNOLD (Matthew
UNIVERSITIES IN
—— REPORTS ON
1852-82. Ed. by L
—— A FRENCH E
EDUCATION AND

BLAKISTON (J. R
ON SCHOOL MANA

CALDERWOOD
ING. 4th Edit.

COMBE (George).-
CIPLES AND PRA
GEORGE COMBE.

CRAIK (Henry).—
TION TO EDUCATI

FEARON (D. R.
6th Edit. Cr. 8vo

FITCH (J. G.).-
SCHOOLS AND T
printed by permiss

GLADSTONE (J.
FROM AN EDUCA
3rd Edit. Cr. 8vo

:ESSURE IN HIGH
With Introduction
'NE. Cr. 8vo. 3s. 6d.

[EALTH AND EDU-

).—POLITICAL AND
s. 8vo. 8s. 6d.

RNING AND WORK-

ICAL AND SE-
ON. Crown 8vo.
Nov. 1891.

—EDUCATION AND
8vo. 6s.

ING.

HOMSON (A.W.)
MECHANICS. Part
Cr. 8vo. 10s. 6d.

RAPHICAL DETER-
IN ENGINEERING
l. 8vo. 24s.

l.).—APPLIED ME-
· General Introduc-
tructures and Ma-
18s.

H.) and SLADE
PLIED MECHANICS.

, W.).—THE ME-
. Cr. 8vo. 8s. 6d.

·THERMODYNAMICS
AND OTHER HEAT-

ENTARY TREATISE
:O STEAM AND THE
:ed. Cr. 8vo. 4s. 6d.

A HISTORY OF THE
2l. 2s. net.

E PRACTICAL ME-
STRAINS ON GIR-
3SES. 8vo. 7s. 6d.

N SERIES.
CS.)

F ACTION.
'HV.)

' LETTERS.
'HV.)

EN, Twelve.
'HV.)

See ART.)
TERATURE, p. 20.)

:e ART.)
:ILOSOPHY, p. 27.)

The.
:GV, p. 35.)

rose.
'URE, p. 18.)

GARDENING.

(*See also* AGRICULTURE; BOTANY.)

BLOMFIELD (R.) and THOMAS (F. I.).—
THE FORMAL GARDEN IN ENGLAND. Illustrated. Ex. cr. 8vo. 7s. 6d. net.

BRIGHT (H. A.).—THE ENGLISH FLOWER
GARDEN. Cr. 8vo. 3s. 6d.
—— A YEAR IN A LANCASHIRE GARDEN. Cr.
8vo. 3s. 6d.

HOBDAY (E.). — VILLA GARDENING. A
Handbook for Amateur and Practical Gardeners. Ext. cr. 8vo. 6s.

HOPE (Frances J.).—NOTES AND THOUGHTS
ON GARDENS AND WOODLANDS. Cr. 8vo. 6s.

WRIGHT (J.).—A PRIMER OF PRACTICAL
HORTICULTURE. 18mo. 1s.

GEOGRAPHY.

(*See also* ATLASES.)

BLANFORD (H. F.).—ELEMENTARY GEO-
GRAPHY OF INDIA, BURMA, AND CEYLON.
Globe 8vo. 2s. 6d.

CLARKE (C. B.).—A GEOGRAPHICAL READER
AND COMPANION TO THE ATLAS. Cr. 8vo. 2s.
—— A CLASS-BOOK OF GEOGRAPHY. With 18
Coloured Maps. Fcp. 8vo. 3s. ; swd., 2s. 6d.

DAWSON (G. M.) and SUTHERLAND (A.).
ELEMENTARY GEOGRAPHY OF THE BRITISH
COLONIES. Globe 8vo. 3s.

ELDERTON (W. A.).—MAPS AND MAP-
DRAWING. Pott 8vo. 1s.

GEIKIE (Sir Archibald).—THE TEACHING OF
GEOGRAPHY. A Practical Handbook for the
use of Teachers. Globe 8vo. 2s.
—— GEOGRAPHY OF THE BRITISH ISLES.
18mo. 1s.

GREEN (J. R. and A. S.).—A SHORT GEOGRA-
PHY OF THE BRITISH ISLANDS. Fcp. 8vo. 3s. 6d.

GROVE (Sir George).—A PRIMER OF GEO-
GRAPHY. Maps. 18mo. 1s.

KIEPERT (H.). — MANUAL OF ANCIENT
GEOGRAPHY. Cr. 8vo. 5s.

MILL (H. R.).—ELEMENTARY CLASS-BOOK
OF GENERAL GEOGRAPHY. Cr. 8vo. 3s. 6d.

SIME (James).—GEOGRAPHY OF EUROPE.
With Illustrations. Globe 8vo. 3s.

STRACHEY (Lieut.-Gen. R.).—LECTURES ON
GEOGRAPHY. Cr. 8vo. 4s. 6d.

TOZER (H. F.).—A PRIMER OF CLASSICAL
GEOGRAPHY. 18mo. 1s.

GEOLOGY AND MINERALOGY.

BLANFORD (W. T.). — GEOLOGY AND
ZOOLOGY OF ABYSSINIA. 8vo. 21s.

COAL: ITS HISTORY AND ITS USES. By
Profs. GREEN, MIALL, THORPE, RÜCKER,
and MARSHALL. 8vo. 12s. 6d.

DAWSON (Sir J. W.).—THE GEOLOGY OF
NOVA SCOTIA, NEW BRUNSWICK, AND
PRINCE EDWARD ISLAND; or, Acadian Geo-
logy. 4th Edit. 8vo. 21s.

GEIKIE (Sir Archibald).—A PRIMER OF GEO-
LOGY. Illustrated. 18mo. 1s.
—— CLASS-BOOK OF GEOLOGY. Illustrated.
Cr. 8vo. 4s. 6d.

GEOLOGY AND MINERALOGY—*contd.*

GEIKIE (Sir A.).—GEOLOGICAL SKETCHES AT HOME AND ABROAD. Illus. 8vo. 10*s.*6*d.*
—— OUTLINES OF FIELD GEOLOGY. With numerous Illustrations. Gl. 8vo. 2*s.* 6*d.*
—— TEXT-BOOK OF GEOLOGY. Illustrated. 2nd Edit. 7th Thousand. Med. 8vo. 28*s.*
—— THE SCENERY OF SCOTLAND. Viewed in connection with its Physical Geology. 2nd Edit. Cr. 8vo. 12*s.* 6*d.*

HULL (E.).—A TREATISE ON ORNAMENTAL AND BUILDING STONES OF GREAT BRITAIN AND FOREIGN COUNTRIES. 8vo. 12*s.*

PENNINGTON (Rooke).—NOTES ON THE BARROWS AND BONE CAVES OF DERBYSHIRE. 8vo. 6*s.*

RENDU—WILLS.—THE THEORY OF THE GLACIERS OF SAVOY. By M. LE CHANOINE RENDU. Trans. by A. WILLS, Q.C. 8vo. 7*s.*6*d.*

WILLIAMS (G. H.).—ELEMENTS OF CRYSTALLOGRAPHY. Cr. 8vo. 6*s.*

GLOBE LIBRARY. (*See* LITERATURE, p. 21.)

GLOSSARIES. (*See* DICTIONARIES.)

GOLDEN TREASURY SERIES.
(*See* LITERATURE, p. 21.)

GRAMMAR. (*See* PHILOLOGY.)

HEALTH. (*See* HYGIENE.)

HEAT. (*See under* PHYSICS, p. 29.)

HISTOLOGY. (*See* PHYSIOLOGY.)

HISTORY.
(*See also* BIOGRAPHY.)

ANDREWS (C. M.).—THE OLD ENGLISH MANOR: A STUDY IN ECONOMIC HISTORY. Royal 8vo. 6*s.* net.

ANNALS OF OUR TIME. A Diurnal of Events, Social and Political, Home and Foreign. By JOSEPH IRVING. 8vo.—Vol. I. June 20th, 1837, to Feb. 28th, 1871, 18*s.*; Vol. II. Feb. 24th, 1871, to June 24th, 1887, 18*s.* Also Vol. II. in 3 parts: Part I. Feb. 24th, 1871, to March 19th, 1874, 4*s.* 6*d.*; Part II. March 20th, 1874, to July 22nd, 1878, 4*s.* 6*d.*; Part III. July 23rd, 1878, to June 24th, 1887, 9*s.* Vol. III. By H. H. FYFE. Part I. June 25th, 1887, to Dec. 30th, 1890, 4*s.* 6*d.*; sewed, 3*s.* 6*d.* Part II. 1891, 1*s.* 6*d.*; sewed, 1*s.*

ANNUAL SUMMARIES. Reprinted from the *Times.* 2 Vols. Cr. 8vo. 3*s.* 6*d.* each.

ARNOLD (T.).—THE SECOND PUNIC WAR. By THOMAS ARNOLD, D.D. Ed. by W. T. ARNOLD, M.A. With 8 Maps. Cr. 8vo. 5*s.*

ARNOLD (W. T.).—A HISTORY OF THE EARLY ROMAN EMPIRE. Cr. 8vo. [*In prep.*

BEESLY (Mrs.).—STORIES FROM THE HISTORY OF ROME. Fcp. 8vo. 2*s.* 6*d.*

BLACKIE (Prof. John Stuart).—WHAT DOES HISTORY TEACH? Globe 8vo. 2*s.* 6*d.*

BRETT (R. B.).—FOOTPRINTS OF STATESMEN DURING THE EIGHTEENTH CENTURY IN ENGLAND. Cr. 8vo. 6*s.*

BRYCE (James, M.P.).—THE HOLY ROMAN EMPIRE. 8th Edit. Cr. 8vo. 7*s.* 6*d.*—*Library Edition.* 8vo. 14*s.*

BUCKLEY (Arabella).—HISTORY OF ENG LAND FOR BEGINNERS. Globe 8vo. 3*s.*
—— PRIMER OF ENGLISH HISTORY. 18mo. 1

BURKE (Edmund). (*See* POLITICS.)

BURY (J. B.).—A HISTORY OF THE LATE ROMAN EMPIRE FROM ARCADIUS TO IREN A.D. 390—800. 2 vols. 8vo. 32*s.*

CASSEL (Dr. D.).—MANUAL OF JEWIS HISTORY AND LITERATURE. Translated Mrs. HENRY LUCAS. Fcp. 8vo. 2*s.* 6*d.*

COX (G. V.).—RECOLLECTIONS OF OXFOR 2nd Edit. Cr. 8vo. 6*s.*

ENGLISH STATESMEN, TWELVE (*See* BIOGRAPHY, p. 4.)

FISKE (John).—THE CRITICAL PERIOD AMERICAN HISTORY, 1783—89. Ext. 8vo. 10*s.* 6*d.*
—— THE BEGINNINGS OF NEW ENGLAND or, The Puritan Theocracy in its Relations Civil and Religious Liberty. Cr. 8vo. 7*s.* 6
—— THE AMERICAN REVOLUTION. 2 VO Cr. 8vo. 18*s.*
—— THE DISCOVERY OF AMERICA. 2 VO Cr. 8vo. 18*s.*

FRAMJI (Dosabhai). — HISTORY OF TH PARSIS, INCLUDING THEIR MANNERS, CU TOMS, RELIGION, AND PRESENT POSITIO With Illustrations. 2 vols. Med. 8vo. 3

FREEMAN (Prof. E. A.).—HISTORY OF TH CATHEDRAL CHURCH OF WELLS. Cr. 8v 3*s.* 6*d.*
—— OLD ENGLISH HISTORY. With 3 Colour Maps. 9th Edit., revised. Ext. fcp. 8vo.
—— HISTORICAL ESSAYS. First Series. Edit. 8vo. 10*s.* 6*d.*
—— —— Second Series. 3rd Edit., wi Additional Essays. 8vo. 10*s.* 6*d.*
—— —— Third Series. 8vo. 12*s.*
—— —— Fourth Series. 8vo. 12*s.* 6*d.*
—— THE GROWTH OF THE ENGLISH CONST TUTION FROM THE EARLIEST TIMES. Edit. Cr. 8vo. 5*s.*
—— COMPARATIVE POLITICS. Lectures at t Royal Institution. To which is added "T Unity of History." 8vo. 14*s.*
—— SUBJECT AND NEIGHBOUR LANDS VENICE. Illustrated. Cr. 8vo. 10*s.* 6*d.*
—— ENGLISH TOWNS AND DISTRICTS. Series of Addresses and Essays. 8vo. 14
—— THE OFFICE OF THE HISTORICAL PR FESSOR. Cr. 8vo. 2*s.*
—— DISESTABLISHMENT AND DISENDO MENT; WHAT ARE THEY? Cr. 8vo. 2*s.*
—— GREATER GREECE AND GREATER B TAIN: GEORGE WASHINGTON THE E PANDER OF ENGLAND. With an Appen on IMPERIAL FEDERATION. Cr. 8vo. 3*s.* 6
—— THE METHODS OF HISTORICAL STUI Eight Lectures at Oxford. 8vo. 10*s.* 6*d.*
—— THE CHIEF PERIODS OF EUROPEAN H TORY. With Essay on "Greek Cities und Roman Rule." 8vo. 10*s.* 6*d.*
—— FOUR OXFORD LECTURES, 1887; FIF YEARS OF EUROPEAN HISTORY; TEUTO CONQUEST IN GAUL AND BRITAIN. 8vo.
—— HISTORY OF FEDERAL GOVERNMENT GREECE AND ITALY. New Edit. by J. BURY, M.A. Ex. crn. 8vo. 12*s.* 6*d.*

FRIEDMANN (Paul). (*See* BIOGRAPHY.)

GIBBINS (H. de B.).—HISTORY OF CO MERCE IN EUROPE. Globe 8vo. 3*s.* 6*d.*

HISTORY—*continued.*

POOLE (R. L.).—A History of the Huguenots of the Dispersion at the Recall of the Edict of Nantes. Cr. 8vo. 6s.

RHODES (J. F.).—History of the United States from the Compromise of 1850 to 1880. 2 vols. 8vo. 24s.

ROGERS (Prof. J. E. Thorold).—Historical Gleanings. Cr. 8vo.—1st Series. 4s. 6d.—2nd Series. 6s.

SAYCE (Prof. A. H.).—The Ancient Empires of the East. Cr. 8vo. 6s.

SEELEY (Prof. J. R.). — Lectures and Essays. 8vo. 10s. 6d.
—— The Expansion of England. Two Courses of Lectures. Cr. 8vo. 4s. 6d.
—— Our Colonial Expansion. Extracts from the above. Cr. 8vo. 1s.

SEWELL (E. M.) and YONGE (C. M.).—European History, narrated in a Series of Historical Selections from the best Authorities. 2 vols. 3rd Edit. Cr. 8vo. 6s. each.

SHUCKBURGH (E. S.).—A School History of Rome. Cr. 8vo. [In preparation.

STEPHEN (Sir J. Fitzjames, Bart.).—The Story of Nuncomar and the Impeachment of Sir Elijah Impey. 2 vols. Cr. 8vo. 15s.

TAIT (C. W. A.).—Analysis of English History, based on Green's "Short History of the English People." Cr. 8vo. 4s. 6d.

TOUT (T. F.).—Analysis of English History. 18mo. 1s.

TREVELYAN (Sir Geo. Otto).—Cawnpore. Cr. 8vo. 6s.

WHEELER (J. Talboys).—Primer of Indian History, Asiatic and European. 18mo. 1s.
—— College History of India, Asiatic and European. Cr. 8vo. 3s.; swd. 2s. 6d.
—— A Short History of India. With Maps. Cr. 8vo. 12s.
—— India under British Rule. 8vo. 12s. 6d.

WOOD (Rev. E. G.).—The Regal Power of the Church. 8vo. 4s. 6d.

YONGE (Charlotte).—Cameos from English History. Ext. fcp. 8vo. 5s. each.—Vol. 1. From Rollo to Edward II.; Vol. 2. The Wars in France; Vol. 3. The Wars of the Roses; Vol. 4. Reformation Times; Vol. 5. England and Spain; Vol. 6. Forty Years of Stewart Rule (1603—43); Vol. 7. The Rebellion and Restoration (1642—1678).
—— The Victorian Half-Century. Cr. 8vo. 1s. 6d.; sewed, 1s.
—— The Story of the Christians and Moors in Spain. 18mo. 4s. 6d.

HORTICULTURE. (*See* Gardening.)

HYGIENE.

BERNERS (J.).—First Lessons on Health. 18mo. 1s.

BLYTH (A. Wynter).—A Manual of Public Health. 8vo. 17s. net.
—— Lectures on Sanitary Law. 8vo. 8s. 6d. net.

BROWNE (J. H. Balfour).—Water Supply. Cr. 8vo. 2s. 6d.

CORFIELD (Dr. W. ⸺ and Utilisation o⸺ Revised by the Aut⸺ Parkes, M.D. 8vo. ⸺

GOODFELLOW (J.).—⸺ of Bread. Cr. 8vo.⸺

KINGSLEY (Charles) cial Lectures. Cr⸺
—— Health and Ed⸺

MIERS (H. A.) and C⸺ Soil in Relation to⸺

REYNOLDS (Prof. C⸺ and How to keep i⸺ Edit. Cr. 8vo. 1s. 6⸺

RICHARDSON (Dr. ⸺ City of Health. ⸺
—— The Future of⸺ Cr. 8vo. 1s.
—— On Alcohol. C⸺

HYMN ⸺
(*See under* Th⸺

ILLUSTRAT ⸺

BALCH (Elizabeth). ⸺ English Homes. ⸺

BLAKE. (*See* Biogr⸺

BOUGHTON (G. H.)⸺ (*See* Voyages and T⸺

CHRISTMAS CARO⸺ Colours, with Illumin⸺

DAYS WITH SIR R⸺ LEY. From the *Sp⸺* Hugh Thomson. C⸺ uncut edges, paper la⸺

DELL (E. C.).—Pict⸺ Engraved by J. D. C⸺

GASKELL (Mrs.).—C⸺ by Hugh Thomson⸺ with uncut edges pap⸺

GOLDSMITH (Olive⸺ Wakefield. New ⸺ trations by Hugh ⸺ Austin Dobson. C⸺ Uncut Edges, paper ⸺

GREEN (John Ric⸺ Edition of the Sh⸺ English People. I⸺ 1s. each net. Part I. ⸺ II. 12s. each net.

GRIMM. (*See* Books⸺

HALLWARD (R. F.)⸺ dise. Music, Verse, ⸺

HAMERTON (P. G.)⸺ Etchings and Photog⸺
—— Large Paper Editi⸺

HARRISON (F.).—A⸺ nor House, Sutto⸺ 4to. 42s. net.

IRVING (Washingto⸺ From the Sketch Book⸺ Caldecott. Gilt ed⸺ with uncut edges, p⸺ Paper Edition. 30s. ⸺
—— Bracebridge H.⸺ dolph Caldecott. ⸺ 6s.—Also with uncut⸺
—— Old Christmas⸺ Hall. *Edition de* ⸺

INGSLEY (Charles).—THE WATER BABIES. (*See* BOOKS FOR THE YOUNG.)
— THE HEROES. (*See* BOOKS for the YOUNG.)
— GLAUCUS. (*See* NATURAL HISTORY.)

ANG (Andrew).—THE LIBRARY. With a Chapter on Modern English Illustrated Books, by AUSTIN DOBSON. Cr. 8vo. 4s. 6d.
—Large Paper Edition. 21s. net.

YTE (H. C. Maxwell). (*See* HISTORY.)

AHAFFY (Rev. Prof. J. P.) and ROGERS (J. E.). (*See* VOYAGES AND TRAVELS.)

EREDITH (L. A.).—BUSH FRIENDS IN TASMANIA. Native Flowers, Fruits, and Insects, with Prose and Verse Descriptions. Folio. 52s. 6d. net.

LD SONGS. With Drawings by E. A. ABBEY and A. PARSONS. 4to, mor. gilt. 31s. 6d.

ROPERT (J. L.). (*See* ART.)

TUART, RELICS OF THE ROYAL HOUSE OF. Illustrated by 40 Plates in Colours drawn from Relics of the Stuarts by WILLIAM GIBB. With an Introduction by JOHN SKELTON, C.B., LL.D., and Descriptive Notes by W. ST. JOHN HOPE. Folio, half morocco, gilt edges. 10l. 10s. net.

ENNYSON (Lord H.).—JACK AND THE BEAN-STALK. English Hexameters. Illustrated by R. CALDECOTT. Fcp. 4to. 3s. 6d.

RISTRAM (W. O.).—COACHING DAYS AND COACHING WAYS. Illust. H. RAILTON and HUGH THOMSON. Cr. 8vo. 6s.—Also with uncut edges, paper label, 6s.—Large Paper Edition, 30s. net.

URNER'S LIBER STUDIORUM: A DESCRIPTION AND A CATALOGUE. By W. G. RAWLINSON. Med. 8vo. 12s. 6d.

ALTON and COTTON—LOWELL.—THE COMPLETE ANGLER. With Introduction by JAS. RUSSELL LOWELL. 2 vols. Ext. cr. 8vo. 52s. 6d. net.

LANGUAGE. (*See* PHILOLOGY.)

LAW.

ERNARD (M.).—FOUR LECTURES ON SUBJECTS CONNECTED WITH DIPLOMACY. 8vo. 9s.

IGELOW (M. M.).—HISTORY OF PROCEDURE IN ENGLAND FROM THE NORMAN CONQUEST, 1066-1204. 8vo. 16s.

OUTMY (E.). — STUDIES IN CONSTITUTIONAL LAW. Transl. by Mrs. DICEY. Preface by Prof. A. V. DICEY. Cr. 8vo. 6s.
— THE ENGLISH CONSTITUTION. Transl. by Mrs. EADEN. Introduction by Sir F. POLLOCK, Bart. Cr. 8vo. 6s.

HERRY (R. R.).—LECTURES ON THE GROWTH OF CRIMINAL LAW IN ANCIENT COMMUNITIES. 8vo. 5s. net.

ICEY (Prof. A. V.).—INTRODUCTION TO THE STUDY OF THE LAW OF THE CONSTITUTION. 4th Edit. 8vo. 12s. 6d.

NGLISH CITIZEN SERIES, THE. (*See* POLITICS.)

HOLLAND (Prof. T. E.).—THE TREATY RELATIONS OF RUSSIA AND TURKEY, FROM 1774 TO 1853. Cr. 8vo. 2s.

HOLMES (O. W., jun.).—THE COMMON LAW. 8vo. 12s.

LIGHTWOOD (J. M.).—THE NATURE OF POSITIVE LAW. 8vo. 12s. 6d.

MAITLAND (F. W.).—PLEAS OF THE CROWN FOR THE COUNTY OF GLOUCESTER, A.D. 1221. 8vo. 7s. 6d.
—— JUSTICE AND POLICE. Cr. 8vo. 3s. 6d.

MONAHAN (James H.).—THE METHOD OF LAW. Cr. 8vo. 6s.

PATERSON (James).—COMMENTARIES ON THE LIBERTY OF THE SUBJECT, AND THE LAWS OF ENGLAND RELATING TO THE SECURITY OF THE PERSON. 2 vols. Cr. 8vo. 21s.
—— THE LIBERTY OF THE PRESS, SPEECH, AND PUBLIC WORSHIP. Cr. 8vo. 12s.

PHILLIMORE (John G.).—PRIVATE LAW AMONG THE ROMANS. 8vo. 6s.

POLLOCK (Sir F., Bart.).—ESSAYS IN JURISPRUDENCE AND ETHICS. 8vo. 10s. 6d.
—— THE LAND LAWS. Cr. 8vo. 3s. 6d.
—— LEADING CASES DONE INTO ENGLISH. Cr. 8vo. 3s. 6d.

RICHEY (Alex. G.).—THE IRISH LAND LAWS. Cr. 8vo. 3s. 6d.

SELBORNE (Earl of).—JUDICIAL PROCEDURE IN THE PRIVY COUNCIL. 8vo. 1s. net.

STEPHEN (Sir J. F., Bart.).—A DIGEST OF THE LAW OF EVIDENCE. 6th Ed. Cr. 8vo. 6s.
—— A DIGEST OF THE CRIMINAL LAW: CRIMES AND PUNISHMENTS. 4th Ed. 8vo. 16s.
—— A DIGEST OF THE LAW OF CRIMINAL PROCEDURE IN INDICTABLE OFFENCES. By Sir J. F., Bart., and HERBERT STEPHEN, LL.M. 8vo. 12s. 6d.
—— A HISTORY OF THE CRIMINAL LAW OF ENGLAND. 3 vols. 8vo. 48s.
—— A GENERAL VIEW OF THE CRIMINAL LAW OF ENGLAND. 2nd Edit. 8vo. 14s.

STEPHEN (J. K.).—INTERNATIONAL LAW AND INTERNATIONAL RELATIONS. Cr. 8vo. 6s.

WILLIAMS (S. E.).—FORENSIC FACTS AND FALLACIES. Globe 8vo. 4s. 6d.

LETTERS. (*See under* LITERATURE, p. 20.)

LIFE-BOAT.

GILMORE (Rev. John).—STORM WARRIORS; or, Life-Boat Work on the Goodwin Sands. Cr. 8vo. 3s. 6d.

LEWIS (Richard).—HISTORY OF THE LIFE-BOAT AND ITS WORK. Cr. 8vo. 5s.

LIGHT. (*See under* PHYSICS, p. 29.)

LITERATURE.

History and Criticism of—Commentaries, etc.—Poetry and the Drama—Poetical Collections and Selections—Prose Fiction—Collected Works, Essays, Lectures, Letters, Miscellaneous Works.

History and Criticism of.
(*See also* ESSAYS, p. 20.)

ARNOLD (M.). (*See* ESSAYS. p. 20.)

BROOKE (Stopford A.).—A PRIMER OF ENGLISH LITERATURE. 18mo. 1s. — Large Paper Edition. 8vo. 7s. 6d.
—— A HISTORY OF EARLY ENGLISH LITERATURE. 2 vols. 8vo. 20s. net.

LITERATURE.

History and Criticism of—*continued.*

CLASSICAL WRITERS. Edited by JOHN RICHARD GREEN. Fcp. 8vo. 1s. 6d. each.
DEMOSTHENES. By Prof. BUTCHER, M.A.
EURIPIDES. By Prof. MAHAFFY.
LIVY. By the Rev. W. W. CAPES, M.A.
MILTON. By STOPFORD A. BROOKE.
SOPHOCLES. By Prof. L. CAMPBELL, M.A.
TACITUS. By Messrs. CHURCH and BRODRIBB.
VERGIL. By Prof. NETTLESHIP, M.A.

ENGLISH MEN OF LETTERS. (*See* BIOGRAPHY, p. 4.)

HISTORY OF ENGLISH LITERATURE. In 4 vols. Cr. 8vo.
EARLY ENGLISH LITERATURE. By STOPFORD BROOKE, M.A. [*In preparation.*
ELIZABETHAN LITERATURE (1560—1665). By GEORGE SAINTSBURY. 7s. 6d.
EIGHTEENTH CENTURY LITERATURE (1660—1780). By EDMUND GOSSE, M.A. 7s. 6d.
THE MODERN PERIOD. By Prof. DOWDEN. [*In preparation.*

JEBB (Prof. R. C.).—A PRIMER OF GREEK LITERATURE. 18mo. 1s.
—— THE ATTIC ORATORS, FROM ANTIPHON TO ISAEOS. 2 vols 8vo. 25s.

JOHNSON'S LIVES OF THE POETS. MILTON, DRYDEN, POPE, ADDISON, SWIFT, AND GRAY. With Macaulay's "Life of Johnson" Ed. by M. ARNOLD. Cr. 8vo. 4s. 6d.

KINGSLEY (Charles). — LITERARY AND GENERAL LECTURES. Cr. 8vo. 3s. 6d.

MAHAFFY (Prof. J. P.).—A HISTORY OF CLASSICAL GREEK LITERATURE. 2 vols. Cr. 8vo.—Vol. 1. THE POETS. With an Appendix on Homer by Prof. SAYCE. In 2 Parts.—Vol. 2. THE PROSE WRITERS. In 2 Parts. 4s. 6d. each.

MORLEY (John). (*See* COLLECTED WORKS, p. 23.)

NICHOL (Prof. J.) and McCORMICK (Prof (W. S.).—A SHORT HISTORY OF ENGLISH LITERATURE. Globe 8vo. [*In preparation.*

OLIPHANT (Mrs. M. O. W.).—THE LITERARY HISTORY OF ENGLAND IN THE END OF THE 18TH AND BEGINNING OF THE 19TH CENTURY. 3 vols. 8vo. 21s.

RYLAND (F.).—CHRONOLOGICAL OUTLINES OF ENGLISH LITERATURE. Cr. 8vo. 6s.

WARD (Prof. A. W.).—A HISTORY OF ENGLISH DRAMATIC LITERATURE, TO THE DEATH OF QUEEN ANNE. 2 vols. 8vo. 32s.

WILKINS (Prof. A. S.).—A PRIMER OF ROMAN LITERATURE. 18mo. 1s.

Commentaries, etc.

BROWNING.
A PRIMER ON BROWNING. By MARY WILSON. Cr. 8vo. 2s. 6d.

CHAUCER.
A PRIMER OF CHAUCER. By A. W. POLLARD. 18mo. 1s.

DANTE.
READINGS ON THE PURGATORIO OF DANTE. Chiefly based on the Commentary of Benvenuto da Imola. By the Hon. W. W. VERNON, M.A. With an Introduction by Dean CHURCH. 2 vols. Cr. 8vo. 24s.

HOMER.
HOMERIC DICTIONARY. (*See* DICTIONARIE:
THE PROBLEM OF THE HOMERIC POEM By Prof. W. D. GEDDES. 8vo. 14s.
HOMERIC SYNCHRONISM. An Inquiry in the Time and Place of Homer. By t Rt. Hon. W. E. GLADSTONE. Cr. 8vo. 1
PRIMER OF HOMER. By the same. 18mo. 1
LANDMARKS OF HOMERIC STUDY, TOGETH WITH AN ESSAY ON THE POINTS OF CO TACT BETWEEN THE ASSYRIAN TABLE AND THE HOMERIC TEXT. By the sam Cr. 8vo. 2s. 6d.
COMPANION TO THE ILIAD FOR ENGLI READERS. By W. LEAF, Litt.D. Crov 8vo. 7s. 6d.

HORACE.
STUDIES, LITERARY AND HISTORICAL, THE ODES OF HORACE. By A. W. VE RALL, Litt.D. 8vo. 8s. 6d.

SHAKESPEARE.
A PRIMER OF SHAKSPERE. By Prof. DO DEN. 18mo. 1s.
A SHAKESPEARIAN GRAMMAR. By Re E. A. ABBOTT. Ext. fcp. 8vo. 6s.
SHAKESPEAREANA GENEALOGICA. By G. FRENCH. 8vo. 15s.
A SELECTION FROM THE LIVES IN NORTH PLUTARCH WHICH ILLUSTRATE SHAKE PEARE'S PLAYS. Edited by Rev. W. V SKEAT, M.A. Cr. 8vo. 6s.
SHORT STUDIES OF SHAKESPEARE'S PLOT By Prof. CYRIL RANSOME. Cr. 8vo. 3s. 6 —Also separately: HAMLET, 9d.; MA BETH, 9d.; TEMPEST, 9d.
CALIBAN: A Critique on "The Tempes and "A Midsummer Night's Dream." I Sir DANIEL WILSON. 8vo. 10s. 6d.

TENNYSON.
A COMPANION TO "IN MEMORIAM." I ELIZABETH R. CHAPMAN. Globe 8vo. 2
ESSAYS ON THE IDYLLS OF THE KING. I H. LITTLEDALE, M.A. Cr. 8vo. 4s. 6d
A STUDY OF THE WORKS OF ALFRED LOF TENNYSON. By E. C. TAINSH. New E Cr. 8vo. 6s.

WORDSWORTH.
WORDSWORTHIANA: A Selection of Pape read to the Wordsworth Society. Edite by W. KNIGHT. Cr. 8vo. 7s. 6d.

Poetry and the Drama.

ALDRICH (T. Bailey).—THE SISTERS' TR GEDY: with other Poems, Lyrical and Dr matic. Fcp. 8vo. 3s. 6d. net.

AN ANCIENT CITY: AND OTHER POEM Ext. fcp. 8vo. 6s.

ANDERSON (A.).—BALLADS AND SONNET Cr. 8vo. 5s.

ARNOLD (Matthew). — THE COMPLET POETICAL WORKS. New Edition. 3 vol Cr. 8vo. 7s. 6d. each.
   Vol. 1. EARLY POEMS, NARRATIVE POEM AND SONNETS.
   Vol. 2. LYRIC AND ELEGIAC POEMS.
   Vol. 3. DRAMATIC AND LATER POEMS.
—— COMPLETE POETICAL WORKS. 1 VO Cr. 8vo. 7s. 6d.
—— SELECTED POEMS. 18mo. 4s. 6d.

USTIN (Alfred).—POETICAL WORKS. New Collected Edition. 6 vols. Cr. 8vo. 5s. each.
    Vol. 1. THE TOWER OF BABEL.
    Vol. 2. SAVONAROLA, etc.
    Vol. 3. PRINCE LUCIFER.
    Vol. 4. THE HUMAN TRAGEDY.
    Vol. 5. LYRICAL POEMS.
    Vol. 6. NARRATIVE POEMS.
— SOLILOQUIES IN SONG. Cr. 8vo. 6s.
— AT THE GATE OF THE CONVENT: and other Poems. Cr. 8vo. 6s.
— MADONNA'S CHILD. Cr. 4to. 3s. 6d.
— ROME OR DEATH. Cr. 4to. 9s.
— THE GOLDEN AGE. Cr. 8vo. 5s.
— THE SEASON. Cr. 8vo. 5s.
— LOVE'S WIDOWHOOD. Cr. 8vo. 6s.
— ENGLISH LYRICS. Cr. 8vo. 3s. 6d.
— FORTUNATUS THE PESSIMIST. Cr. 8vo. 6s.

ETSY LEE: A FO'C'S'LE YARN. Ext. fcp. 8vo. 3s. 6d.

LACKIE (John Stuart).—MESSIS VITAE: Gleanings of Song from a Happy Life. Cr. 8vo. 4s. 6d.
— THE WISE MEN OF GREECE. In a Series of Dramatic Dialogues. Cr. 8vo. 9s.
— GOETHE'S FAUST. Translated into English Verse. 2nd Edit. Cr. 8vo. 9s.

LAKE. (See BIOGRAPHY, p. 3.)

ROOKE (Stopford A.).—RIQUET OF THE TUFT: A Love Drama. Ext. cr. 8vo. 6s.
— POEMS. Globe 8vo. 6s.

ROWN (T. E.).—THE MANX WITCH: and other Poems. Cr. 8vo. 6s.
— OLD JOHN, AND OTHER POEM Crown 8vo. 6s.

URGON (Dean).—POEMS. Ex.fcp.8vo. 4s.6d.

URNS. THE POETICAL WORKS. With a Biographical Memoir by ALEXANDER SMITH. In 2 vols. Fcp. 8vo. 10s. (See also GLOBE LIBRARY, p. 21.)

UTLER (Samuel).—HUDIBRAS. Edit. by ALFRED MILNES. Fcp. 8vo.—Part I. 3s. 6d.; Parts II. and III. 4s. 6d.

YRON. (See GOLDEN TREASURY SERIES, p. 21.)

ALDERON.—SELECT PLAYS. Edited by NORMAN MACCOLL. Cr. 8vo. 14s.

AUTLEY (G. S.).—A CENTURY OF EMBLEMS. With Illustrations by Lady MARION ALFORD. Small 4to. 10s. 6d.

LOUGH (A. H.).—POEMS. Cr. 8vo. 7s.6d.

OLERIDGE: POETICAL AND DRAMATIC WORKS. 4 vols. Fcp. 8vo. 31s. 6d.—Also an Edition on Large Paper, 2l. 12s. 6d.
— COMPLETE POETICAL WORKS. With Introduction by J. D. CAMPBELL, and Portrait. Cr. 8vo. 7s. 6d.

OLQUHOUN.—RHYMES AND CHIMES. By F. S. Colquhoun (née F. S. FULLER MAITLAND). Ext. fcp. 8vo. 2s. 6d.

OWPER. (See GLOBE LIBRARY, p. 21; GOLDEN TREASURY SERIES, p. 21.)

RAIK (Mrs.).—POEMS. Ext. fcp. 8vo. 6s.

E VERE (A.).—POETICAL WORKS. 6 vols. Cr. 8vo. 5s. each.

OYLE (Sir F. H.).—THE RETURN OF THE GUARDS: and other Poems. Cr. 8vo. 7s.6d.

RYDEN. (See GLOBE LIBRARY, p. 21.)

MERSON. (See COLLECTED WORKS, p. 21.)

EVANS (Sebastian). — BROTHER FABIAN'S MANUSCRIPT: and other Poems. Fcp. 8vo. 6s.
— IN THE STUDIO: A Decade of Poems. Ext. fcp. 8vo. 5s.

FITZ GERALD (Caroline).—VENETIA VICTRIX: and other Poems. Ext. fcp.8vo. 3s. 6d.

FITZGERALD (Edward).—THE RUBÁIYAT OF OMAR KHÁYYÁM. Ext. cr. 8vo. 10s. 6d.

FOAM. Pott 8vo. 2s. 6d. net.

FO'C'SLE YARNS, including "Betsy Lee," and other Poems. Cr. 8vo. 6s.

FRASER-TYTLER. — SONGS IN MINOR KEYS. By C. C. FRASER-TYTLER (Mrs. EDWARD LIDDELL). 2nd Edit. 18mo. 6s.

FURNIVALL (F. J.).—LE MORTE ARTHUR. Edited from the Harleian MSS. 2252, in the British Museum. Fcp. 8vo. 7s. 6d.

GARNETT (R.).—IDYLLS AND EPIGRAMS. Chiefly from the Greek Anthology. Fcp. 8vo. 2s. 6d.

GOETHE.—FAUST. (See BLACKIE.)
— REYNARD THE FOX. Transl. into English Verse by A. D. AINSLIE. Cr. 8vo. 7s. 6d.

GOLDSMITH.—THE TRAVELLER AND THE DESERTED VILLAGE. With Introduction and Notes, by ARTHUR BARRETT, B.A. 1s. 9d.; sewed, 1s.6d.—THE TRAVELLER (separately), sewed, 1s.—By J. W. HALES. Cr. 8vo. 6d. (See also GLOBE LIBRARY, p. 21.)

GRAHAM (David).—KING JAMES I. An Historical Tragedy. Globe 8vo. 7s.

GRAY.—POEMS. With Introduction and Notes, by J. BRADSHAW, LL.D. Gl. 8vo. 1s. 9d.; sewed, 1s. 6d. (See also COLLECTED WORKS, p. 22.)

HALLWARD. (See ILLUSTRATED BOOKS.)

HAYES (A.).—THE MARCH OF MAN: and other Poems. Fcp. 8vo. 3s. 6d. net.

HERRICK. (See GOLDEN TREASURY SERIES, p. 21.)

HOPKINS (Ellice).—AUTUMN SWALLOWS: A Book of Lyrics. Ext. fcp. 8vo. 6s.

HOSKEN (J. D.).—PHAON AND SAPPHO, AND NIMROD Fcp. 8vo. 5s.

JONES (H. A.).—SAINTS AND SINNERS. Ext. fcp. 8vo. 3s. 6d.
— THE CRUSADERS. Fcp. 8vo. 2s. 6d.

KEATS. (See GOLDEN TREASURY SERIES, p. 21.)

KINGSLEY (Charles).—POEMS. Cr. 8vo. 3s. 6d.—Pocket Edition. 18mo. 1s. 6d.—Eversley Edition. 2 vols. Cr. 8vo. 10s.

LAMB. (See COLLECTED WORKS, p. 22.)

LANDOR. (See GOLDEN TREASURY SERIES, p. 22.)

LONGFELLOW. (See GOLDEN TREASURY SERIES, p. 22.)

LOWELL (Jas. Russell).—COMPLETE POETICAL WORKS. 18mo. 4s. 6d.
— With Introduction by THOMAS HUGHES, and Portrait. Cr. 8vo. 7s. 6d.
— HEARTSEASE AND RUE. Cr. 8vo. 5s.
— OLD ENGLISH DRAMATISTS. Cr. 8vo. 5s. (See also COLLECTED WORKS, p. 23.)

LUCAS (F.).—SKETCHES OF RURAL LIFE. Poems. Globe 8vo. 5s.

LITERATURE.

Poetry and the Drama—*continued.*

MEREDITH (George). — A READING OF EARTH. Ext. fcp. 8vo. 5*s.*
—— POEMS AND LYRICS OF THE JOY OF EARTH. Ext. fcp. 8vo. 6*s.*
—— BALLADS AND POEMS OF TRAGIC LIFE. Cr. 8vo. 6*s.*
—— MODERN LOVE. Ex. fcap. 8vo. 5*s.*
—— THE EMPTY PURSE. Fcp. 8vo. 5*s.*

MILTON.—POETICAL WORKS. Edited, with Introductions and Notes, by Prof. DAVID MASSON, M.A. 3 vols. 8vo. 2*l.* 2*s.*—[Uniform with the Cambridge Shakespeare.]
—— —— Edited by Prof. MASSON. 3 vols. Globe 8vo. 15*s.*
—— —— *Globe Edition.* Edited by Prof. MASSON. Globe 8vo. 3*s.* 6*d.*
—— PARADISE LOST, BOOKS 1 and 2. Edited by MICHAEL MACMILLAN, B.A. 1*s.* 9*d.*; sewed, 1*s.* 6*d.*—BOOKS 1 and 2 (separately), 1*s.* 3*d.* each; sewed, 1*s.* each.
—— L'ALLEGRO, IL PENSEROSO, LYCIDAS, ARCADES, SONNETS, ETC. Edited by WM. BELL, M.A. 1*s.* 9*d.*; sewed, 1*s.* 6*d.*
—— COMUS. By the same. 1*s.* 3*d.*; swd. 1*s.*
—— SAMSON AGONISTES. Edited by H. M. PERCIVAL, M.A. 2*s.*; sewed, 1*s.* 9*d.*

MOULTON (Louise Chandler). — IN THE GARDEN OF DREAMS: Lyrics and Sonnets. Cr. 8vo. 6*s.*
—— SWALLOW FLIGHTS. Cr. 8vo. 6*s.*

MUDIE (C. E.).—STRAY LEAVES: Poems. 4th Edit. Ext. fcp. 8vo. 3*s.* 6*d.*

MYERS (E.).—THE PURITANS: A Poem. Ext. fcp. 8vo. 2*s.* 6*d.*
—— POEMS. Ext. fcp. 8vo. 4*s.* 6*d.*
—— THE DEFENCE OF ROME: and other Poems. Ext. fcp. 8vo. 5*s.*
—— THE JUDGMENT OF PROMETHEUS: and other Poems. Ext. fcp. 8vo. 3*s.* 6*d.*

MYERS (F. W. H.).—THE RENEWAL OF YOUTH: and other Poems. Cr. 8vo. 7*s.* 6*d.*
—— ST. PAUL: A Poem. Ext. fcp. 8vo. 2*s.*6*d.*

NORTON (Hon. Mrs.).—THE LADY OF LA GARAVE. 9th Edit. Fcp. 8vo. 4*s.* 6*d.*

PALGRAVE(Prof.F.T.).—ORIGINAL HYMNS. 3rd Edit. 18mo. 1*s.* 6*d.*
—— LYRICAL POEMS. Ext. fcp. 8vo. 6*s.*
—— VISIONS OF ENGLAND. Cr. 8vo. 7*s.* 6*d.*
—— AMENOPHIS. 18mo. 4*s.* 6*d.*

PALGRAVE (W. G.).—A VISION OF LIFE: SEMBLANCE AND REALITY. Cr. 8vo. 7*s.* net.

PEEL (Edmund).—ECHOES FROM HOREB: and other Poems. Cr. 8vo. 3*s.* 6*d*

POPE. (*See* GLOBE LIBRARY, p. 21.)

RAWNSLEY (H. D.).—POEMS, BALLADS, AND BUCOLICS. Fcp. 8vo. 5*s.*

ROSCOE (W. C.).—POEMS. Edit. by E. M. ROSCOE. Cr. 8vo. 7*s.* net.

ROSSETTI (Christina).—POEMS. New Collected Edition. Globe 8vo. 7*s.* 6*d.*

SCOTT.—THE LA[Y] and THE LADY [OF] Prof. F. T. PALG[RAVE]
—— THE LAY OF [THE] G. H. STUART, [M.A.] B.A. Globe 8vo. I. 9*d.*—Cantos I.-[ ] each; sewed, 1*s.* [ ]
—— MARMION. E[DITED BY] MILLAN, B.A. 3[ ]
—— MARMION, and[ ] By Prof. F. T. P[ALGRAVE.]
—— THE LADY O[F] STUART, M.A. [ ]
—— ROKEBY. B[Y] B.A. 3*s.*; sewed[ ]
(*See also* GL[ ]

SHAIRP (John Ca[mpbell]) and other Poems, [Selected] by F. T. PALGRA[VE.]

SHAKESPEARE. [ ] SHAKESPEARE. [ ] and Revised Edit[ ] M.A. 9 vols. 8[vo.]
—— —— *Victoria[n]* DIES; HISTORIE[S] 6*s.* each.
—— THE TEMPEST[ ] Notes, by K. DE[ ] sewed, 1*s.* 6*d.*
—— MUCH ADO AB[OUT] 1*s.* 9*d.*
—— A MIDSUMME[R] sewed, 1*s.* 6*d.*
—— THE MERCH[ANT] sewed, 1*s.* 6*d.*
—— AS YOU LIKE [IT]
—— TWELFTH NI[GHT]
—— THE WINTER'[S]
—— KING JOHN. [ ]
—— RICHARD II. [ ]
—— HENRY V. I[ ]
—— RICHARD III. [ ] 2*s.* 6*d.*; sewed, 2[ ]
—— CORIOLANUS. [ ] sewed, 2*s.*
—— JULIUS CÆSA[R]
—— MACBETH. I[ ]
—— HAMLET. 2*s.* [ ]
—— KING LEAR. [ ]
—— OTHELLO. 2[ ]
—— ANTONY AND [ ]
—— CYMBELINE. [ ]
(*See also* GLOBE [ ] TREASUR[Y]

SHELLEY.—COM[ ] Edited by Prof. [ ] 7*s.*6*d.* (*See* GOLD[ ]

SMITH (C. Barna[ ]

SMITH (Horace).[ ]
—— INTERLUDES. [ ]

SPENSER.—FAI[ ] H. M. PERCIVAL[ ] 2*s.* 6*d.* (*See also* [ ]

STEPHENS (J. [ ] other Poems. C[ ]

STRETTELL (A[ ] IAN FOLK SONGS. [ ]

SYMONS (Arthu[r] Globe 8vo. 6*s.*

TENNYSON (Lord).—COMPLETE WORKS. New and Enlarged Edition, with Portrait. Cr. 8vo. 7s. 6d.—*School Edition.* In Four Parts. Cr. 8vo. 2s. 6d. each.
—— POETICAL WORKS. *Pocket Edition.* 18mo, morocco, gilt edges. 7s. 6d. net.
—— WORKS. *Library Edition.* In 8 vols. Globe 8vo. 5s. each. [Each volume may be had separately.]—POEMS, 2 vols.—IDYLLS OF THE KING.—THE PRINCESS, and MAUD.—ENOCH ARDEN, and IN MEMORIAM.—BALLADS, and other Poems.—QUEEN MARY, and HAROLD.—BECKET, and other Plays.
—— WORKS. *Ext.fcp. 8vo. Edition,* on Handmade Paper. In 10 vols. (supplied in sets only). 5l. 5s. 0d.—EARLY POEMS.—LUCRETIUS, and other Poems.—IDYLLS OF THE KING.—THE PRINCESS, and MAUD.—ENOCH ARDEN, and IN MEMORIAM.—QUEEN MARY, and HAROLD.—BALLADS, and other Poems.—BECKET, THE CUP.—THE FORESTERS, THE FALCON, THE PROMISE OF MAY.—TIRESIAS, and other Poems.
—— WORKS. *Miniature Edition,* in 16 vols., viz. THE POETICAL WORKS. 12 vols. in a box. 25s.—THE DRAMATIC WORKS. 4 vols. in a box. 10s. 6d.
—— WORKS. *Miniature Edition on India Paper.* POETICAL AND DRAMATIC WORKS. 8 vols. in a box. 40s. net.
—— *The Original Editions.* Fcp. 8vo. POEMS. 6s.
MAUD: and other Poems. 3s. 6d.
THE PRINCESS. 3s. 6d.
THE HOLY GRAIL: and other Poems. 4s.6d.
BALLADS: and other Poems. 5s.
HAROLD: A Drama. 6s.
QUEEN MARY: A Drama. 6s.
THE CUP, and THE FALCON. 5s.
BECKET. 6s.
TIRESIAS: and other Poems. 6s.
LOCKSLEY HALL SIXTY YEARS AFTER, etc. 6s.
DEMETER: and other Poems. 6s.
THE FORESTERS: ROBIN HOOD AND MAID MARIAN. 6s.
THE DEATH OF OENONE, AKBAR'S DREAM, AND OTHER POEMS. 6s.
POEMS BY TWO BROTHERS. 6s.
—— *The Royal Edition.* 1 vol. 8vo. 16s.
—— THE TENNYSON BIRTHDAY BOOK. Edit. by EMILY SHAKESPEAR. 18mo. 2s. 6d.
—— THE BROOK. With 20 Illustrations by A. WOODRUFF. 32mo. 2s. 6d.
—— SONGS FROM TENNYSON'S WRITINGS. Square 8vo. 2s. 6d.
—— SELECTIONS FROM TENNYSON. With Introduction and Notes, by F. J. ROWE, M.A., and W. T. WEBB, M.A. Globe 8vo. 3s. 6d.
—— ENOCH ARDEN. By W. T. WEBB, M.A. Globe 8vo. 2s. 6d.
—— AYLMER'S FIELD. By W. T. WEBB, M.A. Globe 8vo. 2s. 6d.
—— THE COMING OF ARTHUR, and THE PASSING OF ARTHUR. By F. J. ROWE. Gl. 8vo. 2s. 6d.
—— THE PRINCESS. By P. M. WALLACE, M.A. Globe 8vo. 3s. 6d.
—— GARETH AND LYNETTE. By G. C. MACAULAY, M.A. 2s. 6d.
—— GERAINT AND ENID. By G. C. MACAULAY, M.A. 2s. 6d.
—— THE HOLY GRAIL. Bs G. C. MACAULAY, M.A. 2s. 6d.
—— TENNYSON FOR THE YOUNG. By Canon AINGER. 18mo. 1s. net. —Large Paper, uncut, 3s. 6d.; gilt edges, 4s. 6d.

TENNYSON (Lord).—BECKET. As arranged for the Stage by H. IRVING. 8vo. swd. 2s. net.
TENNYSON (Frederick).—THE ISLES OF GREECE: SAPPHO AND ALCÆUS. Cr. 8vo. 7s. 6d.
—— DAPHNE: and other Poems. Cr. 8vo. 7s. 6d.
TENNYSON (Lord H.). (*See* ILLUSTRATED BOOKS.)
TRUMAN (Jos.).—AFTER-THOUGHTS: Poems. Cr. 8vo. 3s. 6d.
TURNER (Charles Tennyson).—COLLECTED SONNETS, OLD AND NEW. Ext.fcp.8vo. 7s.6d.
TYRWHITT (R. St. John).—FREE FIELD. Lyrics, chiefly Descriptive. Gl. 8vo. 3s. 6d.
—— BATTLE AND AFTER, concerning SERGEANT THOMAS ATKINS, GRENADIER GUARDS: and other Verses. Gl. 8vo. 3s.6d.
WARD (Samuel).—LYRICAL RECREATIONS. Fcp. 8vo. 6s.
WATSON (W.).—POEMS. Fcap. 8vo. 5s.
—— LACHRYMAE MUSARUM. Fcp.8vo. 4s.6d. (*See also* GOLDEN TREASURY SERIES, p. 22.)
WEBSTER (A.).—PORTRAITS. Fcp. 8vo. 5s.
—— SELECTIONS FROM VERSE. Fp. 8vo. 4s. 6d.
WHITTIER.—COMPLETE POETICAL WORKS OF JOHN GREENLEAF WHITTIER. With Portrait. 18mo. 4s. 6d. (*See also* COLLECTED WORKS, p. 23.)
WILLS (W. G.).—MELCHIOR. Cr. 8vo. 9s.
WOOD (Andrew Goldie).—THE ISLES OF THE BLEST: and other Poems. Globe 8vo. 5s.
WOOLNER (Thomas). — MY BEAUTIFUL LADY. 3rd Edit. Fcp. 8vo. 5s.
—— PYGMALION. Cr. 8vo. 7s. 6d.
—— SILENUS. Cr. 8vo. 6s.
WORDSWORTH. — COMPLETE POETICAL WORKS. Copyright Edition. With an Introduction by JOHN MORLEY, and Portrait. Cr. 8vo. 7s. 6d.
—— THE RECLUSE. Fcp. 8vo. 2s. 6d.—Large Paper Edition. 8vo. 10s. 6d.
(*See also* GOLDEN TREASURY SERIES, p. 21.)

Poetical Collections and Selections.
(*See also* GOLDEN TREASURY SERIES, p. 21 : BOOKS FOR THE YOUNG, p. 41.)

HALES (Prof. J. W.).—LONGER ENGLISH POEMS. With Notes, Philological and Explanatory, and an Introduction on the Teaching of English. Ext. fcp. 8vo. 4s. 6d.
MACDONALD (George).—ENGLAND'S ANTIPHON. Cr. 8vo. 4s. 6d.
MARTIN (F.). (*See* BOOKS FOR THE YOUNG, p. 41.)
MASSON (R. O. and D.).—THREE CENTURIES OF ENGLISH POETRY. Being Selections from Chaucer to Herrick. Globe 8vo. 3s. 6d.
PALGRAVE (Prof. F. T.).—THE GOLDEN TREASURY OF THE BEST SONGS AND LYRICAL POEMS IN THE ENGLISH LANGUAGE. Large Type. Cr. 8vo. 10s. 6d. (*See also* GOLDEN TREASURY SERIES, p. 21 ; BOOKS FOR THE YOUNG, p. 41.)
WARD (T. H.).—ENGLISH POETS. Selections, with Critical Introductions by various Writers, and a General Introduction by MATTHEW ARNOLD. Edited by T. H. WARD, M.A. 4 vols. and Edit. Cr. 8vo. 7s. 6d. each.—Vol. I. CHAUCER TO DONNE ; II. BEN JONSON TO DRYDEN ; III. ADDISON TO BLAKE ; IV. WORDSWORTH TO ROSSETTI.

2

LITERATURE.

WOODS (M. A.).—A First Poetry Book. Fcp. 8vo. 2s. 6d.
—— A Second Poetry Book. 2 Parts. Fcp. 8vo. 2s. 6d. each.—Complete, 4s. 6d.
—— A Third Poetry Book. Fcp. 8vo. 4s. 6d.

WORDS FROM THE POETS. With a Vignette and Frontispiece. 12th Edit. 18mo. 1s.

Prose Fiction.

BIKELAS (D.).—Loukis Laras; or, The Reminiscences of a Chiote Merchant during the Greek War of Independence. Translated by J. Gennadius. Cr. 8vo. 7s. 6d.

BJÖRNSON (B.).—Synnöve Solbakken. Translated by Julie Sutter. Cr. 8vo. 6s.

BOLDREWOOD (Rolf).—Uniform Edition. Cr. 8vo. 3s. 6d. each.
Robbery Under Arms.
The Miner's Right.
The Squatter's Dream.
A Sydney-Side Saxon.
A Colonial Reformer.
Nevermore.

BURNETT (F. H.).—Haworth's. Gl. 8vo. 2s.
—— Louisiana, and That Lass o' Lowrie's. Illustrated. Cr. 8vo. 3s. 6d.

CALMIRE. 2 vols. Cr. 8vo. 21s.

CARMARTHEN (Marchioness of). — A Lover of the Beautiful. Cr. 8vo. 6s.

CONWAY (Hugh). — A Family Affair. Cr. 8vo. 3s. 6d.
—— Living or Dead. Cr. 8vo. 3s. 6d.

CORBETT (Julian).—The Fall of Asgard: A Tale of St. Olaf's Day. 2 vols. Gl. 8vo. 12s.
—— For God and Gold. Cr. 8vo. 6s.
—— Kophetua the Thirteenth. 2 vols. Globe 8vo. 12s.

CRAIK (Mrs.).—Uniform Edition. Cr. 8vo. 3s. 6d. each.
Olive.
The Ogilvies. Also Globe 8vo, 2s.
Agatha's Husband. Also Globe 8vo, 2s.
The Head of the Family.
Two Marriages. Also Globe 8vo, 2s.
The Laurel Bush.
My Mother and I.
Miss Tommy: A Mediæval Romance.
King Arthur: Not a Love Story.

CRAWFORD (F. Marion).—Uniform Edition. Cr. 8vo. 3s. 6d. each.
Mr. Isaacs: A Tale of Modern India.
Dr. Claudius.
A Roman Singer.
Zoroaster.
A Tale of a Lonely Parish.
Marzio's Crucifix.
Paul Patoff.
With the Immortals.
Greifenstein.
Sant' Ilario.
A Cigarette Maker's Romance.
Khaled: A Tale of Arabia.
The Witch of Prague.
The Three Fates.
—— Don Orsino. Cr. 8vo. 6s.
—— Children of the King. Cr. 8vo. 6s.
—— Pietro Ghisleri. 3 vols. Cr. 8vo. 31s. 6d

CUNNINGHAM (
leans: A Vacatic
—— The Heriots.
—— Wheat and 1

DAGONET THE J

DAHN (Felix).—F
M. A. C. E. Cr. 8

DAY (Rev. Lal Be
Life. Cr. 8vo. (
—— Folk Tales of

DEFOE (D.). (See
Golden Treasur

DEMOCRACY: A
8vo. 4s. 6d.

DICKENS (Charl
Cr. 8vo. 3s. 6d. e
The Pickwick P.
Oliver Twist.
Nicholas Nickl
Martin Chuzzl
The Old Curiosi
Barnaby Rudge.
Dombey and Son
Christmas Book:
Sketches by Boz
David Copperfie
American Note
Italy.
—— The Posthum(
wick Club. Illu
Jun. 2 vols. Ex

DICKENS (M. A.
vols. Cr. 8vo. 3

DILLWYN (E. A.).
—— Jill and Jack

DUNSMUIR (Am
Girl. 3rd Edit. (

EBERS (Dr. Georg
Wife. Transl. by
—— Only a Wor
Bell. Cr. 8vo.

"ESTELLE RUSS
Harmonia. 3 vo

FALCONER (Lan
Cr. 8vo. 3s. 6d.

FLEMING (G.).—A
—— Mirage: A N
—— The Head of
—— Vestigia. Gl

FRATERNITY: A
8vo. 21s.

"FRIENDS IN C
of).—Realmah.

GRAHAM (John \
Ancient Rome. C

HARBOUR BAR,

HARDY (Arthur S
Woman: A Nove
—— The Wind of I

HARDY (Thomas)
Cr. 8vo. 3s. 6d.
—— Wessex Tales

HARTE (Bret).—C
—— The Heritag
and other Tales.
—— A First Far
8vo. 3s. 6d.

Author of).—HOGAN,

RRARD. Gl. 8vo. 2*s*.

S, AND THE COUN-
*V*O. 2*s*.

Globe 8vo. 2*s*.

Globe 8vo. 2*s*.

REAT TREASON : A
ndependence. 2 vols.

OM BROWN'S SCHOOL
V.—Golden Treasury
Uniform Edit. 3*s*. 6*d*.
.—People's Sixpenny
d. 4to. 6*d*.—Uniform
y. Med. 8vo. 6*d*.

FORD. Cr. 8vo. 3*s*.6*d*.

THE WHITE HORSE,
OT. Cr. 8vo. 3*s*. 6*d*.

. (*See* ILLUSTRATED

AMONA. Gl. 8vo. 2*s*.

EUROPEANS : A Novel.
s.

d other Stories. Cr.
2*s*.

Cr. 8vo. 6*s*.—18mo.

S. Cr. 8vo. 6*s*. ; Gl.
4*s*.

F THE FUTURE : and
6*s*. ; Globe 8vo, 2*s*.

IARE, THE PENSION
VO. 2*s*.

F A LADY. Cr. 8vo.

In Two Series.

Cr. 8vo. 6*s*.

ES. Pocket Edition.
e.

NDON ; MADAME DE

. EPISODE ; THE PEN-
THE POINT OF VIEW.

Study ; FOUR MEET-
F'S MARRIAGE ; BEN-

F THE FUTURE ; A
ERS ; THE DIARY OF
EUGENE PICKERING.

ITIES. Cr. 8vo. 4*s*. 6*d*.

SAMASSIMA. Cr. 8vo.

OR. Cr. 8vo. 6*s*.

RS ; LOUISA PALLANT ;
ING. Cr. 8vo. 3*s*. 6*d*.

Cr. 8vo. 3*s*. 6*d*.

. Cr. 8vo. 3*s*. 6*d*.

THE MASTER, AND
8vo. 6*s*.

, AND OTHER TALES.

KEARY (Annie).—JANET'S HOME. Cr. 8vo.
3*s*. 6*d*.
—— CLEMENCY FRANKLYN. Globe 8vo. 2*s*.
—— OLDBURY. Cr. 8vo. 3*s*. 6*d*.
—— A YORK AND A LANCASTER ROSE. Cr.
8vo. 3*s*. 6*d*.
—— CASTLE DALY. Cr. 8vo. 3*s*. 6*d*.
—— A DOUBTING HEART. Cr. 8vo. 3*s*. 6*d*

KENNEDY (P.).—LEGENDARY FICTIONS OF
THE IRISH CELTS. Cr. 8vo. 3*s*. 6*d*.

KINGSLEY (Charles).—*Eversley Edition*.
13 vols. Globe 8vo. 5*s*. each.—WESTWARD
HO! 2 vols.—TWO YEARS AGO. 2 vols.—
HYPATIA. 2 vols.—YEAST. 1 vol.—ALTON
LOCKE. 2 vols.—HEREWARD THE WAKE.
2 vols.

—— *Complete Edition*. Cr. 8vo. 3*s*. 6*d*. each.
—WESTWARD HO! With a Portrait.—
HYPATIA.—YEAST.—ALTON LOCKE.—TWO
YEARS AGO.—HEREWARD THE WAKE.

—— *Sixpenny Edition*. Med. 8vo. 6*d*.
each. — WESTWARD HO! — HYPATIA. —
YEAST.—ALTON LOCKE.—TWO YEARS AGO.
—HEREWARD THE WAKE.

KIPLING (Rudyard).—PLAIN TALES FROM
THE HILLS. Cr. 8vo. 6*s*.
—— THE LIGHT THAT FAILED. Cr. 8vo. 6*s*.
—— LIFE'S HANDICAP : Being Stories of mine
own People. Cr. 8vo. 6*s*.
—— MANY INVENTIONS. Cr. 8vo. 6*s*.

LAFARGUE (Philip).—THE NEW JUDGMENT
OF PARIS. 2 vols. Globe 8vo. 12*s*.

LEE (Margaret).—FAITHFUL AND UNFAITH-
FUL. Cr. 8vo 3*s*. 6*d*.

LEVY (A.).—REUBEN SACHS. Cr. 8vo. 3*s*.6*d*.

LITTLE PILGRIM IN THE UNSEEN, A.
24th Thousand. Cr. 8vo. 2*s*. 6*d*.

"LITTLE PILGRIM IN THE UNSEEN,
A " (Author of).—THE LAND OF DARKNESS.
Cr. 8vo. 5*s*.

LYSAGHT (S. R.).—THE MARPLOT. 3 vols
Cr. 8vo. 31*s*. 6*d*.

LYTTON (Earl of).—THE RING OF AMASIS :
A Romance. Cr. 8vo. 3*s*. 6*d*.

McLENNAN (Malcolm).—MUCKLE JOCK ;
and other Stories of Peasant Life in the North.
Cr. 8vo. 3*s*. 6*d*.

MACQUOID (K. S.).—PATTY. Gl. 8vo. 2*s*.

MADOC (Fayr).—THE STORY OF MELICENT.
Cr. 8vo. 4*s*. 6*d*.

MALET (Lucas).—MRS. LORIMER : A Sketch
in Black and White. Cr. 8vo. 3*s*. 6*d*.

MALORY (Sir Thos.). (*See* GLOBE LIBRARY,
p. 21.)

MINTO (W.).—THE MEDIATION OF RALPH
HARDELOT. 3 vols. Cr. 8vo. 31*s*. 6*d*.

MITFORD (A. B.).—TALES OF OLD JAPAN.
With Illustrations. Cr. 8vo. 3*s*. 6*d*.

MIZ MAZE (THE) ; OR, THE WINKWORTH
PUZZLE. A Story in Letters by Nine
Authors. Cr. 8vo. 4*s*. 6*d*.

MURRAY (D. Christie). — AUNT RACHEL.
Cr. 8vo. 3*s*. 6*d*.
—— SCHWARTZ. Cr. 8vo. 3*s* 6*d*.
—— THE WEAKER VESSEL. Cr. 8vo. 3*s*. 6*d*.
—— JOHN VALE'S GUARDIAN. Cr. 8vo. 3*s*. 6*d*.

LITERATURE.
Prose Fiction—*continued.*

MURRAY (D. Christie) and HERMAN (H.). —HE FELL AMONG THIEVES. Cr.8vo. 3s.6d.

NEW ANTIGONE, THE: A ROMANCE. Cr. 8vo. 3s. 6d.

NOEL (Lady Augusta).—HITHERSEA MERE. 3 vols. Cr. 8vo. 31s. 6d.

NORRIS (W. E.).—MY FRIEND JIM. Globe 8vo. 2s.
—— CHRIS. Globe 8vo. 2s.

NORTON (Hon. Mrs.).—OLD SIR DOUG-LAS. Cr. 8vo. 6s.

OLIPHANT (Mrs. M. O. W.).—A SON OF THE SOIL. Globe 8vo. 2s.
—— THE CURATE IN CHARGE. Globe 8vo. 2s.
—— YOUNG MUSGRAVE. Globe 8vo. 2s.
—— HE THAT WILL NOT WHEN HE MAY. Cr. 8vo. 3s. 6d.—Globe 8vo. 2s.
—— SIR TOM. Cr. 8vo. 3s. 6d.—Gl. 8vo. 2s.
—— HESTER. Cr. 8vo. 3s. 6d.
—— THE WIZARD'S SON. Globe 8vo. 2s.
—— THE COUNTRY GENTLEMAN AND HIS FAMILY. Globe 8vo. 2s.
—— THE SECOND SON. Globe 8vo. 2s.
—— NEIGHBOURS ON THE GREEN. Cr. 8vo. 3s. 6d.
—— JOYCE. Cr. 8vo. 3s. 6d.
—— A BELEAGUERED CITY. Cr. 8vo. 3s. 6d.
—— KIRSTEEN. Cr. 8vo. 3s. 6d.
—— THE RAILWAY MAN AND HIS CHILDREN. Cr. 8vo. 3s. 6d.
—— THE MARRIAGE OF ELINOR Cr.8vo. 3s.6d.
—— THE HEIR-PRESUMPTIVE AND THE HEIR-APPARENT. Cr. 8vo. 3s. 6d

PALMER (Lady Sophia).—MRS. PENICOTT'S LODGER: and other Stories. Cr.8vo. 2s.6d.

PARRY (Gambier). -THE STORY OF DICK. Cr. 8vo. 3s. 6d.

PATER (Walter).—MARIUS THE EPICUREAN: HIS SENSATIONS AND IDEAS. 3rd Edit. 2 vols. 8vo. 12s.

RHOADES (J.).—THE STORY OF JOHN TRE-VENNICK. 3 vols. Cr. 8vo. 31s. 6d.

ROSS (Percy).—A MISGUIDIT LASSIE. Cr. 8vo. 4s. 6d.

ROY (J.).—HELEN TREVERVAN: OR, THE RULING RACE 3 vols. Cr. 8vo. 31s. 6d.

RUSSELL (W. Clark).—MAROONED. Cr. 8vo. 3s. 6d.
—— A STRANGE ELOPEMENT. Cr. 8vo. 3s.6d.

ST. JOHNSTON (A.). — A SOUTH SEA LOVER: A Romance. Cr. 8vo. 6s.

SHORTHOUSE (J. Henry).—*Uniform Edition.* Cr. 8vo. 3s. 6d. each.
JOHN INGLESANT: A Romance.
SIR PERCIVAL: A Story of the Past and of the Present.
THE LITTLE SCHOOLMASTER MARK: A Spiritual Romance.
THE COUNTESS EVE.
A TEACHER OF THE VIOLIN: and other Tales.
—— BLANCHE, LADY FALAISE. Cr. 8vo. 6s.

SLIP IN THE FENS, A. Globe 8vo. 2s.

THEODOLI (Marchesa)—UNDER PRESSURE. 2 vols. Globe 8vo. 12s.

TIM. Cr. 8vo. 3s. 6d.

TOURGÉNIEF.—VIRGIN SOIL. Translated by ASHTON W. DILKE. Cr. 8vo. 6s.

VELEY (Margaret
RIES; MRS. AUS
Three Stories. 2

VICTOR (H.).—M
DAYS. Cr. 8vo.

VOICES CRYIN(
NESS: A NOVEI

WARD (Mrs. T. Hu
TON. Cr. 8vo.

WEST (M.).—A B(

WORTHEY (Mrs.)
A Novel. 2 vols.

YONGE (C. M.).—
Cr. 8vo. 12s. (S

YONGE (C. M.) an
—STROLLING PLA

Collected Work
Letters; Mis

ADDISON.—SELE
TATOR." With I
K. DEIGHTON. (

AN AUTHOR'S I
lished Letters
"Inconnue." 2 v

ARNOLD (Matthev
6th Edit. Cr. 8vo
—— ESSAYS IN C
Cr. 8vo. 7s. 6d.
—— DISCOURSES IN

BACON.—ESSAYS.
Notes, by F. G. S
swd., 2s. 6d.
—— ADVANCEMENT
same. Gl. 8vo. B(
(*See also* GOLDEN

BLACKIE (J. S.).—

BRIDGES (John
VILLAGE. Cr. 8v(

BRIMLEY (George

BUNYAN (John).—
FROM THIS WORL
COME. 18mo. 2

BUTCHER (Prof. :
THE GREEK GEN

CARLYLE (Thoma

CHURCH (Dean).
TINGS. Collected
8vo. 5s. each.—
ESSAYS.—II. DAI
—III. ST. ANSI
BACON.—VI. TI
1833—45.

CLIFFORD (Prof.
Essays. Edited
Sir F. POLLOCK.

CLOUGH (A. H.).-
a Selection from I
by HIS WIFE. C:

COLLINS (J. Ch
ENGLISH LITERA'

CRAIK (H.).—ENC
With Critical Intro
and General Intro
Edited by H. CRA
8vo. 7s. 6d.

CRAIK (Mrs.).— (
other Papers. Cr.

CRAIK (Mrs.).—About Money: and other Things. Cr. 8vo. 6s.

—— Sermons out of Church. Cr. 8vo. 3s.6d.

CRAWFORD (F. M.).—The Novel: what it is. 18mo. 3s.

CUNLIFFE (J. W.).—The Influence of Seneca on Elizabethan Tragedy. 4s. net.

DE VERE (Aubrey).—Essays Chiefly on Poetry. 2 vols. Globe 8vo. 12s.

—— Essays, Chiefly Literary and Ethical. Globe 8vo. 6s.

DICKENS.—Letters of Charles Dickens. Edited by his Sister-in-Law and Mary Dickens. Cr. 8vo. 3s. 6d.

DRYDEN, Essays of. Edited by Prof. C. D. Yonge. Fcp. 8vo. 2s. 6d. (See also Globe Library, below.)

DUFF (Rt. Hon. Sir M. E. Grant).—Miscellanies, Political and Literary. 8vo. 10s. 6d.

EMERSON (Ralph Waldo).—The Collected Works. 6 vols. Globe 8vo. 5s. each.—I. Miscellanies. With an Introductory Essay by John Morley.—II. Essays.—III. Poems.—IV. English Traits; Representative Men.—V. Conduct of Life; Society and Solitude.—VI. Letters; Social Aims, etc.

FITZGERALD (Edward): Letters and Literary Remains of. Ed. by W. Aldis Wright, M.A. 3 vols. Cr. 8vo. 31s. 6d.

GLOBE LIBRARY. Gl. 8vo. 3s. 6d. each:
Boswell's Life of Johnson. Introduction by Mowbray Morris.
Burns.—Complete Poetical Works and Letters. Edited, with Life and Glossarial Index, by Alexander Smith.
Cowper.—Poetical Works. Edited by the Rev. W. Benham, B.D.
Defoe.—The Adventures of Robinson Crusoe. Introduction by H. Kingsley.
Dryden.—Poetical Works. A Revised Text and Notes. By W. D. Christie, M.A.
Goldsmith. — Miscellaneous Works. Edited by Prof. Masson.
Horace.—Works. Rendered into English Prose by James Lonsdale and S. Lee.
Malory.—Le Morte d'Arthur. Sir Thos. Malory's Book of King Arthur and of his Noble Knights of the Round Table. The Edition of Caxton, revised for modern use. By Sir E. Strachey, Bart.
Milton.—Poetical Works. Edited, with Introductions, by Prof. Masson.
Pope.—Poetical Works. Edited, with Memoir and Notes, by Prof. Ward.
Scott.—Poetical Works. With Essay by Prof. Palgrave.
Shakespeare.—Complete Works. Edit. by W. G. Clark and W. Aldis Wright. India Paper Edition. Cr. 8vo, cloth extra, gilt edges. 10s. 6d. net.
Spenser.—Complete Works Edited by R. Morris. Memoir by J. W. Hales, M.A.
Virgil.—Works. Rendered into English Prose by James Lonsdale and S. Lee.

GOETHE. — Maxims and Reflections. Trans. by T. B. Saunders. Gl. 8vo. 5s.

GOLDEN TREASURY SERIES.—Uniformly printed in 18mo, with Vignette Titles by Sir J. E. Millais, Sir Noel Paton, T. Woolner, W. Holman Hunt, Arthur Hughes, etc. 2s. 6d. net each.

Balladen und Romanzen. Being a Selection of the best German Ballads and Romances. Edited, with Introduction and Notes, by Dr. Buchheim.

Children's Treasury of Lyrical Poetry. By F. T. Palgrave.

Deutsche Lyrik. The Golden Treasury of the best German Lyrical Poems. Selected by Dr. Buchheim.

La Lyre Française. Selected and arranged, with Notes, by G. Masson.

Lyric Love: An Anthology. By W. Watson.

Newcastle.—The Cavalier and his Lady. Selections from the Works of the First Duke and Duchess of Newcastle. With an Introductory Essay by E. Jenkins.

The Ballad Book. A Selection of the Choicest British Ballads. Edited by William Allingham.

The Book of Praise. From the Best English Hymn Writers. Selected by Roundell, Earl of Selborne.

The Children's Garland from the Best Poets. Selected by Coventry Patmore.

The Fairy Book: the Best Popular Fairy Stories. Selected by Mrs. Craik, Author of " John Halifax, Gentleman."

The Golden Treasury of the Best Songs and Lyrical Poems in the English Language. Selected and arranged, with Notes, by Prof. F. T. Palgrave.—Large Paper Edition. 8vo. 10s. 6d. net.

Scottish Song. Compiled by Mary Carlyle Aitken.

The Song Book. Words and Tunes selected and arranged by John Hullah.

The Sunday Book of Poetry for the Young. Selected by C. F. Alexander.

Theologia Germanica. By C. Winkworth.

Matthew Arnold.—Selected Poems.

Addison.—Essays. Chosen and Edited by John Richard Green.

A Book of Golden Deeds. By C. M. Yonge.

A Book of Golden Thoughts. By Sir Henry Attwell.

A Book of Worthies. By C. M. Yonge.

Bacon.—Essays, and Colours of Good and Evil. With Notes and Glossarial Index by W. Aldis Wright, M.A.—Large Paper Edition. 8vo. 10s 6d net.

Bunyan.—The Pilgrim's Progress from this World to that which is to Come. —Large Paper Edition. 8vo. 10s. 6d. net.

Byron.—Poetry. Chosen and arranged by M. Arnold.—Large Paper Edit. 9s.

Charlotte M. Yonge.—The Story of the Christians and Moors in Spain.

Cowper.—Letters. Edited, with Introduction, by Rev. W. Benham.

—— Selections from Poems. With an Introduction by Mrs. Oliphant.

Defoe.—The Adventures of Robinson Crusoe. Edited by J. W. Clark, M.A.

Golden Treasury Psalter. By Four Friends.

Gracian (Balthasar).—Art of Worldly Wisdom. Translated by J. Jacobs.

Herrick.—Chrysomela. Edited by Prof. F. T. Palgrave.

Hughes.—Tom Brown's School Days.

LITERATURE.

Collected Works; Essays; Lectures; Letters; Miscellaneous Works—*contd.*

GOLDEN TREASURY SERIES—*contd.*

KEATS.—THE POETICAL WORKS. Edited by Prof. F. T. PALGRAVE.

LAMB.—TALES FROM SHAKSPEARE. Edited by Rev. ALFRED AINGER, M.A.

LANDOR.—SELECTIONS. Ed. by S. COLVIN.

LONGFELLOW. — BALLADS, LYRICS, AND SONNETS.

MOHAMMAD.—SPEECHES AND TABLE-TALK. Translated by STANLEY LANE-POOLE.

PLATO.—THE REPUBLIC. Translated by J. LL. DAVIES, M.A., and D. J. VAUGHAN. —Large Paper Edition. 8vo. 10s. 6d. net.

— THE PHAEDRUS, LYSIS, AND PROTAGORAS. Translated by J. WRIGHT.

— THE TRIAL AND DEATH OF SOCRATES. Being the Euthyphron, Apology, Crito and Phaedo of Plato. Trans. by F. J. CHURCH.

SHAKESPEARE.—SONGS AND SONNETS. Ed. with Notes, by Prof. F. T. PALGRAVE.

SHELLEY.—POEMS. Edited by STOPFORD A. BROOKE.—Large Paper Edit. 12s. 6d.

SIR THOMAS BROWNE.—RELIGIO MEDICI, LETTER TO A FRIEND, &c., AND CHRISTIAN MORALS. Ed. W. A. GREENHILL.

THEOCRITUS.—BION, AND MOSCHUS. Rendered into English Prose by ANDREW LANG.—Large Paper Edition. 9s.

THE JEST BOOK. The Choicest Anecdotes and Sayings. Arranged by MARK LEMON.

WORDSWORTH.—POEMS. Chosen and Edited by M. ARNOLD.—Large Paper Edition. 10s. 6d net.

HARE.—GUESSES AT TRUTH. By Two Brothers. 4s. 6d.

LONGFELLOW.—POEMS OF PLACES: ENGLAND AND WALES. Edited by H. W. LONGFELLOW. 2 vols. 9s.

TENNYSON.—LYRICAL POEMS. Selected and Annotated by Prof. F. T. PALGRAVE. 4s.6d. —Large Paper Edition. 9s.

— IN MEMORIAM. 4s. 6d.—Large Paper Edition. 9s.

GOLDSMITH, ESSAYS OF. Edited by C. D. YONGE, M.A. Fcp. 8vo. 2s. 6d. (*See also* GLOBE LIBRARY, p. 21; ILLUSTRATED BOOKS, p. 12.)

GRAY (Thomas).—WORKS. Edited by EDMUND GOSSE. In 4 vols. Globe 8vo. 20s.— Vol. I. POEMS, JOURNALS, AND ESSAYS.— II. LETTERS.—III. LETTERS.—IV. NOTES ON ARISTOPHANES AND PLATO.

GREEN (J. R.).—STRAY STUDIES FROM ENGLAND AND ITALY. Globe 8vo. 5s.

HAMERTON (P. G.).—THE INTELLECTUAL LIFE. Cr. 8vo. 10s. 6d.

— HUMAN INTERCOURSE. Cr. 8vo. 8s. 6d.

— FRENCH AND ENGLISH: A Comparison. Cr. 8vo. 10s. 6d.

HARRISON (Frederic).—THE CHOICE OF BOOKS. Gl. 8vo. 6s.—Large Paper Ed. 15s.

HARWOOD (George).—FROM WITHIN. Cr. 8vo. 6s.

HELPS (Sir Arthur).—ESSAYS WRITTEN IN THE INTERVALS OF BUSINESS. With Introduction and Notes, by F. J. ROWE, M.A., and W. T. WEBB, M.A. 1s. 9d.; swd. 1s. 6d.

HOBART (Lord).—ESSAYS AND MISCELLANEOUS WRITINGS. With Biographical Sketch. Ed. Lady HOBART. 2 vols. 8vo. 25s.

HUTTON (R. H.).—ESSAYS ON SOME OF THE MODERN GUIDES OF ENGLISH THOUGHT IN MATTERS OF FAITH. Globe 8vo. 5s.

— ESSAYS. 2 vols. Gl. 8vo 5s. each.—Vol. I. Literary; II. Theological.

HUXLEY (Prof. T. H.).—LAY SERMONS, ADDRESSES, AND REVIEWS. 8vo. 7s. 6d.

— CRITIQUES AND ADDRESSES. 8vo. 10s. 6d.

— AMERICAN ADDRESSES, WITH A LECTURE ON THE STUDY OF BIOLOGY. 8vo. 6s. 6d.

— SCIENCE AND CULTURE, AND OTHER ESSAYS. 8vo. 10s. 6d.

— INTRODUCTORY SCIENCE PRIMER. 18mo. 1s.

— ESSAYS UPON SOME CONTROVERTED QUESTIONS. 8vo. 14s.

JAMES (Henry).—FRENCH POETS AND NOVELISTS. New Edition. Gl. 8vo. 5s.

— PORTRAITS OF PLACES. Cr. 8vo. 7s. 6d.

— PARTIAL PORTRAITS. Cr. 8vo. 6s.

KEATS.—LETTERS. Edited by SIDNEY COLVIN. Globe 8vo. 5s.

KINGSLEY (Charles).—COMPLETE EDITION OF THE WORKS OF CHARLES KINGSLEY. Cr. 8vo. 3s. 6d. each.

WESTWARD HO! With a Portrait.
HYPATIA.
YEAST.
ALTON LOCKE.
TWO YEARS AGO.
HEREWARD THE WAKE.
POEMS.
THE HEROES; or, Greek Fairy Tales for my Children.
THE WATER BABIES: A Fairy Tale for a Land Baby.
MADAM HOW AND LADY WHY; or, First Lesson in Earth-Lore for Children.
AT LAST: A Christmas in the West Indies.
PROSE IDYLLS.
PLAYS AND PURITANS.
THE ROMAN AND THE TEUTON. With Preface by Professor MAX MÜLLER.
SANITARY AND SOCIAL LECTURES.
HISTORICAL LECTURES AND ESSAYS.
SCIENTIFIC LECTURES AND ESSAYS.
LITERARY AND GENERAL LECTURES.
THE HERMITS.
GLAUCUS; or, The Wonders of the Sea-Shore. With Coloured Illustrations.
VILLAGE AND TOWN AND COUNTRY SERMONS.
THE WATER OF LIFE, AND OTHER SERMONS.
SERMONS ON NATIONAL SUBJECTS: AND THE KING OF THE EARTH.
SERMONS FOR THE TIMES.
GOOD NEWS OF GOD.
THE GOSPEL OF THE PENTATEUCH: AND DAVID.
DISCIPLINE, AND OTHER SERMONS.
WESTMINSTER SERMONS.
ALL SAINTS' DAY, AND OTHER SERMONS.

LAMB (Charles).—COLLECTED WORKS. Ed., with Introduction and Notes, by the Rev. ALFRED AINGER, M.A. Globe 8vo. 5s. each volume.—I. ESSAYS OF ELIA.—II. PLAYS, POEMS, AND MISCELLANEOUS ESSAYS.—III. MRS. LEICESTER'S SCHOOL; THE ADVENTURES OF ULYSSES; AND OTHER ESSAYS.— IV. TALES FROM SHAKESPEARE.—V. and VI. LETTERS. Newly arranged, with additions.

— TALES FROM SHAKESPEARE. 18mo. 4s. 6d.

LITERATURE.

Collected Works; Essays: Lectures; Letters; Miscellaneous Works—*contd.*

YONGE (Charlotte M.).—*Uniform Edition.* Cr. 8vo. 3s. 6d. each.

SCENES AND CHARACTERS.
CHANTRY HOUSE.
A MODERN TELEMACHUS.
BYE WORDS.
BEECHCROFT AT ROCKSTONE.
MORE BYWORDS.
A REPUTED CHANGELING.
THE LITTLE DUKE, RICHARD THE FEARLESS.
THE LANCES OF LYNWOOD.
THE PRINCE AND THE PAGE.
P'S AND Q'S: LITTLE LUCY'S WONDERFUL GLOBE.
THE TWO PENNILESS PRINCESSES.
THAT STICK.
AN OLD WOMAN'S OUTLOOK.

LOGIC. (*See under* PHILOSOPHY, p. 27.)

MAGAZINES. (*See* PERIODICALS, p. 26).

MAGNETISM. (*See under* PHYSICS, p. 28.)

MATHEMATICS, History of.

BALL (W. W. R.).—A SHORT ACCOUNT OF THE HISTORY OF MATHEMATICS. 2nd Ed. Cr. 8vo. 10s. net.
—— MATHEMATICAL RECREATIONS AND PROBLEMS. Cr. 8vo. 7s. net.

MEDICINE.

(*See also* DOMESTIC ECONOMY; NURSING; HYGIENE; PHYSIOLOGY.)

ACLAND (Sir H. W.).—THE ARMY MEDICAL SCHOOL : Address at Netley Hospital. 1s.

ALLBUTT (Dr. T. Clifford).—ON THE USE OF THE OPHTHALMOSCOPE. 8vo. 15s.

ANDERSON (Dr. McCall).—LECTURES ON CLINICAL MEDICINE. Illustr. 8vo. 10s. 6d.

BALLANCE (C. A.) and EDMUNDS (Dr. W.). LIGATION IN CONTINUITY. Illustr. Roy. 8vo. 30s. net.

BARWELL (Richard, F.R.C.S.). — THE CAUSES AND TREATMENT OF LATERAL CURVATURE OF THE SPINE. Cr. 8vo. 5s.
—— ON ANEURISM, ESPECIALLY OF THE THORAX AND ROOT OF THE NECK. 3s. 6d.

BASTIAN (H. Charlton).—ON PARALYSIS FROM BRAIN DISEASE IN ITS COMMON FORMS. Cr. 8vo. 10s. 6d.

BICKERTON (T. H.).—ON COLOUR BLINDNESS. Cr. 8vo.

BRAIN : A JOURNAL OF NEUROLOGY. Edited for the Neurological Society of London, by A. DE WATTEVILLE, Quarterly. 8vo. 3s. 6d. (Part I. in Jan. 1878.) Vols. I. to XII. 8vo. 15s. each. [Cloth covers for binding, 1s. each.]

BRUNTON (Dr. T. Lauder).—A TEXT-BOOK OF PHARMACOLOGY, THERAPEUTICS, AND MATERIA MEDICA. 3rd Edit. Med. 8vo. 21s.—Or in 2 vols. 22s. 6d.—SUPPLEMENT, 1s.

BRUNTON (Dr. T. Lauder).—DISORDERS OF DIGESTION : THEIR CONSEQUENCES AND TREATMENT. 8vo. 10s. 6d.
—— PHARMACOLOGY AND THERAPEUTICS ; or, Medicine Past and Present. Cr. 8vo. 6s.
—— TABLES OF MATERIA MEDICA : A Companion to the Materia Medica Museum. 8vo. 5s.
—— AN INTRODUCTION TO MODERN THERAPEUTICS. Croonian Lectures on the Relationship between Chemical Structure and Physiological Action. 8vo. 3s. 6d. net.

BUCKNILL (Dr.).—THE CARE OF THE INSANE. Cr. 8vo. 3s. 6d.

CARTER (R. Brudenell, F.C.S.).—A PRACTICAL TREATISE ON DISEASES OF THE EYE. 8vo. 16s.
—— EYESIGHT, GOOD AND BAD. Cr. 8vo. 6s.
—— MODERN OPERATIONS FOR CATARACT. 8vo. 6s.

CHRISTIE (J.).—CHOLERA EPIDEMICS IN EAST AFRICA. 8vo. 15s.

COWELL (George).—LECTURES ON CATARACT : ITS CAUSES, VARIETIES, AND TREATMENT. Cr. 8vo. 4s. 6d.

ECCLES (A. S.).—SCIATICA. 8vo. 3s. 6d.

FLÜCKIGER (F. A.) and HANBURY (D.). —PHARMACOGRAPHIA. A History of the Principal Drugs of Vegetable Origin met with in Great Britain and India. 8vo. 21s.

FOTHERGILL (Dr. J. Milner).—THE PRACTITIONER'S HANDBOOK OF TREATMENT ; or, The Principles of Therapeutics. 8vo. 16s.
—— THE ANTAGONISM OF THERAPEUTIC AGENTS, AND WHAT IT TEACHES. Cr. 8vo. 6s.
—— FOOD FOR THE INVALID, THE CONVALESCENT, THE DYSPEPTIC, AND THE GOUTY. 2nd Edit. Cr. 8vo. 3s. 6d.

FOX (Dr. Wilson). — ON THE ARTIFICIAL PRODUCTION OF TUBERCLE IN THE LOWER ANIMALS. With Plates. 4to. 5s. 6d.
—— ON THE TREATMENT OF HYPERPYREXIA, AS ILLUSTRATED IN ACUTE ARTICULAR RHEUMATISM BY MEANS OF THE EXTERNAL APPLICATION OF COLD. 8vo. 2s. 6d.

GRIFFITHS (W. H.).—LESSONS ON PRESCRIPTIONS AND THE ART OF PRESCRIBING. New Edition. 18mo. 3s. 6d.

HAMILTON (Prof. D. J.).—ON THE PATHOLOGY OF BRONCHITIS, CATARRHAL PNEUMONIA, TUBERCLE, AND ALLIED LESIONS OF THE HUMAN LUNG. 8vo. 8s. 6d.
—— A TEXT-BOOK OF PATHOLOGY, SYSTEMATIC AND PRACTICAL. Illustrated. Vol. I. 8vo. 25s.

HANBURY (Daniel). — SCIENCE PAPERS, CHIEFLY PHARMACOLOGICAL AND BOTANICAL. Med. 8vo. 14s.

KLEIN (Dr. E.).—MICRO-ORGANISMS AND DISEASE. An Introduction into the Study of Specific Micro-Organisms. Cr. 8vo. 6s.
—— THE BACTERIA IN ASIATIC CHOLERA. Cr. 8vo. 5s.

LEPROSY INVESTIGATION COMMITTEE, JOURNAL OF THE. Edited by P. S. ABRAHAM, M.A. Nos. 2—4. 2s. 6d. each net.

LINDSAY (Dr. J. A.). — THE CLIMATIC TREATMENT OF CONSUMPTION. Cr. 8vo. 5s.

MACLAGAN (Dr. T.). — THE GERM THEORY. 8vo. 10s. 6d.

MACLEAN (Surgeon-General W. C.). — DISEASES OF TROPICAL CLIMATES. Cr. 8vo. 10s. 6d.

MACNAMARA (C.). — A HISTORY OF ASIATIC CHOLERA. Cr. 8vo. 10s. 6d.
—— ASIATIC CHOLERA, HISTORY UP TO JULY 15, 1892 : CAUSES AND TREATMENT. 8vo. 2s. 6d.

MERCIER (Dr. C.). — THE NERVOUS SYSTEM AND THE MIND. 8vo. 12s. 6d.

PIFFARD (H. G.). — AN ELEMENTARY TREATISE ON DISEASES OF THE SKIN. 8vo. 16s.

PRACTITIONER, THE : A MONTHLY JOURNAL OF THERAPEUTICS AND PUBLIC HEALTH. Edited by T. LAUDER BRUNTON F.R.S., etc. ; DONALD MACALISTER, M.A., M.D., and J. MITCHELL BRUCE, M.D. 1s. 6d. monthly. Vols. I.—XLIX. Half yearly vols. 10s. 6d. each. [Cloth covers for binding, 1s. each.]

REYNOLDS (J. R.). — A SYSTEM OF MEDICINE. Edited by J. RUSSELL REYNOLDS, M.D., In 5 vols. Vols. I.—III. and V. 8vo. 25s. each.—Vol. IV. 21s.

RICHARDSON (Dr. B. W.). — DISEASES OF MODERN LIFE. Cr. 8vo.
—— THE FIELD OF DISEASE. A Book of Preventive Medicine. 8vo. 25s.

SEATON (Dr. Edward C.). — A HANDBOOK OF VACCINATION. Ext. fcp. 8vo. 8s. 6d.

SEILER (Dr. Carl). — MICRO-PHOTOGRAPHS IN HISTOLOGY, NORMAL AND PATHOLOGICAL. 4to. 31s. 6d.

SIBSON (Dr. Francis). — COLLECTED WORKS Edited by W. M. ORD, M.D. Illustrated. 4 vols. 8vo. 3l. 3s.

SPENDER (J. Kent). — THERAPEUTIC MEANS FOR THE RELIEF OF PAIN. 8vo. 8s. 6d.

SURGERY (THE INTERNATIONAL ENCYCLOPAEDIA OF). A Systematic Treatise on the Theory and Practice of Surgery by Authors of various Nations. Edited by JOHN ASHHURST, jun., M.D. 6 vols. Roy. 8vo. 31s. 6d. each.

THORNE (Dr. Thorne). — DIPHTHERIA. Cr. 8vo. 8s. 6d.

WHITE (Dr. W. Hale). — A TEXT-BOOK OF GENERAL THERAPEUTICS. Cr. 8vo. 8s. 6d.

ZIEGLER (Ernst). — A TEXT-BOOK OF PATHOLOGICAL ANATOMY AND PATHOGENESIS Translated and Edited by DONALD MACALISTER, M.A., M.D. Illustrated. 8vo.—Part I. GENERAL PATHOLOGICAL ANATOMY 12s. 6d.—Part II. SPECIAL PATHOLOGICAL ANATOMY. Sections I.—VIII. and IX.—XII. 8vo. 12s. 6d. each.

METALLURGY.
(See also CHEMISTRY.)

HIORNS (Arthur H.). — A TEXT-BOOK OF ELEMENTARY METALLURGY. Gl. 8vo. 4s.
—— PRACTICAL METALLURGY AND ASSAYING. Illustrated. 2nd Edit. Globe 8vo. 6s.

HIORNS (Arthur H.). — IRON AND STEEL MANUFACTURE. Illustrated. Globe 8vo. 3s. 6d.
—— MIXED METALS OR METALLIC ALLOYS. Globe 8vo. 6s.
—— METAL COLOURING AND BRONZING. Globe 8vo. 5s.

PHILLIPS (J. A.). — A TREATISE ON ORE DEPOSITS. Illustrated. Med. 8vo. 25s.

METAPHYSICS.
(See under PHILOSOPHY, p. 27.)

MILITARY ART AND HISTORY.

ACLAND (Sir H. W.). *(See* MEDICINE.)

AITKEN (Sir W.). — THE GROWTH OF THE RECRUIT AND YOUNG SOLDIER. Cr. 8vo. 8s. 6d.

CUNYNGHAME (Gen. Sir A. T.). — MY COMMAND IN SOUTH AFRICA, 1874—78. 8vo. 12s. 6d.

DILKE (Sir C.) and WILKINSON (S.). — IMPERIAL DEFENCE. Cr. 8vo. 3s. 6d.

HOZIER (Lieut.-Col. H. M.). — THE SEVEN WEEKS' WAR. 3rd Edit. Cr. 8vo. 6s.
—— THE INVASIONS OF ENGLAND. 2 vols. 8vo. 28s.

MARTEL (Chas.). — MILITARY ITALY. With Map. 8vo. 12s. 6d.

MAURICE (Lt.-Col.). — WAR. 8vo. 5s. net.
—— THE NATIONAL DEFENCES. Cr. 8vo.

MERCUR (Prof. J.). — ELEMENTS OF THE ART OF WAR. 8vo. 17s.

SCRATCHLEY — KINLOCH COOKE. — AUSTRALIAN DEFENCES AND NEW GUINEA. Compiled from the Papers of the late Major-General Sir PETER SCRATCHLEY, R.E., by C. KINLOCH COOKE. 8vo. 14s.

THROUGH THE RANKS TO A COMMISSION. New Edition. Cr. 8vo. 2s. 6d.

WILKINSON (S.). — THE BRAIN OF AN ARMY. A Popular Account of the German General Staff. Cr. 8vo. 2s. 6d.

WINGATE (Major F. R.). — MAHDIISM AND THE EGYPTIAN SUDAN. An Account of the Rise and Progress of Mahdiism, and of Subsequent Events in the Sudan to the Present Time. With 17 Maps. 8vo. 30s. net.

WOLSELEY (General Viscount). — THE SOLDIER'S POCKET-BOOK FOR FIELD SERVICE. 5th Edit. 16mo, roan. 5s.
—— FIELD POCKET-BOOK FOR THE AUXILIARY FORCES. 16mo. 1s. 6d.

MINERALOGY. *(See* GEOLOGY.)

MISCELLANEOUS WORKS.
(See under LITERATURE, p. 20.)

MUSIC.

FAY (Amy). — MUSIC-STUDY IN GERMANY Preface by Sir GEO. GROVE. Cr. 8vo. 4s. 6d

MUSIC—*continued.*

GROVE (Sir George).—A DICTIONARY OF MUSIC AND MUSICIANS, A.D. 1450—1889. Edited by Sir GEORGE GROVE, D.C.L. In 4 vols. 8vo. 21s. each. With Illustrations in Music Type and Woodcut.—Also published in Parts. Parts I.—XIV., XIX.—XXII. 3s. 6d. each; XV. XVI. 7s.; XVII. XVIII. 7s.; XXIII.—XXV., Appendix. Edited by J. A. FULLER MAITLAND, M.A. 9s. [Cloth cases for binding the volumes, 1s. each.]

—— A COMPLETE INDEX TO THE ABOVE. By Mrs. E. WODEHOUSE. 8vo. 7s. 6d.

HULLAH (John).—MUSIC IN THE HOUSE. 4th Edit. Cr. 8vo. 2s. 6d.

TAYLOR (Franklin).—A PRIMER OF PIANOFORTE PLAYING. 18mo. 1s.

TAYLOR (Sedley).—SOUND AND MUSIC. 2nd Edit. Ext. cr. 8vo. 8s. 6d.

—— A SYSTEM OF SIGHT-SINGING FROM THE ESTABLISHED MUSICAL NOTATION. 8vo. 5s. net.

—— RECORD OF THE CAMBRIDGE CENTENARY OF W. A. MOZART. Cr. 8vo. 2s. 6d. net.

NATURAL HISTORY.

ATKINSON (J. C.). (*See* ANTIQUITIES, p. 1.)

BAKER (Sir Samuel W.). (*See* SPORT, p. 32.)

BLANFORD (W. T.).—GEOLOGY AND ZOOLOGY OF ABYSSINIA. 8vo. 21s.

FOWLER (W. W.).—TALES OF THE BIRDS. Illustrated. Cr. 8vo. 3s. 6d.

—— A YEAR WITH THE BIRDS. trated. Cr. 8vo. 3s. 6d.

KINGSLEY (Charles).—MADAM HOW AND LADY WHY; or, First Lessons in Earth-Lore for Children. Cr. 8vo. 3s. 6d.

—— GLAUCUS; or, The Wonders of the Sea-Shore. With Coloured Illustrations. Cr. 8vo. 3s. 6d.—*Presentation Edition.* Cr. 8vo, extra cloth. 7s. 6d.

KLEIN (E.).—ETIOLOGY AND PATHOLOGY OF GROUSE DISEASE. 8vo. 7s. net.

WALLACE (Alfred Russel).—THE MALAY ARCHIPELAGO: The Land of the Orang Utang and the Bird of Paradise. Maps and Illustrations. Ext. cr. 8vo. 6s. (*See also* BIOLOGY.)

WATERTON (Charles).—WANDERINGS IN SOUTH AMERICA, THE NORTH-WEST OF THE UNITED STATES, AND THE ANTILLES. Edited by Rev. J. G. WOOD. Illustrated. Cr. 8vo. 6s.—People's Edition. 4to. 6d.

WHITE (Gilbert).—NATURAL HISTORY AND ANTIQUITIES OF SELBORNE. Ed. by FRANK BUCKLAND. With a Chapter on Antiquities by the EARL OF SELBORNE. Cr. 8vo. 6s.

NATURAL PHILOSOPHY. (*See* PHYSICS.)

NAVAL SCIENCE.

KELVIN (Lord).—POPULAR LECTURES AND ADDRESSES.—Vol. III. NAVIGATION. Cr. 8vo. 7s. 6d.

ROBINSON (Rev. J. L.).—MARINE SURVEYING, AN ELEMENTARY TREATISE ON. For Younger Naval Officers. Illustrated. Cr. 8vo. 7s. 6d.

SHORTLAND (Admiral).—NAUTICAL SURVEYING. 8vo. 21s.

NOVELS. (*See* PROSE FICTION, p. 18.)

NURSING.

(*See under* DOMESTIC ECONOMY, p. 8.)

OPTICS (or LIGHT). (*See* PHYSICS, p. 28.)

PAINTING. (*See* ART, p. 2.)

PATHOLOGY. (*See* MEDICINE, p. 24.)

PERIODICALS.

AMERICAN JOURNAL OF PHILOLOGY, THE. (*See* PHILOLOGY.)

BRAIN. (*See* MEDICINE.)

ECONOMIC JOURNAL, THE. (*See* POLITICAL ECONOMY.)

ECONOMICS, THE QUARTERLY JOURNAL OF. (*See* POLITICAL ECONOMY.)

NATURAL SCIENCE: A MONTHLY REVIEW OF SCIENTIFIC PROGRESS. 8vo. 1s. net. No. 1. March 1892.

NATURE: A WEEKLY ILLUSTRATED JOURNAL OF SCIENCE. Published every Thursday. Price 6d. Monthly Parts, 2s. and 2s. 6d.; Current Half-yearly vols., 15s. each. Vols. I.—XLVII. [Cases for binding vols. 1s. 6d. each.]

HELLENIC STUDIES, THE JOURNAL OF. Published Half-Yearly from 1880. 8vo. 30s.; or each Part, 15s. Vol. XIII. Part I. 15s. net.

The Journal will be sold at a reduced price to Libraries wishing to subscribe, but official application must in each case be made to the Council. Information on this point, and upon the conditions of Membership, may be obtained on application to the Hon. Sec., Mr. George Macmillan, 29, Bedford Street, Covent Garden.

LEPROSY INVESTIGATION COMMITTEE, JOURNAL OF. (*See* MEDICINE.)

MACMILLAN'S MAGAZINE. Published Monthly. 1s.—Vols. I.-LXVII. 7s. 6d. each. [Cloth covers for binding, 1s. each.]

PHILOLOGY, THE JOURNAL OF. (*See* PHILOLOGY.)

PRACTITIONER, THE. (*See* MEDICINE.)

RECORD OF TECHNICAL AND SECONDARY EDUCATION. (*See* EDUCATION, p. 8.)

PHILOLOGY.

AMERICAN JOURNAL OF PHILOLOGY, THE. Edited by Prof. BASIL L. GILDERSLEEVE. 4s. 6d. each No. (quarterly).

PHILOLOGY—continued.

CORNELL UNIVERSITY STUDIES IN CLASSICAL PHILOLOGY. Edited by I. FLAGG, W. G. HALE, and B. I. WHEELER. I. THE *C U M*-CONSTRUCTIONS : their History and Functions. Part I. Critical. 1s. 8d. net. Part II. Constructive. By W. G. HALE. 3s. 4d. net.—II. ANALOGY AND THE SCOPE OF ITS APPLICATION IN LANGUAGE. By B. I. WHEELER. 1s. 3d. net.

GILES (P.).—A SHORT MANUAL OF PHILOLOGY FOR CLASSICAL STUDENTS. Cr. 8vo.

JOURNAL OF SACRED AND CLASSICAL PHILOLOGY. 4 vols. 8vo. 12s. 6d. each.

JOURNAL OF PHILOLOGY. New Series. Edited by W. A. WRIGHT, M.A., I. BYWATER, M.A., and H. JACKSON, M.A. 4s. 6d. each No. (half-yearly).

KELLNER (Dr. L.). — HISTORICAL OUTLINES IN ENGLISH SYNTAX. Globe 8vo. 6s.

MORRIS (Rev. Richard, LL.D.).—PRIMER OF ENGLISH GRAMMAR. 18mo. 1s.

—— ELEMENTARY LESSONS IN HISTORICAL ENGLISH GRAMMAR. 18mo. 2s. 6d.

—— HISTORICAL OUTLINES OF ENGLISH ACCIDENCE. Extra fcp. 8vo. 6s.

MORRIS (R.) and BOWEN (H. C.).—ENGLISH GRAMMAR EXERCISES. 18mo. 1s.

OLIPHANT (T. L. Kington). — THE OLD AND MIDDLE ENGLISH. Globe 8vo. 9s.

—— THE NEW ENGLISH. 2 vols. Cr. 8vo. 21s.

PEILE (John). — A PRIMER OF PHILOLOGY. 18mo. 1s.

PELLISSIER (E.).—FRENCH ROOTS AND THEIR FAMILIES. Globe 8vo. 6s.

TAYLOR (Isaac).—WORDS AND PLACES. 9th Edit. Maps. Globe 8vo. 6s.

—— ETRUSCAN RESEARCHES. 8vo. 14s.

—— GREEKS AND GOTHS: A Study of the Runes. 8vo. 9s.

WETHERELL (J.).—EXERCISES ON MORRIS'S PRIMER OF ENGLISH GRAMMAR. 18mo. 1s.

YONGE (C. M.).—HISTORY OF CHRISTIAN NAMES. New Edit., revised. Cr. 8vo. 7s. 6d.

PHILOSOPHY.

Ethics and Metaphysics—Logic—Psychology.

Ethics and Metaphysics.

BIRKS (Thomas Rawson).—FIRST PRINCIPLES OF MORAL SCIENCE. Cr. 8vo. 8s. 6d.

—— MODERN UTILITARIANISM ; or, The Systems of Paley, Bentham, and Mill Examined and Compared. Cr. 8vo. 6s. 6d.

—— MODERN PHYSICAL FATALISM, AND THE DOCTRINE OF EVOLUTION. Including an Examination of Mr. Herbert Spencer's "First Principles." Cr. 8vo. 6s.

CALDERWOOD (Prof. H.).—A HANDBOOK OF MORAL PHILOSOPHY. Cr. 8vo. 6s.

FISKE (John).—OUTLINES OF COSMIC PHILOSOPHY, BASED ON THE DOCTRINE OF EVOLUTION. 2 vols. 8vo. 25s.

FOWLER (Rev. Thomas). — PROGRESSIVE MORALITY : An Essay in Ethics. Cr. 8vo. 5s.

HARPER (Father Thomas).—THE METAPHYSICS OF THE SCHOOL. In 5 vols.—Vols. I. and II. 8vo. 18s. each.—Vol. III. Part I. 12s.

HUXLEY (Prof. T. H.).—EVOLUTION AND ETHICS. 8vo. 2s. net.

KANT.—KANT'S CRITICAL PHILOSOPHY FOR ENGLISH READERS. By J. P. MAHAFFY, D.D., and J. H. BERNARD, B.D. 2 vols. Cr. 8vo.—Vol. I. THE KRITIK OF PURE REASON EXPLAINED AND DEFENDED. 7s. 6d. —Vol. II. THE PROLEGOMENA. Translated, with Notes and Appendices. 6s.

—— KRITIK OF JUDGMENT. Translated by J. H. BERNARD, D.D. 8vo. 10s. net.

KANT—MAX MÜLLER. — CRITIQUE OF PURE REASON BY IMMANUEL KANT. Translated by F. MAX MÜLLER. With Introduction by LUDWIG NOIRÉ. 2 vols. 8vo. 16s. each (sold separately).—Vol. I. HISTORICAL INTRODUCTION, by LUDWIG NOIRÉ, etc.—Vol. II. CRITIQUE OF PURE REASON.

MAURICE (F. D.).—MORAL AND METAPHYSICAL PHILOSOPHY. 2 vols. 8vo. 16s.

McCOSH (Rev. Dr. James).—THE METHOD OF THE DIVINE GOVERNMENT, PHYSICAL AND MORAL. 8vo. 10s. 6d.

—— THE SUPERNATURAL IN RELATION TO THE NATURAL. Cr. 8vo. 7s. 6d.

—— INTUITIONS OF THE MIND. 8vo. 10s. 6d.

—— AN EXAMINATION OF MR. J. S. MILL'S PHILOSOPHY. 8vo. 10s. 6d.

—— CHRISTIANITY AND POSITIVISM. Lectures on Natural Theology and Apologetics. Cr. 8vo. 7s. 6d.

—— THE SCOTTISH PHILOSOPHY FROM HUTCHESON TO HAMILTON, BIOGRAPHICAL, EXPOSITORY, CRITICAL. Roy. 8vo. 16s.

—— REALISTIC PHILOSOPHY DEFENDED IN A PHILOSOPHIC SERIES. 2 vols.—Vol. I. EXPOSITORY. Vol. II. HISTORICAL AND CRITICAL. Cr. 8vo. 14s.

—— FIRST AND FUNDAMENTAL TRUTHS. Being a Treatise on Metaphysics. 8vo. 9s.

—— THE PREVAILING TYPES OF PHILOSOPHY : CAN THEY LOGICALLY REACH REALITY? 8vo. 3s. 6d.

—— OUR MORAL NATURE. Cr. 8vo. 2s. 6d.

MASSON (Prof. David).—RECENT BRITISH PHILOSOPHY. 3rd Edit. Cr. 8vo. 6s.

SIDGWICK (Prof. Henry).—THE METHODS OF ETHICS. 4th Edit., revised. 8vo. 14s.

—— A SUPPLEMENT TO THE SECOND EDITION. Containing all the important Additions and Alterations in the Fourth Edition. 8vo. 6s.

—— OUTLINES OF THE HISTORY OF ETHICS FOR ENGLISH READERS. Cr. 8vo. 3s. 6d.

THORNTON (W. T.). — OLD-FASHIONED ETHICS AND COMMON-SENSE METAPHYSICS. 8vo. 10s. 6d.

WILLIAMS (C. M.) —A REVIEW OF THE SYSTEMS OF ETHICS FOUNDED ON THE THEORY OF EVOLUTION. Cr. 8vo. 12s. net.

PHILOSOPHY.
Logic.

BOOLE (George). — The Mathematical Analysis of Logic. 8vo. sewed. 5s.

CARROLL (Lewis).—The Game of Logic. Cr. 8vo. 3s. net.

JEVONS (W. Stanley).—A Primer of Logic. 18mo. 1s.

—— Elementary Lessons in Logic, Deductive and Inductive. 18mo. 3s. 6d.

—— Studies in Deductive Logic. 2nd Edit. Cr. 8vo. 6s.

—— The Principles of Science: Treatise on Logic and Scientific Method. Cr. 8vo. 12s. 6d.

—— Pure Logic: and other Minor Works. Edited by R. Adamson, M.A., and Harriet A. Jevons. 8vo. 10s. 6d.

KEYNES (J. N.).—Studies and Exercises in Formal Logic. 2nd Edit. Cr. 8vo. 10s. 6d.

McCOSH (Rev. Dr.).—The Laws of Discursive Thought. A Text-Book of Formal Logic. Cr. 8vo. 5s.

RAY (Prof. P. K.).—A Text-Book of Deductive Logic. 4th Edit. Globe 8vo. 4s. 6d.

VENN (Rev. John).—The Logic of Chance. 2nd Edit. Cr. 8vo. 10s. 6d.

—— Symbolic Logic. Cr. 8vo. 10s. 6d.

—— The Principles of Empirical or Inductive Logic. 8vo. 18s.

Psychology.

BALDWIN (Prof. J. M.).—Handbook of Psychology: Senses and Intellect. 8vo. 12s. 6d.

—— Feeling and Will. 8vo. 12s. 6d.

—— Elements of Psychology. Cr. 8vo. 7s. 6d.

CALDERWOOD (Prof. H.). — The Relations of Mind and Brain. 3rd Ed. 8vo. 8s.

CLIFFORD (W. K.).—Seeing and Thinking. Cr. 8vo. 3s. 6d.

HÖFFDING (Prof. H.).—Outlines of Psychology. Translated by M. E. Lowndes. Cr. 8vo. 6s.

JAMES (Prof. William).—The Principles of Psychology. 2 vols. Demy 8vo. 25s. net.

—— Text Book of Psychology. Cr. 8vo. 7s. net.

JARDINE (Rev. Robert).—The Elements of the Psychology of Cognition. 3rd Edit. Cr. 8vo. 6s. 6d.

McCOSH (Rev. Dr.).—Psychology. Cr. 8vo. I. The Cognitive Powers. 6s. 6d.—II. The Motive Powers. 6s. 6d.

—— The Emotions. 8vo. 9s.

MAUDSLEY (Dr. Henry).—The Physiology of Mind. Cr. 8vo. 10s. 6d.

—— The Pathology of Mind. 8vo. 18s.

—— Body and Mind. Cr. 8vo. 6s. 6d.

MURPHY (J. J.).—Habit and Intelligence. 2nd Edit. Illustrated. 8vo. 16s.

PHOTOGRAPHY.

MELDOLA (Prof. R.).—The Chemistry of Photography. Cr. 8vo. 6s.

PHYSICS OR NATURAL PHILOSOPHY.
General—Electricity and Magnetism— Heat, Light, and Sound.

General.

ANDREWS (Dr. Thomas): The Scientific Papers of the late. With a Memoir by Profs. Tait and Crum Brown. 8vo. 18s.

BARKER (G. F.). — Physics: Advanced Course. 8vo. 21s.

DANIELL (A.).—A Text-Book of the Principles of Physics. Illustrated. 2nd Edit. Med. 8vo. 21s.

EVERETT (Prof. J. D.).—The C. G. S. System of Units, with Tables of Physical Constants. New Edit. Globe 8vo. 5s.

FESSENDEN (C.).—Elements of Physics. Fcp. 8vo. 3s.

FISHER (Rev. Osmond).—Physics of the Earth's Crust. 2nd Edit. 8vo. 12s.

GUILLEMIN (Amédée).—The Forces of Nature. A Popular Introduction to the Study of Physical Phenomena. 455 Woodcuts. Roy. 8vo. 21s.

KELVIN (Lord).—Popular Lectures and Addresses.—Vol. I. Constitution of Matter. Cr. 8vo. 7s. 6d.

KEMPE (A. B.).—How to draw a Straight Line. Cr. 8vo. 1s. 6d.

LOEWY (B.).—Questions and Examples in Experimental Physics, Sound, Light, Heat, Electricity, and Magnetism. Fcp. 8vo. 2s.

—— A Graduated Course of Natural Science. Part I. Gl. 8vo. 2s.—Part II. 2s. 6d.

MOLLOY (Rev. G.).—Gleanings in Science: A Series of Popular Lectures on Scientific Subjects. 8vo. 7s. 6d.

PHYSICAL REVIEW. Bi-Monthly. July, August. 8vo. 2s. 6d. net.

STEWART (Prof. Balfour). — A Primer of Physics. Illustrated. 18mo. 1s.

—— Lessons in Elementary Physics. Illustrated. Fcp. 8vo. 4s. 6d.

—— Questions. By T. H. Core. 18mo. 2s.

STEWART (Prof. Balfour) and GEE (W. W. Haldane).—Lessons in Elementary Practical Physics. Illustrated.—General Physical Processes. Cr. 8vo. 6s.

TAIT (Prof. P. G.).—Lectures on some Recent Advances in Physical Science. 3rd Edit. Cr. 8vo. 9s.

Electricity and Magnetism.

CUMMING (Linnæus).—An Introduction to Electricity. Cr. 8vo. 8s. 6d.

DAY (R. E.).—Electric Light Arithmetic. 18mo. 2s.

GRAY (Prof. Andrew).—The Theory and Practice of Absolute Measurements in Electricity and Magnetism. 2 vols. Cr. 8vo. Vol. I. 12s. 6d.—Vol. II. 2 parts. 25s.

—— Absolute Measurements in Electricity and Magnetism. Fcp. 8vo. 5s. 6d.

GUILLEMIN (A.).—Electricity and Magnetism. A Popular Treatise. Translated and Edited by Prof. Silvanus P. Thompson. Super Roy. 8vo. 31s. 6d.

HEAVISIDE (O.) — ELECTRICAL PAPERS. 2 vols. 8vo. 30s. net.

KELVIN (Lord). — PAPERS ON ELECTROSTATICS AND MAGNETISM. 8vo. 18s.

LODGE (Prof. Oliver). — MODERN VIEWS OF ELECTRICITY. Illust. Cr. 8vo. 6s. 6d.

MENDENHALL (T. C.). — A CENTURY OF ELECTRICITY. Cr. 8vo. 4s. 6d.

STEWART (Prof. Balfour) and GEE (W. W. Haldane). — LESSONS IN ELEMENTARY PRACTICAL PHYSICS. Cr. 8vo. Illustrated. — ELECTRICITY AND MAGNETISM. 7s. 6d.
—— PRACTICAL PHYSICS FOR SCHOOLS. Gl. 8vo. — ELECTRICITY AND MAGNETISM. 2s. 6d.

THOMPSON (Prof. Silvanus P.). — ELEMENTARY LESSONS IN ELECTRICITY AND MAGNETISM. Illustrated. Fcp. 8vo. 4s. 6d.

TURNER (H. H.). — EXAMPLES ON HEAT AND ELECTRICITY. Cr. 8vo. 2s. 6d.

Heat, Light, and Sound.

AIRY (Sir G. B.). — ON SOUND AND ATMOSPHERIC VIBRATIONS. Cr. 8vo. 9s.

CARNOT—THURSTON.—REFLECTIONS ON THE MOTIVE POWER OF HEAT, AND ON MACHINES FITTED TO DEVELOP THAT POWER. From the French of N. L. S. CARNOT. Edited by R. H. THURSTON, LL.D. Cr. 8vo. 7s. 6d.

JOHNSON (Amy). — SUNSHINE. Illustrated. Cr. 8vo. 6s.

JONES (Prof. D. E.). — HEAT, LIGHT, AND SOUND. Globe 8vo. 2s. 6d.
—— LESSONS IN HEAT AND LIGHT. Globe 8vo. 3s. 6d.

MAYER (Prof. A. M.). — SOUND. A Series of Simple Experiments. Illustr. Cr. 8vo. 3s. 6d.

MAYER (Prof. A. M.) and BARNARD (C.).— LIGHT. A Series of Simple Experiments. Illustrated. Cr. 8vo. 2s. 6d.

PARKINSON (S.). — A TREATISE ON OPTICS. 4th Edit., revised. Cr. 8vo. 10s. 6d.

PEABODY (Prof. C. H.). — THERMODYNAMICS OF THE STEAM ENGINE AND OTHER HEATENGINES. 8vo. 21s.

PERRY (Prof. J.). — STEAM : An Elementary Treatise. 18mo. 4s. 6d.

PRESTON (T.). — THE THEORY OF LIGHT. Illustrated. 8vo. 15s. net.
—— THE THEORY OF HEAT. 8vo.

RAYLEIGH (Lord). — THEORY OF SOUND. 8vo. Vol. I. 12s. 6d. — Vol. II. 12s. 6d.

SHANN (G.). — AN ELEMENTARY TREATISE ON HEAT IN RELATION TO STEAM AND THE STEAM-ENGINE. Illustr. Cr. 8vo. 4s. 6d.

SPOTTISWOODE (W.). — POLARISATION OF LIGHT. Illustrated. Cr. 8vo. 3s. 6d.

STEWART (Prof. Balfour) and GEE (W. W. Haldane). — LESSONS IN ELEMENTARY PRACTICAL PHYSICS. Cr. 8vo. Illustrated.— OPTICS, HEAT, AND SOUND.
—— PRACTICAL PHYSICS FOR SCHOOLS. Gl. 8vo. — HEAT, LIGHT, AND SOUND.

STOKES (Sir George G.). — ON LIGHT. The Burnett Lectures. Cr. 8vo. 7s. 6d.

STONE (W. H.). — ELEMENTARY LESSONS ON SOUND. Illustrated. Fcp. 8vo. 3s. 6d.

TAIT (Prof. P. G.). — HEAT. With Illustrations. Cr. 8vo. 6s.

TAYLOR (Sedley). — SOUND AND MUSIC. 2nd Edit. Ext. cr. 8vo. 8s. 6d.

TURNER (H. H.). (See ELECTRICITY.)

WRIGHT (Lewis). — LIGHT. A Course of Experimental Optics. Illust. Cr. 8vo. 7s. 6d.

PHYSIOGRAPHY and METEOROLOGY.

ARATUS. — THE SKIES AND WEATHER FORECASTS OF ARATUS. Translated by E. POSTE, M.A. Cr. 8vo. 3s. 6d.

BLANFORD (H. F.). — THE RUDIMENTS OF PHYSICAL GEOGRAPHY FOR THE USE OF INDIAN SCHOOLS. Illustr. Cr. 8vo. 2s. 6d.
—— A PRACTICAL GUIDE TO THE CLIMATES AND WEATHER OF INDIA, CEYLON AND BURMAH, AND THE STORMS OF INDIAN SEAS. 8vo. 12s. 6d.

FERREL (Prof. W.). — A POPULAR TREATISE ON THE WINDS. 2nd Ed. 8vo. 17s. net.

FISHER (Rev. Osmond). — PHYSICS OF THE EARTH'S CRUST. 2nd Edit. 8vo. 12s.

GEIKIE (Sir Archibald). — A PRIMER OF PHYSICAL GEOGRAPHY. Illustrated. 18mo. 1s.
—— ELEMENTARY LESSONS IN PHYSICAL GEOGRAPHY. Illustrated. Fcp. 8vo. 4s. 6d.
—— QUESTIONS ON THE SAME. 1s. 6d.

HUXLEY (Prof. T. H.). — PHYSIOGRAPHY. Illustrated. Cr. 8vo. 6s.

LOCKYER (J. Norman). — OUTLINES OF PHYSIOGRAPHY : THE MOVEMENTS OF THE EARTH. Illustrated. Cr. 8vo, swd. 1s. 6d.

MELDOLA (Prof. R.) and WHITE (Wm.).— REPORT ON THE EAST ANGLIAN EARTHQUAKE OF APRIL 22ND, 1884. 8vo. 3s. 6d.

PHYSIOLOGY.

FEARNLEY (W.). — A MANUAL OF ELEMENTARY PRACTICAL HISTOLOGY. Cr. 8vo. 7s. 6d.

FOSTER (Prof. Michael). — A TEXT-BOOK OF PHYSIOLOGY. Illustrated. 5th Edit. 8vo.— Part I. Book I. BLOOD : THE TISSUES OF MOVEMENT, THE VASCULAR MECHANISM. 10s. 6d.—Part II. Book II. THE TISSUES OF CHEMICAL ACTION, WITH THEIR RESPECTIVE MECHANISMS : NUTRITION. 10s. 6d.—Part III. Book III. THE CENTRAL NERVOUS SYSTEM. 7s. 6d.—Part IV. Book III. THE SENSES, AND SOME SPECIAL MUSCULAR MECHANISMS.—BOOK IV. THE TISSUES AND MECHANISMS OF REPRODUCTION. 10s. 6d. —Appendix, by A. S. LEA. 7s. 6d.
—— A PRIMER OF PHYSIOLOGY. 18mo. 1s.

FOSTER (Prof. M.) and LANGLEY (J. N.). —A COURSE OF ELEMENTARY PRACTICAL PHYSIOLOGY AND HISTOLOGY. Cr. 8vo. 7s. 6d.

GAMGEE (Arthur). — A TEXT-BOOK OF THE PHYSIOLOGICAL CHEMISTRY OF THE ANIMAL BODY. Vol. I. 8vo. 18s. Vol. II.

PHYSIOLOGY—*continued.*

HUMPHRY (Prof. Sir G. M.).—THE HUMAN FOOT AND THE HUMAN HAND. Illustrated. Fcp. 8vo. 4s. 6d.

HUXLEY (Prof. Thos. H.).—LESSONS IN ELEMENTARY PHYSIOLOGY. Fcp. 8vo. 4s. 6d.
—— QUESTIONS. By T. ALCOCK. 18mo. 1s.6d.

MIVART (St. George).—LESSONS IN ELEMENTARY ANATOMY. Fcp. 8vo. 6s. 6d.

PETTIGREW (J. Bell).—THE PHYSIOLOGY OF THE CIRCULATION IN PLANTS IN THE LOWER ANIMALS AND IN MAN. 8vo. 12s.

SEILER (Dr. Carl).—MICRO-PHOTOGRAPHS IN HISTOLOGY, NORMAL AND PATHOLOGICAL. 4to. 31s. 6d.

POETRY. (*See under* LITERATURE, p. 14.)

POLITICAL ECONOMY.

BASTABLE (Prof. C. F.).—PUBLIC FINANCE. 12s. 6d. net.

BÖHM-BAWERK (Prof.).—CAPITAL AND INTEREST. Trans. by W. SMART. 8vo. 12s.net.
—— THE POSITIVE THEORY OF CAPITAL. By the same Translator. 12s. net.

BOISSEVAIN (G. M.).—THE MONETARY QUESTION. 8vo, sewed. 3s. net.

BONAR (James).—MALTHUS AND HIS WORK. 8vo. 12s. 6d.

CAIRNES (J. E.).—SOME LEADING PRINCIPLES OF POLITICAL ECONOMY NEWLY EXPOUNDED. 8vo. 14s.
—— THE CHARACTER AND LOGICAL METHOD OF POLITICAL ECONOMY. Cr. 8vo. 6s.

CANTILLON.—ESSAI SUR LE COMMERCE. 12mo. 7s. net.

CLARE (G.).—A B C OF THE FOREIGN EXCHANGES. Cr. 8vo. 3s. net.

CLARKE (C. B.). — SPECULATIONS FROM POLITICAL ECONOMY. Cr. 8vo. 3s. 6d.

DICTIONARY OF POLITICAL ECONOMY, A. By various Writers. Ed. R. H. I. PALGRAVE. 3s.6d. net. (Part I. July, 1891.)

ECONOMIC JOURNAL, THE. — THE JOURNAL OF THE BRITISH ECONOMIC ASSOCIATION. Edit. by Prof. F. Y. EDGEWORTH. Published Quarterly. 8vo. 5s. (Part I. April, 1891.) Vol. I. 21s. [Cloth Covers for binding Volumes, 1s. 6d. each.]

ECONOMICS: THE QUARTERLY JOURNAL OF. Vol. II. Parts II. III. IV. 2s. 6d. each. —Vol. III. 4 parts. 2s. 6d. each.—Vol. IV. 4 parts. 2s.6d. each.—Vol. V. 4 parts. 2s.6d. each.—Vol. VI. 4 parts. 2s. 6d. each.

FAWCETT (Henry).—MANUAL OF POLITICAL ECONOMY. 7th Edit. Cr. 8vo. 12s.
—— AN EXPLANATORY DIGEST OF THE ABOVE. By C. A. WATERS. Cr. 8vo. 2s. 6d.
—— FREE TRADE AND PROTECTION. 6th Edit. Cr. 8vo. 3s. 6d.

FAWCETT (Mrs. H.).—POLITICAL ECONOMY FOR BEGINNERS, WITH QUESTIONS. 7th Edit. 18mo. 2s. 6d.

FIRST LESSONS IN BUSINESS MATTERS. By A BANKER'S DAUGHTER. 2nd Edit. 18mo. 1s.

GILMAN (N. P.).
TWEEN EMPLOYER
8vo. 7s. 6d.

GOSCHEN (Rt. Ho
AND SPEECHES ON L

GUIDE TO THE
EVERY-DAY MATT
PERTY AND INCOME

GUNTON (George)
GRESS. Cr. 8vo. 6

HORTON (Hon. S
POUND AND ENGLA
SINCE THE RESTOP

HOWELL (George)
CAPITAL AND LABO

JEVONS (W. Stanley
CAL ECONOMY. 18
—— THE THEORY O
3rd Ed. 8vo. 10s.
—— INVESTIGATION:
NANCE. Edit. by H

KEYNES (J. N.).—1
OF POLITICAL ECO

MARSHALL (Prof.
ECONOMICS. 2 vols.
—— ELEMENTS OF F
Crown 8vo. 3s. 6d.

MARTIN (Frederic
LLOYD'S, AND OF
GREAT BRITAIN.

PRICE (L. L. F. R.
ITS ADVANTAGES,
CULTIES. Med. 8v

SIDGWICK (Prof. H
OF POLITICAL ECON

SMART (W.).—AN
THEORY OF VALUE

THOMPSON (H. :
WAGES AND ITS API
HOURS QUESTION.

WALKER (Francis .
POLITICAL ECONON
—— A BRIEF TEX
ECONOMY. Cr. 8vc
—— POLITICAL ECO
—— THE WAGES Q
8s. 6d. net.
—— MONEY. New Ed
—— MONEY IN ITS F
INDUSTRY. Cr. 8v
—— LAND AND ITS R

WALLACE (A. R.).—
Cr. 8vo. 2s. 6d.

WICKSTEED (Ph. :
ECONOMIC SCIENCE
THEORY OF VALUE

POI
(*See also* H

ADAMS (Sir F. O.:
(C.)—THE SWISS CC

BAKER (Sir Samue
QUESTION. 8vo, s

BATH (Marquis of).—OBSERVATIONS ON BULGARIAN AFFAIRS. Cr. 8vo. 3s. 6d.

BRIGHT (John).—SPEECHES ON QUESTIONS OF PUBLIC POLICY. Edit. by J. E. THOROLD ROGERS. With Portrait. 2 vols. 8vo. 25s. —Popular Edition. Ext. fcp. 8vo. 3s. 6d. —— PUBLIC ADDRESSES. Edited by J. E. T. ROGERS. 8vo. 14s.

BRYCE (Jas., M.P.).—THE AMERICAN COMMONWEALTH. 2 vols. New Edit. Ext. cr. 8vo. Vol. I. 12s. 6d.

BUCKLAND (Anna).—OUR NATIONAL INSTITUTIONS. 18mo. 1s.

BURKE (Edmund).—LETTERS, TRACTS, AND SPEECHES ON IRISH AFFAIRS. Edited by MATTHEW ARNOLD, with Preface. Cr. 8vo. 6s. —— REFLECTIONS ON THE FRENCH REVOLUTION. Ed. by F. G. SELBY. Globe 8vo. 5s.

CAIRNES (J. E.).—POLITICAL ESSAYS. 8vo. 10s. 6d. —— THE SLAVE POWER. 8vo. 10s. 6d.

COBDEN (Richard).—SPEECHES ON QUESTIONS OF PUBLIC POLICY. Ed. by J. BRIGHT and J. E. THOROLD ROGERS. Gl. 8vo. 3s. 6d.

DICEY (Prof. A. V.).—LETTERS ON UNIONIST DELUSIONS. Cr. 8vo. 2s. 6d.

DILKE (Rt. Hon. Sir Charles W.).—GREATER BRITAIN. 9th Edit. Cr. 8vo. 6s. —— PROBLEMS OF GREATER BRITAIN. Maps. 3rd Edit. Ext. cr. 8vo. 12s. 6d.

DONISTHORPE (Wordsworth). — INDIVIDUALISM: A System of Politics. 8vo. 14s.

DUFF (Rt. Hon. Sir M. E. Grant).—MISCELLANIES, POLITICAL AND LITERARY. 8vo. 10s. 6d.

ENGLISH CITIZEN, THE.—His Rights and Responsibilities. Ed. by HENRY CRAIK, C.B. New Edit. Monthly Volumes from Oct. 1892. Cr. 8vo. 2s. 6d. each.

CENTRAL GOVERNMENT. By H. D. TRAILL.

THE ELECTORATE AND THE LEGISLATURE. By SPENCER WALPOLE.

THE LAND LAWS. By Sir F. POLLOCK, Bart. 2nd Edit.

THE PUNISHMENT AND PREVENTION OF CRIME. By Col. Sir EDMUND DU CANE.

LOCAL GOVERNMENT. By M. D. CHALMERS.

COLONIES AND DEPENDENCIES: Part I. INDIA. By J. S. COTTON, M.A.—II. THE COLONIES. By E. J. PAYNE.

THE STATE IN ITS RELATION TO EDUCATION. By HENRY CRAIK, C.B.

THE STATE AND THE CHURCH. By Hon. ARTHUR ELLIOTT, M.P.

THE STATE IN ITS RELATION TO TRADE. By Sir T. H. FARRER, Bart.

THE POOR LAW. By the Rev. T. W. FOWLE.

THE STATE IN RELATION TO LABOUR. By W. STANLEY JEVONS.

JUSTICE AND POLICE. By F. W. MAITLAND.

THE NATIONAL DEFENCES. By Colonel MAURICE, R.A.   [In the Press.

FOREIGN RELATIONS. By S. WALPOLE.

THE NATIONAL BUDGET; NATIONAL DEBT; TAXES AND RATES. By A. J. WILSON.

FAWCETT (Henry).—SPEECHES ON SOME CURRENT POLITICAL QUESTIONS. 8vo. 10s. 6d. —— FREE TRADE AND PROTECTION. 6th Edit. Cr. 8vo. 3s. 6d.

FAWCETT (Henry and Mrs. H.).—ESSAYS AND LECTURES ON POLITICAL AND SOCIAL SUBJECTS. 8vo. 10s. 6d.

FISKE (John).—AMERICAN POLITICAL IDEAS VIEWED FROM THE STAND-POINT OF UNIVERSAL HISTORY. Cr. 8vo. 4s. —— CIVIL GOVERNMENT IN THE UNITED STATES CONSIDERED WITH SOME REFERENCE TO ITS ORIGIN. Cr. 8vo. 6s. 6d.

FREEMAN (E. A.). — DISESTABLISHMENT AND DISENDOWMENT. WHAT ARE THEY? 4th Edit. Cr. 8vo. 1s. —— THE GROWTH OF THE ENGLISH CONSTITUTION. 5th Edit. Cr. 8vo. 5s.

HARWOOD (George).—DISESTABLISHMENT: or, a Defence of the Principle of a National Church. 8vo. 12s. —— THE COMING DEMOCRACY. Cr. 8vo. 6s.

HILL (Florence D.).—CHILDREN OF THE STATE. Edited by FANNY FOWKE. Crown 8vo. 6s.

HILL (Octavia).—OUR COMMON LAND, AND OTHER ESSAYS. Ext. fcp. 8vo. 3s. 6d.

HOLLAND (Prof. T. E.).—THE TREATY RELATIONS OF RUSSIA AND TURKEY, FROM 1774 TO 1853. Cr. 8vo. 2s.

JENKS (Prof. Edward).—THE GOVERNMENT OF VICTORIA (AUSTRALIA). 8vo. 14s.

JEPHSON (H.).—THE PLATFORM: ITS RISE AND PROGRESS. 2 vols. 8vo. 21s.

LOWELL (J. R.). (See COLLECTED WORKS.)

LUBBOCK (Sir J.). (See COLLECTED WORKS.)

PALGRAVE (W. Gifford). — ESSAYS ON EASTERN QUESTIONS. 8vo. 10s. 6d.

PARKIN (G. R.).—IMPERIAL FEDERATION. Cr. 8vo. 4s. 6d.

POLLOCK (Sir F., Bart.).—INTRODUCTION TO THE HISTORY OF THE SCIENCE OF POLITICS. Cr. 8vo. 2s. 6d. —— LEADING CASES DONE INTO ENGLISH. Crown 8vo 3s. 6d.

PRACTICAL POLITICS. 8vo. 6s.

ROGERS (Prof. J. E. T.).—COBDEN AND POLITICAL OPINION. 8vo. 10s. 6d.

ROUTLEDGE (Jas.).—POPULAR PROGRESS IN ENGLAND. 8vo. 16s.

RUSSELL (Sir Charles).—NEW VIEWS ON IRELAND. Cr. 8vo. 2s. 6d. —— THE PARNELL COMMISSION: THE OPENING SPEECH FOR THE DEFENCE. 8vo. 10s. 6d. —Popular Edition. Sewed. 2s.

SIDGWICK (Prof. Henry).—THE ELEMENTS OF POLITICS. 8vo. 14s. net.

POLITICS.

SMITH (Goldwin).—CANADA AND THE CANA-DIAN QUESTION. 8vo. 8s. net.

STATESMAN'S YEAR-BOOK, THE. (See below under STATISTICS.)

STATHAM (R.). — BLACKS, BOERS, AND BRITISH. Cr. 8vo. 6s.

THORNTON (W. T.).--A PLEA FOR PEASANT PROPRIETORS. New Edit. Cr. 8vo. 7s. 6d.
—— INDIAN PUBLIC WORKS, AND COGNATE INDIAN TOPICS. Cr. 8vo. 8s. 6d.

TRENCH (Capt. F.).—THE RUSSO-INDIAN QUESTION. Cr. 8vo. ~s. 6d.

WALLACE (Sir Donald M.).—EGYPT AND THE EGYPTIAN QUESTION. 8vo. 14s.

PSYCHOLOGY.

(See under PHILOSOPHY, p. 28.)

SCULPTURE. (See ART.)

SOCIAL ECONOMY.

BOOTH (C.).—A PICTURE OF PAUPERISM. Cr. 8vo. 5s.—Cheap Edit. 8vo. Swd., 6d.
—— LIFE AND LABOUR OF THE PEOPLE OF LONDON. 4 vols. Cr. 8vo. 3s. 6d. each.— Maps to illustrate the above. 5s.

FAWCETT (H. and Mrs. H.). (See POLITICS.)

GILMAN (N. P.). — SOCIALISM AND THE AMERICAN SPIRIT. Cr. 8vo. 6s. 6d.

HILL (Octavia).—HOMES OF THE LONDON POOR. Cr. 8vo, sewed. 1s.

HUXLEY (Prof. T. H.).—SOCIAL DISEASES AND WORSE REMEDIES: Letters to the "Times." Cr. 8vo. sewed. 1s. net.

JEVONS (W. Stanley).—METHODS OF SOCIAL REFORM. 8vo. 10s. 6d.

PEARSON (C. H.).—NATIONAL LIFE AND CHARACTER: A FORECAST. 8vo. 10s. net.

STANLEY (Hon. Maude). — CLUBS FOR WORKING GIRLS. Cr. 8vo. 3s. 6d.

SOUND. (See under PHYSICS, p. 29.)

SPORT.

BAKER (Sir Samuel W.).—WILD BEASTS AND THEIR WAYS: REMINISCENCES OF EUROPE, ASIA, AFRICA, AMERICA, FROM 1845—88. Illustrated. Ext. cr. 8vo. 12s. 6d.

CHASSERESSE (D.).—SPORTING SKETCHES. Illustrated. Cr. 8vo. 3s. 6d.

EDWARDS-MOSS (Sir J. E., Bart). — A SEASON IN SUTHERLAND. Cr. 8vo. 1s. 6d.

STATISTICS.

STATESMAN'S YEAR-BOOK, THE. Statistical and Historical Annual of the States of the World for the Year 1893. Revised after Official Returns. Ed. by J. SCOTT KELTIE. Cr. 8vo. 10s. 6d.

SURGERY. (See MEDICINE.)

SWIMMING.

LEAHY (Sergeant).—THE ART OF SWIMMING IN THE ETON STYLE. Cr. 8vo. 2s.

THI

The Bible—History
The Church of En
—The Fathers—H
tures, Addresses,

Th
History of the Bible-
THE ENGLISH B
Critical History
Translations of
EADIE. 2 vols.
THE BIBLE IN THE
Bp. WESTCOTT.

Biblical History—
BIBLE LESSONS.
Cr. 8vo. 4s. 6d.
SIDE-LIGHTS UPO
Mrs. SYDNEY BU
STORIES FROM TH
CHURCH. Illust.
BIBLE READINGS
TATEUCH AND
By Rev. J. A. (
THE CHILDREN'S
STORIES. By M
1s. each.—Part
New Testament
THE NATIONS A
KEARY. Cr. 8v
A CLASS-BOOK O
TORY. By Rev. D
A CLASS-BOOK O
TORY. By the s
A SHILLING BOO
HISTORY. By th
A SHILLING BOO
HISTORY. By th

The Old Testament-
SCRIPTURE READ
FAMILIES. By
1s. 6d. each: al
each. — GENESI
JOSHUA TO SOL
PROPHETS.—TH
TOLIC TIMES.
THE PATRIARCHS
OLD TESTAMEN
Cr. 8vo. 3s. 6d.
THE PROPHETS A
TESTAMENT.
THE CANON OF T
Prof. H. E. RYL

The Pentateuch—
AN HISTORICO-CR
ORIGIN AND CO
TEUCH (PENTA
JOSHUA). By P
by P. H. WICKS

The Psalms—
THE PSALMS CHRO
By FOUR FRIEN
GOLDEN TREASU
Edition of the a
THE PSALMS. Wi
By A. C. JENN
LOWE, M.A. 2 v
INTRODUCTION TO
THE PSALMS.
2nd Edit. 2 vol

Isaiah—
ISAIAH XL—LXVI
phecies allied to
ARNOLD. Cr. 8v

Isaiah—

ISAIAH OF JERUSALEM. In the Authorised English Version, with Introduction and Notes. By MATTHEW ARNOLD. Cr. 8vo. 4s. 6d.

A BIBLE-READING FOR SCHOOLS. The Great Prophecy of Israel's Restoration (Isaiah xl.—lxvi.). Arranged and Edited for Young Learners. By the same. 18mo. 1s.

COMMENTARY ON THE BOOK OF ISAIAH: Critical, Historical, and Prophetical; including a Revised English Translation. By T. R. BIRKS. 2nd Edit. 8vo. 12s. 6d.

THE BOOK OF ISAIAH CHRONOLOGICALLY ARRANGED. By T. K. CHEYNE. Cr. 8vo. 7s. 6d.

Zechariah—

THE HEBREW STUDENT'S COMMENTARY ON ZECHARIAH, Hebrew and LXX. By W. H. LOWE, M.A. 8vo. 10s. 6d.

The New Testament—

THE NEW TESTAMENT. Essay on the Right Estimation of MS. Evidence in the Text of the New Testament. By T. R. BIRKS. Cr. 8vo. 3s. 6d.

THE MESSAGES OF THE BOOKS. Discourses and Notes on the Books of the New Testament. By Archd. FARRAR. 8vo. 14s.

THE CLASSICAL ELEMENT IN THE NEW TESTAMENT. Considered as a Proof of its Genuineness, with an Appendix on the Oldest Authorities used in the Formation of the Canon. By C.H. HOOLE. 8vo. 10s. 6d.

ON A FRESH REVISION OF THE ENGLISH NEW TESTAMENT. With an Appendix on the last Petition of the Lord's Prayer. By Bishop LIGHTFOOT. Cr. 8vo. 7s. 6d.

THE UNITY OF THE NEW TESTAMENT. By F. D. MAURICE. 2 vols. Cr. 8vo. 12s.

THE SYNOPTIC PROBLEM FOR ENGLISH READERS. By A. J. JOLLEY. Cr. 8vo. 3s. net.

A GENERAL SURVEY OF THE HISTORY OF THE CANON OF THE NEW TESTAMENT DURING THE FIRST FOUR CENTURIES. By Bishop WESTCOTT. Cr. 8vo. 10s. 6d.

GREEK ENGLISH LEXICON TO THE NEW TESTAMENT. By W. J. HICKIE, M.A. Pott 8vo. 3s.

THE NEW TESTAMENT IN THE ORIGINAL GREEK. The Text revised by Bishop WESTCOTT, D.D., and Prof. F. J. A. HORT, D.D. 2 vols. Cr. 8vo. 10s. 6d. each.—Vol. I. Text.—Vol. II. Introduction and Appendix.

SCHOOL EDITION OF THE ABOVE. 18mo, 4s. 6d.; 18mo, roan, 5s. 6d.; morocco, gilt edges, 6s. 6d.

The Gospels—

THE COMMON TRADITION OF THE SYNOPTIC GOSPELS. In the Text of the Revised Version. By Rev. E. A. ABBOTT and W. G. RUSHBROOKE. Cr. 8vo. 3s. 6d.

SYNOPTICON: An Exposition of the Common Matter of the Synoptic Gospels. By W. G. RUSHBROOKE. Printed in Colours. In Six Parts, and Appendix. 4to.—Part I. 3s. 6d. —Parts II. and III. 7s.—Parts IV. V. and VI., with Indices, 10s. 6d.—Appendices, 10s. 6d.—Complete in 1 vol. 35s.

INTRODUCTION TO THE STUDY OF THE FOUR GOSPELS. By Bp. WESTCOTT. Cr. 8vo. 10s. 6d.

THE COMPOSITION OF THE FOUR GOSPELS. By Rev. ARTHUR WRIGHT. Cr. 8vo. 5s.

The Gospels—

THE AKHMIM FRAGMENT OF THE APOCRYPHAL GOSPEL OF ST. PETER. By H. B. SWETE. 8vo. 5s. net.

Gospel of St. Matthew—

THE GREEK TEXT, with Introduction and Notes by Rev. A. SLOMAN. Fcp. 8vo. 2s. 6d.

CHOICE NOTES ON ST. MATTHEW. Drawn from Old and New Sources. Cr. 8vo. 4s. 6d. (St. Matthew and St. Mark in 1 vol. 9s.)

Gospel of St. Mark—

SCHOOL READINGS IN THE GREEK TESTAMENT. Being the Outlines of the Life of our Lord as given by St. Mark, with additions from the Text of the other Evangelists. Edited, with Notes and Vocabulary, by Rev. A. CALVERT, M.A. Fcp. 8vo. 2s. 6d.

CHOICE NOTES ON ST. MARK. Drawn from Old and New SOURCES. Cr. 8vo. 4s. 6d. (St. Matthew and St. Mark in 1 vol. 9s.)

Gospel of St. Luke—

GREEK TEXT, with Introduction and Notes by Rev. J. BOND, M.A. Fcp. 8vo. 2s. 6d.

CHOICE NOTES ON ST. LUKE. Drawn from Old and New Sources. Cr. 8vo. 4s. 6d.

THE GOSPEL OF THE KINGDOM OF HEAVEN. A Course of Lectures on the Gospel of St. Luke. By F. D. MAURICE. Cr. 8vo. 3s. 6d.

Gospel of St. John—

THE GOSPEL OF ST. JOHN. By F. D. MAURICE. Cr. 8vo. 3s. 6d.

CHOICE NOTES ON ST. JOHN. Drawn from Old and New Sources. Cr. 8vo. 4s. 6d.

The Acts of the Apostles—

THE OLD SYRIAC ELEMENT IN THE TEXT OF THE CODEX BEZÆ. By F. H. CHASE. 8vo. 7s. 6d. net.

GREEK TEXT, with Notes by T. E. PAGE, M.A. Fcp. 8vo. 3s. 6d.

THE CHURCH OF THE FIRST DAYS: THE CHURCH OF JERUSALEM, THE CHURCH OF THE GENTILES, THE CHURCH OF THE WORLD. Lectures on the Acts of the Apostles. By Very Rev. C. J. VAUGHAN. Cr. 8vo. 10s. 6d.

The Epistles of St. Paul—

THE EPISTLE TO THE ROMANS. The Greek Text, with English Notes. By the Very Rev. C. J. VAUGHAN. 7th Edit. Cr. 8vo. 7s. 6d.

THE EPISTLES TO THE CORINTHIANS. Greek Text, with Commentary. By Rev. W. KAY. 8vo. 9s.

The EPISTLE TO THE GALATIANS. A Revised Text, with Introduction, Notes, and Dissertations. By Bishop LIGHTFOOT. 10th Edit. 8vo. 12s.

THE EPISTLE TO THE PHILIPPIANS. A Revised Text, with Introduction, Notes, and Dissertations. By the same. 8vo. 12s.

THE EPISTLE TO THE PHILIPPIANS. With Translation, Paraphrase, and Notes for English Readers. By the Very Rev. C. J. VAUGHAN. Cr. 8vo. 5s.

THE EPISTLES TO THE COLOSSIANS AND TO PHILEMON. A Revised Text, with Introductions, etc. By Bishop LIGHTFOOT. 9th Edit. 8vo. 12s.

THE EPISTLES TO THE EPHESIANS, THE COLOSSIANS, AND PHILEMON. With Introduction and Notes. By Rev. J. LL DAVIES. 2nd Edit. 8vo. 7s. 6d.

3

THEOLOGY.
The Bible—*continued*.

The Epistles of St. Paul—
THE FIRST EPISTLE TO THE THESSALO-
NIANS. By Very Rev. C. J. VAUGHAN.
8vo, sewed. 1s. 6d.
THE EPISTLES TO THE THESSALONIANS.
Commentary on the Greek Text. By Prof.
JOHN EADIE. 8vo. 12s.

The Epistle of St. James—
THE GREEK TEXT, with Introduction and
Notes. By Rev. JOSEPH B. MAYOR. 8vo. 14s.

The Epistles of St. John—
THE EPISTLES OF ST. JOHN. By F. D.
MAURICE. Cr. 8vo. 3s. 6d.
— The Greek Text, with Notes, by Bishop
WESTCOTT. 3rd Edit. 8vo. 12s. 6d.

The Epistle to the Hebrews—
GREEK AND ENGLISH. Edited by Rev.
FREDERIC RENDALL. Cr. 8vo. 6s.
ENGLISH TEXT, with Commentary. By the
same. Cr. 8vo. 7s. 6d.
THE GREEK TEXT, with Notes, by Very
Rev. C. J. VAUGHAN. Cr. 8vo. 7s. 6d.
THE GREEK TEXT, with Notes and Essays,
by Bishop WESTCOTT. 8vo. 14s.

Revelation—
LECTURES ON THE APOCALYPSE. By F. D.
MAURICE. Cr. 8vo. 3s. 6d.
THE REVELATION OF ST. JOHN. By Rev.
Prof. W. MILLIGAN. Cr. 8vo. 7s. 6d.
LECTURES ON THE APOCALYPSE. By the
same. Crown 8vo. 5s.
DISCUSSIONS ON THE APOCALYPSE. By the
same. Cr. 8vo. 5s.
LECTURES ON THE REVELATION OF ST.
JOHN. By Very Rev. C. J. VAUGHAN.
5th Edit. Cr. 8vo. 10s. 6d.

THE BIBLE WORD-BOOK. By W. ALDIS
WRIGHT. 2nd Edit. Cr. 8vo. 7s. 6d.

History of the Christian Church.
CHURCH (Dean).—THE OXFORD MOVE-
MENT, 1833—45. Gl. 8vo. 5s.
CUNNINGHAM (Rev. John).—THE GROWTH
OF THE CHURCH IN ITS ORGANISATION AND
INSTITUTIONS. 8vo. 9s.
CUNNINGHAM (Rev. William). — THE
CHURCHES OF ASIA : A Methodical Sketch
of the Second Century. Cr. 8vo. 6s.
DALE (A. W. W.).—THE SYNOD OF ELVIRA,
AND CHRISTIAN LIFE IN THE FOURTH CEN-
TURY. Cr. 8vo. 10s. 6d.
HARDWICK (Archdeacon).—A HISTORY OF
THE CHRISTIAN CHURCH : MIDDLE AGE
Edited by Bp. STUBBS. Cr. 8vo. 10s. 6d.
—— A HISTORY OF THE CHRISTIAN CHURCH
DURING THE REFORMATION. 9th Edit., re-
vised by Bishop STUBBS. Cr. 8vo. 10s. 6d.
HORT (Dr. F. J. A.).—TWO DISSERTATIONS.
I. ON ΜΟΝΟΓΕΝΗΣ ΘΕΟΣ IN SCRIPTURE
AND TRADITION. II. ON THE "CONSTAN-
TINOPOLITAN" CREED AND OTHER EASTERN
CREEDS OF THE FOURTH CENTURY. 8vo.
7s. 6d.
KILLEN (W. D.).—ECCLESIASTICAL HIS-
TORY OF IRELAND, FROM THE EARLIEST
DATE TO THE PRESENT TIME. 2 vols.
8vo. 25s.

SIMPSON (Rev. W.).—AN EPITOME OF TH
HISTORY OF THE CHRISTIAN CHURCH. 7t
Edit. Fcp. 8vo 3s. 6d.
VAUGHAN (Very Rev. C. J.).—THE CHURC
OF THE FIRST DAYS : THE CHURCH O
JERUSALEM, THE CHURCH OF THE GEN
TILES, THE CHURCH OF THE WORLD. C
8vo. 10s. 6d.
WARD (W.).—WILLIAM GEORGE WARD AN
THE OXFORD MOVEMENT. 8vo. 14s.
—— W. G. WARD AND THE CATHOLIC RE
VIVAL. 8vo. 14s.

The Church of England.
Catechism of—
CATECHISM AND CONFIRMATION. 18mo
1s. net.
A CLASS-BOOK OF THE CATECHISM O
THE CHURCH OF ENGLAND. By Rev. Cano
MACLEAR. 18mo. 1s. 6d.
A FIRST CLASS-BOOK OF THE CATECHISI
OF THE CHURCH OF ENGLAND. By th
same. 18mo. 6d.
THE ORDER OF CONFIRMATION. Wit
Prayers and Devotions. By the same
32mo. 6d.

Collects—
COLLECTS OF THE CHURCH OF ENGLANI
With a Coloured Floral Design to eac
Collect. Cr. 8vo. 12s.

Disestablishment—
DISESTABLISHMENT AND DISENDOWMENT
WHAT ARE THEY ? By Prof. E. A. FREE
MAN. 4th Edit. Cr. 8vo. 1s.
DISESTABLISHMENT ; or, A Defence of th
Principle of a National Church. By GE
HARWOOD. 8vo. 12s.
A DEFENCE OF THE CHURCH OF ENGLAN
AGAINST DISESTABLISHMENT. By ROUN
DELL, EARL OF SELBORNE. Cr. 8vo. 2s. 6
ANCIENT FACTS AND FICTIONS CONCERNIN
CHURCHES AND TITHES By the sam
2nd Edit. Cr. 8vo. 7s. 6d.

Dissent in its Relation to—
DISSENT IN ITS RELATION TO THE CHURC
OF ENGLAND. By Rev. G. H. CURTEI
Bampton Lectures for 1871. Cr. 8vo. 7s. 6

Holy Communion—
THE COMMUNION SERVICE FROM THE BOO
OF COMMON PRAYER. With Select Read
ings from the Writings of the Rev. F. D
MAURICE. Edited by Bishop COLENSO
6th Edit. 16mo. 2s. 6d.
BEFORE THE TABLE : An Inquiry, Historica
and Theological, into the Meaning of th
Consecration Rubric in the Communio
Service of the Church of England. B
Very Rev. J. S. HOWSON. 8vo. 7s. 6d.
FIRST COMMUNION. With Prayers and De
votions for the newly Confirmed. By Re
Canon MACLEAR. 32mo. 6d.
A MANUAL OF INSTRUCTION FOR CONFIR
MATION AND FIRST COMMUNION. Wit
Prayers and Devotions. By the same
32mo. 2s.

Liturgy—
AN INTRODUCTION TO THE CREEDS. B
Rev. Canon MACLEAR. 18mo. 3s. 6d.
AN INTRODUCTION TO THE THIRTY-NIN
ARTICLES. By same. 18mo. [*In the Pres*
A HISTORY OF THE BOOK OF COMMO
PRAYER. By Rev F. PROCTER. 18
Edit. Cr. 8vo. 10s. 6d.

Liturgy—

AN ELEMENTAY INTRODUCTION TO THE BOOK OF COMMON PRAYER. By Rev. F. PROCTER and Rev. Canon MACLEAR. 18mo. 2s. 6d.

TWELVE DISCOURSES ON SUBJECTS CONNECTED WITH THE LITURGY AND WORSHIP OF THE CHURCH OF ENGLAND. By Very Rev. C. J. VAUGHAN. Fcp. 8vo. 6s.

A COMPANION TO THE LECTIONARY. By Rev. W. BENHAM, B.D. Cr. 8vo. 4s. 6d.

Devotional Books.

EASTLAKE (Lady). — FELLOWSHIP: LETTERS ADDRESSED TO MY SISTER-MOURNERS. Cr. 8vo. 2s. 6d.

IMITATIO CHRISTI. Libri IV. Printed in Borders after Holbein, Dürer, and other old Masters, containing Dances of Death, Acts of Mercy, Emblems, etc. Cr.8vo. 7s.6d.

KINGSLEY (Charles). — OUT OF THE DEEP: WORDS FOR THE SORROWFUL. From the Writings of CHARLES KINGSLEY. Ext. fcp. 8vo. 3s. 6d.

—— DAILY THOUGHTS. Selected from the Writings of CHARLES KINGSLEY. By HIS WIFE. Cr. 8vo. 6s.

—— FROM DEATH TO LIFE. Fragments of Teaching to a Village Congregation. Edit. by HIS WIFE. Fcp. 8vo. 2s. 6d.

MACLEAR (Rev. Canon). — A MANUAL OF INSTRUCTION FOR CONFIRMATION AND FIRST COMMUNION, WITH PRAYERS AND DEVOTIONS. 32mo. 2s.

—— THE HOUR OF SORROW; or, The Office for the Burial of the Dead. 32mo. 2s.

MAURICE (F. D.). — LESSONS OF HOPE. Readings from the Works of F. D. MAURICE. Selected by Rev. J. LL. DAVIES, M.A. Cr. 8vo. 5s.

RAYS OF SUNLIGHT FOR DARK DAYS. With a Preface by Very Rev. C. J. VAUGHAN. D.D. New Edition. 18mo. 3s. 6d.

SERVICE (Rev. J.). — PRAYERS FOR PUBLIC WORSHIP. Cr. 8vo. 4s. 6d.

THE WORSHIP OF GOD, AND FELLOWSHIP AMONG MEN. By Prof. MAURICE and others. Fcp. 8vo. 3s. 6d.

WELBY-GREGORY (Hon. Lady). — LINKS AND CLUES. 2nd Edit. Cr. 8vo. 6s.

WESTCOTT (Rt. Rev. Bishop). — THOUGHTS ON REVELATION AND LIFE. Selections from the Writings of Bishop WESTCOTT. Edited by Rev. S. PHILLIPS. Cr. 8vo. 6s.

WILBRAHAM (Francis M.). — IN THE SERE AND YELLOW LEAF: THOUGHTS AND RECOLLECTIONS FOR OLD AND YOUNG. Globe 8vo. 3s. 6d.

The Fathers.

DONALDSON (Prof. James). — THE APOSTOLIC FATHERS. A Critical Account of their Genuine Writings, and of their Doctrines. 2nd Edit. Cr. 8vo. 7s. 6d.

Works of the Greek and Latin Fathers:

THE APOSTOLIC FATHERS. Revised Texts, with Introductions, Notes, Dissertations, and Translations. By Bishop LIGHTFOOT. —Part I. ST. CLEMENT OF ROME. 2 vols. 8vo. 32s.—Part II. ST. IGNATIUS TO ST. POLYCARP. 3 vols. 2nd Edit. 8vo. 48s.

THE APOSTOLIC FATHERS. Abridged Edit. With Short Introductions, Greek Text, and English Translation. By same. 8vo. 16s.

THE EPISTLE OF ST. BARNABAS. Its Date and Authorship. With Greek Text, Latin Version, Translation and Commentary. By Rev. W. CUNNINGHAM. Cr. 8vo. 7s. 6d.

Hymnology.

BROOKE (S. A.). — CHRISTIAN HYMNS. Gl. 8vo. 2s.6d. net.--CHRISTIAN HYMNS AND SERVICE BOOK OF BEDFORD CHAPEL, BLOOMSBURY. Gl. 8vo. 3s. 6d. net.—SERVICE BOOK. Gl. 8vo. 1s. net.

PALGRAVE (Prof. F. T.). — ORIGINAL HYMNS. 3rd Edit. 18mo. 1s. 6d.

SELBORNE (Roundell, Earl of). — THE BOOK OF PRAISE. 18mo. 2s. 6d. net.

—— A HYMNAL. Chiefly from "The Book of Praise."—A. Royal 32mo, limp. 6d.—B. 18mo, larger type. 1s.—C. Fine paper. 1s.6d. —With Music, Selected, Harmonised, and Composed by JOHN HULLAH. 18mo. 3s.6d.

WOODS (Miss M. A.). — HYMNS FOR SCHOOL WORSHIP. 18mo. 1s. 6d.

Sermons, Lectures, Addresses, and Theological Essays.

ABBOT (F. E.). — SCIENTIFIC THEISM. Cr. 8vo. 7s. 6d.

—— THE WAY OUT OF AGNOSTICISM; or, The Philosophy of Free Religion. Cr. 8vo. 4s. 6d.

ABBOTT (Rev. E. A.). — CAMBRIDGE SERMONS. 8vo. 6s.

—— OXFORD SERMONS. 8vo. 7s. 6d.

—— PHILOMYTHUS. A discussion of Cardinal Newman's Essay on Ecclesiastical Miracles. Cr. 8vo. 3s. 6d.

—— NEWMANIANISM. Cr. 8vo. 1s. net.

AINGER (Canon). — SERMONS PREACHED IN THE TEMPLE CHURCH. Ext. fcp. 8vo. 6s.

ALEXANDER (W., Bishop of Derry and Raphoe). — THE LEADING IDEAS OF THE GOSPELS. New Edit. Cr. 8vo. 6s.

BAINES (Rev. Edward). — SERMONS. Preface and Memoir by Bishop BARRY. Cr. 8vo. 6s.

BATHER (Archdeacon). — ON SOME MINISTERIAL DUTIES, CATECHISING, PREACHING, Etc. Edited, with a Preface, by Very Rev. C. J. VAUGHAN, D.D. Fcp. 8vo. 4s. 6d.

BERNARD(Canon). — THE CENTRAL TEACHING OF CHRIST. Cr. 8vo. 7s. 6d.

BETHUNE-BAKER (J. F.). — THE INFLUENCE OF CHRISTIANITY ON WAR. 8vo. 5s.

—— THE STERNNESS OF CHRIST'S TEACHING, AND ITS RELATION TO THE LAW OF FORGIVENESS. Cr. 8vo. 2s. 6d.

BINNIE (Rev. W.). — SERMONS. Cr. 8vo. 6s.

THEOLOGY.

Sermons, Lectures, Addresses, and Theological Essays—*continued*.

BIRKS (Thomas Rawson).—THE DIFFICULTIES OF BELIEF IN CONNECTION WITH THE CREATION AND THE FALL, REDEMPTION, AND JUDGMENT. 2nd Edit. Cr. 8vo. 5s.

—— JUSTIFICATION AND IMPUTED RIGHTEOUSNESS. A Review. Cr. 8vo. 6s.

—— SUPERNATURAL REVELATION; or, First Principles of Moral Theology. 8vo. 8s.

BROOKE S. A.).—SHORT SERMONS. Crown 8vo. 6s.

BROOKS (Bishop Phillips).—THE CANDLE OF THE LORD: and other Sermons. Cr. 8vo. 6s.

—— SERMONS PREACHED IN ENGLISH CHURCHES. Cr. 8vo. 6s.

—— TWENTY SERMONS. Cr. 8vo. 6s.

—— TOLERANCE. Cr. 8vo. 2s. 6d.

—— THE LIGHT OF THE WORLD. Cr. 8vo. 3s. 6d.

BRUNTON (T. Lauder).—THE BIBLE AND SCIENCE. Illustrated. Cr. 8vo. 10s. 6d.

BUTLER (Archer).—SERMONS, DOCTRINAL AND PRACTICAL. 11th Edit. 8vo. 8s.

—— SECOND SERIES OF SERMONS. 8vo. 7s.

—— LETTERS ON ROMANISM. 8vo. 10s. 6d.

BUTLER (Rev. Geo.).—SERMONS PREACHED IN CHELTENHAM COLL. CHAPEL. 8vo. 7s. 6d.

CAMPBELL (Dr. John M'Leod).—THE NATURE OF THE ATONEMENT. Cr. 8vo. 6s.

—— REMINISCENCES AND REFLECTIONS. Edited by his Son, DONALD CAMPBELL. M.A. Cr. 8vo. 7s. 6d.

—— THOUGHTS ON REVELATION. Cr. 8vo. 5s.

—— RESPONSIBILITY FOR THE GIFT OF ETERNAL LIFE. Compiled from Sermons preached 1829—31. Cr. 8vo. 5s.

CANTERBURY (Edward White, Archbishop of).—BOY-LIFE: ITS TRIAL, ITS STRENGTH, ITS FULNESS. Sundays in Wellington College, 1859—73. Cr. 8vo. 6s.

—— THE SEVEN GIFTS. Primary Visitation Address. Cr. 8vo. 6s.

—— CHRIST AND HIS TIMES. Second Visitation Address. Cr. 8vo. 6s.

—— A PASTORAL LETTER TO THE DIOCESE OF CANTERBURY, 1890. 8vo, sewed. 1d.

CARPENTER (W. Boyd, Bishop of Ripon).—TRUTH IN TALE. Addresses, chiefly to Children. Cr. 8vo. 4s. 6d.

—— THE PERMANENT ELEMENTS OF RELIGION. 2nd Edit. Cr. 8vo. 6s.

CAZENOVE (J. Gibson).—CONCERNING THE BEING AND ATTRIBUTES OF GOD. 8vo. 5s.

CHURCH (Dean).—HUMAN LIFE AND ITS CONDITIONS. Cr. 8vo. 6s.

—— THE GIFTS OF CIVILISATION: and other Sermons and Letters. Cr. 8vo. 7s. 6d.

—— DISCIPLINE OF THE CHRISTIAN CHARACTER; and other Sermons. Cr. 8vo. 4s. 6d.

—— ADVENT SERMONS, 1885. Cr. 8vo. 4s. 6d.

—— VILLAGE SERMONS. Cr. 8vo. 6s.

—— CATHEDRAL AND UNIVERSITY SERMONS. Cr. 8vo. 6s.

CLERGYMAN'S SELF-EXAMINATION CONCERNING THE APOSTLES' CREED. Ext. fcp. 8vo. 1s. 6d.

CONGREVE (Rev. AND PLEADINGS FC NOBLER THOUGHT: Cr. 8vo. 5s.

COOKE (Josiah P., CHEMISTRY. Cr. 8

COTTON (Bishop).— ENGLISH CONGREC 8vo. 7s. 6d.

CUNNINGHAM (CIVILISATION, WIT TO INDIA. Cr. 8vo

CURTEIS (Rev. G. OBSTACLES TO CF Boyle Lectures, 188

DAVIES (Rev. J. I AND MODERN LIFE

—— SOCIAL QUESTI(VIEW OF CHRISTIAI

—— WARNINGS AGA fcp. 8vo. 2s. 6d.

—— THE CHRISTIAN

—— ORDER AND G THE SPIRITUAL CC SOCIETY. Cr. 8vo.

—— BAPTISM, CON LORD'S SUPPER. A

DIGGLE (Rev. J. MANLINESS. Cr. 8

DRUMMOND (Pro TO THE STUDY OF

DU BOSE (W. P.). THE NEW TESTAM! Cr. 8vo. 7s. 6d.

ECCE HOMO: A S WORK OF JESUS CF

ELLERTON (Rev. MANHOOD, AND I LIVES. Cr. 8vo. 6

FAITH AND CON VERIFIABLE RELIG

FARRAR (Ven. Arch *form Edition*. (Monthly from Dece SEEKERS AFTER G ETERNAL HOPE. Sermons. THE FALL OF MAN THE WITNESS OF Hulsean Lectures THE SILENCE AND \ IN THE DAYS OF T College Sermons. SAINTLY WORKERS EPHPHATHA; or, MERCY AND JUDGM SERMONS AND AD AMERICA.

—— THE HISTORY Bampton Lectures,

FISKE (John).—MA THE LIGHT OF HIS

FORBES (Rev. Gra GOD IN THE PSALM

FOWLE (Rev. T. BETWEEN REVEAL(COURSE AND CON! Cr. 8vo. 6s.

FRASER (Bishop).—Sermons. Edited by John W. Diggle. 2 vols. Cr. 8vo. 6s. each.

HAMILTON (John).—On Truth and Error. Cr. 8vo. 5s.
—— Arthur's Seat; or, The Church of the Banned. Cr. 8vo. 6s.
—— Above and Around : Thoughts on God and Man. 12mo. 2s. 6d.

HARDWICK (Archdeacon).—Christ and other Masters. 6th Edit. Cr. 8vo. 10s. 6d.

HARE (Julius Charles).—The Mission of the Comforter. New Edition. Edited by Dean Plumptre. Cr. 8vo. 7s. 6d.

HARPER (Father Thomas).—The Metaphysics of the School. Vols. I. and II. 8vo. 18s. each.—Vol. III. Part I. 12s.

HARRIS (Rev. G. C.).—Sermons. With a Memoir by C. M. Yonge. Ext. fcp. 8vo. 6s.

HUTTON (R. H.). (See p. 22.)

ILLINGWORTH (Rev. J. R.).—Sermons preached in a College Chapel. Cr. 8vo. 5s.
—— University and Cathedral Sermons. Crown 8vo. 5s.

JACOB (Rev. J. A.).—Building in Silence : and other Sermons. Ext. fcp. 8vo. 6s.

JAMES (Rev. Herbert). — The Country Clergyman and his Work. Cr. 8vo. 6s.

JEANS (Rev. G. E.).—Haileybury Chapel : and other Sermons. Fcp. 8vo. 3s. 6d.

JELLETT (Rev. Dr.).—The Elder Son : and other Sermons. Cr. 8vo. 6s.
—— The Efficacy of Prayer. Cr. 8vo. 5s.

KELLOGG (Rev. S. H.).—The Light of Asia and the Light of the World. Cr. 8vo. 7s. 6d.
—— Genesis and Growth of Religion. Cr. 8vo. 6s.

KINGSLEY (Charles). (See Collected Works, p. 22.)

KIRKPATRICK (Prof.).—The Divine Library of the Old Testament. Cr. 8vo. 2s. net.
—— Doctrine of the Prophets. Cr. 8vo. 6s.

KYNASTON (Rev. Herbert, D.D.).—Cheltenham College Sermons. Cr. 8vo. 6s.

LEGGE (A. O.).—The Growth of the Temporal Power of the Papacy. Cr. 8vo. 8s. 6d.

LIGHTFOOT (Bishop).—Leaders in the Northern Church : Sermons. Cr. 8vo. 6s.
—— Ordination Addresses and Counsels to Clergy. Cr. 8vo. 6s.
—— Cambridge Sermons. Cr. 8vo. 6s.
—— Sermons preached in St. Paul's Cathedral. Cr. 8vo. 6s.
—— Sermons on Special Occasions. 8vo. 6s.
—— A Charge delivered to the Clergy of the Diocese of Durham, 1886. 8vo. 2s.
—— Essays on the Work entitled "Supernatural Religion." 8vo. 10s. 6d.
—— On a Fresh Revision of the English New Testament. Cr. 8vo. 7s. 6d.
—— Dissertations on the Apostolic Age. 8vo. 14s.

MACLAREN (Rev. A.).—Sermons preached at Manchester. 11th Ed. Fcp. 8vo. 4s. 6d.
—— Second Series. 7th Ed. Fcp. 8vo. 4s. 6d.
—— Third Series. 6th Ed. Fcp. 8vo. 4s. 6d.
—— Week-Day Evening Addresses. 4th Edit. Fcp. 8vo. 2s. 6d.
—— The Secret of Power ; and other Sermons. Fcp. 8vo. 4s. 6d.

MACMILLAN (Rev. Hugh).—Bible Teachings in Nature. 15th Edit. Globe 8vo. 6s.
—— The True Vine ; or, The Analogies of our Lord's Allegory. 5th Edit. Gl. 8vo. 6s.
—— The Ministry of Nature. 8th Edit. Globe 8vo. 6s.
—— The Sabbath of the Fields. 6th Edit. Globe 8vo. 6s.
—— The Marriage in Cana. Globe 8vo. 6s.
—— Two Worlds are Ours. Gl. 8vo. 6s.
—— The Olive Leaf. Globe 8vo. 6s.
—— The Gate Beautiful : and other Bible Teachings for the Young. Cr. 8vo. 3s. 6d.

MAHAFFY (Prof. J. P.).—The Decay of Modern Preaching. Cr. 8vo. 3s. 6d.

MATURIN (Rev. W.).—The Blessedness of the Dead in Christ. Cr. 8vo. 7s. 6d.

MAURICE (Frederick Denison).—The Kingdom of Christ. 3rd Ed. 2 vols. Cr. 8vo. 12s.
—— Expository Sermons on the Prayer-Book, and the Lord's Prayer. Cr. 8vo. 6s.
—— Sermons Preached in Country Churches. 2nd Edit. Cr. 8vo. 6s.
—— The Conscience : Lectures on Casuistry. 3rd Edit. Cr. 8vo. 4s. 6d.
—— Dialogues on Family Worship. Cr. 8vo. 4s. 6d.
—— The Doctrine of Sacrifice Deduced from the Scriptures. 2nd Edit. Cr. 8vo. 6s.
—— The Religions of the World. 6th Edit. Cr. 8vo. 4s. 6d.
—— On the Sabbath Day ; The Character of the Warrior ; and on the Interpretation of History. Fcp. 8vo. 2s. 6d.
—— Learning and Working. Cr. 8vo. 4s. 6d.
—— The Lord's Prayer, the Creed, and the Commandments. 18mo. 1s.
—— Sermons Preached in Lincoln's Inn Chapel. 6 vols. Cr. 8vo. 3s. 6d. each.
—— Collected Works. Cr. 8vo. 3s. 6d. each.
Christmas Day and other Sermons.
Theological Essays.
Prophets and Kings.
Patriarchs and Lawgivers.
The Gospel of the Kingdom of Heaven.
Gospel of St. John.
Epistle of St. John.
Lectures on the Apocalypse.
Friendship of Books.
Social Morality.
Prayer Book and Lord's Prayer.
The Doctrine of Sacrifice.

MILLIGAN (Rev. Prof. W.).—The Resurrection of our Lord. 2nd Edit. Cr. 8vo. 5s.
—— The Ascension and Heavenly Priesthood of our Lord. Cr. 8vo. 7s. 6d.

MOORHOUSE (J., Bishop of Manchester).—Jacob : Three Sermons. Ext. fcp. 8vo. 3s. 6d.
—— The Teaching of Christ : its Conditions, Secret, and Results. Cr. 8vo. 3s. net.

MURPHY (J. J.).—Natural Selection and Spiritual Freedom. Gl. 8vo. 5s.

MYLNE (L. G., Bishop of Bombay).—Sermons Preached in St. Thomas's Cathedral, Bombay. Cr. 8vo. 6s.

THEOLOGY.

Sermons, Lectures, Addresses, and Theological Essays—*continued.*

NATURAL RELIGION. By the Author of "Ecce Homo." 3rd Edit. Globe 8vo. 6s.

PATTISON (Mark).—SERMONS. Cr. 8vo. 6s.

PAUL OF TARSUS. 8vo. 10s. 6d.

PHILOCHRISTUS: MEMOIRS OF A DISCIPLE OF THE LORD. 3rd. Edit. 8vo. 12s.

PLUMPTRE (Dean).—MOVEMENTS IN RELIGIOUS THOUGHT. Fcp. 8vo. 3s. 6d.

POTTER (R.).—THE RELATION OF ETHICS TO RELIGION. Cr. 8vo. 2s. 6d.

REASONABLE FAITH: A SHORT ESSAY By "Three Friends." Cr. 8vo. 1s.

REICHEL (C. P., Bishop of Meath).—THE LORD'S PRAYER. Cr. 8vo. 7s. 6d.
—— CATHEDRAL AND UNIVERSITY SERMONS. Cr. 8vo. 6s.

RENDALL (Rev. F.).—THE THEOLOGY OF THE HEBREW CHRISTIANS. Cr. 8vo. 5s.

REYNOLDS (H. R.).—NOTES OF THE CHRISTIAN LIFE. Cr. 8vo. 7s. 6d.

ROBINSON (Prebendary H. G.).—MAN IN THE IMAGE OF GOD: and other Sermons. Cr. 8vo. 7s. 6d.

RUSSELL (Dean).—THE LIGHT THAT LIGHTETH EVERY MAN: Sermons. With an Introduction by Dean PLUMPTRE, D.D. Cr. 8vo. 6s.

RYLE (Rev. Prof. H.).—THE EARLY NARRATIVES OF GENESIS. Cr. 8vo. 3s. net.

SALMON (Rev. George, D.D.).—NON-MIRACULOUS CHRISTIANITY: and other Sermons. 2nd Edit. Cr. 8vo. 6s.
—— GNOSTICISM AND AGNOSTICISM: and other Sermons. Cr. 8vo. 7s. 6d.

SANDFORD (Rt. Rev. C. W., Bishop of Gibraltar).—COUNSEL TO ENGLISH CHURCHMEN ABROAD. Cr. 8vo. 6s.

SCOTCH SERMONS, 1880. By Principal CAIRD and others. 3rd Edit. 8vo. 10s. 6d.

SERVICE (Rev. J.).—SERMONS. Cr. 8vo. 6s.

SHIRLEY (W. N.).—ELIJAH: Four University Sermons. Fcp. 8vo. 2s. 6d.

SMITH (Rev. Travers).—MAN'S KNOWLEDGE OF MAN AND OF GOD. Cr. 8vo. 6s.

SMITH (W. Saumarez).—THE BLOOD OF THE NEW COVENANT: An Essay. Cr. 8vo. 2s. 6d.

STANLEY (Dean).--THE NATIONAL THANKSGIVING. Sermons Preached in Westminster

TAIT (Archbp.).—THE PRESENT CONDITION OF THE CHURCH OF ENGLAND. Primary Visitation Charge. 3rd Edit. 8vo. 3s. 6d.
—— DUTIES OF THE CHURCH OF ENGLAND. Second Visitation Addresses. 8vo. 4s. 6d.
—— THE CHURCH OF THE FUTURE. Quadrennial Visitation Charges. Cr. 8vo. 3s. 6d.

TAYLOR (Isaac).—THE RESTORATION OF BELIEF. Cr. 8vo. 8s. 6d.

TEMPLE (Frederick, Bishop of London).—SERMONS PREACHED IN THE CHAPEL OF RUGBY SCHOOL. Second Series. Ex. fcp. 8vo. 6s. Third Series 4th Edit. Ext. fcp. 8vo. 6s.
—— THE RELATIONS BETWEEN RELIGION AND SCIENCE. Bampton Lectures, 1884. 7th and Cheaper Edition. Cr. 8vo. 6s.

TRENCH (Archbishop). — THE HULSEAN LECTURES FOR 1845—6. 8vo. 7s. 6d.

TULLOCH (Principal).—THE CHRIST OF THE GOSPELS AND THE CHRIST OF MODERN CRITICISM. Ext. fcp. 8vo. 4s. 6d.

VAUGHAN (C. J., Dean of Landaff).—MEMORIALS OF HARROW SUNDAYS. 8vo. 10s. 6d.
—— EPIPHANY, LENT, AND EASTER. 8vo. 10s. 6d.
—— HEROES OF FAITH. 2nd Edit. Cr. 8vo. 6s.
—— LIFE'S WORK AND GOD'S DISCIPLINE. Ext. fcp. 8vo. 2s. 6d.
—— THE WHOLESOME WORDS OF JESUS CHRIST. 2nd Edit. Fcp. 8vo. 3s. 6d.
—— FOES OF FAITH. 2nd Edit. Fcp. 8vo. 3s. 6d.
—— CHRIST SATISFYING THE INSTINCTS OF HUMANITY. 2nd Edit. Ext. fcp. 8vo. 3s. 6d.
—— COUNSELS FOR YOUNG STUDENTS. Fcp. 8vo. 2s. 6d.
—— THE TWO GREAT TEMPTATIONS. 2nd Edit. Fcp. 8vo. 3s. 6d.
—— ADDRESSES FOR YOUNG CLERGYMEN. Ext. fcp. 8vo. 4s. 6d.
—— "MY SON, GIVE ME THINE HEART." Ext. fcp. 8vo. 5s.
—— REST AWHILE. Addresses to Toilers in the Ministry. Ext. fcp. 8vo. 5s.
—— TEMPLE SERMONS. Cr. 8vo. 10s. 6d.
—— AUTHORISED OR REVISED? Sermons. Cr. 8vo. 7s. 6d.
—— LESSONS OF THE CROSS AND PASSION; WORDS FROM THE CROSS; THE REIGN OF SIN; THE LORD'S PRAYER. Four Courses of Lent Lectures. Cr. 8vo. 10s. 6d.
—— UNIVERSITY SERMONS, NEW AND OLD. Cr. 8vo. 10s. 6d.
—— THE PRAYERS OF JESUS CHRIST. Globe 8vo. 3s. 6d.
—— DONCASTER SERMONS; LESSONS OF LIFE AND GODLINESS; WORDS FROM THE GOSPELS. Cr. 8vo. 10s. 6d.
—— NOTES FOR LECTURES ON CONFIRMATION. 14th Edit. Fcp. 8vo. 1s. 6d.
—— RESTFUL THOUGHTS IN RESTLESS TIMES. Crown 8vo. 5s.

WELLDON (Rev. J. E. C.).—THE SPIRITUAL LIFE: and other Sermons. Cr. 8vo. 6s.

WESTCOTT (Rt. Rev. B. F., Bishop of Durham).—ON THE RELIGIOUS OFFICE OF THE UNIVERSITIES. Sermons. Cr. 8vo. 4s. 6d.
—— GIFTS FOR MINISTRY. Addresses to Candidates for Ordination. Cr. 8vo. 1s. 6d.
—— THE VICTORY OF THE CROSS. Sermons Preached in 1888. Cr. 8vo. 3s. 6d.
—— FROM STRENGTH TO STRENGTH. Three Sermons (In Memoriam J. B. D.). Cr. 8vo. 2s.
—— THE REVELATION OF THE RISEN LORD. 4th Edit. Cr. 8vo. 6s.
—— THE HISTORIC FAITH. Cr. 8vo. 6s.
—— THE GOSPEL OF THE RESURRECTION. 6th Edit. Cr. 8vo. 6s.
—— THE REVELATION OF THE FATHER. Cr. 8vo. 6s.
—— CHRISTUS CONSUMMATOR. Cr. 8vo. 6s.
—— SOME THOUGHTS FROM THE ORDINAL. Cr. 8vo. 1s. 6d.
—— SOCIAL ASPECTS OF CHRISTIANITY. Cr. 8vo. 6s.
—— THE GOSPEL OF LIFE. Cr. 8vo. 6s.
—— ESSAYS IN THE HISTORY OF RELIGIOUS THOUGHT IN THE WEST. Globe 8vo. 5s.

WICKHAM (Rev. E. C.).—WELLINGTON COLLEGE SERMONS. Cr. 8vo. 6s.

WILKINS (Prof. A. S.).—THE LIGHT OF THE WORLD: An Essay. 2nd Ed. Cr. 8vo. 3s. 6d.

WILLINK (A.).—THE WORLD OF THE UNSEEN. Cr. 8vo. 3s. 6d.

WILSON (J. M., Archdeacon of Manchester).—SERMONS PREACHED IN CLIFTON COLLEGE CHAPEL. 2nd Series, 1888–90. Cr. 8vo. 6s.
—— ESSAYS AND ADDRESSES. Cr. 8vo. 4s. 6d.
—— SOME CONTRIBUTIONS TO THE RELIGIOUS THOUGHT OF OUR TIME. Cr. 8vo. 6s.

WOOD (C. J.).—SURVIVALS IN CHRISTIANITY. Crown 8vo. 6s.

WOOD (Rev. E. G.).—THE REGAL POWER OF THE CHURCH. 8vo. 4s. 6d.

THERAPEUTICS. (See MEDICINE, p. 24.)

TRANSLATIONS.

From the Greek—From the Italian—From the Latin—Into Latin and Greek Verse.

From the Greek.

AESCHYLUS.—THE SUPPLICES. With Translation, by T. G. TUCKER, Litt. D. 8vo. 10s. 6d.
—— THE SEVEN AGAINST THEBES. With Translation, by A. W. VERRALL, Litt. D. 8vo. 7s. 6d.
—— THE CHOEPHORI. With Translation. By the same. 8vo. 12s.
—— EUMENIDES. With Verse Translation, by Bernard Drake, M.A. 8vo. 5s.

ARATUS. (See PHYSIOGRAPHY, p. 29.)

ARISTOPHANES.—THE BIRDS. Trans. into English Verse, by B. H. KENNEDY. 8vo. 6s.

ARISTOTLE ON FALLACIES; OR, THE SOPHISTICI ELENCHI. With Translation, by E. POSTE M.A. 8vo. 8s. 6d.

ARISTOTLE.—THE FIRST BOOK OF THE METAPHYSICS OF ARISTOTLE. By a Cambridge Graduate. 8vo. 5s.
—— THE POLITICS. By J. E. C. WELLDON, M.A. 10s. 6d.
—— THE RHETORIC. By same. Cr. 8vo. 7s. 6d.
—— THE NICOMACHEAN ETHICS. By same. Cr. 8vo. 7s. 6d.

ARISTOTLE.—ON THE CONSTITUTION OF ATHENS. By E. POSTE. 2nd Edit. Cr. 8vo. 3s. 6d.

BION. (See THEOCRITUS.)

HERODOTUS.—THE HISTORY. By G. C. MACAULAY, M.A. 2 vols. Cr. 8vo. 18s.

HOMER.—THE ODYSSEY DONE INTO ENGLISH PROSE, by S. H. BUTCHER, M.A., and A. LANG, M.A. Cr. 8vo. 6s.
—— THE ODYSSEY. Books I.—XII. Transl. into English Verse by EARL OF CARNARVON. Cr. 8vo. 7s. 6d.
—— THE ILIAD DONE INTO ENGLISH PROSE, by ANDREW LANG, WALTER LEAF, and ERNEST MYERS. Cr. 8vo. 12s. 6d.

MELEAGER.—FIFTY POEMS. Translated into English Verse by WALTER HEADLAM. Fcp. 4to. 7s. 6d.

MOSCHUS. (See THEOCRITUS).

PINDAR.—THE EXTANT ODES. By ERNEST MYERS. Cr. 8vo. 5s.

PLATO.—TIMÆUS. With Translation, by R. D. ARCHER-HIND, M.A. 8vo. 16s. (See also GOLDEN TREASURY SERIES, p. 20.)

POLYBIUS.—THE HISTORIES. By E. S. SHUCKBURGH. Cr. 8vo. 24s.

SOPHOCLES.—ŒDIPUS THE KING. Translated into English Verse by E. D. A. MORSHEAD, M.A. Fcp. 8vo. 3s. 6d.

THEOCRITUS, BION, AND MOSCHUS. By A. LANG, M.A. 18mo. 2s. 6d. net.—Large Paper Edition. 8vo. 9s.

XENOPHON.—THE COMPLETE WORKS. By H. G. DAKYNS, M.A. Cr. 8vo.—Vols. I and II. 10s. 6d. each.

From the Italian.

DANTE.—THE PURGATORY. With Transl. and Notes, by A. J. BUTLER. Cr. 8vo. 12s. 6d.
—— THE PARADISE. By the same. 2nd Edit. Cr. 8vo. 12s. 6d.
—— THE HELL. By the same. Cr. 8vo. 12s. 6d.
—— DE MONARCHIA. By F. J. CHURCH. 8vo. 4s. 6d.
—— THE DIVINE COMEDY. By C. E. NORTON. I. HELL. II. PURGATORY. III. PARADISE. Cr. 8vo. 6s. each.
—— NEW LIFE OF DANTE. Transl. by C. E. NORTON. 5s.
—— THE PURGATORY. Transl. by C. L. SHADWELL. Ext. cr. 8vo. 10s. net.

From the Latin.

CICERO.—THE LIFE AND LETTERS OF MARCUS TULLIUS CICERO. By the Rev. G. E. JEANS, M.A. 2nd Edit. Cr. 8vo. 10s. 6d.
—— THE ACADEMICS. By J. S. REID. 8vo. 5s. 6d.

HORACE: THE WORKS OF. By J. LONSDALE, M.A., and S. LEE, M.A. Gl. 8vo. 3s. 6d.
—— THE ODES IN A METRICAL PARAPHRASE. By R. M. HOVENDEN, B.A. Ext. fcp. 8vo. 4s. 6d.
—— LIFE AND CHARACTER: AN EPITOME OF HIS SATIRES AND EPISTLES. By R. M. HOVENDEN, B.A. Ext. fcp. 8vo. 4s. 6d.
—— WORD FOR WORD FROM HORACE: The Odes Literally Versified. By W. T. THORNTON, C.B. Cr. 8vo. 7s. 6d.

JUVENAL.—THIRTEEN SATIRES. By ALEX. LEEPER, LL.D. New Ed. Cr. 8vo. 3s. 6d.

TRANSLATIONS—continued.

LIVY.—BOOKS XXI.—XXV. THE SECOND PUNIC WAR. By A. J. CHURCH, M.A., and W. J. BRODRIBB, M.A. Cr. 8vo. 7s. 6d.

MARCUS AURELIUS ANTONINUS.—BOOK IV. OF THE MEDITATIONS. With Translation and Commentary, by H. CROSSLEY, M.A. 8vo. 6s.

SALLUST.—THE CONSPIRACY OF CATILINE AND THE JUGURTHINE WAR. By A. W. POLLARD. Cr. 8vo. 6s.—CATILINE. 3s.

TACITUS, THE WORKS OF. By A. J. CHURCH, M.A., and W. J. BRODRIBB, M.A. THE HISTORY. 4th Edit. Cr. 8vo. THE AGRICOLA AND GERMANIA. With the Dialogue on Oratory. Cr. 8vo. 4s. 6d. THE ANNALS. 5th Edit. Cr. 8vo. 7s. 6d.

VIRGIL: THE WORKS OF. By J. LONSDALE, M.A., and S. LEE, M.A. Globe 8vo. 3s. 6d. —— THE ÆNEID. By J. W. MACKAIL, M.A. Cr. 8vo. 7s. 6d.

Into Latin and Greek Verse.

CHURCH (Rev. A. J.).—LATIN VERSION OF SELECTIONS FROM TENNYSON. By Prof. CONINGTON, Prof. SEELEY, Dr. HESSEY, T. E. KEBBEL, &c. Edited by A. J. CHURCH, M.A. Ext. fcp. 8vo. 6s.

GEDDES (Prof. W. D.).—FLOSCULI GRÆCI BOREALES. Cr. 8vo. 6s.

KYNASTON (Herbert D.D.).—EXEMPLARIA CHELTONIENSIA. Ext. fcp. 8vo. 5s.

VOYAGES AND TRAVELS.

(*See also* HISTORY, p. 10; SPORT, p. 32.)

APPLETON (T. G.).—A NILE JOURNAL. Illustrated by EUGENE BENSON. Cr. 8vo. 6s.

"BACCHANTE." THE CRUISE OF H.M.S. "BACCHANTE," 1879—1882. Compiled from the Private Journals, Letters and Note-books of PRINCE ALBERT VICTOR and PRINCE GEORGE OF WALES. By the Rev. Canon DALTON. 2 vols. Med. 8vo. 52s. 6d.

BAKER (Sir Samuel W.).—ISMAILIA. A Narrative of the Expedition to Central Africa for the Suppression of the Slave Trade, organised by ISMAIL, Khedive of Egypt. Cr. 8vo. 6s.
—— THE NILE TRIBUTARIES OF ABYSSINIA, AND THE SWORD HUNTERS OF THE HAMRAN ARABS. Cr. 8vo. 6s.
—— THE ALBERT N'YANZA GREAT BASIN OF THE NILE AND EXPLORATION OF THE NILE SOURCES. Cr. 8vo. 6s.
—— CYPRUS AS I SAW IT IN 1879. 8vo. 12s. 6d.

BARKER (Lady).—A YEAR'S HOUSEKEEPING IN SOUTH AFRICA. Illustr. Cr. 8vo. 3s. 6d.
—— STATION LIFE IN NEW ZEALAND. Cr. 8vo. 3s. 6d.
—— LETTERS TO GUY. Cr. 8vo. 5s.

BOUGHTON (G. H.) and ABBEY (E. A.).—SKETCHING RAMBLES IN HOLLAND. With Illustrations. Fcp. 4to. 21s.

BRYCE (James, M.P.). — TRANSCAUCASIA AND ARARAT. 3rd Edit. Cr. 8vo. 9s.

CAMERON (V. L.).—OUR FUTURE HIGHWAY TO INDIA. 2 vols. Cr. 8vo. 21s.

CAMPBELL (J. F.).—MY CIRCULAR NOTE Cr. 8vo. 6s.

CARLES(W. R.).—LIFE IN COREA. 8vo. 12s. 6d.

CAUCASUS: NOTES ON THE. By "WANDERER." 8vo. 9s.

CRAIK (Mrs.).—AN UNKNOWN COUNTRY. Illustr. by F. NOEL PATON. Roy. 8vo. 7s. 6d.
—— AN UNSENTIMENTAL JOURNEY THROUGH CORNWALL. Illustrated. 4to. 12s. 6d.

DILKE (Sir Charles). (*See* pp. 25. 31.)

DUFF (Right Hon. Sir M. E. Grant).—NOTES OF AN INDIAN JOURNEY. 8vo. 10s. 6d.

FORBES (Archibald).—SOUVENIRS OF SOME CONTINENTS. Cr. 8vo. 6s.
—— BARRACKS, BIVOUACS, AND BATTLES. Cr. 8vo. 7s. 6d.

FULLERTON (W. M.).—IN CAIRO. Fcp. 8vo. 3s. 6d.

GONE TO TEXAS: LETTERS FROM OUR BOYS. Ed. by THOS. HUGHES. Cr. 8vo. 4s. 6d.

GORDON (Lady Duff).—LAST LETTERS FROM EGYPT, TO WHICH ARE ADDED LETTERS FROM THE CAPE. 2nd Edit. Cr. 8vo. 9s.

GREEN (W. S.).—AMONG THE SELKIRK GLACIERS. Cr. 8vo. 7s. 6d.

HOOKER (Sir Joseph D.) and BALL (J.).—JOURNAL OF A TOUR IN MAROCCO AND THE GREAT ATLAS. 8vo. 21s.

HÜBNER (Baron von).—A RAMBLE ROUND THE WORLD. Cr. 8vo. 6s.

HUGHES (Thos.).—RUGBY, TENNESSEE. Cr. 8vo. 4s. 6d.

KALM.—ACCOUNT OF HIS VISIT TO ENGLAND. Trans. by J. LUCAS. Illus. 8vo. 12s. net.

KINGSLEY (Charles).—AT LAST: A Christmas in the West Indies. Cr. 8vo. 3s. 6d.

KINGSLEY (Henry). — TALES OF OLD TRAVEL. Cr. 8vo. 3s. 6d.

KIPLING (J. L.).—BEAST AND MAN IN INDIA. Illustrated. Ext. cr. 8vo. 7s. 6d.

MAHAFFY (Prof. J. P.).—RAMBLES AND STUDIES IN GREECE. Illust. Cr. 8vo. 10s. 6d.

MAHAFFY (Prof. J. P.) and ROGERS (J. E.).—SKETCHES FROM A TOUR THROUGH HOLLAND AND GERMANY. Illustrated by J. E. ROGERS. Ext. cr. 8vo. 10s. 6d.

NORDENSKIÖLD. — VOYAGE OF THE "VEGA" ROUND ASIA AND EUROPE. By Baron A. E. VON NORDENSKIÖLD. Trans. by ALEX. LESLIE. 400 Illustrations, Maps, etc. 2 vols. 8vo. 45s.—*Popular Edit.* Cr. 8vo. 6s.

OLIPHANT (Mrs.). (*See* HISTORY, p. 11.)

OLIVER (Capt. S. P.).—MADAGASCAR: AN HISTORICAL AND DESCRIPTIVE ACCOUNT OF THE ISLAND. 2 vols. Med. 8vo. 52s. 6d.

PALGRAVE (W. Gifford).—A NARRATIVE OF A YEAR'S JOURNEY THROUGH CENTRAL AND EASTERN ARABIA, 1862-63. Cr. 8vo. 6s.
—— DUTCH GUIANA. 8vo. 9s.
—— ULYSSES; or, Scenes and Studies in many Lands. 8vo. 12s. 6d.

PERSIA, EASTERN. An Account of the Journeys of the Persian Boundary Commission, 1870-71-72. 2 vols. 8vo. 42s.

PIKE (W.)—The Barren Ground of Northern Canada. 8vo. 10s. 6d.

ST. JOHNSTON (A.).—Camping among Cannibals. Cr. 8vo. 4s. 6d.

SANDYS (J. E.).—An Easter Vacation in Greece. Cr. 8vo. 3s. 6d.

SMITH (G.).—A Trip to England. 18mo. 3s.

STRANGFORD (Viscountess). — Egyptian Sepulchres and Syrian Shrines. New Edition. Cr. 8vo. 7s. 6d.

TAVERNIER (Baron): Travels in India of Jean Baptiste Tavernier. Transl. by V. Ball, LL.D. 2 vols. 8vo. 42s.

TRISTRAM. (See Illustrated Books.)

TURNER (Rev. G.). (See Anthropology.)

WALLACE (A. R.). (See Natural History.)

WATERTON (Charles).—Wanderings in South America, the North-West of the United States, and the Antilles. Edited by Rev. J. G. Wood. Illustr. Cr. 8vo. 6s.—People's Edition. 4to. 6d.

WATSON (R. Spence).—A Visit to Wazan, the Sacred City of Morocco. 8vo. 10s. 6d.

YOUNG, Books for the.

(See also Biblical History, p. 32.)

ÆSOP—CALDECOTT.—Some of Æsop's Fables, with Modern Instances, shown in Designs by Randolph Caldecott. 4to. 5s.

ARIOSTO.—Paladin and Saracen. Stories from Ariosto. By H. C. Hollway-Calthrop. Illustrated. Cr. 8vo. 6s.

ATKINSON (Rev. J. C.).—The Last of the Giant Killers. Globe 8vo. 3s. 6d.
—— Walks, Talks, Travels, and Exploits of two Schoolboys. Cr. 8vo. 3s. 6d.
—— Playhours and Half-Holidays, or Further Experiences of two Schoolboys. Cr. 8vo. 3s. 6d.
—— Scenes in Fairyland. Cr. 8vo. 4s. 6d.

AWDRY (Frances).—The Story of a Fellow Soldier. (A Life of Bishop Patteson for the Young.) Globe 8vo. 2s. 6d.

BAKER (Sir S. W.).—True Tales for my Grandsons. Illustrated. Cr. 8vo. 3s. 6d.
—— Cast up by the Sea: or, The Adventures of Ned Gray. Illus. Cr. 8vo. 6s.

BUMBLEBEE BOGO'S BUDGET. By a Retired Judge. Illust. Cr. 8vo. 2s. 6d.

CARROLL (Lewis).—Alice's Adventures in Wonderland. With 42 Illustrations by Tenniel. Cr. 8vo. 6s. net.
People's Edition. With all the original Illustrations. Cr. 8vo. 2s. 6d. net.
A German Translation of the same. Cr. 8vo. 6s. net. -A French Translation of the same. Cr. 8vo. 6s. net. An Italian Translation of the same. Cr. 8vo. 6s. net.
—— Alice's Adventures Under-ground, Being a Facsimile of the Original MS. Book, afterwards developed into "Alice's Adventures in Wonderland." With 27 Illustrations by the Author. Cr. 8vo. 4s net.

CARROLL (Lewis).—Through the Looking-Glass and what Alice found there. With 50 Illustrations by Tenniel. Cr. 8vo. 6s. net.
People's Edition. With all the original Illustrations. Cr. 8vo. 2s. 6d. net.
People's Edition of "Alice's Adventures in Wonderland," and "Through the Looking-Glass." 1 vol. Cr. 8vo. 4s. 6d.
—— Rhyme? and Reason? With 65 Illustrations by Arthur B. Frost, and 9 by Henry Holiday. Cr. 8vo. 6s. net.
—— A Tangled Tale. With 6 Illustrations by Arthur B. Frost. Cr. 8vo. 4s. 6d. net.
—— Sylvie and Bruno. With 46 Illustrations by Harry Furniss. Cr. 8vo. 7s. 6d. net.
—— The Nursery "Alice." Twenty Coloured Enlargements from Tenniel's Illustrations to "Alice's Adventures in Wonderland," with Text adapted to Nursery Readers. 4to. 4s. net.—*People's Edition.* 4to. 2s. net.
—— The Hunting of the Snark, An Agony in Eight Fits. With 9 Illustrations by Henry Holiday. Cr. 8vo. 4s. 6d. net.

CLIFFORD (Mrs. W. K.).—Anyhow Stories. With Illustrations by Dorothy Tennant. Cr. 8vo. 1s. 6d.; paper covers, 1s.

CORBETT (Julian).—For God and Gold. Cr. 8vo. 6s.

CRAIK (Mrs.).—Alice Learmont: A Fairy Tale. Illustrated. Globe 8vo. 4s. 6d.
—— The Adventures of a Brownie. Illustrated by Mrs. Allingham. Gl. 8vo. 4s. 6d.
—— The Little Lame Prince and his Travelling Cloak. Illustrated by J. McL. Ralston. Cr. 8vo. 4s. 6d.
—— Our Year: A Child's Book in Prose and Verse. Illustrated. Gl. 8vo. 2s. 6d.
—— Little Sunshine's Holiday. Globe 8vo. 2s. 6d.
—— The Fairy Book: The Best Popular Fairy Stories. 18mo. 2s. 6d. net.
—— Children's Poetry. Ex. fcp. 8vo. 4s. 6d.
—— Songs of our Youth. Small 4to. 6s.

DE MORGAN (Mary).—The Necklace of Princess Fiorimonde, and other Stories. Illustrated by Walter Crane. Ext. fcp. 8vo. 3s. 6d.—Large Paper Ed., with Illustrations on India Paper. 100 copies printed.

FOWLER (W. W.). (See Natural History.)

GREENWOOD (Jessy E.). — The Moon Maiden: and other Stories. Cr. 8vo. 2s. 6d.

GRIMM'S FAIRY TALES. Translated by Lucy Crane, and Illustrated by Walter Crane. Cr. 8vo. 6s.

KEARY (A. and E.). — The Heroes of Asgard. Tales from Scandinavian Mythology. Globe 8vo. 2s. 6d.

KEARY (E.).—The Magic Valley. Illustr. by "E. V. B." Globe 8vo. 4s. 6d.

KINGSLEY (Charles).—The Heroes; or, Greek Fairy Tales for my Children. Cr. 8vo. 3s. 6d.—*Presentation Ed.,* gilt edges. 7s. 6d.
Madam How and Lady Why; or, First Lessons in Earth-Lore. Cr. 8vo. 3s. 6d.
The Water-Babies: A Fairy Tale for a Land Baby. Cr. 8vo. 3s. 6d.—New Edit. Illus. by L. Sambourne. Fcp. 4to. 12s. 6d.

BOOKS FOR THE YOUNG—*continued.*

MACLAREN (Arch.).—THE FAIRY FAMILY. A Series of Ballads and Metrical Tales. Cr. 8vo. 5s.

MACMILLAN (Hugh). (*See* p. 37.)

MADAME TABBY'S ESTABLISHMENT. By KARI. Illust. by L. WAIN. Cr. 8vo. 4s. 6d.

MAGUIRE (J. F.).—YOUNG PRINCE MARIGOLD. Illustrated. Globe 8vo. 4s. 6d.

MARTIN (Frances).—THE POET'S HOUR. Poetry selected for Children. 18mo. 2s. 6d.
—— SPRING-TIME WITH THE POETS. 18mo. 3s. 6d.

MAZINI (Linda).—IN THE GOLDEN SHELL. With Illustrations. Globe 8vo. 4s. 6d.

MOLESWORTH (Mrs.).—WORKS. Illust. by WALTER CRANE. Globe 8vo. 2s. 6d. each.
"CARROTS," JUST A LITTLE BOY.
A CHRISTMAS CHILD.
CHRISTMAS-TREE LAND.
THE CUCKOO CLOCK.
FOUR WINDS FARM.
GRANDMOTHER DEAR.
HERR BABY.
LITTLE MISS PEGGY.
THE RECTORY CHILDREN.
ROSY.
THE TAPESTRY ROOM.
TELL ME A STORY.
TWO LITTLE WAIFS.
"US": An Old-Fashioned Story.
CHILDREN OF THE CASTLE.
—— A CHRISTMAS POSY. Illustrated by WALTER CRANE. Cr. 8vo. 4s. 6d.
—— FOUR GHOST STORIES. Cr. 8vo. 6s.
—— NURSE HEATHERDALE'S STORY. Illust. by LESLIE BROOKE. Cr. 8vo. 4s. 6d.
—— THE GIRLS AND I. Illust. by L. BROOKE. Cr. 8vo. 4s. 6d.

OLIPHANT (Mrs.).—AGNES HOPETOUN'S SCHOOLS AND HOLIDAYS. Illust. Gl. 8vo. 2s. 6d.

PALGRAVE (Francis Turner).—THE FIVE DAYS' ENTERTAINMENTS AT WENTWORTH GRANGE. Small 4to. 6s.
—— THE CHILDREN'S TREASURY OF LYRICAL POETRY. 18mo. 2s. 6d.—Or in 2 parts, 1s. each.

PATMORE (C.).—THE CHILDREN'S GARLAND FROM THE BEST POETS. 18mo. 2s. 6d. net.

ROSSETTI (Christina). — SPEAKING LIKENESSES. Illust. by A. HUGHES. Cr. 8vo. 4s. 6d

RUTH AND HER FRIENDS: A STORY FOR GIRLS. Illustrated. Globe 8vo. 2s. 6d.

ST. JOHNSTON (A.). — CAMPING AMONG CANNIBALS. Cr. 8vo. 4s. 6d.
—— CHARLIE ASGARDE: THE STORY OF A FRIENDSHIP. Illustrated by HUGH THOMSON. Cr. 8vo. 5s.

"ST. OLAVE'S" (Author of). Illustrated. Globe 8vo.
WHEN I WAS A LITTLE GIRL. 2s. 6d.
NINE YEARS OLD. 2s. 6d.
WHEN PAPA COMES HOME. 4s. 6d.
PANSIE'S FLOUR BIN. 4s. 6d.

STEWART (Aubrey).—THE TALE OF TROY. Done into English. Globe 8vo. 3s. 6d.

TENNYSON (Hon. Hallam).—JACK AND THE BEAN-STALK. English Hexameters. Illust. by R. CALDECOTT. Fcp. 4to. 3s. 6d.

"WANDERING WILLIE" (Author of).—CONRAD THE SQUIRREL. Globe 8vo. 2s. 6d.

WARD (Mrs. T. Humphry).—MILLY AND OLLY. With Illustrations by Mrs. ALMA TADEMA. Globe 8vo. 2s. 6d.

WEBSTER (Augusta).—DAFFODIL AND THE CROÄXAXICANS. Cr. 8vo. 6s.

WILLOUGHBY (F.).—FAIRY GUARDIANS. Illustr. by TOWNLEY GREEN. Cr. 8vo. 5s.

WOODS (M. A.). (*See* COLLECTIONS, p. 17.)

YONGE (Charlotte M.).—THE PRINCE AND THE PAGE. Cr. 8vo. 3s. 6d.
—— A BOOK OF GOLDEN DEEDS. 18mo. 2s. 6d. net. Globe 8vo. 2s.—*Abridged Edition.* 1s.
—— LANCES OF LYNWOOD. Cr. 8vo. 3s. 6d.
—— P'S AND Q'S; and LITTLE LUCY'S WONDERFUL GLOBE. Illustrated. Cr. 8vo. 3s. 6d.
—— A STOREHOUSE OF STORIES. 2 vols. Globe 8vo. 2s. 6d. each.
—— THE POPULATION OF AN OLD PEAR-TREE; or, Stories of Insect Life. From E. VAN BRUYSSEL. Illustr. Gl. 8vo. 2s. 6d.

ZOOLOGY.

Comparative Anatomy—Practical Zoology—Entomology—Ornithology.

(*See also* BIOLOGY; NATURAL HISTORY; PHYSIOLOGY.)

Comparative Anatomy.

FLOWER (Sir W. H.).—AN INTRODUCTION TO THE OSTEOLOGY OF THE MAMMALIA. Illustrated. 3rd Edit., revised with the assistance of HANS GADOW, Ph.D. Cr. 8vo. 10s. 6d.

HUMPHRY (Prof. Sir G. M.).—OBSERVATIONS IN MYOLOGY. 8vo. 6s.

LANG (Prof. Arnold).—TEXT-BOOK OF COMPARATIVE ANATOMY. Transl. by H. M. and M. BERNARD. Preface by Prof. E. HAECKEL. Illustr. 2 vols. 8vo. Part I. 17s. net.

PARKER (T. Jeffery).—A COURSE OF INSTRUCTION IN ZOOTOMY (VERTEBRATA). Illustrated. Cr. 8vo. 8s. 6d.

PETTIGREW (J. Bell).—THE PHYSIOLOGY OF THE CIRCULATION IN PLANTS, IN THE LOWER ANIMALS, AND IN MAN. 8vo. 12s.

SHUFELDT (R. W.).—THE MYOLOGY OF THE RAVEN (*Corvus corax Sinuatus*). A Guide to the Study of the Muscular System in Birds. Illustrated. 8vo. 13s. net.

WIEDERSHEIM (Prof. R.).—ELEMENTS OF THE COMPARATIVE ANATOMY OF VERTEBRATES. Adapted by W. NEWTON PARKER. With Additions. Illustrated. 8vo. 12s. 6d.

Practical Zoology.

HOWES (Prof. G. B.).—AN ATLAS OF PRACTICAL ELEMENTARY BIOLOGY. With a Preface by Prof. HUXLEY. 4to. 14s.

HUXLEY (T. H.) and MARTIN (H. N.).—A COURSE OF PRACTICAL INSTRUCTION IN ELEMENTARY BIOLOGY. Revised and extended by Prof. G. B. HOWES and D. H. SCOTT, Ph.D. Cr. 8vo. 10s. 6d

THOMSON (Sir C. Wyville).—THE VOYAGE OF THE "CHALLENGER": THE ATLANTIC. With Illustrations, Coloured Maps, Charts, etc 2 vols. 8vo. 45s.

THOMSON (Sir C. Wyville).—THE DEPTHS OF THE SEA. An Account of the Results of the Dredging Cruises of H.M.SS. "Lightning" and "Porcupine," 1868-69-70. With Illustrations, Maps, and Plans. 8vo. 31s.6d.

Entomology.

BUCKTON (G. B.).—MONOGRAPH OF THE BRITISH CICADÆ, OR TETTIGIDÆ. 2 vols. 33s. 6d. each net; or in 8 Parts. 8s. each net.

LUBBOCK (Sir John).—THE ORIGIN AND METAMORPHOSES OF INSECTS. Illustrated. Cr. 8vo. 3s. 6d.

SCUDDER (S. H.).—FOSSIL INSECTS OF NORTH AMERICA. Map and Plates. 2 vols. 4to. 90s. net.

Ornithology.

COUES (Elliott).—KEY TO NORTH AMERICAN BIRDS. Illustrated. 8vo. 2l. 2s.

—— HANDBOOK OF FIELD AND GENERAL ORNITHOLOGY. Illustrated. 8vo. 10s. net.

FOWLER (W. W.). (See NATURAL HISTORY.)

WHITE (Gilbert). (See NATURAL HISTORY.)

INDEX.

MACMILLAN AND CO., LONDON.

J. PALMER, PRINTER, ALEXANDRA STREET, CAMBRIDGE.

10/50/8/93